Dear Little Black Dress Reader,

Thanks for picking up this Little Black Dress book, one of the great new titles from our series of fun, page-turning romance novels. Lucky you — you're about to have a fantastic romantic read that we know you won't be able to put down!

Why don't you make your Little Black Dress experience even better by logging on to

www.littleblackdressbooks.com

where you can:

- ❦ Enter our **monthly competitions** to win **gorgeous** prizes
- ❦ Get **hot-off-the-press** news about our latest titles
- ❦ Read **exclusive** preview chapters both from your **favourite** authors and from brilliant new writing talent
- ❦ Buy **up-and-coming** books online
- ❦ Sign up for an essential slice of romance via our **fortnightly email** newsletter

We love nothing more than to curl up and indulge in an addictive romance, and so we're delighted to welcome you into the Little Black Dress club!

With love from,

The *little black dress* team

Five interesting things about Kristin Harmel:

1. I wanted to be a rock star but realized by the age of nine that I couldn't actually sing, which I figured might be a problem.

2. My favorite place to write is in Paris, where I lived a few years ago. I could see the Eiffel Tower from my living-room window!

3. I have also lived in New York, Los Angeles, Boston and Miami, and now live in Orlando.

4. I write for one of the biggest celebrity magazines in the United States and have interviewed Matthew McConaughey, Ben Affleck and Sarah Jessica Parker, among others.

5. I am only 5 feet tall!

How to Sleep with a Movie Star
and
The Art of French Kissing

Kristin Harmel

Copyright © 2006, 2007 Kristin Harmel

The right of Kristin Harmel to be identified as the Author of the Work has been asserted by her in accordance with the Copyright, Designs and Patents Act 1988.

HOW TO SLEEP WITH A MOVIE STAR first published in the USA in 2006 by 5 SPOT
An imprint of GRAND CENTRAL PUBLISHING

First published in Great Britain in 2007
by LITTLE BLACK DRESS

THE ART OF FRENCH KISSING first published in the USA in 2008 by 5 SPOT
An imprint of GRAND CENTRAL PUBLISHING

First published in Great Britain in 2007
by LITTLE BLACK DRESS

First published in this omnibus edition in 2008
by LITTLE BLACK DRESS

An imprint of HEADLINE PUBLISHING GROUP

A LITTLE BLACK DRESS paperback

2

Apart from any use permitted under UK copyright law, this publication may only be reproduced, stored, or transmitted, in any form, or by any means, with prior permission in writing of the publishers or, in the case of reprographic production, in accordance with the terms of licences issued by the Copyright Licensing Agency.

All characters in this publication are fictitious and any resemblance to real persons, living or dead, is purely coincidental.

978 0 7553 4816 9

Typeset in Transit511BT by Avon DataSet Ltd, Bidford-on-Avon, Warwickshire

Printed and bound in Great Britain by Clays Ltd, St Ives plc

Headline's policy is to use papers that are natural, renewable and recyclable products and made from wood grown in sustainable forests. The logging and manufacturing processes are expected to conform to the environmental regulations of the country of origin.

HEADLINE PUBLISHING GROUP
An Hachette Livre UK Company
338 Euston Road
London NW1 3BH

www.littleblackdressbooks.com
www.headline.co.uk
www.hachettelivre.co.uk

How to Sleep with a Movie Star

To Mom, whose strength, wisdom, and kindness have always been an inspiration. I can never thank you enough. Everything I am, I owe to you.

Acknowledgments

A giant 'Thank you!'
   To Mom, to Karen and David, the best sister and brother I could ask for, and to Dad, Grandma, Grandpa, Donna, Pat, Steve, Grandma from Texas, Anne, Fred, Merri, Derek, Jessica, Gregory, and my entire family.

To my literary agents, Elizabeth Pomada and Michael Larsen, my film agent, Andy Cohen, Jim Schiff at Warner Books, and to my fabulous editor, Amy Einhorn, whose patience, kindness, and amazing editorial eye have made this whole experience a wonderful one.

To *People* magazine's wonderful Miami bureau chief Mindy Marques (who is a joy to work with); former bureau chief Joseph Harmes; my University of Florida editor (and the world's best boss) Steve Orlando; and my first editor, Al Martino, all of whom believed in me and taught me so much.

To my wonderful friends, many of whom are guinea pig readers for this book: Kara Brown, Kristen Milan, Lauren Elkin, Ashley Tedder, Megan Combs, Amber Draus, Cris Williams, Josh Henchey, Michael Ghegan, Jessica Cudar, Heather McWilliams, Martin Pachcinski, Gillian Zucker, Courtney Harmel, Stacie Beck, Jen Rainey, my Rock Boat girls (Matie, Amanda, Gail, and Michelle), Lana and Joe Cabrera, Megan McDermott, Samantha Phillips, Lindsay Soll, Amy Tan, Joan and Arde, Kristin Weissman, and Pat Cash.

To all the great people I've worked with, including: Cecilia Gilbride and Jane Chesnutt from *Woman's Day*; Gina Bevinetto from *Organic Style*; Liesl O'Dell and Cinnamon Bair from the UF Foundation; Lori Rozsa, Leslie Marine, Steve Helling, and Linda Trischitta from *People* magazine; Rebecca Webber, Caroline Bollinger, and Sarah Robbins from *Glamour* magazine; Nancy Steadman from *Health* magazine; Kate Kelly, Dorre Fox, Susan Soriano, and Christine Porretta from *American Baby*; Tara Murphy and Kelly Vahaly Long (two of the nicest publicists on the planet); Meghann Foye from *Woman's Day*; Pulitzer Prize-winning photographer John Kaplan; Anne Rach, Troy McGuire, Andrea Jackson, John Brown, Clayton Morris, Mitch English, and Dao Vu from *The Daily Buzz*; all my editors at *People*; my *Glamour* poll girls, the folks at *The Daily Buzz*, and all the great people I've worked with over the years.

To Matthew McConaughey, Ben Affleck, John Corbett, Joshua Jackson, Jay Mohr, Andre Benjamin (from OutKast), Ken Block (from Sister Hazel), and John Ondrasik (from Five for Fighting) for being truly nice people – the kind of celebs who make my job so enjoyable.

In memory of Don Sider, a fabulous mentor and one of the greatest journalists – and nicest people – I've ever known, and Jay Cash, the best childhood friend I could have asked for. You'll always be my superhero.

And to all you single gals out there: value yourselves. *Be* yourselves. Your Mr Perfect may not be a movie star, but believe me, he's out there. Never settle. And make sure you wind up with a guy who deserves someone as wonderful as *you*.

Cover Stories

10 Reasons to Have a One-Night Stand

Surely nothing good had ever come out of a one-night stand.

Except in a one-night stand, you actually got to have sex. Which was more than I could say for myself right now. It had been twenty-nine days. *Twenty-nine days*.

Which would be okay if I were single. But I had a boyfriend. A live-in, sleep-in-my-bed boyfriend. That made the twenty-nine-days figure rather pathetic.

It wasn't helping that the headline '10 Reasons to Have a One-Night Stand' was splashed across the top of my computer screen. I stared at the words blankly, wondering if they were purposely taunting me. I didn't necessarily agree that there were ten or even five reasons that anyone should consider such a thing, but that wasn't the biggest problem.

It would be bad enough to be *reading* a self-esteem-stomping, flaky article about going out and getting laid by a random guy. It was worse when I was the one who had to actually *write* the article.

Besides, in my past experience, there was no reason in the world anyone should encourage that kind of thing. You always woke up the next morning with a hangover, dark circles under your eyes, and a strange guy in your bed who was bound to mumble something like, 'You were great last night, Candi, baby,' when your name was clearly Claire.

I must have been mumbling my protests audibly, for Wendy, *Mod* magazine's assistant features editor, popped up over the wall of my cubicle, an eyebrow arched. The first time I'd laid eyes on her a year and a half ago on my first day at *Mod*, she had looked somewhat nondescript to me. Then she'd smiled at me for the first time, and I was nearly blinded by a seemingly endless display of pearly whites. I'd been powerless to keep from grinning back. If you put Julia Roberts's smile on a younger Kathy Bates's face, you'd come pretty close to approximating Wendy, who had quickly developed into my closest friend.

Since she had dyed her hair red, the latest in a bimonthly series of shades that had little to do with her natural color, she'd looked suspiciously like she was beginning to channel the hamburger queen who shared her name. Today I was momentarily distracted by the neon-green scarf she had tied around her neck, which seemed to have nothing to do with her fitted black tee from Nobu, one of New York's trendiest restaurants, or her pleated red schoolgirl skirt. But I'd long since given up trying to figure out Wendy's style.

'Problem?' she asked wickedly. I couldn't resist responding to her mile-wide smile. I grinned back.

She knew I was having a problem all right. I'd unleashed a flood of complaints this morning about *Mod*'s editor in chief, Margaret Weatherbourne, as the elevator whisked us silently up to the forty-sixth floor. Beneath her seemingly flawless Upper East Side exterior, Margaret had been a bit off-kilter since the release of the recent circulation figures that had put our biggest competitor, *Cosmopolitan*, at 3 million while *Mod* stayed steady at 2.6 million. She had been spotted more than once mumbling words that wouldn't befit her classy persona in the general direction of *Cosmo*'s offices eleven blocks up Broadway.

At our weekly editorial meeting on Monday, she had announced that this was war. If it was the last thing she did, we would beat *Cosmopolitan* in circulation next quarter.

So I suppose it shouldn't have completely blindsided me when she called me into her office at 6 p.m. last night to tell me she'd had a brilliant idea and wanted to crash the August issue with a story about how wonderful one-night stands were for a twenty-first-century girl's self-esteem. Apparently this would be a circulation-raising feat that would restore Margaret to the status of Supreme Fashion Goddess of New York.

'But they're *not* good for self-esteem,' I said flatly. The magazine was going to press on Monday morning, which meant that I'd have to turn around her latest ridiculous idea in less than forty-eight hours if I had any hope of having a weekend free from work.

Besides, I was just about the last person on the *Mod* staff who should be writing the article. Sure, I'd had my share of wickedly fun one-night stands in college but I'd like to think that at twenty-six, I was past that. Besides, there was the fact that I'd been dating my boyfriend, Tom, for over a year now. (Even if he didn't *technically* appear to be sleeping with me at the moment. I was convinced it was just a fluke, or maybe a phase.)

So what did I know about one-night stands?

It wasn't even my department. As *Mod*'s entertainment editor, I was responsible for all of the magazine's celebrity profiles. But my reputation as the 'nice girl' had seemingly convinced Margaret that I would take on impossible projects without putting up a fight.

Note to self: Plan to reconsider reputation as the nice girl.

'Yes they are,' Margaret said. Her green eyes blazed, and for a moment I thought I would see fire shoot from her nostrils.

'One-night stands?' I asked finally.

'One-night stands,' she echoed cheerfully. She waved a

slender hand in the air with a dramatic flourish. 'They're so in. They give the woman the power.' I grimaced. Like she'd know. The only thing that had given her 'the power' was that her mother's fourth husband (whom she still called 'Daddy' – despite the fact that she was in her forties) owned Smith-Baker Media, *Mod*'s parent company.

'Power?' I repeated. I tried to think back to a time when one of my college one-night stands had made me feel powerful, but I was at a bit of a loss. Margaret glared at me.

'Just do it, Claire,' she said firmly. 'The magazine is closing in four days, and I want this article in there. And you'll write it.' Before I could open my mouth to ask the obvious, she said with unmistakable finality, 'Because I said so.'

That's how I'd landed at my desk on a Thursday morning with a headache and a seemingly impossible task before me. The fact that I seemed to have no recent experience in the field of sex or anything sex *related* was only making matters worse.

'That screen still looks pretty blank to me,' Wendy said over the cubicle, winking at me as I slumped over my keyboard and banged my head against my desk. Wendy had wrapped August earlier in the week – we all had – and was already working on September. Other than the layout people, who were rushing at the last minute to include room for the one-night-stand article and splash a teaser for it across the cover, I was the only *Mod* staffer scrambling to finish up for August on such a tight deadline.

'What can you say about a one-night stand?' I moaned, rolling my eyes at Wendy. It was pretty much common knowledge that I was the least sexually advanced of anyone in *Mod*'s offices, due to an inexplicable dating drought B.T. (Before Tom). Wendy, on the other hand, was to sexual liberation what Manolo Blahnik was to shoes – a fearless leader and trendsetter, not to mention a face for a movement.

'Oh, *I* could say plenty,' Wendy said, tossing her red curls over her shoulder and readjusting her Day-Glo scarf.

'I mean, *I* could go out and do field research. Think *Mod* would pick up the tab?' She winked again at me. 'In fact, I have a hot date tonight. Maybe I can test your theory then.'

'A date? With a waiter?' I asked innocently. Wendy nodded excitedly, and I rolled my eyes.

'Pablo,' she said, putting her right hand over her heart and doing a little twirl. 'From Caffe Linda on Forty-ninth Street. He's *so* sexy.'

'You think anyone in an apron who takes your order and brings you food is sexy,' I muttered, trying not to smile. Wendy laughed. Around the office, we called her a 'serial waiter dater', a title she wore as proudly as Miss America wore her crown. Wendy was an aspiring chef who was convinced that culinary greatness would one day be magically bestowed upon her if she ate out every night at Manhattan's top restaurants, sampling the creations of the city's best chefs.

As a result, she barely had enough money for rent and was in massive credit card debt, but she had an endless supply of waiters whom she somehow managed to seduce somewhere between her salad course and dessert. I still couldn't figure out how she did it. I was thinking of asking her for lessons.

'See, I'd be the perfect one to write this article,' Wendy said. Well, I couldn't argue there. 'Hey, you can write me off if you want, but my first piece of advice would be to drop Tom and go out and do some field research.' Wendy raised an eyebrow at me. 'How often do you get to explain a one-night stand to yourself by saying that you just *had* to do it for work?'

'You just want me to drop Tom,' I said, wrinkling my nose at her. Wendy had never liked him. I trusted her – she was my best friend – but that didn't mean she was always right. And even if she was getting laid a lot more than I was, I didn't necessarily want to live like her, hopping from one man's bed to the next in a dizzying array that read like a *Zagat*'s guide.

Although on day 29 of my inadvertent reborn-virgin status, I had to admit, there was a certain appeal to her dating philosophy.

My friends back home in suburban Atlanta, where I had spent my entire childhood, were marrying off left and right, and at almost twenty-seven, I was experiencing the first symptoms of feeling like an old maid. Of course by New York standards, I was years too young to worry about marriage. But by the standards of the South I was already over the hill, matrimonially speaking. At friends' weddings (which now seemed to take place on a bimonthly basis), I was already hearing the sad whispers and standing on the receiving end of the pitying glances reserved for the eternally unmarriageable.

I had confided last month to the most recent of my newly-wed friends that I thought Tom might be 'The One'. And I really did feel that way, don't get me wrong. After all, we were both writers, he made me laugh, we had lots of fun together . . . It seemed so logical.

Of course, this was mere hours after my mother had taken me aside and reminded me, 'Claire, you can't be too picky, you know. You're not getting any younger.'

Thanks, Mom.

'He doesn't even have a job,' Wendy said simply, snapping me out of the beginnings of a daydream about my own nuptials.

'He's writing a novel,' I said, shrugging with what I hoped looked like nonchalance. 'He needs the time to work on it. He's a really great writer, you know. He's always working really hard on it at home.'

Wendy sighed.

'And it's totally normal that he doesn't want to sleep with you?' she asked gently. As my best friend, Wendy had, of course, heard the full and unfortunate details of my dry spell.

'It's just a phase,' I muttered. 'Anyhow, I think maybe he has a sleeping disorder or something. I mean, he sleeps all the time. Maybe it has nothing to do with me. Maybe I should suggest that he see a doctor.'

'Maybe,' Wendy said after a moment. She smiled at me mischievously. 'Or maybe you should just go out and test this one-night-stand theory.'

I rolled my eyes and turned resignedly back to the computer, trying to ignore her giggles. I gritted my teeth and tried to think about sex, which wasn't too hard, considering it had absorbed just about every one of my waking thoughts for the past few weeks.

By the end of the day, I had managed to dash off two thousand words that didn't sound much different from any of the nearly identical 'How to Please Your Man' articles we pushed on readers each month.

This isn't *exactly* what I visualized doing when I graduated from college. But thankfully, the atmosphere wasn't anything like that of the high fashion magazines where a few of my classmates from college worked. They had all been promptly assimilated and now had matching haircuts, matching Fendi and Louis Vuitton bags for every season, and wardrobes that consisted only of the most expensive and trendy designer clothes. Margaret just asked that we look presentable, polished, and stylish, which I usually didn't have a problem with, even on my admittedly meager salary.

After all, I had to look the part if I was going to interact with the fabulously wealthy A-list set. I'd made the mistake my first year at *People* of dressing professionally but without much of a stylish edge, and I'd quickly learned my lesson. Spending a bit more on designer items – even if I could afford just a scarf to pair with less impressive non-designer threads – would go a long way. When you were an actress decked out in tens-of-thousands-of-dollars of diamonds, strutting down the red carpet, there was just something about a reporter wearing a Gucci scarf that made you just a bit more likely to stop and chat. Sad, right? But those were the rules of the game.

And the articles. Sheesh, the articles. Don't get me wrong – I love what I do. I love getting inside people's heads (even if those heads often belong to vacuous celebrities) and finding out what they're thinking, what they're worrying about, what makes them tick. So the job as senior celebrity editor of *Mod* fits me with a perfection that might surprise you, considering I originally had my sights set on the lofty literary world of *The New Yorker*.

But it's the other articles, the in-between assignments that a Prada-clad Margaret dumps on my desk at the last minute, that drive me crazy. I mean, there are only so many ways you can address your readers' 'Most Intimate Sex Questions' (clue: they're not so intimate any more when 2.6 million women are reading about them); the truth behind 'How to Drop Those Last Five Pounds' (um, exercise and eat less – duh); and the ever-popular 'How to Know If He Likes You' (well, men who like a woman usually want to sleep with that woman – wait, should I be taking notes here?).

I became an editor because I love to write. And I took this job at *Mod* because I really like one-on-one interviews and profiles. As a little girl, I loved reading my grandmother's celebrity magazines: *People*, *The Enquirer*, *Star*. The lives of the beautiful people in the pictures seemed so glamorous, so exciting. Perhaps that was what had drawn me to celebrity journalism to begin with, although after several years of working in the field, I knew better than to think that everything was as it appeared to be.

At *People*, where I worked before I started at *Mod*, I'd made a name for myself in the business by breaking two major stories in the same year: the biggest celebrity breakup of the decade, the split between movie star Clay Terrell and pop princess Tara Templeton (thanks to the friendly relationship I'd developed after numerous interviews with the down-to-earth Clay); and the story of musical diva Annabel Warren's breast cancer diagnosis. (I had also interviewed her numerous times, so when the cancer rumors broke, mine was the only call she decided to take.) As a result, *Mod* had come looking for me. Margaret dangled a higher salary – and much more important, the chance to work on lengthy honest-to-goodness human interest profiles – and I was sold. And just like that, I became the youngest senior celebrity editor in the business.

I loved the job, but the move had made me some quick enemies. In the ever-gossipy world of magazines, a rumor had circulated (and lingered for six months) that I'd slept with Margaret's boss, Bob Elder, the president of Smith-Baker Media. Of course I hadn't, but professional jealousy tends to rage when someone several years shy of thirty snags a dream job that scores of women were after. I hadn't done anything wrong to get here. I certainly hadn't slept with Bob Elder, who was pushing sixty and was easily three times my weight. I had just done my job. And ironically, this wasn't *my* dream job at all, anyhow.

When I was an English major at the University of Georgia I wouldn't have suspected that four short years later, I'd be enthusiastically asking pop stars whether they wear boxers or briefs. Or asking actresses whether they feel like Sevens, Diesels, or Miss Sixtys lift their already-perfect butts better (as if Gwyneth Paltrow and Julia Roberts *had* butts to lift).

Speaking of perfectly sculpted women poured into designer clothing, I was snapped out of my reverie by the approach of a heavy cloud of perfume as Sidra, Sally, and Samantha all glided by in the hallway, as if on cue, on three pairs of Jimmy Choos I couldn't have walked in if I tried.

Wendy and I called them 'the Triplets'. Somehow, miraculously, the three rulers of the fashion department roost all had names that began with an S, were pencil thin, abnormally tall, and had painfully pointy noses that seemed to match the painfully pointy toes of their stilettos.

They all looked perpetually polished, as if they visited a beauty salon each morning before they appeared at the office, which was entirely possible since they normally didn't grace us with their presence until after 11 a.m. There was never a hair out of place, never an inch of face without perfectly applied makeup, never a moment when their noses weren't fixed permanently in the air.

I caught pieces of their conversation as they passed.

'Oh . . . my . . . God,' Sidra DeSimon, *Mod*'s coldly beautiful fashion and beauty director, said, sounding remarkably like Chandler's ex-girlfriend Janice, from *Friends*. I wondered momentarily just how one managed to develop a voice that nasal. 'She was carrying a Louis Vuitton bag from *last season*.'

Sally and Samantha both gasped at this apparent mortal sin.

'Last season?' Sally asked incredulously, scurrying after Sidra.

'Ugh.' I could see Samantha shudder in horror before they disappeared around the corner.

I made a face as I choked on the cloud of Chanel No. 5 they left swirling in their wake.

How they managed to afford the latest in designer fashions on editorial salaries was beyond me. I suspected that, like many of the stick-thin, model-tall fashionistas who inhabited the hallways and abused the expense accounts of the country's top women's magazines, all three Triplets were trust-fund babies. It didn't hurt that their penchant for $2,000 pants and the latest Jimmy Choos, Manolo Blahniks, or Prada boots was assisted by their access to the magazine's fashion closet and a ream of eager-to-please designers they probably had on speed-dial.

Sidra, the oldest of the Triplets and their fearless leader, was a bit of a legend in the New York editorial world. She claimed to have dated George Clooney for a month or so in the mid-nineties and had used that fact as a sort-of job reference throughout the rest of her career. She was known to frequently drop 'When George and I were dating...' into various conversations where the words really didn't belong.

For George's part, he denied that he knew her. That hadn't stopped her from dragging his name through the mud to her advantage — and to the endless delight of the New York gossip scene. Her name was a Page Six staple.

For reasons I still hadn't entirely figured out, Sidra had developed an instant dislike for me the moment I'd set foot through *Mod*'s doors a year and a half ago. The more I got to know her, the more I suspected it was a case of clear-cut professional jealousy. I was fifteen years her junior, and I was just one step below her on the editorial chain.

My few attempts during the first month to ingratiate myself with a quick chat were met immediately with a cold shoulder, and to date, we'd never even had an actual conversation. Half the time she refused to even acknowledge my existence, and otherwise she badmouthed me around the office. My coworkers, thankfully, knew her well enough that her complaints tended to go in one ear and out the other.

Unfortunately, she also loved badmouthing me to people at other magazines who didn't quite know how catty and bizarre she was. Once, at a Fashion Week celebrity fashion show, I even overheard her telling a senior editor from *In Style* that I was a delusional intern who liked to pretend that I was *Mod*'s celebrity editor, and it was best to just ignore me and play along.

As the director of fashion and beauty for *Mod*, Sidra oversaw Sally and Samantha, who were clearly being groomed to become her clones. So far, it was working out. Sally, the fashion editor, didn't yet understand that dressing models in Gucci and Versace couture didn't quite fly with most *Mod* readers, who didn't make enough money in a decade to buy the clothes that Sally would order for one shoot. Not exactly the best way to compete with *Cosmo* in the circulation trenches.

Samantha, the beauty editor, was responsible for the magazine's makeup tips. She was apparently equally confused, failing to realize that not everyone had the high cheekbones, full lips, and flawless complexion that she did. Of course, not everyone had the good fortune to be sleeping with Dr Stephen McDermott, Manhattan's premier 'Dermatologist to the Stars', either.

The only way to tell the Triplets apart, I sometimes thought, was by the fact that Sidra was the only one who had already invested $20,000 in breast implants by Dr David Aramayo, arguably the best plastic surgeon in Manhattan. I was sure that the others weren't far behind. They were doubtlessly working out payment plans now.

I wished that Wendy hadn't gone home already. I would have loved to end the day by trading one-liners about Sidra. It was a favorite pastime of ours. And it was completely harmless, because Sidra liked to pretend, for whatever reason, that she had no concept Wendy and I even existed, despite the fact that we had attended editorial meetings together for the last eighteen months. If we didn't exist, then I figured our derogatory comments didn't matter much.

I looked back at my computer screen, which still appeared to be taunting me. A one-night stand actually sounded frighteningly good at the moment. Hell, even Sidra, who had all the warmth and sex appeal of the iceberg that took out the Titanic, was probably getting laid more often than I was.

On that note, I printed out the two thousand words I'd managed to choke out throughout the day. It was 6:30. On the off chance that Margaret was lurking somewhere in the nearly empty office, I knew I'd better get home before she could blindside me with another ridiculous assignment.

How to Live Together Happily Ever After

Okay, day 30. I was getting worried. And this *Mod* assignment was starting to make me just a little desperate.

'Is there something wrong with me?' I whispered to Wendy over the wall of my cubicle the next morning. 'I mean, there's obviously something wrong if my boyfriend suddenly stops wanting to sleep with me.'

'No way,' Wendy said, just like I knew she would. 'My question would be, is there something wrong with him? What red-blooded American man doesn't want to have sex?'

Okay, so she had a point.

'Tom,' I muttered. But it wasn't exactly like he was *refusing* to sleep with me. It was just that he always seemed to be too busy or asleep when I was ready to go. Our timing was off. That was it.

Last night, day 29 had turned into night 30 with Newly Celibate Tom. That's two-and-a-half-dozen sexless nights for all of you who are keeping track. I'd even pulled out the big guns, slinking into the bedroom in a red teddy and a garter belt, feeling ridiculous.

'You're going to be cold in that,' he'd said briefly, glancing up from the television for a millisecond before refocusing his attention on a rerun of *Gilligan's Island*, which, as you can imagine, created quite the conundrum for me. Was he into Mary Ann or Ginger? Pigtails, or evening gowns? You'd think the teddy would trump both.

Apparently not.

'You'd better put something on, sweetie,' Tom added a moment later without glancing up. I gulped and tried again, leaning seductively into the doorframe, wobbling a bit in my stilettos.

'Tom,' I'd said in my best sexy Ginger voice (he'd probably pick Ginger over Mary Ann). I'd paused, unsure of what to say next. 'Uh, I have something I want to show you,' I said throatily. I batted my eyelashes at him flirtatiously as he looked up.

'Do you have something in your eye, Claire?' he'd asked before turning his attention back to the Professor's latest ingenious invention, which Mary Ann appeared to be giggling about. 'There's some Visine in the medicine cabinet if you need it,' he'd added helpfully.

I'd heaved a sigh, stomped back to the bathroom, and changed into a T-shirt and sweatpants while Tom sang along with the *Gilligan's Island* theme song in the other room. He hadn't even looked up when I stormed by him and threw myself into bed, huffing and puffing pointedly.

It hadn't always been this way. Tom and I had chemistry from the beginning, which I suppose led to my willingness to tumble into bed within a week of meeting him at a writers' seminar in the East Village. But with Tom I felt something instantly, something between an animal and an intellectual attraction, which I didn't know could coexist. He had this gorgeous, kind of tousled floppy hair that seemed to scream 'struggling intellectual writer' and the way he kissed always left me breathless.

The seminar, a free program put on by the Eastside Writers' Group, had been about how to write a novel. I was impressed that Tom was already halfway through a draft of what he called 'a slice of Americana mixed with a slice of suspense and a slice of intellectualism.' All those slices left me a bit woozy, more than a bit awed, and hungry for more. After all, the closest I'd come to writing anything fictional was a short story I had to write for a college lit class. I'd gotten a C+. Here was this Prince Charming who gave great massages, could talk about anything from politics to poultry seasonings, and he was doing the one thing I'd always wanted to do with my life.

I was instantly in love. I stood by him a month later when he decided to quit his job peddling medical supplies in order to write full-time, and I'd been only too happy to let him move into my rent-controlled apartment a month after that so that he wouldn't have to worry about making ends meet while he wrote the Great American Novel. Sure, I was a bit hurt that he still hadn't let me read any of it. And I was a bit surprised that it was taking so long to write, but we were in love. And the sex was great. Or it *had* been, before it started to decrease in frequency a few months ago. Then again, he seemed more and more worried about his book. And I figured it probably bothered him a bit that he had lived with me for almost a year and hadn't been able to contribute to the bills at all. The few times we'd gone out to dinner and he had offered to pay, his credit card had been rejected, and I had to pick up the check. I didn't mind, though. I knew he'd pay me back when he sold the book.

'You deserve better, you know,' Wendy said gently, breaking into the slow-motion replay in my head. 'I've always said that. But I know you think he's right for you.'

'He *is* right for me,' I said. He was, really. He was cute, and smart, and nice. He made me laugh. 'Maybe he's just going through a rough spot or something. I'm sure it's just our timing, you know? He's always up late working on his novel, and I'm fast asleep by the time he comes to bed. And I'm up hours before he is in the morning.'

I paused.

'Unless . . .' I sighed. 'You don't think I've put on a lot of weight recently, do you?'

'Are you kidding me?' Wendy asked, rolling her eyes at me and grinning. 'You look gorgeous, as usual.'

'I don't feel very gorgeous,' I mumbled, looking down at my stomach, which wasn't nearly as flat as I remembered it. I shuddered and tried not to picture Tom raptly staring at the television while I tried to gyrate sexily against the doorframe.

'Jeffrey thinks you look just like Christina Aguilera,' Wendy said triumphantly. I wrinkled my nose. I didn't quite know how to take the comparison from *Mod*'s art director.

'Pre- or post-"Dirty"?' I asked skeptically.

'Pre-,' Wendy reassured me. 'Like from her *Mickey Mouse Club* days. You know, when she was cute and thin, and had all that long blond hair.'

'So you're saying I look like a sixteen-year-old *Mickey Mouse Club* kid?' Hmm, this was not so good for the whole sex appeal thing.

'First of all, Jeffrey's saying it. Not me.'

'But you agree?'

Wendy paused.

'I think you look like Christina from the "Lady Marmalade" video.'

Hmm, this was a bit better. But not totally.

'Just because I have a bit of a frizz problem with my hair?'

'No,' Wendy said with a laugh.

'Is it because I wore those slutty boots last time we went out?'

'No.' Wendy giggled. 'But that *was* kinda funny.'

'Glad you were amused.' Actually, my one public attempt at sexy in the last few months had ended in disaster, when I got my heel stuck in a subway grate and smashed face-first into the sidewalk.

'Whatever it is with Tom, it's not you,' Wendy said

firmly. She hesitated for a moment, then added, 'Maybe you're right, and it is just bad timing.'

I shook my head and sighed.

'I bet Christina Aguilera never has this much trouble getting laid,' I muttered.

Note to self: Learn to dance like in that 'Dirty' video. And if there's time, start a public feud with Britney Spears.

Having a live-in boyfriend was a bit like high-stakes poker, I figured. The similarities had begun to dawn on me one insomniac night as I blearily watched three hours of a six-hour *Celebrity Poker Championship* marathon on Bravo.

See, that was the great thing about my job. As *Mod*'s celebrity editor, I was supposed to keep up with what was going on in the kingdom of celebrity, at least to some extent. And I figured that if I couldn't sleep, watching Ben Affleck, Matthew Perry, and Rosario Dawson battle it out in a Vegas casino was *sort of* like working. At least that's what I told myself the next morning, when I hit the snooze button six times in a row and rolled into work an hour late.

Of course, no one noticed. That was the other great thing about my job. People are always late. No one ever notices.

Anyhow, I figure in high-stakes poker, you're supposed to put everything on the line, do your best, and hope that you win. It's kind of the same situation when you take your relationship to the next level and agree to live with a person. You're giving up your independence and your solitude, putting all of your effort into making it work, and hoping for the best. Also, if you're not dealt exactly the hand you expect, you're not allowed to just get up and move to another table.

So I figured I was in it for the long haul with Tom, even if it wasn't going so well now. I mean, sure, I was being dealt a hand full of low cards at the moment – but in gambling, your luck changes all the time, doesn't it? And sure, I was betting everything I had – my heart, my future

– but it had worked out so far. I mean, it had been a great year.

Tom had swept me off my feet (full house!), sent me roses every week (straight!), told me he loved me after just a month and a half of dating (three-of-a-kind!), and moved in a month after that (straight flush!). He was a good guy. He loved me. So what if the sex had dropped off? It was only temporary, I was sure. And any day now, I was sure he'd come up with the royal straight flush: the engagement ring he had hinted at a few times.

Come to think of it, maybe that's why he was acting so strange lately. Maybe he was planning to propose. Maybe he was just nervous, trying to find the right time.

That would explain a lot.

I turned back to the computer and tried to focus. Already, the office was buzzing with activity. Telephones were ringing, editorial assistants were running copy back and forth between editors, and Maite Taveras, the managing editor, was moving from office to office, chatting with senior and assistant editors about the September issue. I'd already told her that we'd have to put off our conversation until Monday.

'You have to turn your full focus to one-night stands, hmm?' she had asked with a laugh, pushing her shining black hair over her shoulder. I knew she shared my low opinion of Margaret and her inexplicable whims.

'Ugh,' I'd moaned, rolling my eyes as she winked at me.

Maite held the third-highest editorial position at the magazine, after Margaret and the executive editor, Donna Foley. Fortysomething and beautiful, Maite had ascended the ranks of women's magazines by being a creative editor, a stickler for detail who always stuck with her writers' original tones. I'd liked her from the day we first met, and since then we'd had a comfortable rapport.

I turned back to the computer and tried to concentrate, but I was having trouble shutting out the rest of the office.

Two of the copy desk assistants, both clad in Earl Jeans and black Bebe tops so similar I could hardly tell them apart, swapped dating stories over the desk in the office they shared, emitting high-pitched sonar giggles every few moments. Anne Amster, the wiry-haired senior features editor, argued with someone on the phone, and a group of senior editors clustered around a bulletin board, one of them jabbing her finger pointedly at a blown-up mock-up of the August cover, saying something insistent in an annoyed squeaky voice.

Then of course there was Chloe Michael, the television and music editor, who was always blasting the latest in pop music from inside the walls of her cubicle. At least she *claimed* it was the latest in pop music. I swore I'd caught her sneakily listening to New Kids on the Block when she thought she'd turned her stereo down low enough to get away with it.

Jeffrey Zevon, the magazine's art director and the sole male on the editorial staff, had been pacing the hallway for the last fifteen minutes, and his nervousness was starting to rub off on me. As always, he was impeccably dressed – a tight black Kenneth Cole ribbed tee with gray Armani slacks that fit his perfect curves like they'd been made for him. ' "Buns of Steel", girl,' he'd confided to me once. 'I swear by those DVDs.' He looked like he belonged at a fashion shoot for *GQ*. His dark hair was speckled with gray, but on him it was salt-and-pepper that said distinguished and sexy.

I watched him as his eyes followed Marla, the fashion department's summer intern. She shuffled down the corridor toward the fashion closet with her eyes downcast and her shoulders slumped. Marla looked like she wanted to disappear. She twirled a finger through her stringy brown curls, her slightly heavy frame covered in a balloon of fabric.

'Poor girl,' Jeffrey murmured mid-stride, finally ending his impatient pacing at the entrance to my cubicle. He shook his head from side to side. 'Tsk, tsk, tsk. Those princesses in fashion do it every time, don't they?'

'Do what?' I asked, my eyes following the self-conscious Marla, then settling back on Jeffrey. I tried to stop imagining the diamond ring that Tom might be picking out at this very moment. Princess cut? Channel set? One carat, or two?

'Torture those poor young girls,' Jeffrey answered, placing a hand on my cubicle wall and leaning forward, apparently oblivious of the admittedly unrealistic visions of Tiffany rings dancing through my head. 'They all come to *Mod* with big dreams of being fashion editors and leave thinking they have to weigh ninety pounds and be six feet tall to succeed.'

'I know,' I said with a sigh. But at *Mod*, they actually *did* have to weigh ninety pounds to make it under Sidra. So poor Marla was completely correct. I wondered if she knew about the last-season designer rule ('Those who recycle last season's fashions aren't worthy to walk the streets of New York,' Sidra had once sniffed). Or how to hold her nose to mimic Sidra's nasal tone.

'They're getting worse,' Jeffrey said in a stage whisper. 'You should see the way Sidra talks to her. And the others, Sally and Samantha. They're just like Sidra. Something's up with them, girl.'

'Something's up?' I repeated skeptically. Jeffrey tended to go just a bit overboard sometimes.

'I don't know what it is, but something's not right in their little designer world,' Jeffrey said. He leaned forward again and grinned mischievously. 'Maybe Sidra finally realized that all the collagen, chemical peels, and silicone in Manhattan can't make her look twenty-five any more.' I laughed.

'About time she realized,' I muttered. It had been a long time since Sidra had looked twenty-five, but I had a feeling she didn't know that.

'You know that's why you piss her off so much, don't

you?' Jeffrey asked, an eyebrow arched. He grinned at me. 'You're everything she wants to be. She's just fifteen years too late.'

I laughed and shook my head.

'Nah,' I said. 'She just hates me because I'm beautiful.' I winked.

Jeffrey laughed – a little too heartily, I might add – then wrinkled his brow in concern and looked somberly at me.

'Really, doll, I'd watch your back,' he said, suddenly dead serious. 'With the executive editor position opening up, she's getting antsy and is bound to start backstabbing anyone she feels threatened by.'

I stared at Jeffrey for a moment, sure I had heard him wrong.

'What?' I asked. 'The executive editor position?'

'You haven't heard?' Jeffrey asked, his eyes sparkling again. He loved being the one to deliver gossip. 'Donna Foley just announced that she's retiring on August fifteenth. The word is that Smith-Baker has decided to let Margaret hand-pick a successor in-house.'

I felt my eyebrows shoot up in surprise. More often than not, magazines hired from the outside to fill major vacated positions. Then again, most magazines didn't have a woman like Margaret, with virtually no editorial skills, at the helm. I suppose that put *Mod* into a different category altogether. It was no wonder we were still struggling.

'Apparently, Margaret has said she's narrowed it down to two people,' Jeffrey said, flicking his eyes around again and arching an eyebrow. 'It's between Maite and Sidra, and they have the summer to prove themselves to her before she makes a final decision.'

I stared at him for a moment, speechless.

'Sidra?' I finally asked, my voice hoarse. It made no sense. Maite Taveras had been in the business for twenty years and was infinitely more qualified for the position. Granted, Sidra had been working in magazines for over a decade, but her experience was all on the fashion side.

I wasn't entirely sure she was capable of stringing together an entire sentence that didn't include a condescending fashion reference.

On top of that, of course, was Sidra's one-sided feud with me. I was no stranger to people snubbing me out of professional jealousy. But Sidra took it to the extreme. She and the other Triplets were always snickering at my fashion choices, and Sidra had even been quoted on Page Six once saying that a 'certain extremely young celebrity editor' at a 'certain women's magazine' had a habit of coming into work 'drunk as a skunk'. I'd confronted her, of course, and she had innocently batted her eyes at me and claimed that she *obviously* wasn't talking about me.

'Sidra,' Jeffrey confirmed with an astonished nod, bringing me back to the present. 'I know. I couldn't believe it either. But apparently Margaret is thinking about taking *Mod* in a more fashion-oriented direction. You know, more *Vogue*-ish. It's her latest plan to compete with *Cosmo*.'

'Unbelievable,' I muttered.

'And can you imagine?' Jeffrey continued, leaning in closer. 'Can you just imagine how drunk with power Sidra would be? She would basically be running the whole magazine. It would be a complete nightmare.'

'I guess it would be,' I murmured, suddenly feeling very uneasy about my job.

'Stranger things have happened,' he said. 'Get ready for some catfights, doll. Sidra can be vicious when she's after something she really wants.'

I finished the one-night-stand piece by 4 p.m., and to be honest, I was pretty proud that I'd managed to make it coherent. Wendy, the die-hard food aficionado, had insisted upon including reason number nine: 'Because it's a good excuse to order breakfast in.'

My personal favorite was reason number three: 'Because you might really hit it off with the guy and begin to develop a relationship.' (Wendy snorted, stifled a laugh, and said something about me living in Never-Neverland.) We'd both agreed that reason number ten was a good kicker: 'Because we all know that getting laid feels pretty damned good.' (Well, I had foggy memories of it feeling good, anyhow. And Wendy helpfully vouched for the statement's veracity.)

Besides, our readers were going to go out and have sex whether I told them to or not. Hooray for them. Maybe I should write Tom an article: 'Ten Reasons You Should Have Sex with Your Girlfriend Who Sleeps Beside You Every Night.'

I knocked lightly on Margaret's door, which was ajar, and let myself into her office.

'Here it is,' I announced grandly, plunking a printed-out, pared-down final draft of the article on her desk. She looked up, surprised, her over-tweaked dark brows arching upward. She lifted a corner of the draft with two perfectly manicured fingernails, looked at it from over the top of her perfect diamond-studded glasses, and reached up to brush a speck of invisible lint from the collar of her perfect Chloe shirt.

'Claire, darling,' she said with that sappy formality and hint of a British accent she'd somehow adopted after a recent trip to Paris. She'd forgotten, apparently, that we all knew she was born and raised in Ohio. 'I must have forgotten to tell you,' she said.

'Forgotten to tell me what?' I asked suspiciously. I held my breath as she did what appeared to be a little pirouette behind her desk. Rarely a meeting went by when she didn't remind the *Mod* staff that her mother, Anabella, had been a prima ballerina. Those of us who valued our jobs refrained from adding that Anabella had peaked with the Dayton City Ballet. Nothing to be ashamed of, but it wasn't like she had performed arabesques and pliés around the world with Baryshnikov.

'I won't be needing this for August after all,' she said casually, finishing her ballerina turn. My jaw dropped as I contemplated two lost and wasted days of my life. 'We'll use it for September, of course, darling. I'm sure it's a great piece.' She tossed the article into a stack of papers on the corner of her immense desk.

'Um, okay,' I said, my eyes following the article to her slush pile and returning to rest uneasily on her.

'But not to worry,' she said brightly. 'We'll be using the space for a feature on Cole Brannon.'

I looked at her in confusion.

'But I haven't done a story on Cole Brannon,' I said blankly. He was the hottest young actor in Hollywood at the moment, and had been for the past few months. He had shared the screen with Julia Roberts, Reese Witherspoon, and Gwyneth Paltrow in the last year, and his movies drew millions of excited women — many of them *Mod* readers — like moths to the light. His tall, muscular frame, eternally tousled brown hair, and sparkling blue eyes had launched many a fantasy.

On top of that, he seemed to have quite the social life, too. He was always being linked in the tabloids — not that you could always believe them — to various A-list actresses. And a certain blond pop princess had been overheard by a Page Six reporter telling a friend over lunch how spectacular he was in bed. Accordingly, *People* magazine had just named him their Most Eligible Bachelor for the year.

Margaret had never even suggested an interview with him. And most of our celeb stories were about women. It was an unwritten rule among the Seven Sisters of women's magazine publishing. Women wanted to read about women.

Although I supposed that any woman with a pulse would want to read about the delicious Cole Brannon too.

'Of course you haven't done a story on him . . . yet,' Margaret said. 'But his publicist has just agreed to let us speak with him, if we put him on the cover of the August issue.'

I tilted my head to the side and squinted at her.

'Just think,' Margaret said, gazing into space, already off in dreamland. 'This could be the major story that helps us pass *Cosmo*. I can see it now. "*Mod* Magazine's Exclusive Interview with Hollywood's Most Eligible Bachelor, Cole Brannon!" The August issue will fly off the newsstands!'

Margaret's eyes were sparkling, and her collagen-injected lips were twisted into a bizarre smile.

'But we're closing the August issue tonight,' I said blankly. That meant all the edits and editorial had to be in.

'But it doesn't ship until Monday morning, darling,' Margaret said, smiling and ignoring my worried expression. 'And your interview with Cole Brannon has been scheduled for tomorrow morning. That gives you two days.'

'Tomorrow morning?' I squeaked. Margaret smiled thinly.

'Yes, *tomorrow morning*,' Margaret mimicked me. 'That will give you two whole days to get it in. I'm sure you'll be able to, darling. After all, I don't want to find out that my decision to make you the youngest senior editor in the business was a mistake . . .'

Her voice trailed off and she looked at me meaningfully. I knew it was a threat. I didn't even bother to pretend I wasn't rolling my eyes.

'Anyhow, I trust you to get all the details right, so I won't be calling the research department in over the weekend,' Margaret said casually. 'You've never gotten a detail wrong before. And besides, did you know we have to pay the researchers overtime if we call them in over the weekend?' Margaret added, sounding astonished. 'It cuts into our bottom line.'

She looked momentarily perturbed. She was such a cheapskate.

'So I'm going to have Sidra DeSimon look it over instead,' Margaret continued breezily. 'This will be a good chance for her to try her hand at editing.'

I could feel my jaw fall.

'Sidra?' I squeaked, suddenly finding it somewhat difficult to breathe. Margaret ignored me.

'Lots of women would love to be in your shoes, Claire,' she said brusquely. 'After all, Cole Brannon is the most eligible bachelor in Hollywood at the moment.'

Which would probably translate into him being my dullest and most egotistical interview of the year so far. The glow of celebrity had long since worn off for me. I ignored Margaret's smile, which was clearly an attempt to soften me up and convince me that we were indeed comrades.

'But . . .' I began. Margaret cut off my protest with a single raised finger and a shake of her head.

'Brunch at Atelier at ten a.m. tomorrow,' she said crisply. I groaned. Brunch. Fantastic. It had to be the worst meal of the day to interview people. Visions of celebs nursing hangovers while sipping Bloody Marys or gulping mimosas, barking hoarse orders at waiters about too-crisp toast or too-runny eggs danced through my head.

Besides, I'd been hoping to spend the weekend with Tom. No one – not even I – could deny any more that our relationship needed some serious work. I did love him, after all, even if he was being a bit odd lately. And now, I would be spending Saturday with Cole Brannon and a looming deadline instead.

I was probably the only woman in America who wouldn't appreciate the trade-off.

'Of course we'll need the copy by Sunday afternoon so that the art department can do layout, Sidra can look it over, and it can be at the printer by Monday morning,' Margaret said.

'But Margaret, I . . .' I began. Again, she cut me off with a raised finger and a clucking sound.

'Thank you very much, Claire, darling,' Margaret said with finality. I opened and closed my mouth without a word, because I knew it would be a waste of breath. 'I'll expect that copy by Sunday afternoon. Have a lovely weekend.'

'You too,' I muttered, defeated, because I couldn't think of anything else to say.

'COLE BRANNON?' Wendy shrieked. I resisted the urge to cover my ears. 'You're having brunch with *Cole Brannon*? At *Atelier*? You are, like, the luckiest girl alive!'

'Hmph,' I grunted. I wasn't really in the mood to indulge Wendy, but I was beginning to realize there was really no way to get out of it. I plunked down in my chair and swiveled toward my computer in silence. I typed in my password and logged in to the news clipping service we subscribed to. I tried to ignore Wendy, who was still standing at the entrance to my cubicle, seemingly bubbling over while she waited for me to look at her. I took my time, avoided her glance for as long as I could, and typed 'Cole Brannon' into the search box. Three hundred twenty-six entries in the last six months. Yikes. This guy had gotten a lot of press, which meant I would be up late doing my research so that I was fully prepared. I finally gritted my teeth and looked up at Wendy.

'*Well?*' she demanded, her eyes as big as saucers.

'Well, what?' I asked, because I really didn't know what she was asking me.

'*Well*, aren't you going to say something? What do you think? It's *Cole Brannon!*'

'I know,' I said. I sighed and tried not to wince. 'And it's not that I'm not excited. I mean, I do think it's cool to meet him. And yeah, I liked him in *Goodnight Kiss*.'

Okay, that was a lie. I'd *loved* him in *Goodnight Kiss* – it was one of my favorite movies – but that was beside the point. I tried to explain.

'It's just that, well, you know – I've told you,' I said, well aware that my words weren't penetrating. Wendy had stars in her eyes with Cole Brannon's name on them. 'They're never what you expect them to be in person.

Sometimes I think I'd rather just see them in their movies or whatever, and not really know what they're like in real life. It kind of ruins it all for me.'

Which was especially disappointing this time because I actually *liked* Cole Brannon. No doubt brunch at one of Manhattan's toniest restaurants would change my opinion. Besides, what if all those rumors about him being a ladies' man and a sex addict – which I didn't entirely believe – turned out to be right?

'They're not all bad,' Wendy pointed out.

'I know,' I admitted, offering a smile as a bit of a truce. 'You're right.'

'Matthew McConaughey, for instance,' Wendy said helpfully.

'He was nice,' I graciously agreed.

'And Joshua Jackson,' she added.

'But who would expect any less from Pacey?' I smiled, but Wendy simply shook her head. This was serious business to her. There was no time for idle *Dawson's Creek* banter.

'Look, you have a date with Cole Brannon tomorrow morning. Can't you get a *little* excited?'

Unfortunately, I was taking a sip of my coffee as she spoke. I nearly choked.

'A date?' I gurgled, my eyes wide and my cheeks suddenly burning. 'It's not a date! I'm interviewing him over brunch!'

'Hmph,' Wendy said. She crossed her arms defiantly over her chest and leaned forward conspiratorially. She winked. 'If I were you, I would tell people that it's a date.'

'Have you been taking cues from Sidra again?' I asked her in mock exasperation. Wendy finally laughed. Sidra DeSimon's involvement with the tabloids was legendary. *Tattletale*, the gossip rag that hit newsstands each Tuesday, always seemed to feature a recollection from her about 'a special moment' she had shared with George Clooney.

Wendy and I still held to the belief that she'd never dated him at all.

'First stop, gossip columnists.' Wendy winked at me. 'Really, though, what else did you have to do this weekend? What could *possibly* be more important than having brunch with Cole Brannon? I mean, it's *Cole Brannon.*'

As if we hadn't already established that. I sighed.

'I was hoping to talk to Tom, you know? Maybe spend some time together to straighten things out.'

Wendy shook her head at me in what looked a lot like disappointment. Of course, on her face, with her wide eyes and toothy grin, it was often impossible to tell which emotion she was trying to project.

'That's it,' she said. 'You're insane, clearly. You want to spend your Saturday with an unemployed creep who won't even sleep with you rather than with *Cole Brannon?* You should be committed!'

I refused to laugh. 'Really, Wendy, I'm serious. It means a lot to me.'

Wendy looked skeptical. I changed the subject before she could launch into an anti-Tom tirade. Lately, her points were hitting too close to home.

'You're a good friend,' I said seriously. I cleared my throat. 'And I appreciate it. Now are you just going to give me a hard time or are you going to help me research Cole Brannon?'

Wendy looked at me for a moment, then grinned.

'Research him?' she said with a sly grin. '*Research* him? I'll give him some research!' She arched an eyebrow seductively.

'Okay, mind out of the gutter,' I chided with a smile. 'That's not even funny.' Wendy laughed.

'Seriously, girl, you're on your own,' she said. She checked her watch. 'You know my rule. Never stay past five o'clock on a Friday unless I absolutely have to.'

'It's a good rule,' I muttered. At this rate, I'd be here all night. Not that there would be anyone missing me at home, from the look of things.

'Now remember,' Wendy said with a mischievous grin, turning off her computer and slipping into her jacket. 'According to *Mod* magazine, which of course should be your first stop for *all* questions of advice, it's great for your self-esteem to have a one-night stand. I think you should try that theory out on Cole Brannon.' She was already down the hall by the time I'd balled up a piece of scrap paper to throw at her. 'Have fun!' Her voice wafted down the hallway as she disappeared around the corner.

I laughed for a moment, then turned back to my computer screen, sighing. I hit Print and heard the printer down the hall whirr to life as it started spitting out the 326 articles I had found about Cole Brannon. It was clear I'd be here for a while.

I sighed again, picking up the phone to call Tom.

'I just wanted to let you know that I'll be a bit later than usual tonight,' I said after he answered on the third ring.

'Oh?' he said, sounding disappointed. 'I'm sorry to hear that. I was going to take you to dinner tonight.'

I felt my heart leap in my chest. I couldn't even remember the last time he had suggested going out to dinner with me.

'I'm really sorry,' I sighed. 'I have to do an interview tomorrow morning, so I'm going to be stuck here for a few more hours doing research.'

'That's too bad,' Tom said.

'Yeah.' I groaned. 'It's Friday! I just want to come home!'

'Don't worry,' said Tom, sounding more cheerful than I'd heard him sound in weeks. 'You'll be home soon enough.'

'I guess,' I said reluctantly, not feeling much better. Then I thought, maybe his sudden cheerfulness was due to the fact that he had found an engagement ring and knew when he was going to propose. A sudden warmth flooded through me, and I grinned.

'If you won't be home in time to go out, would you mind picking up some Chinese?' Tom asked.

'Sure,' I said. My head was suddenly filled with images of Tom seductively feeding me lo mein noodles from perfectly poised chopsticks.

'Okay,' he said. 'I'll see you when you get home. Give me a call before you leave the office, okay, sweetie?'

'Okay,' I agreed. 'See you in a few hours. I love you.'

'See you then,' he said. Then the line went dead.

'Yeah, I love you too, Claire,' I said to myself, placing the receiver in its cradle.

Top 10 Hot Summer Reads

I'm sure you think I'm crazy. Half the women in America would probably kill for a chance to sit down with Cole Brannon.

Well, a few years ago I would have been excited. But that was before I started having to do celebrity interviews every month for *Mod*. They're not as exciting as they sound. It's usually just me sitting across the table from an actor, an actress, or a rock star while they indulge themselves in an empty-headed monologue embodying everything that's wrong with America. I mean, why should I care what Liv Tyler thinks about politics, or how Kylie Dane still struggles with insecurities, or how Winona Ryder really didn't mean it when she slipped some merchandise into her handbag?

The interviews aren't always bad. And the Livs, Kylies, and Winonas of the world all actually seem to be pretty nice people. It's just that after I've gone through a month of back-and-forth tug-of-war with a publicist, rescheduled our interview seven times, listened to briefings about what I can and can't bring up, and finally make it to an interview that has been mysteriously downgraded at the last minute from a two-hour luncheon to a forty-five-minute coffee break, I'm usually on my last nerve. But I paste the smile on anyhow, ask very *Mod* questions, and give our readers a profile of their favorite star.

Then it's back to reality. Sure, we can share a cup of

coffee at a hip, overpriced café, laugh together over raspberry sorbet, commiserate over cappuccino, but then I return to my world, and they return to theirs — and our worlds never intersect again. At the end of the day, I shop at the Gap while they're having their clothes individually designed by Giorgio Armani himself while lounging poolside at his sprawling Lake Como villa. I worry that I won't find anyone else if I break up with Tom, while they worry about whether to date Tom Cruise, Leo DiCaprio or Ashton Kutcher after their current relationship ends. I agonize over spending $1,000 a month for a rent-controlled apartment that's practically falling apart while they spend millions of dollars on their Beverly Hills mansions or Manhattan penthouses and don't think twice about it.

Sure, I'm happy with my life. I don't think I'd ever want to swim in the fishbowl of fame anyhow. But sometimes it can be a bit demoralizing when I have to have a close-up glimpse of how my life looks next to theirs.

So, hot or not — okay, grade-A gorgeous or not — Cole Brannon didn't make the top of my People I Want to Have Brunch with Tomorrow list. Really. He may have been the sexiest guy in Hollywood — quite possibly in all of America — but he was probably just as self-absorbed as the rest of them. Maybe more so. Ego is usually directly proportional to physical attractiveness, and by those standards, Cole's ego should be roughly the size of Texas.

Besides, I'd prefer breakfast in bed with Tom, preferably post-sex, to a boring breakfast with yet another movie star.

Unfortunately, I had to remind myself, breakfast in bed with Tom didn't actually appear to be an option at the moment, however, as Tom had never technically prepared a meal for me in his life. Then of course there was the whole post-sex thing, which seemed equally unlikely. We would actually have to *have* sex at some point in order to be *post*-sex. Details, details.

I finally shut down my computer, grabbed my notes, and called the company car service — the one perk to working late. I could finish my Cole Brannon research at home just as well as I could here.

On the ride downtown, I resisted the workaholic urge to look over my notes and instead looked out the window at the twilit city streaming by me. Manhattan rolled by in waves of yellow taxis, strolling couples, and businesspeople trying to flag down rides home. The hectic glow of Times Square disappeared behind us as we drove, passing the Flatiron Building, then Union Square, where I often bought fresh fruits, vegetables, and bread at the farmers' market on Saturdays. The Virgin Megastore on Fourteenth flashed its bright lights as we drove by, and three-story posters of Madonna, matchbox twenty, Courtney Jaye, and Sister Hazel – all of whom I'd interviewed – kept watch over the city from the windows. As we passed the Strand, I recalled with longing the days when I had time to browse through their endless supply of books for hours, finally settling on a quick read or two to get lost in over coffee in Little Italy. It felt like ages since I'd had that kind of spare time.

Finally, the car turned left on Eighth Street. In a moment, we slowly crossed St Mark's Place, where NYU students and Village funksters decked out in all the colors of the rainbow perused record stores, scanned the endless rows of silver rings, sunglasses, and scarves, or ducked into cheap sandwich shops. As we turned onto Second Avenue, I asked the driver to drop me at one of my favorite Chinese restaurants in the neighborhood, two blocks up from my apartment. It wasn't until I stepped inside that I remembered I'd promised to call Tom before leaving the office.

'I thought you were going to be a few more hours,' Tom said when he answered the phone a couple of minutes later. I grimaced as my stomach growled, triggered by the sweet, spicy smells that now surrounded me. Mr Wong, the store owner, stared at me patiently.

'I figured I'd just finish up reading all these clips at home,' I said, smiling at Mr Wong. 'I wanted to see you.'

'Oh,' said Tom. He was silent for a moment. 'So where are you now?'

'At the Chinese place. What do you want me to get?'

'You're already back?' He cleared his throat. 'That was quick.'

'I guess so,' I said with a shrug. 'Do you want the Szechuan chicken?'

'That sounds good,' Tom said.

'With lo mein, white rice, and an egg roll?' I asked. Man, I knew him well. Either that, or we ordered Chinese way too much. Looking at Mr Wong, who was still staring at me patiently, I realized it was probably the latter. I talked to him more frequently than I talked to my own mother – and he barely spoke English.

'Yeah,' Tom said again. 'Thanks for picking it up. I'll see you in a few minutes.'

The line went dead, and my stomach growled again. I ordered quickly and didn't refuse when Mr Wong, who must have been a mind reader, silently passed me a little bag of crispy noodles to munch on while I waited.

'Dinner has arrived!' I panted, pushing open the door to my apartment and catching my breath after climbing the four flights of stairs. If I hadn't gotten this apartment at a very reduced, rent-controlled price (my dad's cousin Josie had lived here for twenty years before I moved in, and I was lucky enough to share her last name – therefore, somewhat illegally, her rent-control reduction), I definitely would have insisted upon a building with an elevator.

'Hi, Claire.' Tom emerged from the bathroom, drying his hands on a towel. His shirt was half tucked in and looked like he'd been sleeping in it for a week. He looked every bit the part of a stereotypical struggling novelist. 'You're home.'

'Finally!' I exclaimed, setting the brown bag of Chinese food down on the kitchen table and thinking how cute he looked. The maternal instinct in me wanted to tuck his shirt in and spray it with wrinkle releaser. The sex-starved twenty-six-year-old who had been writing about one-night stands for the last forty-eight hours wanted to jump him. My stomach growled and reminded me to put off both alternatives until after I'd eaten. 'What a day!'

Tom crossed the room and kissed me on the top of my head.

'Thanks for getting dinner,' he said. He sat down at the table and started unpacking the contents of the bag, which Mr Wong, who was not only a mind reader but also apparently a mechanical engineer of Chinese food, had assembled perfectly. 'Can you grab me a Coke?'

'Sure,' I said. I grabbed two Cokes – regular for Tom, diet for me – from the fridge and set them down on the table. 'I'm just going to wash up, then I'll be out in a sec.'

'Sure,' said Tom, his mouth already full of lo mein noodles. 'Grab me a napkin too, would ya?'

'Yeah,' I said, reaching under the sink. I grabbed a handful of paper napkins from the cabinet and put them on the table. 'I'll be right back.'

With Tom hungrily slurping lo mein behind me and the crispy noodles doing very little to fill the growling hole in my stomach, I hurried to the bathroom, flicked the light on, and closed the door behind me.

I washed my hands and looked at myself in the mirror carefully. I'd long stopped cursing the freckles that were splashed across my nose and both cheeks. I used to hate them – they didn't quite seem to go with my wavy, hard-to-tame blond hair – but now I thought they were sort of cute. Even if Tom said they made me look like a teenager. At twenty-six, I was anything but.

I sighed and went into the bedroom to change into my favorite University of Georgia T-shirt and a pair of jeans. Stripping off the black A-line skirt and H&M boat neck tee I'd worn to work that day, I frowned as I caught a glimpse of my pasty white shape in our full-length mirror. In the past few months it seemed my thighs had started to thicken, and I'd added a few inches around the waist. Sure, I'd probably put on only five pounds or so, but when you're just five feet tall, every pound seems to show in triplicate. Of course, not one ounce had distributed itself to my breasts. Story of my life. I was still holding strong at the A-cup level.

Maybe the added cellulite in my thighs and pounds around my waist, which were really only noticeable with my clothes off, were the culprits for Tom's seemingly waning interest in me. Geez, didn't I know better? 'You'll never find a man if you don't keep up your appearance.' My mother's voice echoed in my head, as it often did in times of crisis. Easy for her to say. She did an hour of aerobics and an hour of Pilates each day. Of course, she had little else to do. Mortimer, her third husband, was a retired surgeon with one hell of an investment portfolio. He'd insisted she quit her job immediately after she married him, and she had happily agreed.

My stomach growled, reminding me of my original objective. I wriggled into my T-shirt and jeans, smoothed my flyaway blond strands, and, resolving to ignore my reflection for the time being, hurried back into the kitchen to join Tom at the table.

But Tom was already sitting back at his computer, his arms crossed over his chest, staring impassively at the screen. His plate and fork, still covered in remnants of noodles and vegetables, sat in the kitchen sink. His empty can of Coke stood vigil at his spot at the table.

'Thanks for picking up the food, Claire,' he said absently. I stared at the empty box of lo mein noodles that stood in the middle of the table, as if I might have some use for the three or four strands that clung to the inside of the cardboard container. 'It was great.'

I clenched my teeth and helped myself to the portion of chicken and white rice that he apparently hadn't been hungry enough to eat.

I didn't need to eat that much anyhow, I reminded myself. I definitely needed to drop a few pounds. I looked down at my stomach, which growled insistently at me again. So actually, Tom had done me a favor, right? He was inadvertently aiding my diet.

As if to second the motion, he burped complacently, uncrossed his arms, and started typing.

I was still poring over pages and pages of Cole Brannon clips hours later, after Tom had turned in for the night.

'I'm just really worn out,' he explained. 'I'll see you when you come to bed, babe.'

I struggled to keep my eyes open as I read by the light of the table lamp. I was starting to feel annoyed at Cole Brannon, not because he didn't sound like a nice guy (on the contrary, he sounded surprisingly great in his interviews), but because he was now single-handedly depriving me of sleep and time with Tom.

Not that anything was guaranteed any more in my time with Tom. But tonight might have been different. You never know. Maybe day 30 was the charm. I crossed my fingers at the thought, which temporarily made it impossible to turn the pages.

I sighed and returned to reading about Cole Brannon. I was already reading the final interviews, ones he had done just a few weeks ago, and the screen of my laptop was filled with pages of questions for him and notes to myself about topics I hoped to cover the next morning at brunch.

All the papers and magazines seemed to love him. The *Boston Globe* ran a piece by columnist Kara Brown last month that started like this:

> He's larger than life, and in person, Cole Brannon is no less impressive than he is on-screen. He holds doors like his gentlemanly character in *Friends Forever*, laughs at my admittedly poor jokes with the cheerful politeness of his character in *A Night in New York*, and makes intense eye contact with all the skills of his *Goodnight Kiss* charming rogue.

He grins and scribbles his name graciously as giggling teenage autograph seekers approach the table.

'I wouldn't be where I am without them,' says the Boston-born Brannon with a self-effacing shrug.

He certainly sounded nice. But, I reminded myself, he was an actor. It was his job to be able to convince you that his personality was whatever he wanted you to believe.

A short item from MSNBC addressed the recent buzz about Cole Brannon's rumored romance with a married actress:

While rumors of a budding affair with Aussie actress Kylie Dane persist, Cole Brannon denies them.

'She's a lovely woman, and I'm proud to call her my friend,' Brannon said. 'But it's ludicrous to suggest that there is anything more between us. She's married, and I would simply never cross that line.'

He sounded genuine, but he was an *actor*, and rumors get started for a reason. But perhaps it wasn't true — I would give him the benefit of the doubt, as I tried to do for everyone I interviewed. It was only fair. No doubt he would expect a question about Kylie Dane in every interview he did now, anyhow, so he'd be prepared for my nosiness.

This may not seem very journalistically sound, but in a way I regretted that I would have to ask. I was a firm believer that a celebrity's personal life should be, well, personal. But I knew it came with the territory. It was part of being famous. And oddly, the more fame someone achieved for his or her personal exploits, the more fame that person seemed to achieve on-screen or on the *Billboard* charts.

I mean, look at J-Lo and the whole 'Bennifer' debacle. Or Colin Farrell and how quickly his bed-hopping (okay, and his sexy, lopsided grin) had catapulted him to stardom.

As a reporter, I simply couldn't ignore the hottest gossip concerning an actor. I would ask the question as politely and unobtrusively as possible, eyes downcast, feeling guilty.

The actors, in turn, would act annoyed at my intrusion, but I suspected they were secretly pleased that the buzz around them was so prevalent that it would be part of our interview.

The last article in the series of clips was a small Page Six item:

> Despite rumors of a romance with actress Kylie Dane, Cole Brannon was seen earlier this week canoodling with Italian model Gina Bevinetto in the VIP room at BLVD, then joining Rosario Dawson and Scarlett Johansson at the bar.

Yep, I thought as I put the final touches on my questions and notes and hit Print. He was unarguably the hottest star in Hollywood right now, and I was having brunch with him in the morning. I looked at his photograph and felt a momentary and very unfamiliar rush of excitement, but it disappeared just as quickly. It was definitely time for bed.

It was pretty much a given – crossed fingers or not – that there was no excitement awaiting me there.

How to Meet a Movie Star

I was at the Ritz on Central Park South at quarter to ten, fifteen minutes before the scheduled brunch with the hottest guy in Hollywood. I rubbed the sleep out of my eyes as I waited in the entryway to Atelier, the Ritz's premier dining room, and one of the chicest restaurants in New York. And by chic, I mean ostentatious. Pretentious. Showy. Froufrou.

I was surprised, in a way, that Cole Brannon would choose such a place to meet. But who could tell with celebs these days? Maybe his everyday, middle-class Boston-born persona had been replaced with that of a wealthy, caviar-loving Upper East Sider. It figured. I felt embarrassingly out of my element as I shifted from foot to foot and watched a parade of Gucci, Prada, and Escada float by.

I always hated meeting celebrities for meals. On the surface it seemed glamorous. I got to dine out at exclusive restaurants that I wouldn't, in a million years, be able to afford on my own. Once the celebrity had glided in, twenty minutes late and often armed with a makeup artist, a publicist, and a personal assistant, our table would immediately become the center of attention, the glowing core of our own solar system. I'd be the object of envy for dozens of other diners who were no doubt wondering who I was, and why a plain girl like me was dining with Julia Roberts, Paris Hilton, or Gwen Stefani.

Then it became an exercise in futility. The

actor/singer/model in question would nearly forget I was there, even as I asked questions. Instead of making eye contact and truly having a conversation with me, the celeb would multitask like a pro: scanning the room to bask in the adoration of fans, checking pager and cell phone messages, sipping champagne, and whispering to either the personal assistant or publicist, all at once. I always felt like I was somehow intruding on their little private world, despite the fact that *Mod*'s corporate card was paying for the meal for this actor/singer/model and her entourage – and often a doggie bag of food which was, quite literally, for her dog.

So you can imagine why brunch with the gorgeous Cole Brannon didn't excite me quite as much as it perhaps should have. I had no doubt that he would a) be late, b) arrive with an impressive entourage and possibly a model or actress he'd shacked up with the night before, c) be either hung over or simply too bored with me to answer my questions, and d) spend the interview trying to catch a glimpse of his perfect features in the backs of spoons, glossy undersides of serving trays, and the spotless silver carafes the busy waiters bustled by with.

I just wasn't in the mood for yet another prima donna star this morning. But I had a job to do, and I had little choice but to do it.

Ten minutes after arriving at Atelier, I decided out of desperation that I would check in for our reservation and Cole Brannon could join me when he arrived. I was dying for a cappuccino, and I didn't think he'd mind if I got a jump-start on my morning caffeine fix. I asked for a table near the door and watched the entrance intently, so that I'd see him when he came in.

The tables were spread far apart, and the soaring ceiling gave the room an airy feeling. The dark wood and tan fabric melded together in classy (a little nondescript if you ask me) harmony. A myriad of colorful modern art, clearly as expensive as it was bright, lined the walls.

Expressionless waiters bustled back and forth, nearly running, while the wealthy patrons tittered lightly, using precisely the correct silverware from their selections of roughly a dozen utensils. My manners were nowhere near that advanced. After the primary three utensils and the salad fork, I was lost. I slunk down in my chair and tried to blend in with the artwork.

When Cole Brannon still hadn't arrived at 11:00, my cappuccino was gone, and my good humor was wearing off. Celebrities often strolled in a bit late, but a whole hour? When I'd given up a weekend with Tom to slave over a last-minute interview and profile? I'd been all ready to give Cole Brannon the benefit of the doubt – especially since he'd actually sounded *nice* and down-to-earth in the overwhelming majority of clips that were now emblazoned on my brain – but this was testing my patience. I took out my cell phone to dial Cole's publicist, Ivana Donatelli, who had set up this meeting, but I was put through directly to her voice mail. Apparently, she wasn't up either.

Five minutes later, after I'd grumpily waved away yet another attempt by the obsequious waiter to bring me another cappuccino, my cell phone rang. The caller ID said 'Unavailable'. I was sure it was Ivana calling back.

'Hello?' I snapped, knowing that my voice must have sounded almost as peeved as I was beginning to feel.

'Claire?' The male voice wasn't the one I was expecting, but it sounded vaguely familiar all the same. It was far too deep and husky to belong to Tom. But there was something about the way he softened the *r* sound in 'Claire' that rang a bell.

'Yes . . .' I said slowly, still trying to place the somehow familiar intonation.

'It's Cole.' He cleared his throat, and I could feel my eyebrows arch upward in surprise. 'Um, Cole Brannon,' he clarified, as if I might be receiving calls from another man named Cole. Well, this is a first, I thought huffily, squaring my shoulders in annoyance. I'd never actually had a celebrity call me *himself* to cancel, or blow me off, or whatever it was he was about to do.

'Hi,' I said. I couldn't think of anything else to say other than *Where the hell are you?* But that wouldn't be appropriate, now would it? So I bit my tongue and waited.

'Are you here? At the restaurant, I mean?' His voice sounded just as sexy as it always did through the Dolby Surround Sound of theaters, but it wasn't softening me up much.

'Yes, at Atelier,' I said grumpily. 'I'm at a table near the door. *By myself.*' I stressed the last part. 'Where are *you*?' Just because he was a gorgeous movie star, it didn't mean he could stand me up.

'Oh my God.' Cole Brannon started to laugh. Despite myself, the deep, resonating chuckle made me relax a bit. 'You've been here for over an hour!'

'Yes, I have,' I said rather sternly, hating that I loved his deep voice. I reminded myself that I was supposed to be annoyed at him. Then it hit me. 'Wait, how did you know that?'

'Because I've been sitting two tables over from you the whole time!'

To my horror, I suddenly realized that the laughing wasn't coming just from the phone but from a man in a baseball cap, also sitting alone at a table several feet behind me. The cap was pulled low over his eyes, and I hadn't given him a second glance when I'd arrived at the restaurant fifteen minutes early. Celebrities were *never* early, so I was sure I'd beaten Cole that morning. I hadn't given the restaurant more than a cursory glance.

'Hang on, I'm coming over,' Cole said quietly, and I heard my cell phone click off. For a second I couldn't move, and I continued to hold my silent phone to my ear, frozen in embarrassment. By now, my cheeks were fully ablaze, and I wondered if I'd ever felt dumber.

I'd kept the hottest star in Hollywood waiting for more than an hour because I hadn't noticed him. This was a new low in brainlessness, even for me. This definitely topped the sexy-heel-caught-in-the-subway-grate fiasco.

'Hello there,' Cole Brannon said cheerfully, arriving at my side. I looked up warily. For the first time I noticed his brilliant blue eyes and strands of his legendary tousled brown hair peeking out from under his Red Sox cap. In person, his face looked even more perfect than it did on the big screen or in the magazine spreads he'd been featured in. Corny as it sounds, he truly looked like he'd been chiseled by Michelangelo himself.

There was a deep dimple in his chin, and when he smiled, adorable dimples appeared in his perfectly tanned cheeks, too. I usually hated sideburns, but I suddenly loved the way his ran down his jawline, ending evenly at the bottom of his earlobes, in closely trimmed perfection. He had a small cluster of eight or so freckles across the bridge of his nose, which I'd never noticed on-screen, and there was a small, nearly imperceptible scar on the underside of his jaw. I remembered reading in the clips that it was from a football injury he'd suffered in high school.

He was dressed simply in faded jeans (which looked like anything but designer) and a navy collared shirt that stretched perfectly over his well-defined contours.

But what stood out most of all was how good he actually looked close up. I'd been around the merry-go-round of the celebrity world long enough to grasp the fact that people didn't always look as good in person as they did on-screen. Male movie stars always seemed to be shorter in person. Their hairlines always seemed to be receding (I'd even spotted cases of hairplugs up close in two of Hollywood's most popular leading men). Their heads, oddly, tended to seem inordinately large for their bodies. And the faces that looked most perfect on the big screen tended to look so Botoxed in person that they appeared to be expressionless masks.

But Cole was perfect. *Perfect.* His face looked like it

had never had a blemish in its life, his frame was perfectly proportioned, and his eyes really did sparkle with the same intensity they seemed to have on-screen. I'd always assumed that his bright baby blues were a cinematic trick, but here they were, sparkling right at me. There were laugh lines around his eyes and on his forehead, which gave away his lack of Botox experience, and he smiled a smile that looked very real. He had just a bit of dark stubble on his chin, and his dark hair was blissfully hairplug-free.

Up until this moment, I had always thought I was not so superficial as to be taken in by looks. But this was a new situation altogether. This was, without a doubt, the most attractive human being I'd ever laid eyes on. He was stunning.

Of course, I took all this in through eyes lowered in embarrassment.

'Oh my God,' I said, standing up and extending a hand, which I realized was shaking. I was suddenly having a little trouble breathing. 'I am so, so sorry. I didn't notice you there.' I was fiercely aware of my red cheeks. Then I noticed something as Cole finished shaking my hand and grabbed the chair next to mine. He didn't look angry. Instead, he was grinning at me. And laughing. Was I missing something? He even appeared to be laughing *with* me instead of *at* me. But perhaps my laugh-detecting senses were off.

He gestured for me to sit down, and even pushed my chair in before he took a seat.

'Hey, I guess that's an endorsement for the disguise then, right?' he said. As I stared at him, unsure of what to say, it suddenly occurred to me why people sometimes described eyes as 'twinkling'. That's what his blues were doing at the moment.

'I'm . . . I mean . . . Um, wow, I am *so* embarrassed,' I stammered, finally allowing myself a nervous giggle. 'How long have you been here?' Maybe he hadn't been waiting that long after all. Maybe I was less of a jackass than I'd guessed.

'Oh, an hour and a half, or so,' Cole said, still grinning.

I reddened further. Yes, I was definitely a full-fledged jackass.

'Oh no,' I moaned. 'What an idiot I am. I mean, I know what you look like – obviously.' Okay, that sounded dumb. 'And I still didn't notice you.'

Cole laughed again, and I stared in astonishment. He really wasn't mad. I must have been missing something. I half expected his bodyguard to pounce out from behind a potted plant in the corner and kick me out. No celeb I'd ever met would laugh something like this off. But there was something different about Cole Brannon. And there were no bodyguards among the bushes.

Really. I checked.

'Actually, *I* noticed *you*, but I thought to myself, there's no way that's the girl I'm supposed to meet,' Cole said. 'I mean, Ivana told me you were much older.'

Huh? I'd never even met his publicist. Why on earth would she have assumed that? Unless he meant . . .

'I'm not as young as I look,' I said, suddenly defensive. 'I mean, I know I look like a teenager. It's hard not to when you're only five feet tall . . .' I couldn't help but think of Jeffrey's *Mickey Mouse Club* comparison. I realized that Cole was laughing again, so I shut my mouth.

Perhaps I was being a bit overly sensitive.

'I didn't mean that at all!' he exclaimed. My blush deepened. Great, now I was misinterpreting his words. 'And for the record, you don't look like a teenager. You look every bit grown woman to me.' I could feel the blood rising to my face in a full-fledged blush again. 'And wow, five feet tall? That makes me more than a foot taller than you.'

One foot and four inches to be exact, I thought abstractedly, recalling the info on his bio sheet.

'Can I call you Short Stuff? Or maybe Little Lady?' he asked, feigning seriousness. I finally laughed.

'If it will help me get back into your good graces,' I said. I felt the breath go out of me as I heaved a sigh of relief and smiled at him.

'Not that you were ever *out* of my good graces,' he said. 'But I'll keep those nicknames in mind, in case I ever need them.'

I laughed again, and I knew that the ice had been broken. In the space of less than five minutes, this had gone from being the worst-begun interview to being the best. I knew it would be a good morning.

Then again, I suppose that any morning spent with the Adonis-next-door should qualify as a good morning.

'Look,' said Cole, leaning forward conspiratorially. His blue eyes were wide and his perfectly white teeth gleamed just inches from me. 'What do you say we go somewhere else for breakfast?'

'Um, okay,' I said, surprised and a bit disappointed. Geez! Celebrities and their demands! Just when I'd started to think he was different, here he was rearranging the schedule. He'd probably want to go to some place even more expensive. Nobu maybe? Or Tavern on the Green? Great.

'I mean, we can stay if you want.' Cole paused, looking at me with concern as I shook my head. 'But did you look at this menu? I mean, who eats *Eggs en Cocotte with Truffle Jus* for breakfast? What the heck is that, anyhow?'

He looked up from the menu just as a waiter walked by carrying what appeared to be exactly that egg dish (complete with thyme-roasted potatoes and the twenty-five-dollar caviar supplement offered in the menu). We both collapsed in laughter, and my heart mysteriously fluttered as his right arm brushed my left. I shook the feeling off and chided myself. I knew better than to feel giddy about celebrities.

Even if they had gorgeous blue eyes and the most perfect smile I'd ever seen.

'And look at the price!' Cole exclaimed as we finished

laughing, looking back at the menu. 'That was thirty-six dollars of egg that just walked by! Are you kidding me?'

'It is sort of ridiculous,' I admitted. I tilted my head to the side and looked at him intently, trying not to look accusatory. 'But why did you want to meet here, then?'

'Me?' he asked. He shook his head and leaned back in his seat. 'Ha! My publicist Ivana suggested it. It's her favorite restaurant. She wanted to meet us and sit in on the interview, but I see from the looks of it that she must have overslept.' He laughed again, and I realized suddenly that his laugh sounded different in person than it did at the movies. It was richer, fuller, more musical. 'So, what do you say we get out of here before Ivana decides to make an appearance? I need some real breakfast. How about bacon, eggs, and the greasiest hash browns in Manhattan?'

I grinned. 'Lead the way.'

Ten minutes later, after arguing about who would pay for my ten-dollar cappuccino — I finally won by insisting that it was against *Mod*'s policy to let a source pay for anything — we were out on the street, strolling east at the bottom of Central Park. Amazingly, no one had recognized Cole yet. Sixty-story buildings soared around us, and the silence of Central Park was fast disappearing behind us, but we hadn't been rushed by a single fan or even given a second glance. Then again, we were in an area of the city so ritzy that its residents were probably too self-absorbed to notice if a seven-foot green alien with three eyes wandered by.

'Are we going to hail a taxi?' I asked, trying to sound casual. I still couldn't figure out why being with Cole Brannon was making me feel so giddy. I had interviewed dozens of celebs, and I hadn't reacted this way since the first few A-listers I'd talked to. And that had been years ago.

'A taxi?' he said, playfully nudging me. My skin tingled oddly where he'd touched it. 'No way, Little Lady. We're taking the subway!'

'The subway?' I looked up at him incredulously. That was impossible. Every movie star I'd ever known had traveled by limo or chauffeured car – or at the very least, in their own luxury SUV. They never took the subway. Only anonymous nobodies like me took the subway.

'Hell, yeah,' Cole said cheerfully, oblivious of my confusion. He looped his arm playfully through mine for a moment. 'Look at this. No one recognizes me. Isn't this fun?' It was true. I took a quick look around to make sure we were actually surrounded by live, movie-going humans. It looked that way. I was baffled.

'In my defense, you've got that hat pulled so low I can hardly see your face,' I said, grinning up at him. From my vantage point, I had a perfect view of his cleft chin and perfect dimples, which grew even deeper every time he cracked a smile – which was a lot.

'Excuses, excuses,' he said, grinning down at me. 'But hey, you have to hand it to me. Am I the master of disguise or what?'

'That you are,' I said. *Not that looks that good should be covered up*, I wanted to say, but I bit my tongue. After all, I was Professional Claire. *Professional.* I tried to forget that I was also Sex-Starved Claire. It was totally beside the point.

'You are aware, aren't you, that you're part of the disguise?' Cole asked conspiratorially.

'Huh?'

'Well, as far as all these passersby are concerned' – he gestured grandly to the people bustling by – 'you and I are just a young couple out for a romantic stroll.' My cheeks were suddenly on fire. For a moment I forgot that Tom existed, as I realized that indeed I was out on what looked like a romantic amble with Cole Brannon.

Hmm, I could get used to this.

'I mean, all these people are expecting that Cole Brannon would be out with Kylie Dane, not a beautiful young blonde,' he continued, smiling at me as we walked.

My jaw dropped, and I wasn't sure for a moment whether it was because he himself had broached the topic of Kylie Dane, or because he'd referred to me as a beautiful young blonde. (Did Cole Brannon really think *I* was beautiful?) As a result, my response came out as a wordless gurgle, and he laughed again.

'No worries,' he said quickly. He put a hand on my arm and stopped for a minute. I stopped too, and we stood there in the middle of a parting sea of oblivious passersby. He leaned down, his face inches from my right cheek. 'I know you have to ask me about Kylie Dane,' he whispered. I could feel myself blushing again as his breath tickled my ear. In fact, I was surprised that the sheer heat emanating from my face hadn't burned him by this time. 'But it's not true. I swear to God. Really, she's a nice woman, but there's nothing between us. I would never, ever, ever get romantically involved with a married woman. I'm so sick of all the rumors, you know? I mean, this sounds crazy, but it hurts my feelings sometimes.'

I scrambled to dig my pen and notepad out of my shoulder bag and jotted down the words he'd just uttered.

'I mean, I hate that anyone would think I have no morals and would just hook up with someone who's married,' he continued, sounding pained. 'Is she a beautiful woman? Yes. But that doesn't necessarily mean I want to sleep with her. Or that she wants to sleep with me, for that matter. I just don't get how people make this stuff up in the tabloids. And you can quote me on that. All of it. In fact, please do. I hate all this tabloid crap.'

He shook his head and made a face that reminded me so much of a lost little boy that I instantly wanted to cup his face in my hands and tell him everything would be okay. Fortunately, I managed to refrain.

'I mean, she's married to a guy I've worked with, you know?' Cole continued, looking slightly pained as I scribbled. 'Where do these rumors come from?'

He pulled away from my ear, and before he

straightened up to his full six-feet-four, he looked into my eyes. Our noses were a mere few inches apart, and I gulped as I was overcome by a strange tingling sensation. Those lips . . . that I had seen . . . on the big screen . . . were . . . inches . . . from . . . my . . . lips. (I had to catch my breath.)

Then I suddenly remembered Tom and felt guilty that I was having this much . . . fun . . . with a stranger on a Saturday morning when I should have been at home with him instead. I cleared my throat and looked quickly away.

We wound up on Second Avenue and Seventh Street, just five blocks from my apartment, at a twenty-four-hour diner called Over the Moon. I'd been there more than once on my own. The walls had all been painted in bright blues and vibrant whites, and the local artist had added leaping cows in all the colors of the rainbow. In their honor, I had always refrained from ordering a hamburger.

'I love it here,' Cole said as he held the door open. 'I think they triple-fry everything in vats of grease.'

'Ew!' I said, not really meaning it. I loved fried, greasy food too, although I knew that Merri Derekson, the editor of *Mod*'s health section, would probably kick me for saying so. I was sure I was about to consume three days' worth of fat grams. So I kept quiet and insisted my jiggly thighs do the same.

Cole laughed. 'Hey, don't knock it till you've tried it, Short Stuff,' he said. He paused for a moment while I made a face at him, amazing myself with how friendly I was suddenly feeling with the incognito major star. 'Hey now, you're not allowed to stick your tongue out at me! We agreed I could use those nicknames at my discretion.'

'I thought I was already back in your good graces,' I egged him on.

'Simply a technicality, my dear,' he said seriously.

As a server led us to a corner table by the window, I

realized that I kind of liked it when he used the nickname, silly as it was. God, I was ignoring my own cardinal rule of reporting and actually beginning to *like* Cole Brannon. I was giggling at his jokes and feeling slightly woozy in his presence. And I had a boyfriend! What was I thinking?

'Um, excuse me for a moment,' I said as soon as we were seated. 'I need to go to the bathroom.'

'That cappuccino from Atelier got you, huh?' Cole teased.

'Smallest bladder in Manhattan, right here,' I admitted, trying not to blush. He laughed and stood up as I pushed my chair out. I looked at him in surprise.

'Sorry,' he said with a sheepish smile. 'My mom's manners lessons are too ingrained to ignore. I always have to stand when a lady leaves the table, or I'm afraid Mom will jump out and send me to my room.'

I laughed. 'No, it's actually kinda nice,' I admitted. 'I don't think anyone's ever done that before.'

'What?' Cole feigned horror with perfection only a professional actor could achieve. 'For a lady like you? You're kidding. Men must trip all over themselves to charm you.'

I suddenly had a mental picture of Tom slurping down the lo mein noodles I'd just brought home before I'd even had a chance to wash up.

'No, not exactly,' I said. Cole shook his head in astonishment as I turned to walk toward the back of the restaurant, where I hoped to find a bathroom – and regain my vanishing sanity.

I actually did have to go to the ladies' room, but more than that, I needed a moment away from Cole Brannon. I felt that things were spinning a bit out of control.

I liked him. I wasn't supposed to like him. My insides weren't supposed to tingle when he grinned. I wasn't supposed to be acting like a smitten teenager.

There were two things wrong with that. First, obviously, there was Tom. But that wasn't bothering me too much. I'd never cheated on anyone, nor would I ever. I loved Tom.

What concerned me more was that I was letting my professional objectivity slip. It was fine if I found the people I interviewed to be nice and friendly, but this was different. I found myself talking to Cole like I'd known him for years, and I was more comfortable with him than I was with people I saw every day. It was strange. Although I couldn't explain why it was happening, I knew it wasn't supposed to be this way.

Sure, lots of reporters hooked up with the celebs they interviewed – or at least they aspired to. But I had always vowed to myself that I'd never be that kind of reporter. The world of magazines was possibly the most gossipy one in existence. Within five minutes of a reporter's stumbling out of a movie star's hotel suite, editors at *Glamour*, *Vogue*, *In Style*, and *People* would be talking. And you'd always be 'that reporter who slept with Colin Farrell', or 'that reporter who went down on Chad Pennington'. You never got promoted, people whispered about you in the halls, and even the celebs themselves seemed to have some kind of sex-tips wire service – meaning that a third of the interviews you showed up for from then on would include a slew of sexual innuendos and come-ons designed to get you into bed. And it was hard to do a serious interview when you were fending off lascivious stares and groping hands.

Eventually you're forced to quit, because the whole sex stigma affects your work from the bottom up. You can no longer score the best interviews because the publicists all know your reputation. They secretly wish they could be in the position to sleep with movie stars every day, so they're pissed off at you and refuse to answer your calls. Your editors frown upon the reputation you're spreading for the magazine. And the movie stars who *don't* want to sleep with you start the interview off hating you because your exploits make their profession look bad.

It had happened to Laura Worthington, the girl I'd roomed with the first year I lived in Manhattan. She was an editorial assistant at *Rolling Stone*, and she was frustrated because, as the newbie, she was never sent out on exciting assignments. Once in a blue moon she got to cover a party, but most of the time she was responsible for editing the *Billboard* charts, fact-checking the feature editor's always-sloppy work, and calling publicists to verify facts and figures. When the features editor was sick one day and Laura was sent out to interview Kirk Bryant, the floppy-haired, tattooed, and not-at-all-good-looking lead singer of an up-and-coming rock band whose single had just broken the *Billboard* Top Ten, she was thrilled and just a bit star-struck. Thirty minutes into the interview, which he'd conveniently moved from the Four Seasons lobby to his suite on the sixth floor, she was naked on his bed. Forty minutes into the interview, he was zipping up his pants and showing her the door. By the time she got back to the office, other editorial assistants were glaring at her suspiciously, and she realized that she didn't have *quite* enough information to write an article about Kirk, as they hadn't actually *talked* about anything. So she fudged the quotes and sat by the phone for a week, wondering why Kirk Bryant didn't call. Two weeks later she enthusiastically spread her legs ('To help me forget about Kirk,' she told me with a sigh) for Chris Williams, whose band, Mudpile, had just catapulted from obscurity to being the most-requested band on MTV's *Total Request Live*. Of course, she had to make up quotes for that interview too, as there wasn't much time for work-related talk between the sighs and the moans. It was after another year – and eleven rock stars later – that Laura was finally fired. Now she answered phones at a talent agency in L.A. for seven dollars an hour.

I had always vowed that I would keep my emotions completely removed from my job. I wasn't Laura. No crushes allowed. And here I was making googly-eyes at

Hollywood's Most Eligible Bachelor. What was wrong with me?

I chided myself for responding like a rookie to Cole Brannon's charms. After all, it was his job to charm me if he wanted to appear to be a good guy in the media. Maybe he was just a friendly guy who wanted to come across well in *Mod* magazine.

I looked in the mirror and rolled my eyes at myself. I knew better. I needed to grow up and start acting like the professional I was and always had been. I'd done my job, I'd put him at ease. Now it was time for me to stop drooling – surely he saw enough of that every day – and get on with the interview. The sooner I got back to the office to transcribe the interview and type up the article, the sooner I'd get home to Tom, which is where I belonged.

Maybe Tom and I could actually have sex today – on day 31 of the famine – if I made it home early enough. After all, it was a weekend. Surely Tom had slept in, so he couldn't claim exhaustion. Yep, tonight would be the night. The night for some serious lovin'. *Voulez-vous coucher avec moi?* as Christina Aguilera would say.

I smiled at myself in the mirror with new resolve, turned away, and headed back through the bathroom door.

Cole was sitting just where I'd left him, and I tried not to admire the broad contour of his shoulders as I approached from behind. After all, the width of his shoulders and the beautifully sculpted way his whole body fit together were really irrelevant. Right?

'Hey there,' he said cheerfully, standing as I came up beside him. He waited to sit down until I'd settled into my chair. 'I was starting to worry that you'd fallen in.'

I resisted the urge to laugh and instead tried to frown – professionally, of course. I imagine my expression must have come out oddly twisted and meaningless, for I could have sworn I noticed a flicker of confusion cross his eyes.

'Um, no,' I said. I warned myself to ignore those ridiculously gorgeous blue eyes. I needed to be professional. They were probably contacts anyhow, and what kind of vain guy wears colored contacts to brunch? I cleared my throat. 'I've already taken enough of your time. Shall we get on with the interview?'

'Oh no, don't worry about me,' Cole said in that perfect, musical baritone. 'I love it here. It's my favorite restaurant. And I've got nothing else to do today.' He leaned back lazily in his chair and grinned. I resisted the urge to smile back. I was Serious Claire and I would take that role, well, seriously.

'Unfortunately, *I* do,' I said with my best attempt at a frown. 'This article on you is due tomorrow, so that means I have to get most of it written today.'

'On a Saturday?' he asked incredulously. He leaned forward, his blue eyes wide. 'You're kidding me! That's no fun!'

'You're telling me!'

'So there's no escaping the charm of Cole Brannon this weekend, then, is there?' He grinned again. I made another face at him, despite myself.

'No, apparently not.'

'Well, let's get to it, then, Little Lady,' he said. He gestured for our waitress. 'But first we have to order. I can't do an interview on an empty stomach.'

I laughed and looked down at the menu as our waitress approached. I couldn't figure out why I thought it was so cute when he called me 'Little Lady'. There was something in my head that told me his words should offend, but somehow they did anything but. They made me blush.

'Is Marge working today?' Cole asked the waitress who approached our table. I snuck a look up at him as he smiled at her.

'No sir,' she said shyly. 'Today's her day off.'

'That's too bad,' Cole said with a grin. 'You'll have to tell her Cole says "hi".' He turned to me and smiled. 'She's my favorite waitress. Reminds me of my mom.'

I smiled and nodded. This guy seemed so sweet. But was it all an act?

'Know what you want?' he asked me. As if I had to think about it. I always ordered the same breakfast at every diner I'd eaten in for the past several years.

'I'll have two fried eggs, over easy, with hash browns and bacon, fried extra crispy, please,' I said. 'Oh, and can you add cheese to those hash browns, too?'

Cole arched an eyebrow at me.

'I like a woman who can eat,' he said, smiling. 'You know, I'll have the same thing,' Cole said finally. 'Oh, and a big pot of coffee for both of us. She looks like she needs some caffeine, doesn't she?'

'Hey!' I said, mildly insulted for a split second before Cole flashed me another big smile. I grinned back before remembering my vow to be nothing but professional. 'Ahem,' I cleared my throat as the waitress walked away. I was vaguely confused that she didn't seem starstruck, like every other server I'd ever seen wait on a celeb seemed to be. But Cole seemed to be a regular here. Was it possible they were simply used to him? 'Shall we begin?' I asked.

'Ready when you are, boss,' he said, settling his tall frame back into the chair again.

'Mind if I tape this?' I asked, although no one had ever turned me down. 'It helps me make sure that I get every one of your quotes accurately when I'm writing the story later on.'

'Well heck, I don't want to be misquoted,' he said. 'Tape away.'

How to Talk to Your Dream Man

Two hours later I was on my way to the office, trying to stop glowing. I had managed to remain cool and professional throughout the interview – in which Cole had cheerfully covered everything from memories of learning to cook with his dad, to his first tentative foray into acting at Boston College, to his close relationship with his four-year-old nephew Nicholas, to his upcoming movie *Forever Good-bye*, due out Labor Day Weekend.

It was like no interview I'd ever done before. Normally, the actors I interviewed had already done a thousand interviews just like mine before they ever sat down with me. As hard as I tried to make my questions unique and interesting, I usually got cardboard, cookie-cutter answers that sounded just as rehearsed as they probably were. But with Cole, it was different.

He laughed like he meant it. The corners of his eyes crinkled up when I teased him back. He was humble, and it didn't seem fake. He watched me intently while we talked, whereas most other celebs I'd interviewed tended to scan the room repeatedly, rarely focusing their eyes on me. Cole had even opened up and grumbled to me about how he sometimes got annoyed when fans followed him.

'It's not that I mind the fans,' he said sheepishly. 'I really don't. I mean, how cool is it to know there are people out there who've never met you but who like you anyway? But really, I mean, I sign autographs and chat with them for a while, but sometimes there are these girls who follow me, like ten paces behind when I'm at the grocery store or something. It's just awkward, you know? I mean, what do you do? Turn around and ask them to join you? Pretend you don't see them? I never know how to act.'

Cole Brannon was just *real*. There was no facade. There were no pretenses. He wasn't *acting*. And that's something I had never expected.

As we parted ways at the top of the steps to the Eighth Street station, Cole had given me a hug before I descended to the R train.

Now I couldn't stop the scene from replaying again and again in my mind.

'I really enjoyed meeting you, Claire,' he'd said as we stood there on the sidewalk.

'It was nice to meet you too,' I'd said. Then he handed me a piece of paper.

'Here's my cell phone number if you have any more questions,' he said, pressing it into my palm. 'It will be easier than going through Ivana. She's probably still in bed.'

'Um, thanks,' I said, my heart fluttering as I clutched Cole Brannon's number. Was he flirting with me? No, I decided. He was simply being kind because he knew I'd be stuck working on the article all weekend. The biggest movie star in Hollywood couldn't possibly be flirting with *me*.

'Okay then, Little Lady,' he'd said. 'I guess this is where we say good-bye.'

'Yeah, I guess so,' I said. 'Are you going to get back to your hotel all right?'

'I think I can manage without you,' Cole said. He grinned. I could feel my cheeks heat up.

'I didn't mean—'

'I know,' Cole interrupted. 'You're just easy to tease.' Then he hugged me. I mean, he actually reached out and hugged me, engulfing my five-foot frame with his muscular arms and chest, pulling me into an embrace that was much gentler than I would have imagined had I put any thought into what it would feel like to hug Cole Brannon.

Which, I was embarrassed to admit, I had. Was that inappropriate? I tried not to think about it.

I could still feel his arms around me as the subway rattled on belowground.

He's a movie star. He dates other movie stars. And you are not a movie star. I kept repeating the words in my head, just in case I had forgotten.

I arrived at the Forty-ninth Street stop and re-emerged into the daylight, clutching my shoulder bag full of notes and the tape recorder that held my interview with Cole. It had been a wonderful morning, but I was confident that the tape would be all that would remain of it. *Mod* would only do a cover story on an actor once, so I knew the closest I'd ever get to Cole Brannon again was a chance run-in at a movie premiere or a Super Bowl party, where he wouldn't remember my name as I shouted questions at him from behind the ropes of the red carpet.

It was kind of a depressing thought. What a weird world I lived in where sometimes I got to know a person inside and out, only to have them disappear from my life forever. My friends back home envied my access to celebrities. But they never believed me when I told them my job made for the loneliest kind of life.

Three hours later, working at breakneck pace, I had managed to transcribe the entire interview, which added up to a whopping twenty single-spaced pages on my computer screen. Now all that was left was to turn the interview into a two-thousand-word profile of Cole Brannon. It wouldn't take me long, I knew. I'd already started mentally formulating the article, trying to avoid being stirred by Cole's deep voice in my headphones.

He had seemed almost too good to be true. Despite the flashy temptations of Hollywood, he truly seemed like he had remained grounded and normal. He was one of the only movie stars I'd interviewed who still shopped for himself rather than have a personal shopper pick out everything from his coats to his socks. He still got excited when he got free clothes in the mail from publicists trying to get him to wear their clients' products.

'It's like Christmas all the time,' he had exclaimed, shaking his head in wonder. He loved pulling his Red Sox cap low over his eyes, donning a plain, non-designer T-shirt and jeans, and sneaking out alone to movies, dinners, and malls, unrecognized. He was close with his former costars, including George Clooney, Mark Wahlberg, Brad Pitt, Julia Roberts, Jennifer Aniston, Matt Damon, and Tom Hanks, but his best friends were the guys he'd grown up with and a few pals he'd met in college. He loved reading everything from Shakespeare to James Patterson to Dave Barry, but he hated reading celebrity gossip, because it was so unreliable and silly.

'No offense,' he had quickly added. 'I promise I'll read your article about me. But I know it won't be gossip or fluff, you know? It's different.' He loved cooking, surfing, and tuna fishing. And he was scared of spiders, he shyly admitted.

In short, he sounded absolutely normal, and dare I say it, perfect. The only problem I would have was picking and choosing from the many great details. I couldn't fit them all in the article, although I would have loved to.

My fingers were poised over the keyboard and I was just about to start typing when the phone on my desk jangled loudly, breaking the silence.

'Shit,' I cursed under my breath, knocking my mug over and spilling coffee across my desk for the third time that week. I picked up the receiver.

'Hello?' I answered on the second ring, my heart still thumping from the scare.

'Claire!' It was Wendy, and she sounded accusatory. 'You were supposed to call me when you were done interviewing Cole Brannon!'

'Oops,' I said, suddenly guilty. 'I'm so sorry, I forgot.'

'You forgot to call me?' Wendy made a strangled noise. 'So? What happened?'

'What do you mean?' I asked, trying to sound innocent. After all, I was innocent, right? I'd just felt a bit attracted to the guy. It wasn't like I had thrown myself at him. Or slept with him. (Although on second thought, perhaps I should have considered it. Talk about ending my sex drought with a bang! But I digress . . .)

'What was he like?' Wendy asked excitedly, talking a mile a minute. 'Was he nice? Was he as cute in person as he is in the movies? Did he hit on you?'

'Slow down!' I laughed. 'He was very nice. It was a great interview.'

'Blah, blah, blah,' Wendy said. She giggled. 'Interview, schminterview. I don't care. What was he *like*?'

'He was very nice,' I repeated, although I knew Wendy would keep pressing until I gave her more.

'He "very nice"?' Wendy repeated. '*Very nice?* Girl, you gotta give me something else to work with here.'

'Okay,' I agreed after a moment of silence. I sighed. 'He was gorgeous. You wouldn't believe how his eyes look in person. He talks about his mom and his big sisters like they're his best friends in the world – and I think he really means it. He stood up every time I left the table, he laughs all the time, and when he hugged me, it was more gentle than you could imagine.' I was blushing before I finished the sentence. I'd just sounded like a smitten schoolgirl.

Wendy gasped and fell silent for long enough that I started to feel uncomfortable.

'Wendy?' I finally asked gingerly.

'He *hugged* you?' she finally squealed. 'He *hugged*

you?' I cleared my throat and immediately regretted telling her.

'Well, it was just to say good-bye, you know,' I said, trying to backtrack. 'It was nothing. Just a professional hug.'

'A professional hug?' Wendy repeated flatly. 'Claire, c'mon! There's no such thing as a professional hug. He liked you!'

'Yeah, right.'

'Are you kidding me?' Wendy said. 'How often have you been hugged after you do an interview?' Okay, she was right. Never. 'Wake up, honey!'

'No way,' I said firmly. I was sure it didn't mean anything. After all, that would be crazy, right? 'I think that's just how he is. He's like that with everyone. You should read some of the articles about him that I found in the clip files. He charms everyone.'

'He charms the *pants* off everyone,' Wendy corrected quickly. 'Don't you read *Tattletale*?'

I rolled my eyes and tried to pretend that her words didn't bother me.

'I don't believe that,' I said softly. I knew exactly what she was talking about.

Tattletale was so unreliable that our clipping service didn't even include their articles. But I knew gossip well enough to know that it often contained a grain of truth. And the tabloid rag had reported twice in the last month that Cole Brannon was sleeping around with everyone he could get his hands on – from leading ladies to makeup artists to the nineteen-year-old craft service girl who had worked the buffet line on his last movie set.

I didn't believe it. Okay, or maybe I didn't *want* to believe it. *Tattletale* was unreliable. (After all, they were the tabloid that constantly published ridiculous claims from Sidra about her 'time with George Clooney'.) And Cole had seemed so *nice*. It couldn't be true.

Wendy giggled, oblivious of my confusion.

'He's apparently some kind of a sex addict,' she said brightly. 'I mean, he has this reputation for hooking up with anything that walks.'

'I don't believe it,' I repeated in an unconvincing mumble.

'Believe what you will,' Wendy chirped. 'But now that he's midway into charming *your* pants off, I thought I'd better warn you.' She laughed. I blushed, thankful that Wendy wasn't here to see my giveaway reaction. Which meant nothing.

'He's not charming my pants off,' I protested. 'And anyhow, it's not true. He's not like that.'

'Whatever you say,' Wendy said sweetly. I knew she was teasing me, egging me on. She pressed on. 'My friend Diane's friend Matty works at *Tattletale*, and she told me this week they're going to report that Cole Brannon's sleeping with his publicist. Some woman named Ivana, I think.'

I could feel my heart drop in my chest. For a moment, I was entirely speechless.

Suddenly, it all made sense. Ivana had planned to come to brunch with us. Cole had known that she was still in bed. I tried to ignore the fact that I felt betrayed and hurt. What was the matter with me? Was I actually feeling *jealous* of Ivana Donatelli?

'Um, that can't be true,' I stammered. 'He didn't seem like that kind of a guy.'

'And your judgment about men is so good?'

I knew Wendy was referring to Tom, but I ignored her.

'So . . .' Wendy's voice trailed off suggestively. 'I still think you should test your one-night-stand theory on Cole Brannon. Seeing as how he seemed so willing.' She giggled.

'First of all,' I said, 'it's not *my* theory. Secondly, did you forget about Tom?' I hadn't. I looked at my watch. It was 5 p.m. I told him I wouldn't be home until at least ten o'clock, but I was moving along at a remarkable pace. I had a feeling I'd be done with a first draft by 6:30 if I could just get Wendy off the phone. I'd have to come back tomorrow to fact-check and do some final edits, but I was hours ahead of where I thought I would be today. Cole was just so easy to write about.

'Tell you what,' I said finally. 'If Cole Brannon is such a sex addict, *you* go and sleep with him. In the meantime, I'm going to finish up my article and go home to my boyfriend.'

'You're no fun.' Wendy pouted.

'I know,' I said. 'And because I'm so boring, I have to get going. I'll be here forever if I don't get started writing.'

'Okay, okay,' Wendy said, sounding resigned. 'Suit yourself. It's your loss. "Claire Brannon" had such a nice ring to it. Or you could hyphenate. "Claire Reilly-Brannon." What do you think?' I growled at her and she laughed. We said our good-byes and hung up, and I turned back to the computer screen.

I stared at it blankly for a moment, leaning back in my chair. How had I been so foolish? Of course he was sleeping with Ivana. Why should it bother me, anyhow? I had Tom.

Besides, it would be ludicrous to think my affections could ever be returned, if I indeed ever did start developing a Cole Brannon crush. He was the world's hottest movie star. I was the world's plainest, shortest, most boring magazine journalist. We weren't exactly screaming 'compatibility'.

Anyhow, I knew better than to actually start developing a crush on an interview subject. I knew better than to believe that his charm was real. And I also knew I had a boyfriend whom I would never even dream of cheating on. Ever. I knew I could never do that to anyone.

I sighed and leaned forward, ready to start writing. Whether he was a sex addict who liked to sleep around or not, I liked what Cole Brannon had said to me during the interview. I was determined that he would come across well in the article, too.

True to my prediction, I'd finished a draft I was happy with by 6:30. Cole Brannon was easy to write about, partially because his quotes fit so well into the flow of the story, and partially because there was so much to say about him. It was rare to find an actor that well-spoken. Plus, he had elaborated on everything – the interview hadn't been like pulling teeth, like it often was with other celebs – so I had plenty of quotes to choose from. By the time I wrapped up, I was happy with the final product.

I picked up the phone to tell Tom I'd be home early, but I replaced the phone in its cradle before dialing. He'd said he'd be in all day. He wouldn't be expecting me until at least 10 p.m. I'd make it home by 7:00 to surprise him. Maybe tonight would be the night we would start working on making things better between us.

And after all, didn't a surprise homecoming sound like something Ginger or Mary Ann would do? (Was there something ridiculous about the fact that I was comparing myself to Tom's favorite '60s TV characters? I tried not to think about it.)

I flipped off the light over my desk and headed for the office door. This was perfect, I thought as I pushed the button for the elevator. I would surprise Tom and take him out to dinner. Maybe this wasn't a lost weekend after all. We could even work on fixing our problems in the bedroom. I could sleep in as late as I wanted tomorrow, as long as I came into the office in the afternoon to polish and fact-check my copy.

Cole Brannon be damned – Tom and I could be the sex addicts tonight.

I was humming cheerfully by the time I reached the door to our apartment thirty minutes later, after taking the R train downtown to Eighth Street and walking the several blocks over to Second Avenue. I'd thought about making love to Tom the whole way home. Which might account for the strange looks people were giving me as I dreamily walked along, a frighteningly sex-starved look in my eyes.

I had stopped to pick up a bottle of my favorite merlot from the liquor store on St Mark's Place. I knew exactly how the night would go. We would share a few glasses, then head out to Mary Ann's – no relationship to Gilligan's girl – a great Mexican place up the street where we'd gone frequently during the first few months of our relationship. We would talk and laugh over margaritas like we used to, and we'd split one of their giant burrito platters, stuffing ourselves silly with churros and vanilla bean ice cream for dessert. Later, at home, everything would be the way it used to be. We'd sip wine, talk, and make love. It was going to be a great night.

Things were going to be okay. I could feel it.

When I pushed open the door and stepped into the apartment, it was dark except for a sliver of light peeking out from under the bedroom door. I could hear the stereo on in the bedroom and knew instantly that Tom had fallen asleep again. I resisted the urge to laugh. This was bordering on ridiculous. He seemed to sleep eighteen hours a day. No wonder he didn't appear to be making much progress on his novel.

It would work to my advantage this time, though. I laid my bag, the wine bottle, and my notes softly down on the kitchen table and smiled, thinking about what I would do. I was always so rushed and hassled after work. Maybe if I crept in and woke him up gently myself, snuggling up against him, we could make love before we went to dinner, before we opened the merlot. I felt like a sex addict myself as I thought about it. Tonight would be the night that everything would change.

I took out a corkscrew and two wineglasses and put them on the table beside the wine bottle, careful not to make any noise. I took a deep breath and readjusted my Wonderbra to push up my small bosom. In this bra and shirt I actually looked like I had a bit of cleavage. Hooray for the Wonderbra! Tonight it would be my secret weapon in the seduction of Tom.

Cole Brannon was suddenly as far from my mind as he had been before I'd met him. I mean, who needed some A-list movie star when you had a great live-in boyfriend you loved?

I crossed the room and stood by the closed bedroom door for a moment, smiling. The music was so loud. I never understood how men seemed to be able to sleep through nearly deafening sounds. I put my hand on the knob and envisioned for a moment how it would feel to curl up next to Tom. The music selection would have to change, though. Who could make love to 'Born in the USA'? I took a deep breath and turned the knob.

'Hey baby, I'm home,' I said quietly as I pushed the door open. I started to say, 'Did you miss me?' but I'm not sure how many words I got out before I choked on the end of the sentence.

Tom was in bed, all right, just where I'd expected him to be.

What I hadn't expected was the naked brunette, her hair flying as she moved rhythmically up and down on top of him.

'What the hell?' I yelled over the din of the music. Evidently, Tom hadn't missed me much at all. He looked suddenly up at me, red in the face and mouth agape. The brunette turned and looked at me with flickering eyes.

'What *is* *she* doing here?' she squealed, her heavily made-up face flushed. She stopped moving and stared at me. For a moment none of us spoke or moved. Through my utter shock, with Bruce Springsteen pumping at full volume through the stereo – *my* stereo – I was acutely aware that the brunette's big breasts (which surely had to have been surgically enhanced) were still moving slightly up and down, an aftershock from their halted lovemaking.

My mouth was trying to shape something to say, but my brain wasn't cooperating. I was vaguely aware that my mouth was hanging wide open, but there was nothing I could do about it.

'You promised she wouldn't be home until later,' the brunette finally whined. She gestured angrily at me, turning back around to face Tom. I reached over wordlessly and turned off the stereo, plunging us into complete silence. I noticed the brunette hadn't pulled away. Tom was still inside her. I felt like vomiting. 'Well?' the brunette demanded, turning back to glare at me.

'Um, well, er—' Tom stammered, his eyes darting nervously back and forth between us. He paused for what seemed like an eternity, growing redder and redder by the moment.

It suddenly struck me, like a slow-motion revelation, that the brunette looked vaguely familiar. I stared hard at her face for a moment and had a sudden flashback to the *Mod* Christmas party in Margaret Weatherbourne's enormous Upper East Side penthouse. I'd dragged Tom along against his protests. I remembered feeling relieved when I saw him talking animatedly with a curvaceous brunette I didn't recognize, instead of sulking in the corner as he'd been doing most of the night. It hadn't even crossed my mind to be suspicious or jealous. I had assumed she was someone's girlfriend, sister, or wife who was feeling just as out of place at the party as Tom.

And this was her. I was almost sure of it. In my bed. With my boyfriend. Without their clothes. I finally broke the silence.

'I finished early,' I said, surprising myself with my even tone. It took great self-control not to cross the room and begin beating them both to death. 'At the office. Who the hell are you?' Instead of answering, she turned back to Tom. Her brown hair glistened with infuriating perfection, spilling over her narrow and deeply tanned shoulders. Why were mistresses always tan? Was it a prerequisite to sleeping with someone else's boyfriend or husband?

'You said she wouldn't be home until ten,' she said sharply.

'Surprise,' I muttered. I stood stock-still as the brunette rolled off Tom, who was still partially erect. He quickly pulled a sheet over himself, and I gagged on the bile rising in my throat. There were suddenly a million questions racing through my mind as the brunette got up smoothly from the bed and started to get dressed. But all questions were overshadowed by the disgust and shock swirling through my mind. I didn't have the faintest idea how to react.

'How long has this been going on?' I finally asked softly. The brunette, who was much taller and leggier than me, bent down to slip on her shoes. Manolos, I noticed absently. She was wearing $500 shoes and shagging my boyfriend. I wasn't sure why that mattered. Tom greeted my question with silence, his face still the color of tomato sauce.

'Since December,' the brunette finally answered, brushing past me on her way to the bedroom door. Her face was still flushed, her hair disheveled. I felt the air vacate my lungs in a swoosh.

'Since December?' I breathed, looking at Tom. He wouldn't meet my eye.

'What a waste of my goddamned time,' muttered the brunette. She placed a palm on the door and bent down to adjust her left shoe. She turned to glare at Tom, who looked like he was trying to shrink into the sheets, then she finally turned to look at me.

'He kept telling me he was going to leave you,' she said, looking me in the eye, her expression surprisingly calm. 'What bullshit. He's great in bed, though.' She turned away quickly and didn't look back.

Her words echoed in my ears as she tap-tapped to the

front door in her stiletto heels. I stood there in complete silence after she opened and slammed the apartment door behind her. *He's great in bed? He's great in bed?* Hell, not that I would know, lately.

I stared in the general direction of the front door for a moment before slowly turning to look at Tom. He was still wrapped in the disheveled silk bedsheets I'd bought just last month, now curled up against the feather pillows I'd had for years. He stared back at me apprehensively, guilt and fear written all over his face, which suddenly looked ugly and hateful to me. Nothing could have prepared me for walking in and seeing the man I loved deep inside another woman. Another woman with $10,000 breasts, $500 shoes, and silky brown hair that bounced just like the shampoo commercials said it was supposed to.

'Tom . . .' I began finally. The words trailed off into emptiness, because I didn't know what to say. Half of me wanted to leap on top of him and beat him to death, and half of me wanted to break down in tears. My heart pounded rapidly inside my chest, and I could hear the blood rushing inside my head. I wondered for a moment if Tom could hear the pounding, too.

'Claire, I can explain,' he said finally. He looked so uncomfortable I almost wanted to laugh. He reached for his boxers, which lay just to the right of my bed, and awkwardly wriggled them on under the sheets.

'I'm not interested,' I said finally, my voice icy. I was surprised that I was managing to contain my anger. 'I'm not interested in your explanation.'

'But, Claire,' Tom protested. He had tossed back the covers and was reaching for his jeans, which lay crumpled on the floor. 'It didn't mean anything. It's just that you're never around, and . . .'

His voice trailed off – silenced, I suspected, by my icy glare. *Bullshit*, every muscle in my face said. Even caught in the act of cheating on me, he was trying to make it sound like it was my fault.

Suddenly, I felt a cold calm settle over me from out of nowhere, and I smiled at him. He shrank back into the sheets, seeming more alarmed by my smile than by my anger.

'I'm going to leave,' I said slowly, calmly. Inside, my stomach churned. I felt like there was an icy fist wrapped around my heart, squeezing as hard as it could. 'And when I come back, I want everything that belongs to you gone. Every last shred of your crap.'

'Claire, you're overreacting,' he squeaked. I realized suddenly, the concern in his eyes wasn't because he was worried about saving his relationship with me. It was because I was the only woman dumb enough to put a rent-free roof over his head, and he had screwed it up. I was furious at myself for ignoring all the signs. I had wanted so badly to be in a functional relationship, I'd let him use me for almost a year while I blindly believed that he loved me, and was just going through a phase or struggling with his novel.

'*I never want to see you again*,' I said finally, my voice hushed and calm. I had never meant anything more in my life. I took one last look at him: his pathetic, beaten expression, his too-hairy, scrawny chest, his brown eyes that were plain, flat, and emotionless. I hated him. In that instant, I truly hated him. I pushed back the lump in my throat, and without another word, turned on my heel and walked to the front door. I grabbed my shoulder bag, my keys, and the bottle of merlot we were supposed to share. As an afterthought, I grabbed the corkscrew and stuffed it into my bag. I could feel his eyes on my back as I opened the door and slammed it behind me. His stare, which I couldn't see but could somehow feel, sent a chill up my spine.

I waited until I was outside on the street to start crying.

How to Do a Tequila Shot

I didn't know where I was going. Tears ran in hot, salty rivers down my face. I was in a fog as my feet carried me north on Second Avenue and west on Eighth to the N/R subway station. It was quiet this time on a Saturday. As I waited alone for a train, I opened the bottle of merlot with the corkscrew I'd grabbed from the kitchen table on my way out. I struggled with the cork without considering the inappropriateness of opening a wine bottle in the subway. Who the hell cared, anyhow? I was by myself. There was no one there to stop me.

I finally got the bottle open with a satisfying 'pop', tilted it back, and took a giant swig, washing the taste of bile out of my mouth. I didn't bother to take the bottle out of the paper bag, and for a moment I was amused that I must have looked like a well-dressed wino. With a $16.95 bottle of merlot. If there had been anyone there to see me, which there wasn't.

I sat down on one of the dirty benches and waited. I took another swig, and then a deep breath. I regretted it immediately, choking on the stench of oil and urine that hung heavy in the station.

Note to self: No more deep breathing in subway stations.

I drowned the smell with another swig from the bottle.

'How could I be so stupid?' I asked myself aloud after I'd taken a few more gulps. I was greeted with silence. I was already feeling the wine. There was no one else in the station, so I voiced my anger a bit more loudly. 'How could I be so stupid?!' I yelled at the top of my lungs. This time my question was greeted with the echo of my voice off the cold steel of the subway tracks.

A few seconds later, a middle-aged man in a suit descended into the subway station, looking at me like I was crazy as he passed by. He must have heard me yelling. To prove his suspicions correct about my mental state, I took another giant swig from the bottle. I let the smooth, warming wine slip gently down my throat, embracing the burning in my empty stomach as it settled. When I looked up again, he was staring at me. He looked quickly away when our eyes met.

I laughed. I knew what I looked like.

The subway came after what felt like an eternity, and the man in the suit disappeared into another car. I stepped into the door that pulled up right in front of me and settled into a cold, hard plastic seat. As the doors closed, I stared at the man across from me. He was about thirty, Tom's age, and he was alone. I could smell his cologne from across the car, and it looked like he'd just shaved.

I wondered if he was going on a date. Maybe he was going to see his girlfriend. Did she know that men cheated? Someone should warn her. Someone should tell her not to trust him.

I took another swig without taking my eyes off him. His eyes widened in surprise as I tilted the wine bottle up for a refreshing gulp. I wanted to laugh. In my perfectly tailored black pencil skirt and my pink shell – the same outfit I had worn to interview Cole Brannon – I must have looked the complete opposite of someone who would be swigging wine from a brown bag in a subway car.

Yeah, buddy, we're all full of surprises. Nothing is what it seems.

I got off the subway at Forty-ninth Street (my regular stop, out of habit) and stood aboveground, for a moment, just breathing in and out. I felt invisible. I hardly ever came to midtown during the weekends, and it was strange to see the streets so empty. I was used to rush-hour foot traffic as I made my way over to Broadway for work.

I took one last gulp out of the wine bottle and tossed it in a garbage can. It was almost empty anyhow, and I was getting sick of drinking it. I was lucid enough to know that getting drunk wasn't an answer to my problems – in fact, I'd never tried to solve anything that way before – but I didn't see many alternatives. I couldn't go home. I couldn't face Tom again. I couldn't stand to see his face. I hated him. With all my heart. And yet I loved him. With all my heart. I hadn't realized it was possible to feel both things at once.

'Wendy,' I mumbled, suddenly realizing that I could call her. She'd know what to do. I paused for a moment. Would she say, 'I told you so'? Maybe. But probably not. She was my best friend. You were supposed to be able to turn to best friends in times like this, right?

Not that I had ever suspected I would have a time like this.

I fumbled in my big bag, pushing past pages I'd written just this afternoon about Cole Brannon, who was evidently a sex addict. He'd tricked me too. He made me believe he was a nice guy, when in reality he was a sex addict who was sleeping with Ivana Donatelli. And probably Kylie Dane too, despite his convincing protests. They were all scum.

Note to self: Men are scum. Lying scum.

I finally found my cell phone. With shaking hands, I pulled it triumphantly out of the bag. I leaned back against the wall of Katzenberg's Deli, just outside the stairs to the Forty-ninth Street stop, to steady myself. Slowly, carefully, I dialed Wendy's number.

It rang and rang, four times. Then her answering machine picked up. Was she out? Damn. She was one of the last people in America who didn't have a cell phone. There was no other way to reach her.

'This is Wendy,' her voice chirped cheerfully into my

ear. 'Leave me a message, and I'll call you back.' The machine beeped, and I paused for a moment.

'Wendy, are you there? Wendy?' I realized suddenly that my voice was very slurred. Logic told me that drinking almost an entire bottle of wine on an empty stomach in a thirty-minute period would do that. But hindsight is always 20/20, isn't it? 'Wendy, you were right. You were right all along. About Tom. You have to call me, okay? You have to call me. Because I need to talk to you. Please call me, Wendy. On my cell phone. Don't call me at home. Tom's there.'

I was still repeating myself and slurring rather unintelligibly into the phone when her machine cut me off. Damned machine. Didn't it know I needed someone to talk to? I held the phone away from my ear for a moment and stared at it, as if it might tell me where Wendy was. When I realized it wasn't about to impart that information, I sighed and jabbed my finger at the End button. I tossed the phone back in my shoulder bag and leaned against the deli window.

The moment I started to relax, images of Tom straddled by the naked, full-breasted brunette from the Christmas party flooded my brain.

'No,' I said aloud, shaking my head and forcing my eyes open. I didn't want to think about that. Not here, not now. I couldn't.

Suddenly, I knew what to do. I'd go to Metro, the bar Wendy and I went to after work every so often for happy hour. In fact, I'd had my slutty-boot-in-subway-grate debacle outside Metro. But that felt like eons ago. And they probably wouldn't remember me.

In any case, it would be a familiar place to sit down. And I knew I needed to sit down. I also knew I needed a glass of water and probably a nice cold shower, but it was clear that as soon as I sobered up, I'd start thinking about Tom again. I didn't want to do that tonight. I wouldn't think about him, and I wouldn't cry again. The only way I could avoid that was to have another drink. Metro had drinks.

I started walking in the direction of Broadway.

*

Metro was nearly empty when I staggered in the door. It was the first time I'd seen it like that. I'd only been there after work, when the happy-hour crowds threatened to overflow onto Eighth Avenue, which was always creeping by in a blur of taxis outside the darkened plate-glass windows.

I surveyed the room as I stood in the doorway. A young couple was huddled together in a corner booth, looking into each other's eyes. Yuck. Three thirtysomething women laughed and talked in another corner, all holding brightly colored martinis. A fiftysomething couple played pool in the back, and sitting at the bar was a man in a black shirt and a baseball cap, his back to me, deep in conversation with the bartender. I sat down at the opposite end of the bar, as far away from the man as I could get. I knew what I would look like. A single girl all by herself on a Saturday night, already drunk by 9 p.m., sidling up next to the bar.

I'd look like I was trying to pick up a date.

But really, if a guy tried to hit on me tonight, I might just turn around and punch him.

It actually seemed like a good idea. I mulled it over for a moment. I could skip all the steps where he courts me, buys me dinner, buys me gifts, moves in with me, and then cheats on me. I could cut a whole year out simply by slugging him the first time we met.

Too bad I hadn't done that with Tom.

The bartender raised an eyebrow at me and took a few steps closer. His friend, the broad-shouldered man in the black shirt, turned to look at me from the shadows at the other end of the bar. I snarled at him and sent him telepathic messages (which, of course, you're able to do when you're drunk).

Don't even think about it, buddy. Unless you want to get hurt. I have a mean right hook.

'I'll have the usual,' I said as the bartender approached. He looked at me in confusion, and I giggled. I'd always wanted to say that at a bar. 'A Corona,' I said when I was done laughing. 'And a shot of tequila.' If I was going to get drunk – okay, *drunker* – I might as well do it right.

'Can I see some ID?' the bartender asked suspiciously. Damn. I was so sick of looking like I was sixteen. I fumbled in my bag until I found my wallet, which I pulled out triumphantly. It took me another full minute to grasp my driver's license and pull it out from the plastic enclosure.

'Aha!' I exclaimed as the license finally came out. I squinted for a moment until I could read the bartender's name tag. 'Here ya go, Jay,' I said with false cheer. I handed him the ID. He looked at it closely for a second, then handed it back with a strange expression on his face that I couldn't quite interpret. Not that I had the energy to care. Maybe he looked strange simply because he was a man. They were all strange.

'Okay,' he said. I watched him walk down to the other end of the bar, where he reached into the glass-front fridge and pulled out a Corona. He said something to the man in the baseball cap, who turned and looked at me for a moment from the shadows. I growled another telepathic message in his general direction. *What are you looking at? Haven't you seen a drunk girl before?*

'Here's your drink,' Jay the bartender said a minute later, plunking the Corona down in front of me. He reached under the bar for a shot glass and pulled out a bottle of Jose Cuervo.

'Ah, Jose, old friend,' I mumbled, prompting another strange look from the bartender.

He filled the shot glass with the smooth, gold liquid, then reached down for two lime slices. He stuck one into the top of my Corona bottle and handed the other to me. 'Here,' he said. He lifted a glass of soda in a mock toast. 'Cheers.'

I downed the tequila in one gulp and bit hard into the lime, my taste buds balking at the sour taste.

*

Three Coronas, two tequila shots, and four bathroom trips later, I could barely keep my eyes open, but at least I wasn't thinking about Tom. Nope. I was thinking about what I wanted to drink next. I knew I'd end up with either a Corona, a tequila shot, or both, so it shouldn't have been a hard decision, but somehow it was. As I strained my eyes to read the labels of the liquor bottles lining the back shelf – impossible given my drunken stupor – Jay set down a tall, full glass of clear liquid over ice in front of me.

'A drink from the gentleman,' he said, winking at me. Or at least, I thought he winked at me. I couldn't see too well any more. I examined the glass through bleary eyes. Vodka, maybe? Gin? I looked at it closely. I sniffed it. It was water.

'Huh?' I mumbled as he walked away. Gentleman? What gentleman? And wasn't that word an oxymoron? Why had I never thought of that before? Men weren't gentle. They broke your heart. Even the ones who hugged you good-bye. They were probably just sex addicts who wanted to get in your pants.

I looked down the length of the bar. The man in the black shirt and baseball cap was gone. I hadn't noticed him leave. Who had sent me the drink? Was the bartender going crazy? Or was I the only one losing my mind?

'Twice in one day,' said a deep voice suddenly in my ear, startling me. I jumped and nearly fell off the bar stool. A strong hand steadied me.

'Twice in one day, what?' I mumbled crossly, swiveling on my stool to see who stood behind me. I almost swiveled right off the stool, but again, a gentle hand on my lower back kept me in place.

'Twice in one day you sit a few feet away from me, and don't even notice me,' said the voice in my ear. 'I should be insulted.' I blinked as the swivel was complete. It was the guy from the other end of the bar, the guy who'd been looking at me from the shadows. What the hell was he talking about? Was this some kind of new pickup line?

Obviously, I needed to get out more. I was used to the generally cheesy 'So, were you born this beautiful?' lines that men had been using throughout the '90s and the early years of the new millennium. But perhaps things had changed during my time with Tom.

The man looked good – although blurry – in a black shirt and khakis, with a baseball cap pulled low, casting a shadow over the rest of his face. But, I reminded myself, men are scum. Scum. Maybe I should punch him.

I squinted at him, and suddenly I realized that he looked familiar. Really familiar. It took another second for realization to fully dawn.

When it did, I was mortified.

There, in the familiar Red Sox cap, just inches away from me, was Cole Brannon. The movie star. The gorgeous, polite, perfect movie star. The sex-addicted, lying movie star.

He grinned, waiting for me to say something. Damn those twinkling blue eyes. They'd sucked me in once, but now I knew his secret. I squinted at him. *He's a sex addict!* Wendy's words rang in my head.

'Where's Ivana?' I slurred. Aha! That would teach him. *The jig is up, mister. I'm on to you.*

'Huh?' He looked at me closely for a moment, confusion suddenly etched across his perfect face. 'Ivana? My publicist?'

He was playing dumb. How coy. Like I didn't know.

'You know who I mean,' I said, trying to sound accusatory, but probably just sounding drunk.

'Ivana, my publicist?' he repeated. He stared at me for a moment. Then he laughed. 'You know, Claire, she doesn't go everywhere with me. I'm allowed out alone once in a while without a chaperone.'

I tried to make a face at him, but scrunching my eyes up only made me dizzy. I swayed, and he steadied me again.

'Whoa, looks like somebody's had a little too much to drink,' he said softly, his hand still on my back. I liked it there, I realized. But only because it meant I wouldn't fall off the bar stool, which seemed like a pretty real possibility at the moment. Why didn't they put backs on these things?

'Not me,' I mumbled.

'No, of course not,' he said solemnly. He looked suspiciously like he was fighting back a grin. He pulled up the stool next to me, keeping his hand on my back all the while to steady me. 'Is this a typical Saturday night for you, then?'

It took me a minute to realize he was kidding.

'No,' I said stiffly. 'It is not.' I tried my best to sound haughty. 'Is it a typical Saturday night for *you*? What are you doing at my bar?' What *was* he doing here? Of all the bars in Manhattan, why would he have to wind up at the same bar where I was trying to drink my troubles away?

'No, this is *not* a typical Saturday night for me,' Cole said, smiling with what I could have sworn was gentle pity. I was suddenly just lucid enough to feel embarrassed. 'And I didn't realize this was *your* bar.' I made a face because I was pretty sure he was teasing me.

'Jay Cash, there,' he gestured to the bartender, 'is an old college buddy of mine. I usually drop in on him when I'm in New York.' The bartender waved from the other end of the bar as I looked up. Cole looked at me for a minute. 'Your turn.'

'My turn what?' I asked grumpily. I'd already forgotten what we were talking about.

'Your turn to tell me what you're doing here by yourself, getting drunk on a Saturday night,' he said. 'Even if this is *your* bar.' His face was inches from mine. I squinted at him and suddenly noticed that his blue eyes were flecked with gold. How cool.

'I'm not drunk,' I said. He laughed.

'Oh yeah, I can tell,' he said. 'Totally sober.' He picked

up the glass of water and handed it to me. 'Here, have a sip.'

I was too tired to protest. I took a long drink of the water. It actually felt good going down my throat. Better than the tequila.

'Do you want to talk about it?' Cole asked softly as I drank. I didn't answer for a moment, too busy gulping down the water. Cole gently took the glass out of my hand when I was done, setting it back on the bar. I closed my eyes because I could feel thoughts of Tom rushing in, and I wanted to hide from them. Finally, I opened my eyes and looked at Cole. He had an expression of deep concern on that perfectly formed face that I'd seen so many times in movie theaters.

'When I got home from the office today,' I said, speaking slowly because I knew my words were all running together, 'I found my boyfriend in my bed. Having sex. With another woman.' The mental image of the brunette bobbing up and down on him flooded back into my mind with all the clarity of a television show played on Tom's precious high-definition TV that I'd bought him. But I'd never seen *that* kind of thing on Nick at Nite. If Gilligan had gotten it on with Mary Ann, he had done it off-screen. I swallowed hard.

'Oh, no,' Cole breathed. He started rubbing my back with the strong hand he had there to steady me. I closed my eyes for a moment. His touch felt good. 'Claire, I'm so sorry.'

I shrugged, fighting back the tears that had suddenly welled in my eyes.

'I should have known,' I said, sniffing. I felt a single tear escape and roll down my right cheek. 'I'm an idiot.'

'Don't ever say that,' Cole said, gently leaning in. He put an arm around me. I remembered Wendy's words again. *He's a sex addict!* Did he think he was going to have sex with me?

I struggled to pull out of his embrace for a moment, but

then I stopped. What the hell. I could use the help staying upright. I leaned in to him.

'Don't ever say you're an idiot, Claire,' Cole said as he hugged me. 'Your boyfriend, he's the idiot. To cheat on a woman like you . . .' Cole's voice trailed off, and his pity somehow triggered the opening of my floodgates.

'I let him live with me, and he never wanted to have sex with me!' I was rambling now through sniffles and tears. 'And he said he was writing a novel, and he never worked or anything, and he was always in bed, and he treated me like I didn't matter, and I don't know what I was thinking.' I wasn't making much sense as I continued to blubber unintelligibly. I realized that I was crying, hard. Damn. I'd come into Metro to forget about Tom, not to talk about him. But somehow, it was nice to tell someone. Finally. Someone who didn't seem like he was judging me.

Cole pulled me closer and rubbed my back as I sobbed into his shoulder. It felt good to be held. As his hand moved in small, gentle circles, I forgot that I was supposed to have a totally professional relationship with him. I forgot about Tom. I forgot that Cole Brannon was a sex addict. I forgot that he was a movie star who wasn't supposed to remember who I was. Right now, he was just Cole. A friend. My friend who cared and wanted to listen to me.

Finally, I pulled away and tried to steady myself on the bar stool. But suddenly I didn't feel quite right.

'Cole?' I said quietly. Shit. The room was spinning. When had the room started spinning?

'Yes?' he asked with concern, leaning forward.

'I think I'm going to be sick.'

Then I threw up. All over the floor. And Cole Brannon's shoes.

Oops.

'Sorry,' I croaked, ashamed and humiliated. It was the last thing I remember saying before I passed out.

Gossip and Vices

Drinking

Somewhere in the distance, I could hear the phone ringing. I wished someone would make it stop. With each shrill jangle, the throbbing in my head seemed to get worse. I started to open my eyes, but even the smallest sliver of invading morning light turned out to be too much for the powerful ache in the back of my skull. Far off, the phone continued to ring.

'Tom,' I mumbled. 'Tom, can you get that?' There was no reply. Finally, the ringing stopped. I groaned and sank back into the sheets. I wanted nothing more than to drift back to a place where my head didn't throb like I'd been clubbed with a baseball bat.

I pulled the sheets up, still squeezing my eyes tightly shut in a vain effort to block out all the offending sunlight. I shivered, fought back my rising nausea, and reached for my quilted comforter. I pawed around for a moment at the foot of my bed, but I couldn't find it.

'Tom!' I groaned, hating how my stomach swam and my head throbbed with additional force every time I spoke. 'Tom, what did you do with the comforter? I'm cold!' I felt like I was yelling, but I was dimly aware that my words were coming out at a decibel just above a whisper. Any louder, and I feared my head would explode.

I knew I'd woken up from a nightmare, which might begin to account for the throbbing in my head. I couldn't remember much of it. Tom was there, and in the dream I was angry with him. Cole Brannon had been there too, in a bar, which was strange. I couldn't understand why I would be dreaming about him. Even if he was the hottest man I'd ever met.

'Tom!' I moaned again, a bit louder this time. He still didn't answer, and I suddenly realized I could hear the shower running. I couldn't remember hearing it from the bedroom in the past. But perhaps my throbbing headache had given me superhuman hearing.

Finally, I realized that if I wanted the comforter, I'd simply have to crawl out of bed and get it myself. Reluctantly, I forced my eyes open and groaned as the sunlight poured in, blinding me momentarily. Slowly, the room started to come into focus.

Then suddenly, time seemed to stop as I realized that I wasn't in my bedroom at all.

Awe mixed with utter confusion as I slowly blinked at my surroundings, still blurry through my sleepy eyes. My drab and pale bureau, which I'd bought four years ago at a garage sale, had been replaced by a glistening black chest of drawers, topped by a massive oval mirror. Instead of my faded blue gingham curtains over tiny windows, thin white gauze did little to block the sunlight streaming in through giant panes that stretched from floor to ceiling. I was awash in white satin sheets, and the bed they covered was at least twice the size of my double. Beneath me was a seemingly endless sea of plush, snow-white carpeting that covered a floor easily bigger than my whole apartment.

I lay back for a moment, the breath knocked out of me. My head continued to throb and my stomach churned threateningly. But both were overshadowed by the mounting horror I was feeling. I had no idea where I was.

Think, Claire, think. A quick assessment of my physical condition told me I'd gotten drunk last night. But where? With whom? I had never been here before. Had I gone home with a stranger?

That triggered a foggy memory. One-night stands. There was something about one-night stands . . . My God. The article for *Mod*. Had I done it? Had I taken my own misguided advice and had a one-night stand? No, that wouldn't be right. I would never do that to Tom.

Tom. Oh God. Tom.

I closed my eyes, trying to block out the images that suddenly flooded my brain, but it was too late. Tom with the leggy brunette from the Christmas party. Tom *inside* the leggy brunette. That damned Bruce Springsteen singing like nothing was wrong. Me, storming out of the apartment. The bottle of merlot, Metro, the tequila shots, the Coronas.

And Cole Brannon.

Oh no. Cole Brannon.

With rising horror, I remembered seeing him at the bar. Crying on his shoulder about Tom. Letting him hold me and comfort me . . .

Vomiting on his shoes.

Suddenly, I had a very bad feeling about all of this.

As if a director from one of his movies had suddenly yelled, 'Action!' the bathroom door far across the massive bedroom swung open dramatically and Cole Brannon stood in the doorway, clad only in a skimpy white towel wrapped around his waist. His darkly tanned upper body, filled with perfectly toned muscles bulging to get out, gleamed with droplets of water. His perfect washboard stomach drew my stunned eyes tantalizingly toward the top of the low-slung towel, which seemed mere inches away from exposing what it was supposed to be hiding. As our eyes met, Cole grinned and quickly adjusted his towel for more coverage.

'Well hello, sunshine,' he said cheerfully. 'You're awake.' I couldn't move. I just stared. I desperately tried to recall the events of the previous evening. It was hard to think with my head pounding like the bass on a bad rap album. Hard as I strained to remember, though, everything after vomiting was blank.

'I threw up on you last night,' I moaned finally. I was completely humiliated and dimly aware that I was processing my thoughts very slowly. I had puked on the biggest star in Hollywood. This was not how journalists were supposed to behave. I felt sure I'd read that in the *AP Stylebook*.

But instead of looking at me in righteous fury, he laughed.

'Why yes, you did,' he said, the corners of his eyes wrinkling with amusement. He took a few steps closer. 'I must say, that's the first time that's happened. I'm used to journalists kissing my feet, not throwing up on them.'

'Oh my God,' I moaned. I sank back into the pillows and pulled the sheets over my head, wondering if it would be possible to disappear and wake up in my own bed instead.

'I was just kidding,' said Cole's voice with sudden concern, muffled by the covers over my head. 'I really don't mind . . .' I groaned and emerged from the covers. Evidently, it was not possible to teleport home from beneath his sheets.

'No, it's not what you said,' I said finally. 'I just can't believe . . . Oh my God, I have never done anything like this before. Never. And especially not with someone like you.'

'Someone like me, eh?' Cole grinned again. 'And exactly what do you mean by that?' I would have blushed if all the blood in my body hadn't been coursing in throbbing currents through the back of my skull.

'Someone I've interviewed,' I mumbled. 'I don't even know what to say. I'm always so careful to be completely professional. And look at me now.' I groaned. As I spoke, something nagging at the back of my mind came closer to the surface, and I scrunched up my nose in concentration, trying to remember what it was.

'Claire, no worries,' Cole said gently. He crossed the room in a few long strides and sat down beside me on the massive bed. My embarrassment was momentarily overshadowed by the realization that the most attractive man I'd ever seen was mere inches away from me, nearly naked, in a silk-covered bed. Unfortunately, before I had a chance to process that realization, the hyperprofessional-journalist portion of my brain kicked back in.

'I'll lose my job,' I moaned.

'Claire,' Cole began, his voice gentle and soothing. He put a hand on my shoulder and looked so deeply into my eyes that it set my heart pounding. 'I told you. No one has to know. This is between you and me, okay? No one's going to lose their job.'

I glanced down at my lap and received another shock I hadn't been prepared for.

Instead of the pencil skirt and pink blouse I had on last night, I was clothed in a massive gray Boston College T-shirt that certainly didn't belong to me. Before I had time to freak out about the fact that I was no longer wearing my own clothes, the thought that had been nagging me suddenly came into full focus. I could hear Wendy's words replaying in my head.

'Cole Brannon is a sex addict,' her disembodied voice chirped, suddenly loud and clear.

I stared at Cole for a moment in horror, my heart pounding. He was still grinning at me, which made me even more afraid. His grin suddenly looked knowing, almost smug and lascivious.

'Oh my God, did we . . . ?' My voice trailed off. I couldn't even complete the sentence. My heart pounded hard and fast.

'What?' asked Cole, tilting his head to the side and looking at me in confusion.

'Did we . . . ?' I still couldn't say the words. I looked down again at my body, wrapped in one of his T-shirts.

Surely we had. I would have to quit the magazine. I had slept with someone I'd interviewed.

And I didn't even remember it.

'What's wrong?' asked Cole, concern now mixing with the confusion splashed across his face. 'Do you need to throw up again? Are you okay?'

I just stared, the little voice in my head squeaking in horror. *Am I okay? What, did you think that I wanted you just because you were able to drag my unconscious body home?*

I realized suddenly that he was still looking at me in bewilderment. I had to know how it had happened.

'Did we . . . Did we . . .' I couldn't complete the sentence. I looked at him with a mixture of exasperation and shame. 'Did we . . . ? You know!' And suddenly, he did. Realization dawned, and he laughed. He actually *laughed* at me. Had it been that bad?

'Are you asking me if we had sex?' he asked incredulously. It hurt to hear the words, but I nodded anyhow, then squeezed my eyes shut. I braced myself for the words I knew would end my career, my whole professional life as I knew it. He paused, then spoke.

'Claire, you were unconscious all night!'

'What?' As much as I'd braced myself, those were not the words I'd been prepared to hear. He had sex with my unconscious body? What kind of a guy was he? I needed to start taking the tabloid rumors more seriously. I shuddered involuntarily.

'So we . . . ?' I began. I just needed to hear him say it. So I knew that my life was over. He squinted at me.

'No, Claire!' he said finally, looking distressed. 'Of course not!' I blinked and tried to process what he'd said. 'I slept over there,' he added, gesturing to a small love seat near the window that still had a blanket, a sheet, and a pillow strewn across it.

'What?' I asked, confused. It wasn't adding up. I looked

down at the T-shirt and suspiciously back at him. 'But where are my clothes?'

He sighed in exasperation and gave a kind of half laugh.

'You were, um, covered in your own vomit,' he said uncomfortably. I just stared at him. 'I didn't know what to do, so I called the front desk, and they had someone from housekeeping come up and help you change.'

'And you . . . ?' My voice trailed off as I had a sudden mental image of Cole watching my vomit-encrusted clothes being stripped from my jiggly body.

'I stepped outside,' Cole said softly. 'I had the woman come get me when she was done.'

I looked at him for a moment. He was blushing. A new wave of humiliation coursed through me.

'Oh,' I said finally. I didn't know what else to say. 'Thank you.'

'Hey, no problem,' he said breezily. He glanced at me. 'Although I haven't yet decided whether I should be offended by your line of questioning.' This time I could physically feel the blood rushing to my face, which must have meant my headache was starting to subside.

'I'm so sorry,' I said. 'I didn't mean . . . It's just that . . . Well, I mean, I'm not dressed, and I'm in your bed, and . . .' Suddenly it dawned on me. He didn't want to sleep with me. Maybe he *was* a sex addict and I was just too repulsive. My heart sank.

'I prefer my partners to be conscious,' Cole said, as if reading my mind. He winked. 'I try to keep that as at least a minimum standard.'

'Oh,' I said stupidly.

'I'm kidding, Claire,' he said, nudging me gently in the shoulder. 'I'm just giving you a hard time.'

'Oh,' I repeated. I felt like such an idiot. I groaned, closed my eyes, and leaned back into the pillows. I wished I could go back to sleep, wake up, and realize this had all been a bad dream.

'I hope it's okay that I brought you here,' said Cole,

sounding almost shy. I cracked my eyes open and looked at him. 'I didn't know what else to do, and I wanted to make sure you were okay.'

'Thank you,' I said finally. 'I am so embarrassed.'

'No need to be,' Cole said with a dismissive wave of his hand. But he wasn't making me feel much better.

I shuddered. This was horrible. This was more than just a step over the line of professional ethics. This was a pole vault into the next time zone. What was I doing?

'I have to go,' I blurted out suddenly. Cole, still perched on the edge of the bed, looked surprised.

'What?' he asked. 'Where?'

'I just have to go,' I repeated, trying to sound firm.

'Oh, okay,' Cole said. He looked a bit hurt, I thought, but perhaps that was my imagination. 'Well, listen. I had your clothes sent out to be dry-cleaned.' My jaw dropped. 'They should be ready any minute now. Why don't you hop in the shower while I call down to the front desk and see if they can bring them up, okay?'

'I can just shower at home,' I protested weakly.

'You have vomit in your hair,' Cole pointed out wisely.

'Oh,' I said, blushing. That changed things. I looked at Cole for a moment, wrapped in his skimpy towel. A few drops of water still glistened on his body, and his dark hair was damp. I tried to ignore the warm feeling spreading across my abdomen. 'Don't you need to get back into the bathroom?'

'Nah,' he said. 'You go ahead. I'll dress out here.' He grinned. 'No peeking, though.'

I smiled, blushing, and tried not to let my eyes wander down across his tanned, hard body.

'No peeking,' I agreed, trying not to sound as reluctant as I felt.

Twenty minutes later I had taken a quick shower, swallowed two ibuprofen tablets, dried my hair, washed my face, and used the only makeup I had in my purse –

powder, lipstick, and an old tube of mascara – to make myself look somewhat presentable. I was no Gwyneth Paltrow, but I was exponentially more attractive than I'd been when I first stumbled in. Okay, so that was the understatement of the year.

I was still standing with a towel wrapped around me when there was a knock at the bathroom door.

'Your clothes are here,' Cole said through the door, his voice muffled.

'Oh,' I said, startled. I readjusted my towel and tucked in the end tightly to make sure it stayed put. I did a quick check down below and wished that I wasn't showing so much flabby thigh, but at least all the important areas were covered up. 'Um, come in.'

Slowly, the door opened. Cole Brannon stood on the other side of the threshold, holding my perfectly pressed shell and pencil skirt, which hung innocently on a hanger as if they hadn't seen me at my very worst just hours earlier. He looked effortlessly sexy in a pair of dark jeans and a black ribbed T-shirt that traced his contours perfectly. As we stood there in silence, I was conscious of Cole's eyes moving slowly up and down my body. I suddenly felt naked, vulnerable.

'Well, you sure do clean up well, Little Lady,' Cole said finally, his eyes coming to rest on mine. He looked almost embarrassed. 'Here are your clothes, good as new.'

'Thank you so much,' I said quietly, looking down. I took the hanger.

'Now get dressed and get out here to have some breakfast with me,' he said cheerfully.

'Breakfast?' I asked, my eyes widening. 'No, I couldn't.'

'Well, it's already here,' he said with a grin. 'And your coffee is just getting cold.' I opened my mouth to protest, but Cole cut me off before I even began. 'And don't even try to tell me you don't want any coffee. I saw you yesterday morning. I know about your caffeine addiction, Little Lady.'

'Guilty as charged,' I said weakly, forcing a smile. 'I'll be out in a second.'

I quickly pulled on the shirt and skirt, then stared at myself in the mirror.

What had I done? In the past I'd never so much as looked at an actor with lusty eyes, or smiled the wrong way at a rock star. And here I was in the bathroom of Cole Brannon's hotel room after puking on him, sleeping in his bed, and letting him see me wrapped in a tiny towel. I just had to go home. I couldn't let this go any further.

I took a deep breath and opened the bathroom door. Cole Brannon was sitting on the corner of the bed. He grinned at me as I emerged. I quickly forced a frown, but couldn't stop my eyes from darting eagerly around the room.

In front of him a table had been rolled in, and on it were a big pot of coffee, matching crystal pitchers of orange juice and water, and a buffet-sized display of breads, croissants, muffins, Danish, and fruits in every color of the rainbow. The ibuprofen was already kicking in, and my stomach growled, but I ignored it. I had to go. Maybe if I got out of here, we could both eventually forget what had happened. I doubted it, but it was worth a shot.

'Took you long enough,' Cole teased, apparently oblivious of my internal conflict. 'Your coffee's getting cold.' He held out a mug he'd already poured for me. 'Cream and one Sweet'N Low,' he said. I just stared. 'I remembered from breakfast yesterday.'

'Oh,' I said, taken aback. I shook my head and cleared my throat. 'Um, I'm sorry, but I have to go. You were very kind to have helped me out last night.' *And to remember what I take in my coffee.* Cole looked confused. I took a deep breath and started for the door.

'Really, thank you,' I said as I walked, refusing to meet his eye. I could feel him watching me, but I couldn't bear to look. 'But I have to go. I have to go home. Please send me the dry-cleaning bill.'

Eyes downcast, I slipped on my shoes and opened the door. I couldn't resist taking one quick look over my shoulder before I shut it behind me. After all, this was Cole Brannon, America's favorite movie star. He was, among other things, the man who had saved me from myself last night. I felt a horrible pang of guilt as I caught a last glimpse of him staring at me from behind the overflowing table of food. I tried to ignore my rapidly beating heart as I hurried into the hallway.

Bingeing

My heart was still pounding as I stood on Park Avenue minutes later, trying to flag down a taxi. But of course in this city of 8 million people, it always seemed that approximately 7.9 million of them wanted a cab at the same time I did. Today was no exception. I desperately waved my arms in the air, beckoning to cab after unresponsive cab.

I had almost given up and resigned myself to the subway when a driver two lanes away pulled a death-defying move, cutting almost horizontally across Park and screeching to a halt in front of me, missing my toes by mere inches. I yanked open the back door.

'Second Avenue and Second Street,' I said quickly as I heaved myself onto the slick backseat. 'And please hurry.' The driver nodded wordlessly, pulling slowly away from the curb into traffic that was now motionless, stopped at a light. I closed my eyes and leaned back in the seat, willing the light to change and the traffic to move.

But clearly the fates weren't taking requests from me this weekend.

Suddenly, there was a loud knock on the window. Given the luck I'd had in the past twenty-four hours, and the fact that a pounding on your cab in the middle of Manhattan was rarely a good thing, my eyes flew open in alarm. My mind started racing through the horrific possibilities of what would be outside. Perhaps a knife-wielding psychopath. Or a ski-masked robber with a 9mm.

Instead, I looked out the window and saw a crazed-looking man fiddling with the door handle. I gasped.

'That's Cole Brannon,' said the taxi driver in a thick Indian accent. He turned around to look out the window in astonishment.

'Yes, it is,' I agreed slowly. Outside, Cole was mouthing something to me while trying to juggle a mug of coffee, an apple, a banana, a muffin, and a croissant. The driver and I just stared.

Cole gestured to me, a look of desperation on his face as he struggled to rearrange the breakfast items he was carrying. He looked like he was about to start some kind of gourmet circus act.

'Well, open the door for him,' said the cab driver, looking like he was ready to start drooling at any second. 'He's a big star!'

'Do I have to?' I mumbled reluctantly, starting to feel sorry for Cole despite myself. I stifled a giggle as he dropped a banana and looked positively devastated. Around us, traffic started to move – but the taxi driver stayed put, and so did Cole.

'Yes, yes!' the cab driver responded desperately, oblivious of the scores of honking horns now aimed at him. 'You open the door now!' Reluctantly, I reached over and opened the door for Cole, who immediately sighed in relief.

'Claire!' he said, panting from his efforts. 'What took you so long?'

'I have to go home, Cole,' I said, trying to sound stern. Without a word, he handed me the muffin (which looked like blueberry) and the croissant. Still clutching the coffee and the apple, he slid into the taxi, placed the apple on his lap, and swung the door closed behind him.

'Those are for your breakfast,' he said, nodding to the pastries he'd handed me, as if it was the most normal announcement in the world. I looked down at the muffin and the croissant, one in each hand, not sure what to say. 'They'll make you feel better. It's good to eat bread products when you're hungover.'

'Well, thank you, Mr Surgeon General,' I muttered. Cole ignored me.

'And here's an apple, but I'll hold it until you're ready for it,' he pressed on at full speed. 'I brought you a banana too, but I dropped it. And a cup of coffee. But be careful not to spill it.'

The cab driver was staring at us in the rearview mirror. The honking had temporarily subsided now that the light had turned red, and we were once again mired in traffic.

'Hello, Mr Cole Brannon.' The cab driver had apparently mustered the courage to greet his newest passenger. His face was flushed. 'It is an honor to have you in my car.'

'Oh,' said Cole, looking up at the driver as if surprised to see him there. 'Thank you. It's a pleasure to be here.' He sounded like he was graciously accepting an Oscar. I suppressed a laugh. He sounded so earnest. He looked back at me like he was expecting me to say something.

'Um, thank you,' I said finally, looking down at the croissant and the muffin. They *did* look good. 'But Cole—'

'Wait!' Cole interrupted me triumphantly, digging in his pocket. Finally, he pulled out a bottle of water and displayed it for me. 'This is for you, too. It will help your hangover.' I finally gave in and laughed.

'Cole . . .' I began. I didn't know what to say. 'Thank you. But you didn't have to do this.' But somewhere inside of me, where Unprofessional Claire was hiding, I was glad that he had.

'Excuse me, Mr Cole Brannon,' the cab driver cut in again, interrupting the little war that was raging in my head between Professional, Ethical Claire and Recently Dumped, Sex-Starved, A-Movie-Star-Is-Feeding-Me Claire. 'It would be a great honor to have your autograph.'

'Yes, yes, of course,' Cole said graciously. The driver handed him a piece of paper, and he quickly scribbled his name.

'Thank you so much, Mr Cole Brannon,' the cab driver said. He took the piece of paper from Cole just as the light changed.

'Any time,' Cole said with a smile. The cab lurched forward into traffic, and I looked at Cole suspiciously.

'You're coming with me?' I asked.

'Yes,' he said firmly in a voice that made clear it wasn't open for discussion.

'Why?' I asked, squinting at him in confusion as the car crept downtown. I was aware that my heart was suddenly racing, and I didn't know why. Cole shook his head and changed the subject.

'Why did you leave so quickly?' he asked softly. Before I could answer, he nodded at my muffin. 'Eat something,' he commanded like a concerned parent. I looked at him for a moment, shrugged, and took a bite of the muffin. Apparently, he was coming along for the ride whether I liked it or not. Okay, and despite myself, I had to admit: I liked it.

I thought for a moment before I answered Cole's question. What would I say? I finally decided upon the truth.

'I didn't know what else to do,' I admitted after I'd swallowed my third giant bite of muffin. I was hungrier than I'd realized. Cole looked at me with concern and handed me the bottle of water. I took a big sip and handed it back. 'I'm so embarrassed about everything, and I thought maybe if I just left, we could just forget about it, you know? I mean, this isn't me. This isn't the kind of thing I do.'

'I know,' Cole said gently, looking closely at me. 'Do you think I would be doing this now if I thought you did this kind of thing all the time?'

I thought for a second.

'No,' I admitted. He had a point. I took a deep breath. 'It's just that I try so hard to keep those professional boundaries in place, and now look what I've done.'

I sighed and was silent for a moment. The cab inched forward.

'Okay, it's my turn to ask you a question,' I said finally. 'What are you doing here? Why did you follow me?'

Cole looked defensive for a moment, then his face softened.

'I didn't know if your boyfriend would still be at your apartment,' he said finally. He handed me the mug of coffee and steadied my hand as I took a sip. It was perfect – exactly the amount of cream and sweetener I used myself each morning. 'I didn't want you to have to face him alone if he was still there.'

I stared at Cole for a moment over the rim of the mug.

'You followed me in case I had to deal with Tom?' I asked incredulously.

'Yeah,' said Cole with what I could have sworn was a blush. 'I didn't want you to have to be alone with him, you know? He doesn't sound like a very good guy.'

'He's not,' I agreed, smiling at Cole now, despite myself. He was almost too good to be true.

But that was the problem. He *was* the perfect guy – the guy every woman in America probably dreamed of – and I couldn't so much as touch him. I suddenly understood the concept of forbidden fruit.

Not to mention that even if I *did* develop a crush on him, it would be totally useless. I knew from the clips I'd read that his last serious girlfriend had been Kris Milan, the glamorous, willowy model-of-the-moment. Her flawless face looked down over Times Square from not only a Calvin Klein billboard, but also a Burberry perfume board, and an Audi ad. Not exactly in my league.

'Thank you,' I said, realizing I was relieved that he was here with me. I *had* been worried about seeing Tom.

Imagine his surprise if he were still in the apartment and I walked in with Hollywood's most eligible bachelor. 'Really, thanks.'

Cole lowered his eyes.

'You're welcome,' he said softly. He looked back up at me and smiled gently. 'Now eat that croissant, okay? I promise you'll feel better.'

'Okay,' I said finally, smiling at Cole. The cab heaved forward, and Cole sat in silence, watching me eat.

The remainder of the cab ride seemed to take forever, and by the time we reached the corner of Second Avenue and Second Street, I'd polished off all the food Cole had given me, as well as the water and the coffee. As a result, my bladder felt like it was about to burst.

'It was a pleasure to drive you today, Mr Cole Brannon,' said the driver formally as we alighted from the cab. 'And I won't tell anyone about you and your lady friend here. You can trust me.'

Cole grinned at me. I blushed furiously.

'Thank you,' he said seriously to the driver. He handed him the fare plus a twenty-dollar tip. Our starstruck driver simply sat and stared until Cole and I were inside my building.

I dashed for the stairs the moment we pushed past the big entryway. Cole kept pace two stairs behind me. While I huffed and puffed my way up four flights, Cole hardly seemed winded.

'This is me,' I panted as I reached my door. I put the key in the lock and turned it quickly.

But then I stopped, frozen in place.

'You okay?' Cole asked, putting a hand on my arm with a look of concern.

'Yeah,' I said, not really meaning it. I couldn't seem to will myself to open the door.

'Here, let me go in first,' Cole said quietly, putting his right hand over mine. 'In case he's there.' I nodded. Cole gave my shoulder a quick squeeze, turned the knob, and disappeared inside while I waited on the doorstep.

The seconds ticked by so slowly, it felt like I was standing there for hours. Finally, he was back at the doorway.

'He's gone,' he said simply as he pulled the door open for me.

'Oh,' I said, still standing on the threshold.

'Come in,' Cole urged. I looked up at him briefly and he stepped to the side, holding the door open for me. Gingerly, I stepped over the threshold into the kitchen.

Everything looked the same as it had yesterday and the day before, and the day before that. I half expected Tom to come ambling out of the bedroom, lazily claiming to have just finished a day's worth of work on his novel.

But he wasn't there. He'd never be there again.

Once I had used the bathroom, I stood there for a moment, leaning against the counter. Tom's toothbrush was gone from the toothbrush holder we'd shared. His shaving cream had been taken from the medicine cabinet. His razors no longer sat beside mine. He was gone, and I knew I should have been glad. But somewhere deep inside, in a dark corner that shouldn't have any place in a self-respecting girl's heart, I missed him. I hated him with all the fury that had erupted yesterday when I saw him screwing another girl, but I couldn't ignore the part of me that had spent a year desperately trying to make it work. I couldn't shake the guilty feeling that I'd failed, miserably.

I looked at myself in the mirror. I looked awful. I had dark bags under my eyes, and the makeup I'd slapped on in Cole's bathroom had done little to hide the puffy redness that my eyes were still sporting, thanks to the flood of tears the night before. And to cap it all off, I had the most attractive movie star in America standing outside my bathroom door, no doubt thinking how pathetic (not to mention pathetic-*looking*) I was.

I took a deep breath. Cole Brannon had helped me when I was at my most vulnerable, and there was nothing I could do about that. But I was okay now. I was going to be okay. And I had to get him out of here before this went any further.

I tried to ignore the fact that my heart rate was up about 50 per cent thanks to the fact that Cole Brannon – *the* Cole Brannon – was now sitting in my kitchen. I ignored the little uninvited fantasy creeping in at the back of my mind that involved me, Cole Brannon, the kitchen table, and substantially fewer clothes than either of us was currently wearing. I ignored the fact that I was developing one major crush. It was beside the point, not to mention totally inappropriate. And about as likely to develop into anything as winning the lottery.

I closed my eyes once more and vowed that I would send Cole on his way, as politely as possible, before any more damage could be done. Tom had already taken every last shred of my personal dignity. I wouldn't let the situation he'd initiated last night steal my professional dignity too.

'Would you like a cup of coffee?' I asked breezily, emerging from the bathroom. I tried not to think too hard about the fact that Cole Brannon was actually sitting at my kitchen table. In Tom's chair. Talk about an over-adequate replacement.

'Yeah, sure, thanks,' he said. Damn it. He was supposed to say no, and he certainly wasn't supposed to look that sexy when he said it.

'Um, okay,' I said. I should have just been rude. 'I'll put a pot on, okay? But then I'm afraid I'm going to have to take off. I have to get back to the office to finish the story.' There, that was good. I wasn't throwing him out if I actually had somewhere to be, right?

'That story on me, hmm?' Cole asked, leaning back in his chair and grinning. 'It had better be a good one. You better work hard on it. Make me sound good.'

I smiled and wondered how anyone could possibly make him sound bad. He was perfect. I was suddenly sure that the whole sex-addict thing had to have been a false rumor.

'I'm going to go change out of these clothes,' I said. I flipped the switch on the old Black & Decker that had served me well for the past five years. It began gurgling almost immediately, and I could smell the dark-roasted coffee beginning to work its caffeinated magic.

'But the clothes you're wearing are so nicely cleaned and neatly pressed,' Cole teased.

'So true,' I replied. 'But I would love for you to actually realize that I have more than one outfit.'

'Oh, do you? Well, let's see!'

I made a face at him, and we both laughed. I could feel him watching me go as I stepped into my bedroom and shut the door behind me.

The smell of coffee wafted in from the kitchen as I surveyed my room slowly, trying not to think about the scene I'd witnessed here last night, trying not to think about what had happened in the bed I'd shared with Tom for nearly a year now. The room looked just as innocent and welcoming as ever, which struck me as somewhat strange, although I'm not sure what I had expected.

I looked in the closet and was immediately shocked to see that most of Tom's clothes still hung there. From the way he'd cleaned out the bathroom, I assumed he was gone for good and had taken all of his things. I stared for a moment as I realized it meant he'd be making at least one return visit. My stomach turned funny circles as I tried to decide how that made me feel.

As I turned around to survey the rest of the room, an unfamiliar object in the corner of the room caught my eye. I took a step closer.

It was a small Louis Vuitton bag, and it wasn't mine. It lay on its side, half obscured by the faded bureau, its thin strap trailing dangerously toward the bed. I stared warily.

I took a few steps across the room and bent down beside the purse, suddenly feeling choked up and uncomfortable. I weighed it for a moment in my hands and turned it over pensively. I knew instantly that it belonged to the woman with the perfect hair, the perfect breasts, and the perfect legs. Did she have to have a perfect handbag too? Of course she did.

Inside, there was surely an answer to who she was. I had to know. But I wasn't sure I was ready to confront her again, even if this time she'd only be a tiny photo and a name on an ID.

'Cole, can you come in here for a second?' I called out weakly. I sat down on the bed.

'Sure.' I heard his footsteps. He knocked lightly. 'Are you decent?'

'Yeah,' I said absently, still fingering the bag. He cracked the door open slowly and slipped inside.

'You okay?' he asked, looking at me with concern as he joined me on the edge of the bed.

'It's hers,' I said, without answering his question. He knew instantly what I meant. I held the purse out to him and finally looked up. Concern was etched across his perfect face as he put a strong hand gently on the small of my back.

'What are you going to do?' he asked softly.

'Open it, I guess,' I said. I paused for a moment. 'Is that wrong?'

'You have every right to know who she is,' he said softly. 'If you want to.'

'I don't know if I want to.' But I did. If for no other reason than to put a name with the face that had turned my life upside down. More important, I had to know if she had indeed been the woman at the Christmas party. If so, who had she been with? Had one of my coworkers known about Tom's affair all along?

'Want me to do it?' Cole asked gently.

'Yes.' I nodded, relieved that he'd taken over. I was

silent as he unzipped the little purse and reached inside. He pulled out a tiny Louis Vuitton wallet.

He opened it, looked at it for a moment, and silently handed it to me. It was her New York State driver's license, and from the tiny photo on the ID, she looked at me defiantly, almost smirking. Her long hair was dark and shiny, as it had appeared in person yesterday, and her lips were perfectly lined and filled in. Her complexion was creamy and flawless. She looked as if she'd had her makeup professionally done before standing in line at the driver's license bureau.

'Estella Marrone,' I said softly, reading her name. The name didn't ring a bell right away. 'Estella Marrone.' I repeated it once, a bit more softly. There was something familiar about her, but I was sure I'd never heard the name.

'You okay?' Cole asked. He started to rub my back slowly as I stared at the ID. Finally, I nodded.

'Yeah,' I said. I sighed. 'I think I am.' We just sat there for a moment, me staring pensively at her ID, not knowing what to think, and Cole gently rubbing my back.

Suddenly, there was a sharp knock on the front door. I jumped, startled. I wasn't expecting anyone. Cole and I exchanged confused looks.

'It must be Wendy,' I said finally. She had surely been worried when she got my slurred message. 'My best friend,' I clarified. 'Hang on a second. I'll get it.'

I left Cole sitting on the bed while I went to answer the door, suddenly feeling relieved, despite the fact that Cole was still here and the mysterious Estella Marrone's face was dancing around in my head. Wendy was the one person in the world who would know how to take care of this entire situation.

I was actually smiling by the time I reached the door, fully expecting to be blinded by Wendy's toothy smile and amused by today's choice of wacky outfit. I wrestled with the stubborn lock, swung the door open, and smiled into the hallway.

Then I blinked as I realized that it wasn't Wendy on my doorstep at all.

It was Sidra DeSimon.

I stared wordlessly at *Mod*'s fashion director, dressed from head to toe in black leather, despite the fact that it was a warm June day. As usual, her short, dark hair was perfectly slicked back, her eyebrows were perfectly tweezed into sharp lines, and her lipstick was a perfect blood-red. Her perfume filled the hallway.

She stared back at me wordlessly for a moment, looking inexplicably as surprised to see me as I was to see her. My mind began racing.

Oh my God, someone had seen me leave Cole's hotel. Someone had called *Mod*. Margaret had sent the head Triplet here to check and see if the rumor was true. And she would think it was! Cole was in the other room! In my *bedroom*! She would see him, assume the worst, and my life would be over! How had this happened? Finally, she spoke.

'Hello, Claire,' she said, staring at me strangely. She glanced past me into the apartment, and I took a quick step to the right to block her view. I was still confused about her appearance on my doorstep, but I hadn't forgotten about Cole Brannon and his potential to ruin my life if Sidra caught a glimpse of him.

'Can I, um, help you with something?' I asked quickly, hoping to expedite this visit. My discomfort was growing. Sooner or later, Cole was bound to emerge from my bedroom, and I'd have no chance of saving my reputation.

'I didn't know you'd be here,' said Sidra cryptically. I just stared at her. She paused. Then she continued. 'I'm here to pick up my sister's purse.'

I simply stared for a moment, then my jaw dropped. It suddenly clicked, and I realized what I should have known all along. The woman Tom had been sleeping with bore a striking resemblance to Sidra DeSimon. The same thick, dark hair, the same pointed nose, the same high cheekbones (though I would have wagered that they were implants – perhaps by the same plastic surgeon), the same fake breasts. Of course.

'Your sister?' I squeaked.

'That's what I said, isn't it?' said Sidra, looking annoyed. 'Honestly,' she muttered, rolling her eyes and looking at me like I was a half-wit. She reached into her clutch and effortlessly extracted a cigarette, which she proceeded to light, flicking ash on my doorstep and blowing smoke in my face. 'Could we hurry things up here? I don't have all day.'

'Your sister?' I repeated stupidly. Sidra stared at me with blazing eyes. I couldn't move. I took a deep breath.

'Yes, Claire.' She spoke the words slowly, with forced patience, like she was talking to a child. 'My sister, Estella. She left her bag at her boyfriend's apartment, and she asked me to pick it up. Is that really so difficult for you to understand?'

'Her boyfriend?' I choked. 'He was *my* boyfriend. This is *my* apartment.'

'Ah, yes,' Sidra said, still looking bored. She took another long drag from her cigarette. 'I know. Rather awkward.' The corners of her lips twitched, and I suspected she would have been smirking had she not had so much collagen injected recently. Suddenly I wanted to reach out and strangle her. The only thing that stopped me was the realization that it would likely be difficult to get a grip on the slippery leather that covered her body.

'Did they meet . . .' My voice trailed off. I didn't know how to complete the sentence or even why I wanted to know. '. . . at the Christmas party?' I finally finished the thought.

'Yes, Claire,' Sidra said slowly. 'Now are we going to stand here and play twenty questions all day? Or are you just going to give me her handbag? I have work to do today, you know.'

'Oh,' I said, my mind still spinning. This was too much.

'Oh?' Sidra mimicked. 'Look, I have a car waiting outside. I don't have time for chitchat.'

'I'll get the purse,' I said finally. I balled my hands into fists and contented myself by imagining a scenario in which I beat Sidra and Estella to a pulp, perhaps using Estella's Louis Vuitton bag as the weapon of choice. Pummeled to death with Louis Vuitton products. A fitting end to their shallow lives.

But I realized suddenly that Sidra wasn't looking at me any more. She was looking over my shoulder. I knew with horror, before I even turned around, what she was looking at.

'This must be Wendy!' Cole said cheerfully as he emerged, grinning, from the bedroom. He crossed the kitchen in a few steps and was at my side. He placed a gentle, almost protective hand on the small of my back.

'No,' I muttered as Sidra stared. I could practically feel my world crashing down around me. 'This is Sidra DeSimon, the fashion director at *Mod*.'

'Oh,' said Cole, looking confused, but still smiling politely. This was worse than I could have imagined. 'Nice to meet you,' he said, extending his hand. 'I'm Cole.'

'Yes, I know,' said Sidra finally, taking his hand and shaking it slowly. My stomach churned. She turned back to me. 'Well, well, well, what have we here?' she asked, arching an eyebrow at me.

'It's not what it looks like,' I stammered. 'Really, we just got here a few minutes ago, and I barely know him, and . . .' Sidra cut me off, still smiling dangerously.

'Oh, I know what it looks like,' she said. She looked at Cole conspiratorially. 'I used to date George Clooney, you know. How nice to see little Claire here, following in my footsteps.' She tittered lightly. 'Not that *you* would actually date *her*.' She laughed again.

'Why not?' Cole asked. I turned around to look at him and was surprised – and a bit flattered – to realize that his grin had been replaced with an icy glare. 'I think she's wonderful. And it's funny, but I've never heard George mention anything about you.'

I could practically see Sidra's claws coming out. Her eyes flashed, and she prepared to cut into Cole. I interrupted quickly.

'Sidra just stopped by to pick up *her sister's purse*,' I said to Cole, turning around to look at him. His eyes widened.

'But I see I'm interrupting something,' Sidra said mischievously, her mouth twisting as far into a smirk as it was capable of.

'I'll get the purse,' Cole said tightly. He left Sidra and me staring at each other while he disappeared momentarily. She continued to smile knowingly while my stomach again threatened to turn. I distracted myself by returning to the beating-Sidra-with-Louis-Vuitton fantasy.

'Here.' Cole surprised me by tossing the purse at Sidra rather than handing it to her. She deftly caught it and smiled smugly at me.

'I'm sure the editorial staff at *Mod* will be thrilled to hear about this,' she said, a dangerous edge in her voice. She looked back and forth between Cole and me. 'This is just *precious*,' she squealed. She started to back away from the door, but as an apparent afterthought, she turned back around and smiled icily at me once more.

'Claire, dear, one more thing. That shade of lipstick looks absolutely *hideous* on you,' she said, smiling sweetly. 'Just a little tip, from me to you.' She looked at me coolly for a moment, as if challenging me. She dropped her cigarette on my cheery blue and yellow welcome mat, stubbing it out with the toe of her leather stiletto boot. 'Ta-ta, lovebirds,' she said. She spun on her heel and started to clickclack down the hallway and down the stairs. 'Have a lovely day. I know I will.' Her laughter wafted up through the stairwell as she descended and disappeared from view.

Purging

I sat alone in my cubicle, staring vacantly at my illuminated computer screen, my eyes glazing over the words for what must have been the hundredth time. I knew I needed to finish editing the article on Cole Brannon, but I couldn't quite seem to focus. I was worried sick about what Sidra would do with the knowledge that Cole had been in my apartment this morning. It seemed darkly ironic that she was the one who would be responsible for editing my article about him.

I had considered, for a moment, asking that someone else edit the article instead. But then I'd have to reveal the reason why. And how much damage could Sidra truly do to the article itself, anyhow?

The rest of the office was dark. It was almost unheard of in the women's magazine world to be working on a Sunday, but there was little I could do, given Margaret's timing of the article. Besides, given the events of the morning, I had the distinct feeling that I wouldn't be in the women's magazine world much longer. I knew I would be forced to leave in disgrace as soon as Sidra got ahold of Margaret.

I looked at my watch. Wendy would be here any minute. I had finally spoken with her this morning after Cole left. I knew she could tell from my tone that I was in trouble.

I sighed and turned back to my computer screen, which

was still open to the same page. 'COLE BRANNON: HOLLYWOOD'S HOTTEST HUNK OPENS UP ABOUT LOVE, LIFE, AND THE THINGS HE WANTS YOU TO KNOW.' The headline screamed at me, and I grimaced back.

After Sidra had disappeared, taking all hope of my escape from this situation with her (along with Estella Marrone's Louis Vuitton bag), I was too distraught to be polite to Cole any more. It no longer mattered that he was the guy who had cared enough to help me when I needed him. Nor did it matter that he was the most attractive man I'd ever met, or that he was Hollywood's most eligible bachelor. All that mattered was that my life was mere hours away from being ruined.

'None of this is your fault, Claire,' Cole said as we walked down the stairs together.

'Yes it is, Cole,' I said glumly. 'I know better than to do things like this.'

'Like what?' Cole asked gently. 'It's not your fault that this happened.'

'You don't understand,' I said quietly, shaking my head. 'Once Sidra tells Margaret, our editor in chief, I'll be fired. Then Sidra will tell the tabloids. By tomorrow morning, the whole world is going to think I'm sleeping with you.' I blushed as I spoke.

'So?' Cole asked softly. I looked at him desperately.

'So, it will completely ruin my reputation,' I said. 'Don't you understand how it works? I'll always be "that girl". The one who slept with a movie star she was supposed to interview. No one will ever take me seriously again.'

'But we didn't sleep together,' Cole said, looking confused.

'It doesn't even matter at this point.' I sighed. 'A few details from Sidra DeSimon, and the rumor mill will get started. It doesn't have to be true. You know that.'

Cole lowered his eyes for a moment, then looked up at me.

'You can't always believe what you read,' he said softly.

'I know,' I said, exasperated. 'But just having that story circulating around out there . . . It will never be the same for me again. You know how it works.'

'Yes, I do,' he said slowly. 'Listen, I'm really sorry. I didn't mean to cause you any trouble.'

'I know, and I appreciate it,' I said as we reached the ground floor. 'And I'm sorry I'm doing this. It's not your fault. Not at all. I just can't believe Sidra saw us. This whole thing has gotten so out of control.' We walked down the long hallway in silence. Before I pushed the heavy door open to Second Avenue, Cole put a hand on my arm.

'Look, Claire,' he said softly. 'This whole thing, it's going to work out.' I listened, but I shook my head at him. He meant well, but he didn't know what he was talking about. His blue eyes were so earnest and piercing, they reminded me suddenly of the sky on a bright summer day. 'You can't let some creep like that Tom guy make you feel like you're anything less than a great, beautiful woman.'

After an embarrassed pause, blushing furiously, I mumbled, 'Thanks.' But I knew that wasn't enough. My heart was in my throat.

'You know, guys are idiots sometimes,' Cole said. 'Really, Claire, it's not you. And you're better off without someone like that.'

'Thanks,' I said softly. 'I appreciate everything you did for me, Cole. I really do.' He gave me a quick hug and then a light peck on the top of my head, which, despite myself, made my heart skip a beat.

'Call me if you need anything, Claire,' he said. 'Anything at all.' He looked sad as he pushed open the door and disappeared into the blinding sunlight outside. I let the door swing closed behind him, and I stood there motionless for a full minute, wondering what kind of an idiot I was to have kicked Mr Perfect out of my apartment.

*

Now, an hour later, I could still see Cole's blue eyes in my mind as I stared at the article I'd written about him yesterday afternoon, before my world had fallen apart.

Just then I heard the reception door buzz. I turned in time to see Wendy bustle in, her bright purple sundress swirling around her as she rushed toward me. I was so relieved she had arrived, I almost leaped up to throw myself at her.

I just needed a friend to cry to – preferably one who wasn't the biggest movie star in America.

'Are you okay?' she asked across the office, half walking, half jogging to my cubicle. Her face was etched with deep concern. 'What happened?'

Without missing a beat, she yanked a rolling chair out of her cubicle and dragged it quickly over to mine. She tossed her Coach bag on the floor and opened her arms.

'Give me a hug,' she demanded. I stood up and let her envelop me. She held me tightly for a moment as I hugged back, heaving a sigh into her shoulder. Finally, she pulled away, still looking concerned, and we both sat down. 'I'm sorry I didn't get your message until this morning. I was out late. What is it, Claire? It's Tom, isn't it?'

'Among other things,' I muttered. Wendy shook her head.

'What did he do this time?' she asked, looking angry. 'I'm so sick and tired of him hurting you.'

'I caught him cheating on me,' I said flatly. Her eyes widened in surprise. Even Wendy, with all her dire predictions, hadn't seen this coming.

'What?'

'Yep, I actually caught him in the act,' I said, sounding much more cavalier than I felt. 'In my bed, actually having sex with another woman.'

'Oh my God,' Wendy said. 'Claire, I'm so sorry. I knew he was an ass, but I didn't expect . . .'

'Oh, that's not the worst of it,' I continued calmly. 'The

woman was Sidra's sister.' Wendy just stared at me for a moment, looking like she was trying to process the information.

'Sidra DeSimon?' she asked finally, her eyes wide. I nodded. 'You've got to be kidding me. How?'

'They met at the Christmas party.'

'Oh, no.'

'Oh, that's not all,' I said.

'It's not?' she asked incredulously.

'Nope. I left out the part where Sidra came to the door this morning and saw Cole Brannon in my apartment. Now she thinks I'm sleeping with him, and I'm sure I'll lose my job.'

Wendy blinked.

'Cole Brannon was in your apartment?' she finally breathed. I knew she would get stuck on that. 'What happened? What was he doing there?'

So I told her the whole story, relaying it to her with a calmness I didn't feel. She just stared, openmouthed, as I described walking in on Tom, seeing Cole at Metro, waking up in his bed, and then encountering Sidra.

'And now here I am, working on an article about a guy whose appearance at Metro last night will probably ruin my entire career,' I said as I finished, gesturing to my computer. 'And the ironic thing is, this will probably be the last thing I ever write as a journalist.'

'That's not true,' said Wendy, finally clamping her gaping mouth shut. 'You're not going to lose your job. You didn't do anything.'

'But I did,' I said miserably. 'I got drunk and wound up going home with a movie star I'd just interviewed.'

'But you didn't do anything with him,' she protested.

'Do you think that will really matter?' I asked. 'Or that anyone will believe me?' Wendy didn't respond, which was all the answer I needed.

'Look,' Wendy said finally, after we sat there in silence for a moment. 'I'm going to edit your piece for you, okay?

You can sit right there, and I won't change anything without asking you, but you just don't look quite up to it at the moment.' She looked at me with a raised eyebrow. I thought about it for a second and then nodded.

'Okay,' I agreed. 'That would really help me out. If you don't mind.'

'Of course I don't,' Wendy said dismissively. 'Then you're going to come home with me, and stay for a while, okay?' I started to protest, but Wendy held up a hand to silence me. 'Yes, I know I live in a tiny apartment with two roommates and no room to sleep. But it's better than you being in your apartment right now. Bad vibes there. Give it a few days. You don't want to go back there yet.'

She was right. It would have been horrible to try to sleep there with images of Tom and Estella fresh in my mind.

'Okay,' I agreed finally, giving her a grateful smile. 'Hey, thanks.'

'That's what friends are for,' said Wendy, playfully nudging me. 'If Cole Brannon can put you up for the night, so can I.'

'But do you look as good as he does without a shirt on?' I asked with a weak smile.

Thirty minutes later, Wendy had saved my sanity – not that there was much of it left – by editing the Cole Brannon piece for me while I looked mutely over her shoulder. She made only a few changes and she had me verify a few facts from my notes, but otherwise, the piece was much as I'd written it the day before.

'He sounds really nice,' Wendy said softly as she saved the file and closed it.

'He is,' I agreed with just a hint of sadness. I wondered for a moment what he thought of me. No doubt I was his humanitarian project of the year. He'd taken an evening off from shagging movie stars to help some crazy lady who puked on him. How valiant.

I knew he would never look at me the same way he looked at Julia Roberts, Katie Holmes, or any of the other beautiful women he'd acted with. Because I would never look like them. I'd never have their grace, their glamour, or their self-confidence. I was five feet of pure average.

Gambling

It was a cruel twist of fate that left Sidra editing my article on Cole Brannon as part of her competition with Maite for the executive editor position. My only comfort was knowing that she couldn't screw it up too badly or she would be damaging her own reputation and compromising her own editorial credentials. I could imagine the war raging in her head: it must have been difficult for her not to intentionally screw me over, but if she did, it would look like her editing had ruined a perfectly good story.

I'd reviewed Sidra's changes to my article – which were, thankfully, relatively minor – by 8 p.m. and signed off on the copy by 9:00, which meant that the story on Cole was free to make its way onto *Mod*'s pages with my approval. At least one thing had turned out right.

After a nearly sleepless night at Wendy's – I had finally drifted off at about 3:30 a.m., and woke up two hours later in a cold sweat from a nightmare about Tom – I went home quickly to pick up a few changes of clothes. I arrived at *Mod*'s offices at 7 a.m., dreading the next few hours. I was sure I would be out on the street, a cardboard box of my belongings in my arms, by noon.

'Morning, Claire,' said Maite from across the hall as I settled gingerly into my chair.

'Good morning,' I said, sadly waving to her. She smiled, and I smiled back, realizing I was enjoying the last few hours of her respect. Maite had ascended the ladder of women's magazines by being a good writer and a good editor, and by remaining entirely professional – no matter what. Up until today, she'd probably thought the same of me. I knew she would lose all respect for me the moment she found out what had happened.

I turned on my computer and waited silently as it booted up. I sighed loudly enough that Maite poked her head out of her office to look at me.

'Are you okay?' she asked with concern.

'Yes, of course,' I lied. I forced a smile. 'Sorry to bother you.'

'No bother at all,' Maite said, shaking her head and smiling back. 'You look stressed out. Rough weekend?'

'You might say that.'

By 9 a.m., other staffers had started to drift in. Wendy still wasn't here, which didn't surprise me. She'd still been sleeping soundly – snoring, I might add – when I quietly left her apartment. She usually set her alarm for 8:00, but I knew it took her forever to get ready. That face didn't paint itself on every morning, nor did her closet cough up the latest in eccentric outfits without her input.

She would twirl a variety of combinations in front of the mirror for thirty minutes before deciding on something strange and senseless that would somehow look great on her. She'd float into the office by 9:30, long before anyone noticed she was late.

I had a whole pile of work for the September issue on my desk that I should have been working on, but I couldn't bring myself to do it. After all, it would surely be a waste of time. At most, I'd only be here a few more hours before getting fired.

Just then, Maite's phone rang. She chatted for a moment and then turned back around to me.

'That was Margaret,' she said slowly, a strange look on her face. My heart dropped. The editor in chief never called this early. 'The editorial meeting is canceled this morning. She says she won't be in until eleven.' I gulped.

'Um, did she say why?' I asked gingerly. Maite shook her head slowly.

'No,' she said. I gulped and tried not to look guilty. Surely Margaret knew. Sidra had told her. She was probably talking to *Mod*'s lawyers right now, asking how she could legally get rid of me as quickly as possible.

Just then, the speaker on my phone buzzed, signaling an interoffice intercom call.

'Claire, are you there?' The nasal voice of Cassie Jenkins, Margaret's assistant, filled my cubicle.

'Yes, Cassie,' I said into the speaker.

'Margaret would like to see you in her office first thing at eleven.' For a moment I was speechless. This was really it. I was really going to be fired in less than two hours. It was going to be the first thing Margaret did when she walked into the office. She would throw me out with the morning's trash. 'Claire? Are you still there, Claire?' I realized I hadn't answered Cassie.

'Um, yeah, Cassie, I'm here,' I said, my voice strained. 'I'll be there. At eleven.'

'I'll let Margaret know,' said Cassie coolly.

'I wonder what that's about,' Maite said as my intercom buzzed again to signal that Cassie had hung up.

'Um, I don't know,' I lied, looking down, trying my hardest not to look guilty.

'Maybe you're getting promoted,' Maite said cheerfully. 'I keep telling Margaret that you're worth a lot to the magazine. Maybe she finally listened to me.' I looked up at Maite with pained appreciation.

'Thanks,' I mumbled.

At 10:45, I couldn't stand it any longer. Wendy had been in for an hour, and I'd whispered to her about my impending appointment. Her pained and pitying expression had only heightened my fears about what would happen in the dreaded eleven o'clock one-on-one.

'Is there anything I can do, Claire?' she asked softly as the clock inched toward 11 a.m.

'Don't worry,' I said, trying to look brave. 'I'll be fine.'

At T-minus-ten-minutes I slowly pushed my chair back and stood up with a sigh.

'I'm going to the bathroom, Wendy,' I said slowly. 'I'll be back after my meeting with Margaret.' My heart was heavy as I looked around at *Mod*'s offices. My coworkers scrambled from office to office with hands full of paperwork. Phones rang, copy machines whirred, and the comforting click-click of fingers on keyboards surrounded us.

'Want me to come with you?' Wendy asked gently.

'No, I'll be okay,' I said, not really meaning it. I wouldn't be okay. I loved the bustle of the magazine business, the (mostly) friendly camaraderie of the women on staff, the quiet pace of the office when we weren't working on deadline. I loved that at twenty-six I was on my way up, and I had the respect of my colleagues. In ten minutes, that would be taken away from me forever. Because of Tom. Because I'd been stupid enough to believe him.

'Good luck, Claire,' Wendy said. She stood and walked over to my cubicle to give me a hug. 'It's going to be okay.'

'No,' I said, hugging her tightly and pushing back the sudden tears that had welled in my eyes. 'I don't think it is.'

As I began the long walk toward the bathroom on Margaret's side of the building, I felt like a prisoner being marched down the cell block on death row one last time before her execution. I looked at each coworker's face as I slowly marched toward my doom, trying to memorize them. A few looked up and smiled at me as I passed – a few said hello.

Some just looked at me strangely, which I'm sure was due to the fact that I was actually traipsing toward the executive offices with the look of death on my face.

Death did not become me.

In the bathroom I splashed water on my face, dried off with a harsh brown paper towel, and blinked at myself in the mirror. I looked horrible, which would only add fuel to Margaret's fire. She always insisted that we look as presentable as possible – after all, we were employees of *Mod* magazine, and we were supposed to look as chic and stylish as the name of the magazine implied. I was never sure how Wendy got away with the outfits she assembled, but I knew that Margaret always cast a critical eye on anyone who wasn't properly put together.

This morning the bags under my eyes and the stricken expression that I just couldn't shake didn't exactly scream 'mod', if I do say so myself.

I looked at my watch and knew I had to go. It was almost 11:00, and I was on the verge of being late to my own funeral.

Margaret kept me waiting for fifteen minutes before she had Cassie show me into her office. As I waited, the second hand on the Bulova clock on the wall ticked in super-slow motion. Cassie watched me silently from her desk with what looked like a little smirk on her face. It took all my self-control not to make a face at her but to smile wanly, which I did only on the slim chance that I could accumulate some last-minute good karma for the meeting if I showed a little kindness to Margaret's snotty assistant.

At twenty-two, Cassie was a recent college graduate with a useless degree in Classics from some Ivy League school her parents had paid a fortune for. The fact that she was the daughter of a woman in Margaret's social circle had earned her a place at *Mod*, which meant, of course, that Margaret had to fire Karen, her assistant of two years. Cassie had promptly alienated everyone by announcing that her assistantship was just a stepping-stone to getting one of *our* jobs.

Not that it always worked that way. Most of the women who had ascended past the rank of editorial assistant – up the chain to assistant editor, associate editor, then senior editor – knew what they were doing and had been promoted because they were talented, hardworking, and professional. After all, we had a magazine to put out. We couldn't *all* be morons if we were going to get a salable product to the newsstands each month.

The lower ranks of the magazine world were filled with young women like Cassie. They had never really worked a day in their lives and were in the business because their father's friend knew somebody who knew somebody who ran a magazine. The hardest thing about breaking into the magazine business was getting a foot in the door in the first place. Unfortunately, many of those foot-in-the-door positions at the glammest magazines went to women who were too busy getting those feet pedicured to actually bother doing any work. Eventually, most of them wound up quitting after the novelty of having a job wore off and they snagged a rich husband.

As Cassie smirked at me this morning over her spacious desk, I knew she was already planning how she'd fill my shoes once I was released. Well, at least someone would be happy about me losing my job.

The intercom on Cassie's desk buzzed, snapping her out of her smirk and jolting me out of my dark daydream.

'Cassie, please send Claire in now,' Margaret's voice said. Cassie looked up.

'She's ready for you,' she singsonged, smiling evilly. I forced a smile back.

'Thank you, Cassie,' I said politely. With all the grace and courage I could muster, I rose from my chair and walked slowly across Margaret's outer office to the big oak doors that led to her inner realm. I placed my hand on the knob and closed my eyes for a minute, willing myself to be calm.

'Are you going in, or are you going to just stand there?' Cassie honked. I wondered for a moment just how much my karma would suffer if I hit Cassie over the head with a chair on my way out, World-Wrestling style. Hey, at least

I'd leave a legacy at *Mod* beyond the 'She slept with Cole Brannon' gossip that would linger.

Finally, deciding a Cassie smackdown wasn't the way to go, I turned the knob and went in.

Margaret was dressed in a cream-colored tailored pantsuit. Her dark hair was slicked back, and her eyes were heavily made-up. She looked like she would be ready to parade down a fashion runway – if she were six inches taller (and if she hadn't been born with her mother's slightly bulbous nose and too-small chin). I had to give her credit, though – she hadn't used plastic surgery to get rid of these imperfections, and she expertly played up the assets she did have (which of course included her actual *monetary* assets), so she almost always looked untouchably glamorous.

She looked tiny behind her enormous desk, an island in the middle of the spacious room, which was easily the size of three editors' offices put together. Her carpet was a plush cream that matched her pantsuit. Her massive desk and two bookshelves were glistening black, polished each night at her insistence by the janitorial staff. Framed *Mod* magazine covers, blown up to 24 x 30, lined her walls and looked somehow elegant. Last year's June cover, featuring my interview with Julia Roberts, and this year's January cover, featuring my Q & A with Reese Witherspoon, had been recent additions to the Great Wall. I looked at Julia and Reese sadly as I realized glumly that I'd never get the chance to interview people like that again – for anyone.

I really did love my job. I loved getting A-listers like Julia and Reese to let their guard down – if only for a few minutes – so that I could catch a glimpse of who and what they really were. There was just something about humanizing the most untouchable stars that made me feel like I was doing something worthwhile. I wanted our readers to know that the larger-than-life Hollywooders were really people just like them.

'Have a seat, Claire,' Margaret said without looking up.

I gulped, settling into one of the two plush beige chairs that faced her desk. I grimaced as I sank into the cushions.

I braced myself. This was it, the end of the line.

'Claire, thank you for coming on such short notice,' Margaret said, finally looking up from her papers and peering at me over her Prada glasses. This was just like her, to begin politely, to suck me in before she dropped the news that I was fired. As if I wasn't expecting it.

'Of course,' I mumbled. I took a deep breath.

'As you know, Claire, we have a series of professional standards at *Mod*,' Margaret began diplomatically, gazing down at me from her throne. I gulped. Great, I was in for the speech. I knew I'd been wrong, but it wasn't as bad as Margaret thought. I hadn't actually *done* anything with Cole Brannon, contrary to what Sidra had surely told her. I hadn't slept with him. Heck, I hadn't even kissed him – although I was beginning to wish that I had. If I was about to lose my job anyhow, I might as well have gone out with flying colors.

'I'm sure that the other magazines where you worked had similar standards, so you're no doubt familiar with what I'm talking about,' Margaret said. I stared at her until she arched an eyebrow. Oh, she was waiting for a response.

'Yes,' I mumbled. Could this be any worse?

'In order to remain competitive, in order to maintain integrity, each magazine has to live up to certain standards of excellence,' Margaret continued. 'I'm sure you'll agree with me.'

'Yes,' I said meekly. Margaret peered at me for a moment, and I shrank even more – as if that was possible – under the weight of her gaze. She was looking at me so seriously that I knew this was it. I did a mental countdown in my head. Ten more seconds as a *Mod* employee. Nine. Eight. Seven—

'Which is why I'd like to commend you on your great work on the Cole Brannon piece,' Margaret said, suddenly beaming as she interrupted my countdown.

'Huh?' My jaw dropped. Perhaps I was going insane or I'd forgotten to Q-tip my ears that morning.

'You clearly went above and beyond your duty to *Mod* to turn in a great piece that will surely help us in the circulation war against *Cosmopolitan*,' Margaret continued cheerfully. 'August could be the month we surpass them, Claire, thanks to your great work with this piece. I've decided to feature it on the cover. Between your great writing and Sidra's great editing, the piece is an absolute gold mine.'

I simply stared, trying to digest what she was saying. This must have meant that Sidra hadn't said anything after all. Margaret obviously didn't know about my weekend with Cole, or I'd already be out the door with a pink slip. I finally sank back so heavily in relief that I almost disappeared into the chair.

'In fact, Claire,' Margaret continued, 'this will be the first month we feature a man on the cover. We've pushed your Julia Stiles cover back to September. Cole will be our cover face this month.' My jaw dropped again. With the exception of *Good Housekeeping*, with their occasional John Travolta or Tom Hanks covers, women's magazines almost *never* featured men on the cover. Certainly magazines like *Mod*, *Cosmo*, and *Glamour* never swayed from their beautiful-female cover format. I couldn't count the number of times Jennifer Aniston, Courteney Cox, or Gwyneth Paltrow had graced the covers of the magazines in our genre. You'd think that people would get sick of reading about the same people over and over and over again, but somehow they never seemed to.

'Wow,' I said finally, because I sensed that Margaret was waiting for a reaction. I was almost too shocked to speak. Not only had I *not* been fired, which I'd been fully braced for, but Margaret had liked my article on Cole so much that she was taking a risky move – making him the first man in history to appear on the cover of *Mod* magazine.

It surprised me even more that Sidra's editing had pleased Margaret to such an extent. She basically hadn't touched my piece at all. Was it possible she possessed journalistic skills after all? I had thought she was just a talentless spawn of Satan.

I was so shocked that it almost didn't cross my mind to wonder why Sidra hadn't told Margaret about finding Cole in my apartment. No way was Sidra that nice. She had something up her sleeve, and it made me uncomfortable to realize I now had no idea what it was. I had almost felt more comfortable when I was sure she would run immediately to Margaret with the news of my involvement with Cole.

'I'm so confident this cover will do well, Claire, and I am so impressed with your originality and appreciation of your duties at *Mod* that I've decided a little reward is in order,' Margaret said. She smiled at me, and in response, I forced a confused smile of my own. Again, Margaret seemed to be waiting for me to say something.

'Um, thank you?' I said hesitantly. This was too much to take in at once. My article on Cole had been good, but it hadn't been *that* good. Or so I thought. Maybe my perception of the article had been tainted by what happened afterwards. Maybe I had done a better job than I thought.

'So, I've decided to give you a raise,' Margaret said, folding her hands on her desk and leaning forward. 'It's long overdue, I'm sure. You've done great work with us, and I'm simply so impressed with your work with Cole Brannon that I feel you're due.'

'A raise?' I asked. 'Wow. I don't know what to say.' It was like I'd woken up from a nightmare and found myself in a sweet dream.

'Ten thousand more a year.' Margaret beamed. Ten thousand dollars! That was enough to take a trip this year. Enough to finally pay off those mounting credit card bills I'd been doing my best to ignore. One step closer to not feeling quite so much like an impoverished New Yorker.

'Aren't you going to say anything?' Margaret asked. I realized I'd been sitting in utter silence for over a minute while Margaret waited for a response.

'I appreciate this so much, Margaret,' I said finally. 'I worked really hard on the piece, but I had no idea you would like it so much. I'm really flattered.' There, that was good. My shocked brain had actually managed to string together a few sentences.

'There should always be a reward for those who go above and beyond the call of duty,' said Margaret with an odd smile on her face. I stared at her for a moment, finally accepting the praise.

'Thank you,' I said, smiling at Margaret.

'I just want you to know that I appreciate your help in the circulation war,' said Margaret, looking at me with the fierce pride of a general praising her troops. I stifled a laugh. She really did see this as war against *Cosmo*. Oh well, if my on-field battle skills earned me a raise, so be it. With one last tight smile at me, Margaret turned back to flipping through the stack of paperwork on her desk. 'That will be all, Claire,' she said briskly. I nodded and stood up.

'Thanks again,' I said. 'Really.'

Margaret nodded without looking up.

'Just keep up the good work,' she said, still thumbing. She reached for a yellow highlighter and went over a line on the page, now ignoring me. I guess that was it. I was dismissed, with my job, my life, still intact.

Outside Margaret's office, Cassie stared at me from behind her desk, looking almost confused as I grinned at her. But the smile promptly fell from my face as I turned and saw Sidra sitting in the outer room, waiting to see Margaret.

'Oh, hello there,' she said with a smile. 'Tom says hello. He'd like to come by and get some of his things later. That is, if you're not *otherwise occupied*.' She smiled icily, and I suddenly felt sick to my stomach again.

I knew better than to think the issue was a dead one. I

knew she was jealous that Cole Brannon had wound up at my apartment. And I knew that she was the kind of woman who didn't like to be bested – by anyone, in any situation. She would look at Cole's visit with me as a deliberate affront to her. As if I had been trying to top her George Clooney stories.

As I watched Sidra rise from her chair and glide into Margaret's office, I knew with rising certainty she still had something up her sleeve. And somehow, I knew it would be even worse than getting me fired.

Flirting

'What do you think she's going to do?' I asked Wendy over salads at Les Sans Culottes, a French bistro on West Forty-sixth Street. Wendy had insisted on taking me for a 'You didn't get fired' and 'You got a raise' celebratory lunch.

'Sidra?' Wendy asked absently, her attention temporarily distracted by a waiter whose name tag read Jean Michel. 'Cute, isn't he?' she murmured, batting her eyes at him as he looked in our direction. He smiled shyly and turned back to the table he was waiting on.

'Yes, Sidra,' I said, trying not to sound exasperated. I should have known that even lunchtime dining was a pick-up opportunity for the waiter-dating Wendy. 'I know this isn't over. The way she looked at me made my skin crawl.'

'Claire,' Wendy began with a sigh, turning her attention back to me. 'Maybe you're being too sensitive about this. I mean, none of us like her, but maybe she's not *that* evil. Maybe she's just going to keep saying things about Tom to get under your skin, and that will be it.'

'Maybe,' I said, unconvinced.

'So I don't think you have anything to worry about,' said Wendy earnestly. She watched me with concern as I stabbed halfheartedly at a leaf of lettuce.

'I don't know,' I said finally. 'The way she was looking at me . . . but what could be worse than getting me fired?'

'See, you're right!' said Wendy triumphantly. 'If she

wanted to hurt you, she would have just told Margaret, and that would have been the end of it. Why would she want to hurt you, anyhow?'

'Don't be so naive,' I said flatly. 'You've seen the way she looks at me. You've heard the things she says. She hates me for being successful. And now she's jealous of me for other reasons too.'

'What do you mean?' Wendy asked, looking intrigued. She stopped trying to tear off a piece of the crusty baguette that lay between us and finally gave me her undivided attention. After all, Jean Michel had walked back into the kitchen and was nowhere to be seen for the time being.

I shrugged.

'She saw me with Cole Brannon in my apartment,' I said slowly. 'I mean, she's always going on and on about her supposed relationship with George Clooney, right? And here I am, this coworker she already hates because I'm fifteen years younger than her. I have the biggest movie star in Hollywood in my apartment, and it looks like he's spent the night. It looks like I'm actually living her lie.'

Wendy looked at me for a moment, and I could almost see the wheels turning in her head. She looked down at her salad. Then she looked up at me again with a serious expression.

'You might be right,' she said, her voice hushed. Concern was etched across her brow. 'But what could she do to you if she hasn't gotten you fired?'

'I don't know,' I murmured.

We polished off our salads in silence for a few minutes, deep in thought about what Sidra had up her sleeve. Then again, maybe I was just being paranoid and nothing more would happen.

'Enough of this,' Wendy said finally. 'We're supposed to be celebrating your raise!' She looked around and beckoned for our waiter, who came rushing over officiously. 'Two glasses of champagne, please,' she said grandly. She grinned at me.

'Champagne?' I hissed, fighting back a smile. 'We shouldn't drink! We have to go back to work in thirty minutes! And you know I'm a lightweight!'

'Yes, well I think you proved that the other night, as I'm sure Cole Brannon would confirm,' Wendy teased. I blushed, despite myself. 'Anyhow, what the hell, right? You worked all weekend. Who cares if you're a bit off the mark this afternoon? Besides, with all the hell you went through this morning worrying about your job, I think you need something to take the edge off.' I started to protest again, but Wendy held up a hand to silence me. 'I insist,' she said firmly.

'Okay then,' I said, smiling back. 'If you insist.'

The waiter scurried back in a moment with two flutes of bubbly. He set them down on the table and turned to Wendy. 'Anything else, ma'am?' he asked.

'Um, yes,' said Wendy, batting her eyelashes again. 'See that waiter over there?' She gestured to Jean Michel, who was now filling another table's water glasses, his back to us.

'Yes, Jean Michel?' our waiter asked. 'Do you need your water glasses filled? I'd be glad to do that for you.'

'No, no, no,' Wendy said quickly. 'But could you send him over?' The waiter looked confused for a moment; then he seemed to realize what Wendy was getting at.

'Ma'am, he speaks very little English. I don't think—'

Wendy cut him off.

'*Je parle français*,' she said in perfect French. I looked at her in surprise.

'Oh,' said our waiter, looking surprised and humbled. '*Oui, mademoiselle*. I'll get him for you.'

He hurried off in Jean Michel's direction, and I looked at Wendy in amusement.

'Since when do you speak French?' I asked her.

'I don't,' she said, eyeing Jean Michel as our waiter whispered something in his ear and his eyebrows shot up in surprise. He smiled shyly at Wendy and started over in our direction. 'I just learned enough to pick up French waiters,' said Wendy, still smiling at the approaching Jean Michel. She reached up and fluffed her perky red curls. 'I love French restaurants, but I was tired of not being able to talk to the guys who had just come over from France. So I learned pick-up French.'

I arched an eyebrow at her as Jean Michel arrived shyly at our table, his cheeks flushed with color. I had to admit, Wendy had good taste, as much as I teased her about her dating patterns. Jean Michel was tall with dark hair cascading nearly to his shoulders. His features were sharp, and his eyes were big and green.

'*Bonjour, mademoiselle,*' Jean Michel said to Wendy, his voice deep and husky. Wendy smiled.

'*Bonjour,*' she said, again with a perfect French accent. I shook my head in wonder as I watched her work. '*Comment allez-vous?*'

'*Très bien, merci,*' Jean Michel responded enthusiastically, apparently convinced that Wendy spoke his language. He launched into several other rapidly spoken French sentences, which Wendy nodded and smiled at.

'You understand him?' I whispered when he looked away for a moment to check on his other tables.

'Not one word,' she said. She grinned at me. 'But do I really have to?' I shook my head and tried not to laugh as Jean Michel turned eagerly back to us.

'So that's pick-up French,' I said.

'That's pick-up French,' Wendy confirmed with a grin.

An hour later, I was back at work, flipping through clips I'd pulled from our research service. I was supposed to go to a press conference on Thursday for Kylie Dane's new movie, and I wanted to read everything I could about the movie and about her before I showed up for it.

I liked to go into every interview – even press conferences – as fully primed as possible. I was particularly apprehensive about this press conference, because, of course, Kylie Dane had been linked in the tabloids and gossip pages to Cole Brannon. But he had insisted it wasn't true, and I supposed she was as much a victim of the gossip as he was. Still, I couldn't help feeling a tiny twinge of jealousy.

As I flipped through article after article, astonished that I still had a job, I marveled at the media's fascination with everything in a celebrity's life. There seemed to be paparazzi hiding behind every bush, waiting to snap photos of A-listers out to lunch, shopping in Beverly Hills, or whispering in corners with unidentified people of the opposite gender. Everything was speculated upon, feeding rumors that had a habit of sticking around.

Then it hit me.

I got up quickly and crossed over to Wendy's adjoining cubicle.

'Wendy?' I said quickly from her doorway. My palms were already sweating, and my heart was pounding rapidly.

'Hey, girl,' she said, turning around, her curls flying as she turned her head. She smiled at me, her miles of teeth gleaming, not yet realizing that I was on the verge of fullout panic. 'What's up?'

'*Tattletale*,' I said. She looked at me in confusion.

'What?'

'*Tattletale*,' I repeated. 'That's how Sidra is going to get me. With an article in *Tattletale* tomorrow morning. Why just get me fired, when she can embarrass the hell out of me at the same time?'

Wendy simply stared. My heart continued to race, and I felt like I was going to fall over. I put a hand on the wall of Wendy's cubicle to steady myself, waiting for her response.

'You could be right,' she said, her voice hushed. She looked as horrified as I felt. Then she cleared her throat and tried to smile encouragingly at me. 'But that probably won't happen. I mean, who would believe her?'

'*Tattletale*,' I answered quickly. '*Tattletale* would believe her. Enough to print the story anyhow. They don't care if it's true. Just if it sells copies. And that's pretty juicy, right?' *Mod* writer sleeps with hottest movie star in Hollywood?'

'No way,' Wendy said firmly, her face full of forced confidence. She reached out for my hand, giving it a quick squeeze as she smiled at me bravely again. 'The whole magazine world knows Sidra's reputation. You don't really think anyone believes the George Clooney thing, do you?'

'But *Tattletale* still prints it,' I said grimly. 'Every time. Because it sells magazines. And because Sidra is tight with the editors there. She's always quoted in there talking about her *time with George*.'

'You're right,' Wendy muttered finally. She looked down at her lap and then looked up at me again, her brow now furrowed with concern. 'But there's no reason they'd believe her about you, right?'

'What if there are photos?' I asked.

'Photos?'

'Like from when I left his hotel. When he got in the cab with me.'

'But you didn't see any photographers, right?' Wendy asked, looking hopeful. She reached up and pushed her spilling red curls out of her face.

'That doesn't mean they weren't there. Hiding in the bushes or something. You know the paparazzi.'

'Oh, geez,' Wendy said seriously. I knew she didn't want to say it, but I was potentially screwed. Very screwed.

We were silent for a moment. I listened to the blood rushing through my ears as my heart pounded double-time. Wendy nervously chewed her lip.

'You didn't actually leave the hotel with him, though,' she said finally. 'So the best they can do is photos of the two of you together in a cab. Which could be totally innocent.'

'Until Sidra adds in her narration,' I said quickly. 'Until she tells them we had just left the hotel together and were on our way to my apartment to have sex again.'

Wendy was silent for a moment, her brow furrowed in concentration.

'Maybe we're overreacting,' she said finally. 'I mean, maybe Sidra isn't out to get you. She didn't get you fired, right?'

'You know she hates me,' I said.

'It doesn't make any sense,' Wendy said, shaking her head. 'Just because you're a few years ahead of where she was at your age? You'd think she'd be ready to call it even at this point,' Wendy muttered. 'I mean, her sister was screwing your boyfriend, for God's sake.'

I felt unexpected tears rush to my eyes, and I tried to sniff them away before Wendy noticed. Too late.

'God, I'm sorry,' she said quickly. 'I shouldn't have said that. About her sister, I mean.'

'No, no,' I said, wiping my eyes with my hand. I forced a smile. 'I guess it's still fresh, you know?' I didn't want to tell her that part of the problem was the illogical – not to mention embarrassing – feelings I still had for Tom. What was wrong with me? How was it that every ounce of my brain could be telling me one thing and my heart could feel another?

'I know,' said Wendy gently. She got up and hugged me tightly. 'He's an asshole, Claire. Forget about him. He was never good enough for you.'

'I know,' I said. But I didn't know. It wasn't like men were lining up in droves, beating down my door for the chance to have a date with me. And appearances aside, it's not like anything had actually *happened* with Cole Brannon.

The phone in my cubicle rang, snapping me out of my dire self-analysis. Wendy was still looking at me with concern, and I realized I'd been standing in the hallway for at least a whole minute, staring off into space as I thought about what a failure I was as dating material.

'You okay?' she asked as my phone rang a second time. 'Want me to get that for you?'

'No, I'll get it,' I said. I shook my head and snapped myself out of self-pity mode. Fortunately, the cubicles in our office were so small and close together that I could easily navigate from Wendy's office space to mine in time to answer the telephone. I wondered briefly why this morning's raise couldn't have come with an actual office. I made it around the corner after the third ring, diving for the phone.

'Claire Reilly,' I answered, breathless from my dive. I'd knocked a pile of papers on the ground, and I started picking them up, balancing the phone between my shoulder and ear. I was greeted by silence. Perhaps I hadn't reached the phone in time. Great, now on top of everything else, I was missing business calls because I was immersed in self-pity. 'Hello?' I said into the silence.

'Claire?'

My breath caught in my throat as I recognized the voice.

It was Tom. I stopped shuffling the papers and stood stock-still. I didn't answer.

'Claire?' he asked again. His voice sounded desperate, searching. Or perhaps that was just me hoping that he missed me enough to sound desperate. 'Are you there, babe? It's Tom.'

I still didn't answer. Wendy was standing up, looking at me quizzically over the cubicle. She knew something was wrong. I didn't know what to do. What did he want? Should I answer him? Would he ask me to forgive him, to take him back? What would I say?

Still staring at Wendy, as if she could provide an answer to the questions I hadn't asked her, I cleared my throat, but that was as far as I got. I wasn't even sure I wanted to talk to him. I hadn't thought about the possibility of him calling me at work.

'Claire? Are you there?' His voice sounded concerned. But I was too screwed up to deal with this now. I slammed the phone back down without saying a word.

'Are you okay?' Wendy asked, looking at me worriedly. I slowly sat down in my chair, forgetting about the avalanche of papers that had spilled around my feet. 'Who was that?'

'It was Tom,' I said slowly, staring at the phone. I wondered if he'd call back. I realized suddenly that I wanted him to. I wanted him to work at getting back into my life. I wanted him to show me that I was worth that much.

Geez, I was pathetic.

I willed the phone to ring, but it stubbornly stayed silent.

'Good for you,' Wendy said warmly over the cubicle, apparently mistaking my grief for resolve. 'You stay strong, girl. Good for you, for hanging up on him.'

'Yeah,' I said softly, still looking at the silent phone. 'Good for me.'

I felt sick all afternoon and wound up alone in the bathroom at about four o'clock, finally vomiting in the toilet. I realized I was setting some kind of record. I'd thrown up twice in the last few days, which was strange for me, as I hadn't thrown up since the eleventh grade, when I puked right in the middle of Mr Dorsett's American History class. Amazingly, I'd made it all the way through college without ever throwing up once – not even after keg parties, when I was surrounded by vomiting friends. And here I was, for the second time in three days. Someone call the *Guinness Book*.

I rinsed my mouth out in the sink and splashed water on my face, thankful that there were no witnesses to my sorry state. Looking down to make sure that I hadn't gotten any vomit on my clothes, I noticed that my stomach was looking flatter than it had in months. Hey, maybe this was the secret to a slender body – have men break your heart and get rid of all the food you've eaten that day. Excellent. Weight Loss for Losers. Bulimia for the Broken-hearted. I could launch my own diet franchise.

I spit a mouthful of water into the sink, took a deep

breath, and looked at myself in the mirror. I looked awful. My makeup was all gone, thanks to the water I'd splashed on my face. Without it, the dark circles under my eyes were more pronounced, and even my freckles looked pale and boring on my lifeless skin.

I was still assessing myself in the mirror when Wendy burst into the bathroom, a ball of energy, as usual.

'There you are!' she exclaimed as she bustled through the door. 'I've been looking everywhere for you!' Her face darkened as I turned to her. She looked me up and down for a moment. 'Are you okay?'

'I'm fine,' I said, forcing a smile that I hoped looked cheerful. She looked at me doubtfully, but I knew she could read on my face that I didn't want to talk about it. 'What's up?'

She looked at me with concern for another moment, then seemed to decide that the best course of action would be pretending that nothing was wrong. She smiled at me.

'You just had a bouquet of flowers delivered!' she said. 'Let's go see who they're from!' I looked at her, puzzled.

'Are you sure they're for me?' I asked. No one had ever sent me flowers. I know, that's pathetic, right? I'm twenty-six years old and have never gotten flowers from a man. Not once.

In contrast, Wendy seemed to get them from various waiters at least once or twice a month.

'Maybe they're for you,' I said.

'They say "Claire Reilly" on the card,' Wendy said, smiling. 'They are definitely for you!'

I looked at her for a moment, my mind spinning through the possibilities. They had to be from Tom. I'd hung up on him a few hours ago, and he felt so bad that he'd sent me flowers to apologize. The card would say, 'I love you more than life itself,' or something equally devoted. He'd call later and tell me how sorry he was, how wrong he had been, how much he loved me. It would take me a long time to forget what happened, but I could make it work. I'd never even have to tell my disapproving mother that I hadn't been able to hang on to yet another man.

'Well . . .' Wendy said, her voice trailing off. She opened the bathroom door. 'Are you coming? I can't stand the suspense.' She winked at me and I smiled.

'Okay,' I said finally. I followed her out the door and back through the narrow hallway toward the editorial room.

'Who do you think they're from?' Wendy asked excitedly as we walked side by side.

'I don't know,' I said softly. But I did know. I knew they were from Tom. I just didn't want Wendy to know that I was thinking that way or that I cared. She thought that my hanging up on him earlier was a sign of strength, and I preferred that she see me that way. I didn't want her to know I had spent the rest of the day fantasizing about how he'd apologize and beg me to take him back.

I looked at her sideways.

'Maybe they're from Tom,' I said hesitantly.

'Are you kidding me?' Wendy asked sharply. 'Tom has never sent you flowers. He's a complete jackass. Are you delusional?'

'I don't know,' I mumbled. But they were from Tom. I just knew it.

We rounded the corner, and I felt my breath catch in my throat when I saw the display on my desk.

It was the largest arrangement of flowers I'd ever seen. It was easily triple the size of the bouquets that landed on Wendy's desk a few times a month. Three dozen white longstem roses stood upright and slightly angled in a giant vase, accented with an immense violet ribbon. They were flanked by scores of perfect white lilies. As we approached, I could see a small white envelope on the end of a plastic wand protruding from the field of lilies.

'Wow,' I said involuntarily. It was beautiful.

'I know,' Wendy said in awe. 'It's the prettiest bouquet I've ever seen.'

'Wow,' I repeated. We stopped at my desk and I plucked the card from the plastic wand. Wendy waited eagerly beside me, bouncing up and down like a toddler about to receive a cookie. I held the card in my hand for a moment, staring at the flowers and imagining what Tom would say in the note. What would I do after I opened it? Should I call him? Or wait for him to call me?

'Open it, open it,' Wendy said eagerly. I looked at her in amusement. She looked ten times more excited than I was. I wondered how she'd react when she realized the amazing spread was from Tom.

Amanda and Gail, the two assistants who manned the copy desk, drifted over to look at the flowers as I held the card in my hand, letting my imagination run.

'They're beautiful,' Amanda breathed, smiling at me. She reached out to touch one of the roses, then bent down to admire the vase.

'Who are they from?' Gail asked, also smiling as she gently fingered the baby's breath.

'I don't know,' I lied with a smile, forgetting that I'd just been sick mere moments before. Suddenly I felt fine, knowing that somewhere out there, Tom cared. 'Let me open the card.'

Wendy and the two copy assistants waited eagerly as I slit the envelope with my index finger and pulled out the small note card inside. As my eyes scanned the few quick lines on the card, I felt the breath go out of me, my heart dropping in my chest.

'Who are they from? Who are they from?' Wendy asked excitedly. I looked up at the three eager faces clustered around my flowers. I plastered a smile on my face and tried to will my heart to stop racing. I wondered if they noticed the color rising in my cheeks or my suddenly shaky hands stuffing the card back in the envelope.

'They're from my mom,' I said quickly.

'Wow,' Gail said admiringly. 'That's amazing. My mom has never sent me anything like that. You're really lucky.'

'Is it your birthday or something?' Amanda asked. Wendy was silently staring at me. She knew I was lying.

'No,' I said softly. 'It's not my birthday.' They were still grinning at me, so I kept the smile plastered across my face.

I shot a quick glance at Wendy, who was still looking at me suspiciously. 'I, uh, have to go to the bathroom. I'll be right back.'

I stuffed the envelope into my pocket and rushed back down the hallway with Wendy trailing quickly after me. I took a quick look back and saw Gail and Amanda looking at us strangely, but I ignored them. I was sure they'd cluster around the flowers again and in a moment forget I was gone.

'Who are they really from?' Wendy asked, sounding almost accusatory, as we pushed into the bathroom. I silently bent to look under the stalls. Satisfied that we were alone, I took the envelope out of my pocket and handed it to Wendy.

I watched as she opened the envelope and quickly scanned the card. Her jaw dropped, and her eyes widened. She looked up and stared at me in shock. She looked back at the card, up at me, and then back at the card again.

'*Dear Claire,*' she read aloud finally, sounding incredulous. I blushed more as I heard the words read aloud. '*I'm sorry if I caused you any trouble. You're a wonderful woman, and I'm glad to have spent time with you, even if it was under less-than-ideal circumstances. I just wanted to make sure you were okay. Call me if you need anything at all. Best wishes, Cole Brannon.*'

Wendy looked up at me again, shock splashed across her face.

'Cole Brannon?' she squealed. '*Cole Brannon?!* COLE BRANNON sent you flowers?'

'Shhhh . . .' I hushed her quickly. 'Please, I don't want anyone to know.' Wendy ignored me.

'Cole Brannon sent you flowers,' she repeated quietly. This time, it was a statement instead of a question.

'Cole Brannon sent me flowers,' I confirmed softly, my heart still beating rapidly in my chest.

'And he thinks you're a wonderful woman,' she breathed.

'I guess so.' I shrugged, feeling both embarrassed and somewhat elated. I quickly tried to quash the latter feeling, knowing it would do me no good.

'And you didn't even sleep with him,' Wendy said. My eyes widened in shock.

'What? No!'

Wendy looked up at me again. She was holding the card in her hands like it was the Holy Grail.

'He likes you, Claire,' she said finally.

'No, no,' I protested, aware that my cheeks were growing ever redder. 'That's silly. He just feels sorry for me.' Wendy shook her head.

'Men who feel sorry for people don't send flowers,' she said with certainty.

'Maybe men with millions of dollars to blow do,' I said quickly. This was ludicrous. This couldn't be happening. At work, no less. What if someone – what if Sidra – saw the note?

'I don't think so, Claire,' Wendy said. She finally handed the card and envelope back to me. I stuffed them both in my pocket. She was still looking at me with a strange expression on her face.

'It's nothing,' I insisted, not really meaning it. My face was on fire, and I tried not to meet Wendy's eye. 'It doesn't mean anything.'

'I think it means a lot,' Wendy said softly.

I tried not to acknowledge the fact that deep down, I hoped it meant a lot too. But it would be ridiculous to think that anything could ever happen between Cole Brannon and someone like me. Besides, Tom was out there somewhere, and I knew I'd never forgive myself if I didn't at least try again to make it work.

Gossiping

I was up at 5:30 the next morning, the victim of another mostly sleepless night. When I had finally drifted off, I had nightmares about appearing with Cole in the pages of *Tattletale*, where Margaret would see me and instantly fire me, and Tom would refuse to even speak with me again.

My tossing and turning hadn't been helped when Wendy stumbled in, tipsy and mumbling in broken French, just past 2 a.m., after a date with Jean Michel. She must have forgotten that I was sleeping at her place, on a twin air mattress wedged between her full bed and her tiny closet, because she tripped over the edge of the mattress and landed facedown on top of me as she tried to make her way to the laundry hamper in the corner.

After disentangling from her and listening to her soliloquy about the virtues of French men in general, and Jean Michel in particular, I stared at the ceiling and tried not to think about Tom, Cole, or *Tattletale* until dawn began filtering in through Wendy's window.

It wasn't hard to stay awake, despite the fact that I was exhausted. Wendy's snoring was enough to prevent me from drifting off. Besides, every time I closed my eyes I saw Tom and Sidra's sister together in my bed. As I counted down the minutes until daybreak (not nearly as effective as counting sheep, by the way), I grew more and more worried that Sidra's revenge would come in the form of a *Tattletale* article that would forever cost me my reputation. By the time I got up at 5:30, I was sure of it.

I dressed quickly and grabbed my things. *Tattletale* would be on the newsstands already, and I wanted to see it as soon as possible. My heart was pounding as I ran some lipstick quickly across my lips, gave myself one last look in the mirror, and dashed downstairs. There was a newspaper stand two blocks up from Wendy's apartment, and I jogged all the way there, desperately spinning through the possibilities of what I'd find between the covers of the gossip rag.

'One copy of *Tattletale*, please,' I panted as I arrived at the newsstand, breathless from my dash. The vendor was still in the process of cutting the plastic cords binding the stacks of magazines and papers that would soon land in organized piles and displays around his cart. I quickly spotted today's *Tattletale* in the corner.

'We're not open yet,' he said, without turning around. I took a deep breath.

'Please,' I begged. 'I'm desperate. I'll give you . . .' I paused while I rifled through my wallet. 'I'll give you twelve dollars for it.' I quickly counted my change. 'And sixty-three cents.'

The vendor finally turned and looked me up and down.

'You're going to give me twelve sixty-three for a tabloid that will cost you a dollar when I open in thirty minutes?'

'Yes, please,' I said hurriedly, thrusting the money at him. The vendor stared at me for another moment, shrugged, and took the cash from my hand.

'Fine with me,' he said. 'Why do you need this so badly anyhow?' He looked at me critically, his box cutter poised over the pile of magazines. I forced a smile.

'Just an important article, that's all,' I said. He stared at me for another moment. I could no longer stand it. 'Please!' I begged. He rolled his eyes.

'Women,' he muttered under his breath. He finally slashed through the cords, and they fell limp on the sides of the stack. He slowly lifted up a *Tattletale* and stared at the cover before he handed it to me. I was practically bouncing up and down now, trying to restrain myself from reaching out and snatching it from him. 'Harrison Ford and Calista Flockhart Have Lovers' Quarrel?' he asked, reading slowly from the cover. 'Is this what's so important?'

'No, no!' I exclaimed. 'Please! Just give it to me.' The vendor smiled, and I realized that he was enjoying torturing me.

'Clay Terrell Dishes About Tara Templeton's Booty?' he asked slowly, reading another headline. He looked up at me with an arched eyebrow and laughed.

'No!' I exclaimed again. He looked back at the magazine, and I knew he was about to read another headline. I snatched the magazine from his hands before he had the chance to do so. 'Thank you!' I said over my shoulder, ignoring his startled expression and walking away. I had paid twelve dollars and sixty-three cents for a copy of a gossip rag I hated. I didn't need to listen to the vendor's commentary too.

I waited until I'd rounded the corner out of the vendor's sight to rip open the magazine. I leaned in to the side of a building and flipped quickly to the table of contents. My heart sank as I read the fifth item in the highlighted 'Reads of the Week'.

'Cole Brannon's Women: Who's That Girl with Hollywood's Hottest Hunk?'

'Shit,' I said out loud as I flipped to page 18. 'Shit, shit, shit, shit,' I mumbled under my breath, desperately flipping, wondering why pages always stuck together when you needed to see something. It must be Murphy's Law of Magazines. 'Shit, shit, shit.'

I finally flipped past pages 16 and 17 and took a deep breath. This was it. One more flip of the page and my life would be over. There would be pictures of us together and quotes from Sidra. Hell, maybe they'd even found our starstruck cab driver and paid him to tell his story. I took a deep breath and turned the page.

Cole Brannon's now-familiar blue eyes twinkled from a huge photo, splashed in color across the newsprint rag. My heart thumped as I took it all in. His arm was thrown comfortably over the shoulder of a blond woman as they strolled together – she was gazing adoringly up at him as he looked out in the distance.

But the woman wasn't me.

It was Kylie Dane. The married actress.

Whom he had sworn to me that he wasn't seeing.

'What?' I mumbled to myself. I was relieved, of course, but I also had a strange and unexpected feeling that felt suspiciously like jealousy.

But that made no sense. What did I care if Cole Brannon wanted to sleep with Kylie Dane? It wasn't any of my business. I was just mad that he'd lied to me. Yes, that was it. I was mad at myself for believing his lie. I took a deep breath and willed myself to be calm.

The discomfort returned in a flash, though, when I saw the words printed at the bottom corner of the page:

'For more of Cole Brannon's women, turn to page 33.'

'Shit,' I mumbled again. The big photo of Kylie and Cole was just a teaser. She was the biggest star he was sleeping with. On page 33 my cover would be blown, and it would be even worse than I'd originally suspected. I'd be playing second fiddle to one of the sluttiest women in Hollywood. 'Shit, shit, shit.' I flipped quickly through the pages, getting stuck again as I desperately tried to rush to page 33.

I finally found the continued article and stared desperately at the page. It featured three photos of Cole with different women, each complete with its own caption. I quickly scanned each photo, trying to keep my eyes from glazing over.

None of them was me.

I heaved a huge sigh of relief and tried not to feel jealous as I looked at Cole walking through Central Park with a scantily clad Kylie Dane. Cole at dinner in a fancy restaurant with a dark-haired woman identified as Ivana Donatelli, his publicist. Cole locked in an embrace with a perfectly toned, leather-clad Jessica Gregory, the star of TV's *Spy Chicks*.

I slowly flipped the page, just in case the story was continued, but thankfully, the next page just featured a story about Carnie Wilson's weight loss. I resisted the urge to look down at my thighs for comparison.

I flipped back to page 33 again and stared hard at the photos, my heart pounding quickly in anger.

He had lied. I couldn't believe it. He'd made me think he was different. He'd made me think he was a real gentleman and that the stories about him with other women weren't true. He'd looked me in the eye and told me that he'd never get involved with a married woman, but here he was canoodling in Central Park with a practically naked Kylie Dane. In full color. There was no denying it. I wouldn't necessarily believe a story in the often unreliable *Tattletale*, but there was no mistaking what the photos meant.

And Wendy's reports about Ivana Donatelli had been true, too. In the photo Cole was leaning across the small round table to whisper something in her ear, and she was blushing. A bottle of champagne sat between them, and they each had a full flute of bubbly near their elbow. Ivana's sparkling black hair cascaded alluringly over her bare shoulders, coming to rest at the level of the diamond necklace she wore around her slender neck, surely a gift from Cole.

And his pose with Jessica Gregory looked anything but innocent. The *Spy Chicks* star had her arms thrown around his neck. He was picking her up off the ground, lifting her up so that they were nose to nose, gazing into each other's eyes. It looked like they were milliseconds away from locking lips. Her red leather pantsuit clung to the perfect curves of her body, glistening in the light.

I flipped back to pages 18 and 19, where Cole and Kylie

were splashed across two full pages, their arms comfortably around each other. A five-year-old would be able to tell they were more than just friends. She was gazing adoringly up at him, snuggled tightly against his body as they walked. He was pulling her against him, his hand resting on her shoulder as her bosom pressed into his side. He was looking in the direction of the camera, although not right at it. I stared for a moment at his blue eyes, which had seemed so innocent and kind on Sunday.

'Liar,' I mumbled aloud at his picture.

I suddenly felt furious. At myself, and at Cole. How could I have been so stupid as to have been taken in by his charms? To have actually believed, even for a second, that he cared, even remotely? He was an actor. It was his job to make me think what he wanted me to think. And damn it, I'd fallen for it like a rookie, like some silly little reporter who'd never met a celebrity before. Like some silly little lovesick girl. Like someone desperate to be appreciated.

I was such an idiot.

I wouldn't normally have behaved that way. Tom had crushed me, and in a moment of weakness I'd been taken in by a professional con artist's charms. Damn it, he *was* sleeping with half of Hollywood. And I'd been so ready to give him the benefit of the doubt.

I angrily slammed the *Tattletale* closed and stuffed it into my bag. I pulled away from the brick wall I'd been leaning against, brushed my skirt off, and straightened my blouse. I took a deep breath and began walking toward the F train.

'You like him,' Wendy whispered bluntly as she stared at me with wide eyes over the wall that divided our cubicles.

'What?' I asked, making a face at her. 'That's ridiculous. I don't *like* him.'

'Why do you care who he's spotted with in *Tattletale* then?' she asked innocently. Today, her typically outlandish style was toned down a bit with modest, natural makeup colors and slim Diesel jeans. The only clue of Wendy's peculiar fashion sense was the low-plunging neckline of the lime green shirt she wore under a gauzy beige cardigan, and the orange scarf she had tied around her neck.

'It's not that I care who he's in *Tattletale* with,' I said, shooting a dirty glance at the gossip rag protruding from the top of my bag. 'It's just that he lied to me.'

'And made you think he liked you,' Wendy said, finishing my thought.

'No,' I protested. 'I don't care whether he likes me. Why would I care? You know nothing could happen, anyhow.'

'Hmm,' said Wendy, arching an eyebrow at me. 'So you don't care? At all?'

'Nope.'

'Okay.' She winked at me. 'Whatever you say.' I fixed her with a glare. Why did she think I cared? I didn't care about Cole Brannon.

'It just proves that all men are scum,' I said with finality. Wendy arched an eyebrow.

'All men?' she asked. 'I'd agree with you that a vast majority are. But all men? I don't think so.'

'I do,' I muttered. First Tom, now Cole. Lying, cheating scum. I felt angrier at Cole the more I thought about it. Who did he think he was? Just because he was some hot-shot movie star.

'Jean Michel isn't scum,' Wendy said dreamily, batting her eyes and looking off into space.

'Glad to hear it,' I said, trying not to roll my eyes. I wasn't in the mood to hear the virtues of Wendy's waiters today. I didn't know how she did it. *She* dumped *them*. *She* was always the one to lose interest and move on. As long as I'd known her, she'd never been dumped. She'd never been cheated on. She'd never even been treated as anything less than a princess. Why did I attract guys who liked to screw me over and lie to me?

'C'mon, Claire, you can't believe everything you read,' said Wendy gently.

'I don't,' I said firmly. 'But I believe what I see. And those were not innocent pictures. With any of those women.'

'Maybe there's an explanation,' Wendy said quietly.

'And maybe there's not,' I said, looking up at her. 'He lied, Wendy. He's sleeping around with everyone. Anyhow, I'm sick of talking about this. He'll get the complimentary article he wants in *Mod* magazine, and I'll never have to see him again.' Somehow, the words didn't make me feel as good as they should have.

'What about the flowers?' Wendy asked softly. I'd been trying to ignore them all morning, which was pretty difficult considering they were overflowing all over my desk. They still looked perfect, and they smelled beautifully tantalizing. 'Aren't you going to thank him?'

I snorted.

'No,' I said firmly. 'In fact, we're going to pretend this never happened.' I opened my desk drawer and pulled out the card that had come with the flowers – the sweet, sensitive card that was obviously a lie. He didn't care about me. I tore it in half and dropped it into the garbage can. Wendy gasped.

'You're throwing the card away?' she asked.

'I just did,' I said. 'And I don't want to talk about it any more.'

Margaret called an editorial meeting for eleven o'clock that morning, to replace the one she'd canceled the day before. I was relieved in a way, because it gave me an excuse to focus on something other than Cole Brannon. Besides, I was looking forward to thirty minutes without Wendy's half-pitying, half-accusatory glances.

The only downside to the meeting was that Sidra would be there. I'd have to squirm in discomfort as she looked at me smugly, content with the knowledge that I'd been summarily dismissed in the most embarrassing way by a slimy boyfriend who was now screwing her sister.

As I settled into a chair at the oval table, I smiled at Anne Amster, the senior features editor and the only other person to have arrived for the meeting. She was Wendy's direct superior, a fantastic features editor who did a great job of directing her section of the magazine. Like me, she looked much younger than she was and sometimes had trouble being taken seriously by those who didn't know her. Her wiry black hair framed her face in a pixie cut, and her features were sharp and childlike. She smiled back at me.

I hadn't yet been able to decide whether the weekly editorial meetings were actually useful or not. In theory, the senior members of the staff were supposed to discuss the magazine and the articles we were featuring in the month we were currently working on. We were supposed to give progress reports to help debate and decide what direction the magazine would take.

Instead, we pitifully offered suggestions and had them immediately shot down by Margaret while the executive editor, Donna Foley, who would soon be retiring, tried to give us encouraging looks. She would jot down notes about what we said and discuss them with Margaret later. Eventually, the good ideas would end up becoming a part of that month's issue. But of course Margaret would take full credit for them, saying things like, 'I came up with that idea over dinner at Lutèce the other night,' even when there were eight witnesses to the fact that the idea had been proposed by one of us at an editorial meeting. We'd long since learned that it was better to keep quiet and simply be thankful that Margaret was running the *Mod* ship with a little help from those of us who actually knew the magazine industry – even if it was completely thankless help.

Sidra glided in five minutes late, swooping into the empty seat beside Anne, who politely said hello, oblivious of the death looks Sidra was already shooting me. Sidra ignored her greeting, and Anne finally shrugged and shook her head. I had never talked to Anne about the Triplets, but I suspected she wasn't a fan any more than I was.

Today Sidra was dressed in skintight beige leather pants that accentuated her slender hips, and a fitted black top that showed off the curves of her fake bosom.

'It's Gucci,' she said haughtily in response to the other editors' stares. No matter how many times we all saw Sidra, her outfit choices never failed to astonish any of us. I'd never seen her wear the same thing twice, and her clothes were always striking. 'Couture,' she added, tittering lightly. 'George loved it on me.'

I tried not to roll my eyes. We all ignored her.

Before anyone else had a chance to speak, Margaret bustled into the room and glided to the head of the table.

One might think that in a conference room with an oval table, we would align ourselves equally, like the knights of King Arthur's court. I'd thought that when I showed up for my first editorial meeting a year and a half ago, until I noticed that the arrangement of chairs divided the oval nearly in half. Eight of us sat squished into the half closer to the door, while Margaret reigned supreme from the other half, splaying her papers out in front of her and gazing down the table at us, her loyal subjects. We were all subjected to an hour of bumping elbows and fighting for space while Margaret leaned back and enjoyed the room.

'Happy *Mod* morning,' Margaret greeted us with the same silly words she used to open each editorial meeting.

'Happy *Mod* morning,' we all grumbled back, because we knew we'd be the subjects of Margaret's wrath that day if we didn't.

'Let's begin,' Margaret said, contentedly leaning back in her throne. She nodded in Donna's direction. 'Donna?' she said.

Donna sighed. She ran all of *Mod*'s editorial meetings

from her seat in the eight-member throng at the lower half of the oval table.

'It looks like we wrapped up August successfully and on time,' Donna said, reading from her notes, trying not to bump elbows with Jeffrey on her left and Carol on her right. 'As most of you probably know, Margaret made a last-minute decision to sub the Julia Stiles cover with a Cole Brannon cover, which breaks somewhat from *Mod* tradition.' Her voice sounded strained. A few pairs of eyebrows shot up in surprise, and a few editors glanced my way. Sidra and Margaret both looked suspiciously smug.

'According to Margaret,' Donna continued, glancing at her boss, 'Claire's Cole Brannon interview was very intriguing and will have a good chance of increasing our circulation.' I tried not to blush as several heads swiveled toward me. A few editors smiled encouragingly from across the table. 'I didn't have a chance to see it myself, but I'm sure Margaret knows what she's doing.' She didn't sound too sure. My stomach swam uncomfortably.

'The rest of the issue went off without a hitch, just the way we planned it,' Donna continued. 'I talked to Julia Stiles's publicist, and she's okay with us using Julia for the September cover. Her movie is coming out Labor Day Weekend anyhow, so it will be better timing for them. I had to promise another of her clients a Q & A in the September issue, though, so she didn't make a big deal out of this whole thing. Can you do that, Claire?'

I nodded and felt relieved. In this business, timing was everything. If Julia's movie had been scheduled for a late July or August release date, her publicist would be screaming bloody murder right now. Most celebs didn't grant interviews out of the goodness of their hearts. A-listers and most B-listers agreed to features only when they had a movie, TV series, or album coming out, because being featured in a top women's mag was a guaranteed way to increase their fan base. When we had originally agreed with Julia's camp six months ago to feature her this summer, her new movie was scheduled for a late July release, which made the August issue perfect. Thankfully, the release date had been moved to Labor Day Weekend last month, so her publicist had likely been more than willing to make the switch to our September issue.

'Okay, the September issue,' Donna continued. A few editors took out pads of paper and started to jot down notes as Donna spoke. 'According to the ad department, we're going to have four more pages of editorial than we'd counted on, which will be great. I'd like to use one page to expand the fashion section, because Sidra, Sally, and Samantha are shooting on location in Italy this month, and they've promised us a great romantic spread of fall fashions in Venice.'

Sidra nodded without looking up and began filing her nails with a diamond-studded nail file.

'As for the remaining three pages, I'm . . . *we're* . . . open to suggestions.' Donna glanced quickly at Margaret to see if she'd noticed the slip, but she hadn't. She was busy gazing out the window.

'The clouds look like little sheep in the sky today,' Margaret said suddenly. We all looked at her strangely. I stifled a laugh. Sometimes she was like a little child. Donna took a deep breath and continued.

'Claire,' she said. I turned to look at her. 'Margaret and I discussed adding a celebrity Q & A with someone up-and-coming.' Out of the corner of my eye, I caught Sidra's glare. She was no doubt furious that I was getting any extra attention. 'Would you be interested in that? If it works out, we could try to make it a monthly feature. It wouldn't be too tough, just a straight one-page Q & A with a young newcomer. You know, identify the next Brad Pitt. That kind of thing.'

'Sure,' I agreed.

'It was my idea,' Margaret interjected, turning her attention momentarily back to the group. 'Because of

Claire's strong work on the Cole Brannon piece.' She winked at me, and I forced a smile. Donna sighed again and Margaret's attention drifted back out the window.

'Any ideas for the remaining two pages?' Donna asked. She made a note on her pad and looked up.

'How about a two-page feature on the "20 Sexiest Things Women Can Do in Bed"?' Cathy Joseph, the sixty-something copy chief, asked in her perfectly clipped voice. I smiled. It was always strange to hear a woman pushing seventy saying anything at all about sex. But just last month she'd been the one to suggest August's sex feature: '10 New Ways to Have an Orgasm.' I hoped I was still having orgasms at her age. For that matter, I wished I was having them now.

Donna smiled at Cathy.

'Sounds good to me,' she said. Of course it did. Cathy was a forty-year veteran of the magazine business, and it was no coincidence that she was also the fountain of more editorial ideas than anyone else on staff. The funny thing about women's magazines was that once you'd had a subscription to a magazine for five years or so, you would have read every service article ever written. Sure, there were new celebs to feature every month and new spins on old ideas, but women's mags recycled the same hundred or so self-help, sex advice, and to-do articles every few years. For example, there was no doubt in my mind that the '20 Sexiest Things Women Can Do in Bed' wouldn't include a single thing that had never before been mentioned in *Mod* – or in *Cosmo*, *Glamour*, or *Marie Claire* for that matter. After all, creative as we might be, there were a finite number of things one could actually figure out to do between the sheets. I had a sneaking suspicion that Cathy had a pile of women's magazines dating back to the '60s at home, and before every editorial meeting she simply flipped through the stacks and pulled some ideas from the February '68 issue or the July '75 issue. If that was the case, she was smarter than the rest of us.

'Anne?' Donna asked. 'How does the "20 Sexiest Things" idea sound to you?'

As the features editor, Anne would be the one to assign and edit the piece, so she'd have to give her approval.

'Sure,' Anne chirped with a smile. 'I've just started working with a new freelancer who's a regular at *Maxim*. She'd be perfect to work on this if she's available.' Donna nodded and made a note.

'Margaret?' Donna asked, sounding almost timid. Margaret looked up briefly and waved a hand.

'Yes, perfect,' she said. 'I was just about to suggest a similar article. That idea will do.'

'Excellent,' said Donna, making another note. She quickly recapped. 'So one extra page to fashion, one to celebs, and two to features. Okay with everyone?'

She was answered with a chorus of 'fines' and 'okays'. Margaret abstained because she didn't need to give her approval with the masses. Sidra kept quiet because she believed she was too good to speak in unison with any one.

We spent the rest of the meeting outlining and confirming assignments for the September issue. Most articles were already assigned or in the works. Freelancers across the country were already busy tracking down '10 Ways to Land Your Dream Man', '15 Ways to Know if His Love for You Is Real', and '10 Ways to Earn the Promotion You Deserve'. The Triplets were busy putting the final touches on the wardrobes they'd take for their models to wear in Venice.

In the next month I'd have to have five proposals for November celeb cover stories, update my Julia Stiles story for September, find and interview an up-and-coming star for the new Q & A, and include a teaser for Kylie Dane's new movie, which would also come out Labor Day Weekend. Plus, I had to finish a two-page spread with quotes from various celebs about what they'd eaten for dinner the night before (Margaret's idea), and another spread on celeb secrets to finding lasting love.

When the meeting adjourned three minutes before noon, I left feeling relieved that I had a whole pile of work to distract me, and glad that in the last hour I'd thought of Cole Brannon just once. Okay, maybe twice. But the second time hadn't counted. Donna had brought him up.

Not that I cared. It would be ridiculous to care.

Movie Stars

The Starlet

Thursday morning's press conference for Kylie Dane's new movie, *Opposites Attract*, was in a conference room at the Ritz. As I passed the entrance to Atelier, a parade of designer clothes too expensive for me to even consider streamed in and out around me. I tried not to think about Saturday's brunch, but trying to ignore the memory of Saturday was as impossible as trying to make your way to the Rockefeller Center Christmas Tree in December without getting swallowed in a sea of tourists.

Of course I knew there was no Cole Brannon hiding beneath a Red Sox cap in Atelier today. Heck, he was probably backstage at the press event, making out with the married Kylie Dane. I tried to block out the offending mental image.

The press conference was in the meeting room at the far end of the first floor. I took my seat inside, nodding to the other writers I saw at most similar events.

Today's interview session was a small one, geared specifically toward magazines with more than two months' lead time, like ours. Newspapers and weeklies like *People* would get their first crack at Kylie and her costars two weeks before the film's Labor Day Weekend release, to whet moviegoers' appetites at exactly the right time. Reporters for the major monthlies – *Mod*, *Glamour*, *In Style*, *Maxim*, *Cosmo*, and the like – had been invited today so that our presumably glowing praise for the film's stars would appear in our September issues (which actually came out mid-August) at precisely the same time moviegoers were making Labor Day Weekend plans. Amusingly, we wouldn't actually *see* the movie, which was still being assembled in a studio somewhere in Burbank. Yet we were supposed to review and recommend it sight unseen.

The whole dance with the press had been carefully choreographed and planned for maximum benefit to the studio. It was a formula that rarely failed: take one big star, mix with a fair-to-good movie, limit press access to pique interest, and provide senseless snippets from the stars. It all equaled major buzz around movies that, well, weren't even movies yet.

As I waited for the press conference to begin, I told Victoria Lim, *Cosmo*'s entertainment editor and a friend of mine after four years of attending press conferences together, that Tom and I had broken up. As I filled her in on the details, I couldn't help but feel a bit embarrassed, as if I'd done something to invite his infidelity. Had I?

I was secretly pleased when Victoria admitted that she'd never really liked him in the first place. She and her husband Paul had once double-dated with us, and Tom had spent the entire meal lecturing Paul about 'those damned capitalist pigs in Washington'. They had never gone out with us again.

'Well, I could have him whacked, you know,' Victoria said seriously once I'd finished. 'I mean, I know people. I've never heard of anyone who deserved a good whacking more.'

'That I could live with,' I said seriously.

Before I could get too lost in the fantasy, a bleached blonde in a skintight, knee-length red Prada dress appeared on the stage with a sheaf of papers in her hand. Her hair was slicked back and clipped in a twist at the back of her head, and she wore a small name tag that identified her as a publicist on the production company's staff. The whispers and murmurs in the small group of eleven journalists quieted, and we all looked at her expectantly.

'Ladies and gentlemen,' she addressed us formally. I nudged Victoria, who rolled her eyes. She was obviously new. The veteran studio publicists were well accustomed to treating the press like children who needed to be spoon-fed information. They would never address us as ladies and gentlemen, for in their eyes we were *not* ladies and gentlemen – we were gullible children who could and should be manipulated. Hence, the Ritz staffers wandering throughout the room with trays full of canapés, Perrier, and soda – thinly veiled bribes for positive movie reviews. 'My name is Destiny Starr. (Beside me, Victoria stifled a giggle.) Welcome to the Ritz. We have a very exciting morning planned for you today. In just a moment, we'll bring Kylie and Wally out to meet you, but first I'd like to tell you a bit about the plot of the film.'

I zoned out as Destiny launched into a monologue about *Opposites Attract*. I wasn't sure why publicists always opened press conferences this way since presumably, all of us had received a) press packets in the mail weeks in advance with pages of flashy prose about how this would be the best movie of the year, maybe the decade, b) press packets upon arrival at the press conference that told us in more compressed (yet still flashy) prose about how this would be the best movie of the decade, maybe of all time, and c) several phone calls over the last few weeks from studio publicists, allegedly calling to see if we were planning to attend the conference (despite the fact that we'd already agreed by e-mail, fax, and telephone), who would then launch into glowing monologues about how the movie was sure to sweep the Academy Awards and go down in history as the best movie of all time.

Believe me, we'd heard the Academy Award hype speech at every press conference since the dawn of time –

even at the junket for *Gigli*, and we all know how that turned out. As you might imagine, this considerably diminished our faith in the speech.

Indeed, as Destiny described *Opposites Attract*, I could see eyes glazing over around the room as we all slipped into zombie mode, with the exception of a newcomer to our group, a young intern from *Teen People*. She was staring at Destiny with fascination from her seat in the dead center of the second row. She reminded me of myself when I started at *People* four years ago, before I learned that press conferences did little good, except for the opportunity to snag canned quotes from stars – and the free mini quiches, stuffed mushrooms, and chocolate-dipped strawberries that circulated throughout the room. Some press events even offered champagne, but I supposed that 10 a.m. was too early for that sort of thing, even for this Hollywood cast of publicists.

Besides, considering my track record this week, perhaps it would be better to avoid alcohol for a while. At least in the general vicinity of movie stars. Although Kylie Dane's costar in the movie was no Cole Brannon, he did have undeniable sex appeal – and a slightly shady reputation to go along with it. Wally Joiner, a twenty-six-year-old import from Great Britain who was being called the next Hugh Grant, had gotten his share of press over recent exploits involving an affair with a pop star, a threesome with two *Playboy* models, and a night with a roomful of Vegas strippers.

When Destiny finally finished telling us, in fascinated tones and matching canned facial expressions, that the romantic comedy (boy meets girl, boy screws something up – boy must win girl back, boy wins girl back – boy and girl live happily ever after – big surprise) was the early favorite for several categories in this year's Academy Awards, she paused dramatically and announced that the 'talent' would be coming out shortly.

There was silence for a moment, and then we all started

chatting again, as if Destiny had never stepped onstage. None of us (save the enthusiastic *Teen People* intern) had taken a single note, as Destiny had read almost verbatim from the press release we were all handed upon entering the room.

Destiny was back less than three minutes later, having refreshed her deep red lipstick. 'Ladies and gentlemen, I'd like to introduce the two stars of *Opposites Attract*, who of course need no introduction.'

'Then why is she introducing them?' I whispered to Victoria, who giggled.

'Ms Kylie Dane and Mr Wally Joiner!' Destiny said dramatically. She paused, presumably expecting us to clap, but none of us did. It was bad form. Journalists weren't supposed to show any emotion or enthusiasm whatsoever during press conferences, premieres, sporting events, et cetera. In fact, I don't think we were officially supposed to have any feelings at all.

If only that were true, life – and unexpected sleepovers with movie stars – would be much easier.

'Okay, then,' Destiny said, recovering from the apparently unexpected lack of response. She looked back toward the curtain draped across the back of the stage. 'Kylie, Wally, could you come on out?'

Kylie Dane stepped out first from behind the curtain, looking stunning, even in blue jeans and a black shirt. Granted, the jeans were distressed Paper Denim & Cloth, and the shirt was a tiny, glittering number that hugged her curves perfectly, dipping low enough to reveal her tantalizing cleavage and ending high enough to show off her perfectly toned cinnamon-tan stomach. She was wearing impossibly high Jimmy Choo stilettos, making her legs look like they went on forever. She was so slender that I feared we'd lose her if she turned sideways. Her mane of blond hair (which sparkled and bounced in a way mine never had) was professionally tousled and filled with random ringlets that somehow looked perfectly playful and flawlessly sexy at the same time. She smiled demurely as she stepped onto the stage.

'Hello,' she said softly, smiling at the room without really looking at any of us.

I disliked her instantly and tried to convince myself that it was because she seemed aloof. She did, of course – most of them did – but I knew the real reason was that I couldn't erase the image of her walking arm in arm with Cole, grinning up at him with the promise of sex and seduction, from the pages of *Tattletale*. Didn't she have enough already without adding him to the collection?

After all, she was married to Patrick O'Hara, a striking actor twenty years her senior. Her glittering engagement ring, which was roughly the size of a disco ball, sent tiny rays of light flying around the room as she sat gracefully on the velvet-cushioned chair center stage. I squirmed uncomfortably in my hard-backed folding chair and tried not to hate her as little beams from her ring blinded me temporarily.

He is a liar, I reminded myself. *Cole Brannon lied to you. And he's helping Kylie Dane cheat on her husband. He's no different from Tom.*

I gulped and tried to focus on something other than how beautiful and perfect Kylie Dane looked. Which was not easy.

'And Wally Joiner,' Destiny announced. The British actor strode onto the stage, exuding confidence and raw sexiness. His face was unshaven, his gait was purposeful and relaxed, and his faded Levi's and crisp white shirt, with the top three buttons open, worked perfectly together.

"Ello,' he said, sounding so British the accent almost seemed artificial. He slowly laid eyes on each female reporter in the room, smiling devilishly each time he locked eyes with one of us. I heard Victoria next to me emit a little schoolgirl giggle as his burning gaze fell on her, but before he could lock eyes with me, I focused intently on the blank notebook page in front of me.

Sexy as he was, I'd already had my fill of actors for the week, thank you very much.

'We'll just go ahead and take questions, then,' Destiny said after a brief pause, allowing Wally to finish visually assaulting each woman in the room. She looked around the room until her eyes alighted on Karen Davidson from *Glamour*, whose pencil was raised in the air. 'Yes, you,' she said, pointing to Karen.

'Karen Davidson, *Glamour* magazine,' said the sleekly bobbed brunette, identifying herself as we were all asked to do at every press conference. As if the stars cared. I was sure the names went in one ear and out the other. Kylie nodded politely, and Wally leaned forward and winked flirtatiously. Karen tittered. 'This question is for Wally.' She was blushing now. 'You play a nuclear physicist in the movie. Was it difficult for you to learn the ways of nuclear physicism in order to play your role convincingly?'

I leaned over to Victoria.

'Nuclear *physicism*?' I whispered. 'Is that a word?' Victoria stifled another giggle and shook her head.

'Excellent question, love,' Wally said, settling back into his seat, his starched shirt crackling audibly. He appeared to be undressing Karen with his eyes as he talked. And she appeared to be enjoying it. 'Nuclear physicism has always been a passion of mine, you know. So I already had the background, of course. I bloody love all that technical shit. So it was easy for me to just read along with the script and get it all right,' Wally concluded wisely. 'Nuclear physicism is such a vital field.'

Karen Davidson nodded and scribbled furiously. I rolled my eyes. I could just see the article in *Glamour* now. WALLY JOINER IS A CLOSET INTELLECTUAL WHO LOVES NUCLEAR PHYSICS. Sure.

'You,' Destiny said, pointing to Victoria.

'Victoria Lim, *Cosmopolitan* magazine,' Victoria piped up, her voice sounding tiny and childlike. 'And my question is for Kylie.' Kylie nodded, expressionless. 'Kylie, this is the third time you've played a similar role, the helpless female rescued by the strong, intelligent male. Are you worried about being typecast?'

'No,' Kylie said without really meeting anyone's eye. She looked down at her perfectly manicured nails and then seemed to drift into her own little world as she admired her engagement ring. Victoria and I exchanged quick looks. It became apparent that she wasn't planning to elaborate as the uncomfortable silence dragged on.

'Uh, okay,' Victoria said. Destiny looked uncomfortable. This wasn't going well. 'Could you tell me how you feel the roles fit you, then?'

That was good. A nice open-ended question.

Kylie finally looked up, but again, she didn't meet anyone's eye.

'I can fit any role,' she said, her voice full of boredom. She flicked a piece of imaginary lint from her jeans, staring at the ceiling. She pushed a stray ringlet behind her ear and went back to examining her nails. 'That's what talented actors *do.*'

I heard Victoria growl softly next to me, and I felt like laughing. This was such an exercise in futility.

I raised my hand, and Destiny pointed at me.

'Claire Reilly from *Mod*,' I said quickly. I looked at Kylie. 'How do you feel, then, about the example you're setting for young women?' I asked her. Destiny raised an eyebrow, and Victoria snickered next to me. I knew I sounded snide, but I didn't care. 'I mean, are you concerned that they'll think it's okay for women to just be saved rather than saving themselves?'

'It *is* okay,' said Kylie. She sighed and rolled her eyes. I raised an eyebrow.

'So you're saying it's okay for women to just sit around and wait for men to come rescue them?' I prodded.

'That's what I said.' She sighed again and looked over at Destiny. 'This topic is boring me,' she said. 'Can we move on?'

I sat back in my chair and stared at her in amazement. How could this be the woman Cole liked? Whom he'd been linked with? Whom he was pulling close to him in the *Tattletale* photo with such obvious adoration? What was wrong with men?

Then again, it was Kylie Dane who was winning the hearts of thousands of men. I, on the other hand, had lost the only one I'd managed to attract. Perhaps I should take her advice and just sit back, waiting to be rescued by some Prince Charming. It seemed to be working for her. However, Kylie Dane had a few more men throwing themselves at her than I did, which increased her odds of finding that prince among the frogs. I, on the other hand, was just putting together a frog-kissing track record that would make Miss Piggy blush.

The press conference went on like it always did, and I dutifully took notes that suspiciously resembled those of every other movie press conference I'd been to: canned statements galore, zealous praise for the director, demure commentary about how lovely it would be to win an Oscar, and vague references to plot twists the media hadn't been clued in about. I had almost tuned out when a question from the *Teen People* reporter caught my attention.

'Kylie, who is your favorite actor you've ever worked with?' she asked, breathless, young, and excited to be talking to such a big star. She grinned as she waited for an answer, not seeming to realize that Kylie was too aloof to even meet her eye.

I held my breath. *Don't say Cole Brannon. Don't say Cole Brannon.*

'Cole Brannon,' Kylie said after a brief pause. Wally looked surprised, and she shot him a look. 'And Wally Joiner, of course,' she recovered quickly. But the damage was done.

'Not your own husband, Patrick O'Hara?' asked Ashley Tedder from *In Style*.

'Oh, well, of course Patrick,' Kylie said, fixing Ashley

with a glare. Excellent, she finally realized we were all out here and made eye contact with someone.

'So does that mean the rumors about you and Cole Brannon are true?' I heard myself ask. I immediately reddened. Kylie's glare was now fully focused on me. Why had I said that? My self-control button had obviously been deactivated.

'Cole Brannon,' she said through gritted teeth, although I couldn't help but notice she looked secretly pleased, 'is a very, very good friend. A close friend. I'll leave the rest up to your imagination.' She batted her eyelashes, and a few reporters laughed. I turned red again.

Kylie's attention had shifted back to the ceiling, which was good, because I was fixing her with a death stare. She'd leave the rest up to my imagination? What was that supposed to mean?

Obviously, that she was having wild, passionate sex with Cole Brannon.

How could they? What was he thinking?

More important, why did I care? Kylie Dane was beautiful, glamorous, perfect, glowing. I was probably fixed in Cole's mind as short, clunky, pathetic, and covered in tequila-laced vomit.

Not quite the image of loveliness his leading ladies lived up to.

'Kylie Dane and Cole Brannon,' Victoria murmured to me after the press conference, as we were gathering up our belongings. I felt numb. I turned to look at her, trying hard to look like I didn't care. 'God, he's gorgeous,' she bubbled, oblivious of the bizarre expressions surely crossing my face. 'What a couple! Figures he'd go for the most beautiful woman in Hollywood.'

'Yeah,' I said, feeling sick. 'It figures.'

The Leading Man

When I got back to my office, I checked my voice mail and was relieved to see that my luck appeared to be turning around. Not my luck in love, of course. In that area it seemed I was permanently cursed. But at least things were going well professionally. At this point, I'd take what I could get.

I had gotten a call back from Carol Brown, Julia Stiles's publicist, telling me cheerfully that she'd be in all afternoon if I'd like to call her with any additional questions, which meant I'd be able to knock out the changes to the cover story by the end of the day. There was also a message from Mandy Moore's publicist, pitching me a Q & A with her client (which I would push Margaret to accept – our readers loved the multitalented young star), and a message from the publicist for Taryn Joshua, the first celeb I'd chosen to feature in the new up-and-coming stars Q & A that Donna had suggested at Tuesday's meeting. Taryn would be thrilled to participate, her publicist said. I was to call her tomorrow to schedule a 'phoner'. My entire celeb section for next month was falling together perfectly. I could hardly believe it.

I spent the next hour making notes on questions to ask Carol. Then I took a quick lunch break alone. I bought a skim latte in our building's lobby on the way back up to my office and spent the next hour transcribing my notes from the morning's press conference, rolling my eyes childishly every time I heard Kylie's bored voice. I took another break at 2 p.m. to walk Cole's flowers down to the Dumpster, despite Wendy's protests – which, to be honest, weren't too adamant. The French waiter Jean Michel had presented her with a dozen roses at lunch that day, and I think she was secretly a bit relieved that my flowers, which so profoundly overshadowed hers, were gone.

I'd just gotten off the phone with Carol and was starting to revise my Julia Stiles feature when I heard the closest staffer to the reception door squeal in delight. I looked up in time to see two more editorial assistants leap up in tandem and race around the corner, out of my sight.

Wendy and I exchanged confused looks as Amber, the magazine's fact-checker, sprang from her desk and raced toward the door, clapping her hands with glee. More excited squeals emanated from the hallway, just out of our sight, and then Anne Amster raced by us too.

'You won't believe who's here!' she exclaimed as she dashed past. 'Courtney at the front desk just called and told me to get out there! C'mon!'

I looked at Wendy again. She squinted at me.

'What the hell is going on?' Wendy asked with typical bluntness.

'I have no idea,' I murmured. 'I've never seen anything like this.'

Not that the women on our staff didn't act a bit quirky – sometimes downright kooky – on a pretty regular basis. But this display, whatever it was, took the cake.

Staffer after staffer disappeared around the corner with excited squeals. The growing throng, which was now jutting out of the hallway, around the corner, and into the main office, was coming our way. Wendy and I exchanged looks once more and glanced at Maite, who had emerged from her office to watch the frenzy. It was like something from the Discovery Channel. I half expected to see some enthusiastic naturalist round the corner to tell us about the new *Mod* mating ritual or something.

The crowd slowly moved into view. Two interns, clearly starstruck, dropped back from the crowd and looked at each other in excitement, emitting little shrieks before scurrying away. The music editor, Chloe Michael (usually the very embodiment of the word 'cool'), was hopping up and down like a little schoolgirl, thrusting a pen and a sheet of paper toward the center of the throng.

'They've all gone crazy,' Wendy confirmed.

Then he rounded the corner.

There, in the hallway of *Mod* magazine – *my* magazine – thronged by a dozen of my coworkers who had never behaved this way in their lives, was the last person I expected to see in the *Mod* office, today or ever.

It was Cole Brannon.

My Cole Brannon.

Okay, well, really Kylie Dane's Cole Brannon. The Cole Brannon I had totally humiliated myself in front of before realizing he had completely lied to me. The Cole Brannon of coffee-and-croissant fame. The Cole Brannon of embarrassing pity flowers. The Cole Brannon who was way too hot to ever date a girl like me.

I stared at him as he scanned the room, simultaneously scribbling his autograph on pieces of paper thrust in his direction by women too old to be screaming like teenagers. Finally, Cole's eyes landed on me, and he grinned over the throng.

I gave him an involuntary, weak smile in return, then quickly wiped the grin from my face. After all, I wasn't happy to see him. He was a liar, remember? Who cared that he was gorgeous? Certainly not me.

'It's Cole Brannon,' Wendy whispered rather unnecessarily. 'In our office.'

'Yes, it is,' I confirmed flatly. I tried to remind myself that the deep dimples on his tanned face, the sharply defined broad shoulders I had once seen rippling with water droplets, and the perfectly straight, perfectly white smile were totally irrelevant.

Cole grinned at me again over the heads of the women surrounding him as he inched closer to me. Why did my cheeks feel hot? Was I blushing? That made no sense! I was a professional woman with no feelings for this man. Even if he was heart-stoppingly sexy, it meant nothing. I had no feelings for him whatsoever. I could never feel anything for someone who would lie to me. Someone who would sleep with a married woman. Someone who was that hot and totally unattainable.

After all, it would be completely stupid and self-destructive to think that someone like him would ever want to go out with someone like me.

Cole smiled and conversed politely with each of the *Mod* staffers in the throng. Little by little, the pack thinned as staffers got their autographs and wandered away in stunned excitement. Anne Amster even asked for a hug. Cole smiled and gently acquiesced. It was probably just my imagination that Anne's hug hadn't looked as warm, as tight, or as close as the one he'd bestowed upon me.

'He's my favorite movie star,' Anne admitted sheepishly as she flounced gleefully past us on her way back to her desk. Two giggling editorial interns scurried by, signed scraps of paper pressed to their chests.

Finally, Cole had signed his last autograph and was alone – or at least as alone as he could be with an office full of women staring at him. He stood for a moment, looking at me from down the hall. Our eyes locked over the walls of my cubicle. Why was my stomach churning, like it wanted to overturn again?

Suddenly, I was very conscious of how bad this would look. To Maite. To Margaret, if she wandered out. To everyone else in the office. Was Cole Brannon here to see me? Why? Didn't he have something he had to do with Kylie Dane? I fought sudden nausea as Kylie's words replayed in my head.

'I'll leave the rest up to your imagination,' her disembodied voice sneered. Great, I could imagine plenty.

Finally, Cole was at the edge of my cubicle, leaning against the doorway and looking as sexy as he had on Sunday morning. His dark brown locks were as tousled as ever, his cheeks were flushed, and his tall, perfectly proportioned frame looked great in a pair of Diesel jeans and a black button-up shirt.

'Hi,' he said softly, looking down at me with all the energy and emotion he put into meaningful gazes on-screen. I blushed and reminded myself that he wasn't really sexy. Liars couldn't be sexy, could they?

'Hi,' I echoed, trying to remember that I was supposed to be annoyed at him. For lying. For helping Kylie to cheat on her husband. For screwing Ivana Donatelli. For making me think, even for an instant, that I could compare with those women. That I wasn't a nobody.

Okay, that was better. I was starting to feel a bit righteously pissed off instead of just turned on.

I snuck another look around the room. Heads peeked out of offices up and down the hall, staring at us. Phones jangled, but no one was answering. I squirmed uncomfortably. I could practically read their minds as they stared, suspecting us of an affair, suspecting me of compromising my ethics. I looked quickly at Wendy, who raised her eyebrows at me.

'Guess I should have worn the baseball cap, right?' Cole teased, winking at me. I tried to frown at him. 'You know,' he said, apparently thinking I was confused about what he meant. 'To stay undercover?'

'I know,' I said softly. I looked back down at my keyboard and wished I could disappear. Or at least that when I looked up again, Cole wouldn't look so damned gorgeous and irresistible and, well, nice. Because he wasn't. It was all an illusion. I knew the truth.

'Claire!' Wendy hissed from the cubicle next to me. I looked up helplessly. She was staring at me with wide eyes, making faces that seemed to indicate I was supposed to do something.

'Oh,' I said finally. 'This is my friend Wendy.' Wendy raised her eyebrows at me, which I knew was her way of telling me that wasn't what she was getting at. Of course it wasn't. What she wanted was for me to be polite and flirtatious. But she didn't look like she minded being introduced as a consolation prize.

'Oh, so *you're* Wendy,' said Cole enthusiastically. 'Nice to finally meet you.' He took a step forward and reached out a long arm. Wendy stood and shook his hand, her freckled cheeks flushed with color.

I tried to shrink into my chair, fiercely hoping that when I looked up again, Cole would be gone. I closed my eyes for a moment. *Go away! Go away!*

'Sorry to bother you at work,' Cole said, interrupting my thoughts. I opened my eyes. Evidently, he hadn't disappeared.

'What are you doing here?' I asked. For an instant, I could have sworn he looked a bit wounded.

He leaned forward, his voice soft enough not to carry beyond Wendy. The rest of the room strained to hear, but I knew Cole was at least making an attempt to be discreet.

'I didn't have your phone number, and I've gone by your apartment a few times. You weren't there, and I was starting to get worried. I wanted to make sure you were okay,' Cole said. He lowered his voice even further. 'You know. After . . . everything.'

My cheeks were on fire. I couldn't believe what I was hearing. He'd gone by my apartment to look for me? And now he was so concerned that he'd come by my office?

'So you came here?' I whispered. Cole shrugged and looked uncomfortable.

'I was doing a studio shoot in the building for the cover of *Mod*,' he said. 'I figured I would stop by and check on you while I was here.'

I was flattered for a moment before I remembered the dozens of eyes on us. The warmth inside me quickly turned to humiliation and then anger – illogical as that was – as a sudden image of Cole and Kylie in the pages of *Tattletale* sprang to mind.

'Thanks,' I said, knowing my voice sounded cold. 'I appreciate your concern. But I'm fine.' I willed my heart to stop pounding. I wasn't quite sure why it suddenly felt like I'd gotten an 808 bass system installed in my chest.

'Oh,' said Cole. He leaned back and studied my face for a moment. Was it my imagination, or did he look disappointed at the less-than-warm reception? 'Well, I'm glad. I was worried. I never heard from you after I sent those flowers, so I was a bit concerned.'

'Thanks for the flowers,' I said stiffly. He looked hurt, and I instantly softened, despite my best intentions. Okay, he was a liar, but he *had* sent me flowers. Maybe I could be just the teensiest bit nice.

I took a deep breath and exhaled slowly.

'I'm sorry,' I said finally. 'The flowers were very nice. I'm sorry I didn't call. I'm just . . . dealing with a lot here.' *Like trying not to hate you for lying about Kylie Dane,* said the voice in my head. *Like the shame I feel from thinking, even for a moment, that you could be attracted to me. Like the fact that I'm obviously a delusional idiot. Like the realization that I'm probably never going to find anyone who could love me. How's that?*

'I know,' said Cole, who couldn't possibly know what was going through my insanely calibrated brain. 'I mean, I figured. I just wanted to let you know that if you need any help . . .' He paused and looked at me gently. I could have sworn that his blush had deepened. 'Well, I just wanted you to know that you can call me if you need to. Or if you want to talk, or anything.'

'Thanks,' I said. I snuck a look at Wendy, who looked like she was about to faint. The rest of the room was leaning forward in interest. I suddenly felt exposed, humiliated.

'Are you sure you're okay?' Cole looked concerned.

'Yes,' I said sharply, refusing to elaborate. The stares

around the room were growing more intense and, I thought, less friendly. Not that I'd mind if the world thought that Cole Brannon was in love with me.

'Look, we can't talk here,' I said suddenly. I could practically see my reputation crumbling before my eyes.

'Oh,' said Cole, looking surprised. He glanced quickly around the room, then back at me. 'I'm sorry, I didn't mean . . .'

'C'mon.' I stood up quickly, grabbed him by the arm, and dragged him down the hallway. We passed cubicles filled with desperately curious eyes, following our every move. I didn't know where I was taking him until I spotted the door to the men's room at the end of the hall. I paused for a moment and pulled Cole inside, knowing we'd be the only ones there. The odds that the one man on our editorial staff of fifty-two people was using the bathroom at this very moment were slim.

Sure enough, the bathroom was empty, and we were finally alone.

'Look,' I hissed at Cole as the door swung shut behind us, keeping out the prying eyes. 'You can't just come here. What will people think?'

'I'm sorry,' Cole said, looking surprised and a bit wounded. For a moment, I felt a bit guilty, despite myself. 'I just wanted to make sure you were okay. I didn't think . . .' His voice trailed off. He leaned in to the wall and I stepped in front of him, still going.

'It's bad enough that Sidra saw us together and suspected . . . well, you know. But now the whole office has seen us.' I realized I was shaking a finger at him, and I stopped for a moment. I was acting like a disappointed mother. I took a deep breath and felt suddenly embarrassed.

'I'm sorry,' I said with a sigh. 'I just . . . I know you came here because you wanted to help. And I appreciate that. I'm just so afraid of what people will think.'

'Why?' Cole asked softly. As he looked at me, I realized

he wasn't angry about my outburst, but was instead peering at me with what looked like pity. I felt instantly shamed. I didn't want or need his sympathy. I didn't need him to feel sorry for me, then dash off with the lovely Kylie Dane or the coldly beautiful Ivana Donatelli. 'Why does it matter what they think?'

'Because it does,' I answered sullenly, knowing very well that I sounded petulantly childish. 'And because I care about my job and my reputation, and I don't want to risk ruining all that.'

I suddenly felt perilously close to tears as we looked at each other for a moment. He didn't understand. He couldn't possibly understand what it was like to be a young entertainment editor at a major million-circulation magazine, to have to always remain on the up-and-up so that no one thought you were in the position for the wrong reasons.

He couldn't possibly understand what it felt like to catch your boyfriend cheating on you when you'd done everything in your power to make him love you. When nothing you did was enough. When your coworker's plastic sister was more desirable than you. When you knew that no one in their right mind would want you.

I felt as pathetic as I knew Cole thought I was. For a moment, his gentle gaze made me want to hug him, to have him put his arms around me, pull me in to his strong chest, and tell me everything would be all right. But that was ridiculous.

'Have you heard from him?' he asked softly, gently. I blinked.

'Who?'

'Your boyfriend,' he said, looking a bit uncomfortable. He shifted his weight. 'Or your ex-boyfriend or whatever. The guy you walked in on.'

'Oh,' I said. Imagine that. A year of building a relationship had turned him merely into the 'guy I'd walked in on'. Of course I hadn't heard from him. Which would make me look even more pathetic to Cole. I couldn't stand it.

'Um, yes, actually. He called and we talked for a while,' I lied quickly. I glanced at Cole, who looked surprised. I cleared my throat and dove deeper into the fib. I didn't know why I didn't just tell him the truth, but I was already on a roll. 'He sent flowers too. Everything's fine. It was all a misunderstanding.'

Cole was silent for a moment. I mentally kicked myself. Could I have sounded more moronic? A 'misunderstanding'? What on earth did I mean by that?

'Oh,' Cole said finally. I stared at the floor. 'Good. I mean, it sounds like you're, um, working things out.'

'Yep,' I said brightly, digging myself in deeper. I elaborated further. 'I mean, he realized what he was throwing away and how much he really loved me and everything,' I babbled, still not meeting Cole's eye. 'I have to decide whether or not to forgive him, but when someone clearly loves you that much, you know . . .' My voice trailed off, and I snuck a look at Cole. He still looked surprised.

'Oh, well, I'm glad,' he said. He looked like he was avoiding my eye. He was silent for a moment. 'Just as long as he treats you right.'

Well of course he didn't treat me right. He never had.

'It's between me and Tom,' I said stiffly. 'But I appreciate your concern.'

'Of course,' Cole said quickly. 'I mean, I just wanted to make sure, you know, that you knew you could call me if you needed anything. That I'm here for you. But I guess you're okay.'

'I'm great,' I said, flashing him a winning grin. 'Really. I'm great. Life's great.'

'Good.'

'Great.'

There was a moment of uncomfortable silence as we stood in the bathroom. I avoided looking at him. I was suddenly painfully aware that we were mere inches apart.

I was planted firmly in front of him as he leaned against the wall, and I was so close that I could smell his faint cologne and feel his breath ruffling the top layers of my hair. In that moment I had the strange feeling – just for an instant – that I wanted to stay there forever. But that was stupid. He was completely out of my league. And to top it off, he clearly thought I was pathetic.

I quickly cleared my throat and stepped away.

'Look, I appreciate your concern, but you really need to go,' I said brusquely. What was I, crazy? I couldn't let myself feel attracted to him.

Besides, he was having an affair. Just like Tom. It was right there in *Tattletale*'s black and white. Even if they weren't always reliable. But photos didn't lie.

Scumbag.

'I don't need your help, thank you,' I said curtly. 'I'll be just fine, and I'm sure you have much more important things to do.' *Or people to do. Like Kylie Dane.*

Cole looked at me for a moment, his perfect features twisted into an expression of confusion.

'Thank you for all your help on this story,' I continued with forced cheerfulness, trying my best to sound professional and ignore the fact that Cole smelled wonderful, looked wonderful, and sounded wonderful. He *wasn't* wonderful, though. I had to keep reminding myself of that.

'Um, okay, sure, no problem,' he said uncertainly. If I hadn't known better, I would have thought I'd hurt his feelings. But he was an actor, and I was sure he could fake all sorts of emotions. He sure could lie like a pro.

'Fantastic,' I said briskly. I reached out and offered him my hand. He looked blankly at it for a moment, then shook it slowly. I tried to ignore the tingle that ran up my arm when he touched me. 'I'll call your publicist when the article comes out and send over some copies.'

'Okay,' Cole said. He still looked confused. 'Thanks.'

'No problem. Thank *you*.'

And with that, I hurried him out of the bathroom, where a small crowd had clustered just feet away, near the water cooler. Hmm. Taking him into the bathroom to avoid prying eyes probably hadn't been such a hot idea.

Apparently, I didn't need anyone's help to destroy my reputation. I was managing to do it single-handedly. How efficient of me.

'Nice meeting with you, Cole,' I said brightly, as I walked him to the door. To my chagrin, I could feel an involuntary, furious blush heating my face. '*Mod* magazine really appreciates your cooperation.' I was trying to sound as impersonal as possible. We still had quite an audience.

'Nice meeting with you too, Claire,' he said. Was it my imagination, or did he look kind of sad? We paused at the door that opened out toward the reception desk. He leaned in and whispered softly in my ear, 'You will call if you need me, right?' My heart leaped in my chest, but I fought it down.

'I appreciate the offer,' I said firmly. 'But I don't think that will be necessary. I'll be in touch when the article comes out.'

'Oh,' Cole said. 'Okay.' He took a step backward, through the open doorway, still looking perplexed.

'Okay,' I said cheerfully. 'Have a nice day. Thanks for coming by.'

My face hurt as I smiled a smile I didn't mean. Why did I suddenly have the sneaking feeling I'd made a mistake?

The door swung closed behind him, and I saw him glance over his shoulder and look at me one last time as he disappeared toward the elevator bank.

The Hunk

'What the hell were you thinking?' Wendy demanded.
It was just past 6 p.m., and I'd decided to go home to my own apartment tonight. I seemed to be on a roll in the screwing-up-my-life department. I figured I might as well take all my bad karma back to the location where it all started.

But Wendy wasn't letting me off the hook that easily. We walked side by side to the N/R station at Forty-ninth and Seventh Avenue, squished in a private bubble amid the sea of people rushing home from work. Beside us, traffic on Broadway inched south, the drivers trying to cross from east to west honking and trying to maneuver through stopped traffic.

'I don't know what I was thinking,' I said miserably. I shrugged and looked at her out of the corner of my eye.

'So you just told him that you and Tom were back together? And then you told him to get lost?'

'Not in those exact words,' I mumbled.

'Claire! Why?'

'I don't know.' I looked up at Wendy and was instantly silenced by the expression on her face. She was staring at me like I was crazy, which I supposed I was.

'But it was *Cole Brannon*,' she said, drawing out each syllable. 'Cole Bran-non,' she repeated for emphasis, like she was talking to someone with a very small mental capacity. 'You know, Cole Brannon, big movie star, hottest guy in America. That Cole Brannon.'

'I know,' I said softly. Okay, so maybe this hadn't been my brightest move yet.

'And you just told him that you were taken,' Wendy recapped. 'By a man we all know is a total creep.'

'I know,' I said again.

'Why?'

'I don't know.'

'You don't know?'

'No.'

Wendy sighed and looked away for a moment. I cleared my throat and tried to explain.

'He was just there because he felt sorry for me, you know.'

'Oh yeah,' Wendy said, looking at me sharply. 'I get visits at work all the time from movie stars who feel sorry for me.'

'You know what I mean.'

'No, I don't. Guys like that don't just swing by the office because they feel sorry for you. And you just totally blew him off.'

'Whatever,' I said, knowing I sounded like a petulant child. 'What would he want with me? He has Kylie Dane. I'm just this crazy reporter who puked on him.'

Wendy stopped, looking at me in exasperation. Finally, she shook her head.

'You know, did it ever occur to you that he was telling the truth about Kylie Dane?'

'But she said—'

Wendy cut me off.

'I don't care what she said. She might have motives you don't know about. What actress's career wouldn't be helped by being linked with Cole Brannon?'

'But the pictures—'

'Could have a logical explanation,' Wendy completed my sentence. She shook her head again. 'You know, they *are* shooting a movie together. Maybe the picture was from the set. While they were shooting a scene.'

I looked at her.

'What about the pictures with his publicist Ivana?' I persisted. 'Or with Jessica Gregory?'

'The picture with the publicist was probably just dinner,' Wendy said. 'There was nothing romantic about it, really. And you know that Cole Brannon was shooting a guest spot on *Spy Chicks*, Jessica Gregory's show. I'm sure a photographer just got a shot while they were filming outside. Those tabloids can make anything look bad.'

'I guess so,' I conceded. 'But I don't have a good feeling about this, you know? I mean, the thing is, he can have any of those women if he wants to. There's not a reason in the world he'd want to date me. That's just crazy.'

'It's not crazy, Claire,' Wendy said firmly. 'You're not giving yourself enough credit.'

I shook my head, dismissing the compliment. I appreciated her confidence in me, but I knew it was just best-friend blindness. Even Tom – who, let's face it, was a bit of a loser – didn't want me. It was ludicrous to think that Cole Brannon would.

'I'm still not ready to write off the tabloid pictures as meaningless,' I said, deflecting attention from the real issue, my lack of desirability. 'Maybe one picture. But photos of him with all three women? I don't know. I don't think I can believe him when he says that nothing's going on.'

'Not all men are liars like Tom, Claire,' Wendy said, looking at me sharply. I looked down, refusing to meet her gaze. 'You never used to have a problem trusting people.'

'Well, maybe I should have,' I said. I took a deep breath and changed the subject. 'Look, you know how I feel about people thinking I slept my way into my position or something. Do you know how it would look if something happened now between me and Cole? Not that it would even be an option.'

Wendy sighed.

'It's not like you're out trying to get laid by every movie

star you interview,' she said. 'That would be kind of suspicious. But one guy? One guy who you have this connection with?'

'We don't have a connection,' I snapped. 'That's crazy. He's just a guy who I interviewed, and that's it. End of story. I thought he was nice, but obviously he's just like every other man.' Wendy looked at me for a moment and took a deep breath.

'Okay,' she said finally. 'I'm sorry. It's not my business. I just wish someone would look at me the way that man looked at you.'

As we parted at the subway station and went our separate ways, I began to feel vaguely uneasy. But that was silly.

Besides, why would Wendy need men to look at her the way Cole Brannon had looked at me? Men looked at her with lust and an unmasked desire to get her into bed. Cole Brannon looked at me with pity.

I couldn't remember the last time someone had looked at me with lust in his eyes. Least of all my live-in boyfriend, who had spent the last several months screwing someone else.

I had apparently become man-repellent.

The phone rang at 6:45 the next morning, forty-five minutes before my alarm was supposed to go off, and I was rudely awakened from a dream about Cole Brannon. I couldn't remember much of it in those first few seconds that consciousness dawned. But it had been a nice dream, and it hadn't exactly been G-rated. That much I remembered. The thought made me slightly concerned, given the circumstances. I tried to excuse it by telling myself there were thousands of other American women fantasizing about him too.

They just didn't happen to be as sex-starved as me.

And Cole Brannon probably hadn't taken most of them home at night. Or sent them flowers at work. But I digress.

Disappointed that I was now awake and couldn't escape back into the dream world, I reached for the rudely jangling phone.

'Hello?' I answered sleepily.

'Claire?'

The voice snapped me instantly awake. I sat up quickly.

'Tom,' I said, feeling like the breath had been knocked out of me.

'Hi, baby,' he said.

I couldn't speak for a minute. What did he want? Why was he calling? Had he realized that he missed me? That he needed me? That he wanted to come back?

'Hi,' I answered finally. I looked at the clock. 'Tom, it's six forty-five. What are you doing calling me at this time of morning?' I urged myself to sound casual. Casual Claire. Cool, calm, collected Claire. That was me. I took a breath.

'I wanted to make sure to catch you in,' Tom said calmly. 'I've been trying you for a few days, but you haven't been there. Where have you been?'

I opened my mouth to tell him I'd been staying with Wendy; then I reconsidered.

'None of your business,' I snapped. There. Let him wonder. Maybe I was out on dates with men who actually had jobs. Maybe I was out partying until the wee hours of the morning. Heck, maybe I was sleeping with a movie star. Yeah, sure.

'Sorry, you're right,' he said softly. Of course I was right. Even if I wasn't *actually* sleeping with said movie star. I was silent while I waited for him to speak. 'Look, I'm sorry about what happened, Claire. I had no right to . . . You didn't deserve that.'

His voice was soft and slow, and he sounded genuinely remorseful. I was speechless for a minute.

'You're right,' I said finally. He wasn't going to get off the hook that easily. 'I didn't deserve that. Not after everything I've done for you.' Anger welled up inside me.

'I know, Claire, I know,' Tom said softly. 'There's no excuse.'

'No, there's not.' The anger bubbled to the surface. 'Do you have any idea what that was like? Walking in on you like that? Seeing you in my bed with... with... that woman?'

I realized I was squeezing the comforter so tightly with my hand that my circulation was nearly cut off. I slowly unclenched and took a deep breath.

'I know,' Tom said sadly. 'I know, and I am so sorry.' He breathed slowly into the phone, and I felt myself soften a bit in the silence between us. 'Look, can I take you to dinner tonight, Claire?' His question caught me even more off guard. Dinner? Me and Tom? I didn't answer immediately, and he pushed forward. 'I know I'm being really presumptuous here, but I miss you, and I feel like if I can see you in person, maybe I can explain things better.' I still didn't answer. I didn't know what to say. 'I just want to see you, Claire,' he pressed on. 'I miss you so much.'

No way. I knew I shouldn't go. It would just be plain stupid to agree to see him so soon.

'Okay,' I heard myself say. Wait a minute. Had I just agreed to dinner? What was I thinking?

'Great,' Tom said, sounding relieved. I was starting to feel very uncomfortable. Not just because I'd agreed, but also because I'd actually felt my spirits rise when Tom said he missed me. Because I was actually looking forward to the dinner.

Clearly there was something wrong with me. Very wrong.

'Meet me at the Friday's in Times Square at six thirty,' I said tersely. I knew he hated Friday's. Sure, it was a petty way to punish him, but I'd take what I could get.

'Fine,' said Tom agreeably. 'I'll meet you out front at six thirty.'

'Okay,' I said again. My stomach was doing flips, and my heart was doing somersaults. I had a whole acrobatic team using my internal organs for practice. I certainly didn't feel okay.

'Okay, see you then. And Claire?' Tom paused for a moment.

'Yes?' I said finally.

'I love you,' he said softly. My jaw dropped. Then he hung up the phone before I had a chance to answer. I slowly placed the phone back in its cradle and stared at it for a moment.

'You've got a funny way of showing it,' I finally murmured, after Tom was long gone.

'You are not seriously going to go,' Wendy said at lunch as she stared at me over her turkey sandwich. We were sitting in the corner at Cosi, and I'd finally worked up the courage to tell her about Tom's call and the fact that I'd agreed to meet him. I knew she would think I was crazy, and to be honest, I wasn't so sure she was wrong.

As Wendy stared at me incredulously, little drops of lettuce and mustard falling from her freeze-framed sandwich, even more of my confidence slipped away.

'Yes I am,' I said finally.

'Claire,' said Wendy slowly. She put down the sandwich and leaned across the table to take my right hand in hers. 'Why? What could you possibly have to gain?'

'I don't know,' I said slowly. 'But what do I have to lose?'

'A lot,' Wendy said quickly. No way. Wendy was being too harsh, right? 'He's just trying to use you again.'

'No, you're wrong,' I said too quickly. 'He sounded like he was really sorry.'

'Yeah, he's sorry that his source of income has dried up,' Wendy muttered.

'Besides, what else could he want from me?' I said, ignoring her. 'I think he really just wants to talk this time.'

Wendy leaned back in her chair. She studied me for a moment. I wanted her approval. I wanted her to tell me it was okay to meet with him. It was just dinner. I hadn't agreed to marry him or bear his children. Yet.

Not that he'd asked. Not that *anyone* had asked.

'I just think you're going to get hurt,' Wendy finally said. 'But if that's what you want to do, you know I'm here for you.'

I sighed.

'Thank you,' I said softly.

She tilted her head to the side and studied me for a moment.

'You should really call Cole Brannon, you know,' Wendy said softly. I just stared at her.

'I thought we were talking about Tom,' I said finally. Wendy looked down at her sandwich, then back at me again.

'We were. Now we're talking about Cole Brannon.'

'I can't just call him!' I said. That would be nuts. Was she crazy?

'Yes, you can,' Wendy insisted. 'He gave you his cell number. Why can't you?'

'Because,' I said stubbornly. Wendy looked at me, waiting for me to say more, so I did. 'Because he's a movie star. Because he feels sorry for me, and I don't need his pity. Because he's obviously sleeping with Kylie Dane. And his publicist, Ivana. What would he want with me?'

'I don't think that stuff about those women is true,' Wendy said calmly. 'I really don't.'

I shook my head.

'Look,' I said, trying not to sound harsh. 'I'm not going to call him, okay? He gave me his number for work purposes. And besides, I'm not going to hear from him again. I think he got the point.' I tried to feel smug, but instead, I felt just a bit idiotic.

Wendy shrugged. I pretended to ignore her.

'Whatever you say,' she said mysteriously, like she knew something I didn't. I made a face at her and changed the subject.

'How's it going with that French waiter?' I asked.

'Jean Michel,' Wendy filled in dreamily.

'Yeah, Jean Michel,' I said. 'How's that going?'

'Great,' said Wendy, smiling and putting her turkey sandwich back down. 'He's really great, you know. He's not as young as he looks. He's only a year younger than I am, and he's really smart. His English is really coming along well. And I took French in high school, so it's kind of starting to come back to me a bit, you know?'

'That's good,' I said, studying Wendy's freckled face. She was glowing. It had been a long time since I'd seen her like this. She normally liked to hop from waiter to waiter – with an occasional stray investment banker or attorney thrown into the mix – but she'd already been out four times with Jean Michel and was seeing him again tonight.

Had the world turned upside down? Waiter-dating Wendy, finally settling down?

'It's been a long time since I've felt like this,' she said, as if reading my mind. 'I really like him, Claire.'

'I'm happy for you,' I said, and I meant it. 'That sounds great.'

'It *is* great,' Wendy said, flashing me her wide grin. 'He's great. I went out to dinner at Azafran last night while Jean Michel was at work, and you know what? I didn't even look at any of the waiters. It didn't even occur to me. Isn't that weird?'

I reached across the table and squeezed her hand.

'Wow,' I murmured, looking at her closely. 'You didn't even look?'

'No,' said Wendy, looking as surprised as I was. 'I don't think I've *ever* not looked. What do you think that means?'

'Maybe you're in love,' I said.

'Maybe I am,' Wendy agreed softly. She smiled and winked at me. 'Stranger things have happened.'

I don't know exactly what kind of reception I expected at work, but I had expected there would be at least some kind of fallout after Cole's visit. I'd expected to be greeted with the same suspicion that Sidra had looked at me with. Instead, I had a steady stream of coworkers coming by my desk to squeal about how cool it was that Cole Brannon had dropped in to see me.

It didn't seem to occur to any of them that there was anything romantic going on between us. I didn't know whether to be insulted by that or flattered that my coworkers knew I'd never overstep the bounds of professionalism. I finally decided on the latter, and I allowed myself to breathe a huge sigh of relief. I even basked a bit in their jealousy over the fact that 'the Cole Brannon' had sought me out in the office.

'What was he doing here?' Chloe Michael had squealed the moment I walked in.

'Uh, dropping by to confirm a few details of the interview,' I stammered before I had a chance to think.

Chloe had accepted the explanation and it spread like wildfire. A few editorial assistants even dropped by to *thank* me for bringing him by – they'd been thrilled to get his autograph. No one brought up the fact that I had dragged him into the bathroom, which obviously didn't gel with the rest of my explanation.

Details, details.

My relief was cut short, though, when Sidra glided into the doorway of my cubicle at 4:45 that afternoon, on her way out of the building. Her hair had been blown out, and she was dressed in a skintight black designer dress and pointy black Jimmy Choos. In fact, she looked just a bit like the devil himself would look if he were a fashion editor. But maybe that was just me projecting.

'So now we're bringing our lovers by the office, are we?' she singsonged at me. 'I heard about your little encounter with Cole Brannon.' My breath caught in my throat. Yes, she was definitely Satan. Beelzebub in the flesh.

'No,' I sputtered. 'Nothing happened. He was dropping by to answer some questions.'

'Is that what the kids are calling it these days?' Sidra laughed. 'Are your interviews always conducted in the men's room? No *wonder* you got to be a senior editor so fast.'

I blushed furiously and started to protest. Sidra cut me off, batting her long eyelashes at me in faux innocence.

'Oh, and do the movie stars you interview – and refuse to sleep with, according to you – always send you flowers, too?' she asked sweetly.

I was still formulating an answer as she glided away, a smirk plastered across her face. I felt shaken. Obviously, Sidra wasn't done with me yet. I suddenly felt uneasy.

Then it hit me. The flowers. How did she know about the flowers? Wendy was the only one I'd told. Oh no.

'Wendy?' I asked over the cubicle, standing up slowly. I felt a bit sick. 'You didn't tell Sidra about the flowers I got the other day, did you?' I already knew the answer, but it was my last resort before I gave in to believing the worst.

'No, of course not,' she said quickly. She looked at me for a moment, and then her face blanched. 'Why?'

'She knows they were from Cole,' I said flatly. This was not good.

'Oh, no,' Wendy said. 'What did you do with the note?'

'I threw it away,' I said softly.

'Here? In the office?'

I nodded. How could I have been so stupid? We looked at each other for a moment. I closed my eyes, then opened them to stare at Wendy in horror.

'She has the note,' Wendy said finally. I nodded again. 'What do you think she's going to do?'

'I don't know,' I said. 'But it can't be good.'

The Schmuck

Tom was late.

As I stood in the entrance to the TGI Friday's in Times Square at 6:45, I tried not to feel annoyed. After all, he had probably been delayed by traffic or something. He'd be here.

I sank onto a sticky vinyl bench that stretched from the front door to the hostess stand. Around me, tourists with Texas drawls, Southern twangs, and Midwestern inflections crowded in through the big door, between candy-cane-striped pillars. Tray-toting waiters and waitresses with cheerful grins rushed by, their chests lined with buttons that screamed at me to *Give Peace a Chance*, *Tip Your Waiter*, and remember, *Love Makes the World Go 'Round*. I didn't quite believe that last one.

Stupid saying.

As I sat and waited, I tried to be patient. How would it feel to see Tom for the first time since last Saturday night? Would I hate him the moment I saw him?

But at 6:55, when he walked through the front door, I didn't hate him. I loved how he looked in a crisp white button-down shirt, a pair of khakis, and the Kenneth Cole loafers I'd bought for his birthday. I loved how he smiled, his whole face lighting up when he saw me. I loved his stupid crooked grin. And I hated that I didn't hate him.

'Hey, babe!' he said as I stood up beside him. He pulled me into his arms and surprised me with a warm hug.

Simply out of habit I hugged back, before I realized what I was doing and stiffened. 'You're early.'

'Early?' I looked at him incredulously. He looked back, wide-eyed and innocent. 'I'm not early. You're twenty-five minutes late!' He looked shocked.

'What? What are you talking about? We said seven!'

'We said six thirty,' I said, trying to sound calm.

'No, no, I'm positive we said seven,' he said.

'No,' I insisted. I was sure we'd said 6:30. Right? I thought so. But suddenly I wasn't a hundred per cent sure. 'Maybe,' I amended. Tom looked satisfied.

'Great,' he said. He put an arm around me. I thought about resisting, but I didn't. He pulled me close, and despite the fact that I knew it shouldn't, it felt good. 'Let's get a table.'

A hostess whose chest told us to *Knock on Wood*, *Save the Whales*, and *Vote for Kennedy* led us to a table in the middle of the room, afloat in a sea of tourists.

'It's nice to see you, Claire,' Tom said formally after our hostess walked away. I looked at him over the top of my menu for a moment.

'You too,' I mumbled. I returned my attention to the menu, buying myself some time. My emotions were suddenly a mess. I blinked a few times and tried to focus. I was not supposed to be unraveling this early in the evening. I took a deep breath and vowed to get ahold of myself.

While Tom ordered us an appetizer and drinks, I squirmed. A lock of his hair curled across his forehead, falling lightly across his left eyebrow. A week ago I would have reached across the table and tenderly brushed it away, but today I wasn't sure I wanted to touch him.

I wasn't supposed to feel something when I studied his eyes. I wasn't supposed to love the way his mouth curled up at the left corner. I wasn't supposed to love the tiny, nearly imperceptible scar on his right cheek that he'd gotten falling off his bike at the age of eleven. I wasn't supposed to feel my heartbeat pick up when his eyes met mine.

Yet I felt all those things. And that made me an idiot, didn't it?

I looked at him sadly out of the corner of my eye. How had we gotten here? A year ago, when he first moved into my apartment and we were spending every available second together, basking in each other's glow, I thought it would be perfect forever. I thought we'd be together forever. It had never even occurred to me to worry that he would cheat on me one day.

I wondered what he was thinking, what he would say. I wanted him to say magic words that would make everything okay, that would allow us to go back to living our lives as we had before Saturday.

I didn't know what those magic words would be, though, or if they even existed.

And I felt ashamed that any part of me wanted that to happen. I knew deep down that I should have had enough self-respect to walk away, to move on. But he was like an addiction, and I couldn't stop myself.

I was snapped out of my convoluted thought process by the reappearance of our waitress, whose brown curls were tied up in perky pigtails. She set down a Bud Light for Tom and a Coke for me and smiled at us.

'Are you ready to order?' she asked. She turned to me, and I started to open my mouth, but Tom spoke instead. He asked, of course, for the Jack Daniel's steak and shrimp dinner, one of the most expensive items on the menu. I ordered a chicken Caesar salad.

After the waitress took our order, Tom reached across the table for my hand. He squeezed it and held it gently.

'Look, Claire,' he began. He paused and sighed. He squeezed my hand again and looked up at me with soulful eyes. 'I don't even know where to begin,' he said softly. 'I was so wrong. I was so stupid to throw away what we had. I know you can never forgive me, and I don't expect you to, but . . .' His voice trailed off and he gazed at me imploringly. I looked back. I had no idea what to say.

He looked so genuinely pathetic and remorseful that I felt sorry for him. Part of me wanted to squeeze his hand back, smile warmly, and tell him it was okay, that I forgave him. But I didn't forgive him. And it wasn't okay. Maybe someday, but not today.

'Tom,' I began slowly. I didn't pull my hand away, and he continued to hold it gently. I had to admit, I liked the way it felt. I liked his quiet strength and the gentle way he folded his big hand around my little one. I cleared my throat and looked up to meet his eye. 'Why?' I asked finally. I felt suddenly weary. 'Just tell me why.'

He looked at me for a moment, and the uncomfortable silence seemed to drag on forever. My heart was pounding as I waited for his response.

'Why what?' he asked finally, in the same gentle tone of voice. I looked at him sharply. What did he think I was talking about?

'Why would you cheat on me?' I asked in a small voice. He looked away for a moment, then looked back at me with mournful eyes.

'I'm sorry,' he said softly. 'I was totally wrong. I know that. I guess I was just feeling like, I don't know, like you were too busy for me. And I wasn't dealing with that well.' It was true. I knew I was a workaholic sometimes. Maybe I shouldn't have poured so much energy into my career. I felt instantly guilty.

'I'm not saying it was your fault,' he said quickly. 'I'm sure I was being too sensitive, honey.' Was he still allowed to call me *honey*? Why did I still like the sound of the word rolling off his tongue? 'I made a huge mistake because I felt like I wasn't sure that you loved me any more.'

I gasped.

'I never stopped loving you,' I said. My eyes filled with sudden tears. I blinked quickly.

'I know that now,' he said, squeezing my hand. 'And I

know I've gone and screwed it all up. I'm so sorry.'

Our waitress interrupted us by setting down the enormous Friday's Three-for-All that Tom had ordered.

'Enjoy, you two!' She grinned encouragingly at us, as if we were two teenagers on a first date.

We busied ourselves with our food for a minute, avoiding each other's eyes. I pushed a potato skin around on my plate, but I couldn't bring myself to eat it.

'Did you meet her at *Mod*'s Christmas party?' I asked finally. I really wasn't hungry. Tom looked up, surprised, his mouth full. 'Estella,' I clarified. 'Estella Marrone. Did you meet her at the Christmas party?' He looked down and then back at me. He chewed thoughtfully, swallowing loudly.

'Yes,' he said simply, not sounding nearly as guilty as he should have. 'How do you know her name?'

'She left her purse in the apartment,' I said. 'And her sister came to get it.' Anger welled inside me. 'Her sister is Sidra DeSimon, you know. The fashion director at *Mod*. You were sleeping with the sister of one of my coworkers.' I expected his eyebrows to shoot up in surprise, but he nodded and looked guilty.

'I know,' he said. 'I'm so sorry.'

'You knew?' I was incredulous. 'You knew I worked with her sister?'

'Not right away,' he said quickly. 'But yeah, I knew. Not at the beginning, though. I didn't do it on purpose. What a coincidence, right?' He laughed uneasily.

'How is it a coincidence if you met her at *my* Christmas party?' I asked.

He shrugged.

'Well, there were lots of people there you didn't know,' he said sheepishly. 'How was I supposed to know you knew her sister?'

I looked miserably around the table. I was no longer hungry. I swallowed again.

'I am so, so sorry,' Tom said again. 'If I could change things, I would.'

'You'd change that I caught you?' I asked bitterly.

'No,' Tom said solemnly. 'I deserved that. I'd change the fact that it happened in the first place. I had no right. Look what I've thrown away.' He looked as miserable as I felt.

'Oh,' I said finally, because I sensed he was waiting for a response. I didn't have anything else to say. We sat in silence for another moment, but this time there were no menus to distract us. We had only each other and the uncomfortable wall that stood between us.

The waitress came and cleared away our appetizer. I'd barely touched it. A moment later, a server whisked in with our entrees. I avoided Tom's eye as I started to pick listlessly at my salad.

'Can I ask you something?' Tom said finally. I looked up, surprised.

'Okay.' Was he going to ask me to take him back? Ask me to forgive him?

'Are you . . .' He paused and his eyes flicked down at the table and back to me. 'Are you sleeping with Cole Brannon?'

I just looked at him for a minute.

'No!' I answered, appalled. 'Did Estella,' I spat her name, 'tell you that?' He paused again and nodded.

'She said her sister Sidra caught you in our apartment,' he said finally.

'*My* apartment,' I amended, just to be difficult.

I didn't know what to say. I certainly couldn't explain to Tom how pathetic I'd been that night, getting drunk and vomiting on a movie star – all because of him. He didn't need to know he had that kind of power over me. I fixed him with a glare.

'Nothing happened,' I said stiffly. 'It was a work thing.' Tom looked at me for a moment and nodded, seeming to accept the explanation.

'Okay,' he said. 'I believe you.' I simmered silently for a minute, then changed the subject.

'So are you still with her?' I demanded. Tom looked surprised and shook his head.

'No,' he said solemnly. 'No, Claire, I'm not. You're the only one in my heart. You always have been. I just didn't know how to appreciate it before.'

It scared me that the words didn't repulse me. They sent a flush of warmth shooting through my body. I tried to fight it.

'You still have some things in the apartment,' I said icily.

'Do you really want me to move my things out?' he asked softly. I held my breath. Was he asking me to say he could stay? My response was put on hold as our waitress came to refill my Coke and deliver another beer to Tom. She set down our check, and Tom handed her his credit card.

'Claire,' Tom began after the waitress was gone. He again reached for my hand. 'I love you so much. I've never loved anyone as much as I love you And I can never express to you how sorry I am for what I've done.'

My eyes filled with tears, and again, I blinked them back. My heart pounded as we looked into each other's eyes. This was one of those moments you see in Hugh Grant movies. I could practically hear the violin-laced soundtrack. 'I don't expect you to forgive me right away. Maybe you'll never be able to. But I want to try, Claire. I want to try.' I was about to speak when our waitress interrupted us, wrenching my tear-filled eyes away from Tom and his heartfelt message.

'Excuse me,' she said, shifting from foot to foot. 'I'm sorry to interrupt. But, sir, your card didn't go through. Do you have another one?' Tom reached into his pocket and pulled out his wallet. He rifled quickly through and looked up at the waitress.

'Gosh, how embarrassing. No, I don't.' He looked at me. 'Claire? I'm so sorry. Can you get this meal? I'll get the next one?' I swallowed the lump of resentment that had risen suddenly in my throat and nodded. I reached for my wallet and gave the waitress my Visa. She smiled tightly and walked away.

'I'm so sorry, Claire,' Tom said, reaching for my hand again. 'I thought I had paid the balance off, but it must not have been processed yet. I feel like such a jerk.'

'Don't worry about it,' I said tightly, telling myself that he couldn't possibly have done it on purpose. Not when he was about to ask me to take him back. Not while he was in the middle of declaring his love for me. I brushed the thought away and reached for his hand. 'You were saying?'

'Right,' said Tom. He squeezed my hand and cleared his throat. 'Claire, I love you more than anything in the world, and I want to work things out with you. I really do.'

'Me too,' I said softly. I hadn't intended to admit that to him or even to myself. I hadn't known for sure that I'd felt that way until the words were out of my mouth. Had I gone too far? But my heart was pounding, and I knew as I looked at him that I could forgive him. Things could change between us. I still loved him. And now I knew he still loved me. I should have hated him, but I couldn't. I didn't.

'But I know it will take some time,' Tom said slowly. 'I don't expect things to be back to normal right away.'

'Right,' I said softly, astonished that he realized on his own that things couldn't go back to being the way they had been. Just then the waitress returned with my credit card, two copies of the receipt, and a full glass of Coke for me. I signed the receipt, put my card away, and took a small sip. Tom took my hand again.

'So I was wondering . . .' Tom paused and tilted his head to the side imploringly. I leaned forward eagerly. This was it. He was going to beg me to take him back. 'I was wondering if maybe you could loan me some money for a while. Since you threw me out and all. Then we can have some time apart and maybe try to work things out, you know?'

Everything inside me went cold, and I drew my hand

away. I stared at him. He was still looking at me imploringly, an innocent expression on his face.

Suddenly I wanted to reach out and strangle him. Surely it would be justifiable homicide. Any jury would understand.

'You want to borrow money from me?' I asked very slowly, staring at him. Tom shrugged.

'Just a few thousand. To get on my feet, you know.'

'Just a few thousand,' I repeated flatly. Everything inside me had turned to ice.

I looked down at the receipt for the meal I'd just paid for. I couldn't believe it. I'd been so stupid. I'd bought everything he'd said. I'd fallen for it hook, line, and sinker.

Again.

'Yeah,' he said. I glared at him with the most intense anger I'd ever felt. 'You know,' he said, smiling at me with a sappiness that was so obviously fake. 'I heard you got a raise at work. I don't think we should move back in together right away. That might put too much pressure on us. I want you back, and I want to do it right. And since you threw me out and all . . .' He paused and gave an encouraging smile.

'So you want a few thousand dollars,' I said flatly.

He shrugged.

'Give or take,' he said casually.

He winked at me, and suddenly I detested him. I had come here prepared to listen to his explanation and maybe even to reconcile. He had come to try to trick me into giving him a check. I felt physically ill. He pressed on.

'I just want to make things right between us,' he said with a half smile.

I stared at him for a long time, then I smiled at him slowly.

'You know what?' I said. I suddenly felt calm. 'I've been thinking about it. And I want to make things right between us too.'

'Really?' he asked hopefully.

'Oh, yes.' I stood up from the table. In one smooth motion, I picked up my full glass of Coke and flung it into Tom's face, drenching him in a shower of sticky coldness.

He jumped up, his chair clattering to the floor behind him. Around us, people stopped eating and stared, but I hardly noticed.

'What the hell?' Tom demanded furiously, holding his arms out to his side and shaking the soda off. His face dripped with beads of brown liquid, and his hair was drenched. He looked like a drowned rat. A pathetic, hairy, repulsive drowned rat. I smiled.

'I thought you wanted to make things right between us,' I calmly repeated. I shrugged and grinned as he glared at me. 'Well, that was a start.'

Still smiling, I turned on my heel and marched out of the restaurant, my head held high. I'd been foolish to think anything good could ever happen between us again. I knew that now, and I knew I wouldn't turn back.

'You go, girl!' a woman murmured to me as I stormed out of the dining room.

'Thanks,' I said as I kept walking. 'I will.'

The Sexy Siren

Wendy took me out that weekend, and for the first time since last Saturday – maybe even for the first time in a year – I finally felt like things were okay. I didn't need Tom. I didn't need anyone who would treat me like that. And as Wendy's blossoming romance with Jean Michel proved, you never knew when you were going to run into Mr Right.

Or at least *Mr Right Now*. Heck, at this point, I would have settled for Mr Maybe, or even Mr Slim Chance if he actually showed me some attention. But no such luck.

On Sunday, Wendy came over and helped me clean out the closet. Everything that belonged to Tom was thrown in big green garbage bags. Then, on second thought, we went through the bags and pulled out all the items I'd purchased for Tom the times we'd gone shopping and his credit card hadn't gone through. All the shirts I'd bought to surprise him, the ties I'd bought because I was thinking of him, the stain-resistant Van Heusen khakis I'd bought because I was sick of scrubbing ink stains out of his pants before trudging them off to the laundromat. By the time we extracted the clothes I'd bought for him, mounds of shirts, socks, boxers, pants, and ties lay strewn across my living room floor.

Wendy grinned.

'What do you want to do with them?' she asked. I smiled. It wasn't like they belonged to him. He'd gotten them under false pretenses, while pretending to be a faithful, sensitive boyfriend. Which he obviously was not.

'I can think of a few things,' I muttered. We settled on hacking a few of the ties into satisfying little pieces with a pair of scissors, then we bagged up the rest of the clothing to take to Goodwill. As for the clothes Tom had actually purchased for himself, we put them in a heap outside my apartment, and Wendy called to leave a message on his cell phone.

'Your clothes are on Claire's doorstep, and they'll be there only until ten o'clock tonight,' she chirped. 'If you want them, you'll have to come get them before then.' After she hung up the phone, she turned to me. 'You don't need to sit around waiting, wondering when he'll show up. If he doesn't come tonight, those clothes go in the incinerator.'

Wendy called a locksmith who came quickly and changed my locks. He gave me new keys, and Wendy pressed my old key into my palm.

'Throw it in a fountain or something,' she said. 'Maybe it'll bring you good luck.' It couldn't hurt, I had to admit. It would be hard for my luck to get much worse.

We set off for Goodwill, each of us hauling a plastic bag full of things I'd bought for Tom. After we dropped them off, Wendy insisted on treating me to dinner, to celebrate getting rid of Tom once and for all. We took the subway uptown and made a quick trip to Rockefeller Center, so I could throw my old key into the fountain. There it settled, alongside mounds of pennies carrying wishes from their previous owners.

'What did you wish for?' Wendy asked me as we walked away.

'I can't tell you, or it won't come true,' I said playfully. But I had wished that I would never again settle for someone who didn't treat me like I deserved to be treated.

Oh, and I added a wish to have sex again sometime before I hit thirty. After all, a key is bigger than a penny. I figure I was owed at least two wishes.

Over dinner (which Wendy paid for on a credit card that didn't bounce), we laughed and talked, and toasted freedom and self-respect. Cute waiters smiled at me, and I noticed. They smiled at Wendy, and she seemed genuinely oblivious.

How the tables had turned.

Back at my apartment, the doorstep was bare. Tom had come to get his things. Relief swept through me. I didn't owe him another phone call, another encounter, another smidgen of contact in any form.

'To Tom being gone forever,' Wendy said triumphantly, popping the cork in a bottle of champagne we had picked up on the way home.

'I'll toast to that!' I said, raising my glass. 'And to my apartment being *my* apartment again.'

'Well, I was meaning to talk to you about that,' Wendy said, cocking her head to the side and smiling at me. 'Now that Jean Michel and I are officially dating, I won't be eating out quite as much, and I have the feeling I'll have a bit more money for rent. I was wondering if you might be interested in a new roommate?'

'Oh my gosh, yes!' I exclaimed, setting my champagne flute down and hugging her. She hugged me back, and we both laughed and jumped up and down with excitement. 'Really? I would love for you to move in! I can't believe it! Do you mean it? We can turn the office into your bedroom.'

'Really? You sure you want a roommate?'

'Yes! Yes! Yes!' We toasted again.

After Wendy had gone home for the night, I drifted happily into a dreamless sleep.

The phone rang on Tuesday morning at 6:45, jarring me out of only the second pleasant sleep I'd had in months. My first thought was that if it was Tom again, I'd kill him. What was with this new trend of shaking me out of bed at the crack of dawn? I was *not* a morning person.

I grumpily answered the phone and was surprised to hear not Tom's voice, but my mother's.

'How dare you?' she demanded, without even a hello. I sat up in confusion and rubbed my eyes. I looked at the clock again, just to make sure I hadn't imagined the time. Nope, it was now 6:46 a.m. I cleared my throat.

'Um, good morning,' I said sleepily.

'I can't believe you'd embarrass me like this, young lady,' my mother said immediately. 'I am just stunned at your behavior.'

I pulled the phone away from my ear and stared at it for a moment. Then I put it back to my ear. I couldn't imagine what was going on.

'What are you talking about?' I asked finally.

'Don't play innocent with me,' my mother said angrily. I took a deep breath, scanning my brain for any offending activities I might have taken part in, but I came up blank.

'I really don't know what you're talking about,' I said finally.

'Your aunt Cecilia just called me,' my mother said slowly, her voice icy. 'She was on her way to work when she saw a copy of that horrible tabloid *Tattletale*. How dare you embarrass me that way?'

My heart was suddenly pounding although I still had no idea what she was talking about. But I had a sinking feeling in the pit of my stomach. I closed my eyes, and all I could see was a vision of a smug, smirking Sidra DeSimon.

'What was in *Tattletale*?' I asked slowly. This couldn't be good.

'Oh, I think you know,' my mother said coldly. 'If you want to shack up with a movie star, that's just fine with me. But when you tarnish our good family name by being splashed across the cover of a tabloid magazine as Cole Brannon's *sex toy*, that is unforgivable. I did not raise you to be a slut.'

Suddenly, I couldn't breathe.

A sex toy?

Cole Brannon's sex toy?

'Mom, I never did anything with him,' I finally squeaked through a closed throat. My palms were sweaty, my mouth dry. 'I swear. Are you sure it was me? Was Cecilia sure?'

'She's sure,' my mother said, her voice icy. 'You're right on the cover, Claire. How am I supposed to live that down? What am I supposed to say when your eighty-five-year-old grandmother sees you on the cover of a tabloid, looking like a cheap hooker?'

'Oh my God,' I murmured, too stunned to respond to the fact that my own mother was accusing me of looking like a hooker. My heart was racing. I finally spoke. 'This is all a big mix-up, Mom, I swear. I interviewed Cole Brannon, but that's it. *Tattletale* is a tabloid, Mom. It's not real news. You can't believe everything they print.'

'I don't know what to say to you, Claire,' my mother said after a moment's pause. 'You're clearly not the same young lady I raised.'

Her words stung. I took a deep breath and tried again.

'Mom, none of this is true,' I said. 'You have to believe me.'

'I am so disappointed in you,' she said coldly. Then she hung up without waiting for a response. I sat there stunned for a moment, holding the phone to my ear until the dial tone snapped me into action.

'Shit, shit, shit,' I mumbled, jumping out of bed and rushing into the closet. I threw on a pair of jeans and a faded sweatshirt, the first clothes I could find.

I barreled quickly down the four flights of stairs, jogged down the hallway, and burst out onto the street, which hadn't yet begun to bustle with people. I pushed my way inside the convenience store on Second Avenue and Fourth Street, scanned the media rack, and snatched *Tattletale* from its place on the shelf.

I froze as I looked at the cover.

On the upper left corner of the tabloid, there was a black-and-white photo of Cole and me, emerging from the men's room at *Mod*. It looked like a still taken from one of the magazine's security cameras, which meant that someone at *Mod* – no doubt Sidra – had to have sent it in to *Tattletale*. Cole had his arm around me as we emerged from the doorway, and I was looking up at him. It looked damning. But far worse was the headline with it that screamed: MOD EDITOR IS COLE BRANNON'S NEW SEX TOY!

'Ohhhh shit!' I cursed, loud enough for the man behind the counter to look up in surprise.

'Everything okay, miss?' he asked. I grimaced.

'No,' I muttered. With shaky hands, I put a copy of *Tattletale* down on the counter and gave him a dollar for it. 'Everything is *not* okay.'

I stormed out of the store, flipping through the pages as I did. I stopped dead in my tracks as I reached page 32, where there was a whole two-page spread about our 'illicit affair'. Standing there in the middle of the sidewalk, I stared, feeling my chest tighten as I took it all in.

Photos were splashed across the page, along with a small story. There was a picture of the amazing bouquet Cole had sent, and a close-up reproduction of the taped-together card that had come with it – courtesy of Sidra, I'm sure. There was a paparazzi shot of Cole getting into the taxi with me. There was even a photo of me leaving my apartment building alone.

'Cole Brannon Finds New Sex Toy,' the print clearly said. Beneath it, the copy read, '*Mod* senior entertainment editor Claire Reilly is the movie star's latest fling – a *Tattletale* exclusive!'

I was feeling sick as I scanned the snarky text.

Tattletale spies have learned that Hollywood's hottest hunk, Cole Brannon, is getting busy with Claire Reilly, twenty-six, a senior editor at *Mod* magazine, which will be running a cover story about Brannon in their August issue.

'They met when she interviewed him for the August cover story,' says a *Mod* insider. 'She talks about him all the time. She says he's great in bed.'

Ms Reilly has worked at *Rolling Stone* and *People* as a celebrity writer. She brought her talents to *Mod* eighteen months ago when she joined their staff as the senior entertainment editor. She is the youngest senior editor at a top-thirty magazine.

Tattletale has learned that Mr Brannon and Ms Reilly were spotted leaving his hotel together, leaving her apartment together, and ducking into the men's room at *Mod* magazine's New York offices together.

Quickie, anyone?

'They looked quite cozy together,' says cab driver Omar Sirpal, who drove Ms Reilly and Mr Brannon from his hotel to her apartment last week. 'He even fed her breakfast in my taxi.'

Ms Reilly was recently estranged from her live-in boyfriend, so the romance with Mr Brannon sounds a bit like a rebound to us here at *Tattletale*. As for Mr Brannon, it looks like he's fallen head-over-heels for his new sex kitten, who joins the ranks of Kylie Dane and publicist Ivana Donatelli in his cast of lovers.

'He sent her flowers last week,' says our *Mod* source. 'She told everyone in the office who they were from and why he'd sent them. Apparently, he appreciated all the attention she'd been giving him, if you know what I mean.'

What kind of attention might that be? We don't know, but we can guess. Ms Reilly and Mr Brannon were seen heading into the men's room at *Mod* together last Thursday and emerging together fifteen minutes later, looking embarrassed and satisfied, according to our spy.

'We all knew what was going on in there,' says the *Mod* insider. 'If it wasn't obvious enough, we could hear them going at it.'

Who will be the next flame for Hollywood's hottest, busiest bachelor? Check out next week's *Tattletale* to find out.

I stared at the text in horror for a long time after I finished reading it. I read it once more, as if it might have changed to something less damning by the second go-round.

'Oh . . . my . . . God.' I was frozen in the middle of the sidewalk and had no idea what to do next. It would be my word against that of *Tattletale*'s source, who was surely Sidra DeSimon. Everything damning in the text had come directly from her. I was sure of it.

After all, why wouldn't she have run to *Tattletale* once she had damning evidence. They'd pay her big money for a story like this. It would increase her status with them. It would likely thrill her sister Estella. And it would take me down a notch or two.

Basically, I was screwed. Obviously, Sidra hadn't told Margaret about Cole yet, but no doubt Margaret would have been alerted to the *Tattletale* article by the time she got into the office today. After all, the name of her magazine – not to mention my face – was splashed across the cover of one of the country's most prominent tabloids. And although Margaret pretended to be aloof and high-class, we all knew she secretly loved everything from *Star* to the *National Enquirer*. *Tattletale* was always spread across her desk on Tuesday mornings. How could she miss it?

I gulped back the lump in my throat as I realized that I would be fired today. Tears sprang to my eyes at the unfairness of it all.

Even worse, what would Cole think? He'd surely think

I had something to do with this. I was suddenly stiff with embarrassment and disappointment. Sure, he was a liar, but now it would look like I had lied too – and to a trashy tabloid. I was sure he would think I was behind the horrid story of our alleged affair.

I looked up, realizing I was standing in the middle of the sidewalk and that passersby were looking at me like I was crazy. Maybe I was. I quickly snapped the tabloid shut and hurried back down the street to my apartment, still in panic mode.

Forty minutes later, after a tortuously long subway ride to Brooklyn – during which I'd memorized the entire article with a rising sense of panic – I was pounding on Wendy's front door. It seemed to take her forever to answer, but she finally did, dressed in a T-shirt and flannel pants, rubbing sleep out of her eyes.

'Claire!' She yawned, her eyes finally opening all the way. She reached up and smoothed down her frizzy red hair, which had developed into a cross between a halo and an Afro as she slept. 'What are you doing here?'

Without a word, I thrust my copy of *Tattletale* at her. She took one look at the cover, and when she looked back at me, she was wide-awake.

'Oh no,' she said softly. 'Is it as bad as it looks?'

I nodded slowly.

Wendy quickly flipped the magazine open. She gasped as she saw the two-page spread. Her eyes scanned the short article; then she looked up at me in horror.

'This is awful,' she said softly.

'I know,' I said. She took one last look at the magazine and handed it back to me. 'What am I going to do?'

'I don't know,' she said. We just looked at each other for a moment; then she straightened up, gesturing for me to follow her inside. I felt like I was in a trance.

'At least it'll piss Tom off,' Wendy said helpfully as I followed her down the hall to the kitchen. I tried a weak smile.

'At least there's that,' I agreed. I sighed and looked back down at the tabloid in my hands. 'This is Sidra's work.' Wendy and I sat down at her kitchen table. When she looked up at me, her face was hard.

'It has to be,' she agreed.

'Why is that woman out to get me? It isn't enough that her sister stole my boyfriend?'

'Actually,' Wendy clarified, 'her sister did you a service, if you think about it.'

'True,' I said sourly. My hands felt icy, and I could hear the blood rushing through my ears. My body was suddenly tense.

'I have to do something,' I said. Wendy looked at me and nodded. I looked down at *Tattletale*, then back at her. 'But what? What am I supposed to do?'

'I don't know,' Wendy said quietly.

We weren't any closer to reaching a solution when we boarded the subway to work thirty minutes later, but at least I felt better knowing that I wasn't alone. I knew I'd have to brace myself for stares and whispers as I walked into the office, but Wendy had promised to walk in beside me and shoot deadly looks at anyone who said anything inappropriate.

'I'll probably get fired today, you know,' I said miserably as the subway rattled on belowground. Wendy and I were wedged together between a portly woman in an oversized suit from the '80s and a tall man who had a pointy nose and suspenders pulling his pants up above his waist. All around us, newspapers flipped open and closed as New Yorkers prepared themselves for a day at work. I tried to look down and hide my face as I noticed a few copies of *Tattletale* open in the car.

'You don't know that,' Wendy said firmly. But her words weren't much comfort.

When we entered the office at just past 9 a.m., all eyes were indeed on me, as I'd expected them to be. I was totally mortified. Wendy squeezed my arm gently as we began the long walk down the corridor to our adjoining cubicles.

'It's going to be okay,' she whispered as copies of *Tattletale* lined our way. Dozens of pairs of eyes peered at me from over the top of the tabloid.

It was like walking into that dream where you show up at your office naked. But somehow it was worse – and I was wide-awake.

I wanted to run, screaming down the hallway that it wasn't true, that it was all a lie. But as Wendy had reminded me, protesting too much would only make it look like I had something to hide. So instead, I settled for holding my head high and pretending I didn't notice the stares, the whispers, the eyes burning holes in my back. Wendy kept a gentle hand on my arm until we reached my cubicle.

'Just ignore them and try to get your work done, okay?' she said softly as I sat down. I nodded. Easier said than done.

As I picked up my phone to play my voice mail, I was surprised to hear that I already had twelve messages. It was only just past nine in the morning. I blanched as I listened to the first one.

'Hello, Ms Reilly,' the voice began. 'This is Sal Martino, a producer at *Access Hollywood*. We're very interested in your story. As you of course know, Cole Brannon is huge news right now. Call me back at 212-555-5678 as soon as you can.'

The second message was from *Hollywood Tonight*.

'This is Jen Sutton from *Hollywood Tonight*,' she began in a high, chirpy voice. 'Like, what a great story. We love it. Young, high-powered editor swept off her feet by Hollywood's hottest hunk. We'd love to get Robb Robertson out there to interview you right away. You're hot news right now, girl! Call me at 212-555-3232.'

The remaining ten messages were along the same lines. Sal Martino had called back twice. The *National Enquirer* was offering to pay me for my story. *Access Hollywood* wanted to send Billy Bush out to interview me. Page Six wanted something exclusive. Even the city's NBC affiliate wanted in on the action, requesting that I let them send a camera crew to my apartment that night to do a live shot for the eleven o'clock news. I groaned as I hung up the phone in horror. I could practically feel my world crumbling beneath my feet.

I was about to stand up and walk over to Wendy's cubicle when my phone rang. I grabbed it quickly.

'*Mod* magazine, Claire Reilly speaking,' I answered.

'Oh, Claire, I cannot believe I caught you in,' chirped a voice that I instantly recognized from my voice mail. 'This is Jen Sutton, from *Hollywood Tonight*.' She paused, waiting for me to respond.

'Hello,' I said finally.

'Hey, girl!' Jen continued cheerfully. 'I am, like, so jealous of you. This is so cool! You're, like, one of us. A journalist, breaking all the rules to sleep with the hottest guy in Hollywood. That's so awesome!'

'But I didn't—' I started to protest, but Jen rambled on like she hadn't heard me.

'Robb Robertson is so excited about this story,' she chirped. 'You know Robb, right? He's, like, our most well-known reporter, and he is so all over this story. You are so hot right now, girl.'

'But I didn't—' Again, my protest was cut off. Did she ever stop for air?

'Everyone wants your story,' she went on, her voice climbing an octave – perhaps from lack of oxygen. 'We can promise you star treatment. We'll make you up, send you through wardrobe, the whole nine yards. It'll be so glam.' Finally, she stopped and waited for a response. I drew in a breath.

'No,' I said. 'I didn't sleep with him. I didn't sleep with Cole Brannon. Nothing happened, I swear.' Jen was silent for a minute.

'We'll even let you see the questions ahead of time,' she bubbled on like she hadn't heard what I'd said. 'I know Robb seems kind of tough on TV and all, but we'll let you see the question list, and I'll make him promise not to spring anything on you, okay?'

'No,' I said firmly. Was she deaf? 'Not okay. There's no story! I didn't sleep with Cole Brannon.' Jen was silent for another moment.

'Whatever you say,' she said, her voice suddenly icy. 'But we're going with the story whether you cooperate or not.'

'But how? There's nothing to support it!'

'We're a professional news organization,' Jen snapped back. 'We'll find something. Give me a call if you change your mind before four p.m.' Then she hung up. I was left stunned, holding the handset.

'What was that?' Wendy asked over the cubicle, looking concerned.

'*Hollywood Tonight*,' I said, looking at her in horror. 'They're going to report the story whether I cooperate or not. And I have messages from just about everyone else on my voice mail.'

'Oh no,' said Wendy softly.

'Oh yes.'

My heart nearly stopped when my intercom buzzed at ten o'clock. It was Cassie, snarling at me that Margaret wanted to see me immediately. Apparently my boss didn't want to waste any time putting me in my place.

'Want me to come?' Wendy asked.

'No.' I sighed. 'This is something I have to deal with myself.'

I stood up slowly from my chair and started down the hallway to meet my fate.

The Cold-Hearted Snake

My walk to Margaret's office was somewhat anticlimactic, as I'd made a similar trek just last week, when I'd also been convinced I was about to be fired. Today, I felt a grim certainty that this really would be the end of the line for me.

I'd probably never work in magazines again.

Instead of keeping me waiting, Margaret had Cassie usher me in immediately.

As I sat down in one of the huge chairs facing her desk, shrinking down to the size of a child, the fear that I'd managed to push away started to return. Margaret looked down at me, perfect in a rose tailored suit, her dark hair blown out. We sat in silence for a moment. By the time she finally opened her mouth to speak to me, my heart was beating so hard I was afraid she could hear it. To my own ears, it sounded like the pounding of a battle drum, although I kept reminding myself that I wasn't actually going to battle. It sure felt like I was.

'So I assume you've guessed by this point that I've seen this morning's *Tattletale*,' Margaret said flatly, opening our meeting without any ado.

'Um, yes.' Boy, I was articulate this morning.

'And I assume that you, too, have seen it,' she added unnecessarily. This time, I just nodded, unable to speak, thanks to the lump that had risen in my throat.

'Uh-huh,' I finally gurgled, because she seemed like

she was waiting for a verbal response before going on. She looked me carefully up and down as my heart pounded more quickly. My palms felt sweaty, and I could feel droplets of nervous sweat cropping up along my hairline. The hair on my arms was standing up, and I was trying hard not to squirm. I felt like crawling under my chair and hiding from what was to come.

'You've been working for me eighteen months now,' Margaret said slowly, as my heart continued to pound. 'So I'm quite sure you know that when I assign a story for *Mod* magazine, I expect my writers and editors to conform to certain standards.' I nodded again.

'Uh-huh,' I gurgled again. She was silent for another moment. I could feel rivulets of sweat starting to drip down my back.

'This article in *Tattletale* would not have been my idea of how my writers and editors should be behaving, however,' she said slowly, her dark eyes boring into me. I squirmed uncomfortably.

'I know,' I said. 'I'm so sorry. But I swear I didn't sleep with Cole Brannon.'

Margaret waved her slender hand dismissively. She looked like she hadn't heard me.

'In any case, I've given this a lot of thought,' she said. She held up a copy of *Tattletale*, and I looked away. I closed my eyes and braced myself to be fired.

'Claire, this is pure genius,' Margaret said from somewhere off in the distance. I sat there confused for a moment, my eyes still scrunched closed. I felt sure I had become delusional or, at best, that I'd heard her wrong. But when I finally opened my eyes, blinking twice, I was greeted by a big grin splashed across Margaret's face.

'Huh?' I asked, dumbfounded. Margaret's smile just widened. Had she gone crazy? Maybe it was that Mad Cow disease I'd heard about.

'This is the best publicity we could have asked for, Claire!' the mad cow enthused. She tapped the cover of

Tattletale for emphasis. 'This is wonderful! When the magazine comes out next month, everyone will rush out to buy it and get the story behind your romance with Cole Brannon! It's not what I would have expected from you, Claire, but I love it.'

I couldn't grin back. I was flabbergasted.

'But I didn't do anything,' I said finally. This was too bizarre to take in. I wrinkled my brow and studied her in consternation.

'Oh, Claire, no need to be modest with me,' Margaret pushed on, steamrolling right over my words. 'I must admit, I am a bit disappointed at being scooped by a tabloid, but what a great way to get the *Mod* name out there. I've already gotten calls from some of the company's biggest investors, and they're all terribly intrigued.'

'Great,' I said weakly. I was baffled. I forced a wan smile.

'Do you know what this means, Claire?' Margaret asked, leaning forward hungrily. I shook my head slowly. She licked her lips and grinned at me. 'It means we're going to pass *Cosmopolitan*, Claire. For the first time in *Mod*'s history. We're going to pass *Cosmopolitan* in circulation for our August issue. Thanks to your fling with Cole Brannon, Claire, *Mod* will fly off the newsstands.'

'But . . .' I tried to formulate a response, but my brain didn't seem able to connect with my mouth.

'Because of your hard work, Claire, I've decided to give you another raise,' Margaret said, beaming. I started to protest, but Margaret interrupted me. 'I wish more of my editors would take your kind of initiative, Claire. Well done.'

I opened and closed my mouth wordlessly a few times, like a fish. Then I just kept it closed as Margaret chattered on about circulation figures, flings with celebrities, and her own crush on Robert Redford that she always wished she'd pursued. I sat stunned until she was finished. I valiantly issued one last denial, then sat back mutely as she rolled over that one too, dismissing it with a tinkling laugh. I was completely flabbergasted by the time she ushered me enthusiastically out of her office, asking me to keep up the good work.

'Oh my gosh, are you okay?' Wendy rushed out of her cubicle to embrace me in the hallway as I walked back to my desk like a zombie. I didn't respond right away, because I was still in shock. Wendy took my silence and my battle-weary demeanor to mean the worst. 'Oh my gosh, she fired you, didn't she? God, Claire, I am so pissed off. I'm going in there right now to quit myself.' She looked angry and defensive, and she reached down to give me another tight hug.

'No,' I finally said. I felt like I was walking in a fog.

'No what?' asked Wendy, confused. 'Hey, are you okay?' I didn't answer. I looked down and then back at Wendy.

'No, I didn't get fired,' I said finally. I watched her eyebrows shoot up in surprise.

'What happened, then?' she asked. The answer to this still confused me.

'I got another raise,' I said slowly. 'I don't know what just happened.'

By noon I'd stopped answering my phone, because every single call I had taken was from a reporter or a producer looking for the 'real' scoop on my love affair with Cole Brannon.

I realized by lunchtime that the calls were much more than just an annoyance. None of the dozens of people I'd heard from today took me seriously. In the space of a few hours, I'd somehow gone from being a reporter worthy of respect – even if you didn't believe *Mod* was a bastion of great journalism – to a common tramp who was bent on climbing the ladder of celebrity, who'd gotten lucky by landing Cole Brannon on the first rung.

In other areas of the corporate world, women

sometimes made their way to the top by sleeping with their bosses. In the magazine world, it was just as effective to sleep with someone powerful or prominent outside the company – an actor, a politician, a rock star – and let them pull the strings for you.

And now, the world was sure it was true in my case. I had been so careful to always be and appear appropriate. And now it looked like I'd just climbed the ladder with the help of Cole Brannon – instead of my own hard work.

During lunch, which I took alone at my desk after silencing the ringer on my office phone and turning off my cell phone, I thought about Cole Brannon and wondered whether he'd seen today's *Tattletale* yet.

He was probably furious at me. I chewed nervously on the nail of my index finger. He would be mortified. He didn't date women like me. He certainly didn't sleep with women like me. And now he probably thought that I'd lured him into the bathroom just to get a good shot for the cover of *Tattletale*.

I shouldn't have cared, of course. He had lied to me and was probably off somewhere sleeping with a married actress. But I couldn't let it go.

Breathing hard, I pulled open my desk and rummaged through until I found the notebook I had used as a backup when I interviewed Cole last Saturday. I flipped through until I found the piece of paper with the cell phone number he'd given me. The one I swore to myself I'd never use. But this was an emergency. I had to tell him the *Tattletale* story wasn't my doing.

Nervously, I dialed the number, noticing abstractedly that he still had a 617 area code – from Boston – instead of a 323 from L.A., or a 646 from Manhattan, as I would have expected.

As the phone rang twice, time seemed to slow down. I could feel my heart pounding, my palms sweating, my mouth going dry. Maybe I shouldn't be calling him. Maybe I should hang up.

'Hello?' a sleepy female voice answered midway through the third ring. I was too surprised to say anything for a moment. I looked down at the phone to see if I'd dialed correctly. Indeed, I had. 'Hello?' said the voice again, sounding a bit perturbed.

'Uh, hello,' I finally said. 'I'm looking for Cole.' Why was a woman answering his phone? More important, why was it making me feel so jealous?

'Who's calling?' snapped the woman on the other end.

'This is Claire Reilly,' I said timidly. There was silence on the other end. Finally, the woman laughed, low and deep in her throat.

'Well, if it isn't Claire Reilly,' the woman said with what sounded like an edge of anger. 'Claire, this is Ivana Donatelli. Cole's publicist. I'm sure you know who I am.'

I gulped and started to sweat. What was she doing there? Why was she answering his cell phone? Maybe I was right, and the *Tattletale* photos of her and Cole together *had* meant something. Now I felt like an idiot. It would look like I was calling him because I was infatuated or something.

'Hi, Ivana,' I said, trying to sound as friendly and innocuous as possible. 'I was just calling about—'

'*Tattletale*.' Ivana completed my sentence for me.

'Yes, I—'

She cut me off.

'I was going to call you about that too,' she said smoothly. 'But I see you've beaten me to it.' I couldn't read her tone of voice. It was very even, not hinting at what she was thinking.

'I was just calling to apologize to Cole,' I stammered. 'I swear, I had nothing to do with this. Nothing happened with me and Cole, and I wanted him to know that—'

She cut me off sharply again.

'Cole and I just got out of bed, Claire,' Ivana said smoothly. My heart dropped in my chest. 'He's in the shower, so I'm afraid he can't take your call at the moment.

Besides, I think you've had quite enough to do with Cole Brannon.'

'But . . .' I started to protest weakly. My God, they *were* sleeping together.

'I believe he'll draw whatever conclusions he will about you and your moral character,' she continued smoothly. 'As for me, I'd appreciate it if you'd refrain from contacting either one of us in the future.'

'No, Ivana, you don't understand,' I said quickly. 'I swear, I had nothing to do with this. Let me explain . . .'

'No, let *me* explain,' she said, her voice suddenly taking on a menacing tone. 'I am disgusted with you. I am disgusted at your willingness to take such blatant advantage of my generosity in granting you an interview with Cole. You'd better hope to God that your little story in *Mod* is perfect, or I'll have my lawyers on your ass faster than you can imagine.'

'But—'

'Now you listen to me,' she said, cutting me off, her voice slow and deliberate. 'Never call me again. Never contact Cole again. I can't imagine a reporter behaving more unprofessionally, and I am disgusted by you. If you ever contact either of us, I will make it my mission to make your life miserable, understood?'

'But . . .'

'Cole Brannon would never look twice at a woman like you,' she hissed. 'Good day, Ms Reilly.' She hung up the phone before I could say another word. I sat stunned for a good few minutes. I had no idea what else to do.

Cole Brannon hated me. I was sure of it. And he *was* sleeping with Ivana Donatelli after all. I could hardly believe it. I had just started to believe that it was possible he was telling the truth. But I should have known better.

I fought back the tears that welled in my eyes. But eventually, they overflowed. There's only so much one person can take in a single morning.

*

At just past 4 p.m., after a dozen more voice mails from various reporters and producers had pushed me beyond the limits of my patience, I did what I should have done a week before. I stood up with all the fury I had accumulated over the course of the day, and, without saying anything to Wendy or anyone else, I marched directly to the fashion department to find Sidra.

'Well, look who's here,' she purred as I turned the corner into her office. She was wearing a black pantsuit and five-inch heels – she had her long legs stretched out, her feet propped up on her desk, when I stormed in.

'What the hell do you think you're doing?' I demanded without any pretense. My voice didn't sound like my own, but then again, I wasn't feeling much like myself.

Sidra looked me slowly up and down, then a slow smile spread across her lips (which looked like they'd been injected with another shot of collagen in the past few days). She slowly swung her legs down to the floor. I clenched and unclenched my fists.

'I can't imagine what you're talking about,' she said, batting her eyes innocently. She lazily reached over with one long, perfectly manicured finger and pressed a button on her intercom. 'Sally, Samantha,' she said, still looking at me with a little smile. 'Come into my office. You'll never believe who's here. It's *Tattletale*'s new "It" girl!' She removed her finger from the intercom and looked me pensively up and down. 'You certainly don't *look* like an "It" girl,' she said with a sly smile.

'Screw you,' I said. I was so angry, it was hard to breathe. Sidra raised an eyebrow in mock surprise.

'What?' she asked innocently. 'Profanity from the mouth of Cole Brannon's new love interest? How inappropriate!'

Just then, Samantha and Sally appeared in the doorway, standing so close together they looked like Siamese twins. Like their fearless leader, they were both decked out from head to toe in fashionable black – Sally in Prada, Samantha in Escada. I wondered for a moment if Sidra called them each morning to issue a Triplet Dress Code for the day. That would explain why they all arrived at the office late, nearly always looking like they'd come off the couture assembly line.

'Claire!' Samantha purred. 'We just couldn't believe it . . .'

'. . . when we saw you in *Tattletale*.' Sally finished the sentence that had apparently initiated in the brain they shared.

'I know,' Sidra joined in with a smirk. 'It was quite a shock to all of us. I never would have expected such a thing.'

'Just stop it!' I barked, feeling my face heat up with anger. 'Do I look stupid? I know you did this!'

'What?' Sidra feigned shock. '*Moi?* Why on earth would you think such a thing?'

By this time, Samantha had walked over to Sidra's left side, and Sally flanked her right side. For a moment, as I stared at them in their matching black designer uniforms, they reminded me eerily of old pictures of Saddam Hussein and his two evil sons.

'I don't know,' I responded. 'I don't know why you would do it. Jealousy maybe?'

'*Me?* Jealous of *you?*' Sidra's laugh was cold and heartless. She was immediately joined by lifeless chuckles from her two disciples.

'Why are you out to get me?' I demanded. I was starting to feel outnumbered again. It reminded me slightly of elementary school, and I had sudden vague memories of being ganged up on and excluded from kickball games by the 'cool' kids. Sidra laughed again.

'My, my, my, this is going to your head, I think,' she said coolly. 'The universe doesn't revolve around you, Claire, dear. Just because something happens, it doesn't mean anyone's out to get you.'

'Why, then?'

'You're playing with fire,' Sidra said, leaning forward, her voice low and menacing. 'And you're going to keep getting burned until you learn to walk away.' Sally and Samantha nodded their agreement as Sidra leaned back, looking satisfied with herself.

'What are you talking about?' I asked. I could hear my voice rise an octave to soprano. 'I'm not playing with anything. I never was. If I remember correctly, your sister was screwing my boyfriend. You know as well as I do that I didn't sleep with Cole Brannon.'

'Oh, it didn't look like that to me,' Sidra said, smiling knowingly at me. Samantha and Sally tittered in unison. I clenched my fists by my sides.

'This had better be the end of this,' I said finally. I exhaled and felt suddenly weary. 'Fine, you've gotten me back for whatever offense you've imagined. But now we're even, okay? Whatever I've done to you has surely been canceled out by this.'

'I still don't know what you're talking about,' Sidra singsonged slyly. I ignored her.

'Just stop this now,' I said wearily. 'I'm serious. You've gotten what you wanted. I'm mortified. Pat yourself on the back. Mission accomplished.' As Sidra and I stared at each other, our eyes locked in some kind of juvenile staring contest, I felt some of the anger go out of me. This was ridiculous. We were grown women, and we were acting like schoolchildren at war on the playground. 'Just leave me alone, Sidra,' I said finally. 'I'll stay out of your way if you stay out of mine.'

'Deal,' she said icily. As I turned and started to walk away, she called after me.

'Oh, Claire? Would you like me to give your regards to Tom?'

I froze in my tracks but didn't turn around.

'He's having dinner at my parents' house tonight,' she continued. 'My sister thought it was time she brought him home to meet the family.'

The words hit me like a cold slap across the face.

'Yes, give him my regards,' I said softly without turning around. I couldn't. I wouldn't.

I walked away, leaving Sidra and her designer henchmen behind in their weird little world that I wanted no part of.

The Ingenue

The night the *Tattletale* story appeared had to have been the worst night of my life. Wendy was nice enough to stay with me, but even her comfort didn't help much when I saw my face splashed across *Access Hollywood*, *Entertainment Tonight*, and two editions of the local news. Friends I'd gone to high school with in Georgia called, drawling in excited tones about how they couldn't believe 'Little Clairey Reilly' had hooked up with Cole Brannon. My mother called to chastise me yet again, just in case I hadn't gotten the point that morning, and even my little sister Carolyn called to tell me, 'Everybody knows, Claire. It's just soooo embarrassing for me.'

Life eventually started returning to a semi-normal state. I never heard from *Access Hollywood* or *Entertainment Tonight* again, and although I kept a close eye on Page Six and *Tattletale* for the next few weeks, there wasn't another mention of me. I started to breathe more easily.

Although my mother hadn't apologized, she was at least starting to act more normal. Well, normal for her, which might not necessarily qualify as normal in anyone else's world. Still, she was back to her old ways, nagging me about finding a husband before I hit thirty (geez, I still had four years to go!), picking at me for being so career-oriented, and criticizing me for putting on a few pounds.

The next few weeks of work, however, were hellish. There was a sudden chill in the air when it came to me securing celeb interviews for *Mod*. Publicists who had always called right back were suddenly no longer available; interviews that had been set in stone were mysteriously canceled; and I caught coworkers gossiping about me in the break room three times.

On top of that, it was pretty rotten to have everyone believe I'd gotten laid by the hottest guy in America when in reality, I hadn't had sex in so long I probably wouldn't remember how to any more.

Each week I struggled to meet deadlines I'd never had a problem with before. I spent hours waiting by the fax machine for responses to interview requests – sometimes for *faxed* interview answers from celebs who were suddenly 'too busy' to talk to me – and I worked late most days to overcompensate for the fact that my career seemed to be going steadily downhill.

Perhaps the worst work-related fallout from the whole Cole incident was that Margaret still seemed to believe the *Tattletale* story and treated me as though she expected my behavior to mirror that which the tabloid had attributed to me.

When I told her I was having trouble securing an interview with Orlando Bloom, who really shouldn't have been a problem, she had winked at me and said, 'I'm sure *you* can come up with a way to convince him.' When Jerry O'Connell canceled an interview with me, Margaret suggested wearing sexier lingerie. With Hugh Grant, her suggestion was to show a bit more cleavage.

It had been the same story for every male star I'd failed to snag in the past six weeks, and my continued denials that anything had happened between Cole and me seemed to always fall on deaf ears. Margaret had even referred to me twice in staff meetings as 'our little *Mod* vixen'. I had turned a decidedly un-vixen-like shade of red.

June and the first half of July were good months – outside of work, at least. Wendy moved in a week after the *Tattletale* article, like she'd promised, and I quickly discovered she was the best roommate I'd ever had. When she got home from work before I did – which was most nights, thanks to the increasing difficulty of my job – she often cooked dinner for us, and Jean Michel usually joined us when he had the night off. Her meals were always delicious, and she swore that all of her recipes were from scratch.

'I want to open my own restaurant someday,' she told me shyly. It always amazed me when I walked into my apartment and was greeted by the steamy smells of spices, meats, and baking bread.

The summer was a hot one. Wendy and I spent weekend days sunning and sipping lemonade in the Sheep Meadow in Central Park, riding the subway out to the ridiculous attractions of Coney Island, or wading into the water at Sea Bright or Highlands along the Jersey Shore.

As the weeks dragged on, I couldn't seem to shake being bothered by the fact I hadn't heard from Cole. Not once since the *Tattletale* article. I knew he thought it was my fault, which broke my heart. But he was obviously sleeping with Ivana. I knew I shouldn't care. But I did care. Too much.

He'd been nothing but nice with me, taking care of me when I got drunk, comforting me about Tom, and even coming by my office to make sure I was okay. And now he thought I'd paid him back by telling the tabloids that we had slept together. I'd probably embarrassed him beyond words. For a Hollywood star, it was probably mortifying to have everyone think you slept with some frumpy Plain Jane with a low-paying job, A-cup breasts, and clothes bought on sale at the Gap. I was definitely not normal Hollywood fare. He was used to sleeping with women like Kylie Dane – tall, curvaceous, flawlessly complexioned, perfectly dressed – or women like Ivana – coldly beautiful, oozing wealth, with flashing eyes and a throaty, sexy voice. It was stupid to think he'd even looked twice at me. The realization made me feel even more plain and boring than I already did.

It didn't help that everywhere I turned, I seemed to see him. He was on billboards all over the city. His face was on the sides of buses, and early trailers for his movie were on TV. Some nights I'd be flipping through the channels and see a rerun of the night he was on *Saturday Night Live*, or a romantic comedy in which he played the lead. It was like having salt rubbed in my wounds, and each time, I remembered with guilt how I'd left things with him. I'd practically told him I never wanted to see him again. After he'd gone out of his way to make sure I was okay.

I'd started dreaming about him sometimes, which scared me. I was sure it was because he seemed to surround me and because guilt over how things had ended still weighed on my unconscious. I finally talked myself into believing that when *Mod*'s August issue came out in a few days with my cover story about him, that would be it. I would send him several copies of the magazine along with a polite and formal note via his publicist, as I always did each month for the celeb featured on the cover. Then I could forget him once and for all. The article would be out. The *Tattletale* rumor was old news. I would no longer have any kind of connection to Cole Brannon.

The thought should have made me feel relieved, but it didn't.

And that scared me.

Journalism 101

Cover Stories

The second Wednesday in July started out like any other day, except perhaps a bit better. Two publicists called in the morning to confirm interviews with the actresses they represented, I'd already secured commitments from Molly Sims and Kirsten Dunst for the covers of the November and December issues, and I was almost done with the latest article Margaret had assigned me: 'How to Make Him Fall for You in Less Than a Week.'

I was feeling so good, I was barely worrying about the fact that the August issue would be released that day.

After all, it would almost be a relief to have my decidedly unsexual Cole Brannon article hit newsstands so I could be done with him once and for all. Maybe once the article was out, he would stop haunting my thoughts. I was still acutely aware that I hadn't heard from him. I knew he hated me.

The first copies, which would arrive bound in stacks of twenty-five, hadn't arrived by 12:30. I ducked out to lunch without worrying too much about it.

I had already paid for my Styrofoam container of salad and was sitting at an uncomfortably small table – wedged in the back of the Paris Cafe on Broadway and Forty-fifth Street – when Wendy called me on my cell phone.

'You'd better get back here,' she said as soon as I picked up. Her tone sounded nervous, and I sensed something ominous behind her words.

'What's wrong?' I asked, wondering if something had happened between her and Jean Michel. I had been afraid it was too good to last.

'Where are you now?' she asked instead of answering my question.

'At the Paris Cafe. Do you need me to come back?'

'Meet me in the courtyard outside our building as soon as you can,' she said tersely. 'I'll be right down.' She hung up before I could say another word. My heart pounding, I quickly threw out the remainder of my salad, grabbed my purse, and pushed my way out of the restaurant onto Broadway. As I waited to cross the street, I could see Wendy standing outside the building, her carrot hair blowing in the wind. In her hands, she held a magazine, which I guessed was the August issue of *Mod*. She was looking around nervously and hadn't spotted me yet.

'Hey,' I said, coming up behind Wendy and startling her. She jumped and turned quickly around, her eyes wide. I tried a smile. 'What's the big emergency?'

Wendy didn't smile back, which had to have been a first. A strange gnawing began in the pit of my stomach as I took in her nervous posture, her wide eyes, her serious expression. I strained to see the magazine in her hands, sensing that it was central to whatever was wrong, but she held the cover just out of my view.

This couldn't be good.

'Let's sit down,' she said finally, taking my arm and leading me to one of the cement planters in front of the building. I obediently sat and waited for Wendy to speak.

'Are you okay?' I finally asked. She looked at me for a moment, and without saying a word, thrust the magazine into my hands, a look of grim resignation on her face.

Sometimes in the movies, when something terrible is about to happen, the characters suddenly see everything in slow motion. A bullet inches toward a person's head, and he's able to watch it come, contemplating his life before it strikes him dead. A train is about to run over a young family in their car, but they're frozen in place, watching the barreling steam engine come toward them so slowly it feels like they could get out and run a mile before it hits.

In the first moment that I looked at the cover of the August issue of *Mod*, it felt like time had suddenly slowed for me too. In the mere seconds it took for me to scan the cover, the world seemed to suddenly stop moving. The sudden and intense rushing in my ears blocked out all the sounds I'd normally hear on a summer day: chattering theatergoers streaming into a matinee at the Winter Garden Theater across Broadway, honking traffic inching impatiently and loudly southward. Instead of noise, there was just emptiness.

'Claire? Claire?' I could hear Wendy's concerned voice, but it sounded very far away. My eyes were locked on the cover of *Mod*, which I kept reading and rereading, just to make sure I wasn't seeing things. Each time I squeezed my eyes closed and opened them again, I hoped against hope that the words would have vanished. But they didn't. They were still there, in vivid, unmistakably permanent bright blue ink.

'Claire? Are you okay? Say something!' Wendy finally reached over and gently shook me. I looked up at her in a daze.

'There's been some mistake,' I said softly, my voice barely above a whisper. I couldn't think of anything else to say. I couldn't have imagined this.

I looked at the cover once again, taking in the beautiful curves of Cole Brannon's shoulders, the suggestive gleam in his eyes, the arch of his eyebrows, the moistness of his lips, which were parted in just the faintest smile. It was one of the best pictures I'd ever seen of him. For one crazy moment, I was sure that if I just focused on his picture and nothing else, everything would be okay.

Then inevitably, my eyes were drawn back to the glaring blue headline splashed just beneath the level of his shoulders. The right margin was filled with the usual *Mod* fare: '35 Ways to Lose Weight', '20 Sex Tricks to Try This Month', '50 Fashion Finds for Fall'. But I barely saw them. Beneath Cole Brannon, who looked perfect and just slightly mischievous beneath the graceful *Mod* logo, a horrible headline screamed out in block letters. I knew it would make the magazine fly off shelves across the country.

HOW TO SLEEP WITH A MOVIE STAR: OUR WRITER'S
ONE-NIGHT STAND WITH COLE BRANNON —
A *Mod* exclusive by Claire Reilly

'Oh my God,' I whispered finally. I looked up at Wendy in horror. Her eyes were wide with concern, and her forehead was creased with pity. 'How . . . ? What . . . ?'
'I don't know,' she said seriously. 'Claire, I don't know.'
I just stared at her.
I couldn't think. I couldn't move. I couldn't breathe.
'And inside?' I choked on the words. 'Is it just as bad?'
Wendy hesitated for a moment, then nodded solemnly.
Numbly, I flipped the magazine open, turned to the table of contents, and quickly found the article. Right in the middle of the page was a huge, blown-up, grainy picture of Cole hugging me good-bye at the doorway to my apartment building. It didn't look familiar, but it had to have been from the morning that Sidra had caught us. It was the only time Cole and I had been together visibly, as he was leaving my apartment. It wasn't a professional shot — clearly, from the slightly out-of-focus blur and nearly imperceptible tilt to the left, it hadn't been taken by a member of the paparazzi. At least their photos came out straight and clear. Sidra must have come back with a camera after she'd left my apartment that day.

The text was even more damaging than the photo. I began to read, my heart racing.

> For years, men have been the ones to spring one-night stands on unsuspecting women, taking them

in their arms and murmuring sweet nothings, making them believe in love at first sight and all the other things that come true in fairy tales.

I realized in horror it was the hastily written lead to the last-minute '10 Reasons to Have a One-Night Stand' article Margaret had assigned just days before the Cole Brannon interview. My breath came in ragged gasps as I read on.

Because we believe in their promises, we've had our hearts broken and our feelings trampled. But who's to say we can't turn the tables on the men and take control? Ladies, you have the power to go after a one-night stand yourself and to turn the tables by breaking *his* heart.

'Oh no,' I murmured as I read on, feeling ill. Suddenly, the one-night-stand article transitioned into the third paragraph of the Cole Brannon cover story I'd written.

One glance at Cole Brannon, and it was immediately clear how he'd managed to charm his leading ladies on-screen and off. His smile lit up the room, his laugh was kind and genuine, and his handshake firm and gentle.

Then the article deviated horrifyingly into something written by someone else.

I knew I had to have him from the moment I first saw him.

I gasped. The article rapidly switched tracks again, back to the lead of my one-night-stand article. I was amazed at how seamlessly it all seemed to flow together, making it sound like I'd really written about a one-night stand with Cole.

Why have a one-night stand? For one thing, it's a great way to stroke your own ego, especially when the one-night stand is with a guy you've had your eye on.

I recognized the first reason on my hastily assembled top-ten list – which I'd written tongue-in-cheek – cringing at my own words. Now they'd been turned against me, and I was horrified by the next line, the implication of which was obvious.

Like most women in America, I'd had my eye on Cole Brannon for quite a while, making him the perfect person to share a one-night stand with.

I moaned in horror.

It's been rumored that Brannon has been having an affair with his *On Eagle's Wing* costar Kylie Dane, a report he flatly denies.
'I'd never do that,' he told *Mod*. 'She's a nice woman and I enjoy working with her, but there's nothing between us. I would never, ever, ever get romantically involved with a married woman.'

I recognized the quote he'd given me on the street after we left Atelier. The next line, not my own, made me cringe again.

So he sounded single, and with the arch of his eyebrow and the smile he shot me, I began to understand that he was getting at something else. Like he was available. To me.

'Oh my God!' I moaned to Wendy, who was sitting quietly at my side with a frozen look on her face. 'I would never have written this! I would never have even thought it!'
'I know,' she said softly. I read on, horrified.

One of the top reasons for a one-night stand: because we all know that getting laid feels pretty damned good.

I blanched, recognizing my tongue-in-cheek reason number ten from the original article, which Wendy and I had expected Margaret would primly edit out. No such luck, apparently.

And who better to get laid by than the hottest star in Hollywood?

'No!' I wailed to Wendy, finally looking up from the article. 'I can't believe this!'
'I know,' she said miserably. 'Me neither. It's horrible.'
I read on. Altogether, there were four whole pages, blending my one-night-stand article with the Cole Brannon feature, tied seamlessly together with damning words I'd never written. It ended just as badly as it had begun.

As we parted ways in the doorway to my apartment, I looked at him tenderly and remembered the best thing about a one-night stand: you might really hit it off with the guy and begin to develop a relationship.

'No!' I moaned, looking at Wendy. It was the third reason on my original list, the one she'd teased me about.

Time will tell with Cole Brannon. He's the kind of man any woman would fall in love with. I'm sad to say, I'm one of those women. But no matter what happens down the road, I'll always have the memory of our one-night stand.

I closed the magazine as soon as I'd read the last line, handing it immediately back to Wendy. Maybe if I got rid of it, it would be like it had never happened. I couldn't handle having it in front of me any more. This made the *Tattletale* disaster look like child's play. This was the worst thing I could have imagined.

'What do I do?' I finally whispered to Wendy.

'I don't know,' she said, for once at a loss for words.

'It was Sidra, wasn't it?' I asked flatly. I was suddenly beyond furious.

'It had to have been,' Wendy agreed. She hesitated and then added, 'She's the one who did the editing.'

'But I *saw* her edited version,' I whispered.

'She must have come back and changed it later that night, after you signed off on it,' Wendy said. 'This is perfect for her. She gets back at you for supposedly sleeping with a *real* movie star and wins the executive editor position over Maite with her genius editing debut.'

'Oh my God,' I said softly, looking at Wendy in horror. Of course she was right. I was an idiot for not realizing it on my own. 'This is going to increase our circulation, and it's going to look like it was Sidra's editing that did the trick.'

Wendy looked at me gravely.

'I have to do something,' I said finally. Wendy nodded.

'You could sue, you know,' she said softly. I looked at her in surprise. The thought of legal action against *Mod* had never occurred to me. Wendy read the reluctance in my eyes. 'You know, this is the kind of thing you're *supposed* to sue for. It wouldn't be a frivolous suit. You almost have to, or it will be like you're agreeing that it all happened and that you wrote this.'

'You really think so?'

'Enough is enough,' said Wendy firmly. 'This is definitely defamation of character, or libel, or slander, or one of those things. I'm sure of it.'

I looked at her for a moment. My mind was spinning.

'Okay,' I said finally. 'I'll do it.' I was quiet for another moment as I realized what else I had to do. I stood up and looked sadly at Wendy. 'Now I have to go quit.'

'Me too,' said Wendy. She threw an arm around me. 'At least we can be unemployed together.'

'You don't have to quit!' I exclaimed.

'But I want to,' she replied instantly. 'This was a really terrible thing for them to do, and I can't work there any more knowing they'd treat you like this.'

We were silent during the elevator ride up to the forty-sixth floor. I don't know what was going through Wendy's mind. I was trying to keep mine on the task at hand, but it kept drifting dangerously back to Cole, and I realized with a sinking feeling that if he didn't hate me already after the *Tattletale* mess, this *Mod* article would certainly seal the deal.

What was worse, he would never know. He'd probably always think I had set out to hurt him. It looked like I had used him to get ahead. He had trusted me, for whatever reason, and taken care of me in a way that no man had before or since. And look what had happened to him because of it.

'I'll let you go first,' Wendy said softly as we stepped off the elevator and through the reception doors. 'Good luck,' she added as we rounded the corner. She handed the rolled copy of *Mod* to me.

'Thanks,' I said under my breath. We turned another corner and came to Margaret's outer office, where Margaret's assistant Cassie sat smirking at me, a copy of the August issue in her hand.

'Well, this is embarrassing,' she said coolly. I ignored her.

'Is Margaret in?' I asked.

'Yes, but she's on the phone,' Cassie said, but I was already blowing past her on the way to Margaret's pretentious oak doors. 'Hey, wait, you can't go in there like that . . .' Cassie yelled behind me as I yanked Margaret's doors open and stepped inside.

'Claire!' Margaret exclaimed as I slammed the doors behind me, tense with anger. She said something quickly into the phone and hung up. 'Well, this is an unexpected surprise,' she said. She sounded a bit nervous, and I didn't blame her. 'Have a seat,' she added, gesturing graciously to the chairs in front of her desk.

'I think I'll stand,' I said slowly, clenching my left fist and squeezing the copy of *Mod* hard with my right hand. Margaret looked from the magazine to me. She opened and shut her mouth wordlessly. Silence hung thick and heavy over us while she squirmed.

'Um, good news!' she said brightly, trying to break the uncomfortable stillness that had descended. 'That was the president of the company. Circulation is already shooting through the roof. The issue is creating major buzz. We've already gotten calls from CNN, Fox News, the *New York Times*, the *Los Angeles Times*, and Reuters. This is huge. Congratulations, Claire!'

She looked at me hopefully, awaiting a response. It was clear from her expression that she wanted me to be as excited as she was, to spring forward and congratulate her. But as I continued to glare, she started to squirm again. It seemed to dawn on her that I wouldn't be popping any bottles of celebratory bubbly with her today.

'Why?' I asked finally. I'd had it. She looked at me in confusion for a moment.

'Why did circulation go up?' she asked, tittering nervously. 'Well, Claire, your article was just wonderful, and it's the talk of the town, and—' I cut her off.

'No,' I said slowly. 'I'm asking why you did this to me.'

She looked worried again.

'Why did I do what?' she asked, sounding confused.

'This,' I said. I held up the magazine and jabbed my finger at the screaming headline below Cole's picture. 'Why did you do this to me?'

'Why, Claire,' Margaret said innocently. 'I thought you'd be pleased.' I simmered in silence for a moment, formulating my next words carefully.

'You thought I'd be *pleased*?' I asked, nearly choking on the last word. 'Margaret, this is a *lie*. You've libeled me. You've libeled Cole Brannon. There's no excuse for this.'

'What are you talking about?' asked Margaret weakly. Concern appeared to be creeping onto her face. 'Sidra told me you'd be a little upset, but she assured me it was true.'

'But I didn't sleep with Cole Brannon,' I barked.

Margaret laughed. She actually laughed.

'Claire, dear,' she said patronizingly. Her artificially light tone wasn't doing enough to mask the nervous expression she still wore on her face. 'Is that what this is about? I know you've slept with Cole Brannon. You don't have to lie to me about *that*, dear. There's nothing to be ashamed of.'

'I didn't sleep with Cole Brannon,' I said, drawing each word slowly out. 'I didn't shack up with him. I didn't kiss him. I didn't even bat my damned eyes at him. Do you understand that? I can sue *Mod* for millions. Do you understand that you can't do this to someone?'

The moment I said the word 'sue', all the color had drained from Margaret's face. She suddenly looked terrified and uncertain.

'Claire, you can't be serious,' she said uneasily. She had started to tremble, and the false British accent had slipped away. 'Sidra told me she caught you with Cole Brannon in your apartment. That you'd slept with him.'

'I've told you, time and time again, that I haven't,' I said firmly.

'Yes, I know,' said Margaret quickly. 'But I thought . . . well, I assumed . . . that you were just being modest, or that you were worried about your job. Besides, by the time it came up, because of that *Tattletale* thing, the magazine was already at the printer.' She tilted her head and looked at me in nervous confusion. 'Are you really telling me you didn't sleep with him?'

She looked genuinely surprised. For a moment, I felt almost sorry for her. She was way out of her league. It hadn't even occurred to her that the article could be a lie. She had known I'd be mortified, but she hadn't cared.

But now that she knew she was in potential legal hot water – very hot water – she looked like a frightened child.

'I'm really telling you I didn't sleep with him,' I said softly. She looked shocked and scared. 'Which I would have told you again that day if you'd bothered to ask,' I added.

'But Sidra said . . .' she protested weakly, looking sick.

'Sidra wants the executive editor position – not to mention the salary bump and the power that go with it – more than anything in the world,' I said quietly. 'This was how she planned to get it. Look, circulation is through the roof. And it looks like it's because of a story she edited.'

'But . . .' Margaret's voice trailed off and she stared at me. 'But you wrote this article.'

'No,' I said firmly. 'I wrote a profile of Cole Brannon. Sidra completely rewrote it by combining it with that stupid one-night-stand article you assigned.' It was the rudest I'd ever been to Margaret. I had always longed for the day that I could tell her how ridiculous she and her assignments were. I just never thought it would happen like this.

'No, that can't be,' Margaret whispered, looking horrified. I stared her down.

'I've got the original – the version that I signed off on – saved on my computer and printed out in my files,' I said icily. 'I'll get it for you if you need to see it.'

'No,' Margaret said finally. Her shoulders slumped in defeat. 'I believe you. But why would she do this to you?'

'Sidra has hated me since the day you hired me as a senior editor,' I said, giving her the short version. 'On top of that, Sidra's sister was sleeping with my boyfriend. Sidra came by to pick up her sister's things one morning, in time to see Cole Brannon in my apartment. He was there because he knew I'd caught my boyfriend cheating on me, and he was making sure I was okay. He's a nice guy. I've never slept with him. I've never even kissed him. Sidra knows that.

'But it gave her the perfect idea for how to get promoted,' I continued. 'After all, she's been lying about sleeping with George Clooney for years. It wasn't a major leap for her to come up with this and pull all the right strings to make the lie sound real.'

I paused, and Margaret stared.

'But why would she do this to *me*?' she asked in a very small voice. I could tell that she believed my explanation about Cole, at long last, and was now scrambling to save her own hide. But it was too little too late. I shrugged and thought about it for a moment.

'She doesn't care about you or anyone else,' I said slowly. 'She wants to be the executive editor, and she'll do whatever it takes to get there.'

'No, that can't be possible,' Margaret whispered, looking frightened and pathetic. But I knew from her expression that she didn't believe her own words. It was, in fact, very possible.

'I'm suing the company,' I said, ignoring the horrified expression that crossed Margaret's face. I suddenly felt calm. 'And I'm going to sue Sidra directly, too.' The plan was crystallizing as I said the words. Margaret's flat eyes flickered a bit. 'You're going to have to testify against her, because it needs to be clear that this was her doing,' I said firmly. 'Otherwise, you're going to be the only one who's in trouble for this.'

'Yes, yes, of course,' Margaret mumbled. I felt very weary.

'I'm going home now,' I said finally. I dropped the magazine on her desk. It was over. Just like that. Everything I'd worked for.

'Claire, I don't know what to say,' Margaret said hastily, trying to smooth things over. Her eyes shone with pathetic desperation. I knew she was terrified of losing her job, which was probably Sidra's plan all along. 'I can make it up to you. I swear. How about a promotion? Managing editor, maybe?'

I shook my head slowly.

'I quit, Margaret,' I said slowly. 'There's no way in the world I'd work with this magazine again.'

I walked calmly through the big oak doors and found Wendy standing there.

'Did you do it?' she whispered. 'Did you quit?'

I nodded. Wendy stuck her head inside the office, where Margaret still stood, shell-shocked.

'I quit too!' she singsonged. Margaret just looked at her with eyes that had already glazed over, and Wendy pulled the doors closed behind her. Cassie stared at us with an open mouth.

'Oh, and you?' Wendy addressed Cassie like she was an afterthought. She grinned at me and looked back at the slack-jawed assistant. 'When Margaret loses her job, which is a pretty sure thing once Claire files a lawsuit against the magazine, you're going to be out of a job, too. Everyone here knows you're a worthless suck-up. All those times you've deliberately misplaced copy that we've sent to Margaret, all those times you've conveniently forgotten to pass important messages along to assistant editors, all those times you've smirked at editorial assistants and told them it didn't matter how hard they worked because you'd be promoted before they were . . . Well, don't think any of us will forget about that. I give you three weeks before you're crawling back to your daddy.'

I laughed as Cassie's eyes widened.

'But it was quite a pleasure working with you, Cassie,' Wendy added brightly. I laughed again.

'All right, that does it,' Wendy said cheerfully, turning back to me. She patted me on the back. 'Let's clear out our desks and go get a drink.'

I smiled at Wendy. I may have lost my boyfriend, my job, and my reputation, but at least I still had the greatest friend in the world.

Actual Malice

My whole world had just come crashing down, and I didn't have the faintest idea of how to rebuild it.

I felt numb as I sat alone in the backseat of a taxi headed down Broadway. Wendy had stayed behind in midtown to meet Jean Michel, but after a few drinks, all I wanted was to go home.

I closed my eyes and let the world swim around me as I pressed my forehead against the cool window.

As the cab rolled on, I suddenly knew what I had to do. I had to call Cole Brannon and apologize. For everything. For all the things I'd said and done. I needed to tell him that I hadn't written the article in *Mod*. That I hadn't had anything to do with the article in *Tattletale*. That I'd made a horrible mistake by pretending he didn't mean anything to me. That my sense of professional ethics had been useless and misguided. That I was basically the biggest fool on the planet.

As soon as I walked into the privacy of my apartment, I dialed Cole's cell number with trembling fingers and held the phone up to my ear.

It rang once, then an automated message told me that the number was no longer in service, blaring in my ear.

My eyes filled with tears. I didn't know why he had disconnected his cell number. Had it been because of me? Because he hated me so much after the *Tattletale* and *Mod* stories that he never wanted to hear my voice again? That was ludicrous. But I had no idea how else to reach him.

I sat there for a second and considered what to do. The only connection I had to Cole was through Ivana, his publicist. But the last time I called, I'd caught them in bed together. The thought made me sick, but I knew I didn't have a choice. I *had* to get word to Cole that the *Mod* thing hadn't been my responsibility.

I flipped through the notepad from Cole's interview to find Ivana's cell number, which she had given to Margaret when she set up the interview between me and Cole.

She answered the phone after the first ring.

'Ivana?' I said timidly. There was silence on the other end. 'It's Claire Reilly, from *Mod*.'

The silence, almost stifling, dragged on.

'Claire Reilly?' she asked finally. Her voice sounded cold and shaken. 'I thought I told you never to contact me again.'

'I know,' I said softly, trying not to react to her words. I had to reach Cole. Even if it meant swallowing my pride. Come to think of it, I didn't have much pride left any more, did I? 'I was calling because—'

She cut me off.

'You bitch,' she said flatly. My eyes widened, and I sucked in a deep breath as she continued. 'I hope you don't think you can get away with this. Cole Brannon would never sleep with a woman like you.'

'I know,' I said miserably. Boy, did I know. 'I didn't . . .'

'Fuck off,' she said coldly. Then she hung up, and I was left staring at the phone.

I slowly set down the handset and sat there numbly for a moment. Okay. That had gone a bit worse than expected. I didn't know what else to do, only that I had to get to Cole.

I rummaged through the box of papers I'd grabbed from my desk at *Mod* until I came across the press release for *Forever Goodbye*, his upcoming movie due out Labor Day Weekend, which had the name and number of the film's press rep at the bottom. Thankfully, it was an L.A. number. It would only be 3:30 there.

I dialed and asked for the publicist, Leeza Smith. I was connected immediately.

'Leeza? This is Claire Reilly, from *Mod* magazine,' I said, realizing only after the words were out of my mouth that I actually was no longer from *Mod* magazine. That was a strange thought.

My introduction was greeted by a long silence.

'I saw the magazine today,' Leeza finally said, stiffly. 'The August issue,' she added, as if I hadn't understood that the first time. I cleared my throat.

'Then you'll understand why I need to get in touch with Cole Brannon,' I said. I felt stupid the moment the words were out. I opened my mouth to issue a denial, to tell Leeza that I hadn't written the article, that I'd never slept with Cole Brannon or even claimed to, but she was already laughing.

Her peals of laughter were high-pitched and squeaky, and she sounded almost hysterical. I could feel myself turning red as I waited for her to finish. When her laughter finally died down, I started to protest, but she cut me off.

'Are you delusional?' she asked sharply. She laughed again. 'Do you really think anyone is going to allow you near Cole Brannon again?' She was still laughing as she hung up.

I fought back tears as I put the handset back in its cradle. I tore the press release into little pieces and angrily shoved them into the trash can next to my desk. It was worse than I thought. I shook my head and forced myself to think. I had to get to Cole. I had to tell him that the *Mod* story wasn't my doing.

'Think, Claire, think,' I mumbled to myself. Then it hit me. Jay, the bartender. Cole's friend from college who worked at Metro. He'd know where to find Cole. Better yet, he knew who I was, and he knew what had happened that night at his bar. He had to have realized that I hadn't slept with Cole. I hadn't even been conscious.

I hailed a taxi outside, asking the driver to hurry. Still, it took us twenty-five minutes to fight through traffic to Eighth Avenue and Forty-eighth, where I immediately rushed inside Metro.

It was much more crowded than it had been the last time I'd been there. It was, after all, the middle of the week, and 7:30 meant the end of happy hour crowds. I pushed my way to the bar and quickly looked for Cole's friend. I didn't see him.

'What can I get you?' asked a tall, lanky bartender as I looked frantically around.

'I'm looking for Jay!' I said quickly, trying not to sound too desperate.

'Jay who?'

'Jay.' I paused. I knew Cole had mentioned his last name. I racked my brain. 'Jay Cash, I think. He's a bartender here.'

'Oh,' he said. 'I don't know. I'm new, hang on.' The lanky bartender went and whispered something to a short blonde, who came over once she'd finished pouring a martini.

'You're looking for Jay?' she asked.

'Yes,' I said. 'Please, do you know where I can find him?' I knew I sounded desperate and probably looked crazy. The girl hesitated before shaking her head.

'I'm sorry, but he quit about a month ago. I don't know where he went.'

'Do you know where he lives? Or how to find him? Or anything?'

''Fraid not.' The bartender shrugged. 'I think he's opening his own bar or something.'

I thanked her and rushed home, where I flipped open the white pages and dialed every Jay Cash in the phone book. None of them was Cole's friend Jay.

So this was it. I had exhausted my options. I had no other way to reach Cole Brannon.

*

The next day I visited Dean Ryan, a media lawyer, and was encouraged to see his eyes widen when I told him the whole story about the *Mod* article. He said this sounded like an airtight libel case, because Sidra's work met the definition – a false statement of fact about a person that is printed or otherwise broadcast to others – without a shadow of doubt.

'If Mr Brannon wants to sue, he shouldn't have a problem either,' Dean told me as he looked over his notes. 'Public figures, such as government officials or, in Mr Brannon's case, celebrities, have to prove actual malice – that is, that the defendant knew the statement was false, or recklessly disregarded the truth. If he can prove that Ms DeSimon knew she was lying, which shouldn't be too difficult, then he, too, should have an airtight case against both her and the publishing company.

'Your case will be even easier,' Dean said, his eyes gleaming. 'In general, private individuals such as yourself must show only that the defendant was negligent in order to prove libel. Ms DeSimon was not only negligent, but she obviously acted with malice and complete disregard for the truth. There isn't an attorney in the world who could successfully defend against a case like this. If you'll excuse the expression, Ms Reilly, you've got both Ms DeSimon and *Mod* magazine by the balls.'

Dean looked up at me and smiled, his bleached teeth sparkling in the fluorescence of his office.

'You're going to be a very rich woman,' he said.

As I left Dean Ryan's office, I felt a bit better – but not as much as I had expected to. While I felt I was doing *something*, it didn't help me out that much. I didn't care much about the money. I'd already lost my job and my reputation. No amount of cash would bring that back. But I supposed that a successful lawsuit would probably mean the end of Sidra's career too – and that, at least, gave me a bit of satisfaction.

*

In the next few weeks, I tried to forget Cole Brannon. I really did. It seemed like I would have so much on my mind that there wouldn't be room to worry about him, but of course that wasn't true. The fact that my entire life had seemed to crumble before my eyes did little to assuage the guilt I felt about embarrassing Cole.

Wendy got a job as an assistant chef at a new upscale restaurant called Swank that was opening in the East Village, and I knew she was thrilled.

'I don't miss working in magazines at all,' she told me after her first week. 'I can't believe I stuck it out there as long as I did.'

'I thought you liked the job,' I said.

'I did,' she said. 'But I didn't love it. This, I love.'

I had less luck as I hit the job trail, which was starting to worry me. I had enough money to cover August's rent, and having Wendy as a roommate certainly lessened the financial burden, but I wouldn't be able to pay September's rent if I didn't find something soon.

I spent hours each day perusing the job listings on mediabistro.com, scanning the classified ads in the *New York Times*, and calling the major publishers, asking about openings. I sent out several résumés every day and followed up with phone calls.

Everywhere I turned, everyone seemed to know who I was. Did anyone *not* read *Mod*? The answer was always embarrassingly the same.

'We prefer to hire people with better reputations,' I would sometimes hear. Or, 'The name Claire Reilly might carry a connotation we don't want our magazine to have.' And those were the people who bothered to explain. I had a few people hang up when I called and gave my name. A few simply laughed me off the phone. One human resources director actually did return my call – but only to ask for the real lowdown about how Cole Brannon was in bed. I was humiliated.

Then the editor in chief of *Chic*, the newest entry into the crowded women's magazine field, called and asked me to come by her office the next day. I arrived ten minutes early and was shown in thirty minutes late.

'So you're Claire Reilly,' announced Maude Beauvais as her assistant shut the door behind me. She was in her late fifties and looked like she should have been wearing a housecoat and slippers rather than the tailored suit (two sizes too small) she was squeezed into. Her hair was bleached an unnatural shade of blond, and her makeup was caked on so thickly that I wondered how she could move her face beneath it. She wasn't at all what I'd expected as the figurehead of a trendy new magazine. But she said she might have an opportunity for me, so I was determined to listen with an open mind.

'Nice to meet you, Ms Beauvais,' I said, stepping forward and shaking her hand.

'And you,' she said with a nod. She gestured for me to sit down, and she did the same. 'Call me Maude.' I nodded, waiting for her to begin.

'Because you've had several years of experience covering celebrity events, I thought we'd give you a try here at *Chic*,' Maude said as soon as we were both sitting down. 'That is, if you're interested.'

'Yes, yes, of course I am,' I said. I probably sounded too eager. But I couldn't help it. I was. Impending poverty will do that to you.

'I understand you're having difficulty getting hired elsewhere,' she said bluntly.

'Yes, ma'am,' I admitted. Great. The whole journalism world knew I was a loser.

'That's why I'm hoping you'll be open to my offer. I don't have the budget to hire another staffer right now, but I need someone experienced who can cover celebrity events. You know, press conferences here and there, charity events, things like the Grammys and the MTV Movie Awards.'

I gulped back my disappointment and nodded.

'I'd like to hire you as a stringer, to do just that,' she said. 'We'll pay you twenty-five dollars an hour, and I can promise you at least ten hours of work per week. Most weeks, it will be closer to fifteen or twenty hours.'

'Okay,' I said timidly. I'd never been a stringer. I'd always had a salaried job, and I knew from dealing with the freelancers I'd overseen at *Mod* that the life of a stringer was often difficult and the pay was spotty. But spotty pay was better than no pay. 'I'll do it,' I said. It wouldn't be work that I loved. But a job was a job. And I needed one.

'Fantastic,' Maude said. Then she leaned forward. 'We need to have a little discussion before we sign anything, though.'

'Um, okay.'

'I don't know what things were like at *Mod*,' she began. 'And of course, *Chic* looks at *Mod* as a big sister in the business, a magazine that sets a lot of standards for us. But the thing is, we actually do have our own set of standards here at *Chic*, and those standards don't include sleeping with celebrities.'

I reddened. I'd heard the words often enough not to be surprised, but I couldn't help feeling disappointed.

'I didn't sleep with Cole Brannon,' I mumbled. 'That's why I quit *Mod*. It was something they made up.' Maude smiled pityingly at me. I knew she didn't believe me.

'Yes,' she said dismissively, waving her hand in the air. 'In any case, that won't be acceptable behavior here at *Chic*. I assume you'll understand this.'

'Yes, yes of course,' I mumbled.

'Fine, then,' she said. 'I've already alerted human resources that you'll be coming up. They're on the thirtieth floor. Just take the elevator up and ask for Lauren Elkin. She'll walk you through all the paperwork. Give me a call tomorrow morning, and we'll talk about your first assignment.'

We shook hands, and I left Maude Beauvais's office

feeling shamed. The Cole Brannon story was going to follow me everywhere and haunt me for the rest of my life. I was no longer Claire Reilly, celebrity writer. I was Claire Reilly, the girl who shagged a movie star.

After two weeks at *Chic*, I absolutely hated it. I didn't have a choice, though. I continued to send out my résumé, and I continued to get rejected. Twenty-five dollars an hour from Maude Beauvais was the best I could do.

I was sent out a few nights a week to wait patiently behind the ropes at the opening of a new restaurant, a Broadway play that Anthony Hopkins was supposed to be attending that night, a charity concert for homeless kids in Indonesia at which Angelina Jolie was supposed to make an appearance. Night after night, I shot ridiculous *Chic* questions at B-list stars I hardly recognized. I asked former members of boy bands whether they preferred boxers or briefs. (It was boxers, hands down.) I asked aging actors whom I recognized vaguely from the '80s about the most romantic thing they'd ever done for someone. ('I let my girlfriend lick chocolate off my naked body,' was one particularly repulsive answer.) I asked soap actresses what their favorite books were and why. (One even responded, 'I read a book once . . .' before her voice trailed off and she wandered away with a dreamy expression on her face.)

At least I was getting paid. Most weeks, I worked fifteen to twenty hours, so while the paychecks that rolled in weren't excessive, they were enough to scrape by on while I decided what to do with my life.

The whole experience with Cole Brannon and *Mod* had changed everything. I loved to write, but I knew I could no longer work in a world ruled by flaky celebrity gossip. As my days with *Chic* dragged on the truth became more and more clear. This wasn't my world. It never had been.

It was a strange feeling to wake up at age twenty-six and realize that the career I'd been working on night and day, using all my time and energy for the last four years, wasn't the one for me. That the career I'd dreamed of since I was a little girl was no more than an illusion. I had somehow talked myself into believing that I was above the whole celebrity gossip scene, even that I helped counteract it by providing a *real* glimpse into the lives of the oft-gossiped-about A-listers whose careers millions of us followed. But it wasn't true. I was just perpetuating the cycle. I felt an immense sense of sadness, loss, and shame. It was like the last four years of my life meant nothing.

And suddenly, I had no idea what I wanted to do with my life. In one fell swoop, the life I had thought I knew – great boyfriend, great job, great sense of self-worth – had vanished. And to make it even worse, it was like the rose-colored glasses I hadn't even known I was wearing had shattered, leaving me to realize that everything I'd believed was never true in the first place. I'd never had the life I thought I had.

I had never felt so alone or so confused.

On the third Friday in August I was home alone, sitting in front of the TV, stuffing my face with Chunky Monkey ice cream, and trying to figure out how many spoonfuls it would take to add a pound of fat to my already-heavier tummy. Some people lost their appetite when they were stressed out and as a result, shed unwanted pounds. I, on the other hand, found comfort in massive quantities of ice cream and Doritos.

Wendy had tried to set me up on some blind dates, but I just wasn't interested. Who needed a man when I had Ben & Jerry? I was convinced that my relationship with those two was far more fulfilling than any other relationship could be.

Work had to be my focus, despite hating my job and the fact that I was dreading the breast cancer benefit I had to cover for *Chic* the next night. What a lousy way it would be to spend a Saturday night, standing on the red carpet outside the Puck Building in SoHo, waiting in the August heat for an unimpressive parade of B-listers to show up and respond to my stupid questions. I'd be once again reminded of my station in life when the doors to the theater shut, leaving me on the outside looking in.

The eleven o'clock news had just ended and I was in the middle of trying to decide whether to sulk while watching David Letterman or Jay Leno (yes, my life has come to this), when the voice-over for the *Late Show with David Letterman* came on, announcing that Cole Brannon would be one of tonight's guests.

I choked on a particularly chunky bite of Chunky Monkey. I slowly put down the remote and stared at the screen.

I watched, glued to the television, an unfamiliar pain stabbing at my heart, as Cole strode onto the *Late Show* stage twenty-five minutes later. His brown hair was tousled, as usual, and the dark Diesel jeans and tight Rolling Stones shirt he wore clung perfectly to the contours of his body. Women in the audience continued to scream for a long time after he sat down, and he grinned and politely said, 'Thank you, thank you.'

Why had my throat closed up? This wasn't normal.

'They seem to like you,' David Letterman said, smiling at Cole after the last scream had finally died out. Cole laughed, and his face crinkled up in the same way it had for me at Over the Moon months before. I felt sick. What was it about Cole Brannon and instant nausea?

'Well, I like them too,' Cole said with a charming smile. The audience erupted in screams and squeals again, and Cole and Letterman laughed.

'So I haven't had you on the show for months. What have you been keeping busy with?' asked Letterman. I held my breath and prayed he wouldn't mention the *Mod* article.

'Just shooting some films, getting ready to promote the movie I have coming out in two weeks,' Cole said calmly.

Sure. He probably hadn't thought about me once. Why would he?

'*Forever Goodbye*,' Letterman added.

'That's the one,' Cole said with a dimpled grin.

'So it opens Labor Day Weekend?' Letterman asked.

'Yeah,' Cole said. 'The New York premiere is next weekend, but it'll be in wide release the following week.'

'Great!' Letterman said. 'Can you tell us a bit about it?'

As Cole described the plot of the film – a wartime romance in which his character's letters home to his young wife provide a backdrop to tragedy – I watched as his lips moved. The sound of his voice did something to me. His smiles reminded me of the ones he'd given me. His tender sadness as he described the movie's plot reminded me of the gentle way he'd looked at me that Sunday morning in my apartment, when he knew my heart was breaking over Tom. I felt terrible as I thought about how I'd repaid his kindness. With coldness. With forced nonchalance. And with a horrible article in *Mod*.

The show went to commercial break, and I stared at the screen with eyes that had glazed over. I felt like a zombie. It wasn't that I had forgotten about Cole in the previous month, but I'd been so good at forcing myself to ignore all reminders of him. And now here he was, impossible to ignore.

Suddenly, I knew I had to get away from him. I was confused enough about my life already without trying to decipher why I felt so attracted to this man who was off-limits and who obviously detested me – for good reason. I flicked off the TV, stuck the Chunky Monkey back in the freezer (where it would be attacked again shortly), grabbed my purse, and headed out the front door before I could think about where I was going.

I just knew I couldn't stay in the apartment where Cole had once looked at me with those gentle eyes and that kind smile I'd been too stupid to appreciate.

*

I didn't know where I was going as I walked north on Second Avenue, but I wound up at Over the Moon for the first time since I'd eaten there with Cole. In a strange twist of irony, apparently intended to make me even more miserable, the restaurant now sat in the shadow of a giant *Forever Goodbye* billboard. As I sipped decaf coffee and waited for my eggs, my well-done bacon, and hash browns with cheese, a thirty-foot Cole Brannon looked down on me from high above Second Avenue.

'He's a cutie, isn't he?' asked my waitress. She was a plump, gray-haired woman with deep laugh lines, friendly eyes, and a name tag that read 'Marge'. She nodded out the window at the billboard as she refilled my coffee.

'Yes, he is.' I sighed miserably. It felt like so long ago that we'd sat here together.

'He's a sweet boy, too,' Marge said. I looked up sharply. 'He comes in here a lot, you know. Can you believe it? To our restaurant?'

'He does?' My breath caught in my throat.

'Sure,' she said. 'Especially in the last few months. Although I haven't seen him in about three weeks now.'

'He comes here?' I asked, my voice high as I still tried to process it. The waitress smiled gently, apparently convinced that she'd come across his biggest fan.

If only she knew.

'He sure does,' she said, leaning forward conspiratorially. I noticed she had a Boston accent, an endearing removal of the letter *r* from the ends of her words. 'Whenever he's in New York. And he always asks for me. Every time.' She looked at me proudly. I just stared.

'Does he . . . say anything . . . about, um . . .' I stammered, not sure what I was hoping for. The waitress winked at me.

'I wish I could tell you he seems available, honey, but he's been pining away over some girl who lives in the neighborhood.'

My eyebrows shot up and I suddenly felt breathless.

'What?' I croaked.

'Some girl who lives just down the street,' Marge continued, oblivious of my reaction. 'Now, can you believe that? The biggest star in Hollywood pining away over some girl who lives in the East Village.' She shook her head and smiled.

'Where did he meet her?' I squeaked. Marge shrugged.

'Some magazine thing, I think,' she said. I gulped. She couldn't mean me. It was impossible.

'But what about Kylie Dane?' I asked quickly. 'I thought he was dating her. I mean, I read it somewhere.' I cleared my throat. I didn't want to sound too eager. But the waitress seemed more than happy to gossip. I was her only customer at this late hour, and she was probably trying for a bigger tip. Believe me, I'd give her one.

'He was so frustrated about that,' she said. She gestured to the empty seat across from me. 'Do you mind?'

I shook my head mutely and she sat down, setting the pot of coffee on the table.

'He never dated that Kylie Dane woman,' Marge said, wrinkling her nose. 'He thought they were friends, until he realized her publicist was selling paparazzi shots of the two of them together, telling the press they were an item. And it was all that Kylie Dane's idea! Can you imagine?'

'Are you sure?' I asked.

'Of course I'm sure,' Marge said proudly, puffing out her chest. 'He says I remind him of his mother. He talks to me all the time. The same thing happened with his publicist, you know. People kept shooting pictures of them together, and the rumors got started.'

'Really?' I squeaked. 'But he really is dating his publicist, isn't he?' I cleared my throat and backtracked a bit. 'I mean, that's what I've read. In the newspaper.'

'You really know a lot about Cole Brannon, don't you?' Marge looked amused. She smiled at me. 'Big fan, huh?' I paused, then nodded. Maybe she'd continue if she thought I was just a crazy Cole Brannon aficionado. 'Nah, he was never dating her. It bothered him, you know. That publicist of his is a strange bird, if you ask me. She was in here once and kept stroking his arm, and he looked so uncomfortable. She didn't even want him to talk to me.'

'Really?' I said again, because I didn't know what else to say. But I wanted her to go on.

'The next time he was in, I told him he should fire her,' the waitress continued. 'She gave me the creeps. But he said something about her being the sister of someone he'd known in college. He felt loyal to her for some reason. He's too damned nice for his own good, you know. But she seemed crazy, and I know crazy when I see it, honey.'

'Sounds like it,' I murmured. My heart was pounding. Could Marge be right? Could Cole have been telling the truth about Kylie and Ivana after all?

'The worst thing is, the same thing happened with that magazine girl in the Village too,' Marge continued. I blanched, and my heart sank. 'He really liked her. He thought she was different. But she wrote some article in her magazine about sleeping with him. And he never slept with her. He's a real gentleman, you know.'

'Maybe it was a misunderstanding,' I said so quietly, it was barely audible. I could feel the blood rushing to my cheeks in a furious blush. Marge laughed, and I blinked back my embarrassment.

'Yeah, that's real likely,' she said with a snort. 'Anyhow, he was real upset after that. I haven't seen him since. Poor boy. He thought he'd finally found someone who he really connected with. Someone who didn't want to use him. He should have known better, I guess.' I felt the blood drain from my face. I looked at her miserably.

'Thanks,' I said finally.

'Always happy to gossip, sweetheart,' she said with a wink. 'I'll go see if your food's up. And hey, cheer up, honey. Whatever's bothering you can't be that bad.'

'You'd be surprised,' I murmured as she walked cheerfully away.

I sat at Over the Moon through two shift changes, drinking coffee and looking out the window at a Cole Brannon I could never have.

I thought about my life and what I was doing with it. I thought about Tom and thanked God he was gone. I thought about my job and considered switching career tracks altogether. I wondered for a long time how I'd managed to screw things up so badly.

But most of all, I thought about Cole – which wasn't hard to do as he silently kept watch over the city, right outside the window.

The Red Carpet

I was exhausted. I stood along the ropes of the red carpet outside the Puck Building Saturday evening after a sleepless night, thrusting my tape recorder toward a seemingly endless parade of the same faces I saw every week at these events. Tonight's was a black-tie benefit to raise funds for breast cancer research, and I'd dutifully pinned my pink ribbon on the collar of my white blouse. My legs were sweating in my gray boot-cut pants, and I was contemplating taking off my ridiculously uncomfortable heels to stand barefoot on the sidewalk. The only thing that stopped me was a huge wad of recently chewed gum about six inches from my left foot. Who knew what else lined the streets of New York?

As was the case with most minor events, the breast cancer benefit had attracted only a few members of the media. Several paparazzi photographers with big flashbulbs lined the carpet – they were ubiquitous in New York – but there were only three reporters other than me. One was from the *New York Post* – they covered everything that might potentially involve even a minor celebrity. Another was from *Stuff* magazine, as there was a rumor Brittany Murphy might show up, and she was, well, hot stuff. The third was Victoria Lim, my old friend from *Cosmo*, who had spent the first half hour apologizing profusely for not having called. She'd been busy with a freelance project she was doing for

Vanity Fair, and work at *Cosmo* had her swamped.

She was sympathetic about the Cole Brannon story in *Mod* and assured me that she didn't believe it. She had avoided the question when I asked her if it was a source of gossip at *Cosmo*. Then she quickly changed the subject to tell me about a fashion show she'd been to the week before, where the models had actually paraded down the runway in trash bags and stilettos.

'I thought that whole grunge look went out in, like, 1995,' she said.

'Is that even grunge?' I asked skeptically.

'I don't know,' she admitted. 'What else do you call models in trash bags? Seemed pretty grungy to me.'

The breast cancer benefit dinner was being organized by Maddox-Wylin, a small book publisher, so I didn't expect much of a celebrity turnout for the $1,000-a-head meal, catered by the four-star Luigi Vernace restaurant. But Susan Lucci was there. Katie Holmes had a table. Breast cancer survivor Kate Jackson (one of Charlie's original Angels) came with a friend, followed by Olivia Newton-John moments later.

As the celebrities made their way gracefully down the red carpet, I held out my tape recorder and asked *Chic* questions that made me feel silly. They all answered them politely and moved on. I was starting to feel better, knowing that Maude Beauvais would be pleased with tonight's unexpected treasure trove of celeb quotes.

And then I saw him, getting out of a limousine.

It was Cole Brannon.

He was coming toward me on the red carpet, and for a moment I thought I was hallucinating.

But he wasn't a mirage.

There he was, larger than life, striding from his limousine toward the theater. Flashbulbs went off all around us, and there was an excited buzz to the media crowd. He was the biggest star to arrive that night.

I was suddenly breathless and moderately woozy,

which I couldn't entirely attribute to the sleepless night and lack of energy I'd suffered from in the last twenty-four hours. I suddenly understood the expression 'He took my breath away.'

He was stunning in a tuxedo, his broad shoulders filling it out perfectly. He smiled for the cameras and made his way down the red carpet. The reporter from *Stuff* asked him a few soft questions and giggled at his answers. The girl from the *Post* asked him something and he shook his head, then said something softly to her, flashing her his gorgeous smile. A photographer shouted at him, asking why he was at the benefit. He answered in a low voice that his mother was a breast cancer survivor.

Then he turned and saw me.

I froze as our eyes met, and he seemed to freeze, too. I hadn't expected this. I wasn't prepared for it. A sudden stillness fell over the media crowd as Cole and I stood staring at each other for what felt like a small eternity. My face was on fire, and I could hear the whispers around me as photographers and reporters reminded each other that I was the girl who'd slept with Cole Brannon and written about it for *Mod* magazine.

Finally I spoke, breaking the silence between us. My heart beat so quickly, I feared it would jump out of my chest.

'Hi,' I said softly.

'Hi,' he said uncertainly, a guarded look on his face as he continued to stare at me. I took a deep breath and tried to slow my pounding heart.

'Cole, I am so sorry about the article in *Mod*,' I said, my words tumbling out quickly, almost on top of each other. I knew my face was bright red, and I could feel myself shaking. Cole was silent. He just looked at me. I couldn't read his expression. 'I swear to you, Cole, I had no idea. I didn't write that article. One of the other editors there wrote it, I swear to you.'

Still looking at me, he was frozen in place, and he

hadn't said a word. I wanted him to say something, to tell me he believed me, to tell me he forgave me, but he didn't. I took a deep breath and glanced around. Flashbulbs were going off all around us, but suddenly I didn't care. Photos of us would probably land on tomorrow's nighttime entertainment shows – and in Tuesday's *Tattletale* – and rumors would crop up that something was going on between us again. But I ignored all of that. I needed him to know that I would never have hurt him intentionally. This was my one chance.

'You have to believe me, Cole,' I pleaded, probably sounding as desperate and pathetic as I felt. 'I had nothing to do with the *Tattletale* thing either. I swear to God. I am so sorry that all of this happened.' I looked at him desperately, miserably hoping he'd say something. He was silent for another moment.

'I knew the *Tattletale* thing wasn't you,' he said finally. 'Usually their stories aren't true.'

I sighed with relief, then realized he hadn't said anything about the *Mod* article. He looked cold and distant, and I longed to reach across the rope and hug him, like we'd hugged that day that felt like years ago. But I knew I couldn't. It was like a huge valley had opened up between us, and I didn't have what it took to cross it.

'I tried to call you,' I said slowly. He looked surprised.

'You did? When?' It occurred to me, just for a moment, that it had to be a good sign he was still standing there.

'After the *Tattletale* thing,' I said desperately. 'And after the *Mod* article came out. I tried your cell, but it had been disconnected. I tried the studio publicist, I tried finding your friend Jay, the bartender. I even tried calling Ivana.' He studied me for a moment. I knew I was being judged. My knees felt weak.

'She never told me,' he said softly, looking at me curiously. My heart was pounding. He looked like he was going to say something. My palms were sweaty, and I suddenly felt very hot and a bit dizzy. I blinked a few times and was again aware of the crowd around us, watching our every move and straining to hear our words. Cole leaned in closer, his breath whispering past my ear and sending a tingle through my whole body.

'Ivana told me I wasn't the first actor you'd done this kind of thing with,' he said gently. 'She told me you had a reputation for things like this. I didn't know what to think.' He pulled away, looking at me with sad eyes. I gasped.

'What?' I sputtered. 'Cole, I swear to you that's not true. I've never done anything like that, I swear. This whole story has ruined my life. You have to believe me.'

He looked at me skeptically.

'Cole,' I said desperately. 'I quit *Mod* the moment the story came out. I swear to you I had nothing to do with it.'

'You quit?' he asked, looking genuinely surprised. For the first time since he'd seen me, his face had started to relax a bit. But before I could answer, Ivana was at his elbow. I hadn't even seen her coming. Her long, dark hair was tied back in a slick, glamorous ponytail, and she was dressed in a tight red gown. A huge diamond sparkled around her neck.

'It's time to go now, Cole,' she said, coldly taking his elbow and steering him away from me. 'You stay away from him,' she hissed under her breath at me. She was shooting daggers at me with her eyes, which were icy and dangerous. Cole gave me one last confused look over his shoulder and allowed himself to be led away.

I had a sick feeling as I watched him go that it would be the last I would see of him. His appearance at the benefit had caught me off guard, and I hadn't said all the things I'd wanted to say. I hadn't been able to convince him that I was telling the truth. He hadn't believed me.

'You okay?' asked Victoria gently, snapping me back to reality. She squeezed my elbow lightly, and I looked up to see a dozen pairs of eyes staring at me. The reporter from the *Post* was furiously scribbling something in her notebook. I willed myself not to cry in front of the cameras.

'I'm fine,' I lied. I took a deep, ragged breath. Then I realized something. 'I can't do this anymore,' I said softly. It suddenly seemed so clear. Had I been living in a fog for the last few years?

'Do what?' asked Victoria.

'This,' I said gesturing around me. 'This whole stupid celebrity thing. It's not real.'

None of it was what it seemed. None of it was real. And none of it mattered. Who cared whom Nicholas Cage was sleeping with, whom Nicole Kidman had been spotted with, or where Ben Affleck had been seen out on the town? Why did it matter? What was I doing here, in the middle of this useless circus?

'What am I doing?' I murmured aloud to myself.

Just then, Chris Noth, whom I adored as Mr Big on *Sex and the City* and as Mike Logan on *Law & Order* before that, stepped from a limousine that had pulled to the curb. The cameras swung toward him, and even Victoria turned away to try catching the latest star to arrive. For a moment I looked at him, debonair and polished in a slick gray suit, smiling that crooked smile that had always seemed so seductive. Suddenly, I didn't care any more. The feeding frenzy he'd created with his mere arrival seemed so ridiculous, even though I'd been one of those hungry feeders for the past four years.

There was nothing here for me any more.

Without regret, I turned and walked away.

Wendy was working the late shift that night, so the apartment was dark when I got home. I poured myself a glass of pinot grigio and changed into sweatpants, a Bulldogs T-shirt, and my ridiculous-looking-but-comfortable Cookie Monster slippers. I sat down on the couch with my laptop, rewound the cancer benefit interview tape, and put on a pair of headphones.

An hour and a half and two glasses of wine later, I had finished transcribing all the celebrity quotes. I e-mailed them to Lauren Elkin, who edited *Chic*'s celeb section, and to Megan Combs, who handled celebrity fashion for *Chic*. I knew they'd both be able to use a lot of the quotes.

For the next hour, I worked on composing a carefully worded e-mail to Maude Beauvais, thanking her for her kindness in giving me a job as a stringer, but telling her that I could no longer work for her. When I hit Send a few minutes past midnight, I felt like a weight had been lifted from my shoulders. I didn't know what I was going to do for work, but I promised myself it would be something that didn't depend on gossip, celebrity, and the whims of publicists.

I turned the computer off, kicked off my slippers, put my feet up on the couch, and turned on the TV. I flipped aimlessly through the channels until I found *The Blind Man*, starring Cole Brannon, just starting on TNT. Thanks to my sleeplessness the night before, I drifted off before the second commercial break.

I dreamed of Cole Brannon.

I woke up to a series of knocks on our front door the next morning. I groaned and opened one eye, squinting at the clock on the wall. It was only 7:30. In the morning. On a Sunday. I rolled back over on my stomach, pulled the blanket over my head, and hoped that whoever it was would go away.

But the knocking continued.

'Wendy!' I mumbled halfheartedly. But I was already awake. There was no use in waking her up too.

The knocking had turned to an insistent pounding by the time I dragged my protesting body off the couch.

'Hang on!' I yelled at whoever was on the other side of the door. 'It's seven thirty on a Sunday morning, for God's sake!'

I slipped into my Cookie Monster slippers and shuffled hostilely toward the door. Whoever it was had some nerve beating down our door at the crack of dawn. Didn't they know there was a depressed, unemployed woman here who needed her beauty sleep?

Mumbling under my breath, I shuffled across the kitchen, not bothering to stop and fix my hair or straighten my T-shirt.

I unlatched the several locks, swung open the door, and blinked into the hallway as my eyes adjusted to the light. Then I gasped.

It was Cole Brannon.

I froze. I couldn't move. I just stared for a moment, my jaw hanging slack, my hand frozen to the doorknob.

'Oh my God,' I mumbled finally. I reached a horrified hand up to my head and realized the worst was true. I was sporting the worst bedhead known to mankind. My shirt was wrinkled and falling off one shoulder, and I was wearing Cookie Monster slippers. I probably had a string of drool dried across my face too. I reached up to touch the corner of my mouth, and sure enough, I did. I groaned.

'Good morning,' said Cole softly. He wasn't smiling. He was wearing old jeans and a wrinkled T-shirt, and his blue eyes were bloodshot. He looked shaken.

'Oh my God,' I said again. Could this be any worse? I looked like I'd been run over by a train – or at least by a bunch of head-hunting Muppets who had left their conquests behind on my feet. I reached up again and smoothed my hair down as well as I could, but I knew it hadn't helped much.

I took a deep breath in, then exhaled deeply. I needed to get ahold of myself.

'Would you like to come in?' I asked. I cast a furtive glance over my shoulder, trying to make sure that the apartment wasn't too messy and that I hadn't unconsciously scribbled 'I love Cole Brannon', or something equally mortifying.

The coast appeared to be clear.

'Um, no,' Cole said, surprising me. He took a breath. 'I just need to know if you meant what you said last night.'

He hesitated. 'About not having anything to do with that *Mod* article.'

I exhaled and closed my eyes for a moment. When I opened them again, Cole was looking at me anxiously. I looked him right in the eye.

'I swear to God, Cole,' I said. 'I'd swear on the *Bible* if I had one in front of me. I swear on . . .' I looked around quickly for something to swear on. 'I swear on Cookie Monster,' I said, pointing to my slippers, cringing the moment I'd said it. I sounded like an idiot.

Cole looked at me for a moment, and I could feel a blush creeping up my cheeks. Why did I always seem to say and do the stupidest things around him? There was a moment of silence. Then he surprised me by laughing.

'It's a pretty serious thing to swear on Cookie Monster,' he said gravely.

'I know,' I said, trying to match his serious expression with one of my own. 'That's how you know I mean it.'

Cole looked at me for a moment and sighed. We were still in the doorway, and I felt awkward and strange. I knew he was trying to decide whether or not to believe me, and there was nothing I could do but stand there and wait for his judgment.

'Look,' said Cole finally. 'You know Ivana, my publicist?'

I nodded reluctantly, biting my tongue before I could tell Cole exactly what I thought of Ivana. It wouldn't be pretty.

Cole took a deep breath and looked at me nervously.

'I want to believe you, Claire, I really do,' he said seriously. 'But Ivana is friends with one of your coworkers. A woman named Sandra or Sidra or something, I think.' I gasped. 'The thing is, this woman told Ivana that you told your whole office you'd slept with me. That was after the *Tattletale* thing, and I didn't really believe it at the time. Then when I saw the article in *Mod*, Claire, I thought maybe it was true.'

I sighed. I could feel my eyes filling with tears at the unfairness of it all.

'Sidra is the woman who came to the door,' I explained softly. I could hardly believe she'd taken her baseless vendetta against me this far.

'The door?' Cole asked, looking confused.

'The morning you were here, and we'd just found the purse,' I explained softly. 'The woman whose sister was sleeping with Tom.'

Realization dawned on his face slowly.

'Oh,' said Cole softly. He looked stunned. I nodded.

'She's the one who rewrote the article for *Mod*,' I said. Cole just stared at me. I pressed on. 'She's up for the position of executive editor, and she was assigned to edit my piece on you. It never even occurred to me that she would do something like this. But this is how she planned to get promoted. And she hated me, because I was more successful at twenty-six than she was by thirty-six. She couldn't stand it.'

Cole continued to stare at me, a mixture of doubt and horror on his face.

'I've already filed a lawsuit against Sidra,' I said, surprising myself by delivering my monologue so calmly. 'And I've tried to call you, Cole. But Ivana called me names and hung up on me.'

'She did?' Cole asked, looking genuinely startled. 'You told her you weren't responsible for the *Mod* article?'

'Or the *Tattletale* one.' I paused. 'She told me to . . .' I paused again and took a breath. 'She told me to *fuck off* and hung up.'

Cole looked embarrassed. I was quiet for a moment. I took a deep breath. I had to tell him how I felt. I had to come clean.

'Cole, I just need you to know that I didn't do this. I'm so sorry that all of it has happened, and I'm sorry for any embarrassment it's caused you. And I'm so sorry that I blew you off like I did. You were so kind to me, and I didn't appreciate it at the time. Then I believed all the stuff in *Tattletale* about you sleeping with all of those women, and then I thought you'd lied about Kylie Dane. Then this happened...'

My voice trailed off. I didn't know where my rambling was going. I had tears in my eyes again, and Cole looked pained.

'But I didn't,' he said sadly. 'I didn't lie to you, Claire.'

'I know,' I said. I took another deep breath. 'I know that. But then I called you to apologize for the *Tattletale* thing, and Ivana answered early in the morning and said you were in the shower, and that the two of you were sleeping together – but then the waitress at the Over the Moon told me that wasn't true, but I didn't know what to believe, and it was too late anyhow.'

I paused for a breath. Cole was just staring at me. I plunged back into my monologue.

'You were so nice, and I didn't know what to think,' I rambled, quickly, feeling a blush heating my face. 'I mean, you're Cole Brannon. And I'm, like, nothing. I'm just this plain, boring girl who worked for a magazine you probably hate. And I never wanted anyone to think that I slept with the people I interviewed or anything, because I've worked so hard to get where I am – and I never did it by doing anything inappropriate.'

He continued to stare at me in impassive silence.

I sucked in a deep breath and continued. The words were pouring out of my mouth like they had a life of their own.

'I liked you so much, but I knew nothing could ever happen, because that would be crazy – because, I mean, someone like you could never like someone like me, but I couldn't help myself from having these totally inappropriate feelings for you – even though I knew it was impossible. And I know it's just silly to think you'd ever be able to feel anything for me when you have women like Kylie Dane and Ivana Donatelli around you all the time. I knew you just felt sorry for me, and that's why you sent flowers, and that's why you came by – and it made me feel even worse to know that not only could you never possibly fall for me, but you realized exactly how pathetic I was.'

He stared at me for another moment, and suddenly, the silence felt oppressive. I didn't know what was going on in his mind, but his face betrayed a storm of emotions.

'You're not pathetic,' he said finally, looking troubled. 'I never thought you were. You're not plain, and you're not boring. I thought you were really something special. Something different.' His voice trailed off, and he looked confused. I felt tears well up in my eyes.

'I'm just really sorry,' I finally whispered.

'I have to go,' he mumbled suddenly. Before I could say another word, he had turned away and was hurrying down the stairs, his eyes downcast. I watched him until he disappeared, listening in the hallway until I heard the front door of the building open and slam closed. I knew he was gone.

I slid down the doorframe and started to cry.

Celebrity Sightings

The next six days passed without another word from Cole. I stayed home a lot, pathetic as that was, just in case he decided to come back. I felt like a preteen waiting by the phone, convinced that her big crush was going to call. But my big crush, or whatever he was, never called and never dropped by. By Saturday, I was sure he wouldn't again. I'd done everything I could to convince him. I'd finally had the chance to tell him everything I wanted to tell him, and he'd made his decision. He had decided to stay away. I wouldn't forget the look of disappointment on his face as he backed away from me into the hallway.

I'd decided midweek that if I couldn't get Cole to forgive me, the least I could do was set the other aspects of my life right. So I'd applied for a job as an associate features editor at *Woman's Day*, where Jen, a friend of mine from college, worked. There, I'd be about as far away from celebrity writing as possible, and it actually sounded good to me to edit and write about '15 Ways to Spring-Clean' and '20 Family Vacations You Can Take on a Budget'. I'd been called in for an interview the following Monday, and I was elated.

I dropped by my attorney's office on Wednesday to check on the progress of my lawsuit, and Dean Ryan sounded hopeful. He had looked over the case and had come up with a dollar figure that he thought I could reasonably sue *Mod* for.

It was over a million dollars.

But that wouldn't bring Cole Brannon back to my door. It was too late for that.

On Saturday morning, Wendy had gotten up early and disappeared before I woke up, leaving a note saying she'd be gone all day. She had comforted me all week, telling me she was sure that the Cole Brannon thing would somehow work out, but I suspected she was probably drained from playing counselor and needed some time away. I felt sorry for burdening her.

I went shopping for the first time in months and splurged on a new pair of Seven jeans and two new Amy Tangerine tees I'd had my eye on. After all, if Dean Ryan was right, I'd be a millionaire soon. However, even the shopping spree and the dollar signs dancing in front of my eyes did nothing to cheer me up. I grabbed a soft pretzel from a street vendor on the way home.

I was watching *Pretty Woman* on DVD, alone – in sweatpants, on the sofa, with a Healthy Choice frozen dinner on my lap – when there was a knock at the door. It was 6:45. I froze for a moment, hoping against illogical hope that it was finally Cole Brannon.

But that was ridiculous. Tonight was the New York premiere of *Forever Goodbye*, his new movie, and of course Cole would be there. If I hadn't quit *Chic* last week, I would have been there too, standing along the ropes of the red carpet – because a star like Cole would draw an A-list crowd eager to be photographed and interviewed. I could have returned to *Chic* with pages of celebrity quotes in reply to their silly questions. But instead of having a chance to see Cole Brannon again, I was snuggled up on my sofa in sweatpants and a Braves T-shirt, feeling pathetic.

Nonetheless, the knock at the door made me hope against hope that maybe Cole Brannon had swung by on his way to the Loews Lincoln Square Theater to tell me he believed me after all.

Yes, I was bordering on delusional. But who else would be at my door? None of my friends just dropped by unannounced.

There was another knock. I could feel the color rise to my cheeks, and suddenly, I was having trouble breathing. I looked in the mirror, smoothed my flyaway hair, and thanked myself for putting on makeup that morning. But when I opened the front door with a pounding heart, half expecting to see Cole's tall frame filling the doorway, I was once again disappointed. More than you can imagine.

Instead of Cole, it was Tom. Talk about a letdown.

'Hi, Claire,' he said quietly. His clothes were rumpled, and he looked like he badly needed a haircut. He looked pathetic and beaten, but I wasn't moved by his appearance.

'What are you doing here?' I snapped.

'Estella and I broke up,' he announced.

'I thought you'd broken up months ago, like you told me that day at Friday's,' I said. I'd known for a long time that he'd been lying about that, but I pushed him anyhow. He reddened.

'Um, no,' he said.

'So, you lied,' I said.

'Yeah,' he admitted. He nervously tugged at the bottom of his T-shirt. 'Can I come in?'

'No,' I said, moving to block the doorway as he looked hopefully inside. 'I don't think you can. Why don't you just tell me what you want. You'd better not be asking me for money, because, so help me God, Tom – I'll kill you.'

Tom looked scared for a minute. I felt a rush of satisfaction.

'Um, no,' he stammered. 'Actually, no, I wasn't going to ask you for money. I, uh, remember what happened last time.'

I had a mental image of Tom standing in the middle of Friday's, drenched in twenty ounces of ice-cold soda. It was a good memory.

'Well, what then?' I demanded. I was quickly losing my patience.

'Look, Claire, I wanted you to know that I'm sorry about everything. I was a real jerk.'

'No kidding.'

'No, really, let me finish.' Tom took a deep breath and drew himself up to his full height, which wasn't that impressive. As I looked at him, I wondered vaguely how I'd ever found him attractive. His nose was too big, his eyes were too small, his hair was stringy, and his teeth were crooked. I could no longer imagine what I'd ever seen in him. 'I know I treated you really badly, and you didn't deserve that at all. I just want to make it up to you.'

I stared at him in disbelief for a moment and finally shook my head.

'Are you kidding me?' I asked, incredulous. 'How are *you* going to make any of this up to *me*?'

He played nervously with the hem of his shirt again for a moment, tugging at a thread that had come loose. Then he looked at me again.

'I heard you were going to sue Sidra,' he said. 'Apparently your lawyer sent her a summons to appear in court.'

'So?' I said petulantly.

'So I thought that if I offered to testify, it might help.'

I gazed at him coolly for a moment.

'What could you possibly have to say that would help me?' I asked finally. He seemed to consider the question for a moment.

'I overheard Sidra and Estella talking about how to ruin your career,' Tom said finally. I raised an eyebrow. Part of me wanted to reach out and wring his neck for doing nothing to prevent my downfall, but I was too interested in what he had to say.

'Go on,' I said. Tom sighed and looked at his feet.

'Estella was pissed that I was so upset about your walking in on us. She thought I was still in love with you or something.'

'Were you?'

Tom's hesitation was all the answer I needed.

'Um, yes?' he said finally.

'Don't bullshit me,' I snapped. Tom sighed again.

'Anyhow, she knew her sister worked with you, and after Sidra saw you with Cole Brannon that morning, she suggested to Sidra that she spread a rumor that you'd slept together. Just to other people at work, you know, to make you so embarrassed that you would quit.'

I frowned. This wasn't news to me.

'And the *Tattletale* thing?' I asked. 'Was that her too?'

Tom nodded.

'Why?' I demanded.

'That was just because she was jealous of you,' Tom said with a knowing smile. 'I don't think she really dated George Clooney, you know.'

'Yeah, no kidding,' I said dryly. 'And how is it that you know all of this?'

'She can't keep her damned mouth shut,' he said sourly. 'She was always over at Estella's, bragging about what she did.'

He paused.

'So would that information help you?' he asked finally, arching an eyebrow at me.

'I believe it would,' I said, remaining expressionless. I knew him well enough to know what would come next. 'So you're just going to get up there and testify or give a deposition or whatever, just out of the goodness of your heart?'

'Yeah,' Tom said, smiling at me. He hesitated for a moment, then leaned in closer. 'Well, I mean, it would certainly help if you could give me a little bit of money to help me out right now. Estella threw me out, and I could kind of use a little bit of cash, just for the short term.'

'No,' I said instantly, without even thinking about it. Tom looked angry.

'I don't have to testify, you know,' he said, looking

surprised. Evidently he'd expected I'd shower him with cash once I heard what he had to say.

'Actually,' I said brightly, 'you do have to testify.'

'No, I don't.'

'Um, yes, actually you do,' I said slowly. 'See, it's called a subpoena. It will be delivered to you by my lawyer, and it's going to say that you have to testify or get thrown in jail.'

Tom blanched. I smiled.

'Now see, the problem with getting thrown in jail is that you appear to have no money. And I'm not coming to bail you out. But look on the bright side,' I continued innocently. 'Of course, it would be great inspiration for your next novel. You *are* writing a book, right?'

Tom coughed.

'You'd really subpoena me?' he asked.

'I sure would,' I said, smiling at him. 'You got me into this, now you're going to help get me out of it.'

Tom stood on the doorstep and glared at me for a moment.

'Fine,' he muttered finally. 'See you around.' He turned and walked away, and I smiled as I watched him go.

Moments later, I was feeling better than I had in a while, curling back up on the couch with my Healthy Choice dinner and the remote control. I'd rented *Pretty Woman* and *Ghost*, and pathetic as it was, I was looking forward to a night alone with two of my favorite flicks.

I tried not to think about how miserably I had screwed things up with Cole. I knew that one day I'd get over it. For the first time I could remember, everything else in my life had finally fallen into place.

I knew that Tom's information would help my case against Sidra, because it would actually be solid testimony from a witness. She'd never work in magazines again.

As for Tom, he was clearly just as scummy and shameless as ever – but in a way, that was comforting. It reinforced the reasons why I was no longer with him, and it made me feel like the world had some order to it.

I had just gotten up to throw out the plastic TV dinner tray and pop some popcorn when there was another knock at the door. Damn it. What did Tom want *now*?

'What is it?' I yelled toward the door as I turned away from the microwave. 'Haven't you done enough?'

I padded to the door in my beloved Cookie Monster slippers, my hands balled in fists at my side. Couldn't he just leave me alone? He'd taken a year of my life from me. He didn't deserve another millisecond of my time. As I pulled the door open angrily, my eyes flashing, I was fully prepared to tell Tom off once and for all.

But the man at the door wasn't Tom.

It was Cole Brannon.

In my doorway.

Larger than life, in a gray Armani suit and a black tie.

I almost fell over.

'Hey,' he said simply. I just stood there and stared. I had completely given up hope that I'd ever hear from him again.

I opened and closed my mouth, but my voice didn't seem to be working. Actually, nothing seemed to be working. I knew I should step aside and let him in, but I couldn't quite move. I didn't know what to say.

'You okay?' he finally asked, looking at me with concern. I nodded slowly.

His presence filled the doorway and the whole hallway. I noticed dully that he was holding a dozen red roses in his hand. The pieces of this puzzle weren't falling together.

'Here,' he said as he watched my eyes dart back and forth between the roses and his perfect face. 'These are for you.'

Silently, I took the roses from him, staring blankly back and forth between the flowers and Cole. I felt numb.

'Thank you,' I said finally. I was tongue-tied and frozen

on the spot, vaguely aware that I was processing everything slowly.

'You're welcome,' he said politely, as if this wasn't the strangest exchange in the world. There was a moment of awkward silence as I wondered what I was supposed to say.

'Um, can I come in?' Cole finally asked.

'Oh,' I said dully. 'Yes.' I moved aside to let him past me, painfully aware of my dusty apartment and my disheveled appearance.

I shut the door behind him and then just stood there. I couldn't seem to think of what to say or do. I didn't know what he wanted.

Cole took a deep breath and turned to me. He looked like he was about to say something important. I waited, my heart beating faster.

'Aren't you going to put those in water?' he asked finally, gesturing to the roses.

'Oh,' I said, caught off guard. I'd expected some sort of important revelation or something, not a handy household reminder about what to do with flowers. 'Yes. Hang on.' I bent down and rummaged around under my sink, pushing past plastic bottles of Mr Clean, Windex, and Fantastik until I found a vase. I pulled the vase out and filled it with water, putting the roses gently inside. I turned around. 'Um, thank you.'

'You're welcome,' said Cole again. He paused and looked at me closely. He took a deep breath. 'I, um . . .' His voice trailed off and he looked nervous. He was still standing in the entryway, near the kitchen, but I couldn't quite bring myself to move and offer Cole a seat inside. I was too baffled. 'I came by on Wednesday, and you weren't here.'

My mind raced for a moment. Wednesday? Where had I been Wednesday? That was the day I'd gone to see my lawyer. But Wendy had promised she'd stay in while I was gone, just in case Cole Brannon came by. Had she gone out for a few minutes?

I made a mental note to strangle her later.

'You did?' I asked finally.

'Yeah,' he said. 'Your friend Wendy – well, your roommate Wendy, I guess – was here. She told me you'd gone to see your lawyer.'

'Wait,' I said, sure I'd heard him wrong. 'You talked to Wendy?' He nodded. How could she not have told me? I'd spent the week thinking that Cole Brannon hated me, and I'd spent hours moaning about it to Wendy. 'She never told me,' I said, slightly dazed.

'I know,' said Cole. I looked at him with confusion. 'I asked her not to.'

'Oh,' I said stupidly, completely lost.

'She told me that you quit *Chic* and don't want to do celebrity reporting any more,' he said. I nodded wordlessly, wondering if this was going anywhere other than pointing out my current state of unemployment.

'So I figured that if you're not working with celebrities any more, we wouldn't be violating any of your professional standards if I, um' – Cole paused for a moment and looked at me shyly – 'if I asked you on a date tonight.'

I just stared. I must have heard him wrong.

'What?' I asked. I hadn't meant to be quite that abrupt. I was just having trouble getting my tongue to cooperate with my brain to form more than one syllable at a time.

'To my movie premiere,' Cole added, looking vaguely uneasy. 'Would you come with me?'

I fought the urge to look around for hidden cameras. Maybe CBS was debuting yet another reality show in the fall, *Who Wants to Trick a Pathetic, Unemployed Journalist*. Yippee, I'd be the star.

'What?' I said again, simply because I couldn't think of anything else to say.

'I was hoping you'd be my date,' Cole repeated, looking a bit nervous. Clearly this wasn't going as well as he'd hoped.

I blurted out the first words I could think of. 'But I don't have a nice dress.'

Cole laughed and a bit of the concern fell from his face.

'Well, I got you one, if that's okay,' he said. I stared at him. He paused for a moment and went on. 'I mean, no pressure or anything, but I do have a dress if you want to go,' he said quickly. 'But only if you want to. I know I was kind of a jerk to walk away like I did on Sunday morning, so if you don't want to go, that's okay.'

'No,' I said slowly. 'You weren't a jerk. I just thought you hated me.'

Cole looked wounded.

'No,' he said. 'I've never felt like that about you. I just didn't know how to react after that whole *Mod* thing and after the things Ivana had said . . .' His voice trailed off. 'I, um, I fired her. I should have believed you from the beginning.'

'Really?' I asked.

'Really,' Cole confirmed. He took a deep breath and smiled at me. 'Now are you going to go out with me? Or am I going to have to grovel and beg?'

I stared and then finally smiled.

'I'd love to go,' I said softly.

'Good,' Cole said. 'I'm not very good at the groveling and begging. But I can work on it.' He flashed me a wide smile, and took his cell phone out of his pocket. I stared at him. This was like some kind of a dream.

Wait, maybe it *was* a dream. I *had* been dreaming of him an awful lot. Just in case, I pinched myself. 'Ow!' I said. Cole looked startled.

'What?' he asked, sounding alarmed.

'Nothing,' I said slowly. This was real. This was really *real*. I felt like I might faint.

Cole flipped his phone open and started scrolling through his digital phone book.

'Hi there. Can you bring the dress up now?' he said into his cell. He listened for a moment, then grinned. 'Yeah, she said yes.' He smiled at me and listened for another moment. 'I know. It *did* take her a long time. See you in a second, okay?' Then he hung up.

'Who was that?' I asked.

'Your dress,' he said with a grin. 'It will be arriving shortly.'

I looked at him, puzzled.

'Who was that on the phone?' I asked.

'You'll see,' he said mysteriously.

I was startled a moment later to hear a key turn in the lock. Cole winked at me and walked to the door to help open it. Wendy's freckled face and wild hair emerged through the doorway, nearly hidden behind an immense mound of gold silk.

I barely saw her. My eyes were glued to the dress, which was one of the most beautiful things I'd ever seen.

As Cole held it up, the silky fabric reflected the light, making it appear to glow with a life of its own in the middle of my fluorescent kitchen. It was sleeveless and elegant, and the neckline plunged low, but not too low, in the shape of an upside-down teardrop. The top was fitted and slender, and the bottom of the dress billowed out gently while a few thin layers of tulle underneath gave it shape. It was a deep color of gold that I knew immediately would look perfect on me.

'It's beautiful,' I breathed, nearly hypnotized by the glowing dress, knowing that my words didn't come close to doing it justice.

'I know,' said Wendy, beaming. She was still breathing quickly, trying to regain her composure after carrying the dress up the stairs. I finally focused on her in disbelief. 'I picked it out,' she said. Cole laughed.

'*We* picked it out,' he corrected. Wendy rolled her eyes.

'Yeah, yeah, okay,' she said. She winked at me. 'Actually, Cole picked it out. I just okayed it.'

'Unbelievable,' I said, still in awe.

'We'll have to do it again sometime,' said Cole. He

smiled at Wendy, who laughed. Then he turned to me. 'Well? Aren't you going to try it on?'

He gently handed me the dress, and in a daze, I let Wendy lead me into my bedroom.

'I can't wait to see it on you!' she squealed.

A hurried five minutes later, Wendy finished buttoning the back of my dress and turned me around to face the mirror.

'Oh my God,' I breathed.

'You're gorgeous,' she said. The dress fit every curve of my body perfectly, hugging my waist to make it look suddenly slender, cinching perfectly across my chest to lift my bosom, plunging perfectly at the neckline to give the illusion of more cleavage than I really had. My skin, faintly tan thanks to the weekends Wendy and I had spent at the beach, looked dark and smooth against the rich gold color.

'It's perfect,' I murmured.

'Oh, I almost forgot,' Wendy said, bending to rummage through her bag. She emerged triumphantly a moment later with two gold strappy sandals that matched the dress exactly. She handed them to me with a grin.

'I picked these out for you,' she said. 'Cole loved 'em.'

'They're Manolo Blahniks,' I said softly, looking back and forth between the shoes and Wendy's face.

'I know,' she said with a grin. 'If Sidra DeSimon could only see you now. And those are yours to keep.'

'Oh my God,' I said. I was in a daze as I bent to put the stilettos on my feet. For a moment I wished my pedicure was more up to date. But it didn't seem to matter much in the grand scheme of things.

'You are one hot mama,' said Wendy cheerfully as I straightened back up. I looked in the mirror. The shoes completed the outfit perfectly. 'That movie star in our living room won't be able to take his eyes off you.' She winked at me, and I grinned back at her reflection in the mirror.

Twenty minutes later, Wendy had expertly applied my

makeup and put my hair up, leaving a few curly tendrils tumbling down to frame my face. She led me to the door and gave me a quick hug before she opened it.

'You deserve this, sweetie,' she said into my ear as she opened the door.

'You look amazing,' Cole said, his eyes wide, as Wendy and I came out of the bedroom. He stood up from the sofa. 'I don't even know what to say.'

'Thank you,' I said, smiling back at him. It was finally dawning on me that this was all happening, that I wasn't hallucinating or imagining things. Cole was very real as he crossed the room and put his arms gently on my elbows, admiring me at arm's length.

'You are so beautiful,' he said, staring at me like he was seeing me for the first time. I blushed.

He stood there for a moment, just looking at me, and my heart pounded in anticipation. Then he leaned down and kissed me gently on the lips. I moaned softly without meaning to as my lips parted and his tongue gently searched my mouth for the first time. I forgot for a moment that Wendy was standing there, and I put one hand on Cole's back and the other on the back of his head as he folded me tightly into his arms. I felt the softness of his hair and the stiffness of his jacket with my hands, and I felt like I was drowning in him. In a moment, he pulled away, leaving me wanting more. Slowly, I opened my eyes.

This was better than all those dreams I'd had about Cole Brannon.

And it was real.

'I've been wanting to do that for a while,' he said, his voice husky as his blue eyes bored into mine.

'Me too,' I agreed.

The Velvet Ropes

The premiere seemed to go by in a blur. The moment our limo pulled up in front of the Loews Lincoln Square Theater, flashbulbs began exploding around us in a seemingly endless galaxy of light. I blinked and tried to adjust my eyes to the constant pop-pop of the cameras.

'Are you okay?' Cole asked, squeezing my hand, as we stepped out of the car. I thought about it for a second.

'Yes,' I said finally. 'Yes, I am.' And I was. The flashbulbs were nearly blinding me, and for a moment, it occurred to me to be worried about being caught with Cole. After all, photos of us together would be everywhere tomorrow morning. But for once, I didn't care what the pictures looked like or what the tabloids and gossip columns would say. I wasn't doing anything wrong, nothing that should have embarrassed me. I was just a girl out on a date with a guy.

It seemed almost superfluous that the guy happened to be the center of the Hollywood universe.

It was almost surreal to be on the *other* side of the red carpet – across the ominous velvet ropes from the snapping flashbulbs, the jutting tape recorders, and the jabbering reporters as they elbowed each other out of the way, following each star's progress down the carpet with wide eyes and eager looks on their faces. It had never occurred to me what we must have looked like from the celebrities' perspective. But now that I was in their shoes – Manolos, to be exact – I suddenly understood how annoying we, the media, must seem. I suddenly felt like a caged animal in a zoo with a throng of overeager, impolite children fighting to get my attention, to distract me or freak me out in some way.

'Weird, isn't it?' Cole murmured in my ear. 'You never quite get used to it.'

'Wow.' It was all I could think of to say.

'It's okay,' Cole said softly. 'Just be yourself. It gets easier.'

So I stopped and smiled for the cameras while Cole squeezed my hand tightly. I blushed when he leaned over to give me a quick peck on the lips, clearly not caring that it had been captured on a dozen rolls of film.

I glowed when he stopped to tell a reporter from the *New York Times* that yes, my name was Claire Reilly, and yes, this was an actual date. I smiled when he told a reporter from *Tattletale* that their magazine was trash and they'd been wrong about us months ago, but could print whatever they wanted today. I flat out laughed (demurely, of course) when he told a reporter from the *Los Angeles Times* that they might want to have their legal reporter call him if they wanted an interesting story about *Mod* magazine and a certain fashion director.

Then I saw her, and I couldn't stop myself from laughing.

It was Sidra DeSimon.

She was standing along the ropes of the red carpet, flanked by Sally and Samantha, trying to get a better view of the stars walking toward the theater. She was dressed in a black gown and chunky silver jewelry, her hair piled on top of her head. She had a notepad in her hand and was evidently reporting for *Mod* – which was quite strange, as I'd never actually seen Sidra on a reporting assignment, of all things. Stranger yet was the fact that she was the only reporter on the line dressed like a wannabe star. She looked like she thought she was going to the premiere herself, or at the very least, like she was hoping she'd be plucked from the crowd by an actor who had somehow neglected to bring a date. Fat chance.

When she saw me, it was almost cartoonish the way her face fell and her eyes widened in shock. Cole was holding my hand tightly, and I couldn't erase the grin from my face. Even when I saw Sidra. She would never ruin an evening for me again.

'What are *you* doing here?' she hissed at me as Cole stopped to talk to a reporter from *Entertainment Weekly*.

'Oh, I'm on a date,' I said breezily, loving every second of it.

'With . . .' Her voice trailed off and she looked like she was about to choke. 'With Cole Brannon?' Her voice rose an octave as she squeaked out his name.

'Well, yes,' I said, calmly raising an eyebrow at her. 'Does that surprise you?'

'I just thought . . . I thought . . .' she stammered. 'You and Cole Brannon aren't *dating*!'

I smiled at her.

'But, Sidra,' I said innocently. 'Wasn't it you who told *Tattletale* I was sleeping with him? And then printed it in *Mod*?'

'But we both know it wasn't true,' she sputtered. 'You never slept with Cole Brannon. You know I made that up.'

'Really?' I asked calmly. I turned to the reporter from *Entertainment Weekly*, who had stopped chatting with Cole and was now listening intently to our conversation. 'Is that still on, by any chance?' I asked him calmly, gesturing to his mini recorder, which was pointed our way.

'It sure is,' he said, grinning at me. 'And I just heard every word of that. Want a copy?' I smiled and nodded. Cole quickly scribbled my address and phone number down for the reporter, promising him a phone interview this week. Sidra's face had suddenly turned as red as the carpet.

'But, I didn't mean . . .' Sidra stammered. 'I mean, I think you know that—'

I cut her off. Cole was now back at my side, his arm protectively around my waist, pulling me gently toward him. I could feel his body stiffen as he looked at Sidra.

'It was so lovely to see you, Sidra,' I said calmly. I winked at Sally and Samantha, who glowered back at me. 'But I really must run. I have a premiere to attend.'

'But . . .' Sidra sputtered.

'Oh, don't worry,' I said cheerfully. 'I'll be in touch. Through my lawyer. Oh, and give my regards to George next time you see him. Wait, where is he tonight?'

'He's busy,' Sidra muttered, her voice barely audible.

'What a shame,' I said. Cole pulled me closer, his arm still protectively around me. I knew that Sidra couldn't hurt me any more. Ever again. 'Have a lovely evening,' I said to all three Triplets, who were looking back at me with matching expressions of hatred and awe.

Then Cole and I turned away, without looking back. Once we'd walked through the doors, Cole turned to me.

'You okay?'

'I'm better than okay.' I grinned.

'I have the feeling that woman is going to regret the day she crossed you,' Cole said, pulling me closer.

'You know, I think so too,' I said with a smile.

The movie was wonderful. The war scenes were breathtakingly vivid, the script was beautifully written, and the acting was heart-wrenchingly on target. The movie was an early favorite for the Oscars, and after seeing it, I could see why.

But even better than the movie itself was the way Cole slipped his arm gently around my shoulder midway through the second scene, and the way he squeezed me comfortingly, pulling me closer to him each time there was a sad moment in the film. I loved how he looked at me for my reaction after each major moment. I could hardly believe it when he reached over almost unconsciously and softly kissed the top of my head during a romantic scene.

After the premiere, we went back to my place. Wendy had conveniently disappeared to spend the night at Jean Michel's, and she appeared to have cleaned the apartment for the first time in history. I couldn't have asked for a better friend.

Cole and I opened a bottle of chianti and sat on the couch, talking and laughing for hours, away from the paparazzi, away from the prying eyes of curious onlookers. By the end of the evening, I'd forgotten that I was supposed to be intimidated by him, that I was supposed to feel out of my element being on a date with a movie star.

When the bottle was empty and I was full of liquid courage, I asked Cole if he wanted to stay.

He said yes.

We moved into my bedroom, where the ghost of Tom no longer haunted me. We spent what felt like an eternity exploring each other's bodies. Beneath the tux, beneath the movie star image, beneath all the layers of professionalism that had existed between us, he was the gentlest man I'd ever known.

That night, in the privacy of my own bedroom, far away from the prying eyes of the paparazzi, Sidra DeSimon, and *Mod* magazine, I fulfilled the tabloid prophecy.

I finally *did* sleep with a movie star.

When I woke up the next morning, sunlight streaming in the windows, Cole was already awake, watching me. He smiled and kissed my eyelids, then the tip of my nose, then my mouth. We made love again, slowly, languidly, and I knew I'd never let him walk out the door again.

Epilogue

Eight Months Later

I stepped out of my attorney's office with a very nice check in my hand and some very good news dancing through my head. Sidra had just been fired from *Mod*. The *New York Post* would be running the story the next day – she had been ordered by the court to pay me $100,000 in punitive damages, which I figured would put quite a dent in her designer clothing budget.

The victory against Sidra made me feel the most triumphant, but as I clutched the check in my hand, I couldn't help but feel pretty good about my victory over *Mod* too. My attorney had already taken his percentage of the award, but he'd left me with a sizable check. I already knew what I was going to do with it. I opened the envelope and snuck another look at the mind-blowing figure.

$2,400,000.

$2.4 million. It was my portion of the settlement that *Mod* magazine had offered to avoid being dragged through court.

Margaret had, of course, been fired, too. It made me feel a bit bad, because I knew she had believed Sidra's lies and hadn't intentionally libeled me. But now the former managing editor Maite Taveras was running the magazine, and it had finally undergone the jump in circulation that Margaret had obsessively pursued for years.

The day Maite got her promotion, she'd called to offer me my job back, but I politely declined. I loved writing for

Woman's Day, where there was no catty competition, no backstabbing, and no gossip. The staff worked nine to five and went home at the end of the day with smiles on their faces. I could never go back to *Mod*, regardless of who was running the show.

I was humming as I turned into the HSBC Bank branch in Union Square to complete a transaction I'd set in motion a month ago, when my attorney had called to tell me the amount of the settlement. My first thought had been, *What am I going to do with $2.4 million?* I couldn't imagine spending all that money over the course of a lifetime. But I knew someone who would benefit from a percentage of it, and there was no one who deserved it more.

By the time I emerged from the bank an hour later, I had deposited the check into my account and used a portion of it to complete a real estate transaction. My real estate agent Elizabeth met me at the title agency next door. Together, we reviewed the documents and put a 50 per cent down payment on The Space, a restaurant in the East Village whose owner was retiring. Wendy had commented more than once how it was the perfect location for the little French bistro that she'd always dreamed of owning. Now her dream would come true. She'd been the only one to stand by me throughout the tabloid nightmares of the previous summer, and this was the best way I knew to pay her back.

I would give it to her as a wedding present when she married Jean Michel next month in a small ceremony at Les Sans Culottes.

After I left the bank I walked through Union Square, breathing in the sweet aroma of banana bread and carrot cake from one of the stalls set up in the farmers' market. Apple cider simmered at the next stall over – tempting, even in the early May heat.

I stopped into the Starbucks on the east side of the square for a Mocha Frappuccino. While I waited in line, I flipped absently through the *New York Post* and fantasized about Wendy getting a stellar restaurant review in the paper. The words 'Next please' from behind the counter snapped me back to the present, and I lowered the paper to look at the guy in the green hat and apron behind the Starbucks counter.

But instead of ordering my Mocha Frappuccino, I started to laugh. Hysterically. The guy behind the counter turned beet red.

'What can I get you?' he asked stiffly.

'Oh my God,' I managed to choke out. People around me were looking at me like I was crazy, but I didn't care.

The guy behind the counter was Tom.

'It's not that funny,' he said angrily, his face on fire.

'Actually, it is,' I said between giggles. 'So I'm guessing the novel didn't quite work out?'

'No,' Tom mumbled. He looked terrible. He'd put on at least twenty pounds, and most of it had settled in a potbelly that poked out beneath the apron. His hair was so long that it skimmed his shoulders in stringy waves, and his skin was pale and washed out.

'*Was* there even a novel, Tom?' I asked. He paused for a moment and looked down at his feet.

'No,' he mumbled, almost inaudibly. I laughed again and realized how far I'd come in the year since I'd been with him. I could hardly imagine that he'd ever been a part of my life.

'I'll have a tall Mocha Frappuccino, please,' I said finally.

'Fine,' he said glumly. He turned away to put the order in, then turned back to me. 'That'll be three dollars and sixteen cents.'

I silently handed him a five-dollar bill, stifling another giggle. As he handed me back a dollar and change, he suddenly froze. Instead of giving me my change, he grabbed my left hand and turned it over.

'You're wearing an engagement ring,' he said slowly, an odd expression in his eyes. I smiled.

'Yes,' I said. 'Yes, I am.' He turned my hand over to get a closer look. The two-carat stone, princess cut and flawless, set in Tiffany platinum, sparkled alluringly on my ring finger.

'Who is he?' he asked glumly. I turned my hand back over and took my change.

'No one you know,' I said brightly with a smile on my face. 'Nice to see you again.' Then, leaving him staring at me with an open mouth, I made my way to the end of the counter where I picked up my Frappuccino. I left Starbucks without looking back.

As I walked down Broadway a few minutes later, slurping the last few sips of my drink and still giggling to myself about Tom, my cell phone jangled in my purse. I dug for it and pulled it out. I checked the Caller ID, smiled, then flipped it open.

'Hey, sweetie,' I said as I answered the phone.

'Hey, honey,' said Cole. 'Did you get the check?'

'Yep,' I said brightly.

'And did you buy the restaurant?' he asked.

'Yeah,' I said. 'Wendy is going to be so surprised.'

Cole laughed, and I marveled for a moment at how the sound of his voice always made me feel warm and tingly inside. Since the night of his premiere, he'd been spending as much time as possible in New York, and he was no longer staying at the hotel where I'd woken up, mortified, nearly a year ago. On his New York visits now, he squeezed into my double bed with me, and I always woke up with his strong arms wrapped protectively around me. He'd flown me out to L.A. on the few weekends he was stuck on movie sets, and in December, I'd taken him home to Atlanta to meet my mother and sister. We had spent Christmas in Boston with his mother, father, his two sisters, and his nephew. I loved them all instantly, and I'd left feeling like I was already a member of the family.

Cole had proposed to me just three weeks ago on bended knee at Over the Moon. His favorite waitress,

Marge – who I supposed was somewhat responsible for salvaging the chance of a relationship between us – delivered the ring, which I found baked into a slice of strawberry cheesecake, my favorite dessert. We had celebrated quietly that night over champagne at my apartment with Wendy, Jean Michel, and Cole's bartender friend, Jay. We even invited Marge, who showed up with a giant takeout box full of crispy bacon, eggs, and hash browns with cheese ... the meal that had started it all between me and Cole.

No one had leaked the engagement to the media yet, although there was a tabloid rumor that I had been spotted wearing an engagement ring. I felt like Jennifer Garner to Cole's Ben Affleck, which was absolutely ludicrous. Who would have thought that the media would one day be interested in what I was wearing on my left hand?

'I have a surprise for you too,' said Cole mysteriously as I cradled the phone on my ear and sipped my Frappuccino. 'Go pick up a *Tattletale* and turn to page fifteen, okay?'

I groaned.

'*Tattletale*?' I said. 'You know I don't read that trash.'

'No, trust me, you'll like this,' he said, still sounding cryptic. 'It's kind of an engagement present from a friend of mine. Call me back once you've seen it.'

'If you insist,' I agreed with a shrug.

I ducked into the next convenience store I came across and paid a dollar for the last copy of *Tattletale* on the rack. I took it outside with me and flipped to page 15.

As soon as I got there, the hysterics that had started moments ago at Starbucks returned. Once again, I looked like a lunatic to passersby, laughing so hard that tears were falling from the corners of my eyes.

Cole's 'friend' was George Clooney, and he had taken out a full-page ad in *Tattletale*. In it, he'd included a terrible picture of Sidra DeSimon, who appeared to be snarling at the camera. Underneath it, in block letters, were the words:

I DID NOT DATE THIS WOMAN.

EVER.

THIS AD WAS PAID FOR BY GEORGE CLOONEY.

I was still laughing hysterically when I called Cole back.

'That is the funniest thing I've ever seen!' I choked out through giggles.

'I know,' said Cole, who was laughing too. 'When I ran into him last week and told him about our engagement, I told him all about what had happened with Sidra, and he said it was the last straw. He was sick of her using his name to get attention. He swears up and down he's never even met her.'

'This is too funny!' I gasped through my laughter.

'Okay, gorgeous, I have to run,' Cole said softly as his laughter finally subsided. 'I'll be in by nine, okay?'

'I can't wait to see you,' I said softly.

'Dinner at Swank, then?'

'Yes,' I said. 'I'll call Wendy and make sure we have a reservation. Have a safe flight, okay?'

'You bet,' Cole said. He paused for a moment. 'Oh, and are those reporters still following you, honey?'

'Yes.' I laughed. 'Every day.' You had to admit, it was funny. When I was working as a celebrity editor, I never dreamed that one day I'd have a throng of tabloid journalists camping out on *my* front doorstep, demanding to know whether the diamond ring on my finger meant that Cole Brannon was finally off the market.

'You should tell them,' Cole said after a pause. 'I want them to know. I want the world to know.'

'Me too,' I said softly.

'I can't believe we're getting married,' Cole said. 'I don't think I've ever been happier.'

'Me neither.'

'Claire?' Cole said after a pause. 'I love you. I really do.'

'I know,' I said. 'I love you too.' We said our good-byes, and I snapped the phone shut.

As I walked the rest of the way home, the sun shone down on the city, bathing the streets with soft light. Around me, taxis whizzed by, stores overflowed with customers, and people brushed by me up and down the street, hurrying to their destinations. I walked along slowly with a smile on my face, knowing it no longer mattered what any of them thought of me. My life had become more perfect than I could have imagined.

As I turned the corner from Third Street onto Second Avenue, the crowd of paparazzi (who had been clustered on my doorstep since rumors of the diamond ring on my left hand had leaked out) fumbled with their cameras. There were several cries of 'It's her! It's her!' Flashbulbs exploded around me in a blinding array, and I was suddenly at the center of the media storm that had been following me for weeks.

'Claire, is it true you're engaged to Cole Brannon?' shouted one reporter as I made my way to the front door of my building.

'Did he really propose, Claire?' yelled another as I pushed through the throng.

I paused for a moment, like I always did, still somewhat taken aback by the attention. Then I did something I'd never done before.

I stood there and smiled. With a tabloid clutched in one hand and my handbag dangling from the other, I stood and faced the press that had first haunted me almost a year before. And for the first time in my life, I didn't care what any of them thought or what their publications printed about me.

'Yes,' I said finally. The throng immediately hushed into silence. 'Cole Brannon and I are getting married. He proposed three weeks ago.'

There was a moment of silence, and then the questions came in an avalanche of noise and the flashbulbs clicked away like a swarm of psychotic fireflies. I soaked it all in for a moment, realizing how liberating it was to simply tell the truth. To simply be me. To have nothing to hide, nothing to be ashamed of.

I gestured for quiet, and the throng immediately hushed again.

'We love each other very much,' I said, knowing I was no longer afraid of what they thought of me, what they printed about me. I knew who I was, and I had everything I'd ever needed. 'And I've never been happier in my life.'

As the bulbs exploded again in what looked like a fireworks display just for me, I smiled at the cameras and knew that everything in my world was finally the way it was supposed to be.

About the Author

I used to think I'd be a famous rock star. I had big plans. My stage name would be Mystica, I'd start a pop rock group called the Popsicles, and fans across the world would know my hit song 'Why Did You Leave Me?' Of course I was eight years old, practicing for my big gigs on a Star Stage and a Fisher-Price tape recorder, and my 'hit song' was a three-chord little number I'd written on the piano. Then it dawned on me: I can't sing. I mean, I really, really can't sing. As in, I scare people away. So as you may guess, singing stardom was not in the cards for me.

But from the ashes of my Mystica dream (which is revived from time to time in drunken karaoke sessions that everyone regrets) came the beginnings of a writing career that I would fall in love with. Now I contribute regularly to a variety of magazines, including *People*, which has been an incredible experience. I've interviewed Holocaust survivors, civil rights activists, people who have shaped the history of the 20th and 21st centuries, and, of course, the people you would expect me to talk to for *People* magazine: movie stars, rock stars, and celebrities from all walks of life.

I'll admit to developing little harmless crushes on some of the people I've interviewed: Matthew McConaughey, Joshua Jackson, Mark McGrath, and Jerry O'Connell, among others. But unlike the title of the book suggests, I've never slept with any of them! I swear! Not even close. But *How to Sleep with a Movie Star* sprang from the thought of

'What if?' What if I crossed the line and threw professionalism out the window (something I'd never do)? Or worse, what if someone *thought* I had acted inappropriately with someone I'd interviewed and started a rumor saying that I had slept with a source for a story? My career would be over! In this book, Claire Reilly, a twenty-six-year-old magazine editor a lot like me, has to face just that type of issue.

In addition to *People*, I contribute regularly to *Glamour* and *Health* and am 'The Lit Chick' on the nationally syndicated morning show *The Daily Buzz*. Check out my website at www.KristinHarmel.com, and please write in and say hello! If I don't write back right away, I'm probably out shoe-shopping!

The Art of French Kissing

To Lauren Elkin, my Paris roommate, my great friend and one of the best writers I know.

To those who have brought Europe alive for me, especially Jean-Michel Colin, David Ahern, Dusty Millar, Katharine Vincent, Jean-Marc Denis and Marco Cassan.

And of course to my wonderful mom, who introduced me to Europe for the first time.

Acknowledgments

A special thank you to Lauren Elkin, my wonderful friend who first lured me to Paris and has let me sleep on her futon each time I've been tempted to return. She's also a great writer, and I was fortunate enough to have her give me early feedback on this book. Thanks also to Amy Tangerine (extremely talented superstar designer and fantastic friend), who is a great cheerleader and one of the people whose opinion I trust wholeheartedly on early drafts. A thousand thank yous to Gillian Zucker, my trusted friend whom I admire both as a person and a professional (and who lets me call her second bedroom 'home' when I'm in LA!). I owe you a drink (or several dozen) at Vito!

Thanks, as always, to Mom, Dave, Karen and Dad and the rest of my fantastic family. I truly think I'm related to some of the warmest, most wonderful people in the world.

I owe a huge debt of gratitude to my fabulous editors Karen Kosztolnyik and Rebecca Isenberg for helping beat this novel into shape, and to my wonderful agent Jenny Bent for listening to me ramble about all the ideas that pop into my head. Thanks also to my film agent, Andy Cohen, who I'm happy to call my friend; to all the folks at Warner Books, especially Elly Weisenberg (congratulations!!!), Emily Griffin, Caryn Karmatz Rudy and Brigid Pearson; and to my UK editor Cat Cobain and her assistant Sara Porter. And as always, thanks to my first editor, Amy Einhorn.

I'm also fortunate enough to have met some of the nicest writers in the entire world. Thanks especially to Sarah Mlynowski for being so generous with her time and advice, to Alison Pace for giving me a New York couch to sleep on and taking me on walks with the fabulous Carlie, and to Sarah, Alison, Lynda Curnyn and Melissa Senate for the friendship and support you've all provided. Thanks also to the wonderful writers (and wonderful women) Jane Porter, Laura Caldwell, Brenda Janowitz, Johanna Edwards and Liza Palmer.

Thanks to my many wonderful, amazing friends, especially Kristen Milan, Kara Brown, Kendra Williams, Wendy Jo Moyer, Megan Combs, Amber Draus, Lisa Wilkes, Ashley Tedder, Don Clemence, Michelle Tauber, Willow Shambeck, Melixa Carbonell, Wendy Chioji, Mindy Marques, Courtney Jaye, Michael Kovac, Ryan Dean, Michael Johnson, Brendan Bergen, Ben Bledsoe, Jamie Tabor, Andrea Jackson, Lana Cabrera, Joe Cabrera, Pat Cash, Courtney Harmel, Janine Harmel, Steve Helling, Emma Helling and Cap'n. Thanks also to my occasional fellow junketeers and to my mediabistro.com students.

And thanks to you, the reader, for coming along on this journey with me! I love your emails, so keep 'em coming!

Our wedding was supposed to be in September.

I'd already been to my final dress fitting. I'd chosen my bridesmaids, picked out my flowers and booked a caterer. The invitations were printed up and all ready to be mailed. We'd chosen a band. We'd talked about what we would name the kids we'd have some day. I'd filled pages and pages with scribbles: *Mr and Mrs Brett Landstrom. Brett and Emma Landstrom. Brett Landstrom and his wife, Emma Sullivan-Landstrom. The Landstroms.* I could already envision the future we'd have together.

And then one day, it all fell apart.

It was a hot, muggy Tuesday evening in April, and I'd left work at three so that I could make a special dinner for Brett to celebrate our first anniversary of moving in together. I cleaned off our patio table, bought fresh flowers and cooked his favorite meal – grilled chicken stuffed with artichokes, sun-dried tomatoes and caprino cheese, served over angel hair pasta with homemade marinara sauce. Perfect, I thought as I poured a glass of Chianti for each of us.

'Looks good,' Brett said, strolling out through the sliding

glass doors to the porch at six o'clock. As he stepped outside, he loosened his tie and unbuttoned the top button on his shirt, which of course made him look even sexier than usual, in a haphazard way. It was a good sign, I thought, that I found him just as attractive as I had the day I'd met him. I hoped he felt the same way.

I beamed at him. 'Happy anniversary,' I said.

Brett looked baffled. 'Anniversary?' He raked a hand through his dark, wavy hair. 'Anniversary of what?'

My smile faltered a bit. 'Moving in together,' I said.

'Oh.' He cleared his throat. 'Well, happy anniversary to you, too.' He folded his six-foot-two frame into the chair closest to the sliding glass door and took a sip of wine. He swished it around in his mouth for a moment, nodded approvingly and swallowed.

I smiled, sat down across from him and passed him the salad bowl, which was full of chopped lettuce, olives, pepperoncinis, tomatoes, freshly squeezed lemon juice and feta cheese. He sniffed it approvingly before spooning some onto his plate. 'Greek,' he said, his hazel eyes crinkling at the corners.

'Yes,' I said with a smile. 'Your favorite.'

I was determined that I'd be better at this – cooking, cleaning, and basically being a domestic goddess – after we were married. Brett's mother (who, mind you, didn't work and employed both a cook and a maid) had already reminded me several times, with a stiff smile on her face, that her son was accustomed to having dinner on the table when he got home from work and a house that was neat, tidy and virtually spotless. I knew the subliminal message was that I wasn't quite up to par.

Evidently, I was supposed to be a full-time housekeeper

and a full-time cook at the same time I balanced my full-time job.

'So,' I said after a few minutes of dead air between us. Brett had begun eating already and was making *mmmmm* noises as he chewed. I hesitated for a moment. 'Have you had a chance to work on your invitation list yet?'

All I needed from Brett was a list of the names and addresses of the family members he wanted to invite, and I'd already asked him four times. I knew he hated planning things and looked at our wedding prep as a burden, but considering that I had booked the minister and the band, gone to all the caterer tastings, met five times with the wedding planner and picked out the invitations, all by myself, I didn't think I was being too demanding.

'Not yet,' Brett mumbled, his mouth full of chicken.

'Okay,' I said slowly. I tried to remind myself that he was busy at work. He had just started on a big case, and he worked longer hours than I did. I forced a smile. 'Do you think maybe you can get it to me by Sunday?' I asked sweetly, trying not to sound like I was nagging. 'We really have to get those invitations in the mail.'

'About that,' Brett said. He ran his fork round the edge of his plate, picking up the last strands of pasta and taking one last big bite before pushing the plate away, toward the center of the table. He took another long sip from his wine glass, draining it. 'I think we need to talk.'

'About the invitation list?' I asked. I thought we had already agreed that we would include everyone we wanted to invite. After all, my father had promised to pitch in as much money as he could, and Brett's parents were, to put it mildly, loaded. They lived just fifteen minutes from us in Windermere, the Orlando suburb where Tiger Woods and some of the *NSYNC guys owned sprawling mansions. The Landstrom estate was just as grand, and they had already announced that money was no object in planning the perfect wedding for their only child.

'Not about the list,' Brett said. He drummed his fingers on the table. 'About the wedding.'

'Oh.' I wasn't totally surprised. Brett and I had had some minor disagreements over things like whether we'd have the ceremony on the beach in St Petersburg or in his parents' huge back yard (I had deferred to him, and we were planning a garden wedding), and whether we were going to have a traditional vanilla cake or a cake with a different flavor in every layer (we'd gone plain vanilla, which Brett's mother had practically insisted on).

'What is it?' I asked. 'Is it the seating? We can go with the plush folding chairs if you want. It's not really a big deal.' I'd been partial to white wooden benches, which I thought would look beautiful in his parents' rose garden. But it wasn't about the location or the cake or the seating, was it? What was important was that I was going to spend my life with Brett.

'No.' He shook his head. 'The benches are fine, Emma.'

'Oh,' I said, somewhat stunned. It was the first time he had deferred to my opinion without an argument. 'That's great. So what did you want to talk about, then?'

He glanced away from me. 'I think we should call the wedding off,' he said.

I was sure, at first, that I'd heard him wrong. After all, he'd said the words nonchalantly, as if he just as easily could have been telling me that the stock market was down or that rain was expected the next day. And after dropping his bombshell, he had simply reached for the wine bottle, refilled his glass and glanced inside at the TV, which had been strategically turned so that Brett could see the Braves baseball game through the sliding glass door while we ate.

'What?' I asked. I shook my head and forced an uncomfortable laugh. 'That's so weird. I could have sworn you just said we should call the wedding off.'

'I did,' Brett said, glancing at me and then looking away again, back to the Braves game inside. He took another sip of his wine and didn't elaborate. I felt the blood drain from my face, and all of a sudden my throat felt very dry. I gulped a few times and wondered why it felt like all the air had suddenly been sucked out of the space around me.

'You did?' I finally asked, my voice squeaking a bit as it rose an octave.

'No offense or anything, Emma, but I don't think I love you any more,' he said casually. 'I mean I love you, of course, but I don't know if I'm *in* love with you. I think maybe we should go our separate ways.'

My jaw dropped. I mean, it actually felt like it came unhinged and fell open on its own.

'Whaaaa . . .' My voice trailed off. I couldn't seem to get my mouth to cooperate with me. I was so shocked that I could hardly form words. 'What?' I finally managed. 'Why?'

'Emma,' Brett began, shaking his head in that condescending manner he seemed to have adopted when talking to me lately (it was the same way his father often talked to his mother, I'd noticed). 'It's not like I can explain why I feel the way I do about things. Feelings change, you know? I'm sorry, but I can't control that.'

'But . . .' I began. My voice trailed off because I hadn't the faintest idea what to say. A thousand things were racing through my mind, and I couldn't seem to get a handle on any of them. How could he have stopped loving me? Had our whole relationship been a lie? Was he cheating on me? How would I tell my parents that the wedding was off? What was I supposed to do now?

After an uncomfortable moment, Brett filled the silence. 'You know, Emma, it's for the best, really. You didn't want to stay in Orlando anyhow.'

My jaw dropped. 'But I *did* stay in Orlando!' A little flash of anger exploded inside me all of a sudden. 'I turned down that job offer. For *you!*'

Just three months earlier, I'd been offered the job of my dreams — as the head of PR for a new alternative rock label under the Columbia Records umbrella in New York. I'd talked it over with Brett, and he'd told me in no uncertain terms that he would never consider moving; his life always had been, and always would be, here in Orlando. So I'd reluctantly turned the job down (after all, I was engaged, and my fiancé should come first, right?), and as a result, I was still working the same less-than-fulfilling job as a PR coordinator for Boy Bandz, the thriving Orlando-based record label whose latest creation, the boy band 407, had just landed at number four on the *Billboard* pop charts with their song 'I Love You Like I Love My Xbox 360'.

'Well, Emma, that was your choice,' Brett said, shaking his head and smiling slightly, as if I'd said something childish. 'You can't really blame me for choices you've made in your life.'

'But I made the choice for *you*,' I protested. My head felt like it was spinning. This couldn't be happening.

'And I'm supposed to marry you out of a sense of obligation?' he asked. He stared at me. 'Come on, Emma. That's not reasonable. We make our own choices in life.'

'That's not what I'm saying!'

'That's what it sounds like you're saying,' he said. He looked almost smug. 'And that's not fair.'

I stared at him for a long moment. 'So that's it, then?' I managed to say. 'After three years?'

'It's for the best,' he continued smoothly. 'And don't worry, you can take as long as you want to move out. I'm going to go stay with my parents to give you some time.'

I gaped at him. I hadn't even considered that I'd have to move out. But of course I would. That's what happens when people break up, isn't it? 'But where will I go?' I asked in a small voice, hating how desperate and unsure I sounded.

Brett shrugged. 'I don't know. Your sister's?'

I shook my head once, quickly, pressing my lips tightly together. No way. I couldn't stand the thought of having to slink up to Jeannie's door and admit that I'd lost Brett. Eight years my senior, she was married to the passive, mousy Robert, and they had a three-year-old son who was the most spoiled child I'd ever seen. I couldn't bear to think what she'd smugly say about Brett leaving me. *Failure*, she would call it. *Another failure for Emma Sullivan.*

'Well, I don't know, Emma,' Brett said, sounding exasperated. He raked a hand distractedly through his hair, which was starting to grow too long. He needs a haircut, I thought unguardedly for a millisecond, before I realized that it would no longer be my responsibility to remind him of such things. 'You could go stay with one of your friends,' he said. 'Lesley or Mona or Amanda or someone.'

Hearing their names – the names of three of the girls who were meant to be my bridesmaids – sent a jolt through me.

Brett blinked at me a few times and looked away.

'Obviously you understand why you need to move out.'

'Because it's *your* place,' I said through gritted teeth. I could feel my eyes narrow. It had been a point of contention between us for the last year. Brett, with his bigger salary, had made the down payment on our metrowest Orlando house. Each month, we split the mortgage payment, but Brett was the only one with his name on the deed. The few times that I had complained that the arrangement didn't seem fair to me – after all, I was paying half the mortgage but earning no equity – Brett had smiled at me and reminded me that once we were married, all of our assets would be shared anyhow, so what was the point in worrying about something so inconsequential now?

It had all sounded so reasonable at the time.

'Right,' Brett responded, not even having the decency to look embarrassed. 'We'll figure something out about the mortgage, Em. I'm sure I owe you some money back since you've made some contributions over the last year. I'll talk to my father and see what we can do.'

I gaped some more. *Contributions?*

'Anyhow, I'm sorry, sweetheart,' Brett continued. 'This is really hard for me too, you know. But in all honesty, it's not you. It's me. I'm sorry.'

I almost laughed. Really. And perhaps I would have if I hadn't been absorbed in fantasizing about stabbing him with the knife I'd used to cut the bread.

'You'll be okay?' Brett asked after a moment of silence.

'I'll be fine,' I mumbled, suddenly furious that he would even ask, as if he cared at all.

I didn't know what else to do the next morning when I woke alone in an empty, king-size bed that was no longer half mine. I was numb; I felt like I was in the middle of a bad dream.

So I did what I did every morning: I got up, I showered, I blew my hair dry, I put on my make-up, I picked out a sensible outfit, and I went to work. At least there was solace in routine.

The offices of Boy Bandz Records were in an old converted train station in downtown Orlando, just a block from where Brett's law firm was located. Sometimes, we would run into each other on Church Street as he went to get lunch at Kres with a colleague or I went to pick up a greasy slice of pizza from Lorenzo's. I prayed that I wouldn't run into him today. I didn't think I could handle it.

I sat down at my desk just before eight thirty and stared numbly at my computer screen. It was as if I had lost all ability to function. I had a million things to do today – a press release about the 407 boys, a CD mailing for O-Girlz (the girl band our company's president, boy band impresario Max Hedgefield, had just launched), several media calls to return – but I couldn't imagine doing something as banal as work when my life had just fallen apart.

Just past ten, Andrea, my boss, stopped by my desk. I had just put in my third series of Visine drops that morning, in an attempt to mask my bloodshot eyes. I hoped that the tactic was working. I knew how the emotionless Andrea despised it when her employees brought their personal problems to work.

'Great job with the 407 account,' she said. They were named '407' because Max Hedgefield – whom everyone called 'Hedge' – had apparently run out of silly phrases to string together and had thus resorted to using the area code for Orlando, the birthplace of modern boy bands.

'Thanks,' I said, forcing a smile at her through blurry eyes. I had done a good job, and I knew it. One of our 407 boys had decided to come out of the closet the week their album was released, and I thought I had handled the resultant media storm gracefully. Thank goodness Lance Bass had blazed the way for boy-loving boy banders everywhere. Danny Ruben, the out-and-proud lead singer of our band, had been welcomed by the media with open arms, and as a result of all the publicity, 407's album had climbed the charts even more quickly than expected.

'We need to talk about something,' Andrea said. She looked down at her left hand and examined her perfectly manicured fingernails intently.

'Okay.'

Maybe, I thought to myself with a little jolt of hope, I'm about to be promoted. After all, I certainly deserved it. I'd been with the company for four years, and although I was running the 407 and O-Girlz accounts by myself, I was only a PR coordinator. I'd heard rumors lately about a company reorganization, and I had my fingers crossed that I was next in line to move into a PR managing director position, which came with a substantial pay bump.

'Emma, sweetie,' Andrea chirped, glancing now at the perfect nails on her right hand, 'Hedge has decided to downsize a little bit, so I'm afraid we're going to have to let you go.'

I could feel my vision cloud up, despite the Visine. I stared at her in disbelief.

'What?' I must have heard her wrong.

'Don't worry!' she went on brightly, glancing away. 'We're offering four weeks' severance, and I'd be happy to write you a nice letter of recommendation.'

'Wait, you're *firing* me?' I asked in disbelief.

Andrea looked back at me and smiled cheerfully. 'No, no, Emma, we're laying you off,' she said, carefully enunciating the last three words. 'It's a totally different thing! I'm very sorry. But we'd appreciate it if you could have your desk cleared out by noon. And please try not to make a scene.'

'A . . . a scene?' I stammered. What did she think I was going to do, throw my computer at the wall? Not that that would necessarily be a bad idea, come to think of it.

She leaned forward and lowered her voice conspiratorially. 'You're just so well liked around here, Emma,' she said. 'It would be bad for company morale if you created a scene, you know. Please, for the good of Boy Bandz. We truly are sorry we have to let you go.'

I tried to wrap my mind around what she was saying. I felt numb, like someone had just smacked me across the face.

'But . . . why?' I asked after a moment. My stomach was tying myself into strange, tight knots. I worried for a moment that the granola bar I'd eaten on the way to work was about to make a reappearance. 'Why me?'

Andrea looked momentarily concerned and then flashed me a bright smile. 'Emma, dear, we're just downsizing,' she said. 'It's nothing personal, I assure you. You're very overqualified for your current position, and there's simply no room for growth here. Besides, I'm sure you'll find another job in a jiff! I'll be happy to be a reference for you, of course.'

I didn't bother reminding her that Boy Bandz was the only record label in town. Or that it would now be impossible to work for Columbia Records in New York after I'd rejected their more than generous offer three months ago. All of a sudden, my life was completely falling apart.

'Oh,' I said finally. I wasn't sure what else to say. It seemed my brain was suddenly working in slow motion.

'Out by noon, Emma,' Andrea repeated. 'Please, no scenes. And again, I'm sorry.'

I opened and closed my mouth, and when no words came out, I forced myself to nod at her to acknowledge my comprehension.

I didn't panic. I wanted to, but I didn't. Instead, I numbly cleaned out my desk, went home and cried for the rest of the day.

When I woke from a troubled half-slumber the next morning, exhausted and confused, I tried my best to pull myself together. I logged onto the computer, went to orlandosentinel.com and searched for PR jobs. There were eleven posted and, foolishly optimistic, I applied for all of them, faxing my résumé from a nearby Kinko's and dragging back home around noon, feeling useless and confused.

In the next two weeks, which I mostly spent holed up in the house, refusing to talk to any of my friends, I was called in for six interviews. Unfortunately, I burst into tears during five of them (not that this was normal for me in the slightest; I blame it on the post-Brett trauma). In the sixth interview, the one in which I hadn't cried, I knew I wasn't going to be hired when the man interviewing me asked why I wanted to work as a PR rep for J. Cash Steel, and I couldn't come up with a single reason because, well, I really didn't want to work for a steel manufacturer.

Brett called three times in the two-week period, asking me in a monotone voice if I was okay. I was confused by his uncharacteristic concern until he finally revealed his real reason for calling at the end of the second week.

'Look, I know you lost your job, Em,' he said the last time he called. 'And I'm sorry to hear that. But I'd love to move back into my place. Any idea when you might be ready to move out?'

I'd called him a name that my mother had once washed my mouth out with soap for using. Then I slammed the phone down so hard that it cracked.

That afternoon, I finally picked up the damaged (but still functioning) phone to call my three best friends, the girls who were supposed to be my bridesmaids. They hadn't called since I'd split from Brett, but I hadn't called them either. I hadn't wanted to talk about it. I knew they'd be shocked to hear that he'd left me, and I was looking forward to being consoled by them.

At least they'll stand by me, I said to myself before I dialed Lesley's number. At least I can count on them not to hurt me.

Wrong again.

'I feel terrible telling you this,' Lesley said, after she'd mentioned casually that she'd known about the dissolution of my engagement since last week, 'but I thought you'd want to know.'

'Okay . . .' I waited for her to go on, wondering why she hadn't called or come by if she'd known for a week that Brett and I had split.

'Well . . . maybe I shouldn't tell you,' she said quickly, her breath heavy on the other end.

I sighed. I didn't have the energy to play games.

'Whatever it is, Lesley, I'm sure it pales in comparison to everything else in my life right now.' After all, what could be worse than having your engagement broken off and then being fired the next morning?

'Well, if you're sure . . .' Lesley said. She paused. 'All right then. I don't know how to tell you this, so I'm just going to say it. Amanda has been sleeping with Brett.'

Okay. So clearly *that* could be worse than having your engagement broken off and then being fired the next morning.

I opened my mouth to say something but no words came out. I suddenly felt like my whole chest had been hollowed out. I couldn't breathe.

After a moment, Lesley spoke again. 'Emma?' she said. 'Are you there?'

'Urghrhgrgh.' I gurgled nonsense.

'Are you okay?'

'Uhrhghrh.' I couldn't seem to formulate words.

'Listen, Emma, it's not like you two were still together when it happened,' Lesley rushed to fill the silence. 'Amanda says the first time they hooked up was three nights after Brett moved out. I think he just needed a place to stay, you know? And one thing led to another.'

I felt sick. For a moment, I really thought I might throw up.

'You knew about this?' I asked in a whisper after swallowing hard a few times. 'Did Mona know too?'

'Well . . . yes.'

'How long have you known?'

Silence.

'Lesley, *how long*?'

'Since last week.'

'I'm going to kill her,' I breathed, suddenly hating Amanda with every bone in my body.

'Emma, don't say that,' Lesley said sweetly. 'After all, you have to admit, it was over between you and Brett.'

I couldn't even find the words to respond. I gagged on the sour taste that had risen in the back of my throat.

'You're *defending* her?' I whispered once my vocal chords worked again.

'No, no, not exactly,' Lesley said quickly. 'I'm just saying to look at it logically. It's not like Brett cheated on you with her or anything.'

'But—'

'Really, Emma,' Lesley interrupted. 'Mona and I have talked about it, and we really don't think Amanda has done anything wrong. I mean, it's a sticky situation, but I'm sure you'll feel better about it in a week or two, once you've had some time to think about it. Let's all meet for dinner this week, and we can talk about it. I know Amanda would love to see you.'

I was aghast. 'I have to go.' I hung up before Lesley could hear me cry.

I called my sister Jeannie next, illogically hoping for some sort of consolation. Six years earlier, our father had moved to Atlanta with his twenty-years-younger new wife, and three years ago, our mother had moved to California with her twenty-years-older new husband, so Jeannie was the only family member I had close by. Unfortunately, we were as different as night and day, and Jeannie's idea of a good conversation was one in which I was nearly reduced to tears thinking of all my shortcomings.

Perhaps this time, I thought, she will comfort me. After all, isn't that what sisters are for?

'Seriously, Emma,' she said instead after I'd explained everything. I could hear her three-year-old son Odysseus yelling something in the background, and she sighed loudly. 'Brett's just going through a *thing*. It's perfectly natural before a guy gets married. It's just cold feet.'

'Jeannie, did you hear what I said?' I said slowly, not quite sure that she was understanding me. 'He's *sleeping* with one of my *best friends*!'

'Emma, you're overreacting.' She sighed again. 'You *always* overreact. Robert got cold feet before our wedding too, but I talked some sense into him. Men just need a little persuading sometimes.'

'But Jeannie . . .' I started to protest.

'Emma, really, you need to stop being so high-maintenance,' interrupted my sister, the most high-maintenance person in the world. 'And do your best to persuade him to take you back. You're almost thirty, for goodness sakes. You're running out of options. I was married at twenty-three, you know.'

'Yes, you keep reminding me.' Disgusted, I hung up and picked up the phone again to call the only remaining close friend I had – Poppy, whom I'd roomed with in London during a summer internship eight years earlier. She had relocated to Paris three years ago to work for Colin-Mitterand, an international entertainment PR company based in France, and last year she had gone freelance and opened her own boutique firm. Now, I knew, she had been hired to do PR for KMG, an international record label based in Paris.

I crossed my fingers before dialing the last digit of her phone number. If she couldn't be supportive, I didn't know where else to turn.

'Your friend Amanda did *what*? That horrid little tart!' she exclaimed in her clipped British accent after I explained everything.

I breathed an enormous sigh of relief, and the beginnings of a smile tugged at the corners of my mouth. 'You have no idea how relieved I am to hear you say that.'

'You don't need a friend like that!' Poppy said hotly. 'Nor the others, for that matter. How dare they stand up for her?'

I felt a surge of relief. 'You're right,' I said.

'And frankly, sweetie, Brett never sounded like much of a winner either,' she continued. 'He always was a bit of a spoiled mummy's boy. Good riddance! Now you can focus on your work!'

'Not exactly,' I mumbled. I took a deep breath and closed my eyes. 'I was fired.'

'What?' Poppy's voice rose an octave. 'Fired?'

'Well, laid off,' I said. 'But it's basically the same thing.'

'Oh bollocks,' Poppy said. She paused. 'Listen, Emma. We're going to figure things out for you, I promise. I have an idea. Let me see what I can do. I'll call you back tomorrow. Okay, luv?'

I felt momentarily buoyed by her enthusiasm, but there was a part of me that didn't want to let her off the phone. After all, she seemed to be the only sane, supportive person in my life at the moment.

She called back the next day, as promised.

'Look, Emma, I think I have the solution to all your problems,' she said cheerfully.

'Okay . . .' I blew my nose, wiped my tears and put the cap back on the carton of Blue Bell mint chocolate-chip ice cream I'd been eating. I was grateful no one was there to see me consuming my fourth pint of ice cream that day. I felt a bit sick all of a sudden.

'I talked to Véronique, my liaison at KMG, and I have some good news for you,' Poppy said cheerfully, obviously oblivious to my ice-cream stomach pangs. 'I haven't told you yet, but KMG hired me specifically to do British and

American press for the English-language launch of Guillaume Riche's first album.'

'Guillaume Riche?' I repeated, surprised. Guillaume Riche was, of course, the big French TV star who was best known for his high-profile romances, including reported flings with some of the top actresses at the US box office and a year-long romance with British supermodel Dionne DeVrie, which had ended last year in a dramatic break-up that had been splashed across the cover of celebrity rags everywhere. I'd just read last week in *People* magazine that he was launching an English-language recording career, but I'd had no idea Poppy was involved. 'Poppy, that's great!'

'Yes, well, his personal publicist has quit, which leaves me solely responsible for him through the launch of his album,' Poppy went on quickly.

'That's amazing!' I exclaimed. I felt a swell of pride for my friend, who was obviously doing quite well for herself. Unlike me.

'Right, but our big press event in London in just five weeks away, and I could really use some help,' she said. She paused and took a deep breath. 'I persuaded Véronique that with your experience and connections, you'd be the perfect temporary addition to my team, and she has approved some extra money in the budget for it. So how about it, Emma? Can you come over for a month or so and help me with Guillaume's launch?'

'Come to Paris?' I repeated. I dropped my ice-cream spoon and it clattered loudly to the floor.

'Yes!' Poppy said gleefully. 'It will be such fun! Just a little something to get you through while you look for another job. And I can help you get over Brett!'

It sounded tempting. But there was a gaping hole in her logic. 'Poppy, I don't even speak French!' I reminded her.

'Oh pish posh,' Poppy said dismissively. 'It's no matter. I'll translate for you. And besides, you're working on Guillaume's English launch. I'll have you dealing mostly with British, Irish, American and Australian journalists. It should be a piece of cake for you!'

'I don't know . . .'

'Emma, listen to me.' Poppy was suddenly all business. 'You've lost your fiancé. You've lost your friends. You've lost your job. Do you really have anything else to lose by coming over here for a bit?'

I thought about it for a moment. When she put it that way . . . 'I guess you're right,' I mumbled.

'And let me tell you, Emma, there's no place better to get over a wanker like Brett than in Paris,' she added.

And so, a week and a half later, there I was, on a jet bound for a city I'd only spent a week in nearly a decade ago to work with an old friend I hadn't seen in ages.

Unfortunately, it never occurred to me to ask a single additional thing about Guillaume Riche or why his personal publicist had quit so close to his album launch. If I had, chances are I never would have boarded that plane.

2

The jet glided into Paris's Charles de Gaulle airport an hour ahead of schedule, which I took as a good sign. On the approach, I strained to see out the window, sure that I would see the Eiffel Tower or Notre-Dame or even the winding Seine. Instead, all I could see were strangely geometric pastures and a low-hanging mass of dense, gray clouds that obscured everything as the plane approached the airport. It was disconcerting; this was not the France I remembered. Where were the glittering monuments and the picturesque rooftops?

I'd brought my *Fodor's Exploring Paris* and my *Frommer's Portable Paris* with me on the plane, with the intention of reading both of them cover to cover during the eight-hour flight. It had been eight years since I'd been to Paris; I'd taken a week-long trip there with Poppy at the end of our internship when we were twenty-one. However, between the overweight businessman in the window seat, the airsick woman on the aisle jostling me constantly in my middle seat and the fact that I was moderately scared of flying, I couldn't focus on my guidebooks.

Instead, I thought about Brett.

I missed him. And I hated myself just a little bit for feeling that way.

We'd met three years ago during a Saturday eighties night at Antigua, a club in downtown Orlando's Church Street district. I'd been vogueing to Madonna with Lesley and Mona when a tall, dark-haired guy leaning against the bar caught my eye. He was cute; he had an enticing smile, and he was staring right at me. When 'Vogue' faded and 'Livin' on a Prayer' began pumping from the speakers, I mumbled an excuse to the girls and made my way casually to the bar.

'Hey!' Brett shouted over the din as I landed next to him, pretending, of course, that I'd randomly chosen that very spot to order my vodka tonic.

'Hey,' I responded casually, my heart thudding as I noticed for the first time what beautiful hazel eyes he had.

'Can I buy you a drink?' he asked. I hesitated and nodded. He smiled, his cheeks dimpling. 'I'm Brett,' he said.

'Emma,' I said, taking his hand.

He shook my hand up and down slowly, never breaking eye contact. 'You're beautiful, Emma,' he said. There was something about the way he said it that made me believe he meant it.

After we talked for a half hour and he met Lesley, Mona and Amanda, he asked me if I'd come next door with him to the rooftop bar Lattitudes. We stayed there, at a table under the moonlight, sipping vodka tonics (we had the same favorite drink), discussing movies (we both thought *Annie Hall* and the indie film *Primer* were two of the best films we'd ever seen), swapping concert stories (we'd both been to the last three Sister Hazel shows at the House of Blues) and talking about what we wanted in our futures. We seemed to have so much in common, and the way he gazed intently into my eyes and then smiled slowly made my heart flutter. By the end of the night, I was smitten. We went out on our first date the next night, and a month later, he called me his girlfriend for the first time. It felt perfect.

He was everything I thought I wanted – cute, successful, funny, good with people. My family loved him, and his parents grudgingly seemed to accept me. I thought we went together like peanut butter and jelly. Evidently, I hadn't considered that one of my best friends would one day worm her way into the sandwich.

'*Passeport, s'il vous plaît,*' the gruff voice of the stern-looking customs agent behind the glass cut into my thoughts. Somehow, reminiscing about Brett had carried me off the plane and toward the immigration control area, like flotsam on the sea of arriving passengers.

'Um, yes, of course,' I stammered, fumbling in my bag, past the two unopened Paris books, past my pink iPod loaded with Five for Fighting, Courtney Jaye and The Beatles, past the laptop computer I'd purchased with my holiday bonus last year. Finally, my fingers closed around the thick navy jacket of my gold-embossed American passport, and I pulled it out triumphantly. '*Voilà!*' I exclaimed happily, hoping the agent would appreciate the use of my limited French vocabulary.

He didn't look impressed. He simply grunted, opened my passport and studied it closely. My hair was shorter in the photo, just above my shoulders instead of just below, and since the picture had been taken in the winter, the blond strands were a few shades darker than they were now, in early May, which in Florida meant I'd already had two good months of sun. My current tan was a bit deeper and my freckles were a bit more pronounced. And of course, thanks to four weeks of unlimited cartons of mint chocolate chip (hey, it's how I cope, okay?), I was a good ten pounds heavier than I'd been when the photo was taken. But my general dishevelment was the same. In the picture, I knew, my lipstick had worn off, my lips were cracked and my hair looked like I'd been caught in a wind tunnel. I suspected I didn't look much better today, having just stepped off a transatlantic flight.

'You are visiting?' the guard asked after a moment, his voice so thick with a French accent that it took me a full ten seconds to decipher what he'd said.

'*Oui*,' I said firmly, although it occurred to me a moment after the word was out of my mouth that I wasn't, in fact, a visitor. I was here to work. I wondered if I should tell him.

'For how long?' he asked, remaining stubbornly English-speaking.

'Six weeks,' I replied. Suddenly, that sounded like a very long time, and I had a strong urge to turn back around and make a dash for the departure gates.

The French guard muttered something unintelligible, stamped my passport and handed it back to me.

'You may enter,' he said. 'Enjoy your visit to France.'

And then I was in, being swept along in another tide of people into a country I hadn't seen in years, to start a new life I wasn't prepared for at all.

'Emma! Emma! Over here!'

I spotted Poppy the moment I passed through the doors

on the far side of baggage claim, dragging my two giant purple suitcases behind me.

'Hi!' I exclaimed, feeling even more relieved to see her than I'd expected. I hoisted my laptop case and handbag up on my shoulder and dragged my enormous load of luggage toward her in what felt like slow motion. She was grinning widely and waving like a maniac.

'Welcome, welcome!' she said, clapping her hands excitedly before rushing forward to embrace me. Her shoulder-length, red-streaked dark hair was pulled back in a ponytail, and she was wearing a little too much make-up – which was pretty much how Poppy always looked. Three inches taller than me, she had a wide, ear-to-ear smile, rosy cheeks, enormous sea-green eyes and curves she liked to describe as 'voluptuous'.

Today, she was dressed in a bright purple blouse, a black skirt that looked several inches too short and a size too small, and a pair of forest-green ribbed tights. She was currently giving me the signature Poppy grin, and I couldn't help but smile back, despite my exhaustion.

'Let me help you with your bags,' she said.

With relief, I gave up one of the giant purple rollers to Poppy, who began lugging it toward the airport exit, her face promptly turning beet red from the strain.

'Emma, what on earth do you have in here?' she exclaimed after a moment. 'A body?'

'Yep,' I said. 'I've stuffed Brett into my luggage to dispose of him properly over here.'

Poppy laughed. 'That's the spirit! Give the tosser what he deserves!'

I smiled wanly, wishing that I felt as resentful toward Brett as Poppy evidently did. Clearly I had lost my self-respect, along with my job and fiancé.

As Poppy and I piled into a sleek black taxi and began to make our way toward the city center, I began to relax, soothed by the rhythm of Poppy's chirpy cadence. Somehow, being there with someone so familiar made the whole experience feel that much less foreign, even as everything around me was entirely unfamiliar. Gone were the Fords and Hondas and Toyotas I was used to back home. Instead, the highway was a confused and honking mass of tiny smart cars, compact Peugeots and boxy Renaults as it wove through suburbs that didn't resemble anything I remembered about Paris.

Instead of quaint neighborhoods, rooftops with flowerpot chimney stacks and windowsills framed by flowers, there were factories with smokestacks and enormous, characterless modern apartments with tiny balconies. Clothing lines hung with brightly colored T-shirts and jeans dotted the landscape, interspersed with hundreds of makeshift antennas. This wasn't quite the charming France I had envisioned.

'We're not into the city yet,' Poppy whispered, perhaps catching my worried expression.

'Oh. Right.' I felt moderately appeased.

But then our cabbie, who was mumbling to himself and driving at what seemed like the speed of light, shot off the highway, and the industrial skyline of the eastern suburbs suddenly gave way to my first glimpse of the Gothic towers of Notre-Dame off in the distance.

It was the first time that it hit me – *really* hit me – that I was actually in Paris, a continent away from the only life I'd ever known.

I gasped. 'It's beautiful,' I said softly. Poppy squeezed my hand and smiled.

A few minutes later, as we emerged from a crowded thoroughfare, I glimpsed the rest of the Parisian skyline, and my breath caught in my throat. In the evening light, with the sky streaked with rich shades of sunset pink, the Eiffel Tower was a soft outline against the horizon. I could feel my heart thudding against my ribcage as our taxi wove its ways further into the city, around pedestrians, past stop signs, though streets soaked with history and tradition.

As we crossed the Seine, I could see the sprawling Louvre, the looming Conciergerie, the stately Hôtel de Ville. The fading sunlight melted into the river and reflected back a muted blend of pastels that seemed to glow from beneath the surface. It was, I thought, the most beautiful thing I'd ever seen.

'Welcome to Paris,' Poppy said softly.

Already, I felt a bit like I was coming home.

'So what's Guillaume Riche actually *like*?' I asked once I had settled my bags into the tiny second bedroom of Poppy's small apartment, where I'd be staying for the month. She had misled me *slightly* when she said that her place was a 'spacious two-bedroom flat'. In fact, it couldn't have been more than five hundred square feet, and in the room that would be mine, I could stretch my arms out to the sides and touch both walls at once. Its one saving grace – and it was a huge saving grace – was that it was a mere two blocks from the Eiffel Tower, and if you looked out the living-room window, you could see the graceful iron structure soaring behind the apartments across the courtyard. My throat felt strangely constricted each time I caught a glimpse of it.

'Oh, Guillaume? He has quite a lovely voice,' Poppy said vaguely. 'Would you like a café au lait?'

'I'd love one,' I said with a smile. Poppy walked over to her tiny, crowded kitchen area and busied herself with a bright red espresso maker that hissed and spewed steam when she pressed down on the handle. 'So he's talented? Guillaume Riche?' I tried again. 'I've never heard him sing.'

'Oh yes, he's quite good, really,' Poppy said hurriedly. 'Would you like cinnamon on top? Or whipped cream perhaps?'

I had a nagging feeling that she was purposely avoiding my questions. 'I think it's really cool that you're working with him. He's huge right now,' I said, making a third attempt to bring him up. 'I heard a rumor he was dating Jennifer Aniston.'

'Just a rumor,' Poppy said promptly.

'How can you be so sure?'

Poppy shot me a sly grin. 'Because I'm the one who started it. It's all about building buzz.'

I stared at her, incredulous. 'And the rumor that he wanted to adopt a baby from Ethiopia, like Angelina and Brad?'

Poppy smiled sheepishly. 'I started that one too,' she admitted.

'But that's why the press have started calling him Saint Guillaume!' I exclaimed. 'It's not even true?'

'Not at all,' Poppy said, winking at me.

'So what can you tell me about him?' I asked as we walked into the living room and settled side by side on the sofa with steaming mugs of coffee in our hands. 'Is he as perfect as he always seems in the magazines? Or have you made that up too?' The sofa was lumpy, and I could see water stains on the ceiling, but there was something about the window box of yellow daisies and the quaint rooftops across the miniature courtyard outside that made the apartment seem much more luxurious than it probably was. I took a sip of the café au lait Poppy had made.

'Er . . .' Poppy seemed to be at a loss for words, quite a rare condition for her. 'Yes, he's wonderful,' she said finally. 'Do you fancy a croissant with that café au lait? I picked some up this morning from the patisserie on the corner.'

'That sounds great,' I said, suddenly realizing how hungry I was. Poppy hopped up from the sofa and disappeared into the kitchen, where I could hear the rustling of a paper bag.

I stood up while I waited for her to come back and studied the tall bookcase against the wall, which was overflowing with more than forty of what appeared to be self-help books. I read a few of the spines: *How to Make Men Lust After You, Forty Dates With Forty Men, Boys Love Bitches, Love Them and Leave Them*. I shook my head and smiled. Poppy had always gone overboard on things. I'd had no idea that self-help dating books were her new obsession.

'This is quite a collection you have here,' I said to Poppy as she returned with a pair of delectably flaky-looking croissants on a pale pink plate.

Poppy glanced at the bookcase and smiled proudly. 'I know,' she said. 'They've changed my life, Emma.'

I raised an eyebrow quizzically. 'Changed your life?'

'It's amazing,' Poppy said, her eyes sparkling. She reached out and grasped one of my hands as we sank back into the couch. 'After Darren . . . well, let's just say I went a little nuts.'

I nodded sympathetically. Darren had basically been Poppy's Brett. They'd dated for three years, and when he'd broken up with her four years ago, she'd gone into seclusion for two months, refusing to talk to anyone. I hadn't entirely understood what she was going through at the time, but now . . . well, let's just say that going into seclusion for two months didn't sound like such a terrible plan.

'Well, this book got me through,' Poppy said excitedly, leaping up from the couch and pulling a tattered, pale green book from the shelf. She handed it to me, and I glanced down at the cover. I blinked a few times, registering the words, and then stared at it incredulously.

'*Voodoo for Jilted Lovers?*' I read the title aloud, still gazing at the cover, which featured a photograph of a male doll with dozens of pins sticking out of the general area of his crotch.

'Yes!' Poppy beamed at me and clapped her hands together. 'It was perfect. Every night before I went to bed, I would stick a new pin in my Darren doll. It made me feel so much better!'

'You had a Darren doll?'

'Oh, yes,' Poppy enthused. 'I still have it, in fact!' She vanished into her room for a moment and re-emerged with a little doll, no bigger than her hand. It was dressed in jeans and a green shirt and had a thick shock of yellow hair and a smattering of freckles. 'Whenever I think of him, I simply insert a pin somewhere that's bound to hurt.'

'You do?' I asked. While I looked at her skeptically, Poppy cheerfully pulled a pin from a mug on her desk and stuck it into the Darren doll's belly.

'There!' she said. 'See? Now wherever he is in the world, I'll wager he's having a sudden and inexplicable bout of indigestion!' Poppy looked quite pleased with herself as she held the Darren doll up for me to see. 'Anyhow,' she continued, 'after that, I started thinking, perhaps some of these other books out there would help me too. And, Emma, I am a whole new woman.'

'Oh. Well, that's, um . . . interesting.'

'Emma, it's wonderful,' Poppy bubbled on. She put the poor Darren doll down and reached for another book on her shelf. 'Like in this book, *How to Date Like a Dude*, Dr Randall Fishington explains how to chuck men before they chuck you. It's amazing. And in *Secrets of Desirable Women*,' she continued, reaching for another book and handing it to me, 'the authors explain how to make a man want you by acting like you have no interest at all in them. I thought it would be total rubbish but, Emma, it completely works!'

'It does?' I asked.

'Emma, I've discovered the secret to successful dating.' Poppy smiled and paused dramatically. 'The worse you treat these wankers, the more interested they'll be. If you blow them off, they'll wonder what makes you so special, and they'll fall directly in love with you. And the best thing about dating like this, Emma, is that you always get to chuck the guys before they chuck you. You never get hurt!'

'Well, I guess that sounds good,' I said uncertainly.

'Listen, Emma,' Poppy said. She knelt in front of me and smiled. 'I'm going to change your life this month. I'm going to teach you everything I've learned. You're never going to think of Brett again.'

After I showered, changed and had a second cup of coffee, Poppy and I went out to have dinner at one of her favorite restaurants.

I'd forgotten just how dazzling Paris could be. In the wake of a month that had changed the course of my life and shattered much of what I believed in, I was, perhaps, in dire need of something magical. Maybe that's why I found myself rooted to the spot for a whole minute after Poppy and I emerged from the Métro at the Saint-Michel stop.

'It's so beautiful,' I breathed, staring up in wonder.

Beside me, Poppy put an arm round me and smiled. 'It's the most beautiful place in the world,' she agreed.

Night had fallen, and we were standing in the shadows of Notre-Dame, surely one of the most stunning spots in the city. In the darkness, the cathedral glowed with an ethereal light, both soaring Gothic towers lit from somewhere beneath so that they appeared to shine from within. Between them, a huge circular stained-glass window shone with muted blues and pinks. The illuminated building seemed to go on forever, with a spire rising from its middle and curved, leg-like supports rounding out the back end. The light from the church spilled onto the surface of the river and across the water to the sidewalk on which we stood, bathing everything in a pale light that made all of this feel a little like a dream.

'Wow,' I said softly.

'That's an understatement,' Poppy bubbled. 'Wait until you see where we're eating.'

She led me a block down the quai to a café on the Left Bank. Its yellow and green neon letters spelled out Café Le Petit Pont, and its umbrella-covered terrace looked out at Notre-Dame across a narrow sliver of river.

'It's one of my favorite restaurants in Paris,' Poppy said cheerfully as we waited at the entrance to be seated. 'I never grow tired of this view.'

Indeed, I kept pinching myself throughout dinner, convinced that I couldn't possibly be sitting nonchalantly in a Parisian café, sipping Beaujolais, eating the most delicious coq au vin I'd ever had and looking out on the fabled cathedral of Notre-Dame. Only a month ago, I'd been eating at a patio table with Brett, thinking that I had everything in life I could possibly want. It suddenly felt like the world I had lived in before was very small.

After toasting to my new life in Paris with the last of our bottle of wine, we ordered espresso and apple crumble and giggled our way down memory lane, reminiscing about our summer in London eight years earlier and filling in the gaps of our lives since then. We'd stayed in touch, but there had been lapses here and there – particularly on my side, I was ashamed to admit.

'I guess once I started dating Brett, I let a lot of things

sort of fall by the wayside,' I mumbled, avoiding Poppy's gaze. 'I'm sorry.'

'It's in the past,' she said. She reached across the table and gave my hands a squeeze. 'And so is Brett. Good riddance.'

I tried to smile, but it was harder than it should have been to get the corners of my mouth to cooperate. I took a deep breath.

'So tell me about Guillaume.' I changed the subject, hoping that Poppy would be less hesitant than she'd been at home. After all, it had been a long time since I'd worked with a bona fide celebrity. By the time the Boy Bandz boys made it big, I already knew them for the pimply-faced, spoiled, hormonal kids they were, which sort of reduced their charm factor for me. I was looking forward to working with someone who *People* had named one of the sexiest men alive and who sixty-seven per cent of *Glamour* poll-takers had said reminded them most of a real-life Prince Charming.

'Yes, right, okay,' Poppy said, nodding and looking away. 'We're all very excited about him; he sings in both English and French, and his music makes him the perfect crossover artist. He's sort of Coldplay meets Jack Johnson, with a side of John Mayer and the influence of The Beatles, all with that delicious French accent.'

'Poppy, that's great!' I exclaimed. It was just the kind of project I'd dreamed of during all those years of pushing flavorless boy bands. 'He sounds wonderful.'

'Well, that's the way we're marketing him,' she said, finally smiling and meeting my eye. 'He's supposed to be KMG's next big thing, the deliciously sexy up-and-coming French star. The higher-ups here have decided that they'll be pushing him hard to the British and American markets. Everyone already knows his name because of the whole Dionne DeVrie thing – and of course the Jennifer Aniston rumor has helped enormously – so it's perfect. Together, you and I will be handling his English-language launch, with a big kick-off event in London in just under four weeks. I've been working my bum off for the last two months on this.'

'Wow!' I said. 'This all sounds so exciting!'

'It will be,' she said with a nod. 'It's a big deal, really. We're flying lots of press in from the States. Basically, KMG's big roll-out plan this year is to make Guillaume Riche the next worldwide superstar, starting with the UK and America. It's up to me and you to make that happen.'

'It is?' I asked. I blinked at her a few times. The responsibility sounded huge.

'Don't worry,' Poppy added hastily. 'Everything's already in place. Everyone loves him already because he's a TV star over here, of course, and because of his reputation as one of Europe's hottest bachelors. In fact, we organized a poll of fifty British women and fifty American women just last week, and when asked to name the sexiest Frenchman they could think of, ninety-two per cent of them said Guillaume Riche!'

'And the other eight per cent?' I asked.

'A few said Olivier Martinez, a few named Gerard Depardieu, and one woman, who seemed a bit off her rocker anyhow, kept declaring her love for Napoleon,' Poppy said, grinning at me.

I laughed.

'Plus,' Poppy continued, 'the press think Guillaume's a saint. Along with that whole Ethiopian adoption rumor, we've had him doing lots of charity work in the last five months, and the newspapers and TV shows have started to pick up on it. In the last month alone, he's been featured three times in *OK!* magazine and made *Hello!*'s list of Europe's most eligible bachelors – after he and Dionne broke up, of course. The whole Saint Guillaume thing has really caught on.'

'So how come he's not releasing an album in French?' I asked.

Poppy shrugged. 'Over here, the French love English-language music, so they'll embrace the fact that he sings in English. This way, we can launch him to the UK and America at the same time we're launching his French music career. It's like killing two birds – well, a lot of birds, really – with one stone. And really, it's the Americans and the Brits that drive the world's taste in music. Plus, he grew up speaking English, so he'll be ace in interviews. His father spent some time living in the States before Guillaume was born, I gather.'

'Well,' I said, 'he sounds perfect. I don't even know how to thank you for giving me this job.'

'No matter,' she said, glancing away. 'I really need the help for the next four weeks, believe me.'

We lingered over the apple crumble while a jazz trio began to play inside. The smells, the sounds, the feel of everything here was so different to what I was used to. I could almost forget that somewhere, thousands of miles away, Brett even existed.

I fell right asleep that night, thanks to my jet-lag. When Poppy gently shook me awake the next morning at eight thirty, I felt disoriented, and it took me a moment to remember where I was.

'Wake up, sleepyhead,' she said softly, smiling down at me as I blinked at her with bleary eyes. 'It's Monday morning! Time to get up for work.'

I groaned. 'It's too early!' I moaned. After all, with the time difference, my body was telling me it was just two thirty in the morning.

'Sorry,' Poppy apologized. 'But you're on the French clock now. Rise and shine!'

I dragged myself out of bed, muttering words that Poppy wisely ignored. By the time I had showered, put on a suit and some make-up and appeared in the tiny kitchen forty minutes later, she had a flaky apple tart and a mug of cappuccino waiting for me.

'Eat up,' she said, nodding at the croissant. 'I popped by the patisserie on the corner while you were in the shower. You're going to have a full day, and you'll need the energy.'

'Thanks,' I said, my eyes widening as I sunk my teeth into the flaky pastry. 'This is incredible.'

'Yes, well, be careful with them or you'll gain ten pounds in a month,' Poppy said. She smiled sheepishly and patted her stomach. 'Yes, I confess, I speak from personal experience.'

I laughed.

'Er, Emma?' Poppy asked tentatively. 'Would you be insulted if I offered a suggestion on your outfit?'

'Um, no?' I responded hesitantly. I glanced down at my outfit – a charcoal skirt suit with a crisp pink blouse – and wondered what was wrong with it.

Poppy nodded and looked down at my clothes. 'Your suit?' Poppy shook her head. 'Much too New-York-boardroom. This is a city that dresses up – but the women here do it much more subtly, and in a much more feminine way.'

'Oh,' I said, feeling suddenly foolish. This outfit had made me feel powerful and successful in Orlando. Did I not look feminine? I thought the slender cut accentuated my hips. 'But what am I supposed to wear, then?'

'Give me a moment,' Poppy said with a smile.

In ten minutes she had re-outfitted me in a pair of slender black pants I hadn't had a chance to unpack yet as well as a pale pink blouse with a lacy collar from her own closet. She also loaned me a slim black tortoiseshell headband, which I used to pull back my somewhat unruly blond hair.

'*Voilà!*' she said, standing back to admire her work. 'Now we just need to tone down your eyeshadow and make your lips and cheeks a little rosier, and you'll have transformed into a Parisian woman before our very eyes!'

Poppy's finishing touch was a slender scarf, which she tied expertly round my neck, beneath the collar of the shirt. I had to admit that when I looked in the mirror, even I was surprised at the image looking back at me.

'I *do* look kind of French,' I said in surprise.

'You look lovely.' Poppy beamed at her handiwork. 'Shall we go?'

Poppy's office was located in an old building that looked as though it could have been a series of upscale apartments a century ago. It was directly behind the Musée d'Orsay which, with its Impressionist collection, Poppy promised I'd like more than the enormous Louvre once we had a chance to go. Even from the outside, the museum was impressive. Poppy, reveling in her role as impromptu tour guide, explained that it had been a train station until right around World War II. I could indeed imagine Parisians a century ago bustling in and out of the long, ornate building that stretched for several blocks along the Seine. Two giant glass clocks glowed the hour, casting pale pools of light onto the sidewalk below.

'Here we are,' Poppy said as we entered the old office building. We walked down a narrow hallway and stopped at a broad, gold-leafed door halfway down. She inserted a key in the lock, jiggled it a few times and pushed. I followed her into the office as she flicked on the lights.

'Oh,' I said in surprise as the room lit up. I guess I'd assumed that if Poppy owned a PR firm that handled someone as big as Guillaume Riche, she'd have a bigger office space. Instead, the surprisingly small room we'd just entered had barely enough room to contain the two big desks that faced each other. One, clearly Poppy's, was overflowing with paperwork, photographs and a few self-help books.

The other desk was a bit smaller and had a hard-backed stationary chair instead of a plush rolling one. There was an eight-by-ten black-and-white photograph of the Eiffel Tower pinned to a corkboard beside it, and a computer monitor sat on the desk, but other than that, it was empty.

'We can go shopping this weekend to decorate it,' Poppy said as I took in the bare space. She nudged me and added, 'We'll already be out shopping for your new clothes anyhow.'

I smiled and rolled my eyes at her. Evidently, Poppy had already decided that the wardrobe I'd brought with me was entirely useless.

'I had a business partner for a while, you know,' Poppy said softly after a moment, glancing at the bare desk and then looking away. 'But she's gone.'

'What happened?' I asked. It was hard to imagine that anyone would walk away once they'd landed the Guillaume Riche account.

'I'll tell you later,' Poppy said quickly. 'It doesn't matter. For now, it's just me and you, Emma. I'm really going to need your help.'

The first three days of work went smoothly. Véronique, our liaison at KMG, was out of town on business until Thursday, so I wouldn't get to meet her until the following week. Nor would I get to meet Guillaume – although I spent several hours that week drooling over his chiseled features and muscular physique in the hundreds of photos in Poppy's database. According to Poppy, he was holed up in a hotel room somewhere in Paris, writing his next album.

'You'll meet him just before the junket,' Poppy assured me. 'KMG doesn't like us to bother him while he's creating.'

That week, I had to read over some KMG company literature, sign a bunch of employment papers (I was being paid through KMG's small American branch to avoid the French employment laws) and help Poppy write a press release about the upcoming release of Guillaume's first album, *Riche*, which we were describing (somewhat cornily) as a 'lyrical ode to Paris and the power of love'.

Poppy also caught me up on the plans for Guillaume's London launch, which she and I would be solely responsible for. It sounded amazing. One hundred members of the media would be flown into London from the United States, Ireland, Australia and South Africa (as well as a few high-profile English-speaking music reporters floating around continental Europe). At London's five-star Royal Kensington Hotel, Poppy and I would host a two and a half day media junket, complete with a welcome reception, a surprise live performance and five-minute interviews for every reporter, to officially launch Guillaume Riche and his debut album to the English-speaking world.

Guillaume's first single was due to hit the airwaves next week, so there would be plenty of buzz built around the star by the time the junket took place.

'Emma, this guy is gold,' Poppy said on Tuesday as we laid out photos. We were trying to select two to send out with the advance press packet. 'Millions of women are already in love with him.'

In fact, I'd half fallen in love with him myself by the time we were done poring over his pictures. As I already knew from the dozens of photos I'd seen of him in *People*, *Hello!* and *Mod*, he had dark, shaggy hair, deep green eyes, broad shoulders and the kind of perfectly chiseled features that you expect to see on Michelangelo statues, not real human beings. Women all over the world were already going crazy for him, and his break-up with Dionne DeVrie had only excited the public appetite for him. But would his sound measure up as Poppy had said it would?

Wednesday afternoon, I had my answer. Before we left work for the day, a courier delivered our first copy of the single, 'City of Light', hot off the press, and we loaded it into the CD player at Poppy's desk excitedly. It would be Poppy's first time hearing the final recorded version of the single, but at least she'd sat in on some of Guillaume's studio sessions, which was why she was so awed by him already.

It was my first time hearing Guillaume at all.

The song, which he had written himself, was hauntingly beautiful. Poppy was right, it was reminiscent of Coldplay and Jack Johnson, with perhaps a little James Blunt thrown in, but there was no doubt that Guillaume Riche was in a class all by himself.

'Oh my God,' I said, gazing at Poppy in wonder when the song finished. 'We really do have a star on our hands.'

I'd never felt something so strongly in my life. It suddenly made sense why KMG was willing to invest so much in Guillaume. His voice was incredible, the lyrics were gorgeous and the melody was so pretty it gave me goose bumps. It was a totally new sound, like nothing I'd heard before.

That night, Poppy took me to a bar in the 5th arrondissement called the Long Hop. It was, she explained, a bar that catered to Anglos like us. But, Poppy said with a smile, it was always populated with lots of Frenchmen too.

'It's classic,' she said as we walked through the entryway, beneath the fluttering flags of our homelands. 'They think we British and American girls are *so* gullible and that we'll fall for their smooth-talking. But don't be fooled, Emma. They're just as bad as men anywhere else.'

I gave Poppy a look and didn't bother reminding her that I obviously wasn't here to pick up any guys, French or otherwise. Surely she knew I was in full-on mope-about-Brett mode.

Inside, the Long Hop was dark and smoky, with a hardwood bar framed with a list of chalk-written drink specials, a pool table in the back, a stairway to a small second level, and a room full of twenty-somethings packed in like sardines. Vintage beer posters and signs decorated the shadowed walls, and blonde, study-abroad American girls in jeans and heels tried desperately to look more French by tying scarves round their necks while talking to Frenchmen, who were, amusingly, trying desperately to look more American in jeans, Nike and Adidas shirts and sneakers. Music – mostly in English – pumped from the speakers, making it hard to hear. Half of the dozen flat-screen TVs around the room were tuned to football matches, the other half to a rotating mix of concert footage and music videos. The Eagles' 'Hotel California' ran effortlessly into Fergie's 'London Bridges', which pumped seamlessly into Madonna's 'Material Girl'.

'Let's find a place to sit!' Poppy shouted over the music. 'There are a lot of hot guys here!'

I followed her around the room, where she unabashedly looked guys up and down and returned their glances with a confidently sexy stare. I couldn't imagine ever being able to look at guys that way again. Not that I was sure I ever had. It sounded strange, but it was hard to remember what going out had been like before Brett.

'According to *Smart Woman, Stupid Men*, you have to exude confidence to attract confidence,' Poppy whispered as we walked. I shook my head and tried to hide my amused smile.

We settled on a ledge near the dance floor, and right away Poppy excused herself to get us drinks. She returned – after five minutes of flirtation with a tall, floppy-haired blond bartender – with a gin fizz for herself and a Brazilian lime and sugar cane concoction called a caipirinha for me.

'To your visit to Paris!' Poppy said cheerfully, holding her glass up. 'And to you discovering the art of French kissing!'

I held my glass up and clinked it against hers uncertainly. 'What exactly are you talking about?' I asked after we had both taken a sip. I tried not to feel insulted. 'Things may not have worked out with Brett, but it wasn't because I didn't know how to kiss!'

Poppy laughed. 'No, no!' she said. 'I don't mean actual French kissing. I mean kissing Frenchmen!'

That didn't clarify things at all. 'What about kissing Frenchmen?' I asked. I was starting to get a bad feeling about this.

'Well,' Poppy said dramatically, leaning forward and lowering her voice. 'I've decided that the best way in the world to get over an ex is to date as many Frenchmen as possible and chuck them before they chuck you!'

'You're telling me that you want *me* to date a bunch of Frenchmen?' I repeated incredulously. I looked suspiciously at her glass. What was in that gin fizz of hers?

'Exactly!'

'And then dump them?'

'Precisely!'

'And this is supposed to make me feel better?'

'*Voilà!*'

I took a deep breath. Clearly I wasn't getting through. 'Poppy,' I began patiently. 'In case you've forgotten, I just got out of a three-year relationship with a guy I was engaged to. And I'm only in Paris for six weeks. I'm not exactly looking for another boyfriend here.'

'Who said anything about a *boyfriend*?' Poppy wrinkled her nose at the last word, as if it was somehow distasteful. She paused for a moment and intently studied a tall, dark-haired guy in a striped, collared shirt and designer jeans who passed us by without a glance.

'I thought *you* did,' I said, confused. I focused on pretending that I didn't notice the very attractive dark-haired guy in the striped shirt giving me the eye. Or the blond nursing a Guinness in the corner who was staring at me. Or the muscular black man shooting pool near the dance floor who kept glancing my way and smiling.

'Boyfriends are more trouble than they're worth,' Poppy said with a shrug. 'Who needs them? I'm just talking about a lovely date or a good snog, Emma.'

I couldn't imagine that any of the men at this bar would want to snog me – or do anything else with me for that matter. 'I'm not exactly Audrey Tautou,' I said, rolling my eyes. In fact, with my somewhat stringy blond hair, wrinkle-rimmed blue eyes and less than lithe figure, I was pretty much the polar opposite of the doe-eyed brunette gamine.

'Oh rubbish,' Poppy said, waving dismissively. 'You're gorgeous. Besides, just by virtue of your Americanness, you're fascinating to these men. We Anglos are quite different from French girls, you know. And guess what? These Frenchmen? They're rather fascinating too.'

'They are?' I asked, casting a glance at one cigarette-smoking slender guy, dressed head to toe in charcoal gray, who was giving Poppy – or rather her on-display cleavage – the eye.

'Absolutely,' Poppy confirmed. 'They are nothing like those duffers back home in our countries. They know how to treat women. They wine us, they dine us, they actually fall in love with us without getting all effed up because their friends think they've no bollocks. They speak romance as a second language. If you're going to get back on the horse, Emma, these are the guys you want to saddle up with.'

'But I don't want to get back on the horse,' I said stubbornly.

'Sure you do,' Poppy said. 'You just don't know it yet. And there's no better place to start than right here.'

An hour later, Poppy was deep in conversation with the cigarette-puffing guy in head-to-toe gray, while I was being chatted up by a sandy-haired Frenchman named Edouard.

'Ah, I know Floreeda!' he exclaimed when I told him where I was from. His accent was thick and his speech slow and careful. He blew smoke out of his mouth, took another drag of his cigarette and grinned widely. 'Ze land of Meeckey Mouse, *oui*?'

'Er, yes,' I said, stifling a cough. 'But there's lots more to Florida than that.'

'I know!' he said, his broad smile growing even wider. 'Beaches everyvere! *Le jus d'orange!* Sunshine every day!'

More cigarette puffing from him. More coughing from me.

'Um, something like that,' I said, neglecting to mention the daily storms every summer afternoon or that in Orlando I'd been forty-five miles from the closest beach, or that I drank Tropicana juice, not fresh juice from some mystical grove out back. I imagined it was much like the fact that many Americans envisioned all of France as one big baguette-eating, beret-wearing country surrounding the Eiffel Tower.

'So, you would like to see Paris *avec moi*?' Edouard asked carefully, resting his right hand on the banister behind where I stood and leaning forward in a way that was clearly meant to be seductive but that seemed more like an invasion of my personal space. Not to mention my personal lung capacity. 'I can give you ze tour, *non*?' he asked with another giant exhalation of smoke. He grinned again.

I coughed. 'Um, no thank you,' I said, taking a discreet step backwards. Unfortunately, the whole bar seemed to be swirling with smoke, so stepping out of Edouard's cloud just meant stepping into someone else's. I took a long sip of my third caipirinha of the evening and reminded myself to be polite. 'I just got here today,' I added. 'It will take me some time to settle in.'

'So Saturday, maybe, eh?' he pressed, leaning closer. 'I take you on a peecnic, perhaps? Paris, it is such a romantic city.'

I stared at him for a moment. This was so different than an American conversation, where the guy would have asked for my number, strolled casually away and failed to call for three days – all as a means of expressing interest in me.

'Maybe another time,' I said finally.

'So I can to have your phone number?' he persisted.

I paused. 'Um, why don't you give me yours?'

He frowned. 'That is not normal.'

I shrugged, not quite knowing what to say.

He hemmed and hawed for a moment but eventually scribbled his number on the back of a gum wrapper and handed it to me.

'I hope you will to call me, pretty lady,' he said.

I forced a smile, took the gum wrapper and excused myself, backing out of his haze of smoke as he stared after me, seemingly confused that his advances hadn't been successful.

I walked back over to Poppy, who cheerfully informed the gray-clad guy that we'd both like another drink. As he hurried away, she leaned in and whispered to me, 'So? How'd it go with that guy you were talking to? Any snogging potential?'

I shrugged. 'He had bad breath. And he smoked the whole time I talked to him.'

Poppy laughed. 'You'd best get used to that in this city,' she said.

'Great,' I muttered. Now I could add lung cancer to my list of things that would go wrong because Brett had broken up with me.

'Don't take things so seriously,' Poppy chided.

I made a face at her. 'I think I'm ready to head home whenever you are,' I said after a moment, glancing around at the burgeoning crowd of cigarette-smoking Frenchmen on the make and the giggling American girls batting their eyelashes at them.

'No,' Poppy said simply.

'No?' I was sure I'd heard her wrong. 'What do you mean?'

'I mean that you're not going home until you've made a date for tomorrow night.' She fixed me with a firm stare.

'What?' This hadn't been in my plans for the evening. Or for the foreseeable future, for that matter.

'Were you paying any attention to me earlier when I told you about Frenchmen?' Poppy asked, raising an eyebrow.

'All I remember is something about horseback riding,' I said crossly.

Poppy laughed. 'I believe you're referring to getting back on the horse.'

'Whatever,' I mumbled.

'Look, Emma, if you're going to stay with me this month, I'm not going to let you sit around and mope about Brett.' Poppy was suddenly very serious. 'You have to get back out there. In *Secrets of Desirable Women*, Dr Fishington writes that your chances for finding love decrease by six per cent for every week you refrain from dating after a break-up.'

I stared at her for a moment. Although I didn't believe in her self-help mumbo-jumbo, I couldn't help doing the calculations in my head. It had been four weeks since Brett and I broke up. By Poppy's inane theory, that meant that my chances at love had diminished by almost a quarter.

'That's ridiculous, Poppy,' I said, wishing I felt as confident as I sounded.

'Emma, French guys are the best,' Poppy continued, ignoring me. 'It will build your self-esteem. Besides, when's the last time you've just been on a date that you didn't intend to turn into a relationship?'

I opened my mouth to respond but thought better of it. I considered her question for a moment. Even before Brett, every guy I'd dated had turned into a boyfriend, at least for a few months. In fact, I couldn't even remember a time when I'd gone on a series of meaningless first dates. But wasn't dating supposed to be all about finding Mr Right?

'You've just been racing into relationships, haven't you?' Poppy continued, evidently reading my mind. 'The French call it the quest for *l'oiseau rare* – the rare bird, the perfect man. You were like that the summer we lived together, too,' she added triumphantly.

I stared at her. Was she right? I'd gone out on exactly two first dates that summer. One, with a British guy named Michael, had resulted in us having drunken sex at the end of the night and me falling head over heels for him, which scared him away inside of five weeks. The next date I'd had, with a banker named Colin, had resulted in a three-month relationship that he finally broke off after I'd moved back to the States, citing the difficulty of doing long distance.

'So?' I mumbled.

'So . . .' Poppy said, drawing the word out. 'Maybe you need to simply *date* without trying to make it a race to girlfriend status.'

I opened my mouth to protest, but nothing came out.

'You're at your sexual peak, you know,' Poppy added.

'Um, what?' I asked, wondering how this was relevant.

'Yes.' Poppy nodded with confidence. 'According to *Sexy Time* by Dr Boris Sudoko, a woman's sex drive peaks between twenty-nine and thirty-five. Now, I'm not suggesting you sleep with anyone. But there's no better time in your life to feel attractive and sexy. Frenchmen are the best remedy for heartbreak.'

'You realize you're insane,' I muttered.

'Yes, of course.' Poppy thought for a second. The guy in gray was on his way back, balancing three drinks and smiling at Poppy.

'Look,' she said. 'What if I see if this guy Gérard has a friend that he can set you up with? And the four of us can meet tomorrow for a drink? Not a date, just a drink.'

'You know I don't want to,' I said.

'And you know that's mostly irrelevant,' Poppy responded with a smile.

I made a face at her and was about to reply when Poppy's cell phone began ringing to the tune of Gnarls Barkley's 'Crazy'.

'Bollocks,' Poppy cursed. She blushed and, casting a quick look at the approaching charcoal-clothed guy, scrambled for the phone, which was sticking out of her purse. '*Allo?*' she answered, sounding very French. I watched as the color drained from her face. She spoke a few more sentences in rapid French and hung up, looking distressed. 'Bollocks,' she exclaimed again, slamming her fist down on the bar in frustration. The guy in gray glanced at her, set two drinks down and hurried away, shaking his head.

'What's wrong?' I asked with concern.

'It's work,' she said tersely. She reached for the drink the guy had set down for her and took a big swig of it. 'We have to go.'

'Work?' I repeated in disbelief. I checked my watch. 'But it's almost one in the morning!'

'Well, technically we're on call all the time,' Poppy said quickly. She made a face. 'That's what happens when you run your own agency.'

I just stared at her. 'What on earth could we possibly have to do at one in the morning?' At Boy Bandz, I'd been 'on call' two nights a week, but there had never been a middle-of-the-night incident I'd had to respond to. Our boys were usually tucked away in bed by eleven, probably with their nightlights on.

'It's Guillaume Riche,' Poppy said tightly, leaning forward and lowering her voice. 'Véronique from KMG just called. There's apparently been, er, an incident.'

'An incident?' I asked.

'Véronique didn't explain,' Poppy said. 'She just said we needed to get to her office immediately. We need to do some damage control.'

Damage control? I opened my mouth but didn't have time to respond before Poppy grabbed my hand and dragged me toward the exit.

5

'*Merci*,' Poppy said quickly as the cab screeched to a halt in front of KMG's office building, which was just a few blocks from Poppy's office in the 6th. She thrust a handful of bills and coins at the driver and piled quickly out of the cab. I scrambled out after her, trying to compose myself. I was afraid I was failing miserably at that task. I was exhausted, confused and utterly disheveled. I was fairly confident this was not the best way to make a good first impression on Véronique, who, according to Poppy, was currently waiting to brief us inside.

As I hurried a pace behind Poppy toward the building, the enormous, brick-colored front door flew open, and in the entryway a slender, dark-haired woman in inky black skinny jeans, a crisp white blouse and a pile of pearls stood framed there, her arms crossed over her chest.

She said something in rapid French, her voice low-pitched and confident, then, glancing at me, she seemed to realize that she needed to translate.

'You are late!' she exclaimed, her French accent thick as strong espresso and her words coming in sharp staccato.

'Where is Marie?' She glanced at Poppy and then back at me. 'And who are you?'

'Um, I'm Emma,' I replied nervously. I took a step forward and extended my hand. 'Nice to meet you.'

She looked at my hand but didn't shake it. I stood there for a moment, feeling foolish, then lowered my arm back down to my side. I wondered what I had done to offend her in under ten words. Poppy patted me on the shoulder.

'Emma, this is Véronique, our boss,' she said smoothly. 'Véronique, this is Emma, the new publicist I've mentioned to you.'

'Well,' Véronique muttered, looking at me with what appeared to be suspicion. She looked back at Poppy. 'Marie is not responding to my calls,' she said crisply.

'Marie quit last month, remember?' Poppy said wearily. She glanced at me. 'Marie was my business partner,' she said softly. 'The one I mentioned to you. You're sort of, er, replacing her.' I suddenly realized that there was more behind Marie's departure than Poppy had initially led me to believe.

'*Quoi?*' Véronique said sharply. 'Well. This is *monstrueux*. This means that you and the new girl must take care of this on your own!'

'What exactly is happening, Véronique?' Poppy interrupted.

Véronique heaved a weight-of-the-world-on-her-shoulders sigh and rolled her eyes. 'Come with me,' she said.

The moment Véronique turned to walk back into the building, Poppy looked at me with concern and shrugged. 'Guillaume,' she mouthed. I shook my head, not understanding yet what the handsome rock star could have done in the middle of the night to make Véronique so panicked.

After all, Guillaume was practically a saint, wasn't he?

We followed Véronique down a long corridor into a big, open-plan office that looked out of place in such an old building. I'd expected ornate, tiny rooms that had once belonged to businessmen two centuries earlier. Instead, the room felt oddly reminiscent of the Boy Bandz offices back home.

Fluorescent lighting, just as unflattering here as it was Stateside, poured over a dozen desktops, which were separated by cubicle walls into workspaces almost too small to turn around in. The desks were white and modern-looking, and the swivel chairs looked like they had come straight out of Ikea – not at all the ornate, antique desks and chairs I had somehow anticipated. The walls were decorated with twenty-by-thirty framed posters of the bands on the KMG label. I glanced at each of them, orienting myself with the names. La Renaissance. Amélie Deneuve. Jean-Michel Colin. Jacques Cash. TechnoPub. République de Musique.

'Where's Guillaume Riche's poster?' I whispered to Poppy as we hurried to keep up with Véronique.

'He's not up there yet,' Poppy explained. 'His album cover won't be final for another week. Then we'll add him to the wall. Believe me, it will be quite the distraction. He's shirtless on the cover.'

I raised an eyebrow. That sounded like nice workplace scenery.

We followed Véronique into her office, where Poppy and I sank nervously into side-by-side chairs without taking our eyes off her. She was standing before us with clenched fists, looking as if steam might begin shooting from her ears at any moment.

'This is a disaster,' she said, staring first at Poppy, then at me. 'Guillaume is at it again. You must take care of him! What are we paying you for?'

Poppy sighed, and I looked at her in confusion. I was feeling more and more out of the loop by the moment. Just then a phone rang in the outer room, and Véronique made a face.

'Don't move,' she said, fixing us with a glare, as if we might be tempted to climb out a window in her absence. 'I'll be back in a moment.'

Véronique hurried out of the office. I turned to Poppy.

'What exactly is going on?' I demanded.

Poppy averted her eyes. 'Oh yes, Guillaume Riche,' she said with forced casualness. 'There may have been a few things I forgot to mention about him.'

'A few things?' I repeated slowly.

'Er ... yes,' she said, still not meeting my gaze. 'Guillaume sort of has a, um, certain propensity for getting himself into trouble.'

'Trouble?' I was starting to get a bad feeling about this.

'Er, yes,' she said. 'You might say that. All sorts of messes.'

'For example?' I prompted.

Poppy sighed. Her eyes flicked to me and then away again. 'He's been locked in a wine cellar in the south of France,' she said quickly. 'He's been trapped in the dolphin tank at the aquarium in Brittany; he even tap-danced through the prime minister's back yard in the middle of the night. He's a bit batty, you might say.'

'But ... I've never read about any of this!' I exclaimed.

'Good,' Poppy said with a wry smile. 'That means I've been doing my job. Most of the stories were reported in some capacity, but my old colleague, Marie, used to do a wonderful job of coming up with logical explanations for everything.'

My heart – and my hopes of an easy stay in Paris – were sinking like a stone in the Seine. 'But I thought you said he was some kind of saint!'

'That's not *quite* what I said,' Poppy said, averting her eyes. 'What I said was that's how KMG has decided to market him. They did a ton of research with focus groups and all sorts of psychological studies and found that women in our target audience are getting tired of the stereotypical rock 'n' roll bad boy. The market is ripe for something new. Our research showed that positioning Guillaume as a nice guy, the kind of guy you want to take home to your mother, was the best way to make him an international star.'

'Except he's *not* exactly a nice guy?' I filled in flatly.

'No, it's not quite that,' Poppy said quickly. 'He's nice enough. He's just . . . well, let's just say he has a screw or two loose. Which doesn't exactly fit with the image we're trying to project. So far,' she continued, 'we've managed to spin all his little mishaps to make them look like innocent mistakes. The press hasn't caught on. But he can't seem to stop getting himself into trouble.'

Before I could reply, Véronique bustled back into the room, grasping a handful of papers.

'Faxes from just about every reporter we've ever had contact with,' she said sharply, holding up the stack. Poppy and I exchanged glances. 'They all want to know what Guillaume is doing.'

'What *is* Guillaume doing?' Poppy asked, quite sensibly, I thought.

'You mean you don't know?' Véronique demanded. She mumbled something in French that sounded a lot like an expletive. 'Well, I'll tell you then! He's shut himself in a hotel room up in Montmartre with four girls – all of them seemingly underage – and a pile of drugs. It seems a room service waiter called the press, and they're there in droves, waiting for him to come out and get caught.'

Poppy swore under her breath and stood up quickly.

'I expect you to take care of this,' Véronique continued sharply, thrusting a piece of notepaper at Poppy. 'Here's the information about where he is. If Guillaume Riche gets arrested, or winds up looking like he's coaxing young girls into getting high, it's going to be KMG taking the fall. And you'll both be out of a job.'

'I can't lose this job, Emma,' Poppy said, white-faced, as we sat in the back of a cab on the way to Montmartre, the Bohemian quarter of historic Paris that sat atop a small hill and was famous for its miniature windmills and winding roads. She knocked on the divider separating the driver from us. 'Can you go any faster?' she asked loudly. The driver cursed at her in French and threw his hands in the air. Poppy sighed, leaned back in her seat and closed her eyes.

'Poppy, everything will be fine.' I tried to console her. It was disconcerting to see the normally cool, calm and collected Poppy so shaken. 'I'm sure that whatever is happening with Guillaume isn't that bad. We'll work it out.'

Poppy opened her eyes and stared at me bleakly. 'You don't know Guillaume,' she said. 'He's a complete disaster.'

I shrugged. 'I'm sure you're exaggerating.'

Poppy shook her head. 'No, I'm not. That's why Marie quit last month. She'd finally had enough. She was great at this, though. Every scrape he got into, she somehow talked him out of. All I had to do was basically translate whatever nonsense she said and keep the English-speaking journalists happy.'

'So you never had to talk him out of anything yourself?' I asked.

Poppy looked away. 'I'm crap at inventing stories, Emma, I really am. I begged and pleaded with Marie to stay, but she was sick of this and sick of being yelled at by Véronique. I don't know how I'm going to handle this on my own.'

'You're not on your own,' I said softly. I took a deep breath. 'Look, I'll help you.'

Poppy glanced at me. 'You think you can make something up to talk Guillaume out of this?'

I paused. 'Well, I've had to talk the boy band guys out of some ridiculous situations in the past,' I said. There was, for example, the time Robbie Roberts was arrested for shoplifting three pairs of women's panties. Or the time Justin Cabrera was caught naked with his young, blonde high-school math teacher. Or the time Josh Schwartz was caught smoking pot with the rabbi at his little sister's bat mitzvah.

Poppy nodded slowly. 'I just don't know what I'd do if I lost this job. I'd have to close my agency.'

'That's not going to happen,' I said, more firmly than I felt.

'You're my only hope,' she said bleakly. I could see her blinking back tears. We rode in tense silence for a moment. 'Oh no,' she moaned softly as our taxi turned a corner and pulled up at a red light. 'It's worse than I thought.'

My eyes widened as I took in the Hôtel Jérémie, which looked more like a paparazzi cloning factory than a hotel. Spilling out into the street, a whole gaggle of nearly identical-looking disheveled men toting large cameras with complicated looking flashbulbs stood jostling each other.

Even with the cab windows rolled up, I could hear their excited chatter, the clamor of a group of hungry wolves waiting for the kill.

The light changed, and the cab started moving forward again, closer to the Hôtel Jérémie, closer to the hungry pack of predators. Poppy groaned and closed her eyes.

'Can you take us around to the back entrance?' I suddenly asked the driver. My mind was spinning, and I had no idea what sort of situation we'd find this Guillaume in, but it suddenly occurred to me that if we were going to have to explain his way out of this, it might be better if we weren't seen entering the building. We could be his alibi – but only if we could make it look like we'd been there all along.

'*Comment?*' the driver asked, about to turn into the hotel drive, and probably mow down several paparazzi (which didn't seem like such a bad idea at the moment).

Poppy quickly translated my request into French. The cab driver snorted and said something back.

'He says there is just one entrance,' Poppy said, turning to me worriedly.

'Impossible,' I said. 'There has to be a service entrance in the back. Tell him to just drive around the building and we'll find it.'

Poppy hesitated for a moment, opened her mouth as if she was going to say something to me, then shrugged. She said something quickly to the driver, who glared at me for a moment in the mirror then, shaking his head, twisted the wheel sharply to the left and turned down the side street just before the hotel.

'*Voilà!*' the cab driver said, screeching to a halt at the curb of a dark alleyway. '*Vous êtes contente?*' he asked, smirking at me in the rearview. Obviously, sarcasm translated.

'Yes, very content, thank you,' I chirped back. Poppy shot me a look and paid the driver. He screeched away the moment we tumbled out of the cab into the darkness.

'Why did you want to find the back entrance?' Poppy asked as we made our way toward the hotel. 'Shouldn't we just go in and face the music, so to speak? No point in delaying the inevitable.'

'We may need to claim that we've been with Guillaume all along, and therefore the things he's being accused of can't possibly have happened,' I said slowly. 'If that's the case, we can't be seen arriving.'

Poppy was silent for a minute. 'You know,' she said, 'that just might work.'

We found a back door that was slightly ajar and made our way into what appeared to be the hotel kitchen.

'Is there anything else I need to know about Guillaume?' I asked as we hurried through a silent, dimly lit space filled with massive refrigerators, industrial-sized stoves and ovens and a series of prep stations, toward a small sliver of light behind a doorway that I figured was the hotel lobby. 'Other than his apparent clinical insanity?'

Poppy chose to ignore the last part. 'Just that he's actually pretty nice once you get past all the craziness,' she said, hurrying along after me. 'And wildly talented.' She paused and added, 'I know this must feel ridiculous to you.'

'That's an understatement.' I stifled a cry as I smashed my hip bone against the edge of a counter that I hadn't seen in the dark.

'But believe me, Emma, he's going to be so big!' Poppy enthused. 'He really has it all!'

'Including a mental problem,' I muttered as we slipped out of the kitchen and through the darkened dining room, which was closed and silent at this late hour. We silently hurried toward the lobby, keeping our faces turned away from the press mob and trying to look casual. But as soon as we rounded the corner and saw the elevator all the way across the room, we groaned in unison.

'We'll never be able to get to it without the reporters seeing us,' I said.

Poppy nodded and rolled her eyes. She looked around for a moment. 'There's a stairway over there.'

I darted after her. She pulled open the heavy doorway and we both slipped inside.

'I hope you're in shape,' she said as we began to climb. 'Guillaume is in the penthouse suite on the twelfth floor.'

'The twelfth floor?' I groaned, craning my neck to look up at the stairs that seemed to go on forever. 'I didn't think the French built tall buildings.'

'Evidently, they made an exception here,' Poppy said drily. 'It's where Guillaume always stays when he's writing music.'

Six minutes and a dozen excruciating flights of huffing and puffing later, we emerged to find the maroon double doors at the far end of the hall flanked by two enormously beefy, stern-looking men, one of whom had a Salvador Dali-style mustache that looked as if it was designed for twirling, quite an odd sight on a man who looked like he could snap me in half if he so desired.

'Thank God,' Poppy said, still panting from our climb. 'Edgar and Richard are here!'

'Who?' I asked, gazing skeptically at the two strange-looking giants who stood between us and our errant rock star. This was getting weirder by the moment. But Poppy was already striding down the hall toward the enormous men, smiling and saying something in rapid French to the Dali-mustached one. He stared at her for a moment, impassively, then reached out and pulled her into a bear hug. She exchanged a few words with the other beefy guy, who broke into a grin and reached over to muss her hair.

'Emma,' Poppy said, finally pulling away from him and smiling at me. 'This is Edgar.' I reached out hesitantly and shook his massive hand. 'And this is Richard,' she added, gesturing to Edgar's mustache-less twin.

'Nice to meet you.' I shook his hand too and then looked to Poppy for an explanation.

'Edgar and Richard are two of KMG's bodyguards,' Poppy explained, beaming. 'I had no idea they were here! This is fantastic!'

Edgar said something to me in rapid French, and I shook my head.

'*Je ne parle pas français*,' I recited, one of the only French phrases I had memorized, the one that meant, I don't speak French. 'Sorry.'

'It eez not problem,' Edgar said, shaking his head and speaking in slow broken English. 'I taked ze English in ze school. I just tell Poppy that no *journalistes* enter here. Me and Richard, we, how you say, we block ze way.'

'Well, thank you,' I said.

'*Merci beaucoup!*' Poppy beamed. She turned to me. 'We're in luck!'

I raised an eyebrow at her. Somehow, even with this latest turn of events, luck didn't seem like the proper word to apply to a situation that involved standing on the twelfth floor of a hotel, outside a crazed rock star's room, while a gang of hungry reporters waited for us downstairs.

'So, Edgar, can you tell us what is happening?' Poppy asked.

'*Oui*,' he said, nodding solemnly. 'After dinner, Guillaume bring four, how you say, er, young ladies to *la chambre*, er, ze room,' he began.

'You were with him?' Poppy asked.

'*Oui*,' Edgar confirmed. 'KMG ask us to stay with him tonight. But he keep losing us,' Edgar said, rolling his eyes. 'Now, *on est dans un beau pétrin*.'

'What?' I glanced at Poppy for clarification.

'It's an expression that means we're in a fine mess now,' Poppy translated softly.

'You can say that again,' I said.

Edgar looked at me strangely and shrugged. 'Okay. If you wish. *On est dans un beau pétrin*.'

I took a deep breath and reminded myself to be careful using English expressions. 'Edgar,' I said. 'Can you tell us what happened once they got to the room?'

Edgar nodded. 'The music, it go on,' he said, glancing at Richard, who was staring impassively forward. 'And we hear ze laughter from ze room. Guillaume, he order ze food in ze room, and *le serveur* who deliver ze food, he notice ze girls. *Les journalistes*, they arrive twenty minutes later, so we think it was *le serveur* who call them.'

'Did any of the paparazzi make it up here?' Poppy asked.

'*Oui*,' Edgar responded. 'But we make them to go away. Now they wait like – how you say – vultures, down ze stairs. They wait to catch Guillaume and his girls to leave.'

'Do you know what they're doing in there now?' I asked, nodding toward the door. Edgar and Richard exchanged glances.

'*Non*,' Edgar said slowly. He glanced nervously at Poppy.

'It's okay, Edgar,' she said. 'Emma works with me. She's going to try to help get Guillaume out of this. You can be honest with her.'

Edgar stared at Poppy for a moment, then he turned to look at me.

'There are drugs,' he said slowly. 'But there are always drugs. Guillaume, he does not do ze drugs. He never do ze drugs. But the girls, they do ze drugs. Guillaume, he is just crazy. He does not need ze drugs to be crazier. As we say in French, *il est marteau*. And I think he make ze love with ze girls.'

'All the girls?' I asked, incredulously. I wasn't sure whether to be disgusted or mildly impressed.

Edgar laughed. 'I do not know. Is that not what ze rock stars do?'

I cleared my throat. 'So Guillaume *isn't* on drugs. But the girls might be?'

'*Oui*,' Edgar confirmed.

'Which ones?' I asked. 'Which drugs?'

Edgar glanced nervously at Poppy again. '*La cocaine*,' he said finally.

'We're going in,' I said suddenly. Edgar looked at me in surprise.

'We are?' Poppy asked. I sighed and looked at my watch. It was now two thirty in the morning.

'Yes,' I said, trying to sound confident. Edgar and Richard glanced at each other then at Poppy, who shrugged, as if to say, *I guess we'll just have to follow the whims of the crazy American.* That's right. They would.

I raised my hand to the door and knocked. Nothing happened. I waited a moment, cleared my throat and raised my hand to the door again.

'There's no answer,' Poppy pointed out helpfully a moment later, after I'd stood staring at the doorway for what felt like a small eternity, willing some sort of reaction from inside.

'Yes, I see that,' I said and knocked again. Still no reply, although I could have sworn that the decibel level on the blasting music went up a notch or two.

'*Bon, je vais frapper à la porte,*' Edgar said. 'Let me try knocking, Emma.' He pronounced my name Ayma, but as far as I was concerned, he could call me Bob as long as he figured out how to get Poppy and me into Guillaume's suite.

Edgar pounded on the door, so hard that I feared it might actually come crashing off the hinges. Still no answer. So he pounded again, harder and more violently this time. A moment ticked by, and then the music suddenly screeched to a halt.

'*Qui est-ce?*' came a slurred male voice from inside.

Edgar shouted something in rapid French through the door.

'I told him to open ze door, because there are two more ladies who want to join his party,' Edgar whispered.

'Good plan,' I said.

A moment later, the door opened, and framed in the doorway stood the most attractive man I'd ever seen.

I know it's not polite to stare, but I figured that the dark-haired Adonis in front of me was probably used to it. Six feet tall or so, with thick, dark, shaggy hair, emerald-green eyes and a perfectly chiseled face, Guillaume was literally breathtaking. As in, I had to take several deep breaths in order to pretend that I was annoyed at him, not attracted to him. He was a thousand times hotter in person than in any photo I'd ever seen of him. It didn't help me that he was wearing only low-slung jeans, unbuttoned at the top, and that his shirtless physique was absolutely perfect.

'Ah, Poppy!' Guillaume exclaimed, his eyes lighting up as he focused on her. 'You have come to join my party!' He turned his gaze to me and studied me intently before grinning again. 'And you have brought a friend, I see!' he added.

I continued to stare dumbly at him, marveling at the fact that his English was much cleaner and less accented than I would have suspected. Had he been able to pronounce his r's correctly, and had he not drawn out the ends of the words Poppy, party and see so dramatically, I would almost have been able to believe that he was American instead of French. I hadn't expected such English proficiency.

'Emma, meet Guillaume Riche,' Poppy said hastily, nodding at him, then at me. 'Guillaume, this is Emma.'

'Ah, Emma, you are beautiful!' Guillaume replied with a wink that made me blush. He reached forward and planted a kiss on each of my cheeks, French-style. 'Just my type!' He took my hand in his and kissed it.

'I didn't bring her to add to your harem, Guillaume,' Poppy interrupted. He looked questioningly at her and then back at me. 'She's your new publicist.'

Guillaume looked back at me, still clutching my hand. I forced a smile. He studied me for a moment more, then grinned sheepishly.

'Of course!' he exclaimed. 'I knew that. I meant she was just my type of publicist. Really, Poppy. You always suspect the worst.'

'Right,' Poppy muttered. 'I'm sure that's entirely unfounded.'

'So, uh, what exactly is going on here, Guillaume?' I

asked, putting my hands on my hips and trying to sound tough. But Guillaume just looked amused.

'I'm just having some drinks with a few friends, Emma,' he announced brightly, wobbling a bit as he said the words. 'It's totalleeeee innocent.'

'I'm sure,' Poppy said, glaring at him and then poking her head into the hotel room. I followed her gaze inside, where four girls, who may or may not have been eighteen, were flitting around in various stages of undress. One was sniffing and wiping at her nose, which seemed to support Edgar's assertion about the cocaine. My heart sank. Guillaume followed our eyes and shrugged.

'We were just playing a little bit of strip poker,' he added. He arched an eyebrow. 'I'm winning. Good for me!'

'Yes, excellent for you,' Poppy said, glancing past him to glare at a wispy blonde wearing just white panties and a matching cami who glided through the room, toward the bathroom.

'Don't they have underage laws here?' I whispered. Poppy nodded.

'Oh, sweet Emma, they are not underage!' Guillaume exclaimed, apparently having overheard my question. 'I wouldn't be that foolish! I checked all of their IDs before inviting them here!'

I just stared at him, dumbfounded, until Poppy took over.

'Damn it, Guillaume!' she exclaimed. 'You know we're launching your album in less than four weeks! You know how much KMG has invested in you. Do you know how many photographers and reporters are in the lobby waiting to destroy your perfect image?'

'So it's good publicity!' Guillaume exclaimed brightly, wobbling again as he said it. He glanced at me, seemed to have trouble focusing, then shook his head and looked away. 'All press is good press, right?'

'Wrong,' Poppy said firmly. 'You *know* we're trying to portray you as Mr Perfect. Clearly, you're determined to make sure I fail miserably at that task.' She sighed and looked around the room. '*Allez-y!*' she said, making eye contact with each of the girls and clapping commandingly. 'Let's go! Everybody out!'

She spoke a few sentences in French to the girls, who suddenly looked worried and scrambled to put their clothes back on.

'What on earth did you say?' I whispered.

'I told them we had called the police, and they're on their way,' she said. 'Sentences for drug use in France are pretty severe.'

'Poppy!' Guillaume exclaimed, watching dejectedly as the girls scrambled to get dressed. 'You are ruining my fun!'

Poppy fixed him with a glare. 'One of these days, Guillaume, you are going to get into a mess we can't get you out of.'

Guillaume shrugged sheepishly. Then he turned to me and winked, as if I was his conspirator.

I swallowed hard and tried to look annoyed instead of smitten.

6

Ten minutes later, Poppy and I were riding an elevator in silence toward the ground floor with Guillaume wedged between us. Edgar and Richard had helped sneak the girls down the back stairs and out the service entrance by disguising them in bellboy outfits Edgar had found in a storage closet on the eleventh floor.

'I don't see why I can't just sneak out too,' Guillaume grumbled.

'Because,' Poppy said sensibly, 'everyone knows you're here.'

'So?'

'*So,*' Poppy said impatiently, 'the only way to deal with this is to act like it was one giant mistake on the part of the guy who brought you room service. There was nothing unseemly going on in your room at any time.'

'I don't follow your logic,' Guillaume muttered.

'Of course you don't,' Poppy shot back irritably. 'You're completely mad.'

I stared straight ahead, pretending to myself that I wasn't trapped in an elevator with two people who sounded very much like they were involved in some sort of lover's spat.

'I have no idea what to say to the press,' Poppy had confided in me desperately five minutes earlier while we stood outside Guillaume's door, waiting for him to put his shirt back on and make himself look as presentable and presumably sober as possible. 'I'm so bad at this. I can write the press releases and spin all these stupid situations the next day, but I'm terrible at knowing what to say on the spot. That was what Marie was good at.'

'So why don't we take some time to think about it?' I suggested.

'Because we need to go down now to distract attention from the girls leaving,' she said. 'Because if we wait, someone's bound to spot them, and they'll tell the real story.'

'What story will we be telling?' I asked.

'I haven't a clue.' Poppy's face clouded over, and she looked like she was about to cry.

'Okay,' I said slowly. I put a hand on her arm. 'Don't worry. We'll figure something out.'

So while Poppy and Guillaume bickered during the seemingly interminable elevator ride, I tried very hard to stop finding Guillaume attractive and instead tried to formulate a plan.

'Let me handle the talking, okay?' I said, glancing past Guillaume to an exhausted-looking Poppy as the elevator finally touched down on the ground floor. 'Poppy, can you just take care of translating whatever I say into French?'

Poppy stared at me with concern. 'Emma, are you sure?'

'Yes,' I said firmly, although of course I wasn't sure at all.

'I mean, because you don't have to—'

'I know,' I said. 'Don't worry.'

Fortunately, we had time to have this entire conversation,

because the elevator was clearly designed to open as slowly as humanly possible. First the elevator landed, then it locked shakily into place, then the door slowly slid open, and finally we had to push ourselves out of what appeared to be a rusty, gold-chipped cage of some sort, which, in turn, was designed to be heavy, unwieldy and badly in need of WD-40.

By the time we emerged from the gilded cage, with flashbulbs exploding frantically all around us, I was ready. Well, as ready as I was going to be, anyhow.

The media interest in Guillaume was far more intense than I had expected. It was like nothing I'd experienced back home with Boy Bandz, even when the 407 boys were at the height of their popularity. Poppy had always told me that European journalists were relentless, especially when it came to celebrity coverage, but I hadn't expected anything to this degree. There were dozens of clamoring reporters and scores of photographers shouting Guillaume's name.

I am in control, I told myself. Realizing that in this situation, at least, I could take charge of something made me feel a little more like myself again.

Filled with this false confidence, I strode out of the elevator, with Poppy following me, herding a sheepish Guillaume between us.

'*Mesdames et messieurs*,' Poppy said quickly as we approached a makeshift podium off to the side of the lobby. She raised her hands until the crowd of journalists had fallen into an expectant hush. A few flashes went off, and Guillaume grinned for the cameras, as if oblivious to the fact that anyone here could wish him ill. '*Puis-je avoir votre attention, s'il vous plaît?* May I have your attention please?'

The crowd shushed further and waited expectantly. Poppy stared at them for a moment, like a deer caught in the headlights – or, at the least, the flashbulb lights. Then she cleared her throat and glanced at me. Guillaume elbowed me gently in the ribs, and, when I looked at him, he grinned charmingly and batted his thick eyelashes at me. I rolled my eyes and tried not to blush.

'May I present my new colleague, Emma Sullivan,' Poppy said. She glanced nervously at me again and then looked back out at the quieted press corps. 'Emma will be making a short announcement in English. I will be translating to French. Thank you. *Merci beaucoup.*'

She nodded, raised her eyebrows at me and took a step back. I cleared my throat and forced a smile at the twenty or so journalists who were clustered in front of me, looking hungry, tired and eager.

'Good evening,' I said formally, stepping forward.

'*Bon soir*,' Poppy translated behind me. I drew a deep breath and continued.

'It has come to our attention that there have been some rumors this evening about Guillaume Riche's behavior,' I began. Behind me, Poppy translated, and as she finished speaking, several hands shot up in the air. I held up a hand, indicating that I wasn't finished.

'Sometimes, people tell stories for personal gain or call the press for reasons of their own making,' I continued. I debated for a moment whether I should feel badly about calling the room service waiter's honesty into question, but after all, he had been the source of all this madness. And wasn't a hotel guest's private business supposed to remain private? 'I cannot guess at the motives of the individual who called all of you,' I said, pausing so that Poppy could translate after each sentence. 'Or perhaps it was just an innocent mistake. But I assure you, there was nothing unseemly going on in Guillaume Riche's hotel suite this evening.'

Poppy translated in a voice that was growing more confident by the moment, and again, half a dozen hands shot up and the reporters began clamoring. I glanced at them and, without meaning to, locked eyes with a dark-haired thirty-something guy with glasses in the front row who was staring at me with a creased forehead.

He was cute. Very cute. He had classic French good looks: green eyes, thick lashes, darkly tanned skin and a square jaw darkened by stubble. Unfortunately, he was also wearing an expression of deep skepticism, which made him exponentially less attractive at the moment. I could almost read the words *I don't believe you* emanating from him. I cleared my throat and looked away before I accidentally looked guilty.

'This evening, my colleague, Poppy Millar, and I met Guillaume Riche in his hotel suite to go over plans for the highly anticipated launch of his album in Britain and the United States,' I continued, with Poppy hurriedly turning my words into French beside me. I glanced again at the journalist with the glasses, who hadn't looked away, and my resolve faltered a bit. Why was his gaze making me so nervous? 'We've been at it for hours,' I said, 'and I think you'll be very pleased with the result at our big launch party in London three weeks from now.'

Poppy translated while I paused to give myself a mental pat on the back for sneaking a promotion for the upcoming launch in – twice. So far so good.

'The three of us have simply been brainstorming for the past several hours, and I assure you, there hasn't been anyone else in the room,' I concluded. The lie had come out so easily, but I didn't see any other way around the issue. It seemed to be the only way Guillaume could escape from this situation.

More hands shot up, and I took a deep breath and pointed to a sleek, dark-haired woman who looked about fifty.

She asked something in French, her voice tense and clipped.

'She wants to know if you deny the reports that there were four women in the room,' Poppy translated softly.

'Yes, it was just the three of us,' I lied.

'And ze reports that all of you, were, er, without your clothing?' the reporter pressed on in thickly accented English.

'Well,' I said slowly, making sure to appear perplexed by the question. 'The suite was rather warm, and we'd been working for hours. I do admit that Poppy and I took off our jackets and that Guillaume was in a T-shirt.'

'Reports say you were in your underclothes,' the reporter persisted, glaring at me. 'And that there was some sort of card game going on.'

Uh oh, I thought. I forced a smile.

'Um, well, I actually have a camisole underneath my jacket, so it may have looked like I was in underclothes,' I said, keeping my voice slow and patient. 'And as for the cards, yes, you've got us there.' I smiled sheepishly and shrugged. 'We took a break and played . . . er . . . Go Fish.'

The moment the words were out of my mouth, I wanted to smack myself in the forehead. Go Fish? Why had I said that? Who plays Go Fish?

'Go Fish?' asked the man in the front row, the one with the glasses, the dimples and the suspicious expression.

'Yes, it's a card game where—'

'Yes, I know what it is,' the man said in English, sounding surprisingly American for someone who seemed to fit in so well with the European press corps. 'I'm just surprised. I didn't realize Guillaume knew how to play. Guillaume, have you learned Go Fish?'

Guillaume started to respond, and Poppy elbowed him in the ribs.

'Please direct all questions to Emma or me,' Poppy said, fixing the reporter with a stern look.

'I'm sorry,' the reporter said, not sounding sorry in the slightest. 'The whole thing just sounds a little suspicious. In fact, it sounds sort of like Guillaume was probably up there with several girls playing drunken strip poker and that things got out of hand.'

I gulped and glared at the reporter, who was staring evenly back at me with a small smile on his face.

'I'm sorry if that's the impression you got,' I said through gritted teeth, refusing to break eye contact with him, for fear it would make me look like I had something to hide. Which, of course, I did. 'But I'm afraid tonight was simply a rather boring evening of organization and planning on our part. Nothing to get excited about.'

I looked deliberately away from the reporter and scanned the room. 'Are there any more questions?' I called on a few more reporters, whose questions Poppy translated into English for me, and I gave several more safe answers. Yes, Guillaume had been fully clothed the whole time, except for when he had spilled a glass of water and needed to change his shirt. No, we didn't expect this evening to ruin his appeal to younger listeners, because of course nothing had happened. Yes, he was excited to make his English-language debut. No, he wasn't ashamed to be standing here, because of course nothing had happened.

I glanced nervously at the dimpled guy a few times. As he gazed evenly back, I had the uncomfortable feeling that he could see right through me.

'You were great in there!' Poppy whispered to me twenty minutes later as the crowd of reporters reluctantly dispersed and we hustled a subdued Guillaume into a stretch Hummer that Edgar had summoned during our impromptu press conference. Véronique had called Poppy to tell her that she'd got Guillaume a room at the Four Seasons George V Hotel for the night so that he could stay there in seclusion, with Edgar and Richard guarding his room, until the interest in this story had died down.

'I didn't *feel* great,' I grumbled as the Hummer made its way down the darkened, tree-lined Avenue des Champs-Élysées toward the Arc de Triomphe. 'I felt like a liar.'

'You *did* lie,' Guillaume pointed out helpfully. I glared at him.

'I'm aware of that,' I said. 'Which I wouldn't have had to if you hadn't been such an idiot.'

There was a moment of silence, and I could see Poppy's face tense up. I knew I had crossed a line. I immediately regretted it. You simply didn't talk to the talent that way. I held my breath, waiting for Guillaume to freak out and demand that I be fired.

But instead, he started laughing.

'I like you, Emma!' he said, grinning at me. 'You have spunk!'

I could hear Poppy exhale beside me, and even the impassive Richard smiled slightly.

'I shouldn't have said that,' I muttered, glancing at Guillaume. 'I'm sorry.'

'No, you're right,' Guillaume said, still smiling at me. 'I *am* an idiot, as you say. But Emma, it's what keeps things fun!'

'Fun?' I asked.

'After all, if I was some boring guy who didn't know how to have a good time,' Guillaume said with a wink, 'you'd be out of a job!'

7

'So who was that reporter guy last night?' I asked the next morning after Poppy and I arrived at the office. I'd finally put up a few photographs in my cubicle – one of my nephew Odysseus, one of me with my mother and one of me and Poppy from a decade ago.

'Which one?' Poppy asked absently.

'The dark-haired guy with glasses who was staring at me like I was lying?'

'You *were* lying,' Poppy reminded me.

'Yes, but *he* wasn't supposed to realize that,' I said.

Poppy shrugged. 'He always seems to suspect something,' she said. 'Frankly, he's rather a pain. His name is Gabriel Francoeur. He's a reporter for the UPP wire service.'

'The one that provides stories to newspapers around the world?'

'Right,' Poppy said. 'Like the Associated Press. But with better international distribution. Especially in Europe. In other words, Gabriel Francoeur can single-handedly make or break Guillaume Riche. Which means that for the next few weeks, he's your new best friend.'

'He was kind of cute,' I said, glancing away.

Poppy looked at me sharply. 'Yeah, but he's a pain in the arse.'

I ignored her. 'He barely had an accent. Is he American?'

Poppy shook her head. 'No, French, I think. He must have lived in America for a while, though. He does have your Yankee accent, doesn't he?'

Just then, there was a loud buzzing sound from overhead. I jumped, startled.

'What was that?' I asked.

Poppy sighed. 'It's our front door. I keep asking the building to get that bloody buzzer fixed. It sounds like an air raid siren.'

'I didn't even know we had a buzzer,' I said. After all, this was my fifth day here, and not once had anyone appeared at our front door.

'I'm sure it's a delivery,' Poppy said. 'I'm expecting a shipment of eight-by-ten glossies of Guillaume. Can you answer it? I'll get my checkbook. The copy shop always sends the photos COD.'

I crossed the tiny room and pulled open the front door. I blinked a couple of times at the tall, dark-haired figure with glasses in the hallway before it registered who he was.

'Well, speak of the devil,' Poppy said somewhere behind me.

'You two were talking about me, were you?' Gabriel Francoeur said with an innocent grin, glancing past me and into the office. 'I'm sure you were saying only wonderful things.'

'Ah, you know me too well,' Poppy said drily.

Gabriel refocused his attention on me. 'So,' he said. 'You're Emma. Guillaume's new publicist.'

'You're quite observant,' I said, feeling suddenly

uncomfortable. I couldn't shake the feeling of transparency I'd had last night with his eyes boring into me.

Gabriel studied me for a moment and then smiled slowly. 'I pride myself on my powers of perception,' he said.

'Do you?' I asked, trying to affect boredom. I couldn't help but notice his evergreen eyes and the way they sparkled behind his glasses when he looked at me.

'I do,' Gabriel confirmed with a nod. He raised an eyebrow. 'In fact, one of the things I happened to notice last night was that your little story about Guillaume didn't completely add up.'

I struggled not to blush. 'I don't know what you're talking about,' I responded stiffly.

'I'm sure you don't,' Gabriel said, looking amused. We stood there staring at each other for a moment until I began to notice the little waves in his thick, dark hair and the way that I could already see a dark shadow beneath the surface of his strong-looking jaw, although he had clearly shaved this morning. I could feel heat creeping up the back of my neck. I shook my head and glanced away.

'So,' Gabriel finally said, breaking the uncomfortable silence. 'Are you going to invite me in?'

I opened my mouth to say no, but Poppy pre-empted me.

'Of course,' she said smoothly. She elbowed me in the back. 'Come in, Gabriel, of course.'

He nodded, glanced down at me with a smile and moved into the office, brushing against me a bit as he did. I felt a little uninvited shiver run down my spine. Geez, I was attracted to him. How was that possible?

'I don't know why we need to invite him in,' I muttered to Poppy as Gabriel settled himself into my seat at my desk, without even asking.

'Because,' Poppy whispered, leaning close into my ear, 'he basically holds Guillaume's career in his hands. We have to be very, very nice to him.'

'Even if he's a jerk?' I whispered back, eyeing him warily as he ignored us and leaned in to look more closely at the photos on my desk.

'Even if he's a jerk,' Poppy confirmed.

'Good to know,' I said. 'Because he is.'

'Is what?'

'A jerk.'

Poppy looked at me closely. 'Methinks thou doth protest too much,' she said with some amusement.

I made a face and took a few steps closer to Gabriel.

'You're in my chair,' I said bluntly, pointing to the seat he had made himself comfortable in.

'Oh,' Gabriel said. He smiled at me for a moment and then stood up. 'I'm sorry. I didn't realize. I didn't see anywhere else to sit.'

'I didn't realize you'd be staying that long,' I said.

'What Emma is trying to say,' Poppy interrupted smoothly, stepping in front of me, 'is that we would be pleased to help you with whatever you need so that you can be on your way.'

She elbowed me in the ribs, and I shrugged. Gabriel, with all his dark-haired, green-eyed good looks, was starting to make me uncomfortable.

'Ah, I see,' Gabriel said. He glanced at Poppy and then he returned his gaze to me, where it lingered a moment longer than it had to. 'Well, ladies, I was just stopping in as a favor, actually.'

'A favor?' Poppy and I said in unison. We stared at him incredulously.

He looked a bit taken aback by our reaction. 'Hey, I can't be a nice guy?' he asked.

'There's a first time for everything,' Poppy muttered.

Gabriel looked wounded. 'Now that's not fair, Poppy,' he said. 'I'm just doing my job.'

'And we're just doing ours,' I said.

Gabriel glanced at me and nodded. 'I know,' he said. He hesitated a moment and then locked eyes with me. 'That's why I thought you'd appreciate knowing that Guillaume has a big night planned tomorrow at Buddha Bar. You may want to, er, keep an eye on him. He always gets himself into trouble there.'

'He's *never* got into trouble there,' Poppy corrected quickly.

'Ah', Gabriel said, 'so the fire in the men's room there last month . . .'

'Not his fault,' Poppy said, too quickly.

'And the sexual harassment charges from the waitress?'

'A mistake, obviously.'

'Hmm,' Gabriel said. He stroked his chin thoughtfully. 'That's interesting. How about the drug dealer who was arrested there and told the police he'd sold to Guillaume just the night before?'

'He doesn't do drugs,' Poppy said, her voice tight. Oddly, Gabriel still looked amused.

'How is it,' I interrupted, 'that you know that Guillaume is going to Buddha Bar tomorrow night?'

'I have my sources,' Gabriel said, fixing me with an even stare.

I cleared my throat. 'And you're just here out of the goodness of your heart?'

He laughed. 'Not entirely,' he said. 'I was sort of hoping that you two might remember this next time around. And that you might consider being a bit more honest with me in the future.'

'That's it?' Poppy asked.

'Well, that, and an exclusive first listen to his album,' he said. I could tell he was trying to sound nonchalant. 'So that the UPP gets first dibs on reviewing it.'

Poppy shook her head. 'You're a real piece of work, Gabriel,' she said.

Gabriel shrugged. 'I'm just doing my job.'

'To be honest,' Poppy said, 'I don't actually believe that you have a source that says Guillaume will be at Buddha Bar. I think you're making it up.'

Gabriel looked a little troubled. 'Okay,' he said. 'Suit yourself. Don't say I didn't warn you.'

He glanced at Poppy and then turned his attention back to me.

'Emma,' he said. 'It was a pleasure to meet you. Officially, anyhow.'

He extended his hand. I reluctantly slipped mine into his, noticing immediately how warm and big it was. I expected a handshake, but instead, he raised my hand to his lips and kissed the back of it.

'Ladies,' he said, nodding at us as he lowered my hand slowly back down. He hadn't broken eye contact, and I was startled to feel my heart beating more rapidly. My hand still tingled where he had kissed it. 'Good day. I'm sure I will be seeing you again soon. *Au revoir.*'

With that, he backed out of the office, pulling the door closed behind him.

'Jerk,' Poppy muttered once the door was shut.

'Yeah,' I said, absently holding my hand up to examine the spot where it had just been kissed. 'What a jerk.'

*

Poppy took me to dinner after work that night to celebrate the fact that I had saved her from getting fired the night before – at least temporarily. After first courses of escargot and green salads with a Dijon dressing, I had coq au vin and noodles while Poppy had a steaming bowl of cassoulet – a French stew of beans, sausages, chicken, duck and tomatoes. We split a bottle of house red and shared a crème brûlée for dessert.

'That's the best chicken I've ever had,' I said in awe, patting my full stomach, as we left the restaurant.

Poppy grinned at me. 'This isn't even a particularly good restaurant,' she said. 'I suspect you're going to like France very much, dear Emma.'

I was tired after dinner, but Poppy insisted that we go out again.

'You're never really going to get over Brett, are you, if we sit around the flat moping?' she asked, linking her arm through mine and pulling me along the street. 'Besides, it's a Friday night! The perfect night to go meet guys!'

'How do you figure?' I was almost afraid to ask.

'According to *Take Control of Your Lover's Soul*, Fridays are *the* night that men are most psychologically primed to meet women,' Poppy said. 'It's something about the negative endorphins in their bodies after a long day of work as well as the positive endorphins in their bodies because they know they have two days of relaxation coming up.'

I rolled my eyes. She had a theory for everything.

Against my dwindling protests, we wound up at another English-language pub, the Frog and the Princess, a microbrewery tucked away in a back alley in the 6th arrondissement, near St-Germain-des-Prés.

'So what's the deal with Guillaume?' I asked as we settled into seats at the bar, each of us clutching a glass of Maison Blanche, one of the Frog and the Princess's house brews. Around us, a Justin Timberlake song blared from the speakers, and a handful of college-aged blonde girls in jeans gyrated on the dance floor, which was ringed with nervous-looking guys clutching beers like lifelines. Again, except for the smoke and plethora of smoking Frenchmen, it felt suspiciously like I was back at a bar in the United States.

'You've been dying to ask me that all day, haven't you?' Poppy said.

I nodded and smiled. 'Maybe. So what's the story? Why does KMG put up with stunts like last night?'

'Because he's really something special,' Poppy said. Her face softened a bit. 'You haven't seen him perform yet. But don't worry. You'll understand when you do.'

'I don't know about that,' I said. Although I had to admit that hearing 'City of Light' had blown me away.

Poppy shook her head. 'No, believe me. You think you hate him now. I know; I felt that way too. But as soon as you see him perform, trust me, you'll fall just a little bit in love with him too. That's his charm. That's why he's going to sell millions of records all over the world. That's why he's going to be a bigger star than David Beckham.'

'You're comparing him to a soccer player?'

Poppy feigned horror. 'A soccer player? First of all, it's called football. Secondly, my dear, David Beckham is so much more than a football star. Just as Guillaume Riche is so much more than simply a singer. He will be a household name. Little girls everywhere will have his poster on the wall.'

'Or post offices will have his wanted poster,' I grumbled.

'Oh, he's harmless,' Poppy said dismissively. She laughed, but I could detect a hint of nervousness behind her smile. 'He just keeps us on our toes.'

'Yeah, about that,' I said slowly. 'What about what Gabriel Francoeur said? About Buddha Bar?'

'He was just trying to get under our skin,' Poppy said quickly.

I hesitated. 'Are you sure? I mean, he seemed pretty confident.'

'That's Gabriel for you,' Poppy said. 'He's just messing with our heads. He doesn't have some sort of inside source. That's nonsense.'

'He did seem to know an awful lot about things in the past that never made the papers,' I said carefully.

Poppy shrugged. 'So he's a good reporter. Fine. But we cover all our bases so that even when he's right, his editors won't risk going with the story because we make him sound wrong. I know it drives him crazy. This is probably just his attempt to get even.'

'Probably,' I agreed after a moment. But I wasn't entirely convinced.

'You're moping,' Poppy accused me an hour later when she returned from the bar, where she'd been flirting with a tall blond guy. She was holding two beers, one of which she handed to me.

'I'm just tired,' I said.

'No,' Poppy said. 'You're moping. About Brett. Who is a complete tosser.'

I couldn't help but laugh. Poppy was so matter-of-fact.

'He's not a tosser,' I protested weakly. 'We just weren't right for each other.'

'Oh, come on,' she said, rolling her eyes. 'If he didn't want to be with you, he's a wanker. Plain and simple. You're fabulous. And anyone who can't see that is completely useless.'

'Well,' I mustered a smile, 'I'll drink to that.'

'That's the spirit!' Poppy exclaimed. 'Cheers!' We both took a long sip, then Poppy spoke again. 'Look, I'll make you a deal,' she said. 'If I can get you a date within the next thirty minutes, you have to give this thing a try. You have to start dating again. Not to fall for some smooth-talking French guy, but because it's fun and they know how to say all the right things, and believe me, they know how to kiss. And right now you need that.'

'Poppy—'

'Didn't you have fun last night?' she asked.

'Before or after Guillaume?' I muttered.

She made a face at me. 'Before,' she said. 'Obviously.'

'Seriously, Poppy,' I said after a moment. 'I don't think this is going to work. I'm about the most unglamorous person in Paris right now. Even if I wanted to date, I doubt I'd have much luck anyhow.'

'We'll see about that,' Poppy said with a smile. 'Let me work my magic.'

Unglamorous or not, I somehow had a date twenty minutes later.

'Told you so!' Poppy sing-songed triumphantly as my new Monsieur Right excused himself to go buy us a round of drinks. 'I told you I could get you a date!'

'What did you say to him?' I demanded. Poppy had disappeared into the crowd and returned ten minutes later with Thibault (which sounded like 'T-bone' when he said it), a thirty-something architect who lived nearby. He spoke good English, had deep brown eyes rimmed with thick, dark lashes and was the stereotypical tall, dark and handsome Frenchman. In short, he seemed perfect. And he'd had the charm turned on full force since arriving at our table and asking if I'd like to meet him at noon tomorrow at Notre-Dame for a little tour of Paris.

'I just said that my very beautiful American friend was new in town and hadn't met anyone yet,' Poppy said with a nonchalant shrug. 'He wanted to meet you right away.'

I looked at her skeptically. 'You're kidding me. *That* gorgeous guy wanted to meet *me*?'

Poppy sighed. 'I'm getting a little tired of you selling yourself short. You're a doll, and any man would be lucky to have you.'

I shrugged and looked away. I didn't believe her.

The next morning, after a quick breakfast of cappuccino and pains au chocolat at Café de l'Alma, a little café near our apartment, Poppy and I were standing outside the Galeries Lafayette, the biggest and most famous department store in Paris, when the doors opened at nine thirty. Despite my exhaustion and reluctance to be dragged around what I figured would be an oversized Macy's, I couldn't help but be dazzled when we walked in.

My jaw must have literally dropped, because Poppy started laughing.

'I had the same expression on my face the first time I came here,' Poppy said. 'It's nine floors of pure fashion heaven. If I ever win the lottery, I'm coming here straightaway.'

'Oh my,' was all I could manage in reply.

From where we were standing, I could only see the ground floor, but it was breathtaking. There were colorful clothes, beautiful salespeople and seemingly endless rows of accessories and cosmetics as far as the eye could see, all in dazzlingly bright colors and patterns. I felt like a kid in a candy store. A very big, very beautiful candy store.

But it was the ceiling that really blew me away. Rising above us, nine floors off the ground, was an enormous dome of stained glass and wrought iron, through which the morning light was pouring, illuminating the center arcade. It reminded me of something you might find in an old, exquisitely decorated church, except that here, we were worshipping at the altar of fashion. Each level of the enormous department store overlooked the ground floor in a beautiful, tiered arrangement that made me feel like I was inside a wedding cake. It was like nothing I had ever seen.

'Okay, Wide Eyes,' Poppy said after a moment. 'Stop gawking. Let's get going.'

We had a mission today. Poppy had vowed to help me pick out an outfit for my tour of Paris with Thibault, and we only had two hours before I had to meet him.

'Spending the day with someone creates the perfect opportunity for romance,' Poppy informed me solemnly as we wove our way through endless accessories. 'It's what *Date for the Day* is all about. It's one of my favorite dating advice books.'

I tried not to feel uneasy, thinking about the fact that I was about to go on my first date since Brett.

Poppy took me by the arm and led me past row upon row of jewelry counters, gorgeous handbags, silky hosiery, ornate watches and facial care displays that promised to restore youthful skin to all buyers. I gaped the whole way. I felt sure this was what my heaven would look like. In fact, I even pinched myself once to make sure I hadn't fallen asleep on Poppy's floor and dreamt it all.

'Ouch!' I exclaimed when the pinch did, in fact, hurt. Okay, so I was awake.

Poppy glanced at me. 'No offense, but you should probably stop staring and start acting nonchalant. You'll fit in a lot better. You look very American at the moment, you know.'

I snapped my mouth closed and tried to look casual. Poppy was right. All around me, bored-looking Frenchwomen, who looked far too put together for nine thirty on a Saturday morning, browsed among the endless accessories, looking like they weren't impressed at all to be here. It had to be an act! How could they not feel like dancing gleefully through the aisles, touching scarves and bags and belts in all sorts of rich fabrics and beautiful shapes?

'*Bonjour*,' Poppy said to the woman at the Clinique counter as we walked up. The woman's make-up and hair were impeccable, and her black wrap dress looked perfect. I felt even more frumpy than usual next to her. 'My friend here needs to have her colors done. Do you speak English?'

The woman beamed at me.

'*Oui*, I do speak English, a little,' she said. 'I would love to do your make-up. Have a seat.'

I smiled, feeling suddenly shy, as I sat down in the make-up chair.

'I'll leave you here for a bit,' Poppy said. 'Good luck! I love this counter. They always do such a great job.'

Thirty minutes later, when Poppy returned to retrieve me, I was a whole new person.

The make-up artist, whose name was Ana, chattered

pleasantly in broken English while plucking foundations, blushes, shadows and lipsticks from the enormous counter beside us as if it was second nature. She wouldn't let me look in the mirror until she was done.

'*Voilà!*' she said finally. 'What do you think?'

Ana handed me a mirror. I hardly recognized the woman reflected in it.

Gone were the ubiquitous dark circles beneath my eyes and the reddish shade of my chin, something I'd never been able to correct on my own. My skin looked silky smooth and completely even, yet natural at the same time. My cheeks had a healthy, dewy flush to them, and my lips were a perfect color of pale pink.

'Emma, you're lovely!' exclaimed Poppy, who had just returned to the make-up counter.

'I can't believe it,' I replied. I looked at Ana in astonishment. 'How did you do that?'

She laughed. 'Nothing complicated. I used a little more foundation, a different color rouge and better moisturizer. You're really quite pretty.'

I bought all the make-up on the spot (despite the fact that I hadn't received my first paycheck – but really, how could I not?) and, with a final thank you, followed Poppy upstairs to the women's clothing department.

An hour later, after paying for a sheer pink blouse and a cream-colored tulip skirt that fitted perfectly, I went back to the dressing room to change into my new clothes and then let Poppy help me pick out a pair of shoes to match. We settled on a silky pair of ballet flats in the same color as the new shirt, as I figured I'd need something easy to walk in if I was going to be accompanying my new Frenchman around Paris all day.

Poppy walked me to Notre-Dame by eleven forty-five, and as we parted ways, she gave me a peck on the cheek.

'Your date is going to be fabulous,' she reassured me. 'You look beautiful. Thibault will fall for you in an instant. Trust me, you're going to love your new city. And Paris is going to love you right back.'

P oppy had actually succeeded in getting me excited about my date.

I hadn't expected to feel that way. After all, the Brett wound was still wide open. Being dismissed nonchalantly by the man I'd been with for three years, the man I'd planned to *marry* in September, wasn't exactly the most confidence-inspiring thing.

And while I still felt vaguely like I was betraying Brett in some way (although I knew that was utterly illogical), there was also a part of me that was looking forward to spending the day with someone new. After all, as Poppy had said, it wasn't like I was going to spend my life with this guy. It was just a few hours. And maybe there *was* something to be said for being with someone who made me feel attractive and interesting. I hadn't felt that way around Brett in quite a while.

Despite myself, I had to admit that there was something to Poppy's theory. Or at least to the magic of this city. I couldn't help but feel a bit overwhelmed by the romance of it all as I sat in a little park in front of Notre-Dame, gazing up at the seven-hundred-year-old Gothic church with its stately towers and soaring stained-glass windows.

As I sat there waiting, I let my imagination wander. Perhaps Thibault would arrive with red roses. Didn't Frenchmen always go around giving red roses to their dates in movies? I felt sure he'd give me a peck on each cheek and perhaps gallantly take my small hand in his strong one as he led me into the church, where he had promised we would begin our Parisian tour by climbing the steps to one of Notre-Dame's towers. Perhaps afterwards we'd take a little boat ride on the Seine, followed by a trip to the top of the Eiffel Tower, then dinner in some yummy French restaurant.

I felt a little shiver of anticipation. And then, just as quickly, I felt a pang of guilt. I knew it was ridiculous, but waiting for a romantic date in this romantic city so soon after my break-up made me feel a little like I was cheating on Brett.

'Stop thinking about him. *He* left *you*,' I said aloud, prompting an odd look from the woman on the other end of the bench. She stared at me for a moment. Then she closed the book she was reading, stood up and hurried away.

Okay, so perhaps I should avoid talking to myself in public. Duly noted.

I *hated* that I missed Brett. Poppy would have killed me for saying so, but I would have given anything in that moment to be waiting for Brett to turn the corner of the cathedral to sweep me off my feet, declare how wrong he had been, and take me on a romantic, whirlwind tour of the city of love.

But no, I shouldn't think like that. Brett was in the past. Thibault was in the future.

My French knight in shining armor would be here at any moment.

Except Thibault never showed up.

So much for my supposed confidence-inspiring leap back into the dating pool.

I waited until twelve fifteen before I called Poppy from the cell phone she'd given me yesterday (presumably so that I'd be reachable twenty-four hours a day, so that I could come running whenever Guillaume got himself into a scrape).

'You're kidding,' she said flatly when I announced that my date was a no-show.

'Nope.'

She hesitated for a moment. 'Maybe he's just late. Give him another fifteen minutes.'

So I did. I sat back down on the bench and tried to distract myself by trying to guess the nationality of the tourists who streamed by my perch.

Fifteen minutes came and went. Still no Thibault. I'd been stood up.

Wonderful. I was off to a great start.

I pulled out my phone to call Poppy back. Then I stopped. What was Poppy going to say that would make me feel better? I didn't want to go back to her tiny apartment and mope about my bad luck with guys. I'd done quite enough of that on my own, thank you. And wasn't it Poppy who had gotten me into this mess in the first place? I felt pathetic.

I sighed and stood up from the bench. I didn't need a guy to see Paris with, did I? I'd take myself to lunch and go on my own tour of the city.

Trying not to think about the fact that I'd just been dumped *before* the first date (a new record, even for me), I walked west on the Île de la Cité, then I crossed to the Right Bank over the Pont Neuf, feeling my heart leap a bit as I looked off to the left and saw the tip of the Eiffel Tower soaring above the gleaming water. I should have known better than to spoil my time here by letting Poppy talk me into trying out some dating game.

I found a little café across the street from the water on the Right Bank, just to the left of the bridge. As I ducked inside the dimly lit café, which had burgundy walls and neatly spaced little round tables of dark wood, the waiter at the door said something to me in French, but of course I didn't understand.

I shook my head. '*Je ne parle pas français,*' I mumbled, feeling like an idiot.

He smirked a bit at me. 'Ah, *une americaine*,' he said, as if it was a bad word. 'Sit anywhere.'

'*Merci.*' I nodded and walked to a table for two by the window, overlooking the street outside, which was filled with Parisians and tourists hurrying to and fro on the sidewalk. Off to the left, I knew, was the Hôtel de Ville, Paris's ornate city hall. Off to the right was the enormous Louvre. Perhaps I'd join the crowds and see it after lunch today.

I glanced around the café and noticed several clusters of people close to the bar. One group, obviously American, judging from their baseball caps, sneakers and loudly familiar accents, were chugging beer.

The waiter came and plunked a menu down in front of me without a word. I glanced at it and realized immediately it was all in French.

'Um, excuse me!' I said. The waiter stopped in his tracks and turned. 'Do you have a menu in English?'

He smirked at me some more. 'No. Only French.'

'Oh.' I was temporarily deflated. I reached into my bag, where I kept *Just Enough French*, a little French travel dictionary I'd picked up at the airport before I left the States. I flipped to the *In a Restaurant* section and began to try to decipher the menu. I hadn't thought I'd need it today, I thought glumly. I'd thought I'd have a handsome Frenchman with me to serve as a translator. But no such luck.

'You would like a large Coca-Cola?' the waiter asked a moment later, reappearing at my elbow.

I looked up in confusion. 'No. I'll have a café au lait and a glass of water, please.'

'What? No Coca-Cola?' He smirked some more. 'I cannot believe it.'

'No,' I repeated, puzzled.

'All Americans want Coca-Cola,' he said. He laughed. 'A large Coca-Cola for all Americans!'

Then he pranced away, leaving me staring after him.

'Just ignore him,' said a voice from behind me. I turned and saw a sandy-haired guy with thin-rimmed glasses sitting a few tables away, by himself, with a tattered paperback open in front of him. He looked like he was about my age, and he spoke with a thick French accent. 'There is a certain stereotype of some Americans. It's silly, really.'

I attempted a smile. 'Do we all really order large Coca-Colas?'

'Most of you do, yes.' He grinned. 'You are new in the city?'

I nodded. 'I just got here a week ago.'

'You are dining alone?' he asked. He closed his book and peered closely at me.

I hesitated then nodded. 'Yes. I was supposed to meet someone, but . . . Well, it doesn't matter, does it?'

'May I join you?' he asked. It should have sounded presumptuous, but somehow it didn't. He didn't make a move to stand up, as if waiting for my approval before his next step.

I hesitated. After all, I didn't know this guy at all. And hadn't I just made a self-aware promise to myself to be independent and experience Paris alone for the day?

'I'll help you translate the menu,' the guy prompted with a smile.

I hesitated. I *did* need help. 'Well . . . okay.' I nodded.

He smiled, picked up his book and his mug of coffee and made his way over to my table.

'I'm Sébastien,' he said. He smiled and sat down in the chair beside mine.

Over a deliciously heavy lunch of *magret de canard à l'orange*, incredibly tender duck breast in a Grand Marnier sauce, and a bottle of red Burgundy, Sébastien and I chatted, and as the wine warmed me up, I found myself beginning to enjoy talking with him.

He said that he was thirty-one and a computer programmer who lived in a tiny apartment in the Latin Quarter, the neighborhood directly across the river, which was rife with students and nightlife. Every Sunday, he said, he took a stroll around Paris and chose a different restaurant to try. Today, he had chosen this café, Café Margot. He was three-quarters of the way through a Gérard de Nerval novel and had been looking forward to finishing it over lunch.

'Then why did you let me interrupt you?' I asked.

'You looked like you needed some help with the waiter.' He grinned. 'Once he said Coca-Cola, I knew there was a problem. Plus, I love to practice my English.'

He winked at me, and I could feel myself blushing.

'So,' he said after a moment, 'you have had a tour of Paris, *non*?'

I shook my head. 'No,' I admitted sheepishly. 'I was going to do that today.'

I neglected to mention that I hadn't thought to bring a guidebook along, as I'd assumed I'd be meeting a Frenchman for a romantic tour of the city.

Sébastien looked at me for a long moment. 'I know the perfect place to show you. If you will allow me?'

I studied his face for a moment. He was, after all, a total stranger. But he had translated the menu for me and seemed pleasant enough. And hadn't I promised Poppy that I'd give this dating thing a try? Not that Sébastien's proposal necessarily constituted a date.

Besides, I'd been ready to spend a day with Thibault, who I really didn't know at all either, right? At least Sébastien was right here and wasn't likely to stand me up.

'Okay,' I agreed. 'Where do you want to go?'

'To the most magical *quartier* in Paris,' He leaned forward and smiled at me. 'Montmartre. It is the neighborhood of *les artistes* and the Bohemians. It is Paris as it is meant to be. Plus, from the steps of Sacré-Coeur, you can see all the city. *C'est très impressionnant*. It is magic.'

My only experience with Montmarte so far had been at the Hôtel Jérémie on Thursday night with an insane rock star. That hadn't exactly been magical.

'Please? May I show you my Paris today?' Sébastien's

eyes sparkled as he looked at me imploringly. I hesitated a moment. What did I have to lose?

'Yes,' I said slowly. 'That sounds wonderful.'

And it was.

After lunch – which Sébastien insisted on paying for, despite my protests – we took a long walk up the rue du Louvre, passing the famous museum, which I couldn't take my eyes off. It was absolutely massive; it seemed to go on forever.

'It's the largest art museum in the world,' said Sébastien, who was evidently taking his job as tour guide seriously. He led me up through the 2nd and the 9th arrondissements, pointing out sights along the way, and at the foot of a big hill, he pointed upward.

'That's Sacré-Coeur,' he said. 'Do you know it?'

I looked up at the glistening white Byzantine-looking dome and shook my head. I'd heard of it, of course, and seen it in photographs. I knew it was one of Paris's most famous landmarks. But I was ashamed to admit I didn't know a thing about it.

'It was begun in the late eighteen hundreds after the war with Prussia and was *consacré* after *la Première Guerre Mondiale*, the First World War,' Sébastien said as we walked. 'It is built of stone from Château-Landon. The most amazing thing about the church is that the stone constantly releases *le calcium* – I believe it is the same in your language – which means that it stays forever white.'

The afternoon was amazing. Sébastien took my hand as we rode a funicular up the hill to the top of Montmartre, and I didn't pull away. His palms were soft and his fingers just a little rough as they threaded through mine. We saw the inside of the church, ate sugared crêpes on the church steps as we gazed out over the hazy city, visited the Musée de Montmartre and the Salvador Dali museum and even had a street artist sketch a portrait of us in the Place du Tertre, a square that Sébastien called the tourist center of the *quartier*.

When darkness fell, Sébastien took me to dinner at a tiny place called Le Refuge des Fondues that was like nothing I'd ever seen. The narrow dining room had space for only two very long tables, so everyone in the packed restaurant ate together. After waiting for a spot for twenty minutes, Sébastien and I were shown to the back of the room, where a gruff French waiter had to help me climb on top of the table to get across it. I had to basically straddle the table, hovering over other laughing diners, to the bench on the other side. The second we sat down, we were handed small glasses of kir royale, and the moment we finished those, we were offered red wine – in baby bottles!

'Baby bottles?' I asked Sébastien incredulously, inspecting the bottle that had been handed to me. It even had a nipple!

'This place is a favorite of Americans!' he shouted back over the din.

We talked and laughed over a little feast of olives, cheese cubes, spicy potatoes, and *saucisson*, several wine refills and the most enormous fondue meal I'd ever had. The huge yellow pot of silky white cheese between us never ran dry, and our waiter seemed to be constantly refilling our bread basket. Just when I thought I couldn't eat any more, the waiter brought over dessert – lemon sorbet frozen into hollowed-out lemon halves – and two small glasses of Alsatian sweet white wine, which Sébastien had ordered for us.

'What a perfect day!' I exclaimed as we left the restaurant and walked out onto the winding, cobbled rue des Trois Fréres to make our way toward a main street to find a taxi stand.

'I'm glad you had a nice time,' Sébastien replied. He reached up and touched my cheek gently. My world was spinning a bit, maybe from his touch, maybe from the wine. Either way, when he leaned down to kiss me, it felt amazing.

Is this what I'd been missing in all those years of kissing Brett? No wonder French kissing was named after these guys, I thought. His lips were soft, and as his tongue gently parted my lips and probed my mouth, I could feel my toes curl up in pleasure.

'You taste like lemon,' Sébastien said as he pulled away.

'You taste like wine,' I said with a smile, blinking at him a few times and trying to regain my balance.

'You are so beautiful,' he said, his voice soft.

I could feel myself blush. 'Thank you.' I couldn't remember the last time anyone had said that to me. 'May I ask you something?'

'Anything,' Sébastien replied with a charming smile. He ran a finger slowly down the bridge of my nose, ending at the bow of my lips. I could feel my whole body come alive with goose bumps.

'What made you talk to me at the café today?' I asked. 'What made you want to stop reading your book and spend the day with me?'

Sébastien studied my face for a moment. 'You seemed lost,' he said. 'And,' he hastened to add, 'very beautiful. I would have been foolish not to suggest us spending the day together.'

Although the words sounded vaguely rehearsed, they did

something to me. I couldn't seem to stop smiling. No one had said anything that romantic to me in a long time.

Thirty minutes later, we stood outside the hallway to Poppy's apartment, with Sébastien gazing into my eyes.

'May I come inside?' he asked, brushing the hair back from my face.

'My roommate is there,' I said, my voice full of apology. 'It's a really small place.'

'I cannot spend the night?' Sébastien asked. The question startled me. He'd been a perfect gentleman all day, and the only moves he'd made had been to hold my hand as we strolled and to kiss me after dinner.

'Um, no,' I stammered. 'I mean, there's really not room.'

'But you are American,' he said, looking baffled.

I'm sure my expression was equally confused. I had no idea what he was getting at. 'What does that matter?'

'American girls are usually happy to spend the night,' he said.

I frowned. 'What are you implying?'

He backed off. 'Nothing, nothing,' he said hastily. 'Maybe another day, then? When your roommate is out?' He moved closer and ran his thumb lightly along my bottom lip.

I didn't know what to say. 'Um, maybe.' After all, the kiss had been amazing, even if he was being a little pushy now.

'You will give me your phone number, then?' he asked.

I almost gave it to him. But then I paused. After all, what did I expect would happen with Sébastien? We'd had a nice day, but I wasn't looking for a relationship, was I? I tried to keep Poppy's words in mind. It was okay to go out with someone without turning him instantly into the man of my dreams.

'Why don't you give me yours instead?' I asked. He

looked taken aback, but he acquiesced, scribbling his mobile number down on a piece of paper.

'You will call?' he asked uncertainly. 'I hope you will call.'

'Maybe,' I said. I felt a bit mean. But at the same time, the non-committal answer filled me with a little rush of power. Perhaps it was nice to know that I could go to bed tonight without a stomach full of butterflies, without wondering if the man would call *me*.

'It has been a pleasure spending the day with you, Emma,' Sébastien said formally. He leaned in and kissed me again, a long, lingering, probing kiss this time. I knew it was supposed to make me change my mind. I knew I was supposed to grow weak in the knees and invite Sébastien in despite my earlier refusal. And I very nearly did.

After all, it was the perfect French kiss.

But perhaps that didn't mean anything at all.

'Ah, so you met Sébastien?' Poppy said, eyeing me in amusement the next morning.

I was puzzled by Poppy's reaction. She'd been in bed by the time I arrived home, and I'd been eager to get up the next morning to tell her about my unexpected date the day before. Perhaps, I thought, she'd been right about the potential of these French guys after all.

'What?' I asked. 'You know him? That's impossible.' How could she possibly know a person I'd randomly encountered in a city of millions?

'Let me guess,' Poppy said drily. 'He was tall with glasses. Sitting alone. Reading a novel. Told you he goes to a different café each week?'

I stared. Was she clairvoyant? 'Yes,' I said. 'But how . . . ?'

'I met him my second week in Paris,' she said, the left corner of her mouth curling upward into a smile she was clearly trying to fight. 'I'd been taking a walk near Notre-Dame and it started to rain, so I ducked into Café Margot. He was there, reading a Gérard de Nerval book. The moment he realized I was British, he came right over.'

'What?' My mouth felt dry.

'I didn't realize until I was telling my American friend Lauren about it that it's apparently his routine,' Poppy said. 'He did the exact same thing to her. Wined her, dined her, took her on a tour of Montmartre, got her drunk at that great fondue place up there. Is that what happened to you?'

'Yes,' I said, flabbergasted.

'Right. Me too. And then he walks you home and asks if he can come in?' Poppy finished the story for me.

I gaped at her and nodded silently.

'Well, at least you were smart enough to say *no*,' she said. 'I wasn't so smart. He wound up spending the night.'

'You're kidding,' I said flatly.

'Not at all.' Poppy grinned. 'Nothing happened. But imagine how foolish I felt when I told Lauren the story and found out the same thing had happened to her.'

'Probably just about as foolish as I feel right now,' I muttered.

'Don't feel that way,' Poppy said brightly. 'In fact, I think it just proves my point. That's the game they play, you know. They know exactly how to woo you. But as soon as they get what they want, they're on to the next conquest. You have to jump ship before you get too attached.'

I stared at her, feeling a little ill. 'Are all French guys like this?' I asked in horror.

Poppy laughed. 'No. I believe Sébastien is a rare case. But he's a great example of why you can't believe a word they say. Never. Men just want to tell you lies, whether they're French or American or British. It's universal. At least according to Janice Clark-Meyers, the author of *Different Language, Same Men*.'

I looked at her for a moment. 'You sound awfully bitter,' I said carefully. 'Darren must have really hurt you.'

Poppy looked away. 'No. I'm just a realist.'

Poppy went out Sunday evening to meet some guy for drinks, and I spent the time finally unpacking my two massive suitcases, hanging clothes in my tiny wardrobe and putting away T-shirts, lingerie and nightgowns in the little drawers under my bed.

I was lost in trying to decide whether to put my shoes under my bed or try to buy an over-the-door shoe rack somewhere when the phone rang, startling me.

'Emma, I've missed you,' said Brett's familiar voice on the other end when I picked up. I froze, stunned. It had been nearly six weeks since I'd last seen him, and already his voice sounded unfamiliar to me. 'Your sister gave me your number,' he added. 'It hasn't been the same here without you.'

I breathed into the phone. I didn't know what to say. Had he, by some sixth sense, realized that last night, for the first time, I'd fallen asleep without thinking about him? I'd just been getting used to a life without him.

'Emma? Are you there?'

'Brett,' I said finally, trying to keep the wobble out of my voice. 'Why are you calling?'

'Because I miss you,' he said, sounding wounded. 'Don't you miss me?'

'No,' I said. There was silence on the other end, and I felt guilty, not just for hurting his feelings but because it was a lie. I *did* miss him. But that was pathetic, wasn't it?

'I shouldn't have said the things I did,' he said after a moment. 'I was stupid, and I'm so sorry. It was all a mistake.'

I was silent. I didn't know what to say.

'What about Amanda?' I asked finally.

There was silence and then heavy breathing on the other end of the line.

'You know about that?' he asked in a small voice.

I didn't bother answering. 'You're such an asshole,' I said instead.

'Oh Emma, I'm so, so sorry,' he said quickly, his words tumbling out on top of each other. 'Emma. Please. Can you hear me? I'm sorry. More sorry than you know. It was just a mistake. A huge mistake. I was trying to get over you.'

'That's an interesting technique,' I muttered. 'If it doesn't work out with your fiancée, screw her best friend?'

Brett sighed and continued. 'Emma. Please. I don't know how to tell you how sorry I am. But I love you. I still want to marry you. I just got cold feet, that's all.'

It was exactly what I'd wanted to hear six weeks ago. But now, his words just made me feel empty and confused.

'Emma, will you come home?' Brett asked. 'Please? Give me another chance?'

I walked into the living room and sat down on the sofa, facing the window. Outside, mere yards away, the Eiffel Tower loomed like a reminder of all I had yet to discover in this city.

'No,' I said finally, trying to sound far more confident than I felt. 'I think this is where I belong now.'

I hung up the phone before he had a chance to protest.

'Well, it's what he deserves,' Poppy said at work the next morning as she leaned over me to grab a permanent marker from the other side of the conference table. We had arrived early to work on the layout for the cover of the press folder for Guillaume's London launch. We couldn't agree on the perfect photo to use; I wanted to use one where Guillaume was holding his guitar and smiling, while Poppy wanted to find one where he had his signature sexy sulk.

'Are you sure?' I asked as I took a sip of coffee and studied the display of photos we had laid out in front of us. 'I mean, maybe it just took him a little while to realize what a huge mistake he'd made. Maybe he *did* just get cold feet.'

'You were with the guy for three years,' Poppy recapped. She picked up two of the photos and put them in our discard pile. 'You've been engaged for almost a year. And then suddenly he dumps you and tells you to move out? I don't care whether he's changed his mind or not. Is that really the kind of guy you'd want to be with?'

'I guess not,' I muttered. We worked in silence for a few minutes.

I tried hard to concentrate on the task at hand. Guillaume's single was due to hit airwaves around the world that night, so it was a big day for us. Focus on Guillaume, I told myself. Not on Brett.

'So,' I said lightly, trying to change the subject. 'I guess Gabriel *was* wrong about Guillaume getting into trouble at Buddha Bar last night.'

'I told you he was full of it,' Poppy said.

'You were right,' I said. 'How stupid of me to have believed him.'

'Not stupid,' Poppy said. 'Just naïve. You can't trust these reporters.'

'I'm sure they're saying the same thing about us,' I said.

Poppy grinned. 'Yes, and they're absolutely right.'

We finally agreed on a photo of Guillaume in a Cuban-looking military jacket with sliced-up sleeves that showed off his incredible arm muscles. In the photo, he was holding his custom-made red Les Paul guitar, which he had nicknamed Lucie, after his little sister, and he was giving the camera one of his signature smoldering looks that was practically enough to make any red-blooded woman melt on the spot.

'Okay, I've got to get running to that lunch meeting in London,' Poppy said after we'd called the printer and added the photo to the layout we'd already given them for the press pack, which they'd have printed and ready for us by the end of the week. 'Will you be okay on your own for the afternoon? You have plenty to keep you busy, right?'

Poppy had a one fifteen meeting in London with the president of the British Music Press Association, which she'd spent the last few days preparing for. She'd catch the eleven thirteen Eurostar out of Gare du Nord in time to make it to a restaurant just outside London's Victoria Station for lunch. She'd leave just after three to make it home in time for dinner. It was amazing how quickly you could hop between the two national capitals.

'Of course,' I said brightly. I'd been here a week now, and thanks to eight years of working in the industry, I certainly knew how to handle myself around a PR office. On top of that, I was getting excited about Guillaume's London launch. It would be one of the biggest projects I'd ever been involved in, and I was proud of the work Poppy and I had already done. I had dozens of calls to make to American music journalists that afternoon, and I needed to verify some things with the London hotel where we'd be holding the event in less than three weeks.

'Okay, sweetie,' Poppy said, getting up to grab her handbag, which was a perfect-looking Kelly knock-off. 'Wish me luck. I'll have my mobile on if you need me.'

*

Thirty minutes later, I had made five media calls, all of which went well. I was particularly happy with the chat I'd had with a London-based writer from *Rolling Stone*, who had promised she'd be at the junket.

'Guillaume Riche looks just yummy!' she had exclaimed. 'And the advance copy of "City of Light" you sent me sounds amazing. You really have a star on your hands!'

The call had left me with a warm glow, which is exactly what I was basking in when my phone rang again. Assuming it was one of the British journalists I'd left a message for calling me back, I cheerfully answered the phone, 'Emma Sullivan, Millar PR!'

A deep voice on the other end of the line blurted out several sentences in French.

'I'm sorry,' I said quickly, interrupting the flood of words. Even if I couldn't understand the language, I knew he was upset. *'Je ne parle pas français.'*

I was getting awfully tired of saying that.

'Who eez thees?' the voice asked in thickly-accented English. 'Where eez Poppy?'

'Poppy is away at a meeting,' I said. 'This is her new colleague, Emma. I'm also working on Guillaume Riche's English-language launch. Is there something I can help you with?'

There was dead silence on the other end.

'Yes,' the man said finally. 'Emma, you must hurry. This is Guillaume's manager, Raf. I'm een Dijon, so you are going to have to help me.'

'Help you with what?'

'Guillaume just called me,' Raf said rapidly. 'Emma, he somehow fell asleep een a storage room near ze lifts on the second floor of ze Eiffel Tower last night.'

I gasped. 'What?'

'I'm afraid it eez true,' Raf said. 'The morning cleaning crew discovered heem, and as you can imagine, he eez een a lot of trouble.'

I groaned. 'Could it get any worse?' I asked rhetorically. Only, it turned out the question wasn't so rhetorical after all.

Raf paused for another moment.

'Well, yes, eet could,' he said with a sigh. 'There eez one more thing I may have forgotten to mention. The young lady he was with clearly thought it would be amusing to steal heez clothes while he slept. So it seems he was een ze lift with just heez briefs when ze crew found him.'

'What?!'

'*Mais oui.*'

'Where is he now?' I asked, starting to panic.

'He's een ze Eiffel Tower security office being interrogated,' Raf said, his voice sounding weary. 'But there eez a lot of press outside – ze same journalists who have been bothering heem for a week, mostly. You are going to need to get down there and do some damage control.'

Raf gave me Guillaume's mobile number and told me that I was to call him as soon as I got to the tower, and I'd be escorted up.

'Emma, there eez one piece of good news een all of thees,' Raf added at the end. 'The security guards have not called ze police. They knew who Guillaume was and prefer to handle this privately. So there may be some opportunity there for you to sort things out.'

'Okay,' I said. 'Thanks.'

I hung up and pounded my head on the desk for a moment. This couldn't be happening.

I dialed Poppy's mobile number, but there was no

answer. I tried again. Still nothing. I left her a panicked message explaining the situation. Then I dialed Véronique's number. I was sure that she, or one of the company's in-house PR reps, would know how to handle things.

'Well, you obviously need to take care of this,' she said calmly when I was done recapping my conversation with Raf. Why was it that the French never seemed to panic?

'Me?' I tried to stop myself from freaking out. 'But I can't reach Poppy!'

'Unless I'm mistaken,' Véronique said, her voice cold, 'you are being paid as part of Guillaume's PR team. So if you and Poppy want to keep your jobs, I suggest you hurry down to the Eiffel Tower to solve this little problem before word gets out. Or should I hire another PR firm that is more reliable?'

I sat there in shock for a moment before mumbling a reply, slamming down the phone and hurrying out of the office.

'Oh dear, Emma, I am so sorry I can't be there,' Poppy whispered into the phone when she called me back fifteen minutes later. I was already en route to the Eiffel Tower, and I'd broken out in a cold sweat in the back of the cab. 'I'm already on the train. We've left the station.'

'I understand,' I said through gritted teeth. 'But what am I supposed to do?'

'I don't know,' Poppy whispered back. 'Lie?'

'Yeah.' I shook my head. 'I'm going to get lots of practice with that here, aren't I?'

'Look, I'll call you as soon as I'm done,' Poppy said. 'I'm so sorry to make you handle this on your own.'

I asked the cabbie to swing by the Celio store on the rue

de Rivoli on the way. He waited while I dashed inside to buy Guillaume a shirt, cargo pants and flip-flops. I guessed at his size, assuming that even if the clothes weren't exactly right, he'd appreciate wearing something other than his underwear when he was escorted outside.

Ten minutes later, the cab drew to a halt in front of the Eiffel Tower.

'You will love it!' the driver said, turning round to me with a smile. Obviously he'd mistaken me for a carefree tourist. 'It is ze best tourist sight in Paris. You must go up to ze top.'

'Uh huh,' I said, counting out his fare with trembling hands. I could feel sweat beading at my brow.

'Oh no, do not be nervous!' he exclaimed. 'I see you are transpiring.' I guessed he meant 'perspiring'. 'But do not worry,' he went on encouragingly. 'There are guard rails. It is completely safe.'

'*Merci beaucoup*,' I mumbled, pressing a handful of bills into his hand. 'Keep the change.'

'Just take deep breaths and you will be fine, *mademoiselle*!' the car driver shouted behind me as I slammed the door and began my dash across the courtyard to the entrance. 'It is nothing to panic about!'

Unfortunately, before I reached the tower, I had to pass a horde of journalists, who were clustered near the base of the tower's west pillar. Gabriel was the only one who spotted me as I tried to sneak by.

'Emma!' he shouted out. The other reporters, snapped to attention by his voice, spun to face me too. Suddenly, I was in the center of a storm of questions that were being hurled toward me far faster than I could respond to them.

'Is it true that Guillaume Riche is in custody inside the Eiffel Tower?'

'Was he drunk?'

'Has he been taken to jail?'

'Will this delay his album launch?'

'Does KMG have an official statement?'

'No,' I muttered, trying to make my way past them.

'What about the allegation that he was trapped in the tower overnight?' Gabriel's mysteriously American-sounding voice rose above the others. 'Are you denying it?'

'I don't know what you're talking about.' There was hardly room to move as I elbowed through the crowd. I quickly explained who I was to one of the guards, who thankfully spoke enough English to understand. He radioed someone, and in a moment he reluctantly ushered me through and pointed me toward the south pillar of the tower.

'What about the allegation that he's naked?' Gabriel yelled after me as I began to stride away, trying to stop myself from panicking.

'Not true.' I stopped and glared at Gabriel. Who did he think he was anyhow?

'Then what are you doing here if there's nothing going on?' Gabriel asked smugly. His deep green eyes sparkled triumphantly behind his thin-rimmed glasses. He grinned at me, and I was disappointed to realize that his dimples were just as charming, even when he was annoying the heck out of me. Which was unfortunate, because I really wanted to dislike Gabriel Francoeur.

'Er ... we're doing a promotional thing for his single, "City of Light", which you'll all have a chance to hear very soon,' I said, thinking quickly. I glanced at Gabriel and then at the other journalists. 'I'm sorry you all appear to have been misinformed again.'

With that, I began striding toward the entrance.

'If there's nothing wrong,' I could hear Gabriel shouting behind me, 'then bring Guillaume out to talk to us when you're done inside!'

I ignored him and tried to swallow the lump in my throat. I clutched the Celio bag tighter. How could I bring him out past the media horde if he was in custody? I was in serious trouble here. I had no idea how I would talk the security guards out of having Guillaume charged.

After a quick consultation with a security manager outside the tower, I was escorted sixty meters up to the first level by elevator. I hardly had time to marvel at the fact that, for the first time in years, I was once again inside one of my favorite buildings in the world. I barely noticed the intricate, criss-crossing geometric ironwork of the tower as we were whisked quickly upwards toward what I suspected would be a much crazier scene than the Hôtel Jérémie last week.

My security escort led me down a series of hallways on the first floor and into a small office behind the Eiffel Tower's post office, where I was introduced to two of the security guards who had Guillaume in custody.

'Where is he?' I asked wearily. Smirking, one of the guards gestured toward a closed door at the back.

'*Bonne chance, mademoiselle,*' he said.

The guard opened the door for me, and for a moment I just stood there, staring.

Inside the small, mostly bare room, Guillaume was sitting in a plastic chair, naked but for a pair of faded Hanes briefs, which were red with a thick white band round the waist. He had one leg crossed casually over the other and was reading a tattered copy of *Fear and Loathing in Las Vegas*. And, as if things couldn't get any stranger, he was wearing a black top hat. A black cane with a white tip was propped against the chair.

'*Allons-y,*' the officer urged. Let's go. I gulped and stepped inside. The officer slammed the door behind me with a definitive bang, and Guillaume looked up. He stared at me for a moment as if trying to place me, then blinked a few times and grinned.

'Ah, *bonjour*, Emma!' he said brightly, as if I had just dropped in on him in his penthouse as opposed to a security cell in the Eiffel Tower. He snapped his book shut and set it down. 'You are looking lovely this morning.'

I tried to control my impulse to blush – and also my impulse to stare at his mostly naked body. 'Guillaume, what on earth are you doing?'

'It's not my fault, Emma,' he said with a casual shrug. He tipped his top hat to me and lazily stood up. I blinked a few times and looked away. After all, it was irrelevant that his was the nicest body I'd ever laid eyes on, right?

'I'm sure you're totally innocent, once again,' I said drily. I thrust the Celio bag at him. 'Please get dressed, Guillaume,' I said, still trying not to look too closely.

He looked at me for a moment then took the bag from me. He peered inside and his face lit up. 'Emma!' he exclaimed. 'You brought me clothes! How nice! And I didn't get you anything! How rude of me!'

I looked at him. He was smiling happily at me, as if there was nothing in the world wrong with the present situation.

'Yeah, I'm a real angel,' I muttered. I looked him up and down. 'What exactly were you doing, anyhow?'

Guillaume regarded me blankly. 'I was doing a dance number, Emma,' he said.

'A *dance* number?'

Guillaume nodded. 'Want to see?'

'Not particularly,' I said.

Guillaume smiled and shook his head. 'Oh, Emma, where is your sense of adventure?'

'I don't know,' I muttered. 'Where are your clothes?'

He ignored me. 'I was just seeing what it was like to be Fred Astaire. You're American. You should appreciate that, right?'

With that, he stood up, dropped the bag full of clothing on the ground and picked up the cane.

'Guillaume—'

He held up a hand. 'Do not interrupt the artistic process, Emma.'

He closed his eyes, breathed in and out and whispered, 'Zen.' Then, wearing just his red-and-white briefs and his top hat, he began to do a little barefoot tap dance, singing some sort of song about Park Avenue and Rockefellers, waving his cane around grandly.

I stared in horrified awe as he pranced back and forth in the little cell, swinging his cane, tipping his hat, kicking his legs up and dancing around me until he concluded on his knees, the top hat in one hand and the cane in the other. He looked at me hopefully, and I sensed that I was supposed to applaud.

Instead, I shook my head slowly. 'You are seriously insane,' I said.

Guillaume pouted, dropping his hat and cane dejectedly to the floor. 'Aw, Emma, I'm just having a little fun.'

I closed my eyes for a moment and took a deep breath. 'Okay, Guillaume, wonderful,' I said. 'Now seriously, would you put some clothes on and let me deal with this?

Otherwise, you're going to be performing your next dance routine at the local jail.'

'I was going to suggest you join me,' Guillaume sulked. 'You'd be great dancing with me to "Cheek to Cheek". It's my favorite Astaire song, you know.'

'Maybe some other time,' I said. 'Now please? Get dressed!'

Guillaume looked a bit disappointed, but he picked up the Celio bag, pulled a shirt out and shrugged. 'Whatever you say, Emma,' he said sadly as he began to pull the shirt on over his head. I lingered a second longer than I needed to (hey, it's not every day you get to see the world's most handsome man in his underwear, okay?), then I made my way back out to the main office where I asked who was in charge. The Eiffel Tower security chief offered me a seat and called over the two other guards who were standing in the room.

'I'm so sorry about this,' I said, after introducing myself and apologizing for my lack of French proficiency. 'What happened?'

In broken English, the security manager described how a guard who had just started his morning shift had found the nearly naked Guillaume fast asleep in a room near the tower's south pillar. They couldn't imagine how he had snuck in, as security at the tower had been tight since 2001. It had taken the guard several minutes to wake up the snoring Guillaume, and then he had alerted his superior and escorted Guillaume to the security office. That's when Guillaume began doing his little tap dance routine.

'He continued to say he was Fred Astaire,' said one of the guards, scratching his head. 'And he began to sing a song about tomatoes, tomahtoes, potatoes and potahtoes.'

'That is when I realized that it wasn't just some bum,' the security manager interrupted, leaning forward conspiratorially. 'It was Guillaume Riche! One of the biggest celebrities in France!'

I sighed. 'Yes. That's why an incident like this could really be a problem for his image, you understand.'

The security guard exchanged glances with his two deputies. 'I thought so,' he said with a nod, looking back at me. He lowered his voice. 'That's why we're prepared to . . . negotiate.'

I looked at him blankly. 'Negotiate?'

His eyes darted from side to side then settled on me. '*Oui*,' he said. 'We can do a little, how you say, exchange? And we can forget that this happened. We have not called the police yet.'

'Okay,' I said slowly, not quite understanding what he meant by an 'exchange'. 'But the police obviously know there's something going on, right? I mean, there are dozens of reporters outside.'

'*Oui*,' the security chief said. 'But we are willing to say that this was all a misunderstanding. We can say that Guillaume Riche had our permission to be here.'

'You would do that?' I asked.

'*Oui*,' he said. 'If we can reach an agreement.' He rubbed his hands together and winked at me.

'And if he promises to put his trousers on,' one of the guards muttered.

'And not to dance any more,' said the other. All three men nodded vigorously.

Suddenly I understood.

'Are you talking about a bribe?' I asked incredulously.

The three men exchanged looks.

'A bribe?' the security chief asked. 'What does this mean? I do not know this word.'

Okay, so obviously he was going to play dumb. I took a deep breath and nodded. 'Let me see what I can do,' I said. 'I need to talk to Guillaume, okay? I'm sure we can work this out.'

'*Oui, mademoiselle,*' the security chief said, still looking confused.

I asked them to hold on for a moment. I knocked on Guillaume's door. 'Are you dressed?'

'Do you want me naked?' he shouted back. I rolled my eyes and opened the door. Thankfully, he had managed to find his way into the T-shirt and cargo pants. And at least he had one of the flip-flops on his feet. He was holding the other one in his hands, examining it as if it was the key to the universe. 'It's amazing how they put these things together,' he said, gazing at the flip-flop in awe. Inexplicably, he was also still wearing the top hat.

I shook my head. There was seriously something wrong with the guy. 'Guillaume, I think the security guards are asking for a bribe to let you out of this,' I said. I felt a little ill; I couldn't believe that I was about to resort to bribery to extract my insane client from a potentially disastrous situation. I wondered vaguely what the penalties were in France for such an offense. I sighed. 'Do you have any money on you?'

I realized as soon as the words were out of my mouth what a ridiculous question it was. Of course he didn't. He didn't have any clothes on until I'd brought him the Celio garb. Where would he keep his money?

But clearly I had underestimated Guillaume Riche.

'Of course,' he responded with a shrug. 'I always keep some cash in my underwear.'

'You . . . you do?' I had no idea whether he was kidding.

'Of course,' Guillaume said. He reached down the front of his pants, felt around for a moment and pulled out a thick fold of bills. 'Do you want to borrow some?' he asked pleasantly, holding up the bills. I stared. 'To buy a souvenir or something?'

'Um, no, not a souvenir.'

Guillaume shrugged and tossed the fold of bills to me. I caught it reluctantly, trying not to think about the fact that it had spent the night down his briefs. I tried to remember that desperate times called for desperate measures, and if being responsible for a naked, top-hatted rock star trapped in a major monument wasn't a desperate time, I didn't know what was.

'I don't know how much is there.' He shrugged. 'Take what you want. I don't care.'

While he returned his attention to his apparently intriguing flip-flop, I looked down at the bills in my hands. My eyes widened when I realized that the bill on top was a hundred. I quickly counted the rest.

'Guillaume, you keep twenty-eight hundred euro in your underwear?' I asked after a moment, looking up at him in confusion.

He shrugged. 'So what?' he asked. 'You never know what you might need a little cash for.'

He smiled at me like nothing was wrong.

I shook my head. 'Um, okay.' I didn't know what to make of this guy.

'"Night and day . . ."' Guillaume suddenly broke into song again and began to dance around.

'Guillaume!' I said sharply.

He abruptly stopped dancing. 'What, you do not like Fred Astaire? That was "Night and Day", one of his greatest hits.'

'No, Fred Astaire is fine,' I said through gritted teeth. 'I just need to handle this situation. So can you stop dancing for a moment and talk to me?'

Guillaume shrugged. 'Okay.'

'Great.' I took a deep breath. 'So I can have this money?' I asked, holding up the bills.

'That's fine.' Guillaume nodded and smiled at me. 'Whatever you want, Emma. You should buy a souvenir. To remember this day.'

'I think I'll pass on that,' I said drily.

I knocked on the door to the security office and slipped inside, holding the roll of bills in my hand. The eyes of all three guards widened as I held it up.

'Okay, I have twenty-eight hundred euro here,' I said.

'*Mademoiselle*, where did you get that?' asked one of the guards.

'You don't want to know,' I said.

'*Mademoiselle*,' the security chief said slowly. 'I think you misunderstand. You are trying to make a *pot-de-vin*?'

'What?' I asked. I rapidly translated the words in my head. 'A pot of wine?'

'No, no,' he said, looking troubled. 'It is an expression. It means to, eh, to try to get somebody to do something by giving them the money?'

'A bribe?' I asked. We seemed to be talking in circles.

'I do not know that word,' the guard said. 'But in France, *mademoiselle*, it is *illegal* to trade money for a favor.'

'Oh,' I said, reddening. 'I thought that's what you were asking for.'

'No, no, *mademoiselle*!' the security guard said, shaking his head violently. I glanced at the other two guards, who were staring at the money rather more lustfully than their boss. 'I meant that perhaps we could trade a favor for a favor, so to speak.'

'A favor?' I asked hesitantly. I jammed the wad of bills into my pocket, feeling like an idiot.

'*Oui*,' the chief said. He glanced at the other guards and then back at me. 'Could it be arranged to have Guillaume Riche play a private concert for my daughter and her friends? I would be the best father in the Île-de-France.'

'And my daughter too,' said one of the guards. 'She would also like to go to the private concert.'

'I do not have a daughter,' the youngest guard said. 'But my girlfriend, she would like to see Guillaume Riche.'

I stared at the three of them for a moment.

'You just want Guillaume to perform a private concert?' I asked.

'At my house,' the security chief said boldly. 'My wife will even cook him dinner.'

I sighed and closed my eyes for a moment. 'I think that can be arranged.'

Twenty minutes later, after extracting a promise from a reluctant Guillaume that he would do a private concert for the security guards' loved ones, I was on my way downstairs in an elevator, my Celio-clad rock star in tow.

'Here,' I said, thrusting a piece of paper at him. I'd spent five minutes jotting down some notes while he signed autographs for the starstruck security staff. 'This is what you're going to say to the media.'

'I have to make a statement?' he whined. 'C'mon, Emma! I just want to go home and go to bed.'

'You should have thought of that before you wound up naked in the Eiffel Tower,' I said.

'I wasn't naked,' he pointed out with a grin. 'I had my briefs on. *And*,' he added pointedly, 'a top hat.'

'You are the strangest person I've ever met,' I muttered. 'Anyhow, unless you want me to go out there and tell the truth, you're going to have to read this.'

'You're very tough, Emma,' he said sullenly. 'You know that?'

I sighed. 'Can we lose the top hat too, Guillaume?'

He shook his head sadly, removed the hat from his head and handed it over, along with the cane.

I led Guillaume outside to the wall of reporters. The moment they spotted us, they started clamoring and shouting. I tried to avoid locking eyes with Gabriel, who was in the front of the crowd, staring at us in disbelief.

'Guillaume and I have a statement to make, and then we won't be taking any questions,' I said firmly. The crowd quieted down a bit. 'This has all been a mistake. Guillaume will be filming scenes for his "City of Light" music video here, and he was simply scouting out locations. There was a miscommunication, which is why I wasn't here with him. "City of Light",' I added, throwing in a promotional plug, 'is the first single from Guillaume's debut album, *Riche*. I have no doubt you'll be blown away. It's the story of a man meeting the woman of his dreams in Paris, which is why this location makes so much sense for the video shoot. The song will hit radio stations across the world this evening, for the first time. Now,' I concluded, 'Guillaume has a few words to say to you.'

Guillaume looked at me for a moment, then he shook his head, looked down at the piece of paper I had given him and began to speak.

'I regret that I was locked accidentally into the Eiffel Tower last night while scouting locations for the "City of Light" video,' he read slowly and stiffly. It was obvious his words were scripted. I cringed and snuck a look at the media. Some of the reporters looked skeptical (especially Mr Skepticism himself in the front row), but all appeared to be listening and jotting down notes. 'I feel terrible that all of you have come here to report on what isn't really a story. It was an unfortunate incident, and I'm sure you'll understand when you see the video next month. Thank you for your concern.'

'Thank you very much,' I added quickly. 'Please direct all questions to my office.'

The reporters started shouting out questions, but I ignored them and hustled Guillaume toward the dark-windowed limo idling at the curb. I'd called Poppy before coming down and asked her to order one for us. It was the least she could do from her cushy seat on the Eurostar.

'Nice job, Emma!' Guillaume said admiringly once the car pulled away from the curb and the Eiffel Tower began to disappear behind us. He had put his top hat back on his head and was fiddling with his cane.

I rolled my eyes and shook my head. 'Guillaume, what were you doing in the Eiffel Tower without your clothes anyhow?'

He looked puzzled. 'You know, I haven't the faintest idea,' he said slowly. 'One minute I was drinking manzana with a girl I met at Buddha Bar. The next thing I knew, I was waking up without my clothes with some security guard staring at me. Rather embarrassing, you know.'

'You were at Buddha Bar?' I asked, startled. I thought back to Gabriel's warning.

'*Oui*,' Guillaume said. 'Although it's all a blur, really.'
'You are unbelievable,' I muttered.
'Thank you!' Guillaume said brightly.
I shot him a look. 'That wasn't a compliment,' I said.
He grinned and tipped his hat to me. 'I know.'

10

I filled Poppy in on everything when she returned from London late that afternoon, and she apologized about a thousand times for not being there to help out.

'It's fine, Poppy,' I said. 'Really.' And I meant it. Knowing that I could handle a situation like that changed something inside of me. Perhaps I hadn't been giving myself enough credit – for anything.

That night, all the news stations in Paris ran reports on Guillaume's Eiffel Tower incident, and they showed clips of him addressing the media. He looked even more handsome on TV, and I knew that girls all across the world, wherever this was being aired, were probably swooning and saving up their money to buy his album. Poppy translated what the anchors were saying, and it was all good. Guillaume's debut album, which would be mostly in English, was one of the most highly anticipated releases of the year, one anchor said. His good looks already had girls around the globe plastering his poster on their walls, said another. A third network's anchor interviewed the president of the Club d'Admirateurs de

Guillaume Riche – the Paris-based Guillaume Riche Fan Club.

'He has a *fan club*?' I asked incredulously.

'He has three hundred and forty-one fan clubs around the world, at the last count,' Poppy said mildly. 'Including one in a remote village in Siberia where they don't even get TV reception. It's mind-boggling.'

That night, for the first time, Poppy and I heard 'City of Light' on the radio while we were eating the pre-made meals from French supermarket chain Champion that we'd heated up. We both squealed and jumped out of our seats.

'He's really on the radio!' Poppy exclaimed, jumping up and down.

'He sounds fantastic!'

We went out that night to celebrate at the Long Hop and, thanks to my ebullience over the quick save at the Eiffel Tower, I didn't even protest when Poppy brought two cute guys back from the bar along with our cocktails. Poppy quickly disappeared into another corner of the bar to flirt with Alain, the sandy-haired, slightly freckled one she'd evidently chosen. That left me with Christian, who was tall with bushy dark brown hair, glasses and a slightly crooked nose. He was cute, nice and spoke great English. By the time we went home that night, Poppy had persuaded me to go on a double date with her and the guys later that week.

The next morning, the e-clipping service Poppy subscribed to had found 219 hits for the name 'Guillaume Riche' in the last twenty-four hours, and even the *New York Times* had dedicated five paragraphs to describing the 'misunderstanding' that had ensued when a false tip led the press to believe 'rising rock star and international playboy

Guillaume Riche' was trapped inside the Eiffel Tower without his clothes.

'That report was false,' the security chief was quoted as saying. 'We opened the tower early so Guillaume and his production company could have a tour for their new video.'

The article went on to mention that Guillaume's just-released single was already heating up airwaves across the US and Europe and that his 'Coldplay-meets-Jack Johnson style' (a quote from my press release!) was expected to catch on. 'He's the next big thing,' the paper quoted Ryan Seacrest as saying.

I was still riding high from all the success when Gabriel Francoeur called to rain on my parade.

'Hi, Emma, I'm glad I caught you,' he said when I answered. 'It's Gabe Francoeur from the UPP.'

The smile fell from my face. 'What can I help you with?'

'Nothing big,' he said. 'I just want to see if I can schedule an interview with Guillaume about some of his, um, odd behavior lately.'

'There's nothing odd about his behavior,' I said right away, hating how stiff my voice sounded. 'I'm not sure what you're referring to.'

'Ah.' Gabriel sounded amused. 'Right. I'm sure you're not. But in any case, I'd just need a few minutes of his time. And yours, of course, if you'd like to sit in and comment.'

'I'm afraid that will be impossible,' I said. 'His schedule is really quite busy right now.'

'Really?' Gabriel asked. 'That's funny, because I happen to know that right now he's sitting on the sofa in his apartment, watching cartoons. He doesn't *seem* busy.'

'How would you know that?' Panic prickled at the back of my neck. 'Are you *spying* on him?'

Gabriel laughed. 'No, Emma! Of course not. But a good reporter never reveals his sources. So how about it? An interview?'

'No, really, we're not doing interviews right now.'

He sighed dramatically. 'Okay then,' he said casually. 'I'll just have to go with the story I'm working on about how he keeps getting into unsavory scrapes that his publicity team manages to get him out of.'

'Mr Francoeur, I assure you, that's not true!'

'Call me Gabe,' he said. 'All my American friends do. And Emma, I won't really have another option if I can't get that interview, now will I?'

'Is that blackmail?' I demanded.

'Call it creative negotiating,' he said. He paused and added, 'I'm sure *you* know all about creative negotiating.'

'What?'

'I'm sure you know what I mean.' Gabriel sounded smug, and I felt suddenly uneasy. Did he know about the Eiffel Tower bribes? How would he know? But I couldn't take any chances.

I cleared my throat. 'I'll get back to you about your interview request later this week,' I said stiffly.

'I'll look forward to hearing from you, Emma.'

I hung up feeling like I'd just been outmaneuvered. And I didn't like it one bit.

The rest of the work week was spent studiously avoiding Gabe's calls. He called every morning and every afternoon, like clockwork, and I always made sure to wait until at least eight in the evening to call him back and leave an apologetic gosh-I'm-sorry-I-missed-you-again-but-maybe-we-can-connect-tomorrow message. So far, the avoidance seemed to be working, although I was slightly concerned that all this call-dodging was just going to make him more annoyed at me.

Meanwhile, Poppy and I were working overtime to prepare for the press junket in London. We had a confirmed list of journalists, we had ironed out all the reception details and I was beginning to believe that everything would go off without a hitch. On top of that, Guillaume was staying quiet and hadn't got himself locked half-naked in any major monuments lately.

On Friday, Poppy and I went out on our double date with Alain and Christian, the two guys we'd met at the Long Hop. They took us to dinner at Thomieux, a restaurant in our neighborhood specializing in south-western French cuisine. Afterwards, we went to Bar Dix, which Poppy said was one of her favorite bars. It was like no place I'd ever seen; it was small and had two levels that looked like they'd been carved into the side of a cave. We wound up wedged into a tiny booth in the basement, sharing three pitchers of the best sangria I'd ever had. Poppy and I told stories, and Alain and Christian, both of whom had their arms thrown protectively over our shoulders, laughed and leaned in to give us pecks on our respective cheeks.

As our taxi pulled away from the curb at the end of the evening, leaving the two Frenchmen staring wistfully after us, I turned to Poppy, who was smiling.

'See?' Poppy asked. 'Doesn't it feel good to leave them in the dust?'

'I guess . . .' I responded, my voice trailing off. But actually, it didn't feel that great at all. They seemed like nice enough guys. There was really no reason to reject them.

'Oh, stop worrying,' Poppy said. 'They'd eventually do the same to you anyhow. You're just beating them to the punch. You know what the author of *How to Date Like a Dude* says!'

That weekend, Poppy and I went out a few times, to a disco near the Place de la République and to a Latin American bar near Bar Dix. Both nights, she flirted with guys like crazy in fluent, rapid French, while I blushed and tried hard to make myself understood in English.

On Monday night, Poppy had a date and I was planning to stay home alone and watch *Amélie*, a French movie Poppy had insisted I needed to see. So, figuring that there was no rush, I decided to work late at the office to finish the following week's interview schedule. Hours after Poppy had flitted out the door in a cloud of perfume, I was still hunched over a list of TV reporters who had requested interviews with Guillaume. Suddenly, a deep voice above me startled me so much that I nearly fell off the edge of my chair.

'I figured you'd still be here.'

I looked up in shock and saw Gabe Francoeur smiling down at me. I was so shaken that I stood up too quickly and knocked over a box full of ballpoint pens in the process.

'Sorry,' Gabe said, bending down to help pick up the pens that littered the floor. 'I didn't mean to startle you.'

'Uh, no,' I said. 'You didn't startle me. I just, uh, wasn't expecting anyone. How did you get in?'

'The door was ajar,' he said. I rolled my eyes; Poppy must not have pulled it closed behind her when she left, starry-eyed, for her date. 'Still,' Gabe added, 'I should have knocked. I'm sorry.'

'Yeah, well, whatever,' I grumbled.

Gabe straightened up and handed me the pens he'd retrieved from the floor. I righted the box, put them back inside and tried to give Gabe my best impassive expression.

'So you've been ignoring me?' he said, arching an eyebrow at me.

I cleared my throat. 'Um, no,' I said. 'What would give you that idea?'

'I don't know,' he said. 'Maybe the fact that you're never available, no matter how many times I call?'

'I've been busy,' I said defensively. 'Besides, I've called you back.'

'Yes. This may surprise you, but I'm not generally still in the office after eight in the evening,' he said, looking almost amused. 'But then again, you know that, don't you?'

I ignored him and sat back down in my seat. I gestured half-heartedly to Poppy's chair, which he dragged over so that it was facing me. He settled into the seat.

'So, what is it you want?' I asked, trying to sound mean. 'Clearly it's something important since you've called twenty times.'

'I just wanted to tell you that I don't believe a word of what you've said,' he said pleasantly.

My eyes widened and I stared at him. 'What?'

'About Guillaume. I don't believe you. I know you're covering up for him.'

'Well, it's not really my concern what you do or don't believe,' I sputtered, feeling my temper rise. I hoped it wasn't too obvious that he was making me nervous.

Gabe smiled. 'I realize that,' he said. 'But I'm working on a profile of Guillaume for the UPP. I think he's going to be big in the US. Really big. And don't get me wrong, I think he deserves to be. He's quite talented. I just wanted to let you know that I'm not buying the things you and Poppy are saying. I know you're lying.'

I felt a little sick. I stared at him for a moment. 'So that's it? You don't have a question for me or anything?'

Gabe shrugged. 'Nope. Just wanted to let you know.' He stood up and added nonchalantly, 'Oh, and I'll be needing that interview with Guillaume too.'

'What, I'm supposed to give you an interview now despite everything you've just said?'

He grinned. 'No. You're supposed to give me an interview now *because* of everything I've just said.'

I glared at him.

'And even if I'm right about all of his insanity, certainly a rock star like him should be able to charmingly explain it all, right?' Gabe continued, that same amused look still on his face.

'Well, I . . .' I started to retort, but then I stopped and clamped my mouth shut. I thought about it for a moment. Damn it, I hated to admit it, but he was right. Obviously, Gabe wasn't going to stop until he had some kind of story. 'He's not insane,' I finally said, in a weak attempt to defend my completely nutty client.

'Oh I know,' Gabe nodded. 'He adores the attention, though. And lately, he's been going too far. So about that interview?'

'Fine,' I said through gritted teeth. 'I'll try to schedule something for this coming week.'

Gabe seemed to consider this for a moment. 'Okay,' he said finally.

'Okay,' I echoed. I swiveled back around in my chair to face my computer, hoping that Gabe would disappear.

Unfortunately, he didn't seem to get the hint.

Finally, I rolled my eyes, shut down my computer and said loudly, 'Okay, well, I have to be going now, Gabe. Thanks so much for stopping by!'

'My pleasure,' he said cheerfully. 'I'll give you a ride home.'

I just looked at him. 'What? No, I'll take the Métro.'

'Oh, c'mon, Emma,' he said. 'It's like a hundred degrees outside. And I'm talking centigrade. The Métro will be miserable.'

I shrugged. What was he, Jekyll and Hyde? He was ready to destroy my career one second, and the next, he wanted to drive me home? 'I'll be fine,' I mumbled.

'My car is air-conditioned,' he said, raising an eyebrow.

'I'm sure I'm out of your way.'

'Where do you live?'

'Rue du Général Camou,' I said, knowing that he wouldn't have heard of the tiny side street between Avenue Rapp and Avenue de la Bourdonnais.

Wrong again.

'Oh, fantastic!' he exclaimed. 'I live in the seventh too! What a coincidence. You're just a few blocks from me.'

I gaped at him. I was out of excuses.

'So? Are you coming?' Jingling his car keys, he started toward the door.

In the passenger seat of Gabe's immaculately clean Peugeot, I braced myself for an onslaught of questions about Guillaume, but instead, he made pleasant conversation, asking me where I was from, why I'd come to Paris and where I'd gone to school.

'You went to the University of Florida?' he exclaimed as soon as the words were out of my mouth. 'I can't believe it!'

I looked at him, startled. 'Why?' I asked defensively. How on earth had he even heard of the school? Sure, it was well known in the States thanks to their dominance in

American football and basketball. But how could some guy in France have such strong feelings about my alma mater?

'Because I went there too.'

I was sure I'd heard him wrong. 'What? But you're French!'

'Emma, French people *are* allowed to go to school in the United States, you know,' he deadpanned.

I blushed, feeling stupid. 'I know that.'

'Besides,' Gabe added, 'I have dual citizenship. My father is French. My mother is American. They divorced when I was a baby. I spent summers in Brittany with my dad and the rest of the year in Tampa with my mom.'

'You lived in Tampa?' I stared in disbelief. 'I grew up in Orlando.' The cities were only an hour apart. Gabe laughed.

'That's unbelievable,' he said. 'What a small world.'

'You really went to UF?'

Gabe nodded. 'Yes. I got a journalism degree there ten years ago and then got my master's at the Sorbonne, here in Paris. That's when I decided to move here to work for the UPP. Being bilingual really helps.'

'You graduated from UF ten years ago?' I asked. 'I graduated seven years ago. Also from the journalism school.'

'Wow, we overlapped a year,' Gabe said. 'That's unbelievable. How come I never saw you?'

I shrugged. 'I don't know. Maybe we crossed paths and didn't even know it.'

'No,' Gabe said, staring straight ahead. He made the left turn onto Avenue Rapp. 'I think I would have remembered you.'

My heart fluttered bizarrely for a moment, and I shot a quick glance at him. Maybe he wasn't as bad as he'd initially seemed.

A moment later, Gabe turned right down my street, and I pointed out my building.

'You're right next to the American Library,' he said. 'That's so weird. I come here all the time.'

'You do?'

He nodded. 'Yeah. I'm a big reader. Well, maybe some weekend when I'm over here, we can grab a cup of coffee.'

'Um, maybe,' I said slowly, thinking that, although he seemed nicer than I had expected, I would probably have to wear my ice skates to such a meeting, because it would be a cold day in hell before I voluntarily subjected myself to coffee with Gabe Francoeur. He would no doubt spend the entire time we were together pumping me for information about Guillaume. No thanks. 'Well, thank you for the ride,' I said awkwardly.

'It was great to talk with you, Emma,' he said. 'I'm afraid I have to get going, though. I have dinner plans.'

I felt myself blushing again. 'Oh, of course,' I said. Shoot. *I* was supposed to blow *him* off. Why had he just made me feel like he was eager to get rid of me?

I opened the car door and stepped out. 'Well,' I said awkwardly. 'Thanks again.' I slammed the door behind me.

'No problem!' Gabe said through the open window. 'Cheers!' He gave me a little wave and then sped off without looking back.

11

That night, Poppy came across the gum wrapper Edouard had scribbled his name and number on the first night I'd been to the Long Hop.

'Who's this guy?' she asked, holding the wrapper in the air.

'That chain-smoker I met the first night we went out.'

'You should call him,' Poppy said. 'He seemed nice!'

'You didn't even talk to him,' I said. 'And he smoked like a chimney.'

'Nonsense,' she said firmly. 'He liked you. And I guarantee, he'll be great for your confidence.'

Against my protests, Poppy dialed for me and handed the phone to me. 'Try to sound sexy,' she said. I rolled my eyes.

Edouard sounded surprised to hear from me, but he said that of course he remembered 'ze pretty blonde American girl' and would still love to take me on a romantic picnic in Paris. We agreed to meet on Wednesday night.

'Let's go buy you something to wear!' Poppy said on Wednesday afternoon. We left the office early, and I let her talk me into a black strapless dress from Zara on the rue de

Rivoli and a new pair of way too expensive strappy black heels from the Galeries Lafayette.

'See?' Poppy asked on the Métro on the way home. 'Don't you feel sexier now?'

I had to admit, she had a point. I spent longer than usual that evening blow-drying my hair, applying my make-up and slipping into my dress. By the time I was done, I saw a completely different person in the mirror.

Perhaps the more different I felt, the easier it would be to forget about the life I'd left behind in the States.

'So you said you are new to our beautiful city?' Edouard asked as we walked to his car, his hand resting lightly on the small of my back.

'I'm getting to know it,' I answered.

'And I hope you are loving it so far?'

'I am.'

After a brief drive along the Seine in his little Renault, Edouard parked near the Musée d'Orsay and, with an enormous picnic basket in hand, led me toward the Pont des Arts, the beautiful pedestrian bridge that spanned the river between the Louvre on the Right Bank and the Quai Malaquais on the Left. When we found a spot on the bridge, he pulled a perfectly folded white-and-red checkered picnic blanket out.

'My lady,' he said, gesturing to it after he'd spread it neatly, aligning the corners with the planks of the bridge.

'Can I help?' I asked, watching him in awe.

He smiled at me. 'Just relax and enjoy.' He pulled out an iPod and mini-speakers and turned it on. 'I've organized some selections from Serge Gainsbourg, to introduce you to one of our country's legends,' he said. Soft jazz music began to waft from the speakers as Edouard lit a cigarette and busied himself pulling perfectly packaged foods from the basket and setting them up in front of us. I stared as the picnic materialized; he seemed to have brought at least a dozen dishes, some of which I'd never even seen before.

'You did all this for me?' I asked as he uncorked a bottle of red wine and began to fill two glasses. 'You barely even know me yet!'

He shrugged and stubbed his cigarette out on the bridge. He exhaled a mouthful of smoke and smiled. 'You said you hadn't had a proper Parisian picnic yet,' he said. 'I know no better place to start than here.'

His chain-smoking aside, it felt like something out of a dream. To the west, the Eiffel Tower rose gracefully over the Seine, and to the east, I could see the twin towers of Notre-Dame. To the north, the enormous, palatial Louvre seemed to go on forever, and to the south, the beautifully antiquated buildings of Paris dotted the Left Bank. As the sun began to dip low in the sky over the Eiffel Tower, the bright blue of early evening gave way to muted pinks and oranges on the horizon. It was breathtaking, the kind of scene that made me wish fervently I could paint or even take good photographs. It was the kind of evening mere words couldn't describe.

While I looked on in awe, Edouard patiently explained some of the dishes he had brought to share with me. 'This is goose rillette,' he said of the first item. It looked like a grayish, brownish box of mush, but when he spread it on a slice of baguette and I took a bite, I felt like my taste buds were doing a little happy dance on my tongue.

'This is amazing!' I said, my mouth still full. It was salty and sweet all at the same time, and it tasted entirely unfamiliar.

He grinned at me in amusement. 'It's a French specialty,' he said. 'You can't get it in your country.'

Next up were several fresh cheeses, including a herbed chèvre and a strong blue cheese, then a jar of tiny sour pickles called cornichons and a series of little salads, including a shredded carrot one that I couldn't seem to get enough of. There were two kinds of meat pâté, both of which were amazing, and a strange-looking dish that appeared to be hard-boiled eggs wrapped in ham and encased in gelatin but actually turned out to be surprisingly delicious.

By the time we were finished with our meal – which ended in espresso from a thermos and fruit tarts that looked almost too beautiful to eat – the stars were starting to come out, and a crescent moon was rising above Notre-Dame. Thoroughly stuffed, I lay back on the picnic blanket beside Edouard and looked up at the night sky.

'It is beautiful, no?' Edouard said after a moment, puffing on a cigarette.

'It's amazing,' I breathed. I felt like we were in our own little world, although there were passers-by walking to and fro and another couple on a blanket a few yards away making out like hormonal teenagers. The vague, sweet smell of marijuana wafted over from a trio of snickering teenage boys clustered on the other side of the bridge. I turned my head to the side to look at Edouard. 'I think this is one of the most wonderful evenings I've ever had.'

'We are just getting started,' he said. He put his cigarette out and took a sip of water. Then, inching closer to me, he pressed his lips to mine. It was magical, even though I could still taste tobacco on his breath. I kissed him back, spurred on by the food, the wine, the starry night and the romance of it all. He pulled me closer and parted my lips with his tongue, threading one hand tenderly through my hair and stroking the side of my face with the other. It was perfect. I didn't want the moment to end.

I cracked my eyes open as he kissed me and looked up at the night sky with the Eiffel Tower glowing ethereally white in the background. It was a quintessential moment of French romance – exactly what I needed. As I kissed back, I thought about Brett and all I'd left behind in Florida. These last few days, I'd been missing him – and my old life – a lot less. Somehow, Swanson frozen meals eaten in front of the TV while Brett watched Fox News didn't compare to picnicking on a bridge over the Seine while a handsome Frenchman gazed into my eyes and made me feel like the only woman in the world.

I was just falling into the kiss when a rude ringing sound jolted me out of the moment.

'Is that yours?' Edouard asked after a moment, between hungry kisses.

'Is that my what?' I whispered back, wondering who could have been rude enough to leave their cell phone volume up on a bridge meant for picnickers and lovers.

'Is that your *phone*?' Edouard asked, kissing me again and biting my lower lip gently. I shuddered.

'My phone?' I asked vaguely. Then I sat straight up. 'Oh no, it *is* my phone!'

I'd forgotten that I'd left it on. I could feel heat rising to my cheeks.

Just then, the ringing stopped. I breathed a sigh of relief.

'Do you need to see who was calling?' Edouard asked.

'No, I'm sure it's not important.' All I wanted was for him to kiss me again. Fortunately, he acquiesced. Unfortunately, whoever was calling me apparently had different plans for the evening.

'Do you think you'd better answer?' Edouard asked on the fifth series of rings. People around us were starting to stare.

I heaved a sigh and pulled myself reluctantly away from him. I groped in my purse until I found my phone, then I flipped it open. Poppy's name was on my caller ID. I gritted my teeth. 'This had better be important,' I said as I answered.

'I am *so* sorry to interrupt your date,' she said hurriedly. 'But I need your help, Emma. Guillaume has done it again!'

My heart sank. I glanced at Edouard, who was still lying on his side on the picnic blanket, gazing at me hopefully. 'Done what?' I asked.

Poppy sighed. 'All I know is he's hanging from a rope between two apartment buildings in the seventeenth.'

I swore under my breath. 'You're kidding, right?' I asked hopefully. Maybe this was her idea of a joke.

Poppy was silent for a moment. 'I wish I was,' she said. 'Seriously, Emma, could he make our lives any more difficult? His launch is only a week away!'

I glanced at Edouard again. 'Poppy,' I whispered, turning away from him a bit. 'I'm on a date with Edouard!'

'I'm sure he'll understand,' she said quickly. 'Just explain it to him. Tell him you have to go for work.'

'Fine,' I said through gritted teeth. I jotted down the address and promised to meet her there as soon as I could.

'Everything okay?' Edouard asked as I ended the call.

I took a deep breath. 'No,' I said. 'I'm sorry, but I have to go. There's a work emergency I have to help take care of.'

Edouard just stared at me.

'You are leaving?' he asked.

'I'm so sorry.' I glanced around at the remnants of the perfect picnic. 'Really,' I said. 'You have no idea how disappointed I am.'

He stared at me for another moment then shook his head. He stood up without another word and started grabbing empty dishes and tossing them back into the picnic basket, muttering under his breath.

'Edouard?' He was obviously upset, and I couldn't blame him, especially after all the effort he had gone to.

'It's just not natural,' he grumbled as he tossed the last of the dishes back into the basket.

'What's not natural?' I asked, confused.

'This,' he said shaking his head. 'In our country, women do not leave dates early to go to work. Perhaps things are different in America, but here, the women are women and the men are men.'

I stared at him. What did being women and men have to do with anything?

He studied me for another moment then shook his head. 'Let's go to the car.'

'I can find a taxi . . .'

'Nonsense.' His voice was frosty. 'I will drive you.'

He gathered up the blanket, threw out the empty wine bottle and began striding quickly, picnic supplies in hand, back toward the Left Bank, away from our perfect little spot on the perfect little bridge. With Edouard puffing aggressively away on a series of cigarettes, we drove in uncomfortable silence to the 17th, where he found his way to the address on a side street off Avenue Niel that Poppy had given me.

'The avenue is blocked,' Edouard said stiffly as we pulled

up. There were several Paris police officers motioning for drivers to keep going. I groaned. I had no doubt that they were there because of whatever Guillaume had done. Edouard pulled down the next side street and looped around to the top of rue Banville. 'This is as close as the police will let me get.'

'Thank you,' I muttered. 'And again, I'm sorry.'

'You know,' Edouard said, his face stony as he watched me exit the car, 'You will never find a boyfriend if you continue putting your career first.'

I stared at him. 'But I'm not looking for a boyfriend.'

'I'm just giving you some advice,' he said. '*Bonne nuit.*' And with that, he nodded at me stiffly and sped away. I stared after him for a moment.

'Hot date?' came a voice from behind me. I spun around to see Gabe standing there on the curb, watching me with a look of amusement on his face.

'None of your business.' I narrowed my eyes at him.

'Seemed like a nice guy,' Gabe said, raising an eyebrow.

'He was,' I said awkwardly, feeling foolish, wondering how much of the conversation he'd heard.

I brushed past him and into the throng waiting outside. I could feel Gabe following me, but I didn't turn around. When I rounded the corner onto rue Banville, I stopped dead in my tracks.

'He doesn't look too comfortable up there, does he?' Gabe asked, his voice far too cheerful for the situation at hand.

'Oh no,' I muttered. High above the street, which was blocked off by police barricades, Guillaume was dangling by his ankles from a thick rope suspended between two buildings, at least twelve or thirteen floors off the ground.

He was belting out a slurred version of 'City of Light', complete with grandiose arm gestures.

> *Mon amie, mon coeur et mon amour*
> *Won't you show me what our love is for?*

His words rang out, deep and melodic, between the buildings.

'He sounds good,' Gabe said, as nonchalantly as if we were listening to his song on the radio. I turned to glare at him.

Beneath Guillaume were four Parisian fire trucks, one with its ladder extended up a few stories, and several firefighters gazing up at him. But no one seemed to be making a move to get him down.

'Someone has to do something!' I exclaimed, more to myself than anyone else.

'This is France,' Gabe replied cheerfully. 'The *pompiers* will stand around all night and gaze up at him, waiting for someone to tell them what to do.'

'But . . . what if he falls?' I asked.

'Then I guess you'll get your big publicity push,' he said.

I turned around and snapped at him. 'What's *wrong* with you? He could get hurt up there!'

Gabe looked slightly abashed. 'Emma.' He reached out and put his hand on my arm. 'I'm sure he'll be fine. He always is. He's always getting himself into scrapes like this. He loves them. Relax.'

I shook my arm away. 'Go back and wait with the other media,' I muttered. I focused my attention away from him and turned to the police officer standing at the top of the street, keeping the crowds away.

'Hello,' I began politely. He looked down at me, his forehead creasing. 'I'm Guillaume's publicist. May I please get through?'

'*Comment?*' he asked sharply. Darn it. He didn't understand me.

'Um, I'm the publicist. For Guillaume Riche.' I spoke slowly, firmly, keeping eye contact with the police officer, who still looked confused.

'*Comment?*' he asked again. '*Je ne parle pas anglais.*'

Great. I'd found the only Parisian who didn't speak even basic English. Just my luck.

'Um, okay,' I said, trying to seize on whatever French I'd picked up. 'Um, *je* . . . um, *amie* of Guillaume.'

'*Vous êtes une amie de ce fou?*' the police officer asked slowly. I gathered that he was confirming that I was Guillaume's friend. I wished I knew how to say *publicist* in French, as I was certainly no friend of the wacky rock star.

'*Oui,*' I confirmed confidently.

The police officer started to laugh. He shook his head and said something in rapid French that I didn't understand. Then he said in clear English, 'You no come. Too many girl.'

'No, no, I'm not actually a friend,' I started to protest. 'I'm his publicist.' I couldn't for the life of me think how to say the word, so I said the closest thing I could think of. 'Um, *journaliste.*'

Clearly that was the wrong thing to say, because the moment the word was out of my mouth, the police officer began pushing me away and muttering in French.

'No, no, wait!' I protested, realizing too late that I was being pushed back to where the press was being kept waiting. But the officer ignored me.

'Well, hello again,' said Gabe as the officer guided me

forcefully around the corner to join other members of the press pool. 'Do you need some help?' Gabe asked, arching an eyebrow at me and glancing between me and the officer.

I sighed. 'Yes,' I muttered.

Gabe smiled at me — a triumphant smile, if I'm not mistaken — and turned to the officer. He said something in rapid, confident French, and the police officer responded in a low, grumbling voice. Gabe spoke again, and finally the police officer shrugged, took my arm and began guiding me away from the media horde.

'I told him you were Guillaume's publicist and to bring you inside to find Poppy,' Gabe said as the officer pulled me away.

'Thank you,' I said reluctantly through gritted teeth.

'Anytime!' Gabe gave me a cheerful little wave. 'And hey, be careful in there.'

The police officer guided me through the crowd and into the lobby of one of the buildings Guillaume was dangling between. He said something to one of the officers inside, and in a moment another officer appeared to escort me further into the building. I found Poppy around the corner, waiting for me.

'What on earth is going on?' I asked.

Poppy sighed and glanced toward the ceiling. 'Well, the good news is that he's not violating any laws, so for once we don't have to worry about him being arrested. Apparently in this city, you can hang upside down by your ankles thirteen stories above ground and no one minds.'

'Of course you can,' I muttered.

Poppy nodded tersely. 'The bad news is that he's not being particularly responsive to the *pompiers*, and they can't get him down without his cooperation,' she said.

'Oh no.'

'It gets worse,' Poppy said grimly. 'He and some friends tied the ropes themselves. The police have secured the ends, but who knows how well he's knotted onto the rope. Or how long the rope can hold his weight.'

'This is awful,' I said. I thought about it for a moment. 'Have you tried to talk him down?'

Poppy nodded. 'He wouldn't listen. He just kept on singing.'

I hesitated. 'Let me give it a shot,' I said.

'You think he'll listen to you?'

'I think we sort of, um, bonded during that whole Eiffel Tower thing,' I said. 'It's worth a try.'

Poppy shrugged and led me to the elevator, which we took up to the thirteenth floor. When the doors opened, we stepped into a hall filled with police officers, firemen and paramedics, all of whom appeared to be doing nothing but standing around, sipping coffee and smoking cigarettes. Had I not known that a man was dangling above the pavement outside the window, I would have mistaken this for a friendly hall party.

I shook my head, and Poppy led me past them and into a room at the end of the hall. Inside, several officers were gathered around the window, looking just as casual as the people in the hallway. It was as if they dealt with dangling rock stars every day. After a quick glance around the room, I could see the end of a thick length of rope tied to a bed pushed against the wall. I followed the rope to the window and looked outside. Suspended in mid-air, Guillaume was dangling cheerfully, still belting out the lyrics to 'City of Light'. This was insane.

I checked the rope and made sure it looked like it was

securely tied. While Poppy conferred with one of the police officers, I leaned out the window, trying not to think about how dangerous this was for the rock star we were responsible for.

'Guillaume!' I called. I couldn't resist looking down, and when I did, I felt sick to my stomach. Thirteen floors was a long way. Definitely far enough to worry about a splattered rock star on the pavement. In a city where most of the residential buildings topped out below ten floors, how had Guillaume managed to find two buildings beside each other whose height made this stunt so potentially deadly?

Guillaume turned his head slowly toward me. It seemed to take him a moment to focus, but when he realized who I was, a broad grin spread across his face. 'Emma!' he exclaimed cheerfully, as if I had simply surprised him in the recording studio as opposed to suspended in mid-air. 'Hi! You're here! Welcome! Join the fun!'

Below us, a murmur ran through the crowd as it became obvious that Guillaume had stopped singing and was now conversing with someone inside. For a moment, I wondered what Gabe was thinking on the ground below, but just as quickly I banished the thought from my mind. Who *cared* what he was thinking? Why had that been the thought that popped into my panicked brain?

Guillaume was grinning at me broadly. I stared for a moment and sighed. 'Guillaume,' I began wearily. 'What on earth are you doing?'

He looked puzzled for a moment – or at least he appeared to (it was rather hard to tell considering that he was hanging upside down by his ankles). 'Well,' he began. 'I was drinking with a few of the guys from the band. This is Jean-Marc's apartment, you know. He's my drummer. So his girlfriend, her name's Rosine, well, Rosine says wouldn't it be fun if we string a rope between her apartment and his and see if we can get across. That's Rosine's apartment over there.'

He paused and pointed to the window across the street where the rope disappeared into another apartment building. 'So we did that, and then no one else wanted to go first, so I said I would,' Guillaume continued cheerfully. 'So they tied this cord to my foot just in case I fell or something. I guess it's good that they did because, Emma, this rope is slippery. I started across, but about halfway I just couldn't hold on any more. I let go, and, well, here I am. Hanging upside down. By my ankles. By the way, where did Jean-Marc go?' Guillaume asked, suddenly looking around in confusion. 'Where are the other guys?'

I shook my head at him in disbelief. 'They're gone, Guillaume,' I said wearily. I took a deep breath and exhaled slowly, trying to calm myself. 'Look, we have to get you down from there before you get hurt.'

He shrugged absently. 'I don't know. I kind of like it here. I can see the Eiffel Tower, you know!'

That was the cue, in Guillaume's mind at least, to begin singing again.

'Night has fallen on this City of Light!' He belted out the opening line of his single enthusiastically, his baritone still sounding surprisingly perfect, considering that his throat had to be swelling up thanks to all the blood rushing to his head.

The crowd below, which had grown even larger as word had apparently spread that there was a bona fide rock star hanging between buildings, started clapping, cheering and whistling. Guillaume grinned and started singing even more loudly.

'I think of you and tears fill my eyes,' he continued. The crowd below cheered wildly. 'I dream of you when you're not here with me. You're all I've ever wanted and you set my soul free!'

Down below, unbelievably, people started singing along the third time he reached the chorus. By the time he was done, he had a whole group of amateur back-up singers below.

'They love me, Emma!' he shouted to me when he was done. Down below us, the whistles, cheers and catcalls continued.

'Guillaume . . .' I began wearily. But I didn't know what else to say. This guy was clearly a lunatic. And somehow, my PR education hadn't included lessons on how to talk singers with a screw loose down from ropes dangling between buildings in foreign cities. I'd have to get in touch with my college's dean about that; there'd clearly been a gap in the curriculum. 'Guillaume,' I tried again, keeping my voice firm. 'You need to come in now.'

Guillaume studied me for a moment and grinned. 'I have a better idea. Why don't you come out and get me?'

'What?'

'Come out here with me, Emma!'

'Are you crazy?'

'Probably!' Guillaume seemed to be gathering steam. 'But it will be fun! We will sing a duet!'

'There is no way I am going out there with you!' I shot back.

'Then I am not coming in!' Guillaume said. He stuck his bottom lip out stubbornly and crossed his arms over his chest. 'And if something happens to me, it will be your fault.'

I stared at him. 'You can't be serious!'

'I am completely serious, Emma,' Guillaume said. 'I am not coming down until you come out and sing with me.'

I slowly turned around to see a roomful of people staring at me. I locked eyes with Poppy.

'What are you going to do?' she asked softly.

'I don't particularly want to die from falling out of a thirteenth-story window while singing a duet with a lunatic,' I said.

'We can guarantee your safety,' one of the police officers piped up. Poppy and I turned to look at him. He was young, with flushed cheeks and bright blue eyes. 'I mean, the rope itself is secure, and it's thick enough to hold your weight. If you let us hook you onto it, you will not fall.'

I stared at him. 'You really think I should do this?'

The young officer shrugged uncomfortably. 'It is not for me to say, *mademoiselle*. I am only saying that we can keep you safe if you choose to go out there.'

I turned back to Poppy. She looked at me for a long moment. 'It's up to you,' she said finally.

I glanced out the window.

'Are you coming?' Guillaume yelled. 'The view is amazing, Emma! You must come see!'

I thought about it for a moment then turned back to the young officer.

'You promise you can keep me safe?' I asked.

He nodded solemnly. '*Oui*,' he said. 'I can almost guarantee it.'

I pretended I didn't hear the word *almost*.

I walked back over to the windowsill. 'Hang on Guillaume,' I yelled half-heartedly. 'I'm coming!'

*

Fifteen minutes later, after borrowing a spare pair of police pants from the back of a police car so that no one would see up my dress as I dangled above the street, I was trying not to panic. Secured with several ropes and attached to the main rope with a pulley contraption, I slowly inched my way out the window, praying that I wouldn't die.

'Your face looks a little green, Emma!' Guillaume said as I started down the rope toward him.

'I'm afraid of heights,' I said stiffly as I inched closer and closer. The young officer had given me a pair of gloves and showed me how to walk my hands down the rope to get closer to Guillaume. He had promised that even if I lost my grip, I'd be fine; I was attached to both the rope and the window so, allegedly, I wouldn't fall. I might, on the other hand, slide down the rope and smash into the side of the building. I tried not to think about it.

'Afraid of heights?' Guillaume asked. 'That's impossible! Look around! It's so beautiful here!'

I glanced up for a second and realized that he was right. I could see all the way to the Eiffel Tower. But I could also see the Eiffel Tower from my living room, which is where I would have greatly preferred to be at the moment.

Below us, the crowd was murmuring and pointing. Gabe was probably having a field day. This would make one great UPP story.

'Okay, Guillaume,' I said as I made my way to his side. 'Let's just get this over with quickly.'

'You're no fun!' he said. I looked down at him and shook my head. Not only was I dangling beside a rock star on a rope strung over the streets of Paris, but I was head to toe with him, as he was secured to the rope by his ankles.

'Your feet smell,' I retorted.

'That's not very nice.' Guillaume sounded wounded.

'Neither is making me risk my life for you. Now are we going to sing or what?'

'Fine, fine,' Guillaume sighed. 'What would you like to sing?'

I rolled my eyes. 'Whatever, Guillaume! Can you just choose something so we can get down from here?'

I was starting to get more and more nervous. The rope was swaying, and I felt sick to my stomach. I glanced toward the window. Poppy and the young officer were leaning out.

'Are you okay?' Poppy shouted. The officer slipped a comforting arm around her shoulder and Poppy glanced up to bat her eyes at him. Great. Even in the midst of a death-defying tragedy, she was flirting.

'I'm fine!' I shouted back.

'How about "Cheek to Cheek"?' Guillaume asked. I turned my attention back to him. He smiled up at me and patted his cheek, which appeared very red thanks to the fact that blood had been rushing to his head for the past two hours. 'Fred Astaire debuted it in 1935, long before Sinatra got his hands on it!'

'No more Fred Astaire!' I groaned.

'Good point,' Guillaume said thoughtfully. 'I don't even have my top hat with me. I couldn't do it justice.' He thought for a moment. 'Do you know "Jackson" by Johnny Cash and June Carter?'

'No.'

'How about "Islands in the Stream"? Kenny Rogers and Dolly Parton?'

'No!' I exclaimed in frustration. How on earth did he know so many country songs?

Guillaume thought for a moment.

'How about "You're the One That I Want"?' he asked. 'From *Grease*?'

'You've *got* to be kidding me,' I muttered.

'You know it?'

'Yes, I know it,' I said. I just didn't want to sing it.

'Okay, I'll start! This will be beautiful! You are just like Olivia Newton-John!'

I groaned. Guillaume shouted to the crowd. 'For my finale tonight, I will be performing a hit song from the musical *Grease* with my lovely publicist, Emma!'

The crowd below applauded, hooting and hollering like they were at a real concert.

'They love us already!' Guillaume said. 'Doesn't this feel good, Emma?'

'Yeah, it feels just fantastic.' I was still trying not to throw up.

Guillaume cleared his throat and began to sing a familiar line about multiplying chills. Personally, he was giving me the chills at the moment. But that seemed beside the point. I sighed loudly. Guillaume made a face at me and sang the remainder of his verse.

'Your turn!' he urged.

I shot him a look, tried to channel Olivia Newton-John and began singing the female part of the song unenthusiastically.

'Louder, Emma!' Guillaume grinned at me. 'They can't hear you!'

I took a deep breath and continued with the rest of the verse, feeling like a complete idiot.

Down below, the crowd applauded wildly. Miraculously, we managed to make it through all the verses and several renditions of the chorus, ending with a drawn out, 'Ooh, ooh, ooh,' that we sang together as the crowd below us went wild. Dozens of flashbulbs went off and I closed my eyes. I just wanted this night to be over.

'Emma?' Guillaume said after a moment, after the screams had finally receded a bit. 'You know, I'm getting a bit of a headache.'

'Yes, Guillaume,' I said stiffly. 'It's probably because you've been hanging upside down for two hours.'

He appeared to think about this for a moment. Then he shrugged, which, unfortunately, made us both swing wildly from side to side for a moment. I felt like I was going to vomit.

'Maybe you're right, Emma,' he said earnestly after the swinging had slowed. 'It's probably time to come in then, right?'

'Yes, Guillaume,' I agreed. 'I think it's time to come in.'

'Really?' he asked. He seemed to consider this. 'Okay then. Thanks!'

As the young officer had instructed, I asked Guillaume to grab my ankles. He acquiesced, and I shouted inside to let the officers know we were ready. Slowly, three officers pulled on the rope attached to my back so that Guillaume and I, locked in a strange head-to-toe position, were slowly dragged along the length of the rope, via the pulley I'd been connected to. Five agonizing minutes later, Poppy's young officer and two others pulled Guillaume and me to safety.

'That was fun!' Guillaume exclaimed, grinning at me as the police untied his ankles and unhooked him from the rope. There was some yelling outside as the officers in the building across the way discussed how to detach the rope. As soon as Guillaume was free, he reached out and pulled me into a hug. 'You saved me!' he declared in a deep, theatrical voice.

I rolled my eyes and gritted my teeth. 'You're insane.' I didn't mean it facetiously.

'Emma, you were worried about me!' Guillaume said, pulling back and studying my face.

I avoided his glance. 'I was worried about the *album*,' I mumbled.

'No, you were worried about *me*!' Guillaume insisted triumphantly. He turned to Poppy and gave her a hug too. 'Poppy! Emma loves me!' he announced.

Poppy frowned. 'Then she's even crazier than you are.'

After Guillaume had been ushered out a back entrance by Richard and Edgar, who had arrived during my dangling duet, Poppy and I walked outside to where the police were keeping the waiting journalists at bay.

'Do you want to do the talking?' Poppy whispered as we walked.

I just looked at her. 'Are you kidding? I just dangled thirteen stories above Paris singing a duet from a John Travolta musical. I think it's your turn to handle this.'

'Fine,' Poppy nodded. We arrived at the bank of microphones and tape recorders that the reporters had thrown together, and Poppy raised a hand to silence the crowd.

'I'm pleased to announce that Guillaume Riche is perfectly fine and is on his way home with his bodyguards,' Poppy began. 'Thank you all for your concern.'

As she went on to explain that Guillaume's stunt certainly wasn't illegal and certainly wasn't the result of drunken stupidity, I gazed around at the journalists, trying to gauge their reactions. Most were listening and nodding as if Poppy's words were entirely sensible. Were they crazy? There were a few skeptical faces in the crowd. Oddly, Gabe didn't appear to be watching Poppy, although once in a while he scribbled something on his pad. Instead, he appeared to be staring hard at me.

Every time I caught his eye, I glanced quickly away, but he kept right on looking, as if he could see right through me. It was making me feel uneasy.

'This was simply an impromptu demonstration on Guillaume's part,' Poppy concluded, 'to show you how much he enjoys singing with normal women. Like my colleague, Emma.'

I smiled weakly. After a round of questions, each of which Poppy answered quickly and crisply, she finally called on Gabe. I braced myself for something sarcastic.

Instead, looking straight at me, he spoke softly. 'That was really brave, Emma,' he said. 'Are you okay?'

I gulped and nodded. 'Yes, I'm fine,' I said.

After the press conference ended and the reporters began to go their separate ways, Poppy turned to me, looking exhausted.

'Feel like going out for an our-rock-star-isn't-splattered-on-the-pavement celebratory drink?' she asked. She leaned in. 'That cute officer asked me out!' she whispered.

I smiled weakly and shook my head. 'No,' I said. 'I'm sorry. I'm just worn out. I think I'm going to go home and go to bed.'

Poppy nodded. 'I understand.'

I smiled. 'Have fun with Officer McDreamy, though. See you at home.'

We hugged goodbye, and I began walking toward the Porte Maillot Métro stop, which was several blocks away, according to the little *Plan de Paris* map Poppy had loaned me.

There was a chill in the air, and with the uneven cobblestone of some of the sidewalks, I was beginning to doubt the logic of wearing high heels in a city like this. How did Frenchwomen do it, anyhow? I glanced around, hoping I'd see the gleaming light of a taxi somewhere, but the streets were empty. As I walked through the puddles of light cast from the street lamps, my feet ached more and more with each step.

I'd walked four blocks and was just beginning to contemplate whether it would be worse to keep my heels on (I was already getting massive blisters) or to walk barefoot on the grimy streets, when I heard a car horn honk beside me. I turned my head wearily to the right, gritting my teeth against the pain, and was somehow unsurprised to see Gabe sitting there in his little Peugeot, smiling at me.

I stopped walking, and he rolled down his window.

'Need a ride home?'

'No,' I said grumpily. I regretted it the moment the words were out of my mouth. It was another few blocks to the Métro, then, after I got off the train at the closest stop to our apartment, I'd still have to walk all the way home, which meant crossing the Pont de l'Alma and walking halfway up Avenue Bosquet – a good half mile. I'd surely have to have my feet amputated. But I was in no mood to need anyone, particularly Gabe, so I started walking again, pretending to ignore him. Better to go through the rest of my life without sensation in my feet, right?

'Okay,' Gabe said cheerfully. I expected him to speed up and drive off, leaving me and my aching feet in the dust, but instead, as I walked and stared straight ahead, his car crept slowly beside me, keeping pace with me.

Ignore him, I told myself. It's like he's not even there. Don't look.

That worked for a block. But when I turned left onto Boulevard Péreire and Gabe turned with me and continued inching along beside me, I'd finally had enough.

'Stop following me!' I snapped, stopping in my tracks and turning to face him.

'Oh, you're still there?' Gabe feigned surprise. He stopped his car. 'I hadn't noticed.'

I glared at him.

'Oh, come on, Emma,' Gabe said after a moment of smiling at me. His face looked serious now. 'Just get in the car. I know your feet hurt in those shoes.'

'I'm fine,' I said through gritted teeth.

'No, you're not,' Gabe said simply. 'Stop being proud and just get in. I'm going to your neighborhood anyhow.'

I opened my mouth to say something sarcastic in reply, but what was the point? My feet *were* killing me.

'Fine,' I grumbled. I marched over to his car like *I* was doing *him* a favor, yanked the door open and slammed it behind me after I'd flopped into his passenger seat.

'Um, you seem to have shut your dress in the door, Emma,' Gabe said. I glanced at him and was perturbed to see that he appeared to be hiding a smile.

I looked down and realized that in all my righteous indignation, I had, in fact, managed to trap the hem of my dress in the car door. 'Thanks,' I mumbled. I opened the door, pulled my dress in and slammed the door again, fervently hoping that my cheeks hadn't turned too red.

Gabe pulled away from the curb, and I looked out the window, trying to ignore him, which, admittedly, was difficult to do when I was sitting two feet away from him. We drove in silence for a few moments.

'So really, Emma, are you okay?' Gabe asked finally.

I glanced at him and nodded. 'Yeah.'

'I meant what I said back there,' he said. 'That was really brave.'

'Thanks,' I said, surprised.

'And really foolish,' he continued.

I made a face. I should have known his apparent kindness was too good to be true.

'I didn't exactly have a choice,' I said.

'Guillaume would have come down eventually on his own,' Gabe said softly.

'You don't know that,' I protested. 'Maybe I saved his life.'

Gabe was quiet for a moment. 'You know, he's not as crazy as he looks,' he said finally. 'He just enjoys the attention.'

I ignored him and looked out the window. What was he, Guillaume's psychiatrist?

'So, how was that date of yours tonight?' Gabe asked casually as we entered the roundabout that circled the Arc de Triomphe.

I could feel the heat rising in my cheeks again. I blinked a few times. 'None of your business,' I muttered. After all, what was I going to do, admit to him that it had been a horrible failure? That I had thought the guy was perfect until his chauvinistic resentment came pouring out? I glanced up at the Arc, which loomed, big, glowing and impressive, over the street, casting its pools of light every which way.

'No, I suppose it's *not* my business.' Gabe paused and glanced at me as we pulled out of the roundabout and up to a stop sign. 'But you *do* look really pretty in that dress.'

I looked at him in surprise. 'Um, thanks,' I mumbled, feeling like I was on the outside of some inside joke.

'I mean it,' he said softly.

'Oh,' I said awkwardly, not quite knowing what to make of him.

We drove in silence down the crowded Champs-Élysées, and Gabe didn't talk again until he was on Avenue Franklin D. Roosevelt, heading toward the Seine.

'So how about that interview with Guillaume, Emma?' he asked just as the Eiffel Tower came into view on the horizon, off to the right. 'Can you help me out?'

Ah. So *that* was it. That was why he was giving me a ride and pretending he thought I was pretty. Typical. As if I'd be stupid enough to eat up his compliments and respond by giving him carte blanche to harass my client.

Then again, if I was smart enough to realize what his ulterior motives were, why was I feeling disappointed?

'I've told you that I'll book an interview for you,' I said wearily, staring out the window. We were passing the entrance to the tunnel where Princess Diana died, and as always I felt a little twinge of sadness.

'I know,' Gabe persisted. 'But we're all leaving for London next Saturday for the press junket. Why don't you set it up for Tuesday? We can meet for coffee. I don't think Guillaume has any plans.'

I turned to look at him. 'How would *you* know if Guillaume has any plans?'

Gabe had the decency to look a bit embarrassed. 'Well, I wouldn't, exactly. I just meant that no public appearances have been announced or anything. So how about it? I just need a half hour for a UPP write-up. I promise I'll go easy on him.'

I studied his profile for a moment, noting for the first time that there was a small, nearly imperceptible bump on the bridge of his angular nose, probably from a break at some point in his life, as well as a small scar just above his right eyebrow.

'Do you promise the write-up will be positive?' I asked, trying to ignore the fact that I had also just noticed for the first time how long his dark eyelashes were. We were on the Left Bank now, just a few blocks from my apartment. I had to admit, this had been much easier than walking and taking the Métro, even with Gabe's constant questions.

Gabe smiled. 'You know I can't promise that,' he said. 'But I *can* promise you that I'm not going into this with any bad intentions. I just want to ask Guillaume about all these crazy antics lately. But I'll also ask him about the new album, and the much-anticipated launch and everything. You can't ask for better publicity than this, Emma. My story goes out to hundreds of papers around the world.'

'I know,' I grumbled. I tried to weigh in my mind how much harm Gabe could do versus how much extra publicity he could bring us. In the end, I knew I had to grant him the interview, if for no other reason than I had already given him my word. 'Fine,' I said finally. 'I'll call you tomorrow with a time and place.'

Gabe turned left onto my street and came to a stop along the curb.

'Wonderful,' he said. 'Thanks, Emma. Will you be there?'

'Will I be where?'

'At the interview.'

'Oh,' I said. I unbuckled my seat belt. What, did Gabe think I was as crazy as Guillaume? I wasn't going to leave my client alone with some muckraking journalist! 'Of course I'll be there.'

'Great,' Gabe said again. 'I'll look forward to it, then.'

I sighed. What was I supposed to say? 'Um, thanks for the ride.'

'No problem,' Gabe said. 'You're on my way home anyhow.'

I gritted my teeth and stepped out of the car.

'Talk to you tomorrow, Emma!' Gabe said cheerfully as I shut the door behind me. I stood and watched him as he pulled away from the curb and disappeared down Avenue Rapp without looking back.

12

After a few more days of working long hours to prepare for the launch and to do more pre-emptive damage control by sending out releases about all of Guillaume's great charity work, Poppy and I spent the weekend shopping, eating out and, of course, flirting with strangers Poppy picked out at bars. Despite myself, I was starting to enjoy feeling attractive to Frenchmen. It *was* good for my confidence, in a way I had never expected.

On Tuesday, Guillaume and I arrived by taxi at Café le Petit Pont, the same place Poppy had taken me on my first night in Paris, for the interview I'd reluctantly promised to Gabe.

'I promise we'll keep this short,' I said to Guillaume as we sat down at a table in the outside courtyard, facing the river. 'We just have to appease this Gabriel Francoeur guy, and maybe he'll leave us alone.'

'I've heard he's terrible,' Guillaume said with what appeared to be an expression of amusement on his face.

'The worst,' I muttered. I glanced around and saw that most of the people near us were staring at Guillaume, who seemed oblivious to the attention. Several tourists were surreptitiously snapping photos, and others were holding up cell phones to capture his image. No matter how many times I'd been responsible for my Boy Bandz clients in public, I'd never quite got used to the attention that fame brought with it.

'What's wrong?' Guillaume asked me after a moment, leaning across the table.

'Nothing.' I shook my head. 'It doesn't bother you? All these people staring and taking your picture?'

Guillaume glanced around, as if noticing for the first time that we weren't entirely alone in the restaurant.

'Oh,' he said. 'I guess I don't even think about it any more.' He smiled broadly and waved a few times to excited fans. Then he turned his dazzling smile back to me.

When our waiter arrived with a basket of French bread, we both ordered a café au lait, which arrived within seconds. Amazing the kind of service you got when you lunched with a superstar.

'Okay,' I said once we'd each taken a sip. 'Gabriel will be here in twenty minutes. We need to go over some things first.'

'Whatever you say, beautiful Emma,' Guillaume said, flashing me a winning smile. 'Then perhaps we can make sweet music together again, you and me?'

I rolled my eyes. He was so strange sometimes. 'No, Guillaume.'

He pouted. I ignored him.

'So I think it goes without saying that you can't admit to Gabe that you were drunk on any of the occasions he'll be asking you about,' I began.

Guillaume recoiled in mock horror. 'Drunk? Me? Never!'

'Riiiiiiight.'

'Really, Emma, excessive alcohol consumption is wrong,' Guillaume said. He batted his lashes sweetly. 'Drug use is wrong.'

'Oh yeah, I'm sure Gabe will be won over by your puppy dog eyes.'

Guillaume looked confused. 'Puppy dog eyes?'

I realized the expression didn't translate. 'I mean, innocent expression.'

'I am innocent,' Guillaume said. 'I've never hurt anyone.'

I thought about this for a moment. I supposed it was true. All of Guillaume's antics seemed only to harm himself – and of course the PR people who had to clean up the messes he made.

'You know, Emma, your eyes look very blue when you smile,' Guillaume said softly, gazing at me so intently that I started to squirm. 'They are beautiful. Like little pools of sparkling Mediterranean water.'

I could feel my cheeks heating up. 'Okay, Guillaume,' I muttered. 'Let's just stick to preparing for this interview.'

He leaned closer. 'But you are so lovely, Emma,' he said, still staring into my eyes. I felt my heart hammering in my chest. Sure, he was insane. But he was also gorgeous. And there was something about being gazed at by the most handsome man you'd ever seen that made your heart go pitter-patter, even if he was completely nuts.

'Guillaume, cut it out,' I said, hating that he could certainly see that my cheeks were on fire.

'Cut it out?' He looked confused. It was another expression that didn't cross the language barrier.

'I mean, stop it,' I clarified. 'We're here to talk business. I don't know why you're saying these things all of a sudden.'

'I just say what's in my heart, beautiful Emma.' He smiled softly at me, and I tried to tear my eyes away.

I cleared my throat loudly and took a big sip of my café au lait, burning my tongue in the process. I coughed and tried to recover quickly. 'Okay,' I said, all business again. I avoided Guillaume's eyes. He was still staring at me in that unnerving way. 'Here's what you need to say. You need to mention how excited you are to be reaching such a broad, English-speaking audience. You need to say how wonderful it is to be helping to bridge a cultural gap with music. You need to talk about how "City of Light" is about finding love in Paris and how you haven't found your own special woman yet.'

'But *you're* very special, Emma,' Guillaume interjected.

'Please stop.'

'I can't stop my heart from beating for you, can I, Emma?' Guillaume said, reaching out to fold his hand over mine. I yanked my hand away as if his touch had burned me. He grinned.

'Be serious, Guillaume,' I mumbled.

'Okay, I am totally serious now,' he said, furrowing his brow.

'If Gabe asks you about any of the recent incidents you've had – the hotel room, the Eiffel Tower or the whole rope thing the other day – just laugh and explain that it was all a misunderstanding,' I continued, trying to sound as businesslike as possible.

'It *was* all a misunderstanding,' Guillaume said.

'Right.' I nodded. 'Good start. Just explain that the hotel was nothing – just me and Poppy working with you with our clothes on. The Eiffel Tower was simply research for your video shoot. And the rope thing was just a joke gone wrong. Okay?'

'Whatever you say, beautiful lady,' Guillaume said.

'Oh, and one more thing. I know you and Gabe are both French. But can you speak in English, please? So I can make sure to stop Gabe if he's asking anything inappropriate?'

'Anything for you, my dear,' Guillaume said, bowing his head. 'I can never refuse the requests of a beautiful lady.'

Before I had time to respond, I spotted Gabe striding confidently through the front door of Café le Petit Pont. He was scanning the room for us, and I had to admit, he looked really good. He was dressed in a pair of dark jeans and a pale green button-up shirt that made his green eyes stand out sharply behind his glasses, even from across the room. I felt a little shiver run through me, and I pinched myself to get rid of it.

Guillaume waved. Gabe spotted us and came over.

'I'm sorry I'm a few minutes early,' he said as he reached the table. He shook hands with Guillaume and then with me. 'I hope I'm not interrupting anything, like, for instance, the two of you plotting what you're going to say to me.'

I glared at him. Guillaume laughed.

'You've always been so skeptical, Gabe,' he said, raising a finger and moving it side to side in a tsk-tsk motion. I glanced at the two of them.

'You already know each other?' I asked. Somehow, I had expected that Gabe only knew Guillaume from afar, or perhaps from a few small interviews over the last year. But they were behaving as if they had met many times in the past.

'Let's just say we go way back,' Gabe said drily, shaking his head. He sat down in the chair between Guillaume and me and ordered a kir royale from the waiter.

'Ah, drinking in the afternoon, are we?' Guillaume said,

leaning back in his chair and inspecting his café au lait with disdain. He grinned at Gabe. 'A man after my own heart.'

'Says the alcoholic,' Gabe muttered.

'He is not an alcoholic,' I said quickly, 'and I would appreciate you not joking about such a serious matter.' I was already getting a headache. I shot him a withering look.

'Right,' Guillaume said stiffly. I could tell he was fighting back a grin. 'I am not an alcoholic. Everything that has happened has been a – what did you call it, Emma? – a misunderstanding.'

'It *was* a misunderstanding,' I said through gritted teeth.

Gabe stared at me for a long moment. Then, thankfully, he switched gears. 'So Guillaume,' he began, looking away from me and focusing on Guillaume, his pen poised over a pad of paper. 'Tell me about your debut single, "City of Light", and why it's the perfect record to cross over to English-speaking listeners.'

I breathed a sigh of relief as Guillaume started rattling off the perfect answer, describing how love is the universal language and how the song is, at its core, about falling in love, no matter where it takes place, or in what language. His answer was so perfect, in fact, that I was a bit transfixed myself, even though I knew Poppy and I had practically spoon-fed him the words.

Gabe took Guillaume through several questions about the album, about his appeal to English-speaking audiences and about his music career.

The questions were surprisingly innocuous, and I was just starting to get comfortable when Gabe rapidly switched tracks.

'So these three recent incidents – the Hôtel Jérémie, the Eiffel Tower, your little high-wire act over rue Banville –

you claim they were all innocent mistakes?' Gabe asked, leaning forward. I cleared my throat loudly in an attempt to remind him not to press too hard.

'Yes, yes, of course,' Guillaume said, shooting me a look. 'You journalists are always getting it wrong.'

Gabe, clearly sensing a challenge, arched an eyebrow and went in for the kill.

'Oh, so *we're* the ones getting it wrong?' he asked, looking half amused, half pissed off. Uh-oh. 'So I suppose it's relatively commonplace to get locked in the Eiffel Tower without your clothes. Or to get caught in a hotel room with a bunch of naked girls. Or to get drunk or high or whatever and convince yourself that it's just a fantastic idea to hang upside down over a city street fifteen stories up.'

'It was thirteen stories,' Guillaume said, waving a hand dismissively. 'And things aren't always what they appear.' I looked back and forth between them nervously. So far, Guillaume seemed to be doing fine. His answers were nonchalant, non-defensive. Perfect. Then he glanced at me. 'Besides,' he added. 'I have the beautiful Emma here to always come to my rescue.' He smirked at Gabe.

I turned toward Guillaume and fixed him with a glare. What was he doing?

'Yeah, well, maybe if you could control yourself, she wouldn't have to keep disrupting her life to help you,' Gabe snapped immediately.

'Who says it's a disruption?' Guillaume shot back.

'Guillaume—' I started to say, but Gabe cut me off.

'Well, I'd say that making a woman risk her life to come get you down from a stupid high-wire act is a disruption,' Gabe said.

'Gabe!' I interrupted hastily. Guillaume was still

smirking at Gabe, and Gabe looked peeved. 'That's my job. Don't worry about it.'

'Yeah, Gabe. We were singing a duet!' Guillaume said. 'Emma loved it! Why are you so uptight? Is it because you haven't had a girl to sing a duet with in years? Are you jealous?'

Gabe's eyes flashed angrily and he said something to Guillaume in rapid French, and Guillaume laughed and answered. Whatever he said made Gabe look even angrier, and he barked another few unintelligible phrases at my annoying pop star.

'Guys?' I interjected. 'Could we switch back to English?'

'Sorry, Emma,' Guillaume said. 'I was just telling Gabe here that I *do* respect you.'

'And I was telling him that he obviously doesn't,' Gabe retorted, his face stormy. 'Because if he did, he wouldn't be making your life so difficult.'

'Now, Gabe,' Guillaume responded slowly. 'Aren't *you* the one who's making Emma's life difficult? By hounding her so much for an interview with me?' He had a point. I glanced at Gabe, but Guillaume wasn't done. 'In fact,' Guillaume continued with a little grin, 'just a few minutes before you got here, Emma was telling me you were, how did you say it? *The worst*, I think she said.'

Gabe flinched and glanced at me. I felt the blood drain from my face.

'Guillaume!' I chided. He was smirking at Gabe now, pleased to have elicited a reaction. 'I didn't mean it that way, Gabe,' I tried to explain. 'Just that you were hard to deal with sometimes.'

'I wasn't aware I was such a problem, Emma,' Gabe said stiffly. 'I certainly apologize.'

Guillaume hooted with laughter.

'*Oh, I'm so sorry, Emma!*' he mocked. '*I'll never bother you again!*'

'Guillaume!' I exclaimed.

'Don't worry, Emma, it's fine,' Gabe said stiffly. 'He's just being *un imbécile*.' He pronounced the word the French way, but the meaning was obvious.

'Gabe!' I exclaimed. I'd never had a reporter talk to a client that way before, particularly not a client who was already such a big star.

'Don't worry, babe,' Guillaume said, patting me on the arm and glowering at Gabe. 'I can handle this.'

Gabe retorted with something in French that I didn't understand, and Guillaume responded in French too. The two men went back and forth for a moment, with Guillaume smirking, Gabe glaring and me trying desperately to interject, when finally Guillaume interrupted Gabe in English.

'That's it. Interview's over,' he said abruptly, glancing at me. 'I'm tired. Time to go home.'

Gabe checked his watch. 'But I have five more minutes,' he protested.

'No,' Guillaume said. 'I believe your watch must be slow. Right, Emma?'

I sighed and looked back and forth between the two men, both of whom were looking at me expectantly. I felt exhausted.

'Look, Gabe, if Guillaume says he's done, he's done,' I said finally. 'I'm sorry.'

Gabe started to protest, but I held up a hand. 'Guillaume,' I said. 'Since you did guarantee Gabe thirty minutes, and we're only at twenty-five now, would you answer one more question for him please?'

Guillaume tilted his head to the side, closed his eyes as if he was deep in thought and then nodded. 'Yes. Okay. One more question.' He opened his eyes and looked at Gabe.

'Thanks,' Gabe said drily. 'You're too kind.' He looked at his notes and I began visualizing the worst. Perhaps he would ask something about Guillaume's reputation for frequenting strip clubs (something we had, thus far, kept out of the press). Or rumors that he had to go to rehab for a coke addiction before KMG would sign him (something no one, including Poppy and me, had ever been able to verify). But instead, Gabe's face settled into a look of calm. 'So Guillaume, do you talk to all women with the same disrespect you talk to Emma with?' he asked pleasantly.

I choked on the sip of coffee I had just taken. I looked at Gabe, my eyes wide, then I turned to Guillaume, who didn't look offended at all.

Guillaume grinned. 'Just the ones who like it,' he said, winking at me. My jaw dropped.

'Wonderful,' Gabe said tightly. He stood up. 'Nice to see both of you. You can expect an article about Guillaume on tomorrow's UPP wires. Thanks for setting up the interview, Emma. And thank you for your time, both of you.'

My stomach was tying itself into hard knots. 'Gabe, you're not going to write anything bad, are you?' I asked, trying to keep the desperation out of my voice. I didn't know how things had spiraled to such an extent.

'I'll only write what's fair, Emma,' Gabe said, looking hard at me. I gulped. That wasn't good. I knew as well as well as Gabe probably did that *fair* would mean skewering the crazy rocker.

Gabe reached out and shook my hand briskly. 'Until next time,' he said, turning to Guillaume and putting a hand to his forehead in a little salute. Guillaume cheerfully and grandly saluted back. I waved weakly, feeling shell-shocked. 'Have a nice day,' Gabe added. Then he stood up and strode toward the door without looking back.

I waited until he was gone and then turned slowly to Guillaume. 'What was that all about?' I demanded. 'You acted like a jerk!'

Guillaume looked a bit offended. 'Emma! Relax!'

'Relax? You want me to relax? You just ruined an interview with a guy whose story will literally be picked up all over the world! Seriously, Véronique will fire Poppy and me!'

'No one's getting fired,' Guillaume said calmly. He smiled and reached across the table to put a hand on my arm. 'Just relax, Emma. Gabe's article will be fine.'

'You don't know that,' I grumbled. 'What were you thinking?'

'Ah, I was just having a bit of fun,' Guillaume said, shrugging grandly.

'A bit of *fun*?' I repeated.

Guillaume nodded. 'He obviously likes you,' he said, as if it was the plainest thing in the world. I just stared at him. 'I just thought I'd see if I could get under his skin a little,' Guillaume added. 'I guess it worked. Good for me!'

I tossed and turned all night worrying about what horrible things Gabe would write in the UPP article. Would my career be ruined? Would Guillaume's? Exactly how far would Gabe go? Poppy had tried to calm me down by serving a slightly overdone baked chicken for dinner and filling me up with wine, but I only wound up feeling more nervous.

As soon as I got to work early the next morning, I searched the internet for Gabe's story. I saw right away that Guillaume had been mentioned in 123 publications in the last twenty-four hours, and that 119 of them were different versions of the same article (undoubtedly Gabe's, sent over the UPP wires and picked up in entertainment sections worldwide). There would certainly be more additions popping up over the course of the day as papers in the States began to appear. It was only one in the morning in New York and ten in the evening in LA, and many papers hadn't closed yet.

Gulping and steeling myself for the worst, I clicked on *Read Text* and waited for the first article, from the *Sydney*

Morning Herald in Australia, to load. When it came up, it was indeed from the UPP Wire Service, with Gabriel Francoeur's byline. The headline screamed at me from the page.

CONTROVERSIAL CROSSOVER ROCKER OPENS UP ON EVE OF DEBUT ALBUM!

I gulped. I wasn't ready for this. Not yet. Not now. I loved my new job. I was falling in love with Paris. I was even learning to consider that there might be life after Brett. Now, Gabe would probably bring it all to a close. I braced myself and began to read.

> Celeb bachelor Guillaume Riche's debut album hits stores worldwide next Tuesday, and his first single, 'City of Light', is already burning up the charts across Europe as well as in the United States and Australia. But although the buzz about Riche's album is strong and he's already being hailed as 'the greatest European export since The Beatles' by *Rolling Stone* magazine, the eccentric star is perhaps currently better known for his many mishaps than for his music.
>
> From getting trapped in the Eiffel Tower – reportedly without his clothing, although publicists for Riche deny it – to getting trapped in mid-air between two high-rise apartment buildings earlier this week, Riche is anything but your typical rock star.
>
> 'Sure, Ozzie Osborne can eat bats and Pete Wentz can wear eyeliner,' Riche said in an exclusive interview yesterday. 'But no one can be Guillaume Riche.'
>
> Antics aside, though, Riche has the musical muscle to back up his record label's claims that he'll be the

next big worldwide sensation. Not only do his vocals span the range from early Paul McCartney to Coldplay's Chris Martin to John Mayer, but he has a writing credit on all the songs on his much-anticipated album, called simply *Riche*.

'Music just speaks to me,' Riche says. 'And if I can channel that into something that touches other people, then that's a gift, isn't it?'

Born in Brittany, France, to Pierre, an accountant, and Marie, a stay-at-home mom, Riche began taking piano lessons at the age of four and was proficient on piano, guitar, trumpet, saxophone and percussion by the age of seven. He wrote his first song when he was nine, and after spending two months in hospital following a serious car accident that claimed the life of a schoolmate, he was performing in pubs by fifteen. A short stint in jail after a public disturbance charge just before his seventeenth birthday exposed him to famed producer Nicolas Ducellier, imprisoned in the same jail on a drug charge, and Riche's musical formation was complete after working with this mentor for thirty days. His informal recordings lit up the airwaves in northern France around the time he turned eighteen, and he had earned a cult following by twenty. Now, ten years later, after a career in television and achieving fame as an international playboy, he's finally about to make his musical debut on the worldwide stage.

'I'm excited,' Riche says. 'This is quite an opportunity. I think that music is the universal language, so if I can bridge the gap between English speakers and French speakers through my songs, then perhaps that's one step closer to global harmony.'

The article went on to talk about Guillaume's tour plans and to quote several record execs talking about how wonderful 'City of Light' was and how eager the world was to hear the whole album. It concluded with a mention that the upcoming launch in London would be Guillaume's official entry into the music world.

I sat in stunned silence for a moment after reading the article. I couldn't believe it. Not only had Gabe not blasted Guillaume (despite the few early mentions of his antics), but he had actually sounded *positive* about the singer and his music. How could that be after the debacle yesterday?

I re-read the article. It was wonderful, but I was puzzled about something. Where had Gabe got the information about Guillaume's past in Brittany? Sure, it wasn't a secret where Guillaume was from, and in fact a few profiles in the past had mentioned it. But how had Gabe known about Guillaume's parents? Or about his proficiency on so many instruments at such a young age? Or about his thirty days in jail at the age of seventeen? None of that had ever been printed, and I knew that Guillaume's parents, sister and half-brother had never agreed to an interview. Poppy had said they were an extremely private family.

Had Guillaume told Gabe about his background during our interview yesterday, while he was speaking in rapid French? I didn't think there had been enough time for a conversation like that, but perhaps I'd just missed it.

In any case, there was no point in worrying, was there? Gabe had gone easy on Guillaume. We were out of the woods. I breathed a giant sigh of relief.

Poppy took me to lunch that day to thank me for somehow preventing whatever damage Gabe had intended to do, and when we got back to the office, there was an enormous bouquet of white lilies, my favorite flower, sitting in a vase in front of the door.

'I wonder who these are from?' Poppy asked, beaming as she picked them up and unlocked the door. Inside, she set them down on the corner of her desk and opened the attached envelope. 'You know what? I bet they're from Paul, the guy I went out with on Saturday. He seemed like quite the romantic!'

Still smiling, she pulled the card out and scanned it quickly. She blinked a few times, and her smile faltered for a second.

'My mistake, Emma,' she said, handing the envelope over to me. 'The flowers are for you.'

Surprised, I took the card from her and read it.

To Emma: Beautiful flowers for a beautiful woman, the card read.

There was no signature. I could feel my cheeks burning.

'So?' Poppy asked eagerly. 'Who are they from?'

She picked the vase up from her desk and carried it over to mine. I stared at the flowers in confusion for a moment.

'I have no idea,' I said. But even as I said the words, I realized that I was harboring a small hope that they were from Gabe, perhaps to thank me for the interview. But that was ridiculous, wasn't it? Reporters didn't send publicists flowers. And reporters like Gabe probably made it a general rule never to do anything nice at all, except when they were trying to get something out of you.

'Oh, come on,' Poppy said, smiling at me. 'You must have *some* idea.'

'Really, I don't,' I said. 'I don't think many people even know I work here.' I certainly hadn't given my work address to any of the random dates I'd had. As far as I knew, Gabe, Guillaume, the KMG staff, Poppy and my family were the only people who knew where to find me.

'Ooh, a mystery man!' Poppy squealed. 'See? The whole French kissing thing is working already!'

My phone rang a few times that afternoon, and each time I picked it up, I half expected to hear Gabe's voice on the other end, admitting to sending me flowers and apologizing for the blow-up during the Guillaume interview. Maybe he'd even ask me out – not that I would necessarily say yes. But he never called; the calls were all junket-related questions about catering, room accommodation and journalists' flight information.

I was still confused when the phone on my desk jingled again at five that evening.

'Hello?'

'Emma? It's Brett.'

My heart stopped for a second. It had been two weeks since I'd heard his voice. The familiar depth of it sent a jolt through me. My mouth suddenly felt dry.

'Emma?' he asked tentatively after a moment. 'Are you there?'

'I'm here,' I said shakily. 'How did you get my work number?'

'Your sister,' he responded promptly. I made a face. I wished Jeannie would just mind her own business. But then again, she never had; why would I expect her to start now?

'Oh,' I managed.

'So,' Brett began slowly, 'did you get the flowers?'

I felt an unexpected twinge of disappointment. 'Those were from *you*?' I asked.

'Of course, Emma.' Brett sounded surprised. 'Who else

would send you flowers?' He paused, and a thought seemed to occur to him. 'Wait, you're not dating over there, are you?'

'So what if I am?' I responded stubbornly.

He was silent for a moment. 'I'm sure you're just being facetious, Emma,' he said dismissively. 'And I guess I deserve that, don't I?'

Why was he so sure that I couldn't be serious? I felt insulted.

'Look, Emma,' Brett went on before I could respond. 'We really need to talk. You need to know something.'

'What?' In the silence, I could feel my palms beginning to sweat.

Brett spoke slowly and carefully. 'I love you, Emma,' he said. 'I always have. I always will. I just got scared.'

I didn't know what to say. I drew a deep breath.

'Brett, you threw me out,' I said after a moment. 'You slept with one of my best friends.' I looked up and saw Poppy staring at me.

Are you okay? She mouthed the words at me. I nodded and looked down.

On the other end of the line, Brett sighed. 'I know,' he said. 'And I can never tell you how profoundly sorry I am, Emma. It was incredibly stupid and wrong.'

'No kidding,' I muttered.

'Please, Emma, let me make it up to you,' Brett pleaded. 'Come home. This is where you belong. Let me show you how sorry I am. I love you.'

I paused. It was everything I'd thought I wanted. But I was fairly certain that it was too little, too late.

'I'll have to call you back,' I said. I hung up before Brett could respond.

As soon as I hung up, Poppy announced we were going straight to Bar Dix for pitchers of sangrias and a conversation about Brett.

'Maybe he deserves another chance,' I mumbled once we'd ordered a pitcher and begun drinking. I was half hoping that Poppy wouldn't hear me. I drowned my response – and apparently my self-respect – with a swig of sangria, wishing that the buzz would start to set in. No such luck.

'*Another chance?*' Poppy repeated carefully. She took a slow sip of her sangria, never taking her eyes off me. 'Haven't we been over this, Emma?'

I looked down at the table and thought about it for a moment. I knew I sounded crazy. And I knew that Poppy – in all her one-date-and-leave-'em wisdom – would be the last person in the world who would understand where I was coming from. I supposed she was right. But sometimes, unfortunately, there's a difference between what your brain tells you and what your heart feels.

I sighed. 'I know you think I'm crazy,' I said finally. I took a big sip. 'It's just that it's hard to throw away three years without looking back.'

'*You* didn't throw them away,' Poppy said slowly.

I fumbled with my words, trying to explain. 'I know. But can I walk away from him, just like that? He says he made a mistake. Do I refuse to give him a chance just because he screwed up once?'

Poppy shook her head. 'He didn't just screw up, Emma. He slept with *your best friend* after unceremoniously chucking you.'

I could feel tears prickling at the back of my eyes. 'I *know*. But he left her. It only lasted a few weeks. Maybe he was just confused. Maybe I pushed him into getting engaged. Maybe he wasn't ready and he freaked out.'

'Freaking out makes guys do a lot of things,' Poppy said firmly. 'But it doesn't make them move into the beds of your friends. Not if they're decent guys, anyhow.'

As Poppy studied my face, I could read pity in her big green eyes.

It made me sad. I didn't want her to feel sorry for me. But on some level, I knew she was right. I was acting pathetic. But I couldn't stop myself from feeling like maybe it was *my* fault that Brett had been scared away, had gone looking for something else with Amanda. After all, obviously there was something he wasn't getting from me if he was so quick to move on to her. Obviously there was something lacking in me. Or had I simply been too obsessed with work? Or too concerned with dragging him down the aisle?

'Look,' Poppy said after a moment. 'Are you happy? Here, I mean?'

I only had to think about it for a second. 'Yes. I am.'

'Happier than you were in Orlando?'

I thought for a moment. Was I? It was hard to compare. My life here was so different than it had been back home. My job in Paris was stimulating and exciting but at times infuriating and nerve-wracking. But wasn't that better than a nine-to-five job that was the same thing day in and day out? My social life in Orlando had been stable and secure; I was with Brett constantly, and I had my three peas-in-a-pod girlfriends. Here, with Poppy as my social planner, I was going on interesting dates and spending my free nights sitting in cave-like bars sipping sangria. I had to admit, I was having fun.

'Yes,' I said slowly, realizing it for the first time as I said it. 'I guess I *am* happier here.'

'Has he even taken a few days off to come over and apologize to you in person?' Poppy asked. 'To try to win you back?'

'No,' I answered in a small voice.

'And you want to leave this life you love to give a second chance to someone who hasn't exerted any more effort than picking up the phone?'

I stared hard into my glass of sangria as if it was a wishing well that would give me the answers, if only I looked hard enough. But the fact was, I already knew the answers I needed, didn't I?

'No,' I said again. Maybe I just needed to look inside myself and stop placing blame where it didn't belong. Maybe I needed to be a little more like Poppy and learn to take control of my own life instead of letting myself be a doormat. After all, I could do it at work – and I *had* been doing it since I got here. Why was I so seemingly unsure that I deserved to be respected in my personal life?

'But I'm going home in a few weeks anyhow, right?' I asked softly. Maybe all this Paris-driven self-discovery was for naught.

Poppy paused. 'Well, I was going to wait to tell you this,' she said slowly. 'But I've talked to Véronique. And based on all your good work these last few weeks with Guillaume, we'd really like you to stay.'

'What?'

Poppy smiled. 'KMG would like to offer you a longer assignment,' she said. 'That is, if you can stand Guillaume Riche for the next year.'

'A year?' I asked.

'A year,' Poppy confirmed. 'So will you do it? Will you stay?'

*

After Poppy went to bed that night, I sat in the living room for a long time, staring out the window at the Eiffel Tower until the lights went out and the tower faded into the shadows, making me feel all alone again. I looked at my watch. It would only be 8 p.m. back in Florida. I took a deep breath and picked up the phone to call Brett.

'I'm going to stay in Paris for a while,' I said when he answered.

There was silence for a long moment on the other end of the phone. 'Is this some kind of joke?' he asked.

'No,' I said. I tried to put into words how I felt. 'I'm really happy here. I'm finally part of something important. I feel needed.'

Brett was silent for a moment. 'So I guess it doesn't matter if *I* need you,' he said. 'I guess that's just not important?'

'I didn't say that.' I took a deep breath and thought about Poppy's words tonight. 'Besides, if I'm so important to you, why don't you come over here for a while? I'm really happy here. Maybe we could give it a try here.'

'Are you crazy?' Brett asked. 'I don't even speak French.'

'Neither do I,' I said. 'But maybe you could just take some vacation time from work. Take the time you were going to use for our honeymoon even. Come stay with me for a few weeks and see how you like it.'

I was testing him, and I knew it. I was holding out my hand, and if he took it, I was willing to give things a try and admit that Poppy may have been wrong.

'Haven't I been clear with you about the fact that I intend to stay in Florida?' Brett said after a moment. 'If I wouldn't move to New York, why would you think I'd come to France?'

'Because *I'm* here,' I said right away. There was silence on the other end of the line. I struggled to fill it, because that's what the insecure side of me did – rushed to fill in words when the silence between them felt too heavy. 'Besides, you wouldn't have to *move* here. Just come for a little while to see where I'm living. This is my life now, Brett. And I still want you to be a part of it, if you want to.'

I wasn't sure if I meant that last part or not. I felt terribly torn. But I owed him at least that, didn't I? I owed him a chance. It was more than he had given me, but I was trying to live by my rules, not his. At the end of the day, there was comfort in that.

'Emma,' Brett said slowly, as if talking to a child or someone whose mental comprehension abilities were in question. 'I thought you told me you were coming home.'

I looked out at the darkened silhouette of the Eiffel Tower and felt a sense of calm settle over me. 'I know,' I said. 'I think I *am* home.'

14

The thing about Paris is that it's seductive. It's not the men or the dates or even the perfect kisses that have the power to seduce you, as Poppy would have me believe. No, it's the city itself – the quaint alleyways, the picturesque bridges, the perfectly manicured gardens, the rainbow of flowers that bloom everywhere in graceful harmony in the springtime. It's the way the sparkling lights illuminate everything at night, the way the stars dangle over the city as if someone placed them there by hand, the way the Seine ripples softly like a supple blanket stretched between the banks. It's the hidden cafés, the tiny, self-righteous dogs and the cobblestone streets where you least expect them. It's the bright green of the grass, the deep blue of the sky, the blinding white of Sacré-Coeur.

It is perfection. And in perfection, there is seduction. Because maybe if you stay long enough in a city that's so perfect, you'll find perfection in your own life too.

The night before I was scheduled to leave for the junket in London, I worked late and walked home alone, looking forward to a night by myself, for once. Poppy had left for London a day early to visit some friends and work out some last-minute details at the hotel. As I turned down my street and started walking the several yards to my building's front door, I stared up at the Eiffel Tower, which loomed over me from two blocks away. For the hundredth time, I marveled at how lucky I was to live here. How could I honestly live in the shadow of that and consider, even for a moment, leaving to go back to my old life?

I was so focused on the Eiffel Tower that I didn't notice the door to the American Library swing open in front of me. Nor did I notice a man walk out, balancing a tall stack of books that swayed uncertainly to and fro as he looked in the opposite direction. In fact, I didn't notice anything but the Eiffel Tower until I ran smack dab into the man, sending the books flying everywhere.

'Oh!' I exclaimed in horror. 'I'm so sorry! Um, *je suis désolée!* I'm so sorry! Is there anything I can do to . . .'

My voice trailed off in mid-sentence as the man stood up and grinned at me.

'Well hello, Emma,' he said. 'Imagine running into you here. Literally.'

My jaw dropped.

'*Gabe*,' I said stiffly. 'It's you.'

'Indeed it is,' Gabe agreed cheerfully. He looked down at the books lying around us like a pile of rubble. 'I suppose this was your revenge for the little incident in your office with the box of pens?'

'What? No!' I said sharply. 'It was an accident. I didn't mean to run into you!'

'Mmm, so you say,' Gabe said, arching an eyebrow at me.

I stared at him for a moment before I realized that he was

kidding. I smiled reluctantly. 'Hey, I wasn't the only one not looking where I was going, you know.'

'Duly noted,' Gabe said with a mock solemn nod. 'Now, don't you think we'd better clean up this mess?'

I bent to help Gabe pick up all the books. 'Big weekend of reading?' I asked as I stacked the final one – a James Patterson novel – on the sidewalk beside him.

'I don't know about you, but I have a junket to go to,' Gabe said with a little grin. 'This is just some light reading for the train ride over.'

I smiled. 'Good plan.' I paused and looked down. 'Hey, I meant to thank you for the nice article the other day,' I said softly.

'Oh, that?' Gabe waved a dismissive hand. 'No need to thank me.'

'Yeah, but . . .' I paused. 'The interview was a little weird. I know Guillaume was not exactly . . . nice to you. You could have been a little harsher on him in the article. I appreciate you going easy on him.'

Gabe sighed. 'Look,' he said. 'This isn't easy for me to say. The guy's a nutcase. But Guillaume is very talented, Emma, even if he's an obnoxious *bricon*. I didn't say anything that wasn't the truth.'

I just looked at him. After a moment, he rolled his eyes and smiled.

'Fine, fine,' he said. 'Also, my editors make sure I stay nice.'

'Oh,' I said awkwardly. I didn't know why I was suddenly feeling tongue-tied. I realized it was the first time I'd seen Gabe out of work attire. He was dressed casually in dark jeans, a gray T-shirt and maroon Pumas, and I had to admit, he didn't quite look like the annoying journalistic foe I usually thought of him as. He looked great.

'So Emma, I'm glad I ran into you,' Gabe said. 'There's something I've been meaning to ask.'

'Oh?' Inwardly, I groaned. It was just my luck that I'd be cornered on the street by the very journalist who seemed to be a master at getting his way. 'What is it?' I braced myself for him to ask me about Guillaume's mental state. Or his alleged alcohol addiction. Or something equally horrifying.

'Do you rollerblade?' Gabe asked instead. I blinked at him a few times in confusion. Was that code for something embarrassing? Was it some sort of French slang?

'What?' I asked.

'Do you rollerblade?' Gabe repeated.

'Like . . . with roller skates?' I asked tentatively.

He nodded enthusiastically. 'Yes. Do you?'

I stared at him for a moment. With his bright eyes and his big smile, I could swear he looked just as crazy as Guillaume for a moment. I blinked a few times.

'Um, yes,' I said after a moment. 'I mean, I used to rollerblade sometimes in Florida. But . . . why?'

'Excellent!' Gabe exclaimed. He beamed at me. 'You must come skating with me tonight!'

I furrowed my brow at him. 'What?'

'The Paris Roller!' he said excitedly, as if I would know exactly what he was talking about. Of course I hadn't a clue.

'The what?'

'The Paris Roller!' he repeated. 'Every Friday night, twenty thousand people meet in the fourteenth arrondissement and skate all over Paris!'

I stared at him. 'Twenty thousand?' I repeated. 'That sounds insane!'

'It is!' he replied with delight. 'It's the most insane thing ever! It's the biggest group skate in the world. There are dozens of police along to block off the roads. But it's the best way to see Paris, Emma. You must come along!'

I looked at him dubiously. 'You're not pulling my leg?' I asked.

'No, no!' he exclaimed. He dug in his pocket and pulled out a computer printout. 'Look. This is the route for tonight. It comes out each Thursday.'

He handed me the crumpled sheet, and I studied it for a moment. It was a map of Paris that seemed to have been colored over with an interlocking, zany design.

'That's the route,' Gabe said, pointing at the tangled mass of zigzags. 'It's nineteen miles long. It's fantastic! My baby sister Lucie and I used to go every week, but then she moved back home to Brittany to live with our father. So I've been going alone, but it would be perfect for you!'

'Oh,' I said. I didn't know what he wanted me to say. 'So . . . you're asking me to come?' I said. It sounded like a zany idea. But I had to admit, the longer I looked at the piece of paper, the more intriguing it sounded. I'd never considered seeing Paris on rollerblades.

'Yes, yes, you'll love it,' he said. He was grinning like a lunatic.

I narrowed my eyes at him suspiciously. 'Is this just another way to trick me into giving you information about Guillaume?' I asked. 'Or are you going to try to corner me into an interview?'

Gabe looked taken aback. 'No, Emma, I wouldn't do that,' he said, the smile slipping from his face.

I made a face at him. 'I think you would.'

He frowned. 'Emma, I promise,' he said. 'I won't say a word about work this evening.'

'Really?'

'I give you my word,' he said solemnly.

I hesitated. 'I'm just not sure if it's professional,' I said reluctantly.

Gabe looked surprised. 'What do you mean?'

I blushed. 'I don't know. Since you're a reporter and I'm a publicist and everything. Isn't this unethical?'

'Emma,' Gabe said. 'I'm not asking you to spill all your Guillaume Riche secrets or give me exclusive information. I'm asking you to go skating.'

I thought about it for a moment. What did I have to lose? My alternative was spending a night alone. And when would I have a chance to skate all over this city again? It sounded fascinating. And perhaps, if we could stay away from talking about Guillaume for a night, I could curry a bit of additional favor for KMG with Gabe. Obviously, I'd need the extra store of goodwill for the next time Guillaume did something stupid.

'But I don't have skates,' I said.

'Don't worry,' Gabe said. 'My sister left hers at my apartment. If they don't fit, we'll figure out a way to rent you some.'

'Well . . . okay,' I said after a moment. I smiled. 'I guess I'm in.'

'Great!' Gabe said. 'Why don't you meet me in an hour and we'll eat first.'

Against my better judgement, I was at the door of Gabe's apartment in an hour, dressed in jeans and a long-sleeved shirt, as he had suggested. It felt crazy to be there, but I kept reminding myself that it was for the good of Guillaume. After all, if I was friendly to Gabe, he might forgive more of my rock star's wackiness, right? He might be easier to charm the next time Guillaume did something stupid. There was no doubt in my mind that there *would* be a next time.

Plus, I had to admit, I'd spent the last hour getting excited about the Paris Roller. I had looked it up online to make sure that Gabe wasn't making it up, and as wacky as it sounded, it was true. From ten in the evening to one in the morning every Friday, a group of nearly twenty thousand skaters, most of them in their teens and twenties, went roaring north from the Montparnasse station into the heart of Paris, snaking their way past monuments and landmarks in one noisy stampede on wheels.

When Gabe opened the door to his apartment, which was indeed just a few blocks from mine on rue Augereau, he was holding a pair of skates in one hand and a baguette in the other.

'My sister's skates,' he said in greeting, holding up the pink rollerblades. 'And dinner,' he said, holding up the baguette. 'Well,' he amended. 'Part of dinner, anyhow.'

'You cooked?' I asked. I'd assumed we would just grab a sandwich or crêpe on the way.

Gabe shrugged. 'We'll need the energy. Believe me. Besides, it's nothing special. I'm not so great in the kitchen. But I do make a fantastic spaghetti Bolognese, if I do say so myself.'

I laughed. 'It sure smells good,' I said. And it did. The pungent aroma of tomatoes, basil and garlic danced down the hallway toward the door, enticing me in.

'I'll go prepare it,' Gabe said. 'Why don't you try on Lucie's skates?'

While Gabe set the table and chopped up lettuce

for a salad, I slipped my feet into his sister's rollerblades and was a little surprised to find that they fit almost perfectly. I stood up and wobbled a bit. Gabe came over to check on me.

'How do they feel?' he asked.

'Good,' I said. He looked down at the skates and bent to press his fingers into the space just above my toes, like shoe salesmen sometimes did.

'They're a little loose,' he said. 'But I think you'll be okay if you wear a second pair of socks. I'll go get some for you.'

Forty-five minutes later, our stomachs full of spaghetti and our arms full of skates, socks, helmets and pads, Gabe and I left his apartment and started walking toward the Métro stop at La Motte-Picquet Grenelle, about five minutes away.

'So I thought you said you grew up in Florida,' I said to make conversation along the way. 'How come your sister lives in Brittany?' I tried to shift the weight of the skates from one arm to the other as we walked. They were getting heavy.

'She's actually my half-sister,' Gabe said. He glanced over at me. 'Here, let me take those,' he said, coming to a dead stop in the middle of the street. 'I'm sorry. I should have offered.' Despite my protests that he didn't have to, he grabbed my skates and handed me his much lighter helmet and pads to carry. I thanked him, and we started walking again.

'So Lucie is your half-sister on your dad's side?' I asked after a moment.

Gabe nodded. 'Yes. He's still in Brittany. My mother, of course, still lives in Florida. So, as I spent every summer with my dad, I'm close to Lucie.'

I absorbed this for a moment. Then I realized something. 'So when you said in the UPP story that Guillaume had grown up in Brittany, you knew that because you spent summers there as a kid? You knew who he was from when you were younger?'

'Yes,' Gabe said quickly. 'That's right. But I thought you said we weren't going to talk about work tonight.' We had reached the Métro entrance, and before he could say more, we had to scramble to get our Métro tickets out with our hands full. By the time we were through the turnstiles and had boarded the Nation-bound 6 train, Gabe was already on to another subject, asking me where I had lived in college. I let the whole Brittany issue go. After all, he had answered my question; it had been bothering me for days how Gabe had known so much about Guillaume's background.

We joined thousands of other skaters in the Place Raoul Dautry, between the train station and the huge Montparnasse tower, just in time for a brief lecture, in French, from the roller organizers about safety and road rules. Gabe quietly translated for me as I pulled on my knee-pads, the extra socks he had loaned me and his sister's skates. He helped me fasten Lucie's helmet on my head and grinned as he adjusted the strap.

'Why, you look beautiful, Emma,' he said, patting the top of my helmet once he had tightened it on. I made a face at him.

'Yeah,' I said. 'I'm sure I'm really hot with my hair squished into a mushroom shape under a big, hard helmet.' I rolled my eyes.

'You *are* hot,' Gabe said, looking surprisingly serious. I opened my mouth to say something smart in return, but before I could, the whistle blew and we were nearly run over by a sudden onslaught of rollerbladers descending on Paris.

'Let's go!' Gabe grinned down at me. He put a hand on my arm and helped steady me as we made our way into the crush of bodies on wheels. 'You ready?' he shouted over the noise that came from twenty thousand sets of wheels grinding over the pavement in unison.

'Uh-huh!' I nodded nervously, and off we went, swept away in a tide of skaters.

For the next hour and a half, we barely said a word to each other, although Gabe kept looking down to make sure I was with him. I was – and I spent the entire skate in awe. It was the fastest and the hardest I'd ever bladed, but it was next to impossible to fall behind with a tide of thousands to sweep me forward every time my energy faltered. My ribcage vibrated the whole time with the gentle, steady roar of the thousands of wheels around us, and I marveled as we made our way toward the river, passing the Eiffel Tower far off to the left, then up past the impressive Opéra on the Right Bank and then through the 9th up to the Gare du Nord, the station where I'd be catching the Eurostar to London the next morning. We snaked through several neighborhoods I didn't recognize, and everywhere we went, people stood along the sidewalks, cheering and waving as we roared by. I felt like we were part of a parade.

By the time we arrived, breathless and drenched in sweat, in the Place Armand Carrel, a big park in the 19th, on the opposite side of Paris from where we'd started, it was eleven forty-five. I scooted onto the grass and, like thousands of other exhausted skaters, collapsed onto my back.

'That was amazing,' I breathed to Gabe, who was standing over me, looking down in amusement.

'I'm glad you liked it,' he said. 'But you realize we're only halfway done.'

I sat straight up. 'What?'

He laughed. 'This is just the halfway point. We take a break here before we skate back through the Place de la République and over to the Left Bank again.'

I stared at him for a moment. 'Oh,' I finally said. I flopped back down on the ground and closed my eyes. I couldn't imagine another hour and a half of this.

'We can stop here and just take the Métro back if you want,' Gabe said. I cracked open an eye and looked at him. He was still gazing down at me in amusement.

'I'm not a quitter,' I said.

'I didn't say you were,' Gabe said. 'It's just pretty overwhelming the first time. I would completely understand if—'

I cut him off. 'No.' I sat up. 'We're going to finish this course.' I struggled to my feet, but my legs felt like jelly. Gabe grinned and helped me up, taking my hand in his to steady me. His fingers were rough and warm as they folded through mine.

'You sure you want to do this?' he asked.

I looked him in the eye and nodded, my heart pounding. 'Yes.'

We stood there for a moment, looking at each other. I was standing just fine on my own now, but Gabe hadn't let go of my hand. Nor had I pulled away. For a moment, as we stared at each other, I had the crazy feeling that he was about to kiss me. But just as he leaned a little closer, the whistle blew, and the stampede of skaters began again.

'Ready?' Gabe shouted over the din. He squeezed my hand, and I felt a little tingle run through me.

'Ready whenever you are!' I shouted back.

For the next hour and a half, the tide of skaters swept us south through the eastern edge of the Right Bank, through the Place de la Bastille, over the Pont d' Austerlitz and then for miles west along the Left Bank of the Seine before heading south back toward Montparnasse. Gabe didn't let go of my hand.

And, to my surprise, I didn't want him to.

'That was amazing,' I said as we walked up to the front door of my apartment building just past two in the morning. Every bone, every muscle, every tendon and every joint in my body ached, but somehow I felt better than I'd felt in years.

'Yeah, it's pretty fun, huh?' Gabe said, grinning down at me. He set our skates down on the ground and touched my left forearm with his right hand. My skin tingled. 'I'm glad you came with me.'

'Thank you so much for inviting me,' I said. I couldn't believe this was the same Gabe Francoeur who had made my professional life tense and tenuous for the last few weeks. When he wasn't wearing his journalist hat, he was . . . normal. And very nice. Not to mention surprisingly attractive.

'I'm glad I did,' Gabe said. He took a step closer and looked down at me. I suddenly realized that I wanted very much for him to kiss me. 'You're amazing, Emma, you know that?'

In what felt like slow motion, he put both his arms around me and gently pulled me closer. Then he dipped his head and touched his lips softly to mine. A bolt of electricity shot through me; it felt perfect. His lips tasted salty and sweet, all at the same time. He lingered for a few seconds and then pulled away. He quickly straightened his glasses and cleared his throat.

'Well,' he said. He coughed and smiled at me.

'Well,' I echoed, feeling suddenly awkward. It had been the perfect kiss, but it had only lasted a few seconds.

'I, uh, probably shouldn't have done that,' Gabe said, glancing away.

I felt my heart sink. 'Oh,' I said.

'I mean, I wanted to,' he amended quickly. 'It's just that with work and everything . . .' His voice trailed off.

Feeling foolish, I hurried to agree. 'Of course. It was totally unprofessional of both of us.'

'Totally,' Gabe agreed. He paused and glanced down at me. 'But do you mind if I say it was nice?'

I cracked a smile. 'No.' I felt relieved. 'Not if you don't mind me saying that I thought it was nice too.'

'Well,' Gabe said. 'Good.'

'Good,' I agreed nervously.

'So, um, I'll see you tomorrow evening, then?' he said. 'In London?'

'Um, right.' I nodded, trying to look professional. 'Yes, definitely. We look forward to introducing you to Guillaume's music.'

Gabe smiled. 'Right. Well. I'm sure I'll love it.'

'I hope so.'

Gabe studied my face for a long moment. Then he nodded. 'Good night, Emma,' he said.

Then he bent to pick up the skates from the ground and, without another word, strode quickly away.

And despite the fact that I knew I had a long day ahead of me in London for the opening day of the junket, I barely slept at all that night. I could still feel Gabe's fingers woven through mine.

15

I snoozed on the train to London the next morning. Although I was supposed to be keeping an eye on Guillaume in first class to make sure he didn't moon any passers-by or go streaking through the dining car, I figured that Edgar and Richard could handle him for once. I was too exhausted to care.

'Late night, Emma?' Guillaume asked with a suggestive smirk as I settled into my seat.

'I was just rollerblading, Guillaume,' I said wearily. 'Nothing more salacious than that.'

He arched an eyebrow at me. 'I don't know. Rollerblading can be pretty hot and heavy.'

I rolled my eyes. Clearly our definitions of rollerblading differed in some fundamental ways.

Every time I began to doze off, I thought of Gabe's lips pressed against mine, and I felt a mixture of pleasure and guilt. The kiss had been perfect, but publicists weren't supposed to go around kissing journalists, were they? I felt like I had violated some sort of important code of ethics.

Somehow, Brett was back in my mind too, lurking at the

borders of my conscience. Sure, I'd kissed a few guys since I'd been here, at Poppy's insistence. But Gabe was the first I'd actually felt anything for. Even though I knew it was crazy, I still felt a little guilty.

Three hours later, when the limo that had picked us up at Victoria Station dropped us at the Royal Kensington Hotel, I stared in awe for a moment before letting the valet help me out. It was one of the most beautiful places I'd ever seen. Stately and enormous, lined with marble columns, its exterior was softened by lush window boxes and a bevy of flapping flags that soared over the marbled drive. Dozens of bellhops and valets in tuxedo jackets and top hats rushed around outside, opening car doors and effortlessly extracting luggage. If the journalists at the junket were half as impressed as I was, we were already off to a good start.

After I checked in, I went to see Poppy, whose room was beside mine. We did rock-paper-scissors for who would go check on Guillaume and make sure his suite was to his satisfaction (and that he hadn't managed to sneak any teenage girls in during the thirty minutes since checking in). Poppy's rock crushed my scissors, which meant that I had to go.

'I'll be here taking a nice soak in the tub!' Poppy sing-songed as I rolled my eyes and put my shoes back on. She didn't realize that I'd recently become the skating champion of Paris and would have given my left arm for a relaxing soak in a hot bath. 'I'll think of you while I'm relaxing in the bubbles, sipping cava and reading *Glamour*.'

'You're lucky I like you,' I muttered as I slipped out the door and into the hallway.

Poppy and I were in nice enough rooms, but of course our rock star was staying in a suite on the top floor. I couldn't imagine that it *wouldn't* be to his liking, but keeping him happy, especially prior to the press junket, was a vital part of my job. So off I went.

I knocked on his door twice before I heard a rustling inside.

'Who is it?' came Guillaume's muffled voice through the door.

'It's Emma!' I yelled back, attracting a scornful look from a bellhop delivering several Louis Vuitton suitcases to the suite across from Guillaume's. Evidently yelling didn't fit with the decorum of the hotel.

'Just a moment!' Guillaume yelled from inside. I heard footsteps, and a second later he pulled open the door. 'Hi there,' he said, looking down at me with a smile.

I hadn't been sure what to expect when I knocked on his door, but I'd been relatively sure that there would be some form of undress involved. To my surprise, though, Guillaume was fully clothed and actually looked relatively normal in a long-sleeved green T-shirt and a pair of dark jeans. Had I not known he was a lunatic, I might have looked at him and assumed he was simply a normal, good-looking (okay, Calvin Klein billboard perfect) guy.

But alas, he was a crazy person. And my client.

'How are you, Emma?' Guillaume asked, stepping aside and gesturing with his arm. 'Come in, come in.'

'No, I think I'll stay out here,' I said. After all, I'd seen the kind of thing that went on in Guillaume's hotel suites. And I was really bad at poker.

'Whatever you want,' Guillaume shrugged and moved again so that his body filled the doorway. 'How can I help you?'

It was the most normal, civil conversation I'd ever had

with the guy. 'I just wanted to make sure you were okay and that everything with the suite is fine,' I said uncertainly.

'It's better than fine,' Guillaume said. 'It's perfect.'

'Well, good.'

'Good,' Guillaume repeated.

'Is there anything I can get you?' I asked. 'Or anything you need?'

'No, I'm fine.' He studied my face for a moment. 'But can I ask you a question?'

'Um . . . sure.' I braced myself for the worst. He was probably going to ask if Poppy and I were interested in a threesome. Or if I knew where to buy good crack in London. Or if I knew of any monuments he could get naked in. I thought I'd suggest Big Ben.

But his question wasn't anything like that.

'Emma, I just want to know if you're okay,' he said slowly.

I could feel my eyes widen. 'What? Yes, I'm fine,' I said quickly, flashing him a bright smile. 'Why?'

Guillaume shrugged and looked a bit uncomfortable. 'I don't know. You just haven't been yourself today. And you looked upset on the train.'

I was startled. 'Thanks,' I said, forcing another confident smile. 'But I'm fine. Really.'

'Are you sure?' He looked genuinely concerned. I didn't know what to make of him.

'Yes, I'm sure,' I said. I was getting uncomfortable.

Guillaume looked at me for a long time. 'You know, I'm not such a bad guy,' he said. 'I mean, I know I can be a bother sometimes. But I'm not so bad underneath.'

Where was he going with this? 'I know,' I said, my heart hammering just a little.

'I just mean . . .' He paused. 'Well, if there's anything you want to talk about, you can talk to me.'

I think my jaw actually dropped. How could this be the same person I'd performed a death-defying duet with while hanging from a rope strung between two buildings just last week? How could this be the same guy who kept twenty-eight hundred euro in his briefs, just in case?

'Um, well, thank you,' I said. 'That's . . . really nice of you.'

'Yeah, well.' Guillaume shrugged and glanced away. 'Anyhow, try to feel better. About whatever it is.'

'Thank you,' I said, still in partial shock. Guillaume gave me an awkward little hug and a peck on each cheek and closed the door to his suite.

I stood in the hallway for a long time wondering what had just happened.

Six hours later, Poppy and I had briefed a staff of twenty assistants, most of them from a British temp agency specializing in media and public relations. They would all be performing various duties at the cocktail reception that was due to begin in a half hour. A blonde girl named Willow and a brunette named Melixa, for example, had been stationed in the lobby to help streamline media check-in. Two brunettes who looked as if they could have been sisters were upstairs in the media suite, handing out press packs, while two guys were manning the small continental buffet of fruits, pastries, sodas, waters and coffee that sat in the adjoining suite. A girl named Gillian was working as a sort of page, running back and forth between the lobby, the media suites and the ballroom, alerting Poppy and me to any problems. (So far, knock wood, there hadn't been anything more serious than an entertainment writer from the New York *Daily News* being put in a non-smoking room when she had requested smoking.) And several of the assistants were running around backstage in the reception room, making sure that everything was all set for Guillaume's performance tonight.

'I'm really nervous,' Poppy said as the two of us settled into seats at the check-in table outside the reception room. In ten minutes, TV and print journalists would begin arriving for the opening night cocktail party, which would culminate in a surprise three-song set from Guillaume. He'd open, of course, with his hit single, and he'd also be debuting two other songs, including my favorite, '*La Nuit*', a haunting ballad about unrequited love, sung half in English, half in French.

'Me too,' I admitted, riffling through the stack of papers in front of me until I emerged with tonight's media list. Most of the journalists on the two-day junket had arrived tonight, and although I knew that some would skip the reception in favor of wandering around London (not realizing, of course, that Guillaume would play), I figured that ninety per cent of our journalists would be there, which added up to just over a hundred guests.

Poppy and I were both wearing black cocktail dresses, something we had debated about for some time last week while shopping at the Galeries Lafayette. I'd said we should wear suits in keeping with our roles as the business leaders of the evening. Poppy had rolled her eyes at me and said that it was a cocktail party, and thus we should dress accordingly.

'More than half of the journalists we're inviting are men,' Poppy had reminded me with a wink. 'There's nothing wrong with giving them something to look at while Guillaume sings his love songs, yeah?'

By seven thirty, nearly all of the journalists we'd invited had checked in at our table, where Poppy and I welcomed them warmly, made sure they had everything they needed and then sent them inside to a room whose décor Poppy had been planning for months.

The reception room was lined with enormous photos of Guillaume in various outfits and poses, interspersed with blown-up *Riche* album covers. The lights were dim, and disco balls dangling high above cast sparks of light that almost looked like falling snowflakes around the room. Poppy had even taken care of ordering aromatherapy scents to be piped in, so the vague smell of French lavender permeated everything.

'Are you ready to go in?' Poppy asked me at seven forty-five, folding her list of checked-in journalists in half and putting it in her handbag. We hadn't had an arrival in ten minutes, and inside, we could hear enough conversation and laughter to know that the party was in full swing.

I looked at my watch. 'Maybe a few more minutes out here,' I said.

'But we have to go on in fifteen minutes, to introduce Guillaume. Don't you think we'd better have a glass of champagne first?'

I shrugged. 'Just give it a few more minutes,' I said. 'Not everyone is here.'

Poppy looked confused for a second. She glanced at the list. 'We're only missing five people.'

'I might as well wait.'

Poppy looked at me strangely and shrugged. 'Well, *I'm* going inside. Suit yourself.'

Ten minutes later, Gabe still hadn't arrived. Surely he's coming, I thought in frustration. But where is he? And more importantly, why is it bothering me so much?

I sighed and got up from the table, leaving one of the PR assistants in charge in case anyone – like, for example, Gabe – showed up late.

Inside, the reception was going even better than I had anticipated. I grabbed a glass of pink champagne off a tray that went by on the arm of a tuxedo-clad waiter and drank half of it down in one sip, trying to relax. There were roughly a hundred journalists in the room, and glancing around at their faces, I could see that most of them looked content. And why shouldn't they be? There were endless trays of hors d'oeuvres being carried around the room by a fleet of servers, and there were flutes of pink champagne, glasses of Beaujolais, strong mojitos and Riche-tinis (a specialty drink of champagne, vodka, crème de cassis and Sprite that Poppy and I had created for the event) everywhere.

I shook a few hands as I made my way toward the stage to find Poppy. None of the reporters knew they were in for an impromptu concert in a few moments, and I could hardly wait to see their faces when the man of the hour took the stage.

'Were you waiting for someone in particular?' Poppy asked quietly as I slipped behind the curtains to the backstage area. She was standing by herself with her glasses on, reading over the scribbled remarks she planned to make later.

I shook my head and tried not to blush.

'You're not developing a crush on one of the journalists, are you?' she asked.

'No!' I exclaimed defensively.

Poppy looked at me carefully. 'I told you to be careful with these French guys,' she said. 'They'll just break your heart.'

I nodded and tried not to look guilty. It's not like I was *falling* for Gabe or anything. 'I know.'

Poppy took off her glasses and slipped them back into her case. Then she ran a hand through her hair and shoved her notes into her bag. 'You ready?' she asked.

'Ready when you are.'

She nodded, and together we walked out in front of the curtain onto the small stage.

'Hello, everybody, and welcome,' Poppy said into the microphone. The chatter around the room quieted, and a hundred pairs of eyes came to rest on us. I smiled politely as Poppy continued. 'Thank you so much for being here today for an event that we at KMG are very excited about. We're thrilled to launch Guillaume Riche to the world with the debut of his new album, *Riche*, which hits stores Tuesday.'

There was a smattering of applause, and Poppy looked momentarily troubled. I assumed she'd been expecting more.

'Of course you've all probably heard "City of Light", the debut single from Guillaume's album,' she continued. There was more applause this time, and a few whoops and catcalls to boot. Poppy smiled at this. 'Of course as you all know, one-on-one interviews with Guillaume begin tomorrow. Print journalists are in the morning; TV reporters in the afternoon. You should have received your interview time in your check-in packet. Please plan to be in the media suite thirty minutes prior, and make sure you check in with either Emma or me.'

There were nods around the room, and the buzz of chatter started up again softly, as if some of the reporters had decided that Poppy wasn't saying anything of real value. I shot her a look, and she nodded.

'But before I bore you with the details,' she continued, 'I'd like to introduce you to the reason you're all here tonight.' She paused dramatically, and the chatter faded again as the reporters looked at her expectantly. 'Ladies and gentlemen . . . I give you France's greatest export, Guillaume Riche!'

There was a collective startled gasp, and then the clapping began. A moment later, the curtain rolled back and revealed Guillaume's back-up band. They started to play the first chords of 'City of Light', and the room exploded into applause and cheers. Poppy grinned broadly at me as she stepped down and joined me beside the stage.

'They love him!' she whispered.

'How could they not?' I said back, watching as Guillaume, looking deliciously sexy in tight leather pants and a black button-up shirt, emerged from the other side of the stage with a wireless microphone in hand. The cheering and whistling went up an octave, and the applause thickened. Guillaume smiled at the crowd and waved.

'Welcome to London!' Guillaume said with a charming smile, eliciting even more cheers. 'I can't wait to meet you all tomorrow during the interviews!'

Then he launched into the first verse of 'City of Light', and the crowd went wild, which was a very good sign. In my previous experience, I'd found that journalists tended to be a particularly unexpressive lot, as they were supposed to remain objective and judge things without emotion. But this crowd was falling hook, line and sinker for the musical bait Guillaume was casting out, and he was reeling them expertly in with his rich voice, his heartfelt lyrics and his smoldering gazes.

After playing 'City of Light', Guillaume and the band launched immediately into '*La Nuit*', and the decibel level of the crowd skyrocketed as they all realized they were getting the very first exposure to one of Guillaume's new songs.

Poppy gave me a spontaneous hug as we watched the normally staid reporters go wild. 'It's working!' she whispered. I hugged back, just as enthused.

As I gazed out contentedly over the room, I suddenly spotted Gabe toward the back of the crowd, and my heart leapt immediately into my throat. He looked perfect – and very French – in a pair of jeans, a blue Oxford, a charcoal-grey suit jacket and a black scarf, with his dark hair spiked a bit and his face smoothly shaven. He spotted me at the exact same moment I noticed him, and he grinned and raised his hand in a little wave. Then he turned his attention back to the person he was chatting with.

I took a step to my left to see who it was. He was talking to an older, gray-haired man who I didn't remember checking in. Perhaps Poppy had met him.

'Hey.' I nudged her. 'Who's that Gabe is talking to?'

Poppy glanced out at the audience then back at me. 'Ah, so it's Gabe, is it?'

I could feel my cheeks heat up. 'What do you mean?'

'He's the journalist you fancy, is he?' Poppy was grinning at me. She didn't wait for me to respond. 'He's a bit of a pain sometimes, but he *is* a good guy. And rather gorgeous to boot, I admit. Good for you!'

I looked at the floor, feeling like an idiot. 'Yeah, well,

whatever,' I mumbled. 'So do you know that guy?'

Poppy leaned to the side to see Gabe's conversation partner, and when she leaned back, she looked troubled. 'This could be a problem,' she said under her breath. 'That's Guillaume's dad.' She took a step forward to glance at them again. 'Oh bollocks! I told him not to talk to any media! What's he doing talking to Gabriel Francoeur?'

'Oh no,' I said grimly.

'You'd better go over there and interrupt,' Poppy said. I nodded, gave her a worried look and started making my way through the crowd. Just before I reached them, Guillaume's father patted Gabe on the arm, glanced at me and turned to walk away.

'Hi, Emma!' Gabe said quietly, reaching out to kiss me on each cheek. He glanced toward the stage, where Guillaume was still belting his heart out to *'La Nuit'*. It sounded amazing, and everyone in the room seemed to be standing in silence, transfixed by his performance. Except Gabe. Who didn't seem to care. And who seemed to be using the time to chat up the one person we would have liked to keep him away from.

'Hi,' I whispered, trying not to bother any of the other journalists. After all, I didn't want to detract from what was, so far, the perfect performance. 'You arrived okay?'

'Yes, yes,' Gabe said, glancing again toward the stage and then back at me. He smiled. 'Thank you.'

'You were late,' I said. I realized immediately that it sounded like an accusation, and I felt foolish.

But Gabe just smiled again. 'You noticed.'

I cleared my throat and ignored his words. I tried to sound casual. 'So, um, was that Guillaume Riche's father you were talking to?'

Gabe hesitated but didn't look the slightest bit guilty. 'Yes.'

'I thought Poppy told him not to talk to any reporters!' I grumbled, looking crossly at Gabe.

He looked surprised, and, if I'm not mistaken, a little bit wounded. 'Well,' he said after a moment. 'I suppose I'm not just any reporter.'

I lowered my voice. 'You know, just because I let you kiss me doesn't mean you can get away with anything you want now.'

Gabe looked startled. 'I know that, Emma,' he said.

Before I could respond, Guillaume and the band finished '*La Nuit*', and Guillaume began to speak.

'Thank you all so very much,' he said. 'You are a very kind audience. Now, I will play one more song for you. This one is the third song from my album. It will be the second single. It is called "Beautiful Girl". Tonight, I dedicate this song to Emma, my lovely publicist, who keeps coming to my rescue. I hope you are smiling, Emma.'

My jaw dropped and Guillaume and the band launched into the upbeat song about a man who falls in unrequited love with a woman from afar. I could feel my cheeks heat up as several journalists turned to look at me with curiosity.

'Oh, great,' Gabe muttered. 'Now your rock star is dedicating songs to you.'

I glanced at him in surprise. 'He's not *my* rock star,' I stammered.

'Is something going on between you and Guillaume?' Gabe asked, staring at me.

'What? No!'

'Then why is he dedicating songs to you?' It was not an

unreasonable question. Unfortunately, I didn't have a good answer.

'I don't know!' I insisted.

Gabe made a face but didn't respond.

I cleared my throat and looked away, hoping that Gabe would drop the subject. I gazed around the room for a moment while Guillaume played, taking in the rapt, smiling faces of most of the journalists. His charm was so evident in a small, intimate live show. I knew half the female reporters would go back to their rooms tonight fully in love with him.

'So what time is your interview with Guillaume tomorrow?' I asked Gabe as the song wound down, hoping that we could move on to safer conversational topics. But when I looked to my left for Gabe's answer, he had disappeared. I frowned and looked around. He was nowhere to be seen.

Guillaume ended the song with a big grin, a wave and a shouted, 'I'll see you all in a little while!' He strode off stage, and I realized I didn't have time to worry about Gabe or where he had gone. I needed to go find Guillaume so I could escort him briefly through the reception room to meet journalists.

I found Poppy backstage.

'So? What did Gabriel say?' she asked.

'Nothing,' I said, averting my eyes.

She gave me a funny look. 'No, I mean about why he was talking to Guillaume's dad,' she said.

'Oh. Right. Well, he didn't exactly explain.'

'That's weird,' Poppy murmured. Just then, Guillaume appeared with his guitar case in hand.

'I'm ready for the walk-through, ladies,' he said with a grin. 'How did you like the songs?'

'Oh, Guillaume, you were marvelous!' Poppy exclaimed.

'*Merci beaucoup, mademoiselle,*' he said with a little bow. He turned to me. '*Et toi?* Emma, did you like the concert?'

'Yes, Guillaume, you did a great job,' I said.

'And the dedication? What did you think of that?'

'Um . . .' I didn't know what to say. 'It was . . . it was very thoughtful, Guillaume. Thank you very much.'

'You are a beautiful girl,' he said, staring at me. I glanced at Poppy, who was looking intently at Guillaume.

I cleared my throat. 'Um, well, thank you anyhow,' I said quickly. 'So, uh, are you ready for the walk around the room?'

'You take him first,' Poppy piped up, making matters worse. She glanced back and forth between us, then reached out her arms. 'I'll put his guitar away.' Guillaume obediently handed the instrument over, and I made a face at Poppy.

For the next twenty minutes, I led Guillaume around the room and tried to introduce him to the various journalists, all of whom were conveniently wearing 'Hello My Name Is . . .' stickers with their names and affiliations. I was worried at first, because this was the 'get to know the *real* Guillaume Riche' part of the evening, and of course what Poppy and I were trying to conceal was that the *real* Guillaume Riche was, at times, a raving lunatic.

But tonight, miraculously, he stayed normal. He shook hands with the men and chatted them up about football (if they were British), his visits to the United States (if they were American) and about his love of music (if they were from anywhere else). With the women, he turned on the charm to full voltage, talking, laughing and flirting like it was his job, which, I suppose, it was.

Eventually, after Guillaume had shaken hands with all

the journalists and Poppy had wandered off to talk to a British radio host she knew, Guillaume and I made our way over to Guillaume's father, who was standing near the bar in the back of the room, drinking a glass of red wine.

'Emma, have you met my father yet?' Guillaume asked as we approached. I shook my head. 'I would love to introduce you. Come.'

Guillaume's father was about five foot ten with a slender build, thin, trembling hands and green eyes that looked surprisingly bright on a face that had sunk into itself with age. It was easy to see the resemblance between father and son; it was all in the brilliant eyes and the mop of dark hair, although the elder man's hair was peppered with gray. Guillaume said something to his father in French, then I caught my name.

'*Oui, oui, enchanté.*' Guillaume's father smiled at me pleasantly and then leaned forward to kiss me once on each cheek.

'Nice to meet you,' I said, smiling at the older man. 'We are very happy to work with your son.'

'He eez, how you say, very good. Very good talent,' his father said haltingly.

I smiled. 'Yes, absolutely. He's wonderful.'

His father nodded and smiled at me. '*Merci beaucoup,*' he said.

Father and son talked for a few moments in rapid French, then seeming to realize he was excluding me, Guillaume switched to English.

'So you liked the show?' he asked his father slowly.

'*Oui, oui,*' his father said. 'Eet was perfect.'

'Thanks, Papa.' Guillaume smiled. 'And this party? What do you think?'

'Very nice, very nice,' his father said haltingly.

It was so strange seeing Guillaume interact with his dad. He seemed almost . . . normal.

'Guillaume,' the elder man said slowly. 'I talk to Gabriel during your show. He has some, how you say, concern about you.'

My head whipped toward Guillaume. 'Wait, Gabriel *Francoeur*?' I interrupted in surprise. 'Your dad actually *knows* Gabriel Francoeur?'

Guillaume's father started to say something, but then Guillaume interrupted. 'Yes, he does,' he said evenly.

I looked at him in confusion. Brittany was an enormous region. I hadn't thought they would actually know each other. I was about to ask more, but just then Poppy came flouncing up with a handsome, dark-haired man in tow.

'Guillaume!' she bubbled, completely unaware of what she was interrupting. 'I would like you to meet Vick Vincent, London's premier disc jockey and one of the people who has been pushing your record hard. He's an old school chum of mine.'

'I don't know that I like the adjective *old*, Poppy,' Vick boomed in a flawlessly deep deejay voice. 'But indeed I've become one of Guillaume Riche's supporters. Good job, mate.' He clapped Guillaume on the back.

'Thank you,' Guillaume said graciously. He took a small step back. I knew he didn't like to be touched – unless he invited the touching. And he usually only invited touching from females, not pompous male disc jockeys.

I leaned closer to Guillaume. 'You want to call it a night?' I whispered in his ear while Poppy was saying something to Vick.

Guillaume nodded. I looked around to gather his father

up too, but he had vanished. What was it with men and their disappearing acts this evening?

'Where's your dad?' I asked Guillaume.

He glanced around and shrugged. 'Don't know,' he said. 'But he'll find his way. I'm the only one you have to worry about.'

16

The interviews the next day went flawlessly. Once again, Guillaume was on his best behavior, which made me nervous. I was starting to worry that his good-guy routine was too good to be true. I found myself waiting for the other shoe to drop. But so far, so good. Poppy and I took turns sitting in on the interviews all day, so we each heard him say, dozens of times, how pleased he was to be bridging the gap between France and the English-speaking world with his music.

He sang a few verses a cappella for the TV journalists who thought to request it and flirted incessantly so that most of the women, regardless of age or experience, were reduced to giggling schoolgirls within five minutes. He looked handsome, acted charming and came across cool, calm and collected. In short, he was perfect.

'He's a dream!' bubbled one starstruck reporter from *Entertainment Tonight* after she emerged from her interview.

'He's hotter than Justin Timberlake and John Mayer and Adam Levine put together!' exclaimed a reporter from the

Orlando Sentinel. 'And omigawd, he kissed me! I'm never washing this cheek again!'

'What a charmer,' said a red-faced reporter for *The Advocate*. 'I think I'm in love,' he added.

Poppy and I celebrated the success of the day's interviews that evening in the hotel bar with a big dinner and a bottle of wine between us. Most of the journalists would be leaving in the morning, after a lavish breakfast, during which Guillaume would perform a surprise acoustic rendition of 'City of Light'. Then Poppy and I were to escort Guillaume back on the 4.12 p.m. Eurostar train, so as long as we made it past tonight, we'd be through the junket virtually scot-free. Neither of us could quite believe how easy it had all been.

After dinner, Poppy yawned and said she was tired; she was thinking of turning in. I was a bit disappointed; I'd hoped that now that the media weekend was almost over, she'd feel up for a night on the town and I'd be able to see a bit of London. Poppy had given her mobile number to the security director of the hotel so that if there was any sort of problem, we could be reached anywhere. But I'd have to resign myself instead to a night of watching pay-per-view movies on TV from my king-size hotel bed.

Thirty minutes later, I sat in bored silence in my room, flipping aimlessly through muted channels on the television. I found myself thinking of Gabe and feeling disappointed that I hadn't seen more of him. He had somehow managed to change his interview time today without me knowing it, and I'd been taking a lunch break downstairs the entire time he was in the press suite.

I thought about calling him but eventually nixed the idea. After all, what would I say? Still, it felt strange to be all by myself in an unfamiliar city, sitting in a hotel room alone at nine in the evening when Gabe was just a few floors away. All I could think about was how much I wanted to kiss him again.

But evidently he wasn't feeling the same way. If he was, he would have called me, right? Perhaps, said the little self-conscious voice in my head, he was just using you to get access to Guillaume. That couldn't be true, could it?

Just then, the hotel phone in my room began jangling. It startled me, and I whipped my head toward it immediately. It couldn't be, could it? Could Gabe be calling me? It had to be him, right? No one else who would want to call me knew I was here. Heart pounding, I picked up the receiver.

'Emma?' The worried voice on the other end wasn't Gabe's. It was Poppy's.

'Hi,' I said, startled. 'What's wrong? Are you in your room?'

'Er, not exactly. I'm actually out.'

'You're out? I thought you said you were tired.'

'I'm sorry I didn't tell you,' she said. 'I'm kind of on a date.'

'A date?' I was shocked. I hadn't realized that Poppy's dating schemes extended across the Channel.

'Well, yes. I'm sorry. I didn't want to make a big deal of it.'

'But I thought you only dated Frenchmen,' I said, confused. 'Your whole French kissing philosophy and all.'

'Er, right, well, I guess I might have forgotten to mention that Darren still lives in London.' Poppy's voice sounded muffled.

My jaw dropped. 'Darren?' I asked. 'As in ex-boyfriend, voodoo-doll Darren?'

'Er, yes,' Poppy admitted, her voice sounding strained. 'We've sort of been, er, talking lately.'

'Ah,' I said. 'Like, talking talking? Romantically?'

Silence on the other end. 'Maybe,' Poppy said, her voice small.

'What do your books say about getting back with an ex who broke your heart?' I asked accusingly.

Poppy paused. 'I suppose they would advise against it,' she said. 'But you can't always believe everything you read.'

I pulled the receiver away from my ear for a moment and stared at it in disbelief. Poppy was still talking when I tuned back in. 'Anyhow, I feel really badly about this, Emma,' she was saying. 'But I just received a call from hotel security. About Guillaume.'

I groaned. 'What did he do this time?'

'It seems there is some sort of party going on in his room with loud music and such.' Poppy sighed. 'I'm on my way back to help you out. I know it's just dreadful of me to ask you, but would you please go up and try to put a stop to things before they get out of hand? It'll be another thirty minutes till I'm there, at least.'

I closed my eyes and took a deep breath.

'Yes, of course,' I said finally. 'I'll go right now. Don't worry.'

'Emma, you're a gem,' Poppy said. 'I really owe you. I'm getting back there just as soon as I can.'

'Thanks,' I muttered. I forced a smile that I hoped she could hear through the phone. 'Good luck with Darren, okay?'

Grumbling to myself, I threw the covers off the bed, disentangled myself from the sheets and found a pair of jeans, an old Beatles T-shirt and a pair of black ballet flats that were so worn I generally used them as slippers around the house. In front of the mirror, I swiped on some blush as well as a bit of mascara and lipstick so that I would look vaguely presentable. Then, grabbing my room key and sticking it into my back pocket, I reluctantly left and headed for the elevators.

Two minutes later, when the elevator doors opened on the penthouse floor, I could indeed hear loud music blasting from the direction of Guillaume's suite.

'Can't he control himself for *one* night?' I said aloud, throwing in a few expletives for good measure.

I had to pound on the door three times – the third time with all my strength – before the door swung open to reveal Guillaume standing there, in just a pair of jeans, holding a glass of champagne in his hand. His dark hair had gone haywire, shooting off in all directions, and he evidently hadn't shaved since earlier in the day, as he was sporting the beginning of a five o'clock shadow. I tried to tear my eyes away from his body and focus on his face, but that took considerable effort given the obvious solidity of his pecs and the impressive definition of his chest.

I took a deep breath and locked eyes with him.

'Hi, Emma!' Guillaume said with a broad grin. 'You have come to join me?'

'No, Guillaume, I haven't come to join you.' I fixed him with a reprimanding look. 'Honestly, Guillaume, can't you keep the partying to a minimum when you're in a hotel filled with media?'

Guillaume looked confused. 'Partying?' he asked, swirling around the remainder of the champagne in his glass and downing it in a big swig. '*Chérie*, it's just me in here.'

I looked at him suspiciously. There was no way our hard-partying rock star was entertaining *himself* with a room full of blasting music and a bottle of champagne. 'Come on, Guillaume. I'm not here to get you in trouble. But please, whatever girls you have in there, just send them home before the situation gets worse.'

'Emma, I promise you,' Guillaume said, looking me dead in the eye. 'It's just me. I swear on my life.'

I locked eyes with him, and when his gaze didn't waver after a moment, I sighed and shrugged. 'Fine, whatever you say,' I said, not quite believing him. 'But could you turn the music down, at least? Hotel security is getting calls.'

Guillaume stared at me for a long moment then shrugged and disappeared back into his suite, leaving me standing in the open doorway. I waited and waited for what felt like an eternity, but the volume never went down, and Guillaume never returned. I waited a bit more, then, looking from side to side to make sure no one was watching and would get the wrong idea, I left the door ajar and walked into the suite and down the hallway to find Guillaume – or at the very least, to find the volume knob on the stereo, which was currently blasting an old Rolling Stones album.

'Guillaume?' I called out above the music as I made my way down the suite's long hallway and into the living room. 'Where did you go?'

Just before I reached the living room, Guillaume appeared from around the corner, scaring me half to death. I jumped, startled. Guillaume grinned and thrust a full flute of champagne toward me.

'Guillaume? What are you doing?' I demanded, eyeing the bubbly warily. Inside the glass, it fizzed mesmerizingly.

Guillaume thrust the glass forward again insistently. 'Drink up, Emma!' he said cheerfully. 'We must toast!'

'Guillaume, I—'

'Listen, Emma,' he said. 'The hotel gave me two complimentary bottles of this wonderful champagne. Now it's up to you, of course, but if you don't have a drink with me, I'll be forced to drink both bottles myself.'

'Guillaume,' I started to say wearily, but he interrupted again before I could even get to the frustrated eye-rolling.

'We both know what happens when I drink too much, *oui*?' he continued, grinning at me. 'So really, if you think about it, it's in your best interest to drink with me, because that's less champagne for me, now isn't it?'

I started to say something, but the protest got lost in my throat. After all, he was right, wasn't he? I couldn't exactly argue with the more-for-me-equals-less-for-him theory, could I?

'Fine,' I said, reluctantly accepting the glass. 'But only if you promise to turn the music down.'

Guillaume beamed at me. 'As you wish, my dear.' He raised his glass and waited until I reluctantly raised mine too in a toast. 'Here's to you, my dear Emma,' Guillaume said. I made a face as we clinked glasses, and Guillaume looked delighted. He waited until I took a small sip from my glass.

'The volume, Guillaume?' I reminded him.

'Ah, of course, of course!' he said. He dashed toward the living room. The moment he had turned his back, I emptied half my flute of champagne into the potted plant at the end of the hallway. Then I innocently righted the glass and put my lips to the edge as if I'd been sipping it just in time for Guillaume to return.

'Emma, you *do* drink!' he exclaimed, eyeing my glass with delight. 'Very good! Very good!'

I smiled wanly at him.

'Well, aren't you going to come in?' he asked, 'Or do we have to drink standing up in the hall?'

I didn't see that I had much of a choice. With any luck, I could sit beside another potted plant and proceed to get rid of as much of Guillaume's champagne as possible before he could drink it and do something stupid. I followed Guillaume into the living room. He grabbed the open bottle of champagne from where it sat in a bucket of ice, and topped up my glass.

'Have a seat, Emma,' he said, gesturing to the couch. 'Please, make yourself at home. My suite is your suite, my sweet.' He laughed uproariously at his pun.

'Thank you.' I tried to stifle a yawn. It had been a long day, and I should have been falling asleep in my own bed, not playing AA sponsor to my client. This surely wasn't in my job description, although I had to admit that very little of what I'd had to deal with in the past few weeks fell under the umbrella of officially outlined duties.

I sat down on the couch, beside another potted plant, feeling a bit surprised at how comfortable the cushions were.

'So,' Guillaume said, settling down beside me. 'Are you going to tell me what's wrong? Or do I have to begin guessing?'

I looked at him, startled. 'Nothing's wrong. What do you mean?'

Guillaume shook his head knowingly. 'You were sulking today.'

'I wasn't sulking!'

Guillaume laughed. 'Yes, you were. You were sulking. You cannot deny it.'

I sighed. 'It's nothing.' I took a long sip of the champagne

– one sip couldn't hurt – and felt a small tingle of warmth spread over me.

Guillaume watched me closely. His near-nudity was beginning to get to me.

'Could you put a shirt on please?' I asked crossly. I took another sip. After all, if I was going to have to sit here with him and dispose of half his champagne, I would appreciate us both being fully clothed.

But Guillaume only laughed. 'It's hot.' He shrugged. 'Does my body offend you?'

No, I wanted to say. It's making me feel attracted to you.

'No,' I said aloud. 'It just seems weird that you don't have a shirt on.'

Guillaume laughed again, shrugged and made no move to get up to put more clothes on. Instead, he topped up my glass again. Obediently, I took another sip. I was starting to feel the alcohol, but not enough to worry about it. Just enough to relax me a little. And besides, it was all for the greater good anyhow. Every sip I drank was one less that Guillaume could consume.

After a moment of silence, Guillaume tried again. 'So? Are you going to tell me what is bothering you? I just want to help.'

I studied his face for a moment. He certainly appeared genuine. His usual smirk was gone, and he looked concerned.

'Fine.' I sighed and looked away. 'Look, it's just that I'm confused, you know?' I looked back at Guillaume and found him listening to me carefully. I went on. 'I mean, Poppy offered me a permanent job in Paris, working with you, and I think I want to take it. I really do. But I'm not sure it's the right decision.'

'*Pourquoi?*' Guillaume asked, leaning forward with interest. I took another sip of my champagne and glanced away. Really, I hadn't intended to share so much.

I hesitated. 'Because there's a guy at home who I just ended an engagement with.' The words came pouring out. 'Well, I didn't exactly end things with him. He broke up with me. But I think that maybe he thinks he made a mistake. He says he wants to try things again. And we were together three years, you know? I'm really confused. But I don't know that I want to go home. I love Paris. I love almost everything about it. I even love the job, although you make it difficult for me sometimes.'

I stopped, embarrassed. What was in this champagne – truth serum?

Guillaume smiled. 'I'm sorry I make your life difficult,' he said.

'No, it's not that you make my life difficult,' I amended. 'And you will never hear me say this again. But really, I prefer working with you to working with the boy band boys I used to work with. There was nothing exciting about that job.'

I hadn't realized until that very moment how true the words were. I *did* like working with Guillaume, despite – or perhaps even because of – the fact that I never knew what was going to happen next with him. How could it be that I preferred talking my clients down from ropes suspended in mid-air to making excuses for prepubescent boys gone wrong?

I looked down at my glass. Somehow it had become empty. Had I really sipped it all while embarrassingly pouring out my heart? I glanced guiltily at Guillaume. But he wasn't looking at me. He was looking at my glass. Which he was presently refilling. Why did I have the sudden sense that I was the one drinking the majority of the champagne? Somehow, my pour-it-in-the-shrubbery plan seemed to have derailed.

'Well, I'm glad I can make your life more exciting,' Guillaume said, refilling his own glass as well. He upended the bottle in the ice. We seemed to have finished it all. He reached for the other bucket, which held a second bottle of champagne. 'So,' he continued smoothly. 'Do you still love this guy back home? The one you just ended your relationship with?'

I blinked a few times and studied my glass of champagne intently, as though an answer to the question might appear on the surface courtesy of the constantly rising stream of bubbles. But no such luck, evidently.

'I don't know,' I mumbled. I took another sip of champagne as I contemplated the question. 'I don't think I do. No. Not any more. It's confusing. I don't think you can love someone for three years and then just turn it off.'

'Probably not.' Guillaume nodded supportively.

'But I don't think I've been *in* love with him for a long time,' I continued, still wondering vaguely what was possessing me to confide so much in Guillaume when I had barely even admitted these things to myself yet.

Satisfied with my honesty, at least, I leaned back into the comfortable cushions and watched as Guillaume popped the cork on the second champagne bottle and poured us each a fresh glass. The liquid seemed to be disappearing with surprising speed.

'Plus,' Guillaume added nonchalantly, leaning back and taking a sip from his glass, 'you have a crush on a certain UPP journalist.'

'What?' I sat up so quickly that I sloshed a bit of champagne onto my jeans. But I was more concerned at the moment with the fact that my cheeks felt like they were on fire. 'No I don't! I don't know what you're talking about! I don't have a crush on him!'

Had I really been that obvious? I'd hardly realized it myself until just a few days earlier, although I suppose I'd been attracted to him since the moment I'd first spotted him in the Hôtel Jérémie press corps crowd.

'Yes, you do,' Guillaume said simply.

I could feel the heat in my face. I had no doubt I was beet red.

'No, I don't!' I don't know why I felt compelled to deny it. But I couldn't have Guillaume thinking that. I was determined to be one hundred per cent professional. And my idea of professionalism did not include drooling over a cute reporter who seemed determined to be my client's primary adversary.

'Yes, you do.' The words were sing-songed merrily at me this time.

'*No*, I don't!' I felt annoyed now. Had he lured me into his room for the express purpose of making me feel foolish? 'And just what would make you think that, anyhow?' I asked defensively, realizing a bit late that my indignation perhaps wasn't transmitted as clearly as it could have been, given that I was slurring my words pretty severely.

Guillaume rolled his eyes and grinned. 'Wow, I don't know. The way you look at him. The way you're always looking around for him when you can't find him. The way you're blushing now that I am asking you.'

'I'm not blushing,' I said quickly.

'Right. It must just be that the temperature in the room has climbed. Perhaps you're overheating?'

'Don't make fun of me,' I snapped. 'I'm serious. It's not like I'm even looking for a boyfriend or anything anyhow.'

'Oh?' Guillaume asked with some interest.

I had the dim sense I was talking myself into a hole. But I just kept on digging. 'Yes,' I said triumphantly. 'I'm *dating*. According to Poppy, I need to go out with as many Frenchmen as possible, but no more than one date each.'

Guillaume grinned. 'And you sleep with them, yes?'

I shook my head vehemently. 'No, of course not!'

Guillaume looked confused for the first time. 'So what is the point?'

I thought about this for a moment. 'The pursuit of the perfect French kiss, I think,' I said, realizing that I was slurring even more than before. I'd better stop drinking the champagne and go back to the shrubbery plan.

'Can I ask you something?' I asked.

'But of course.' Guillaume smiled.

'What's *with* you, anyhow?' I realized that the words sounded completely tactless, but between my frustration and the champagne, I hardly cared any more. 'I mean, do you have a drinking problem? I've never actually even seen you drink until today. Or are you crazy? Or is it like Gabe says and you just want the attention?'

Guillaume looked surprised. Then a slow grin spread across his face. 'Gabe said that, did he?'

I shrugged. 'Maybe I shouldn't have said that.'

'No, no, it's fine,' Guillaume said. He shook his head. 'It's just typical of him.' He took a deep breath. 'Okay. So you asked whether I was crazy. No, I do not think I am.'

'So it's alcohol then?' I asked.

Guillaume shook his head. 'No. Can I tell you a secret?'

I nodded. 'Yesh.' I had intended to say *yes*, but the champagne was really kicking in.

'I actually don't drink at all,' he said.

'But you're drinking champagne now!' I exclaimed.

'No,' Guillaume said. 'I've been pouring it in the shrubbery.'

My jaw dropped. 'That was my plan!'

Guillaume arched an eyebrow. 'Was it? Hmm. I seem to have executed the plan better than you, then.'

Okay. I had to admit that he was right.

'But why did you ask me to come in and have a drink if you weren't planning on drinking yourself?' I asked.

Guillaume shrugged. 'I was lonely. And you and I never get to talk.'

I stared. 'I'm your publicist. We're not supposed to be sitting around bonding, Guillaume.'

'I know,' he said. 'Still, this has been fun, right? I mean, that thing you were telling me about French kisses? That's pretty interesting.'

'It is?' I couldn't figure out why Guillaume would be so intrigued.

'Indeed,' he said. He scooted a bit closer and smiled. 'So what is it you've discovered?'

'About French kissing?' I asked. 'Well, for one, I think someone needs to tell all the women back in the United States that no one kisses like a Frenchman!'

Guillaume laughed. 'Really?'

'*Mais oui*,' I said with an exaggerated French accent, thinking how much easier it was to speak French while drinking. Hmm, perhaps I would have to begin stashing a bottle of champagne in my desk at work. 'You Frenchmen have really perfected the art of the kiss, you know.'

Guillaume studied my face for a moment. He looked sort of fuzzy around the edges, but I supposed that was because of the alcohol, not because he was actually disintegrating. 'That's very interesting,' he said softly. Then, before I realized what was happening, he leaned over and pressed his lips to mine, softly at first and then, when I didn't protest, with mounting intensity.

Wow, he's a good kisser, I thought vaguely. And being pressed against that amazing body is incredible. My mouth, which apparently had a mind of its own, kissed him back. But wait, I thought suddenly, trying not to sink into the sensation of the kiss. He's my client! What am I doing?

I had just started to pull away when there was a voice from the doorway.

'Guillaume! *Putain de merde!* You're such an asshole!'

I jerked my eyes open, pulled away from Guillaume and whirled around, horrified.

Gabe was standing there in the doorway, fists clenched, staring at us. I felt absolutely horrible – and all of a sudden terribly sober. He wasn't looking at me; he was staring at Guillaume with eyes that flashed with anger. Slowly, I turned back to Guillaume and was surprised to see him smirking, looking rather pleased with himself.

'Oh, Gabe, I wasn't expecting you,' he said casually, as if Gabe had just walked in on us playing bridge or sipping tea or something equally mundane.

I looked slowly back at Gabe. He looked even more furious. He glanced at me, then back at Guillaume. 'That's bullshit, Guillaume,' he said sharply. 'You called my room thirty minutes ago and asked me to come up! You even had a room key delivered!'

'What?' I asked, startled. I whirled back to look at

Guillaume, who looked vaguely guilty but still mostly self-satisfied. Then I turned back to Gabe, who was staring at me. He looked like he was about to say something, but then he shook his head and shut his mouth. His face looked sad, which made me feel terrible.

'Gabe?' I started to say. But he cast one last look at me, turned on his heel and strode quickly back down the hallway.

'Gabe!' I tried again, standing up and staring after him. But the only reply I got was the violent slamming of the door to Guillaume's suite. I stared down the dark hallway for a moment, feeling totally crushed.

Slowly, I turned back to Guillaume. The smirk had finally vanished from his face, replaced with an expression that I could have sworn looked a bit guilty.

'What is wrong with you?' I hissed at him. He shrugged.

'It's nothing, Emma,' he said, waving a dismissive hand, as if I was being high-maintenance, in some way, for reacting to what he'd done. 'Don't worry about it so much.'

I could feel my head throbbing with anger – or was it alcohol? 'You are *such* a jerk!' I exclaimed. I slammed my glass of champagne down on the coffee table. I heard the glass crack, but I didn't care. With one last furious look back at Guillaume, I jumped up and dashed toward the door. I pulled it open and looked frantically out into the hallway. But Gabe was long gone.

Back in my room, still slightly drunk and completely ashamed, I immediately dialed the front desk and asked to be connected to Gabe's room. There was no answer. I tried three more times until the hotel operator suggested, in a tone filled with barely concealed annoyance, that *perhaps* the gentleman I was trying to reach had gone out. I hung up, feeling stupid, and wondered where he could have gone.

Checking to make sure I still had my key, I raced out of the room and took the elevator down to the lobby, willing it to go faster. I emerged on the ground floor just in time to see Gabe striding rapidly out of the hotel, pulling his suitcase behind him.

'Gabe!' I called desperately, pushing past the crowd of people waiting to get into the elevator. 'Gabe, wait!'

But he didn't slow down. Nor did he look back. I dashed after him, pulling up beside him just as he reached the front doors.

'Gabe, where are you going?' I asked, my voice laced with a desperation that made me feel ashamed.

'To the train station,' he muttered without looking at me.

A valet appeared from outside to help Gabe with his bag. 'Where to this evening, sir?' he asked, bowing slightly.

'Victoria station,' Gabe said tersely. 'As soon as possible.'

'I will get you a taxi right away, sir,' the man responded. He hurried officiously away.

'Gabe, I am so sorry,' I said quickly, my words pouring out on top of each other in my desperation. 'Please look at me. Please! Gabe!'

Finally, with obvious reluctance, he looked down at me, his face stony.

'Gabe, I'm so sorry!' I said again. 'It's not what you think!'

'Hey, it's not my business if you want to make out with your client,' he said coldly. 'After all, what woman can resist a rock star?'

'Gabe, please, it didn't mean anything,' I babbled. 'I swear!'

He shook his head as a cab pulled up and the valet approached us with a raised hand. 'It never does,' Gabe muttered.

'What does that mean?' I asked. But he ignored me.

The valet began dragging Gabe's bag away, and he turned away from me to follow.

'Wait!' I exclaimed, desperately searching for any reason to make him stay. 'You can't go! We're hosting a media breakfast in the morning! Guillaume's going to perform again!'

Gabe laughed bitterly. 'I think I know everything I need to know about Guillaume Riche.' He got into the cab and slammed the door behind him. The valet was staring at us, but I didn't care.

'But Gabe—'

'Emma,' he said. 'You're the only reason I came to this junket.'

The words pierced me like a spear through the heart. 'I'm so sorry,' I said in a whisper.

Gabe shook his head. 'No, *I'm* sorry,' he said, looking away from me. 'I should have known better.'

Gabe said something to the driver and then turned his attention forward. As the cab pulled away, Gabe didn't look back.

17

I thought I would die on the spot. I sank to the ground, my head throbbing, my face flushed with shame. The valet was staring at me like I was a lunatic.

Just then, another cab pulled up and Poppy cheerfully alighted with a tall, sandy-haired, completely gorgeous guy in tow. He had his arm slung over her shoulder, and she was giggling about something he was saying. Then, just as they tumbled onto the pavement in unison, she looked up and saw me.

'Emma!' Her eyes registered surprise as she stopped dead in her tracks. She started to smile at me then seemed to realize that something was wrong – perhaps due to the fact that I was currently half crumpled on the sidewalk. 'Emma?' she said again, dropping to one knee next to me. 'Are you okay?'

I shook my head, and although I was biting my trembling lip and trying not to, I burst into tears. I didn't know if they were from the shame or the sense of loss or the copious amounts of champagne. I knew only that I was sitting on the ground in front of one of the nicest hotels in London, trying not to cry in front of my friend and the human incarnation of her voodoo doll.

'Oh goodness, Emma!' Poppy exclaimed in concern, wrapping me in her arms and then pulling back to search my face. 'What's wrong? What is it?'

I glanced up at the man with Poppy – presumably Darren – and flushed. 'I'm sorry,' I said to him. I looked at Poppy. 'I'm sorry. Now on top of everything else, I'm ruining *your* night.'

'No, no, not at all,' Poppy soothed, stroking my hair. She glanced up at Darren who was looking at us with concern, but not, I noticed, with any sort of disdain. Poppy stood up slowly and whispered to him. He nodded.

'I'm going to head home,' he said with a casualness I knew was forced. I tried to protest, but he shook his head. 'No, no, it's late. I will see Poppy tomorrow.'

'Emma, this is Darren, by the way,' Poppy said.

I forced a smile at him and stood up from my spot on the ground, feeling silly. I extended a hand, which Darren shook firmly. This both impressed and embarrassed me, as my hand had obviously just been on the ground – not to mention on the surface of my wet, mucky face.

'Nice to meet you,' I said.

'And you as well,' he said pleasantly, as if I wasn't a pathetic mess. 'Poppy has told me a lot about you.'

'Er . . . thank you,' I said, glancing at Poppy.

Darren smiled at me again and then, after a few whispers and kisses with Poppy, he got back into a cab, waved goodbye to both of us and disappeared.

'I'm so sorry I ruined your date,' I moaned as soon as he was gone.

'Nonsense,' Poppy said firmly. 'Now let's go inside, and you can tell me what's wrong.'

She put her arm around my shoulder and guided me back to my room, where we both sat down on the edge of my bed.

'I think I've ruined everything, Poppy,' I declared miserably, once she'd fetched me a box of tissues and a glass of water. 'Guillaume will have a problem with the UPP, I've lost Gabe . . . everything is just so screwed up!'

I found myself pouring out the whole story of what had happened this evening, from the champagne-in-the-shrubbery plan gone awry to Gabe hurtling out of the hotel with his suitcase, slamming the cab door behind him.

'Emma, why didn't you tell me you felt like this about Gabe Francoeur?' Poppy asked when I was done.

'I don't know.' I shrugged uncomfortably. 'I don't think I even realized I did, before the whole roller thing the night before last anyhow. Or maybe I did, but I didn't want to. It's not like it's professional of me to start falling for one of the journalists we work with.'

Poppy shrugged. 'Hey, we live in Paris,' she reminded me gently. 'The city of love. You can't control who you fall in love with.'

I shook my head. 'Anyhow, it doesn't matter. I've totally ruined it. But what's even worse is I've probably ruined Guillaume's relationship with the UPP. I have no idea what Gabe will write, but seriously, Poppy, he could sabotage us. And I don't know that I would even blame him at this point.'

I felt tears prickling at the back of my eyes, and I blinked them back. I was already pathetic enough.

Poppy put a hand on my shoulder. 'It's not your fault, Emma,' she said gently. 'First of all, I don't know that Gabe is necessarily going to do anything. But even if he does, it's really Guillaume's fault, not yours, right?'

I paused. 'No,' I said after a moment. 'I should have known better. I let my personal stuff get in the way. I made a big mistake with Guillaume. I should never have had a drink with him. That was really, really stupid. And then Gabe came in . . .' I stopped and closed my eyes for a moment. I swallowed hard. 'And now he hates Guillaume. He's going to get bad press on the eve of his album release, and it's going to be all my fault.'

'Okay, now you're just being silly,' Poppy said firmly. I looked at her, surprised, as she continued. 'You were trying to do the right thing. And I must say, it sounds a bit like Guillaume lured you into all of this, although I can't imagine why. Guillaume obviously planned for Gabe to walk in on you. And Emma, if Guillaume is so intent on sabotaging himself, there's not much you can do.'

I thought about it for a moment. It *was* very strange, come to think of it, that Guillaume had apparently called Gabe either before or just after I arrived and asked him to come up in thirty minutes. Why would he do such a thing? And if he'd called him, why on earth would he lean in to kiss me if he was expecting a reporter whom he suspected I had a crush on? Was Guillaume *trying* to hurt me? The thought startled and unsettled me.

'Whether it's all my fault or not,' I said finally, 'I wouldn't be surprised if Gabe totally rips him apart in print. And that's going to come down on us. On your firm.' I felt like everything was on the line here, and I'd screwed it up irreversibly. 'I crossed a line, Poppy. I've put everything in jeopardy. I don't think I deserve to be here any more.'

*

I barely slept that night. I tossed and turned thinking about Gabe, worrying about what his article would say and about what would happen to Poppy's company.

After I woke up, I logged onto my computer and was tentatively relieved to find that Gabe hadn't published an article about Guillaume in the last twenty-four hours. It was mildly comforting, but I feared that it was really just delaying the inevitable. In a way, I would have preferred to have everything out on the table that day so that everything could end in a cataclysmic burst of shame instead of under a lingering cloud of tense regret, waiting for the other shoe to drop.

The press breakfast that morning was in the grand ballroom on the second floor, a spacious, soaring room with domed ceilings and smooth, ecru walls. As the reporters – conspicuously minus Gabe – settled into their seats and chattered happily away, a fleet of waiters filled their water glasses, brought them orange juice, coffee and tea and refilled their overflowing pastry baskets. Fifteen minutes after we'd begun, nearly everyone was accounted for.

After the meal, during which Guillaume continually shot me wide-eyed, guilty glances from his table near the stage, he performed 'Charlotte, je t'aime', a love-song from his album. The press were delighted. Then, with his guitar, he did one final acoustic version of 'City of Light' which had the crowd on its feet, applauding wildly, by the time it was over. I met Poppy's eyes as Guillaume strummed his last chords. We both smiled. In the space of two days, our press plan – and the charm and talent of the crazy Guillaume – had won over a room full of a hundred journalists who were paid to be skeptical. We had somehow done the impossible.

Poppy and I said goodbye to all the reporters as they

filtered out of the room. When we finally shut the doors behind us, I leaned back against the wall with a sigh.

'Well, that went perfectly!' Poppy said with a smile. She looked at me carefully. 'Are you okay?'

I forced a smile. 'I'm fine. You're right. It was perfect.'

Just then, Guillaume slipped back into the ballroom. I looked quickly around for an escape route, but alas, he was entering through the only set of doors, and there was no conversation about rugby or cosmetics or cricket that I could join and feign interest in.

I could feel Poppy put a hand on the small of my back. 'It's going to be fine,' she said softly. I nodded, trying to summon some strength.

'Emma,' Guillaume said as he approached. He looked shamefaced. 'Please, Emma, I'm so sorry.'

I could see Poppy glaring at him beside me. I averted my eyes. 'It's fine,' I mumbled. I dismissively waved my hand and hoped he would go away.

Beside me, Poppy took a step forward. 'It is *not* fine!' she declared hotly, putting her hands on her hips and glaring at Guillaume. 'Don't you dare tell him it's fine, Emma! He totally screwed you over!'

Guillaume looked uncomfortable. 'In my defense, I was trying to screw with Gabe, not you.'

'What are you talking about?' Poppy demanded. 'Are you *trying* to destroy your career before it even takes off?'

He ignored her and continued to address me. 'I, uh, didn't realize how much you liked him,' he said. 'I'm really sorry.'

I felt mortified. Great. Not only had Guillaume ended any chance I may have had with Gabe, he was also under the mistaken impression that I was madly in love with the reporter he'd just scared away.

'It's fine, Guillaume,' I said uncomfortably, wishing he would disappear. But quite irritatingly, he didn't. 'Anyhow,' I added, 'it's not like I even liked him that much to begin with.'

The lie felt sour on my tongue, but it wasn't as if I had a choice.

The next morning, the world came tumbling down.

After having taken an evening train back to Paris the night before, Poppy and I arrived at the office early in the morning to see what kind of an impact the junket had made.

At first glance, the coverage was good. The *Boston Globe* ran a glowing profile of Guillaume that said his music was 'like a bottle of fine French wine: smooth, delicious and designed to make you feel good'. The *New York Times* ran a piece about how Guillaume – actor, songwriter, singer and international playboy – was the first real Renaissance man of the twenty-first century. The London *Mirror* ran a front-page story with a headline that screamed: 'Prince William, Watch Your Back! There's a New Bachelor in Town!'

But there was one glaring problem.

There was nothing on the UPP wires about Guillaume. Or about the junket.

'Gabriel didn't file a story,' Poppy said after a few moments of flipping through various sites. She looked at the computer screen, and then at me. 'He didn't file a story,' she repeated.

'Well, at least he didn't file a *bad* story,' I said in a small voice, trying to look on the bright side.

Poppy looked at me for a long moment. 'Right, but there's nothing at all,' she said quietly. 'That means that in spite of all the money KMG poured into this, the junket is conspicuously absent from more than two hundred newspapers around the world.'

I gulped. A knot was beginning to form in the center of my stomach. 'Oh,' I said quietly. In a way, then, no news was even worse than bad news.

The phone rang and Poppy reached distractedly to pick it up. The voice on the other end was so loud that I could hear it from where I was sitting. After a moment, Poppy hung up, her face pale.

'That was Véronique,' she said. 'She wants to see us both immediately.'

'Oh Poppy,' I said. 'I'm so sorry.'

Poppy took a deep breath and tried to smile. 'Don't worry,' she said. 'Not yet, anyhow. Maybe all Véronique wants to talk about is all the great coverage we got.'

Fifteen minutes later, we were walking in the door of KMG, where we were promptly ushered into Véronique's office. After nodding at both of us and telling us to take seats, she sat down behind her desk, crossed her arms silently and looked back and forth between us for what felt like an eternity.

'Poppy,' she finally began in an even tone. 'Do you know how much KMG spent on this junket?'

Poppy gulped. 'Yes,' she said. 'It was quite a lot.'

'Correct,' Véronique said. 'And do you know *why* we spent so much money?'

Poppy gulped. 'To help promote Guillaume.'

'Well, yes,' Véronique said. 'And because *you* insisted that this junket was the way to do it.'

Poppy cleared her throat. 'We got some great coverage,' she said in a small voice.

I chimed in. 'The *Boston Globe* did a great piece. So did the *New York Times*. And the London *Mirror*.'

Véronique glanced at me quickly, as if I were an insignificant annoyance, and then focused her stare back on Poppy.

'I wondered when I got into the office this morning why, with all that money spent on this, Guillaume Riche was missing from hundreds of papers around the world where you had promised there would be coverage.'

There was dead silence for a moment. Poppy glanced over at me and then back at Véronique. She cleared her throat nervously again.

'I can explain,' she said finally.

'No need,' Véronique said crisply, holding up a hand. 'Because I already have this issue answered, you see. When I realized the omission, I thought to myself, *why?* Why is there no coverage in more than two hundred papers Poppy promised would carry news of the junket?'

'Véronique, I—' Poppy began.

'Do not interrupt,' Véronique said, again holding up a hand to silence her. I felt ill and sank down lower in my chair, wondering if it would be possible to simply vanish into the upholstery.

'In any case,' Véronique continued, 'I began calling around and realized that the omissions were all in papers that rely on UPP content. But, I said to myself, I thought there was a UPP reporter on the list for the junket.'

'Véronique, I—'

'Let me finish, Poppy,' Véronique said icily. 'I checked your junket list, and indeed there was a listing for Gabriel Francoeur from the UPP. And, according to your master billing list, he checked in and stayed all weekend. Well,

I thought to myself, perhaps he did not like the music. So I called the UPP Paris bureau chief to find out.'

'You did?' Poppy asked quietly. All the blood had drained from her face. I slid even further down in the chair, feeling like the worst person in the world.

'I did,' Véronique confirmed. 'And do you know what I found out?'

Poppy didn't respond. She just sat there, staring. Véronique's gaze flicked to me. I could feel my cheeks heating up. I tried to keep an innocent face.

'I found out,' Véronique continued, 'that this reporter, this Gabriel Francoeur, did indeed like Guillaume's music. He's the one who has been giving us coverage so far. But his editor said that something happened at the junket that made Monsieur Francoeur return early, saying that he no longer felt he could cover Guillaume Riche impartially.'

'Oh no,' I mumbled. Véronique looked sharply at me.

'*Mais oui*,' she said. 'His editor didn't understand at first either, and he was distressed that he had spent all this money sending one of his top reporters to this junket and had even teased the forthcoming story on the wires, so that papers around the world had created space in their entertainment sections for it. So he pressed Gabriel Francoeur for some sort of an answer.'

Poppy and I exchanged worried looks.

Véronique pressed on, glaring at us. 'The only information Francoeur offered was that something had happened between himself and a publicist *in the employ of KMG*. He wouldn't specify what actually occurred but the incident was apparently so serious that it has made him give up the music features beat for the time being. He has been voluntarily demoted to the international obituary department.'

Véronique paused again and studied us for a moment, first Poppy and then me. I wanted to sink into the floor.

'Would either of you care to explain?' Véronique asked. 'You two are the only two publicists employed by KMG who were at the junket this weekend.'

Poppy opened her mouth, but Véronique rolled right over her, gathering steam as she went.

'Because,' she continued coldly, 'you realize that whatever happened, you have damaged KMG's relationship with one of the most influential media outlets in the world.'

'Véronique, it wasn't really such a big deal,' Poppy said in a small voice.

Véronique glared at Poppy. '*You* do not get to decide what is a big deal to KMG,' she spat. 'That is for *me* to decide. You are just the hired help.'

Poppy was stunned into silence. I glanced at her, and my heart sank to see Poppy, who was rarely at a loss for words, looking so stricken. I had to do something.

'Véronique?' I said quietly. She turned and focused her flashing eyes on me. 'It's not Poppy's fault. It's mine. And for the record, I don't think there's any way in the world that you could possibly accuse Poppy of failing. She got an enormous amount of media coverage for Guillaume. Far more than most record launches. She really did a phenomenal job. The junket was a huge success even if the UPP didn't carry the story.'

'I did not invest so much of my company's money to have it undone by some personal problem between a publicist,' she paused to glare at Poppy, 'and a journalist.'

'It was my fault, Véronique,' I said. Véronique turned her gaze back to me. I braced myself and continued. 'I was the publicist who screwed things up. It was me, not Poppy.'

'Don't do this,' Poppy muttered. But I shook my head at her.

Véronique stared at me. 'Go on,' she said, her voice hushed, her expression unforgiving.

I took a deep breath. 'I behaved in an unprofessional manner with Gabe Francoeur,' I said. 'There was an incident involving him and Guillaume, and I handled it all wrong. It's one hundred per cent my fault, not Poppy's.'

Véronique was silent for a long moment. 'I see,' she said finally.

Poppy and I exchanged looks.

Véronique looked down at her lap and sat there motionless for a moment, as if meditating. When she looked up, her focus was on me. 'I trust I will have your resignation letter by the end of today,' she said softly.

Beside me, I heard Poppy gasp. 'Véronique, I don't really think that's necessary!' she exclaimed.

'As for you,' Véronique said, turning to Poppy, 'you will have one more chance with KMG because of the work you have done so far. But I trust that in the future you won't hire any more publicists who risk our reputation. This is unforgivable.'

'But—'

'Either Emma goes or you both go,' Véronique interrupted.

'It's fine, Poppy,' I said. Poppy opened her mouth to say something else, but I spoke first, turning to Véronique. 'You'll have my resignation by the end of the day. I'm sorry.'

In a daze, I stood up and strode quickly to the door before anyone could see me cry.

18

I wasn't sure what would be harder to leave: Poppy, the friend I'd grown to trust; or Paris, the city I'd grown to love.

Poppy was full of apologies and promises to try to talk Véronique out of her decision. But I'd screwed up, and I knew it. I didn't want to cost Poppy more than I already had. I had the feeling that her own job security was hanging by a string, and I knew that losing the Guillaume Riche account would mean the end of Poppy's business. I would never do that to her. I felt terrible that I had already wrought so much havoc. She had rescued me from my own depression back home, and I had repaid her by putting her agency in jeopardy. Although Poppy kept insisting that it wasn't my fault, I knew that it was. It was unforgivable.

Once Poppy realized that her powers of persuasion weren't going to get me to revise my decision, she gave in and began to say her goodbyes. She took me out to dinner at a different restaurant every night, perhaps to try to convince me to stay in France. But all the crêpes complètes and coq au vin and crème brûlée in Paris couldn't change things.

She even loosened up on the whole French kissing mission, which was a relief. I didn't know whether her relaxing of the rules was due to her pity for me or perhaps over some sort of change that her visit with Darren had wrought in her. But it allowed me to slip back to my old ways of *not* dating, which were much less disaster-prone. After all, if I wasn't dating and I wasn't thinking about kissing Frenchmen, there was no chance of anything going wrong, now was there?

I tried calling Gabe several times that week, but there was never an answer on his work or cell phones, and he didn't return any of the messages I left. *I'm so sorry*, I said in several messages. *It didn't mean anything*. In others, I apologized for my complete lack of professionalism and told him I was leaving for Orlando on Saturday morning. They all had the same general theme: *I'm a jerk. And I'm so sorry I hurt you*.

On my last day of work, Guillaume, who had managed, impressively, to stay out of trouble all week, came by Poppy's office in the afternoon for one final round of apologies.

'Look, Emma, I really like working with you,' he said, sitting down at my desk and widening his already enormous green eyes at me. 'I didn't mean for any of this to happen. I'm so sorry.'

'It's okay,' I said with a nod. And it was. Guillaume was Guillaume, and I should have known better. This was my fault, for the most part, not his. 'I've liked working with you too,' I admitted as an afterthought.

This made Guillaume look even sadder. 'Isn't there anything I can do?' he asked. 'Talk to the people at KMG, maybe?'

'No. What's done is done, I think.' I gave him a small smile. 'But you are really talented. I wish the best for you. I know you'll do well.'

On my last night in Paris, after I'd packed and left one final apologetic message for Gabe, I went to dinner with Poppy at a crêperie near Place d'Italie, where we stuffed ourselves with salads, buckwheat crêpes with cheese, eggs and ham, a bottle of *cidre*, and massive flambéed crêpes Suzettes and cafés doubles for dessert. Outside the window, a parade of Parisians strolled continually by, walking little white dogs, carrying baguettes, chattering away on their mobile phones or tending to small, impeccably dressed little children with pink cheeks and spring coats buttoned all the way to the top.

'I love it here,' I murmured, staring out the window as Poppy counted out a small handful of euro bills and coins for our dinner, which she insisted on paying for.

'So why don't you stay?' Poppy asked softly.

I shook my head and gazed out on the Paris outside our window before answering. 'No,' I said. 'I can't. It's obviously not where I belong.'

After dinner, Poppy suggested heading to Le Crocodile in the 5th for cocktails, but I only wanted to be alone with the city. 'No,' I said. 'I think I'm going to take a walk. I'll see you at home in a little while.'

Poppy and I hugged goodbye and went our separate ways; her to a taxi and me underground to line 7 of the Métro, which I took to Châtelet, seven stops away. I emerged twenty minutes later in a square full of sparkling lights lining centuries-old buildings. The Palais de Justice, the Hôtel de Ville, the Pont de la Cité and Sainte-Chapelle were flooded with soft light and glittered on the surface of the Seine, which was broken only by the occasional silent passing of a boat.

I strolled toward the river in silence, pulling my cardigan around me as a chill crept into the air. All round me, Paris was alive with conversations, smiles, the quiet exchanges between couples, the happy laughter of friends crossing the bridge on the way to a bar or a café in the 5th. As I crossed Pont Neuf and saw the Eiffel Tower glowing over the river to the west, I could feel tears prickling at the back of my eyes. They blurred the searchlight from the top of the tower before I could blink them back.

As I walked further across the Île de la Cité, the massive Conciergerie hulked in the shadows, a reminder of a time of sadness and horror when thousands were imprisoned and met their deaths during the French Revolution. To the left, Notre-Dame basked in its own light across its broad, cobblestone courtyard, its many saints and gargoyles standing silent watch over the hushed clusters of tourists clutching guidebooks and speaking in whispers as they stared up at the fourteenth-century cathedral in awe. Across the bridge on the Left Bank, the green-and-yellow cursive of the Café le Petit Pont glowed like a beacon, reminding me of my first night in Paris with Poppy and the interview I'd supervised between Guillaume and Gabe. Somehow, it all seemed so long ago.

I wandered for hours along the banks of the Seine, weaving down the rue de la Huchette in the Latin Quarter then across the Petit Pont and Pont Notre-Dame bridges and down the rue de Rivoli on the Right Bank. The quaint cobblestone of the Marais gave way to the Pont Marie and then, as I wove back, to the regal buildings of the Place des Vosges, where Victor Hugo once sat and created a hunchback named Quasimodo to ring the bells of Notre-Dame. By the time I had strolled back to the Pont Neuf to take one last look west down the Seine toward the Eiffel Tower, it was past midnight, the tourists had disappeared and I felt like I had the city, or at least the tip of the island, all to myself. The ripples of the Seine kissed the embankment in a soothing tempo, and the moonlight reflected in the river mixed with the light cast from the buildings that had been host to kings and saints and history in all its forms.

I would miss it here. I would miss it a lot.

I took the RER from the Saint-Michel stop back to Pont de l'Alma and walked up Avenue Rapp to our street. As always, the moment I turned right onto rue du Général Camou, the Eiffel Tower loomed enormous at the end of the short lane. Usually, it was a thrill to see it. Tonight, it just felt hauntingly sad. In Orlando, the only thing that had loomed at the end of my street had been a big traffic light. Here, one of the most beautiful monuments in the world sat just feet away, shining with golden light in the darkness.

I didn't sleep that night. I couldn't. I crawled into bed and closed my eyes, but I couldn't bring myself to spend my last hours in Paris that way. Eventually, I got up and walked to the living-room window, where I sat with a bottle of Beaujolais and a crusty baguette, gazing at the Eiffel Tower long after the lights had gone out and it was just a dark silhouette against the distant rooftops of the city.

It was dawn before I realized that there were tears rolling down my cheeks. I wondered how long I'd been crying. As the first birds of the morning began to chirp and the sky turned gradually from inky blue to a blend of sunrise pastels, illuminating the steel of the tower, I got up from the window, took a shower, brushed my teeth and went out for a walk. By the time Poppy and I had finished the pains au chocolat I'd brought home from the patisserie on the corner, along with the espresso she silently made in the kitchen, I still wasn't ready to go. But it was time. Poppy walked me over to the taxi stand on Avenue Bosquet, and with one last hug goodbye, I was on my way. But I wasn't so sure any more that the place I was going was home.

Because Brett had moved back into our old house and because I had no desire whatsoever to see any of my three so-called 'best friends' in Orlando, I had nowhere to go when I got back to the States but to my sister Jeannie's place.

'I told you it was a bad idea to move to Paris,' Jeannie said when she opened the door at her Winter Park home to find me and two giant suitcases waiting on the doorstep at eleven in the evening. She'd been too busy to come and pick me up at the airport, so I'd had to take a cab, at a cost of fifty-five dollars, which was not exactly the way I'd envisioned starting my life as an unemployed American. 'I don't want to say I told you so, but, well . . .' Her voice trailed off and she smiled sweetly at me.

'You know the story, Jeannie,' I answered wearily. After a grueling eight-hour flight from Paris to Detroit, a three-hour layover and then a three-hour flight to Orlando, I was in no mood to argue with my sister.

'You have to admit, it was really immature to go to Paris on some silly whim,' Jeannie said, shaking her head. 'You're going to have to grow up some day, Emma.' I bit my lip, figuring that things would be better all round if I didn't reply. She turned away, leaving me to drag the suitcases inside myself. 'Try to be quiet, Em,' she said over her shoulder. 'Robert and Odysseus are in bed!'

Ah. I wouldn't want to disturb her husband. Or King Odysseus, as I liked to call her spoiled three year old.

Jeannie and I had never been close. After I'd turned about five and was no longer as cute to play with, she had started treating me with a general disdain.

'I'm still Mom's favorite,' she used to whisper to me throughout my childhood. 'She'll never love you as much as she loves me.'

But for all our squabbles and differences, I knew that deep down we loved each other. It was just that she had an opinion about *everything* in my life. Her way was *always* the right way, and she couldn't see that she might not always be correct. In fact, we'd barely spoken since I moved to France, because she was horrified that I had left Brett without trying harder to work things out.

'You have to forgive him if he's made one little mistake,' she kept telling me. 'It's not like Robert has always been perfect. At least Brett makes a lot of money and will provide for you. Where do you think you're going to find someone else like that when you're almost thirty?'

Now, since I'd had no choice but to come crawling back to her and stay in her guest room until I figured out what I was going to do, she had basically been proven right. That night, in the immaculately clean, freshly dusted, Febreeze-scented room that had been prepared for me (complete with Jeannie's perfect hospital corners on the beds), I had a bad feeling about how the next few weeks would go. There was no question about it: I needed to find a job and get out of here as soon as I could.

*

'You know, if you had just tried to work things out with Brett, none of this would have happened,' Jeannie said the next morning as I sat sipping coffee and she sat making airplane noises and 'flying' little spoonfuls of Cheerios toward Odysseus's mouth. Upon each landing, he would wave his arms wildly, shriek and knock cereal and milk flying into the air. It was a little hard to take Jeannie seriously when she had soggy o's in her hair, milk splashed on her cheek and a three year old who seemed wholly uninterested in obeying her.

'There was nothing worth working out,' I said with a sigh.

Jeannie blinked at me blankly. 'But you dated him for three years. And he had a *great* job.'

'No Cheerios!' Odysseus screamed at the top of his lungs, sending another spoonful of cereal flying around the kitchen. 'I want chocolate!'

'Odysseus, sweetie, you can have chocolate later,' Jeannie said in a high-pitched baby voice that drove me crazy. At three, Odysseus was old enough to be talked to like a human being rather than a poodle. 'Now it's time for Cheerios! Open wide for the airplane!'

'Waaaaaaaaaaaah!' Odysseus screamed, his little face turning beet red as he waved his chubby arms around. Jeannie sighed and went over to the pantry to get some Cocoa Puffs. The moment Odysseus saw the box, his screams subsided.

I rolled my eyes. 'Jeannie, it doesn't matter that Brett had a great job,' I said once she had commenced with shoveling spoonfuls of Cocoa Puffs into the contented Odysseus's open mouth. '*He* left *me*. Then he started sleeping with Amanda. How am I supposed to be okay with that?'

'Em, you're almost thirty,' Jeannie said, spooning more chocolate balls into Odysseus's mouth. Chocolate-colored milk dribbled down his chin in little rivers. 'You've got to wise up. If your fiancé's looking elsewhere, maybe there's something you're not doing at home.'

'Oh, come on, Jeannie,' I snapped, feeling suddenly angrier at her than I normally did. 'You can't really mean that! I must not have been screwing him enough so he had to go and sleep with Amanda?'

'Not in front of the baby!' Jeannie snapped.

'Screw, screw, screw!' Odysseus repeated in delight, little globs of mushy chocolate shooting every which way.

'Sorry,' I muttered, glancing guiltily at my nephew. 'But seriously, Jeannie. I can't go back to him.'

Jeannie sighed and put down the spoon. She turned away from Odysseus, who immediately knocked over his sippy cup and began eating fallen Cocoa Puffs off his high chair tray by picking them up with his tongue, in between muttering *screw, screw, screw* thoughtfully to himself.

'Emma, I'm just trying to help you here,' she said. 'God knows Mom and Dad don't have anything useful to say. I'm the only one in this family who seems to know how to make a relationship work.'

I decided to change the subject before I was forced to pour the remaining milk-sodden Cocoa Puffs over Jeannie's perfectly sleek, Winter-Park-wife hair. 'So I think I'm going to see if there's an opening at any of the restaurants on Park Avenue,' I said, referring to Winter Park's shopping and restaurant district.

'You want to *waitress*?' Jeannie asked, her voice rising incredulously.

I shrugged. 'I don't know. It's not like I can go back to Boy Bandz. And there's not really a music industry here, you know? I can start applying for PR jobs, but who knows if that will work out?'

'But waitressing?' Jeannie looked at me with what appeared to be disgust. 'At the age of twenty-nine?'

I bit my lip. I was determined not be drawn into an argument.

'Well,' Jeannie said after a moment. 'I suppose it's a good way to meet rich guys. Just make sure to flirt. A lot.'

I rolled my eyes. 'I'm planning to waitress, not husband-hunt,' I said. 'Besides,' I muttered under my breath, 'I think I'm in love with a French guy who hates my guts.'

'What?' asked Jeannie distractedly. She had turned her attention back to Odysseus, who had finished his Cocoa Puffs and was now flinging chocolate-colored milk around the kitchen.

'Nothing,' I said with a sigh.

'Huband-hut! Huband-hut! Huband-hut!' repeated Odysseus, who had apparently been listening more closely than his mother.

By the end of the week, I had landed a lunch-shift job at Frenchy's, a French-American fusion restaurant on Park Avenue. The owner, Pierre, had been fascinated that I'd just returned from Paris and had given me a job on the spot.

'You know Guillaume Riche?' he asked once he looked at my résumé.

I nodded, wondering why I'd even bothered to put the miserably short-lived job on there.

'*Merveilleux!*' he exclaimed, clearly excited. 'He is a huge star! You have heard his new single, *non*?'

Indeed I had. 'Beautiful Girl', the second single from his album, had just been released and was heating up the airwaves. The internet buzz was that Guillaume could have two songs – 'City of Light' and 'Beautiful Girl' – in this week's Billboard Top Ten. It was incredible.

I talked to Poppy every few days; it was the only thing that kept me mentally afloat. Despite the fact that I spent a small fortune on international phone cards at CVS to call her, it made me feel infinitely better to talk to someone I knew was a true friend. And her stories of crazy dates with unsuspecting Frenchmen made me laugh and forget for a moment that I was a lonely boarder in my sister's house, working at a job that just didn't fulfill me the way music PR had.

Poppy would mention Gabe; she had seen him several times since the junket, and she said he always looked dejected. But I suspected she was just saying that to try to cheer me up.

'I can't talk about him,' I finally told her. 'I need to move on. I need to stop thinking about him.'

Of course that was easier said than done, because everything seemed to remind me of him. It seemed like every time I turned on the radio, I heard 'City of Light' or 'Beautiful Girl'. The second song in particular always made me feel empty inside, because the last time I'd heard it was at the junket where everything had fallen apart.

Poppy kept me informed of Guillaume's progress, and the week after I got the new job, I was at Jeannie's one night watching the eleven o'clock news when I saw a clip of Guillaume waterskiing down the Seine with three police boats chasing him. He was, of course, wearing only his top hat and a pair of SpongeBob Squarepants boxers. I giggled a bit to myself and then groaned in empathy with poor Poppy. I thought I'd be glad that I wasn't there to clean up yet another Guillaume Riche mess. But in a way, seeing him grinning and waving at the cameras as he glided illegally down the Seine, just made me miss him – and the job – even more.

'I have no idea how to get him out of this one,' Poppy confided to me when she called in a panic from her cell phone.

'Just say he was out for some exercise and the boat took a wrong turn,' I advised.

'What about his underwear?'

I thought for a moment. 'Say that he thought it was a bathing suit and apologizes for his error.'

'Emma,' Poppy said. 'You're a genius.'

'I don't think that's the word for it,' I muttered.

Two weeks after I'd got back from Paris, I was sitting in the den with Odysseus, watching Saturday morning cartoons and trying to keep him from licking the carpet (which I suspected was because Jeannie had started using a chocolate-scented vacuum powder to make the house smell like she'd been baking all day). He was babbling to himself in nonsense talk, a habit that I thought was sort of worrisome at the age of three but which Jeannie encouraged by babbling in baby talk right back to him.

'Use your words, Odysseus,' I said, keeping my voice quiet so Jeannie wouldn't hear. She always said that criticism would wound a child's fragile sense of self-esteem. Not that it was my business, but I figured that Odysseus's precious self-esteem would be in grave danger anyhow the moment he began goo-gooing and ga-gaing to kids on the playground who had left infant babble behind in their infancy.

'Goo goo blah goo ga blah,' he said defiantly then went back to licking the carpet.

Just then, the doorbell rang.

'Emma, can you get it?' Jeannie's voice rang out from upstairs. 'I'm a bit busy at the moment!'

'No problem!' I shouted back, relieved that I wouldn't have to worry about Odysseus's vacuum powder consumption or lack of language mastery for at least the next few minutes. Not that it was really my problem anyhow. But as his aunt and his godmother, not to mention someone who loved him, I was concerned about a lot of things.

Straightening my wrinkled T-shirt and combing my fingers through my hair (when had I last washed it anyhow? Somehow, I had stopped caring), I walked down the front hallway and pulled open the front door. My jaw dropped when I saw who was standing there in khakis and a button-down shirt, his brown hair neatly combed, his square-jawed face freshly shaved and a bouquet of red roses in his hand.

'Hi, Emma,' Brett said. He looked me up and down for a moment and appeared vaguely confused. I guessed he hadn't expected a rumpled, unwashed, disheveled version of the previous me.

'What are you doing here?' I blurted out.

Granted, it wasn't the most tactfully phrased query. But really. What *was* he doing here, on my sister's doorstep?

'I heard you were back in town,' he said. He appeared to be studying the wrinkles in my shirt with some consternation.

'You *heard*?' I repeated. I stared at him for a moment and sighed in realization. 'Let me guess. Jeannie called you.'

Brett shrugged. 'Yeah, well,' he said. 'She thought I might want to see you.'

'How nice of her.'

Brett paused. 'I, uh, brought you flowers,' he said, holding out the roses.

I stared at them. 'I can see that,' I said flatly. I made no move to take them. Eventually, he lowered them back down to his side.

'You weren't going to call?' Brett shifted uncomfortably from one foot to the other.

'I didn't think we had much to talk about.'

Brett tried one of his charming smiles, the ones that used to win me over. 'I don't know,' he said. 'I think we have a lot to talk about. Can I come in?'

I sighed and thought about it for a moment. 'Fine.' I turned away and let him follow me down the hallway into Jeannie's living room. Not surprisingly, she was already standing there.

'Oh Brett!' she cooed, shooting me a look. 'How very nice to see you!'

'You too, Jeannie,' Brett said. They gave each other European-style pecks on the cheeks, which made me want to laugh. What looked so natural in Paris, looked pretentious and awkward on the two of them. And they had no idea.

'Well, I'll leave the two of you alone,' Jeannie chirped after a moment. 'I'm sure you have a lot to talk about!' She shot me a meaningful look and added, 'I'd forgotten how perfect you two look together!' She clapped her hands together gleefully, shot me one last look and flounced out of the room, yelling, 'Odysseus! Odysseus! Mommy's coming!' in her ridiculous baby-talk voice.

I rolled my eyes. I needed to get out of here.

I sat down on the living-room couch and gestured vaguely and unenthusiastically for Brett to sit on the love-seat opposite me. Instead, he sat down beside me and looked at me with baleful eyes. 'I'm so glad you've come back, baby,' he said. My stomach turned and I scooted away from him. Brett looked insulted. 'Emma, I've never stopped loving you. You know that.'

'Really?' I said sweetly. 'Were you loving me when you were screwing Amanda?'

Brett's eyes widened and he coughed. 'It didn't mean anything.'

I didn't say anything. I just wished he would leave.

Brett looked annoyed. Evidently, this wasn't going the way he had expected. I suspected that Jeannie had probably led Brett to believe that I thought, as she evidently did, that he was the answer to all my prayers. And Brett had been dumb enough to believe that he could dump me, hook up with my friend, and then come back to me to a blanket of full forgiveness.

'So I guess Paris didn't work out,' Brett said after a moment. He looked a little smug. 'You must have been unhappy there.'

'Actually,' I said, 'it was the happiest I've ever been in my life.'

Brett looked surprised. 'What about when you were with me?'

'As I said,' I repeated calmly, 'being in Paris was the happiest I've been in my life.'

He looked completely baffled, as if the thought that the world didn't revolve around him hadn't even crossed his mind. He stared for a long moment and then cleared his throat. 'Look,' he said. 'We've both made some mistakes here. But don't you think it's time to put that all behind us?'

I was about to respond when Jeannie whisked into the room, balancing Odysseus on her hip. He was waving some sort of little plastic truck around, making *vroom-vroom* noises and smacking the back of Jeannie's head every few seconds. She didn't seem to notice.

'Oh, look at you two, sitting side by side!' she cooed. She bounced Odysseus a few times on her hip. 'Look at Auntie Emma and Uncle Brett!' she said in her baby-talk voice, widening her eyes at her son. 'Aren't they *so* cute together!'

Odysseus glanced at us and then went back to whacking his mother on the head with his truck. 'Screw, screw, screw!' he yelled in delight, evidently recalling his breakfast-hour language lesson.

Jeannie reddened. 'Odysseus!' she said. 'We don't say *screw* in this family!' She shot me an evil look, and I shrugged.

'Screw, screw, screw!' Odysseus insisted.

Brett looked embarrassed.

Jeannie put a hand over Odysseus's mouth so that his babbling was muffled. 'You'll have to excuse him,' she said to Brett. 'He hasn't been himself since Emma got here.'

'No problem,' Brett said uncertainly.

'Anyhow,' Jeannie said smoothly, 'have you asked her yet?' She looked at me and raised an eyebrow.

'Asked me what?' I said apprehensively.

Brett nodded at Jeannie and turned to me. 'I wanted to ask you to consider moving back in with me, Emma,' he said. He glanced at Jeannie, who nodded encouragingly. I felt like I was being ganged up on. 'After all, we were perfect together, don't you think?'

'I used to think so,' I muttered after a moment. 'But that was a very long time ago.'

'Please, Emma,' Brett said. He sidled off the couch and awkwardly knelt beside me on one knee, holding the red roses up like a peace offering. I considered the joy I would derive from beating him over the head with them. But since

I had obviously already begun to corrupt poor, innocent Odysseus with my lack of vocabulary control, I figured that attacking a man with flowers wouldn't exactly be the most responsible thing to do in front of him.

'Please what?' I asked wearily.

'Please consider getting back together with me,' Brett said. 'Please consider moving back in.'

I stared at him with pursed lips.

He shifted uncomfortably and lowered the roses. 'At least have dinner with me tonight, Emma,' he pleaded. 'So that I can have a chance to explain.'

I opened my mouth to respond, but as usual, Jeannie was way ahead of me.

'She'd love to,' she said firmly. I started to protest, but she shushed me. 'Why don't you pick her up at seven? I'll make sure she's ready.'

'Perfect,' Brett said, scrambling to his feet. He laid the roses down on the coffee table and made a beeline for the door, before I could protest. 'Bye, Odysseus!' he said cheerfully, stopping to give my nephew a little peck on the top of his head.

Odysseus responded by whacking Brett with his toy truck.

'Huband-hut! Huband-hut! Huband-hut!' he screamed, as Brett rubbed the back of his head in surprise. 'Screw, screw, screw!'

True to his word, Brett was at Jeannie's door at seven that evening, bearing a brand new bouquet of red roses and dressed in charcoal pants, a pale blue button-down shirt and a dark grey tie.

'You look beautiful, Emma,' he said softly.

I smiled tightly. 'Thank you.' I had to admit, he looked

good too. He always had. But I couldn't say that to him.

'This restaurant we're going to in Thornton Park just opened,' he explained, breaking an uncomfortable silence as he drove. 'I think you'll like it. It's like Ruth's Chris, but nicer.'

I bristled at the mention of the upscale steak restaurant where we'd had our first date three years ago. Unexpected tears prickled at the outside corners of my eyes, and I blinked them back quickly.

Forty-five minutes later, we had ordered – medium-well filet mignon for him and medium-rare for me, with asparagus, garlic mashed potatoes and creamed spinach to share – and the waiter had uncorked and poured a bottle of Pinot Noir for us before disappearing into the kitchen.

Brett raised his glass in a toast. 'To us,' he said, looking me straight in the eye.

I hesitated and lowered my glass. 'I can't toast to that.'

Brett stared for a moment, took a long sip of his wine and then set his glass on the table too. 'Why not?' he asked carefully.

'Are you kidding?' I asked. 'Do you seriously not have any idea why I'd basically hate your guts?'

Brett sighed. 'Emma. You don't *hate* me. Do you?' His eyes were sad, and his regret looked almost genuine. He took another sip of his wine. 'Look, I know how much I hurt you. I know I will always regret it. More than I could ever tell you.'

I shook my head. 'I don't think you regret it at all.'

Brett looked upset. 'That's not true, Emma,' he said. He stared at me. 'Look, it was the biggest mistake I've made in my life.'

'Yeah, well, maybe it was for the best,' I muttered. I took

a long sip of my wine and wished I was anywhere but here. Why had I agreed to this?

'Please, Emma, you need to listen to me,' Brett said. He reached across the table and put a hand on my arm. 'I am so sorry. More sorry than you can possibly imagine. I love you, Emma. I do. I always have. I just got scared, that's all.'

I considered his words. It was the same explanation Jeannie had given me, and in a way, it made sense. 'But if you were scared,' I said slowly, 'why didn't you talk to me? Why didn't you ask to postpone the wedding or something? Why did you dump me and basically just throw me out of your house?'

Brett looked miserable. 'Geez, Emma, I don't know,' he said. 'I've been through this a thousand times in my head. There's just no excuse. All I can say is that I've regretted it every day since. I didn't think I was ready to get married yet, but I am, Emma. I am. Losing you made me realize that.'

I could feel the ice beginning to melt on the outside of my heart. I couldn't forgive him – how could I? – but maybe I could find a way to accept his apology and move on. After all, this was my life now, wasn't it? It wasn't like Gabe Francoeur was going to come walking through the door to sweep me off my feet. I was stuck living in my condescending sister's guest room, estranged from every friend I'd made in this city. That was no way to live.

Our food arrived, and we ate in silence for a few minutes. I could feel Brett watching me between bites.

'Why Amanda?' I asked softly after a while.

Brett swallowed hard but didn't look surprised. He had to have known the question was coming.

'I can't tell you how much I regret that,' he said carefully, his voice soft. He looked straight into my eyes. 'There is no excuse, Emma. I freaked out, and she was right there, and I fell into something I shouldn't have. It was all my fault, and it was a huge, huge mistake.'

'It wasn't *all* your fault,' I mumbled, thinking that it takes two to tango, as the saying goes.

'Well, I should have known better,' Brett said. 'Especially with one of your best friends. I'm so ashamed.'

I took another sip of wine and considered his words. Despite the fact that I'd only taken three bites of my steak, I wasn't hungry any more.

'I'd like to go now,' I said.

Brett looked up in surprise. 'But we're not done eating,' he said.

'I know,' I said. 'I just don't want to be here any more.'

He studied my face then nodded. 'Okay,' he said. 'I know this is hard for you. I appreciate you even giving me the opportunity to explain myself.'

I nodded. I was surprised by how genuine he seemed, and the hatred and anger I'd been clinging to for the last two months were beginning to seem pointless. Yes, he'd hurt me more deeply than I ever would have imagined. But he seemed genuinely sorry and repentant. And it wasn't like *I'd* never made a mistake. If I didn't at least consider his explanation and his apology, wasn't I being just as blind as Gabe?

Thinking of the French reporter – and his refusal to take my calls after the whole incident with Guillaume – made me feel suddenly ill. I excused myself and made it to the restaurant bathroom just in time to throw up what little I had eaten.

That week, I went out twice more with a repentant Brett, and he even stopped by Frenchy's one day at lunch to bring me white lilies, my favorite. There was no doubt that he was doing everything he could to win me back. I just hadn't made up my mind yet.

After all, on the one hand, I'd been so sure two months ago that he was The One that I'd been gleefully planning a wedding with him. Had he not freaked out on me, I probably never would have considered leaving him. Our wedding would be mere weeks away.

But on the other hand, his leaving me had forced me to look at all the things that were wrong with our relationship. He was, at times, condescending and overbearing. He often didn't listen to me and sometimes treated me like a child. But all in all, our relationship hadn't been bad. I knew he loved me – or at least he had, for a time. He seemed to be genuine in his proclamations of love for me now.

Maybe he *had* just made a mistake. Maybe he *did* deserve another chance.

'Are you seriously considering getting back together with

him?' Poppy demanded the day after I'd been out with Brett for the third time. I had finally called to tell her, sheepishly, knowing that she wouldn't react well to the news.

'I don't know,' I mumbled. 'Maybe he deserves another chance.'

'Emma,' Poppy said slowly. 'Perhaps you don't remember. He cheated on you. With your best friend.'

'No,' I protested. 'He didn't exactly cheat. He didn't get together with her until after we broke up. Besides, maybe he just made a mistake. You should see how hard he's trying.'

Poppy made a snorting sound.

'Besides,' I added, 'you've forgiven Darren, haven't you?'

Although she'd still been going out on French-kissing dates here and there, Poppy had been seeing her British ex regularly since the London junket, and I knew that she was beginning to think more seriously about calling off her whole mission to date as many Parisian men as possible.

Poppy was silent for a long moment. 'Emma, it's a different situation,' she said quietly. 'Darren and I both did a lot to hurt each other. We both made mistakes. And who knows what will happen now? We haven't made any decisions. We're just seeing where things go.'

'Maybe that's all I'm doing too,' I said defensively.

'But Emma,' Poppy said, 'it's different. Brett moved on *by sleeping with your best friend*. And you weren't just dating, you were engaged. He kicked you out of *your* house.'

'So?' I asked in a small voice.

'So,' Poppy said gently. 'Don't you wonder what's motivating him now? Why has he changed his mind so quickly? It just doesn't feel right to me.'

*

The day after I talked to Poppy, Brett took me out to dinner again, this time to Seasons 52, a restaurant I loved down on Sand Lake Road. He booked my favorite table alongside the lake out back, and he ordered a bottle of my favorite wine – a smooth petite syrah – and the artichoke and goat cheese flatbread, which I adored.

'See, babe?' he said, after we had started sipping our wine. 'I remember exactly what you like. We just *fit*.'

But Poppy's words had been gnawing away at me for the last twenty-four hours.

'Why?' I asked slowly.

Brett looked confused. 'Why what?'

'Why do we fit?' I asked slowly. 'Why do you think we're so perfect together? And why are you so intent on getting back together with me?'

'Because I love you,' Brett answered promptly. 'Because I made a huge mistake. C'mon, Emma, we've been over this. You know how much I care. You know how I feel.'

I thought for a moment. 'What about your parents?' I asked. 'They never thought I was good enough for you, did they? They wanted you to marry some Ivy League girl or something.'

'That's not true,' Brett said.

'Yes, it is,' I said. 'I know it is. They've always acted like I was a disappointment. Like you could do so much better.'

'Well, why are they so eager to have me get back together with you, then?' Brett asked triumphantly.

I stared at him in surprise. 'Your parents *want* us to get back together?' I had just assumed that Operation Win-Emma-Back had been a secret from them.

Brett nodded vigorously. 'Yes! They've even invited you over to dinner this week. They're thrilled about us.'

'They are?'

Brett nodded again. 'They were mortified when we broke up,' he said. 'They said it made the family look bad. They even stopped paying me my allowance.'

'Your *allowance*?'

Brett blinked a few times, turning scarlet. 'Um, yeah,' he said. 'I guess I never told you. But they gave me some money every month. Something about a tax write-off.'

'How *much* money?' I asked slowly, thinking of all the times Brett had insisted we split the check fifty-fifty when we went out to eat.

Brett paused. 'Five thousand dollars.'

I dropped my fork.

'A *month*?' I asked, my voice cracking as it went up several octaves.

Brett nodded and had the decency to look embarrassed.

I digested this for a moment. 'And they've stopped paying you this allowance?' I repeated. I was starting to feel a little sick. 'Until you get me back?'

Brett nodded again, not seeming to realize he was talking himself into a hole. 'They called it their "grandbaby fund".' He chuckled. 'They're ready for us to get married and start having kids, Emma. I mean, if that doesn't prove to you how much they care about you, I don't know what will.'

'Brett,' I said patiently. 'That's doesn't mean they care about *me*. That means that they care about how our broken engagement made *them* look. And they care about being grandparents. I'm just the quickest route to that.'

Brett tilted his head to the side. 'That's not true. They love you, Emma. Just like I do.'

'Do you really?' I asked flatly. 'Or are you just trying to get me back so that you can win back your allowance?'

Brett opened and closed his mouth, fish-like. 'I can't believe you'd even ask that,' he said after a moment.

Just then, my cell phone rang. Grateful for an excuse to escape the conversation momentarily, I dove for it.

'You're going to answer your phone in the middle of dinner?' Brett made a face.

'Yes,' I said. I checked the caller ID. *Unavailable*. It could be a sales call, for all I knew, but at least it would give me a temporary escape. 'It's an important call.'

I stood up and walked away from the table toward the outside bar area. Knowing that Brett was watching me, I sank down into a lounge chair with my back to him and pressed *send* to answer.

'Emma?' It was Poppy, and she sounded excited. 'Where are you?'

'Out to dinner with Brett,' I mumbled.

'What?'

'Don't ask.' I sighed. 'So what's up? It's late over there, isn't it?' I did the mental math. If it was eight thirty in Florida, that made it two thirty in the morning in Paris. 'Is everything okay?'

'Everything's fine,' Poppy said. I could hear the smile in her voice. 'I'm not in Paris, actually. I'm in your time zone.'

I sat up straight in my lounge chair. 'What? Where?'

'In New York!' Poppy said gleefully.

'In New York?' I repeated. 'What are you doing there?'

'Turns out that Guillaume's waterskiing incident was a success after all,' Poppy said. 'We got calls from all sorts of American media outlets. We just got in tonight, and we're scheduled to do *Today with Katie Jones* tomorrow and *Good Morning America* on Friday!'

'You're kidding!' I exclaimed. 'Poppy, that's wonderful! Why didn't you tell me sooner?'

'I wanted to surprise you,' she said.

'Surprise me?'

She paused. 'I was hoping you would come up and join us.'

My heart sank. 'I'd love to, Poppy. But I can't afford the trip up there now. You know that.'

'Well,' Poppy said. 'Let me put it this way. I've already booked an airline ticket in your name, and you have a room at the Hyatt Grand Central. You'd fly up tomorrow morning, so you'll only have to take a day off work. Frankly, you'd be silly not to come.'

'Poppy—' I started to protest, but she cut me off.

'Emma, Guillaume paid for all of it out of his pocket,' she said. 'He still feels terrible about what happened – as well he should. So you might as well get a free trip on his dime!'

I considered it. She *did* have a point. And if the ticket was already purchased . . .

'All right,' I said slowly. 'I guess I'll be there, then.'

'Brilliant!' Poppy exclaimed. 'Be at the Katie Jones studio on Broadway and Fifty-third at noon tomorrow. I'll leave a ticket for you. We'll have dinner after the show!'

'That sounds wonderful,' I said warmly. 'I don't know how to thank you.'

'I know how you can thank me,' Poppy said.

'How?'

'Come to your senses and walk away from Brett before you get sucked back in,' she said. 'I know you feel like you're lonely and stuck there, Emma. But don't fall back into that. Please.'

I thought about it for a moment. 'You're right,' I said softly.

'Good girl,' Poppy said. 'I'll see you tomorrow, Emma. *Au revoir* for now!'

I sat there for a moment after I hung up. What was I doing? How had I come to a place where I thought Brett was once again the answer to everything? Three weeks' worth of Jeannie's get-back-together-with-him-you-idiot diatribes had turned me into someone different, and the hopelessness of my situation had made me desperate and needy.

But I'd become someone else during my brief time in Paris. Or, more accurately, I'd looked inside for the first time and gotten in touch with *me*. It wasn't the job or the meaningless dates, or even the self-destructive crush I'd had on Gabe. It was that, for the first time in more than three years, I'd learned that being alone really wasn't so bad.

I took a deep breath, stood up and walked back to our table.

'That was really rude, Emma,' Brett said, shaking his head. 'I never answer calls during dinner.'

I looked at him. 'Brett, you used to answer your phone all the time while we were eating.'

'That's different,' he said. 'Those were work calls.'

'Well, actually, this was a work call too.'

'What, that restaurant was calling you?' Brett smirked. 'Important waitress business?'

'No, Poppy was calling,' I said. 'About Guillaume Riche.'

'I thought you were fired from that job.'

I nodded. 'But maybe it's time to fight for what I deserve,' I said. I paused. I was still standing beside the table, and Brett was beginning to look uncomfortable.

'Aren't you going to sit back down, Emma?' he asked. 'People are looking.'

I ignored him. 'I need to ask you something,' I said. '*Why* do you want to get back together with me?'

Brett looked confused. 'Because I love you.'

'Why?' I persisted. '*Why* do you love me?'

'I don't know.' He looked uneasy. 'I just do.'

'Why?' I persisted. 'I mean, why me? Why me instead of Amanda?'

'Let's not bring her into this,' he mumbled.

'I think you already brought her in,' I said with a shrug.

Brett had the decency to look embarrassed. 'I don't know, Emma,' he said, sounding exasperated. 'I love you because you've always been there. I love you because you know me and put up with me. I love you because I know you will be a good mother to our children. I love you because we're perfect together. I don't know what else you want me to say.'

I looked at him for a moment. None of his reasons for loving me had anything to do with *me*. They never had, had they?

'You were right,' I said finally.

Brett nodded, as if this was a given. 'About what?'

'About us.'

Brett smiled. 'Good. Finally! You've seen things my way. So do you want to move back in? Or should we take things slow?'

I shook my head. 'No, I mean you were right the first time.'

'What?'

'When you said we weren't right together. When you kicked me out.'

'Now, wait a minute, Emma.' Brett held up his hand

impatiently and gaped. 'You're being ridiculous here.'

'No,' I said. I shook my head sadly. 'I was being ridiculous to even consider getting back together with you.'

Brett stared at me in disbelief. 'Emma, you're making a huge mistake. Do you know what you're saying?'

'Yes, I do,' I said slowly and calmly. 'I don't want to be with you.'

Brett just stared at me, as if he couldn't understand what he was hearing. 'You're not going to find anyone better than me, you know. Not at your age.'

For some reason, I thought of Gabe, who I quite possibly would never hear from again.

'You know, I think I already have,' I said softly.

I took a cab home, and the moment I walked in the door, Jeannie cornered me in the front hallway.

'Brett called,' she said, putting her hands on her hips and glaring at me.

'Did he? How nice. Did you have a nice chat?'

Jeannie ignored me. 'Do you know what you just did?' she asked, her eyes wide. Upstairs, Odysseus began wailing something unintelligible. Jeannie didn't seem to hear.

'Yes, I know exactly what I did,' I responded calmly. 'I told Brett I didn't want to get back together with him.' I wasn't sure why a recap was necessary, as Jeannie had clearly been filled in already.

'Emma!' Jeannie exclaimed with dismay. 'Why? He's perfect for you!'

I looked at her blankly. 'Why do you say that?' I asked finally. 'Why do you think he's so perfect?'

Jeannie looked a bit taken aback. 'I don't know. Because he's hot and he makes good money?' she said after a moment. 'And he's a pretty nice guy. I mean, really, what more can you ask for?'

I nodded slowly, feeling deeply grateful that although we'd come from the same set of parents, somehow I'd grown up with a completely different set of values. 'Yes, Jeannie,' I said softly. I looked her right in the eye. 'But he's not capable of loving me even remotely as much as he loves himself,' I said. 'And I want to be with someone who loves me and wants what's best for me. Brett will never be that person, because all Brett cares about is Brett.'

Jeannie pursed her lips. 'You are making a *huge* mistake,' she said. 'One of these days, you're going to have to learn that adulthood is about not always getting what you want, you know.' Then, as if my decision not to give Brett another chance was a personal affront to her, she spun on her heel and stormed upstairs.

21

Poppy had booked me on the 7.20 a.m. to LaGuardia, and thanks to traffic it was nearly noon when I arrived at the Katie Jones studio for the two o'clock taping. By the time I was seated, my nerves were fully on edge, but I couldn't explain why. It unsettled me to think of seeing Guillaume again. I'd been trying hard to put what had happened behind me, but he was, of course, at the center of it all.

I felt conspicuously alone as I waited for the show to begin.

'You all by yourself?' asked the overweight man to my right, who was so large that he was sitting in both his seat and half of mine, wedging me against my left armrest. Thankfully, I was on an aisle, so at least I wasn't squashed against a person on the other side too.

I forced a smile. 'Yes.'

'A pretty girl like you?' he asked, the words pouring out in a syrupy drawl. Beside him, his wife giggled and looked at me. 'You don't got no friends?'

I gritted my teeth. 'They're just not sitting with me,' I said.

The man snickered and said something to his wife. I rolled my eyes. It seemed the whole world was in cahoots with Jeannie to remind me of the error of my lonely ways.

The show began at two, and I settled in to watch as Katie Jones opened with a monologue that the Texan next to me found so funny that he shook the whole row of seats with his chortles every few seconds. I was relieved when the jokes were over.

The second half of the show opened with an interview with movie star Cole Brannon, who was starring in the most anticipated release of the summer. When Katie finished talking to the tall, handsome actor, she turned to the camera.

'Hang on, because after the break, we have France's craziest export, Guillaume Riche, who will be playing his top ten hit, "City of Light",' she said, reaching one hand up to smooth her perfect brunette bob. 'And maybe if we're lucky, he'll tell us what it's like to waterski down the Seine in SpongeBob SquarePants boxers and a top hat!'

The crowd laughed, and the house lights went up as the show went to commercial break. I scanned the room for Poppy, but I couldn't find her. On the darkened stage, a crew hurried to set up a drum kit, mics and amps that would be used for Guillaume's performance in a moment. I caught sight of Jean-Marc, Guillaume's drummer, and my heart leapt into my throat. I missed those guys more than I had realized.

After the break, the spotlight shone back on Katie Jones. She grinned into the camera and said dramatically, 'Ladies and gentlemen, Guillaume Riche!'

My heart began to thud wildly the moment the stage lights flashed on, revealing Guillaume standing there. He looked more handsome than ever. He was wearing a button-up shirt with the sleeves ripped just above the biceps to show off his impressive arms, and his tight jeans emphasised the sculptured curves of his legs. His hair was professionally tousled into perfect little wayward spikes; he looked as if he had just got out of bed, clean-shaven and flawless. The guitar he was currently strumming was the perfect last touch; it was emblazoned with the French flag, and the Jodi Head strap said *Riche* down the front in bold, Swarovski crystal letters.

As the crowd went wild with screams and whistles, I smiled. Guillaume Riche had crossed the pond for his first American appearance as a ready-made superstar. The crowds loved him. In fact, there was a girl in front of me who was screaming so loudly that I was fairly sure she was about to hyperventilate. Although I was no longer working with KMG, I felt a little swell of pride for the small role I'd played in his career. This felt better than all the boy bands I'd ever helped unleash on the world.

The band started playing, and when Guillaume started in on the first verse of 'City of Light', I was stunned to hear a chorus of voices in the auditorium join in. Guillaume looked moderately surprised too, but he grinned broadly and turned the enthusiasm up a notch. Around me, scores of girls were on their feet, singing in unison with Guillaume. It was an incredible thing to see. In that moment, I missed working with Poppy so much it hurt; I missed KMG; I missed the buzz and excitement of working on a project that was bound for such success. I even missed Guillaume.

'City of Light' ended with a standing ovation from the crowd, and then Katie Jones joined Guillaume at the mic and promised the audience they'd be back after the break to talk to Guillaume about his breakout success and his penchant for getting into crazy situations.

After the brief commercial break, the house lights faded again, and the spotlights swung toward Katie's interview area, where Guillaume was sitting, one leg crossed over the other, holding a coffee mug and looking very French. I felt another pang that I tried to dismiss.

The crowd went wild for a moment while Guillaume laughed and waved with his free hand. Finally, the screams quieted.

'That's quite a reaction you're getting,' Katie said with her signature slow, toothy grin.

Guillaume smiled back. 'I'm a lucky, lucky man,' he said. A few girls in the audience screamed again, and Guillaume obliged them with another wave.

'Some would say it's talent and not luck,' Katie said. She glanced at her note cards. 'Okay, so it looks like your album is really doing great in the US, right?'

'Yes. It's such a thrill,' Guillaume said. I smiled. They sounded like words right out of Poppy's mouth – and I suspected they were. 'I'm really grateful that everyone is listening to my music. I've always wanted to be a big hit with the American girls.'

The crowd erupted in screams again, and Guillaume blew a few kisses. 'I love American girls, Katie,' he said over the din. 'Too bad you're married.'

Katie smiled again and shook her head. 'So I have to ask you,' she said. 'What's with all these crazy stunts? You were arrested for skiing on the river in Paris last week. And you've gotten locked in the Eiffel Tower? Is that right?'

Guillaume glanced offstage, where I suspected Poppy was standing, shooting him death looks. 'Well, Katie, the

Eiffel Tower thing was a mistake,' he said. I breathed a sigh of relief. Good; he was sticking to the story. 'It was all a misunderstanding. But yes, I admit that the waterskiing thing was a little crazy.'

The audience laughed and Guillaume made an embarrassed face. 'I guess I just felt like having a ski, you know?' he said, widening his eyes into that same puppy dog look of innocence he had tried with me. The audience seemed to eat it right up.

They talked for a moment more about the next single on the album, the inspiration for his songs and his plans for a US tour in the fall. Then Katie peered down at her notes.

'Okay, so Guillaume, I've been told that you have some sort of public apology to make tonight,' she said.

My heart skipped a beat and I sat up a little straighter in my chair (which was hard to do with the Texan sharing my seating space).

'Yes, Katie,' Guillaume said, pulling a slightly sheepish face that I suspected he had practiced in the mirror to achieve maximum cuteness. It worked. 'I'm afraid I've been a bit of a fuck-up.'

The audience laughed, and Katie reminded Guillaume that he couldn't talk like that on American TV. 'I guess that'll be bleeped out,' Katie said with a smile, glancing at the camera.

'Sorry, sorry,' Guillaume said, not looking sorry at all. 'Anyhow. The thing is, I had this great publicist, Emma, for a month.'

My jaw dropped and time seemed to slow down around me.

'She was the only one who seemed to be able to get me out of scrapes without getting too mad at me,' Guillaume continued. I could barely hear him over the rushing sound in my ears. I knew that my face had turned beet red, although of course no one in the audience knew that I was the person he was talking about. Guillaume went on, 'Somehow, she always made it so I came out looking good.'

'She sounds perfect,' Katie said. 'I need a publicist like that.' The audience laughed lightly, and she added, 'So, what's the problem?'

Guillaume looked sheepish. 'Well, the thing is, she liked this reporter named Gabriel, and I *knew* she did,' he said.

'Oh no,' I muttered to myself, prompting a strange look from my Texan seatmate. I barely noticed. My face felt hot and my palms felt suddenly sweaty. Had Guillaume really just announced to the *entire country* that I had an inappropriate crush on a journalist? And this was supposed to make me feel *better*? I wanted to shrink into my seat and disappear.

'Oh really?' Katie prompted, leaning forward with some interest.

'Yes,' Guillaume said, the same sheepish expression on his face.

'Please stop talking,' I muttered under my breath. 'Please stop talking.' But Guillaume apparently wasn't listening to me. The only one who seemed to respond to my words was the Texan who finally scooted an inch or two away from me and gave me a look like he was afraid I was insane.

Onstage, Guillaume continued, undeterred by the *please shut up* mental messages I was furiously sending him. 'See, the thing is, I've been basically trying to screw with Gabe for the last thirty years,' he said.

Wait. What? Thirty years? What was he talking about?

'I'm a bit of a jerk,' Guillaume continued. 'But the thing

is, this time, it actually mattered. It wasn't just harmless. I actually effed things up with Emma and Gabe.'

'Why is it you've been trying to screw things up with this Gabe for the last thirty years?' Katie prompted. Good question, Katie, I thought.

Guillaume shrugged, a mischievous expression playing across his perfect features. 'Ah, it's silly really,' he said. 'It's our stupid brotherly rivalry.'

I gasped. 'Huh?' I said aloud. I couldn't understand what Guillaume was talking about.

'See, he's my half-brother,' Guillaume continued on stage.

'*What?*' I breathed.

Beside me, the Texan was staring at me with alarm. 'You crazy or something, lady?' he asked. He scooted even closer to his wife. I barely noticed.

'But he grew up in the United States with his mom,' Guillaume continued. 'He's a year and a half older than me. So when he'd come spend summers with our dad and me, all the girls went for him since he was bigger, stronger – and half-American. Even all those summer months he spent teaching me to speak better English, and I was still just the boring French kid next door.' Guillaume paused and grinned. 'It's why I had to join a band,' he quipped. 'It's the only way I was ever going to get laid with Gabe around every summer.'

The audience laughed at his joke, but all I could do was stare, my jaw hanging open. 'They're *brothers*?' I whispered to myself. How could it be? How had Gabe never mentioned any of this to me? But it certainly explained a lot – like how Gabe knew so much about Guillaume's background, how he always seemed to know what Guillaume was doing, and how he was the only one who seemed to effortlessly see through my lies about Guillaume's odd behavior.

I thought about it for a moment. Although I never would have put two and two together, it made so much sense. They *did* look alike. But while Guillaume wore his dark hair spiky and sexy, Gabe wore his combed and professional. Where Guillaume's green eyes were framed by thick, dark eyelashes, Gabe's were hidden behind his omnipresent wire-rimmed glasses, but they were more similar than I'd ever realized. Where Guillaume flaunted his body in curve-hugging rock-star wear, Gabe tended to the more professional and reserved, but I suspected that their builds were more similar under those clothes than I had considered. Even their accents when speaking English were similar, although Guillaume's was thicker. Obviously, this could be explained by the fact that they shared a father and that much of Guillaume's English had come from Gabe's tutelage.

Katie was talking as I tuned back in, still riveted by the revelation. 'So,' she was saying, 'I hear from producers that this brother of yours is actually here backstage right now. Can we bring him out?'

I could feel my eyes widen as Gabe, looking even more handsome than I remembered, came striding reluctantly out from stage left, looking embarrassed. He was dressed casually in dark jeans and a gray T-shirt that actually showed off contours of his arms and chest that I had never noticed before under his stiff, button-up shirts. He had never looked better to me.

A producer guided him to the chair beside Guillaume's and quickly clipped a little microphone on the collar of his shirt before scurrying away.

'Hi, big brother,' Guillaume said. Gabe just glared at him. 'Gabe, I'm so sorry. I really am.'

I held my breath as the cameras zoomed in on Gabe's face. Overhead on the monitors, I could see his jaw set. His eyes darted nervously around. I knew he didn't like being the center of attention, and he was obviously uncomfortable on the stage.

'It's fine,' Gabe muttered.

'No, Gabe, it's not,' Guillaume said. The cameras zoomed in on his face, and he looked genuinely upset, although I wouldn't have put it past him to have practiced his remorseful face in the mirror for hours before his TV appearance. 'Emma's a great girl. And I screwed it up for you, before you even had a chance to make a move on her.'

'Yeah, thanks for telling the world that I didn't make a move,' Gabe said, rolling his eyes.

The audience laughed a bit, and Gabe reddened. I felt terrible for him. I couldn't shake the feeling that this was largely my fault.

Guillaume grinned devilishly. 'Speaking of that, Gabe, you have to learn to stop being so shy and actually ask out the women you like.'

The studio audience laughed again, and Gabe blushed as deeply as I suspected I was currently blushing. I felt suddenly short of breath.

'You're not helping your case here, Guillaume.' Gabe looked down at his lap, a grimace playing across his features.

Guillaume shrugged. 'Look, I just wanted to apologize to you. You won't take my calls, so this was my last resort. Listen, no matter how it looked, nothing happened between me and Emma. She was actually in my room talking about *you* when I leaned over and kissed her. It was my fault, not hers.'

Gabe looked up at him, and for the first time there was something in his expression that wasn't embarrassment or anger.

Guillaume continued. 'And Emma, wherever you are,' he said, looking directly into the camera. I sat up in my seat and stared at the monitor above me. 'I owe you an apology too. Now listen to me. I want you to give my brother here a chance, okay? And once you two have worked things out, I need you to come back and be my publicist again. I'll fix everything with KMG. I can't seem to stop getting myself into trouble. I need you.'

The audience laughed again, and I sat there, stunned, frozen to my seat.

Katie, an eyebrow arched, interjected. 'Okay, Gabe, now is there anything you want to say to Emma?'

Gabe turned even redder and shook his head. The audience groaned, and Guillaume looked delighted at his brother's discomfort.

'Come on, big brother, you're on national television in America,' Guillaume urged. 'It's the perfect opportunity to finally make that move on the girl, for once in your life.'

I felt mortified for poor Gabe. But at the same time, I hoped he'd say something. After all, I had no idea how he felt. Would he forgive me? Or was he just as angry at me as he had been?

'Okay,' Gabe said, taking a deep breath. I leaned forward in my seat, my heart pounding. 'I'd just like to tell her . . .' His voice trailed off, and he paused for a moment. Then he looked straight into the camera, and above me on the monitor, it looked like he was talking directly to me. 'I'd like to tell her that I'm sorry I didn't take the time to listen and realize that this was just Guillaume being a jerk again.' He paused and looked at his lap. When he looked up again, his cheeks were a little flushed. 'And also, I think I might be in love with her.'

There was a collective '*Awwww!*' from the audience. I felt like I couldn't breathe. He *loved* me?

'Hey now, watch it, big brother!' Guillaume said with a grin.

'All right guys, you can kiss and make up over the break,' Katie said with a grin. She turned to the camera and added, 'Stay right here to see Guillaume perform "Beautiful Girl", the second single off his album, when we come back.'

The Katie Jones house band played a few chords, and the house lights came back up. I watched, rooted to my seat, as Gabe unhooked his mic, said something to Guillaume and strode offstage.

'Emma?' said a voice above me. I looked slowly up to see Poppy there, smiling down at me. 'Gabe is backstage. Come on.'

I stared up at her.

'You . . . you knew about this?'

Poppy nodded and smiled.

'Guillaume has been planning this for the last week,' she said. 'He really does feel bad. But it went even better than I thought! Did you hear Gabe? He said he loved you!'

I felt like I was in a fog as I got silently to my feet and followed her. The Texan next to me shifted, looked up at me and muttered to his wife, 'Where does she think she's goin'?'

It wasn't until Poppy had shown her pass and we had slipped through a backstage door that I finally found my voice again.

'Poppy,' I said, still feeling very confused. 'Does Gabe know I'm here?'

'No.' Poppy grinned. 'But he's about to find out.'

Poppy led me to the area behind stage left, where I could see Guillaume and his band onstage, getting ready for the show to come back from commercial break so they could launch into 'Beautiful Girl'. Between me and Guillaume, just ten feet away, stood Gabe, with his back to us, watching Guillaume from the wings. I wished I knew what he was thinking. I studied his broad back for a moment, my heart pounding as I tried to think what I'd say to him. I felt nervous and unsure. I stopped dead in my tracks, suddenly paralyzed and rooted to the spot.

Just then, Guillaume, who was adjusting his mic stand, glanced over and spotted me.

'Emma!' he exclaimed in surprise. He grinned and waved.

Gabe whipped his head round and stared. 'You're here,' he said softly after a moment, shock playing across his features.

Before I could respond, the stage lights came back on and I could see Katie Jones standing on the stage.

'Here he is again, ladies and gentleman, Guillaume Riche!' she said enthusiastically. Guillaume's band immediately launched into 'Beautiful Girl', and, still grinning, Guillaume turned his attention away from me and began singing. Gabe continued to stare at me for a moment, then he shoved his hands in his pockets and took a few steps closer.

'Hi,' he said softly. Onstage, Guillaume glanced over and gave us the thumbs-up sign before he went back to the song.

'Hi,' I said nervously. We both stood there in silence for a moment. I was dimly aware that Guillaume was playing, but suddenly everything around me – the music, the bright lights, the people who were beginning to whisper and stare at us – faded into the background. I felt like I was in one of those films where everything is fuzzy and blurred except for the characters in the middle of the scene.

Gabe and I stood looking at each other for what felt like an eternity. A lump had risen in my throat, and I could feel tears prickling at the backs of my eyes. My cheeks were hot, and my heart was pounding. Everything seemed suspended. Then Gabe reached out and touched my arm.

'I'm sorry,' I blurted out, the spell broken. 'I'm so sorry, Gabe. I never meant to do anything to hurt you.'

Gabe studied my face for a moment while my heart pounded double-time. I didn't know what he'd say. Was he trying to decide whether he could forgive me? Whether he could forget what had happened? After all, even though it seemed that Guillaume had conjured the whole situation to get under Gabe's skin, the fact remained that I *had* kissed his brother.

'No,' Gabe said after a moment. '*I'm* sorry. I'm sorry I didn't give you a chance to explain.' He glanced toward the stage for a moment, where Guillaume was playing his heart out to a backdrop of screams from the audience. 'I'm so used to Guillaume getting the girl – for the last ten years, at least – that I just assumed it had happened again.'

'But it didn't,' I whispered.

Gabe gave me a small smile. 'I know,' he said. 'I mean I know that now. But he and I are pretty competitive, and, well, let's just say that the rock star usually trumps the reporter every time in situations like this one.'

I smiled. It didn't take a rocket scientist to figure out that most girls would be more attracted to a flirtatious rock star than a quiet journalist.

But I wasn't most girls.

'I'm sorry too,' I said. 'I never should have let Guillaume kiss me. I . . . it's a lousy excuse, but it was the champagne talking, not me.'

Gabe nodded and touched my arm again softly. I knew he understood. We looked at each other for a moment and then we both turned our attention to Guillaume, who was still making his way through the verses of 'Beautiful Girl' on stage. After a moment, he glanced over at us and grinned.

'So, doesn't this violate some sort of professional ethics?' I asked carefully. 'You covering your brother for the UPP, I mean?'

Gabe shrugged. 'Maybe. But my editor has known about it since day one. The thing is, I've been the chief music reporter for the UPP in Europe for the last five years, way before Guillaume signed a record deal. It wouldn't make sense to take me off a big story like this one.'

'Even if you have an obvious bias?' I persisted.

Gabe smiled. 'If you've noticed, I've been nothing but fair in my articles,' he said. 'Even when I wanted to kill my brother, I still stuck to the facts. As for the reviews about his album, my editor wrote all that. We *did* decide it wasn't fair for me to pass judgement on him.'

I nodded slowly. 'So what now?' I asked as Guillaume launched into the chorus.

Gabe studied my face. 'Will you move back to Paris?' he asked softly. 'Guillaume will make sure you get your job back. I'll fix things between KMG and the UPP. You can pick up where you left off.' He paused and I could see his cheeks turn a bit pink. 'And maybe,' he added in an embarrassed mutter, 'you and I can give things a try and see what happens without my brother getting in the way.'

I gazed up at him for a moment. There suddenly wasn't a doubt in my mind that I'd do it. After all, I'd left Paris because I'd been sure that my own professional error had led to bad press for the star I was being paid to promote. But now that I knew it hadn't been my fault – or at least that it had only been about ten per cent my fault – I knew that I could take the job back in good conscience.

But suddenly, for no reason at all, Brett popped into my mind. Not because I had any interest whatsoever in him. But because the fact that he had always refused to leave Orlando – and his comfort zone – for me was still an open wound.

'What if I want to stay in Orlando?' I heard myself asking Gabe. It was a stupid question; staying in Orlando wasn't even a consideration. But somehow, I needed to hear what Gabe would say.

He looked startled. He thought about it for a moment. 'Well,' he said finally. 'I suppose there's a UPP bureau there I could find a job with.'

I stared at him. 'You would leave Paris?'

He considered this for a moment. 'Paris is my home,' he said. 'But it will always be there. And you might not be. I want to see where things can go with you. And if you want to stay in Orlando, well then, I guess I'll see about moving to Orlando. We could figure something out.'

I felt breathless. Gabe, who I'd only known for a couple of months, was saying the words I never would have heard in a million years from Brett, who I'd been so sure loved me.

'No,' I said finally. 'I'll come back to Paris.'

'Good.' Gabe breathed a sigh of relief and grinned. He glanced at Guillaume. 'Because my idiot brother clearly needs you to keep him out of trouble.'

I laughed. 'That's true. Plus, Paris *is* the most romantic city in the world.'

Gabe rolled his eyes. 'Yes,' he said. 'Guillaume told me all about how you and Poppy are on the hunt for the perfect French kiss.'

I could feel myself blushing. It sounded stupid when he put it that way.

'But do you know who kisses better than Frenchmen?' Gabe continued.

'No,' I said, startled. Why would Gabe be suggesting that there was someone out there who kissed better than his countrymen?

Gabe grinned. 'French-American men,' he said. Then he leaned down to touch his lips lightly to mine. Everything in my body began to tingle.

If I'd thought that the rest of the world had been fuzzy when we were staring at each other a few moments ago, this was a whole new ball game. Everything faded away as my lips parted and Gabe's kiss grew more passionate. It was, in fact, the perfect French kiss, the one I'd been searching for at Poppy's insistence. It had been right here, with Gabe Francoeur, all along.

Gabe pulled me to him, and the rest of the world disappeared. That is, until I heard Guillaume whooping from stage.

'All right, Gabe!' he was cheering into the mic. 'Ladies and gentleman, that's my brother!'

Mortified, I pulled away from Gabe and realized that not only had Guillaume and the band stopped playing while we had been lost in kissing each other, but now a camera was trained on us, capturing our every move. The audience was cheering, and I could see our faces on every monitor overhead. I suspected it wasn't just the lighting that made both of us look bright red.

'Kiss her again, Gabe!' Guillaume encouraged. The audience cheered, and I could hear a few shouts of 'Kiss her! Kiss her!' Gabe and I looked at each other for a long moment.

'I guess we don't really have a choice,' he said with a little smile.

I smiled back. 'I guess not,' I said. Then slowly, with the cameras trained on us and all of America watching, Gabe pulled me into his arms and leaned down. The cheers, the shouts and even the refrain of 'Beautiful Girl' which Guillaume had started playing again, faded into the background as our lips met in the perfect French kiss.

Epilogue

Ten months later

It should have been one of the most beautiful moments of my life.

As the sky deepened to a sunset of pink-streaked royal blue, Gabe and I were floating above Paris in a hot-air balloon, something I had always dreamed of doing. However, as one might suspect with Guillaume in the picture (and Guillaume *always* seemed to be in the picture these days), things weren't quite as idyllic as they should have been. For instance, apparently hot-air balloons were not actually supposed to move into the air space directly above Paris – probably for fear of some sort of disaster involving a balloon impaling itself on the Eiffel Tower or something. But we weren't concerned about the rules at the moment.

We were more concerned about the fact that Guillaume, who was single-handedly manning a second balloon a hundred yards away, was on the way to floating to his certain death.

Below us, Paris rose up around the ribbon of the Seine, a gentle sprawl of cream-colored, centuries-old apartments, little chimneytops, quaint bridges and geometric green parks. We were just west of the city, so the Eiffel Tower jutted gracefully into the sky right in front of us, and had I not been in such a state of panic I would have marveled at just how beautiful it was as it loomed, all one thousand feet of iron gridwork and graceful symmetry, over the glorious green ladder of the Champ-de-Mars, which spread out in a neat rectangle to the foot of the dark-domed École Militaire.

The Arc de Triomphe, the stone masterpiece Napoleon had commissioned two hundred years ago, looked palatial in the waning sunlight as it sat across the river in the center of the busiest roundabout in Paris, twelve avenues radiating like points on a star from its center. The Avenue des Champs-Élysées, lined with trees and sparkling lights, marched away from us toward the center of Paris, ending in the octagonal Place de la Concorde, where I could see the tall, slender, 3,200-year-old Egyptian obelisk that pointed at the sky, framed by two fountains.

Beyond that, the perfectly geometric Jardin des Tuileries was an emerald expanse stretching toward the enormous Louvre, which hulked on the Right Bank, long and limber around I.M Pei's famed glass pyramid. On the Île de la Cité, the island in the middle of the Seine, I could just make out the twin towers of Notre-Dame beyond the Palais de Justice and the spires of Sainte-Chapelle. All along the gently winding river, which sparkled bright blue in the fading daylight, bridges looked like rungs of a ladder from the air.

However, there was hardly time to take in any of the incredible beauty of the city. Instead, I was in a state of panic as Gabe and I, with the help of a hastily hired balloon operator, chased Guillaume through the clouds above Paris. Gabe had called me an hour ago and told me tersely that

Guillaume had taken a hot-air balloon and was currently floating solo above the city. My stomach had twisted into knots, and I'd asked Gabe if he could see if he could arrange for another balloon so that we could go up and try to talk Guillaume down before he killed himself. After all, hot on the heels of the success of *Riche*, Guillaume was just finishing recording his second album and was due to embark on a world tour the week after next. It would be a little difficult for us to fill auditoriums if the headliner was in a body cast or, heaven forbid, splattered on the Paris pavement. I shuddered at the thought.

Guillaume was floating high above Paris, all by himself, without a balloon operator, in a green, yellow and red balloon that he'd evidently somehow stolen from a field just outside Paris. He was cheerfully firing up the propane tank every few minutes, making his balloon rise and gently fall as our balloon, which Gabe had scrambled to hire from a tour site outside the city, floated perilously close so that I'd be in shouting distance. I didn't even want to think about the legal trouble we'd all be in when we landed; we were currently much closer to Paris than we were allowed to be.

'Hi, Emma!' Guillaume's voice wafted across, faint over the wind and the periodic gentle hiss of the propane burner heating the air inside our balloon.

'Guillaume!' I shouted back, fearing that my voice wouldn't carry far enough. 'What on earth are you *doing*?'

I'd just been counting myself lucky, too. I should have known better. But it had been two whole months since a major incident with Guillaume. Sure, he'd done dumb things here and there – swimming in the fountain in the Place de la Concorde (along with his favorite rubber ducky, no less) one afternoon two weeks ago, for example – but nothing life-threatening. Until now. And of course Guillaume wasn't just my insane rock star client any more. He was also the brother of the man I loved, which made me that much more frightened for him.

'Emma!' Guillaume shouted. He sounded surprisingly cheerful for someone who was all by himself in a hot-air balloon and could plummet to his death at any moment. 'I thought you'd never get here! And you've brought Gabe with you? How fantastic!'

'Guillaume!' I shouted back. 'You're going to get yourself killed!'

I turned to Gabe, feeling panic rise inside me. 'We have to help him get down,' I said urgently. 'We have to have our balloon operator tell him how to land.'

Gabe nodded, but he made no move to help or to yell across to Guillaume.

'Gabe!' I exclaimed in exasperation. 'Why aren't you doing anything? Aren't you worried?'

Gabe shrugged. 'Guillaume always manages to get himself out of things,' he said.

I groaned. Sometimes, Gabe was infuriating. Every time I'd been called by my office to respond to a Guillaume emergency, Gabe had behaved as if it was no big deal. One of these days, he was going to be wrong. I wished he'd stop acting as if his charmed brother had nine lives – although I had to admit that, so far, that had proven to be the case after all.

In the ten months I'd been back in Paris, everything had gone relatively smoothly up until now. Véronique had reluctantly given me my old job back, as it appeared that I did, somehow, have the ability to get Guillaume out of the many disastrous scrapes he routinely got himself into. I'd moved back into my old desk at the office and back into the spare room in Poppy's flat, which relieved her to no end, because it meant she had someone to share the rent with. For her part, she was still going out with random Frenchmen occasionally. But Darren had been visiting her every few weeks, and she had confessed just a few days ago that, despite herself, she thought she might actually try to have a relationship with him. I'd even seen a stack of her self-help books in the trash can, under some used coffee grinds, one day last week.

As for me, my string of random Parisian dates had ended, as I was fully absorbed with Gabe. The more I got to know him, the more compatible I knew we were. We had even taken a trip back to the States last month so that he could meet my parents and I could meet his mother, who still lived in Tampa. Jeannie and King Odysseus had even liked him; Odysseus had temporarily ceased the launching of milk-sodden breakfast cereals to play some sort of complicated French patty-cake game that Gabe patiently taught him.

But now, no matter how well things were going, I half wanted to push Gabe out of the balloon. He wasn't exactly helping matters.

'Guillaume!' I yelled across. 'Our balloon operator is going to tell you how to float west out of Paris and then lower your balloon into a field. You *have* to listen!'

I nodded at the balloon operator, who gave me an incredulous look and turned to Gabe. Gabe shrugged and said something to him in French. The balloon instructor spoke rapidly back. In the ten months I'd been in Paris, I'd enrolled in French classes and was rapidly picking up the language of my new home. But my education hadn't progressed enough to allow me to understand the quickly spoken words of someone with a thick accent from the countryside of France who was currently speaking over the hiss of a propane burner.

Gabe said something else in rapid French to the operator and then added, '*Allez-y.*' Go ahead.

The balloon operator heaved a big sigh then shouted several rapid sentences to Guillaume who just grinned in response, waved and yelled, '*Merci, monsieur!*'

'Guillaume!' I exclaimed in frustration a moment later when it became evident that he was making absolutely no attempt whatsoever to land his balloon. 'What's wrong with you? Do you know how hard it's going to be for me to get you out of this, if you don't wind up killing yourself first?'

'Oh, Emma, you worry too much!' Guillaume yelled back cheerfully. He fired his burner up again and his balloon rose a little higher. Our balloon operator shrugged and followed him, trying to stay at an even altitude so that I could scream at him adequately. Not that it was doing any good. At this rate, Guillaume would be floating up toward the upper atmospheric levels within the hour.

'You'll probably wind up in jail if you don't get killed!' I shouted. 'Do you have any idea how much trouble you're probably in?'

'Not really!' Guillaume yelled back. He came to the edge of his balloon and leaned over to look at the ground. I almost had a heart attack as his basket wobbled back and forth. He looked back over at us and grinned. 'Hey, Gabe!' he yelled. 'Don't you have anything to say?'

There. Finally. Maybe my boyfriend would actually step up and try to talk some reason into his lunatic brother for a change.

'Come *on*, Gabe!' I urged softly without turning around. I was still watching Guillaume wobble perilously in his basket. 'Say something!'

'As a matter of fact, there is something I'd like to say!' Gabe finally yelled across to Guillaume.

'It's about time,' I muttered, still watching Guillaume.

'Okay, Gabe!' Guillaume said cheerfully. 'Let's hear it! What is it?'

'I'd just like to ask Emma if she'll marry me!' Gabe shouted back.

It took me a second to register what he'd said. 'What?' My response came out in a gurgle.

'Would you marry me, Emma?' Gabe asked.

I turned slowly round and saw Gabe kneeling awkwardly in the wicker basket of our balloon, holding a little jewelry box with a silver diamond ring inside. My jaw dropped, and my eyes filled with tears. But I quickly blinked them back.

'Gabe,' I said softly. 'This really isn't the time, I don't think. Guillaume's going to get killed up here if we don't talk him down!'

My heart was thudding as I looked down at my boyfriend, who was still kneeling, ring outstretched, smiling at me. It would have been the best proposal I could have imagined, had I not been worried about the fate of Guillaume, floating toward his certain death several yards away. I couldn't believe that Gabe had chosen *now* of all times to ask me the most important question in the world.

'Emma!' Guillaume shouted. I whipped round, feeling guilty that my attention had been distracted from him for a moment.

'What, Guillaume?' I shouted back. 'Are you okay?'

'Did Gabe forget to tell you that I was a hot-air balloon

operator for nine months the year I turned eighteen?' he yelled cheerfully. 'I'm still licensed, you know!'

I just stared at him, uncomprehending. 'What?'

'This is my balloon!' he yelled back. 'Do you like it?'

'*Your* balloon?' I repeated. I stared at him for a moment. 'Do you mean that you planned this whole thing?'

'Maybe!' he shouted cheerfully.

'You didn't steal the balloon?' I asked incredulously. 'You're *not* in danger of floating away into the atmosphere or crash-landing on the Eiffel Tower?'

'No!' Guillaume grinned. 'But it was worth it to see the expression on your face! Sorry to disappoint you, Emma, but I've paid for these balloons, fair and square. And on top of that, I've even got permission from the French government for us to be in this air space. It's amazing the doors that open for you when you're a rock star.'

'Wh-what?'

'Yes!' Guillaume looked triumphant. 'And much as I'd like to stick around to see what my idiot brother has to say to you, I suppose I'll leave the two of you alone. *Au revoir.* See you back on the ground!'

With that, he turned off his burner and his balloon began to float back toward the ground. He waved once more, blew me a kiss and then turned his back to me. Slowly, in a daze, I turned round. Gabe was still kneeling in the basket, holding up the ring.

'So?' he asked softly after a moment. 'Will you? Will you be my wife?'

I smiled at him, completely overtaken by emotion. I blinked a few times. Then I threw my arms round his neck and laughed. 'Of course I will!' I exclaimed. I leaned back and grinned at him. 'Yes! Yes, I'll marry you!'

Gabe breathed a sigh of relief. 'I was hoping you'd say that.' He grinned at me and took the ring out of its box. 'May I?' he asked, holding it up.

I nodded, and he slipped it onto my ring finger. It fitted perfectly. We both watched for a moment as the princess-cut diamond sparkled in the late afternoon sun.

'*Félicitations*.' Our balloon operator, who I'd nearly forgotten about, congratulated us.

'*Merci*.' I beamed at him.

'Your accent is really getting quite good,' Gabe teased. I rolled my eyes.

'I think I still have some work to do,' I said. 'I'm not French yet.'

'Oh, I don't know,' he said with a sly smile. 'You have the kissing part down at least.'

He touched his lips to mine, and I kissed back, feeling the breeze in my hair as our balloon began to descend. Gabe slipped his arm round my shoulders and pulled me close. As the sun began to set and Guillaume's balloon drifted gently downward below us, we held each other tightly and looked over the edge of the basket as darkness fell on the City of Light.

About the Author

Five years ago, I moved to Paris on a whim, just like Emma, the main character of this novel. I didn't speak French. I had only been there once before, on a family vacation. I had never imagined living there. It was the most impulsive thing I'd ever done, and it changed my life.

That summer was a turning point for me in terms of everything. It's hard to explain, but I think that along with encountering delicious pastries, curious cheeses, incredible wines and charming Frenchmen, I also somehow stumbled upon the best, most authentic version of myself. I wrote every day in the Champs de Mars or along the Seine; I shopped with my roommate Lauren, picnicked in the park, experimented with cooking French food in our tiny kitchen (which, unbelievably, overlooked the Eiffel Tower), sampled wines beyond my wildest imagination and fell in love with the city and its people. I started writing my first novel there, and I formed a lifelong friendship with Lauren, who is also a writer. That summer in Paris changed my life.

In this book, you (along with Emma and Poppy) can visit some of the places that meant the most to me. Emma's apartment, beside the American Library on the rue du General Camou near the Eiffel Tower, for example, was the apartment that Lauren and I lived in. Café le Petit Pont, where Emma and Poppy go on Emma's first night in Paris, was one of my favorite restaurants in the city. The Long Hop and Bar Dix were two of my favorite bars. Le Refuge

Des Fondues is, just as Emma finds out, a crazily wonderful fondue restaurant where patrons actually *do* sip wine out of baby bottles.

I thought for a long time that it was Paris that had changed me and instilled in me a new sense of freedom and self-confidence. But I've realized in the years since then that my summer in Paris simply served to bring those things to the surface because, for the first time in my life, I let go and gave myself permission to simply be *me*. You don't need to go to Paris like Emma and me to become a better version of you. You simply need to open your mind, step out of your comfort zone and to believe you can do anything you set your mind to. As the French say, '*A coeur vaillant rien d'impossible.*' *Nothing is impossible for a willing heart.*

As Emma discovers, the 'art of French kissing' isn't about the kisses themselves (although they are admittedly nice!); it's about letting go and giving yourself permission to live and love without fear and without preconceptions about what you *should* be doing. That's the piece of my Paris summer that I try to keep with me always, and every time I see a picture of the Eiffel Tower or hear the beautiful lilt of a French accent, I can't help but smile.

You can find out more about me and my other novels (*How to Sleep With a Movie Star* and *The Blonde Theory*, both from 5-Spot and Little Black Dress, and *When You Wish*, a novel for teens) at my web site, www.Kristin Harmel.com. I'll also post some photos of life in Paris on my site so that you can see for yourself the world that Emma and Poppy call home. Please drop by and say hello!

FIVE PLACES YOU MUST VISIT ON YOUR NEXT TRIP TO PARIS:

Sure, you know you have to go to the Eiffel Tower and Louvre, and you're planning to take a little cruise up and down the Seine. But to get a taste of Paris behind the scenes, follow in Emma's footsteps and check out these perfectly Parisian locales:

1. **Rue Cler:** This cobblestoned pedestrian market street, overflowing with colorful flower stalls, produce stands, bakeries, cheese shops, butchers and wineries, is the perfect place to practice your *bonjours* and *mercis*, soak in the atmosphere of Parisian daily life and pack a picnic to enjoy in the nearby Parc du Champs de Mars, which sits in the shadow of the Eiffel Tower.
2. **Montmartre:** This bohemian Paris neighborhood sits on a hill overlooking the city and is full of mysteriously beautiful winding streets and alleyways, some of which suddenly dead-end in breathtaking vistas over the sprawling city below. Buy a *crêpe au sucre* at the base of the hill and climb up the picturesque steps leading to the glistening Sacre-Coeur church, where you can perch on a step and overlook all of Paris spreading out below you.
3. **The Latin Quarter:** Perhaps my favorite neighborhood in Paris, this area, enveloped by the Seine River and the beautiful Luxembourg Gardens, overflows with little shops, relatively inexpensive restaurants and some of my favorite places, including The Long Hop pub (located at 25–27 rue Frédéric Sauton – a favorite of Emma, Poppy and lots of English-speaking expats) and Café le Petit Pont (located at 1 rue du Petit-Pont), the perfect place to

settle with a bottle of wine and a great meal while overlooking Notre Dame.

4. **Some Favorite Places to Eat:** One of the most famous cafes in Paris, Café Les Deux Magots (at 6 place Saint Germain des Prés) was a favorite haunt of Ernest Hemingway, Simone de Beauvoir and Jean-Paul Sartre. It's a great place to enjoy a *kir* or a rich hot chocolate while watching the world go by. On the other end of the spectrum is The Cockney Tavern (at 39 boulevard Clichy), in the heart of the fascinatingly seedy Pigalle area of the city that is also home to the famed Moulin Rouge. Owned and managed by my friend Jean-Michel, it is, to me, the quintessential Parisian eatery. Drop by and say hello to Jean-Michel!

5. **Great Places Overlooking the Seine:** There's something intensely beautiful and peaceful about finding your own way along the river that runs through the city. Take a book to the Square du Vert-Galant, a tiny, triangular park that juts into the river from the tip of the Île de la Cité, just west of the Pont Neuf bridge, or plan a sunset picnic on the Pont des Arts, a pedestrian bridge that spans the Seine from the Louvre on the Right Bank to the Institut de France on the Left. Enjoy!

little black dress

brings you
fantastic new books like these
every month - find out more at
www.littleblackdressbooks.com

And why not sign up for our
email newsletter to keep
you in the know about
Little Black Dress news!

You can buy any of these other **Little Black Dress** titles from your bookshop or *direct from the publisher*.

FREE P&P AND UK DELIVERY
(Overseas and Ireland £3.50 per book)

Just Say Yes	Phillipa Ashley	£4.99
Not Another Bad Date	Rachel Gibson	£4.99
Hysterical Blondeness	Suzanne Macpherson	£4.99
Blue Remembered Heels	Nell Dixon	£4.99
Honey Trap	Julie Cohen	£4.99
What's Love Got to do With It?	Lucy Broadbent	£4.99
The Not-So-Perfect Man	Valerie Frankel	£4.99
Lola Carlyle Reveals All	Rachel Gibson	£4.99
The Movie Girl	Kate Lace	£4.99
The Accidental Virgin	Valerie Frankel	£4.99
Reality Check	A.M. Goldsher	£4.99
True Confessions	Rachel Gibson	£4.99
She Woke Up Married	Suzanne Macpherson	£4.99
This Is How It Happened	Jo Barrett	£4.99
One Night Stand	Julie Cohen	£4.99
The True Naomi Story	A.M. Goldsher	£4.99
Smart Vs Pretty	Valerie Frankel	£4.99
The Chalet Girl	Kate Lace	£4.99
True Love (and Other Lies)	Whitney Gaskell	£4.99
Forget About It	Caprice Crane	£4.99
It Must Be Love	Rachel Gibson	£4.99
Chinese Whispers	Marisa Mackle	£4.99

TO ORDER SIMPLY CALL THIS NUMBER

01235 400 414

or visit our website: www.headline.co.uk

Prices and availability subject to change without notice.